EVERYMAN'S LIBRARY

EVERYMAN,
I WILL GO WITH THEE,
AND BE THY GUIDE,
IN THY MOST NEED
TO GO BY THY SIDE

FRANÇOIS RABELAIS

Gargantua and Pantagruel

Translated by Sir Thomas Urquhart and
Pierre Le Motteux

with an Introduction by
Terence Cave

———

181

La Ho
9264

CLBS
F

This book is one of 250 volumes in Everyman's Library
which have been distributed to 4500 state schools
throughout the United Kingdom.
The project has been supported by a grant of £4 million
from the Millennium Commission.

First included in Everyman's Library, 1929
Introduction, Bibliography and Chronology © David Campbell
Publishers Ltd., 1994
Typography by Peter B. Willberg

ISBN 1-85715-181-X

A CIP catalogue record for this book is available from the
British Library

Published by David Campbell Publishers Ltd.,
Gloucester Mansions, 140A Shaftesbury Avenue,
London WC2H 8HD

Distributed by Random House (UK) Ltd.,
20 Vauxhall Bridge Road, London SW1V 2SA

GARGANTUA AND PANTAGRUEL

GENERAL CONTENTS

———

INTRODUCTION

Nothing could be simpler at first sight than the narrative sequence of Rabelais's five books. The story of the giant Gargantua is followed by the story of his gigantic son Pantagruel; the Third Book gives centre stage to Pantagruel's companion Panurge (will he or will he not get married?); and the quest for an answer is pursued through ever more exotic terrain in the Fourth and Fifth Books until at last it is resolved at the shrine of Bacbuc, priestess of the Holy Bottle.

The reader may soon find, however, that things are not quite so simple. Why is it that the continuation of the tale announced at the end of the Second Book bears so little relation to what follows? Why does Friar John, Gargantua's cheerful companion in the First Book, disappear in the Second Book, only to return, apparently no older, in the later books? Why does the ageing Gargantua, 'translated into the Land of the Fairies' in the Second Book (chapter 23), also reappear in the Third Book?

An outline of the historical as opposed to the fictional chronology of Rabelais's works will make things clearer. *Pantagruel* (the Second Book in the narrative sequence) was in fact published first, in 1532; *Gargantua* (the First Book) followed some two years later. Having invented Friar John, Rabelais clearly didn't want to lose him, so he is carried over into the later books, where he becomes a foil to Panurge. Furthermore, there is an interval of more than ten years between *Gargantua* and the Third Book, which first appeared in 1546: Rabelais is starting on a new tack, and consistency with the earlier books is a low priority. In retrospect, the continuation promised in 1532 looks like a comic flourish rather than a firm narrative commitment. It is probably also useful to know, although it is not visible in this translation, that the Fourth Book appeared in a brief, truncated form in 1548 and only assumed its full dimensions in 1552, a year before Rabelais died. Finally, the Fifth Book was not printed until 1564; although parts of it may have been composed by Rabelais, the authenticity of the whole is still uncertain.

Another assumption which the reader is not entitled to make is that this translation faithfully represents what Rabelais wrote: it was the work of two late seventeenth-century translators, and a close study would no doubt tell one a good deal about habits of reading and writing, as well as about religious and other preconceptions, in their day. Sir Thomas Urquhart was a Scottish Calvinist, Pierre Le Motteux a Huguenot exile; both translators adapt Rabelais's satire of certain abuses in the Church to the demands of a forthright anti-Catholic sensibility. It would thus be wrong to project the religious attitudes of the late seventeenth-century English Rabelais on to his early sixteenth-century French original. Moreover, the translation is based on a relatively late state of Rabelais's text and thus does not restore passages which the censors forced him to remove or modify. These passages are important if one wants to reconstruct in detail the ideological context in which Rabelais lived and wrote.

The translation is also extremely free. Urquhart's rendering of the first three books is half as long again as the original. Many of the additions spring from a cheerful espousal of Rabelais's copious style: Urquhart adds exuberantly to Rabelais's virtuoso word-lists; expletives, far from being deleted, are multiplied. The consequence is a change of balance in favour of what might be called the ludic aspect of the work. Le Motteux is a little more restrained, but he too makes no bones about adding material of his own.

This being said, the translation remains an extraordinary feat. It is a literary work in its own right, capturing and embroidering on the verve of Rabelais in a way that would be virtually impossible for a modern translator. The linguistic resources available to Urquhart and Le Motteux are much closer to Shakespeare's than to our own; any attempt to recreate that rhetoric now would look absurdly archaic and false. Rabelais is sometimes compared to James Joyce: both are certainly extraordinary wordspinners; yet if Joyce had translated Rabelais he would have transformed him far more comprehensively than did Urquhart and Le Motteux.

The remainder of this introduction will present the work as it appeared in its day. Readers who wish to check the fidelity

of the translation and who have no French can always consult
a more literal modern translation.[1]

*

In chapter 9 of the Second Book – one of the earliest episodes
Rabelais composed – a major new character is introduced. He
appears at first as an enigmatic stranger. When asked who he
is and where he comes from, he replies in a series of foreign
languages (seven modern, three ancient, three invented)
incomprehensible to Pantagruel and his friends – incomprehensible, that is, until Panurge tries the great languages of
antiquity which Pantagruel has just been urged by his father
to acquire. In the end, it turns out that he is French: he comes,
like Rabelais, from 'the garden of France, the Touraine'.
Though it would certainly be an over-simplification to identi-
fy Panurge with the author, this brilliant invention already
displays some essential Rabelaisian characteristics: Panurge
likes fooling or mystifying his audience, and he is above all an
incarnation of linguistic energy. He is a polyglot, and readers
of Rabelais's work will soon find that he too speaks many
languages: literally, in that there are fragments of Latin,
Greek and Hebrew, of Italian and German and other modern
languages scattered throughout the five books, together with a
large number of fantastic and invented words; but also
metaphorically, in that Rabelais's idiom is composed of every
stylistic and linguistic level available to him. Furthermore, the
level often shifts disconcertingly, leaving the reader stranded.
The pleasure of language is thus dramatized on the threshold
of the work, a pleasure which is both social and competitive,
conciliatory and provocative. Pantagruel and Panurge will be
friends for life, but they won't always agree.

There are many strange encounters – and encounters with
strangers – in Rabelais. One of the most famous also belongs to
the first published book. The narrator himself ('Alcofribas
Nasier', a patent anagram) takes shelter from the rain in
Pantagruel's mouth, where he finds a landscape not unlike
that of Europe. He meets a man planting cabbages ('coleworts') and asks him in amazement what he is doing:

I plant coleworts, said he ... Jesus! (said I) is there here a new world? Sure (said he) it is never a jot new, but it is commonly reported, that without this there is an earth, whereof the inhabitants enjoy the light of a Sunne and a Moone, and that it is full of, and replenished with very good commodities; but yet this is more ancient that that. (II.32)

As Erich Auerbach points out in what is still one of the best pieces of critical writing on Rabelais, this is among the earliest examples in European literature of a reversed cultural perspective: the traveller finds that *he* is the foreigner; the exotic other world is the only and natural world for its inhabitants.[2] The theme is also characteristic of Rabelais in this early phase of his career as a comic writer in that the narrator is not daunted or unduly threatened by the grotesque giant-world in which he finds himself: he helps, indeed, to familiarize it. In the Fourth Book, by contrast, the encounters will often be dangerous; the monsters are not easily tamed, and some have to be left where they are or prudently evaded. This is a point we shall return to.

A good way of getting an overall sense of Rabelais's narrative voice is to begin by reading all five prologues. One finds there the same double theme of the familiar and the grotesque, of fascination and repulsion, welcome and exclusion, traced this time through Rabelais's authorial relations with his own readers. His tone is by turns cheerful and aggressive: he advises, warns, pleads, attacks and curses, and in the process he softens the reader up. Either one is a reader of goodwill, a true Pantagruelist, who will understand him and take everything he says in good part, or one belongs to the reviled gang of hypocrites, bigots, censors, whom he chases from the scene at the end of the prologue to the Third Book with curses and growling. Much the same principle of exclusion and inclusion presides over the founding of the Abbey of Theleme in the First Book This great utopian invention, placed under the sign of joy and freedom, in fact depends on a rigorous preliminary sorting out of sheep and goats (see chapter 52, and the inscription on the gate in chapter 54). In the late 1540s, in troubled times, Rabelais wrote a first prologue for the Fourth Book which was later superseded by the prologue translated here, although it left its trace in the dedicatory epistle to Rabelais's patron Odet de Châtillon. In this prologue, the threat of the censors and 'calumniators', a threat to Rabelais's life as well as to his values, is evoked graphically and at length.

Anxiety about censorship is only one of the forms taken by Rabelais's insecurity about how he will be read, although it is a crucial one. It looks as if he was conscious of writing a strange book that his readers might reject with ridicule or disgust, a strangely *mixed* book. In the prologue to the Third Book, he tells the story of the black camel and parti-coloured slave presented by Ptolemy to the Egyptians, who were frightened and offended rather than pleased by this monstrous offering. The anecdote is no doubt defensive, but it should also be read as a challenge to the reader: be ready to be disconcerted, be ready to be shocked out of your habits and prejudices. At the same time, plenty of reassuring images of the author's good will are available, from the promise of amazing therapeutic effects in the prologue to the Second Book to the image of the book as an inexhaustible barrel or cornucopia at the end of the prologue to the Third Book.

*

The strangeness of Rabelais's book has not decreased since it first appeared, and it may well have shifted its ground also. We can't assume that the author's sense of strangeness is quite the same as our own, still less that what was familiar to him was familiar to us. We may fail to laugh at things meant to be funny, and laugh at things that didn't necessarily seem funny at all to Rabelais. We may be shocked by things that Rabelais's censors found innocuous, even though they condemned many passages as indecent, largely where they saw that they themselves were being mocked. And so we have a responsibility to familiarize ourselves, at least in outline, with that other world of early sixteenth-century France in which Rabelais himself appears to us as the planter of cabbages (though not, admittedly, of common or garden ones).

Rabelais's anxieties about readers and censors are clearly in the main ideological. His works were composed during a critical period of change in the religious and political ideologies of Europe, the period we now call the Reformation. In order to understand the situation in France at this time, it is important not to look at it, as Urquhart and Le Motteux did, through Protestant spectacles, or indeed with the kind of hindsight which reduces the conflict to a simple opposition between 'Catholic' and 'Protestant'. In the 1530s, as Rabelais's first comic writings were appearing, Henry VIII was declaring himself head of what came to be called the Church of England. France had its own Gallican policy, which Rabelais will later support with his satire of the Papimanes in the Fourth Book, but – unlike Anglicanism – it was not schismatic. The religious themes of Rabelais's works imply a deep sympathy with a movement of moderate reform which became established in France in the early 1520s and was enjoying a period of great success by 1532. These moderate reformers were known as 'evangelicals' because they insisted on the supreme importance for Christian faith of Scripture, as opposed to the theological doctrine which had been evolved by the Church over more than a millennium. They attacked the excessively formalistic character of late medieval worship, its attachment to 'externals' such as prescribed fasting and other mortifications; they attacked the scandal of the sale of indulgences (pardons), which was another aspect of the same materialistic emphasis; they called in question excessive worship of saints and saw pilgrimages as in the main a futile dereliction of domestic duties in the hope of obtaining a material benefit from some (probably fake) relic; they questioned monasticism not only for its abuses, but also as a denial of human nature which could either stultify or give rise to excesses; and they attacked the vested interests of the Faculty of Theology at the University of Paris, generally known as the Sorbonne, who had for centuries claimed the power to define orthodoxy in their own abstruse philosophical language.

Some evangelicals inclined towards the more extreme theological position of Luther, who had denied any separate efficacy to human 'works' as a means to salvation and insisted on the doctrine of justification by faith. Many of these radical evangelicals moved to Basel or Geneva to escape the censure of the Sorbonne, and eventually joined the fully schismatic Church state established by Calvin in the 1540s. Others followed the more liberal and tolerant lead of Erasmus, who devoted much of his life to promoting moderate, non-schismatic reform in Europe.

The French evangelicals – especially those connected in some way with the court – were greatly assisted by the patronage of Marguerite of Navarre, the sister of King François I. Author of a number of spiritual poems (one of which seems to have incurred the wrath of the Sorbonne in 1533) and of a collection of stories in the manner of Boccaccio called the *Heptameron*, she gave her protection to the most able vernacular writers of the day, who also shared her evangelical views. One of them was Clément Marot, whose witty, fluent poems were still admired by the extremely choosy *literati* of the seventeenth century, and whose translation of some fifty psalms was to form the basis for the French Protestant psalter. Rabelais dedicated his Third Book to Marguerite of Navarre in 1546; but by that time the cause of the evangelicals was in jeopardy. Calvin had begun to mount from Geneva a formidable propaganda campaign in France; Marguerite's influence over her brother was intermittent, in part because he was deeply involved in wars with the Emperor Charles V; the Sorbonne had intensified its campaign against its opponents, all of whom – schismatic or not – it regarded as equally threatening; and the Council of Trent, which had been convoked in 1545 after much delay to solve the religious problem in Europe, soon began to show a conservative bias by reaffirming practices such as prescribed fasting. When François I died in 1547, his son Henri II combined a Gallican policy in matters such as Church revenues and appointments with an actively conservative anti-reformist position. By the time Marguerite herself died in 1549, the cause of the evangelicals was all but extinguished. Just over ten years later – at about the time the Fifth Book was published – the wars of religion began, and the polarization between orthodox Catholics and schismatic Huguenots was complete, although leading moderates continued to try to achieve conciliation throughout the later part of the century.

This brief outline is essential to an understanding of Rabelais as a passionately committed writer. It enables one, for example, to see the point of his satire of Sorbonne theologians (usually referred to obliquely as 'sophists'), of monks and monastic discipline (see I.27 and 40, and the Theleme episode), of pilgrimages (I.38 and 45), and of Papal abuses (IV.48–54), without falling into the now wholly discredited fallacy of assuming him to be either a 'free-thinker' or alternatively a 'Protestant': in the Fourth Book, he attacks Calvin – who had attacked him – no less virulently than he attacks his conservative opponents (IV.32). It explains his frequent quotations from and allusions to Scripture, which often provide a touchstone for moral and spiritual values: the young Gargantua begins his day with Scripture readings and prayer (I.23); Pantagruel quotes St Paul in order to demolish Panurge's defence of debt (III.5); and another Pauline quotation is used against the Gastrolaters (IV.58). It explains, too, the emphasis from beginning to end on evangelical *caritas*, love of and goodwill towards one's neighbour – this is the sense of the quotation in Greek from St Paul on the emblem Gargantua wears (I.8: 'Charity seeketh not her own'; Urquhart has confused matters by adding another, non-scriptural, Greek quotation), and it is applied by Gargantua in his generosity towards Picrochole's vanquished army (I.50), by Pantagruel in his unwavering friendship to the wayward Panurge, and by the Thelemites, who 'entered into a very laudable emulation to do all of them what they saw did please one' (I.57). It is essential to see that the motto of the Abbey of Theleme, 'Do what thou wilt', presupposes that those whose nature is not tainted by some accident of birth will naturally apply the principle of charity: their will ('Theleme' comes from the Greek word for 'will', often used in the New Testament) is directed towards the good of others, so that the whole community lives in harmony.

*

In a celebrated letter to his son Pantagruel (II.8), Gargantua writes that the time when he himself was educated 'was darksome, obscured with clouds of ignorance, and savouring a little of the infelicity and calamity of the Gothes'; now, by contrast, the study of letters

hath by the divine goodness, been restored unto its former light and dignity ... the mindes of men are qualified with all manner of discipline, and the old sciences revived, which for many ages were extinct ... I see robbers, hangmen, freebooters, tapsters, ostlers, and such like, of the very rubbish of the people, more learned now then the Doctors and Preachers were in my time. What shall I say? The very women and children have aspired to this praise and celestial Manna of good learning.

This consciousness of a renewal, of an immense cultural leap, is what we now refer to loosely as 'the Renaissance', a vast and complex development that can only be touched on briefly here.

As perceived and presented by Rabelais, it appears first and foremost as an ambitious educational programme accompanied by a vigorous propaganda exercise. Both are visible in Gargantua's letter, and at greater length in the series of chapters devoted to Gargantua's education in the First Book (remember again that this was written *after* the Second Book): Gargantua's education is an expansion of the outline in the Second Book, and of course makes nonsense of the chronology; the generation gap described in the letter is replaced by the two phases of Gargantua's own education.

Rabelais belongs to a relatively late stage in the development of the Renaissance, and to its northern European variant. This stage is marked above all by the influence of Erasmus, to whom, in November 1532, Rabelais wrote a highly flattering letter in Latin, saying that he owed everything to him. By the early sixteenth century, a good knowledge of Greek as well as of classical Latin was accessible to scholars and regarded as essential; many were also acquiring Hebrew. In 1517, a 'trilingual' college was established at Louvain, and in the same year, François I invited Erasmus to found a similar college at Paris; however, Erasmus declined, and it was not until 1530 that humanist studies were officially launched in Paris with the establishment of four regius professorships in

Greek and Hebrew. It is no doubt this development above all that is being referred to in the educational episodes of Rabelais's first two books.

Rabelais cites classical authors at every available opportunity. He had acquired Greek in the later part of his long period as a Franciscan at the monastery of Fontenay-le-Comte, and his admiration for Greek authors is especially visible in his borrowings from the moral essays of Plutarch and the satirical fantasies of Lucian. But Greek was also the language of the New Testament, and the quotation in Greek from St Paul on Gargantua's emblem is a symptom of the influence of humanist studies in the history of the Reformation: Erasmus' Greek New Testament of 1516 had been a major event, by implication presenting a radical challenge to the official Latin Bible (the Vulgate) by showing that it was philologically unsound, and thus opening the way to new and theologically disturbing readings of Scripture. Equally, Erasmus' desire to make Scripture available to ordinary people was implemented by translations into the vernacular languages: whether Rabelais quotes Biblical texts in Greek or in French, he is being controversial. Hebrew, too, has a presence in Rabelais's writings: Panurge speaks it eloquently, and Hebrew names are used in the Fourth Book.

Rabelais was familiar, in fact, with virtually every strand in High Renaissance intellectual culture. The prologue to the First Book opens with an extended reference to Plato's *Symposium* and the figure of Socrates as an exemplar of ideal wisdom hidden beneath a deceptive exterior; Gargantua's emblem carries, together with the Pauline quotation, the symbolic image of the androgyne, adapted from the *Symposium*. A Christianized reworking of platonist thought – usually known as 'Florentine neoplatonism' because it was founded by the fifteenth-century Florentine scholar Marsilio Ficino – became fashionable in France in the earlier sixteenth century, where it was popularized by handbooks of courtly behaviour such as Baldassare Castiglione's *The Courtier* (1528, translated into French in 1538). With its special blend of the spiritual and the aesthetic – even the sensual – it presented a powerful challenge to the abstract, logic-based Aristotelian philosophy which is now known as 'scholastic' because it was cultivated in the late medieval schools (universities) and above all at the Sorbonne. In this way, neoplatonism and evangelism often join forces in the work of this generation of writers. A complex and beautiful example is provided by the Macreons episode of the Fourth Book, and the later part of the Fifth Book is an allegorical narrative of a kind much favoured by neoplatonist writers.

Even more prominent in Rabelais's writings is his medical knowledge. He had studied medicine at the famous school of Montpellier and was employed by his patrons as a physician, among other things. From the prologue to the Second Book via the Rondibilis episode of the Third Book to the perhaps ironic adage 'Physician, heal thyself' in the prologue to the Fourth Book, this interest is prominently displayed; indeed, Rabelais's overwhelming preoccupation with the body, its functions and malfunctions, is apparent in almost every episode (a powerful example, taken at random, is the descent into Pantagruel's gut to remove an obstruction in II.33). The other great traditional discipline, law, is almost as central: the quarrel between Kissbreech and Suckfist in the Second Book and the Bridlegoose episode of the Third Book are only the most obvious instances; in fact, Rabelais shows throughout a remarkable command of legal process and terminology, turning it to all kinds of comic effect.

These are highly technical matters, where a great deal of erudition is necessary nowadays in order to perceive that Rabelais adopts in medicine as well as in law an advanced position for his day. Without recourse to a well-annotated edition, it is not easy for a modern reader to see where the point lies, still less what exactly the joke is: for example, it seems probable that Rabelais espoused the controversial Galenic theory that sperm originated in the brain, while Bridlegoose's recourse to a throw of the dice to resolve a case where the proceedings have reached a dead end is an evangelical version of a highly reputable principle of Roman law.[3] These warnings of possible misunderstanding are not meant, however, to place a protective wall of erudition round Rabelais's work: as with other great writers, the force of his writing

lies partly in the fact that it is able to turn even misunderstanding to its own account.

*

With this sketch of Rabelais's 'high culture' in mind, it
becomes possible to see the contrast between the earlier and
the later books in sharper relief. In 1532–4, evangelism was at
its zenith, the Sorbonne could be satirized and parodied, if not
with impunity, at least without immediate peril. Rabelais had
abandoned the monastic life in about 1526, and the sense of
liberation is palpable, whether in the self-parodic invention of
the all-too-emancipated Friar John or in the anti-monastic
utopia of Theleme, which is built like the luxurious new
châteaux that were springing up in Rabelais's day in the Loire
valley and elsewhere. Humanist education is presented as
triumphant over scholastic obscurantism; Erasmian optimism
about man's ability to perfect himself morally through education is vividly dramatized; Erasmian toleration and pacifism
are apparent in Grangousier's attempts to defuse the quarrel
with Picrochole. Furthermore, in the old giant's homily first to
the pilgrims, then to Touchfaucet (I.45–6), Rabelais endorses
a far-reaching change which was gradually taking place in the
political and geographical conception of Europe:

The time is not now as formerly, to conquer the Kingdomes of our
neighbour Princes, and to build up our own greatnesse upon the losse
of our nearest Christian brother: this imitation of the ancient
Herculeses, Alexanders, Hannibals, Scipios, Caesars, and other such heroes
is quite contrary to the Profession of the Gospel of Christ . . .

Pilgrimages and crusades continue, but appear increasingly as
outmoded; imperial conquest, connected with the feudal ideal,
is giving way to the notion of a Europe of nation-states; travel
is becoming secularized. The alien is familiarized, in the
meeting between Pantagruel and Panurge or between Alcofrybas and the cabbage-planter, by an exercise of imaginative
sympathy, and the terrain of the first two books is cheerfully
dominated by utopian giants whose power is never seriously
threatened.

Yet the First Book ends on a sombre note, and here again it

is important to stress the chronological rather than the fictional order. The closing episode turns on the sense of a 'prophetic riddle'. Is it merely a joke in which the apparent meaning, heavy with apocalyptic overtones, collapses when Friar John suggests that the solution to the riddle is 'a game of tennis'? Rabelais's readers would have recognized the poem, since it is borrowed from the court poet Mellin de Saint-Gelais. Friar John supplies the meaning Saint-Gelais intended; but Rabelais has added several lines which emphasize the Biblical tenor of the poem, and these lines provide the cue for Gargantua's pathos-laden reading. His premonition of persecution and disaster cannot easily be laughed off. It is not improbable that this episode was written in the immediate aftermath of the notorious 'Affaire des placards' (the poster affair) of October 1534, when a group of radical reformers put up posters in Paris and in a number of provincial towns attacking the traditional form of the Mass. This provoked a particularly aggressive backlash from the religious authorities. Many evangelicals had to flee the country, or at least to lie low, and although the situation subsequently eased again, the event may be seen to mark the end of a period of intense evangelical optimism.

By the time the Third Book was published in 1546, the threat foreseen by Gargantua had been amply realized. The cheerful prologues of the first two books give way to a more sombre and embattled tone, echoing the renewed wars between France and the Empire; the Socrates of the First Book prologue is replaced by the cynic Diogenes, who keeps himself to himself in his legendary barrel. Pantagruel begins to represent and preach a christianized stoic doctrine of indifference to everything that is beyond our control, a doctrine designed to withstand the assaults of a hostile and unpredictable world (III.2 and 10). Instead of the harmonious social world of Theleme, grounded in an ideal evangelical conception of love for others ('charity'), one finds Panurge's brilliant but essentially flawed rhetorical exercise in praise of debt, in other words self-interest. Instead of the exuberant educational programmes of the First and Second Books, a question is posed which seeks an answer in every conceivable form of knowledge but is never satisfied. No doubt this is because the questioner doesn't want to hear the answer he gets: the experts are not, in the main, absurd; but Panurge's perverse and self-preoccupied performance none the less shows that learning cannot solve the deepest moral problems, that it is not a universal panacea. The Erasmian ideal of an encyclopedic learning that leads to moral perfection is fragmented and called in question by human self-love ('philauty': III.29) and human uncertainty; it seems indeed probable that Rabelais had in the interim moved closer to the much more austere view of human nature held by Marguerite of Navarre, to whom, as we saw, the Third Book is dedicated. At the same time, alert as always to the intellectual climate of his day, he places at the centre of his narrative of uncertainty an episode dramatizing the contemporary interest of Parisian scholars in ancient scepticism (III.35–6).

It has often been remarked that in the Third Book the burlesque anagram 'Alcofribas Nasier' is replaced on the title page by Rabelais's own name, and that the Rabelaisian world has shrunk and grown more sober: the comedy of gigantic proportions and disproportions is in abeyance. When giant-size figures reappear in the Fourth Book, they are for the most part ugly, disturbing and threatening, like the ghastly Shrovetide (IV.29–32), who is composed of surreal non sequiturs. Even the human characters may be monstrous: the fanatically intolerant Homenas, who relishes the thought of putting heretics to the torch (IV.48–54), is a much more sinister figure than Picrochole or Janotus de Bragmardo. It is symptomatic also that Pantagruel, far from attempting to attack and defeat these threatening figures, remains evasive or aloof. He retains his moral stature as a prudent observer of ills and abuses, but – unlike Gargantua and his own former self – he no longer conducts zestful and all-conquering campaigns against puny enemies. The world is not so easily set right.

Perhaps the most moving indicator of the change of mood in Rabelais's later books is the double cluster of chapters in which the death of his beloved patron Guillaume Du Bellay, uncle of the famous poet Joachim Du Bellay, is woven deep into the fiction. As we are told in chapter 21 of the Third Book,

'William of Bellay, late Lord of Langey', had died in 1543: the precise place and date are given, almost as if the clock had stopped at that moment. The Fourth Book version supplies instead a roll-call of those present, amid whom Rabelais himself is named. In both versions, the intensely real character of the event is intensified by its other-worldly setting: this is a death-bed scene, where the soul of a great man takes on, as it prepares to leave the body, a numinous quality. The Third Book stresses the prophetic dimension. Divination and prophecy, other-worldly forms of knowledge, are a constant preoccupation of this book, and Rabelais draws on neoplatonist sources to describe, via Pantagruel, how souls close to death are given the power of foretelling the future, and how Du Bellay foretold strange and unlikely things that none the less came to pass. In the Fourth Book, Du Bellay's death is again associated with a neoplatonist theory: the death of 'heroes' (mortals endowed with exceptional gifts and qualities) unleashes cosmic disturbances; the storm that Pantagruel and his friends have just – only just – survived is thus explained, and Pantagruel carries the theme to a point of high pathos by telling the story of the portents accompanying the death of Pan, who is patently here a figure of Christ.

It looks, indeed, as if the death of his patron was for Rabelais the symbol of a calamitous shift both in contemporary affairs and in his own life, represented through metaphors of storm and shipwreck. The storm in the Fourth Book (chapters 18–24) arises after the Pantagrueline crew had met a boatload of clerics going to the Council of 'Chesil', a Hebrew word meaning 'fools': the reference is clearly to the Council of Trent and the sinister direction it was taking, which might have been avoided if a moderate statesman as powerful and charismatic as Guillaume Du Bellay had been there to exercise his influence. In the prologue to the Third Book, Rabelais speaks mysteriously of 'the shipwreck of my former misfortunes'; the image of dangers at sea recurs in both of the 'Du Bellay' episodes; the first, partial version of the Fourth Book ends just after the beginning of the Macreons episode, that is to say just before the reference to Du Bellay, as if the writing of this episode were itself traumatic, creating a rift in the very fabric of the book; and it is of course no accident that the new episode dramatizes old age (the names 'Macreon' and 'Macrobius' refer to length of life). Nowadays we would nervously trivialize such a psychological event by calling it a mid-life crisis; but it was also, as Rabelais clearly saw, a crisis in the history of the Church and of France, and it would be wiser to use – as Rabelais uses it to specify the point Du Bellay's life had reached – the ancient and more potent term 'climacteric'. In many ways, this double episode may be regarded as the nucleus from which both the Third and the Fourth Book sprang.

*

This is one way of reading Rabelais, in which the political, the biographical and the psychological converge to bring alive, with strange intensity, a moment in history. It is poles apart from the tiresomely jolly caricature of Rabelais as a red-nosed boozer for whom no feast is too gargantuan and who, according to taste, is either gloriously liberated from inhibitions about the body and its functions, or grossly obsessed with sexual and lavatorial humour. The caricature was formed early, indeed in Rabelais's lifetime: it was after all a natural response to the self-caricaturing voice of the narrator Alcofrybas Nasier. Some of Rabelais's most loyal readers and commentators have attempted to prove, to his greater glory, that it has never been anything but a legend, that his preoccupation with the body was a phase that he and most of his characters rapidly outgrew, that 'coarse humour' was a smoke-screen behind which he could more safely put forward his deeply serious religious and moral convictions. In support of this view, they quote among other things the prologue to the First Book, where the narrator tells us insistently to look beneath the surface of his work. Others have claimed that this prologue is a parody of the long-standing tradition of allegorical reading, and that the very terms in which Rabelais speaks of a hidden meaning are burlesque. Rabelais is for them a writer of the comic imagination: that is, after all, how he has been read and admired for hundreds of years by readers who knew little and cared less about the precise historical circumstances in which he wrote. If we strip the comic mask from Rabelais and find a committed evangelical humanist, that may be of interest to historians; for those who care for literature, it may seem like throwing a vociferous gargantuan baby out with his bathwater.

In recent years, the debate has focused on the question whether Rabelais was in any sense a 'popular' writer. In his study *Rabelais and his World*, which was not known in the West until the 1960s, the Soviet critic Mikhail Bakhtin brilliantly surveyed the aspects of Rabelais's work which, he argued, originated in popular culture – in the marketplace, in oral culture, and above all in carnival practices, which still provided in the early modern period a safety-valve for people whose everyday lives were strictly controlled by political, religious and social authority. He argued, too, that Rabelais's representations of what Bakhtin calls the 'lower bodily stratum' arise from the popular imagination as embodied in an ancient tradition of narrative which had the function of enabling people to relieve the anxieties of a physically harsh and precarious life. The *Gargantuan Chronicles*, the chap-book from which Rabelais seemed to derive the idea of his own work, is one example among many of this tradition. Bakhtin recognized, in a final chapter which his detractors tend to skate over, that Rabelais participated in an elite, bookish culture, and indeed in the ruling ideology of the period; he also noted that the world of popular imagery is less apparent in the later books. But he insisted that in Rabelais's work, despite the elements of high culture and even despite Rabelais's own intentions, the authentic voice of the people may be heard.

The Marxist colouring of this argument has provoked some violent objections. On almost every page of Rabelais's work there are allusions, quotations, names, words which could only have been identified by a small circle of learned readers; this is often true of whole episodes, not to mention a substantial proportion of the jokes. What would a hypothetical representative of the people have made of the reference to Plato and Socrates and the discussion of allegory in the prologue to the First Book, or of the discussion of the true meaning of the

colours blue and white (I.10), or of the island of the
Macreons? It is also pointed out that, in the second quarter of
the sixteenth century, humour that a Victorian age would
regard as coarse and *thus* plebeian seems to have been appreciated at the highest level of society: it is known that the
Bishop of Paris read Rabelais's works aloud to the King, and
Marguerite of Navarre's *Heptameron*, full as it is of scriptural
reference and moral reflection, also contains many stories in
which sexual behaviour is explicitly described.

Yet this last example works both ways. We know that,
despite the prestige of learned culture at the court of François
I, many members of the court were not themselves learned. It
seems likely that the King himself would have had difficulty
with many of the more obscure allusions. Besides, later generations have not, on the whole, regarded Rabelais as an
impossibly obscure writer. The example of Shakespeare makes
it clear enough that imaginative writing has the power to
operate at several levels, and above all to generate a tide of
meaning on which fragments of obscurity may be carried with
ease: as readers or listeners, we know in general where those
fragments fit in the cultural spectrum, and we get the gist, if
not the whole point. And this applies *a fortiori* to the sixteenth-
century public, who, even if many were relatively uneducated,
were not necessarily stupid and had the advantage of knowing
the cultural topography of their own world. They lived, for
example, in a world where Latin was often used, and where
the Latin had itself been brought close in structure and
pronunciation to the vernacular, and thus would have had
little difficulty in placing the 'kitchen Latin' which is scattered
throughout episodes such as the harangue of Janotus de
Bragmardo (I.17–20). They would also have recognized the
lawyers, doctors and theologians and understood that they
were being caricatured.

Rabelais's case is of course different from Shakespeare's in
that drama does not require literacy. Some scholars have
argued that Rabelais's works were read aloud, privately or
publicly, to those who could not themselves read. The hypo-
thesis is plausible, although the evidence is not substantial.
Even if one assumes that the illiterate would have had no

direct access to the text, that still leaves a considerable number of potential readers who had some degree of education but were not necessarily learned.

This means, I think, that it is wrong to posit an extremely small, hyper-learned circle of readers for Rabelais's work, to argue that it could only have been written for such readers, and then to give exclusive priority to the learned as opposed to the 'popular' aspects of the text. It is no doubt equally wrong to posit an archetypal, transtemporal voice of the people speaking by ventriloquy through an unwitting author. Rabelais's early life was not especially privileged; he was able to make his way into the company of the great and the good by one of the rare channels of social mobility that existed in his day; and it would be absurd to believe that he did not experience even in that milieu, as part of his everyday life, the whole texture of the world he lived in. There are borrowings in Rabelais from oral culture, from old legends of giants and monsters and stories of tricksters and fools, from carnival, drama and other forms of public entertainment. Some of these are inextricably mixed with bookish transcriptions of similar materials (Boccaccio's stories are one example among many); all are also, amazingly, mixed with an inexhaustible supply of materials from the high culture that Rabelais had mastered. What is unique is Rabelais's ability to marshal such diverse elements, to turn this virtuoso concoction into an imaginative encyclopedia of his world.

*

The mixed and many-layered character of Rabelais's writing is in fact an extreme variant of the aesthetic preferences of his period. He lived at a time when the French language was changing rapidly, when the linguistic range available to a writer was unusually extensive: archaisms, neologisms, regional words, foreign words all go into the melting pot, encouraging an inventiveness unparalleled in French literature before or since. The resources of the French language are being stretched in entirely new directions: in the age of François I, translations proliferate – translations of Scripture, of the Greek and Latin classics, of Italian prose and poetry;

jurists, theologians and doctors begin to write in French; before Rabelais died, a new generation of French poets led by Ronsard and Joachim Du Bellay had launched a comprehensive renewal of French poetry. A little later, Montaigne's constantly expanding book of essays (a genre which he virtually invented) covers an enormous range of topics in a flexible, often rambling but always colourful and inventive style. Such writers – like their great humanist predecessor Erasmus, who of course wrote in Latin – cultivated an aesthetic of abundance and diversity. They found their own styles and themes through what was called 'imitation', by which they meant precisely not a slavish copying, but a process whereby the whole range of ancient materials recovered by humanist scholarship was assimilated, digested (their metaphor), and transformed into a new style for a new age.

Rabelais's extraordinary outpouring of fragments of all kinds – quotations, allusions, anecdotes, legends, myths, poems, personifications – is an idiosyncratic and extreme instance of this preference for the inclusive. Indeed, from the Third Book on, the narrative becomes a quest for the truth amid the thickly strewn bric-à-brac of human knowledge and experience. The Third Book is coherent only because it repeats the same scenario over and over again: there are significant groupings of chapters, but no necessary narrative progression. In the definitive Fourth Book (following, it should be remembered, a fragmentary first edition), the chase becomes even more random and discontinuous as the Pantagrueline crew embarks on a voyage through uncharted seas and fabulous archipelagoes, with more than a whiff of the real voyages of discovery which had recently begun to change the world. A powerful embodiment of the work's own character is to be found, once again, in the Macreons episode: Pantagruel and his friends pick their way through a landscape littered with the remains of a lost civilization, with enigmatic inscriptions and pieces of fallen architecture (IV.25). In this way, two contemporary conceptions are profoundly linked: the view of antique culture as a vast necropolis, a treasure-house of fragmentary remnants which can no longer be restored to their original form; and the shattering of a centuries-old world map centred on the Mediterranean basin.

It is true that the Fifth Book provides a conclusion which is wholly consistent in narrative terms with the nature of the quest. The Holy Bottle is found, and it delivers its oracle. But there is an irony here which is also consistent with, say, the Macreons episode, and which Rabelais would surely have appreciated: for us, the Fifth Book is only another fragment, posthumous and of dubious authenticity.

The Rabelaisian mixture is of course especially inclusive and permissive because it is comic. As an encyclopedic comedy, it bears a distant family resemblance both to the *Divine Comedy* and to Balzac's *Comédie humaine*. The comparison has at least the merit that it presents the comic principle as something other than the production of intermittent laughter. Laughter is indeed central to Rabelais's writing, but as a principle which is stated in the prefatory poem of the First Book: 'to laugh is proper to the man'. This poem has sometimes wrongly been taken to mean that Rabelais's work is 'simply' comic, and therefore devoid of serious moral and religious reflection. In fact, the formula surely means the reverse. If laughter is proper to man, a distinctive feature of the human – and this is the philosophical sense of the tag – it becomes a sufficient and even a necessary angle from which to view human activity. Humankind is like Panurge rather than the Pantagruel of the later books – mixed, fallen, fragmented. To speak of man with unmixed seriousness would be a fundamental error; the only seriousness humans deserve, the only seriousness they are capable of, is of a kind indivisible from the comic.

Rabelais is here drawing on an ancient philosophical definition of human nature, of Aristotelian origin, as he draws on Plato in the prologue to the First Book to communicate the bonding of the comic and the serious. He draws a good deal, too, on the satirical fantasy of the late Greek writer Lucian, who was especially popular with humanists of the early sixteenth century (the 'world in Pantagruel's mouth' owes something to Lucian, as does the scene in heaven in the prologue to the Fourth Book). Rabelais is conscious of the

GARGANTUA AND PANTAGRUEL

celebrated model provided by Erasmus' *Praise of Folly*, in which the personification Folly praises herself and her followers in a disconcerting parade of human foibles, some mild and endearing, some pernicious, culminating in an ecstatic Christian folly that combines elements from Plato and St Paul. Folly is reversible: the man who thinks he is wise is the real fool; the one the world considers a fool or a madman may be a saint, or Christ himself. This theme is particularly visible in the Third Book, where Panurge's folly, rooted in 'philauty', is ultimately played off against the inspired folly of Triboullet (III.37–8, 45–6). The theme reappears, of course, in the Shakespearian figure of the fool or jester, who, like the trickster with whom he may often be identified, has an ancient pedigree: Panurge and Autolycus, despite their Greek names, would be recognizable at many levels of culture.

This last example takes us beyond the intellectual and bookish domain, and it is clear that comedy in Rabelais cannot be explained exclusively in terms of the influence of Lucian or Erasmus. Bakhtin was no doubt right in suggesting that the real power Rabelais manages to tap, the power which has made his books an unsurpassed exemplar of comic energy, is visceral: if humankind is comic, that is primarily because the human body seems grotesque, incomprehensible, uncontrollable. Furthermore, all of mankind's aspirations to spiritual and moral values, to high intellectual seriousness, have to pass through this comic body. Not only are they subject to basic human needs – eating, drinking, urinating, defecating, sex – but they are also inextricably mixed up with, even produced by, those needs. Explicitly, this theme runs through Gargantua's educational programme, reappears in the Third Book in Rondibilis' advice to Panurge, and brings the Fourth Book to a climax in a dazzling sequence of episodes connected with the stomach (see especially IV.61–2). Implicitly, it is everywhere.

In Rabelais, comedy is a solvent. It dissolves the dividing lines between areas of experience too often kept apart. The chief of these is the dividing line between comedy itself and seriousness, and it is ironic that Rabelais's readers have so obstinately continued to separate the tipsy master of ceremonies from the high-minded evangelical humanist: his work already, from the start, disallows this polarization and the false choice it imposes. His extraordinary mastery of his diverse materials lies above all in his ability to place them in relation with one another – by analogy, by association, by narrative twists and turns, surprisingly, shockingly, always refreshingly. The odd and disproportionate friendship between Pantagruel and Panurge is just one of these; the strange concatenation of images and reflections and explanations provoked by the thawing words in IV.55–6 is another; the island of Ennasin consists of nothing but connections. It is also not surprising, given the evangelical desire to replace Scripture at the centre of everyday life, that Biblical references are cited in the most unexpected contexts: by Friar John, for example, after a discourse on why the thighs of gentlewomen are always cool (I.39); or in the much more complex instance of the birth of Gargantua (I.6), which can be shown to satirize the official doctrine according to which faith consisted in assent to a set of beliefs prescribed by the Church, in favour of the evangelical understanding of faith as confidence in God's limitless power. In this last example, a theological position which, in Rabelais's day, was more than a matter of life and death (since salvation was believed to depend on it), emerges into the light of day after a journey through the body *in exactly the opposite direction* to the one expected, as if reflecting the violent imaginative effort required by this inversion of perspective. The comedy in such cases is not a thin veneer or a sugaring of the pill; it is the heuristic vehicle of a new insight.

The demolition of monastic walls and other limits in the Theleme episode is a further effect of the unbinding power of the comic imagination. If Rabelais in this instance creates his own division between the select band admitted to the Abbey and those kept out, that is a temporary strategy due to the utopian nature of the episode. Humankind, by and large, is not capable of using that degree of freedom properly, so that the ideal can only be demonstrated at the expense of the very principle the work as a whole most consistently promotes. In the Third Book, we are back in the ordinary mixed world, where the distinctly un-utopian Panurge precisely fails to see how to use his freedom of choice. Freedom, the crossing of barriers, the attempt to see things whole, is never naively presented as a panacea: it makes things more complicated, but the complication is of the essence of mixed human experience.

It is therefore not inconsistent that, in the later books, the exuberantly untrammelled activities of the giants should give way to the search, above all, for a balance amid the many varieties of excess. This theme is prominently advertised in the prologue to the Fourth Book by the Aesopic fable of the woodcutter who loses his axe, and runs as a linking thread through the series of episodes where grotesque images of fasting and feasting are set in opposition to one another. The sequence is crowned by the wonderful episode off the island of Chaneph where Pantagruel answers the futile abstract questions posed by his crew by offering them a copious but frugal feast. What is achieved here is the immensely difficult balance of moderation: moderation not as dull neutrality but as an unbinding of all the energies of body and mind. Thus it is that, as the friends raise their glasses, the wind rises again, the dead calm is broken, and the voyage proceeds under the sign of a winged Bacchus (IV.63–5).

*

Those strange, brilliantly inventive frescoes of the 1552 Fourth Book may well be the last thing Rabelais ever wrote: they certainly contain, in compressed and often enigmatic forms, the quintessence of his creative and moral imagination. At the centre of their thematic tapestry is, once again, language, the medium from which Rabelais drew his power, the medium he loved and explored and turned inside out from one end of his career to the other; the medium, too, within which all barriers may be dissolved and a precarious poetic balance achieved.

It is not difficult to substantiate a reading of the whole work as a reflection on the powers and deficiencies of language, which includes here the use of non-verbal signs. Language, as Rabelais represents it, is ambivalent: on the one hand, it is an endlessly rich mode of communication, a vast reservoir of possible meanings, and a kaleidoscopic instrument for playing with the world; on the other, it may prove dangerously deceptive (as in Panurge's speech on debt), or be degraded (as by scholastics like Janotus de Bragmardo), or simply give out in the face of mysteries too great for it to express. Often, indeed, Rabelais seems to be showing us not only how to use language but also when to recognize that it is superfluous.

This ambivalence is clearly present in the polyglot episode mentioned earlier (II.9), since what Panurge says, in all those incomprehensible languages, is that it should not be necessary for him to speak at all: he visibly needs help – especially food and drink – and Pantagruel's questions are premature if not wholly irrelevant. The Second Book also contains a disputation by signs (chapters 18–20); another occurs in the Third Book (19–20), and in this instance Pantagruel provides a learned gloss on the nature of language itself. More generally, Rabelais's writings again and again exhibit obscure or ambivalent pieces of language, or phenomena which the characters or the reader or both are required to interpret. The First Book begins with a corrupt and obscure poem and ends with an enigma; the Third Book reiterates a question to which a large number of ambivalent replies are given; and the 'frozen words' episode (IV.55–6) dramatizes the very substance of language, sounds that, before they can mean anything, are a rich and strange experience of the senses. This crucial theme can be shown to carry with it a profound reflection on language, derived from both scholastic and humanist traditions and ultimately traceable to Plato and Aristotle.[4] One need only note here that language is indeed, for Rabelais, both medium and message, and that if his work has an ultimate, all-inclusive coherence, it must lie in the inextricable interweaving of the two.

Finally, it is no accident that Pantagruel, in answering his friends off the island of Chaneph, chooses to use not words, but a feast offered explicitly as a speaking sign (see his speech at the end of IV.63). Imagery of the feast or banquet is endemic in Rabelais's work, from the rustic feast of the First Book via the dinner-party given by Grangousier during the Picrocholine war and the symposium laid on by Pantagruel for Panurge in the Third Book to the feasts and anti-feasts of the Fourth Book. In the banquet, the physical and the intellectual are ideally mingled: tongue, lips and teeth both take in food and drink and articulate words.[5] The paradigm of the banquet comes from a venerable tradition of high culture: Plato's *Symposium* and its later Greek descendants such as Plutarch's table-talk were immensely influential in the High Renaissance, and Erasmus' experiments in the genre were among the finest things he ever wrote. Yet this strand merges with an earthier evocation of non-learned feasting, like the *déjeuner sur l'herbe* in the First Book: even Pantagruel's feast at Chaneph retains some of that rustic character, since it seems to consist principally of four huge pies, fruit and of course drink.[6] However the banquet is presented, it remains an inclusive paradigm of human behaviour in which friendship, goodwill, freedom from repressive rules, bodily welfare and the spontaneous exchange of language are brought together. It is in fact a secular sacrament, as Panurge reminds the company in IV.65.

*

No amount of commentary will ever exhaust the sense of Rabelais's work. Words, here again, prove inadequate to do justice to one of the most extraordinary verbal constructions ever produced. In any case, Rabelais shared his contemporaries' distaste for excessive commentary, which he liked to equate with excrement. For most readers, the detailed sense of this, that or the other allusion will matter less than the irresistible dynamism of the text, its capacity to do things with words.

But perhaps it is important to repeat that it isn't just a word-game, and that the reader is not quite free to do what he or she likes with it. It is certainly an open work, which has been read productively in many different ways; it is not didactic, still less authoritarian. Yet it is also traversed by powerful signs of commitment: Rabelais clearly cared deeply about all the issues he touched on. Many of his implied views may seem to us dated, irrelevant, or even offensive: for example, women readers may legitimately feel that Panurge's sadistic treatment of the Parisian lady (II.21-2) is presented by the text in a shockingly indulgent way, and that elsewhere Rabelais seems either deeply uninterested in women or at best,

INTRODUCTION

as in the question of marriage in the Third Book, patronizing. Rabelais's work none the less provides a model in which the overall combination of moral seriousness and openness doesn't depend on any particular view that may be attributed to him. Differences of response of the kind just referred to are historically inevitable, and it should not be assumed that the moral advantage is always on our side. Rabelais is a stranger from another world who speaks a language only just comprehensible to us and whose customs and beliefs are not ours; but this stranger presents us with a propitiatory gift: a living encyclopedia of his culture which can also, if we let it, challenge all the things we ourselves take too much for granted.

Terence Cave

NOTES

1. See below, Bibliography, 'Modern Translations'.
2. Auerbach's essay is listed below in the Bibliography, 'Critical and Historical Studies', together with the other studies referred to in these footnotes.
3. See M. A. Screech, *Rabelais*, pp. 247–50, 265–77.
4. See Screech, *Rabelais*, pp. 377–97, 410–39; also M. Jeanneret, *A Feast of Words*.
5. See Jeanneret, *A Feast of Words*, *passim*.
6. The reference to 'the long train of dishes that came after [the pies]' is an invention of Urquhart's.

SELECT BIBLIOGRAPHY

THE FRENCH TEXT

The following two editions of the complete works of Rabelais are convenient to use:

Œuvres complètes, 2 vols., ed. Pierre Jourda, Garnier, Paris, 1962.

Œuvres complètes, ed. Guy Demerson and others, Seuil, Paris, 1973.

In the second of these, a version in modern French is provided, together with the original text, in parallel columns.

For more advanced study, it is advisable to consult the scholarly editions of the first four books available in the *Textes littéraires français* series (Droz, Geneva) as follows: *Pantagruel*, ed. Verdun Louis Saulnier (1946); *Gargantua*, ed. Ruth Calder and M. A. Screech (1970); *Le Tiers Livre*, ed. M. A. Screech (1964); *Le Quart Livre*, ed. Robert Marichal (1947).

MODERN TRANSLATIONS

Gargantua and Pantagruel, trans. J. M. Cohen, Penguin Classics, first published 1955.

Gargantua and Pantagruel, trans. Burton Raffel, Norton, New York and London, 1990.

The Complete Works of François Rabelais, trans. Donald M. Frame, University of California Press, Berkeley, Los Angeles and Oxford, 1991.

The last of these is to be recommended not only because it contains the complete works but also because the translator was an internationally renowned specialist in French Renaissance studies.

CRITICAL AND HISTORICAL STUDIES IN ENGLISH

AUERBACH, ERICH, *Mimesis: The Representation of Reality in Western Literature*, trans. Willard Trask, chapter 11, 'The World in Pantagruel's Mouth'. First published in German in 1946; first published in this translation by Princeton University Press in 1953; widely available in paperback.

BAKHTIN, MIKHAIL, *Rabelais and His World*, trans. Hélène Iswolsky, first published in Russian in 1965; this translation published by the MIT Press in 1968.

BERRONG, RICHARD, *Rabelais and Bakhtin: Popular Culture in 'Gargantua and Pantagruel'*, University of Nebraska Press, Lincoln and London, 1986. This is included less on its own merits than because it launches a full-scale attack on Bakhtin's interpretation.

BURKE, PETER, *Popular Culture in Early Modern Europe*, New York University Press, 1978 (also available in paperback).

CLARK, CAROL, *The Vulgar Rabelais*, Pressgang, Glasgow, 1983.

COLEMAN, DOROTHY GABE, *Rabelais: A Critical Study in Prose Fiction*, Cambridge University Press, 1971.

FEBVRE, LUCIEN, *The Problem of Unbelief in the Sixteenth Century: The Religion of Rabelais*, trans. Beatrice Gottlieb. First published in French in 1942, reprinted 1968; this translation published by Harvard University Press in 1982.

JEANNERET, MICHEL, *A Feast of Words: Banquets and Table Talk in the Renaissance*, trans. Jeremy Whiteley and Emma Hughes. First published in French in 1987; this translation published by Polity Press in 1991.

KAISER, WALTER, *Praisers of Folly: Erasmus, Rabelais, Shakespeare*, Harvard University Press, Cambridge, Mass., 1963.

SCREECH, M. A., *Rabelais*, Duckworth, London, 1979 (also available in paperback). This comprehensive study of the First to the Fourth Books is by far the best and most reliable guide to the understanding of Rabelais's works in the intellectual and religious context of their age.

CHRONOLOGY

DATE	AUTHOR'S LIFE	LITERARY CONTEXT
1470		
1483	Conjectural date of Rabelais's birth. His father, Antoine Rabelais, was a lawyer from Chinon in the Loire valley. Rabelais's name is particularly associated with the family farmhouse at La Devinière.	First French edition of Boccaccio's *Decameron*.
1492		
1494	Possible alternative date for Rabelais's birth.	Sebastian Brant: *Ship of Fools*.
1506		Johann Reuchlin: *De Rudimentis Hebraicis*.
1510–11	Having previously studied law, Rabelais enters the order of the Observantine Franciscans at the monastery of Le Puy Saint-Martin in Fontenay-le-Comte, where he remains until 1526.	Erasmus: *Praise of Folly* (1511).
1513		
1515		
1516		Sir Thomas More: *Utopia*. Erasmus: Greek New Testament; *Colloquia*; *The Education of a Christian Prince*. Ludovico Ariosto: *Orlando Furioso*. Niccolò Machiavelli: *Art of War*; *Life of Castruccio Castricanie*.
1517		
1518		
1519		
1520–21	Rabelais corresponds with the leading French humanist Guillaume Budé; his first extant letter, in Latin and containing a good deal of Greek, is dated March 1521.	Martin Luther: treatises on *Christian Liberty*, *The Reformation of the Christian Estate*, and *The Babylonian Captivity of the Church* (1520).

First printing press in Paris.

Death of Louis XI; succession of Charles VIII (to 1498). In England, death of Edward IV and murder of the young Edward V and his brother; Richard III becomes king.

Columbus' first landfall in the New World. Conquest of Granada by Ferdinand V.

Charles VIII invades Italy.

Pierre Gringore's tetralogy, *Le Jeu du Prince des Sots et Mère Sotte* plays at Paris on Shrove Tuesday, 1511, with the sanction of Louis XII; the Pope held up to open ridicule.

English army under Henry VIII invades France.

Accession of François I, King of France. French army defeats Swiss at Marignano and captures Milan.

French Concordat with Leo X; Pope grants French king right of nomination to senior ecclesiastical appointments.

Luther makes public his 95 theses against indulgences.

Zwingli becomes people's priest at Zürich.

Charles V elected Holy Roman Emperor in preference to François I and Henry VIII of England.

Luther excommunicated. Field of Cloth of Gold – meeting of François I and Henry VIII. François I founds Bibliothèque royale. Magellan discovers Chile (1520). Diet of Worms; Luther placed under the Ban of the Empire; his writings condemned by the Sorbonne. Occupation of Milan by the forces of Charles V and Leo X (1521).

DATE	AUTHOR'S LIFE	LITERARY CONTEXT
1521–5		
1522		Birth of Joachim Du Bellay. Luther's translation of the New Testament. Huldreich Zwingli: *Archeteles*.
1523		Lefèvre d'Etaples' French translation of the New Testament.
1523–4	Rabelais's Greek studies are clearly advanced: he has translated the first book of Herodotus into Latin, and is also engaged in translating Lucian into Latin. This activity attracts official censure: Rabelais's friend Pierre Amy, who shares his interests, is forced to flee the monastery, and Rabelais changes orders to become a Benedictine at Saint-Pierre-de-Maillezais.	
1524		Birth of Pierre de Ronsard.
1524–5		
1524–6	Under the protection of bishop Geoffroy d'Estissac, Rabelais is able to continue his studies and has greater freedom of movement.	
1525		William Tyndale's English translation of the New Testament printed in Cologne.
1526	Rabelais leaves Poitou and appears to have abandoned holy orders. He may have studied medicine in Paris between 1526 and 1530, and it is probably at this time too that he becomes the father of two illegitimate children, François and Junie, legitimized by the Pope in 1540.	
1527		Death of Machiavelli.

CHRONOLOGY

Bishop Briçonnet, assisted by other French reformers, attempts a programme of moderate reform in his diocese at Meaux, eventually suppressed by the Sorbonne.
Spanish conquest of Mexico completed. Rhodes falls to Turks.

Election of Guilio de' Medici as Clement VII. First public disputation at Zürich; Zwingli's ministry endorsed; programme of Reformation in Switzerland begins.

The Pope and Henry VIII persuade Erasmus to attack Luther on question of free will; Luther replies. Peasant uprisings in Germany.

Defeat of French by army of Charles V at Battle of Pavia; François I taken prisoner.

François I released, but royal children retained as hostages until 1530.
Capuchin Order founded (reformed branch of the Franciscans).

Marguerite d'Angoulême, sister of François I, widowed; marries Henri, King of Navarre. The Västerås Recess establishes Protestant Church in Sweden.

xliii

DATE	AUTHOR'S LIFE	LITERARY CONTEXT
1528		Baldassare Castiglione: *The Courtier*. Erasmus: *Ciceronianus*.
1529		Guillaume Budé: *Commentarii linguae graecae*. Luther's *Catechism*.
1530s and 1540s		Circle of French court writers active under patronage of Marguerite de Navarre, producing poetry, collections of stories, and translations; these include Clément Marot, Bonaventure des Périers, Antoine Héroët, and Marguerite herself.
1530	Rabelais matriculates as a medical student at Montpellier, becoming a bachelor of medicine only two months later.	Tyndale: *The Practice of Prelates*. Zwingli: *De providentia Dei*; *Fidei ratio*.
1531	Rabelais lectures at Montpellier on Hippocrates and Galen.	Machiavelli's *Discourses* published. Sir Thomas Elyot: *The Book of the Governour*. Erasmus: *Apophthegmata*.
1532	Rabelais acts in a farce in Montpellier; publishes editions of various medical works; and publishes his *Pantagruel*, first printed at Lyons. In November, he takes up a post as physician at the Hôtel-Dieu in Lyons; he writes a celebrated letter to Erasmus; and publishes his *Pantagrueline Prognostication* for the year 1533.	Machiavelli's *The Prince* and *The History of Florence* published. Jean Calvin publishes his first work, a commentary on Seneca's *De Clementia*.
1533	Rabelais publishes an expanded edition of *Pantagruel*; also a *Pantagrueline Prognostication* for 1534.	Birth of Michel de Montaigne.
1534	Rabelais travels to Rome for about three months with bishop Jean Du Bellay and works on a topography of ancient Rome. His second comic book, *Gargantua*, appears to date from this year or	Luther completes German translation of the Old Testament. Pietro Aretino: *The Courtesan*.

xliv

CHRONOLOGY

HISTORICAL EVENTS

Sack of Rome by Imperial forces.

Louis de Berquin burnt at the stake for heresy.

François I establishes *lecteurs royaux* in Paris against opposition from the Sorbonne. Diet of Augsburg; Melanchthon draws up Confession of Augsburg, an attempt to conciliate German Catholics and Protestants.

Henry VIII appoints himself head of Anglican Church. Beginning of period of relative success of 'evangelicals' in France, protected by Marguerite de Navarre. Death of Zwingli at the Battle of Kappel.

Alliance of France and England. Jean Du Bellay, moderate reformer, becomes Bishop of Paris. Religious Peace of Nürnberg. Inquisition first established in Lisbon. Conquest of Peru.

Marriage of Henry VIII and Anne Boleyn. The future Henri II marries Catherine de' Medici. Nicolas Cop, Rector of the Sorbonne, publicly expounds doctrine of Justification by Faith in a discourse written by Calvin; François I enjoins the *Parlement* to proceed against the 'accursed heretic Lutheran sect'.
Persecutions cease while François I negotiates alliance with German Protestant Princes; Guillaume Du Bellay in conference with Melanchthon. October: 'Affaire des placards'; temporary repression and flight of evangelicals. Twenty-three burnt for heresy 1534–5. Calvin leaves France, settling in Basel. Ignatius Loyola founds the Society of Jesus (Jesuits) in Paris.

DATE	AUTHOR'S LIFE	LITERARY CONTEXT
1534 *cont.*	possibly early in 1535. A *Pantagrueline Prognostication* for 1535 and an *Almanach pour l'an 1535* also appear.	
1535	Conjectural date of death of Rabelais's father and birth of his son Théodule. He leaves his post at the Hôtel-Dieu in Lyons, and travels to Rome again with Jean Du Bellay. He obtains papal absolution for his 'apostasy' in leaving holy orders without permission.	
1536	Rabelais becomes a secular priest at Jean Du Bellay's abbey at Saint-Maur-les-Fossés when the abbey itself is secularized.	Calvin: *Christianae religionis institutio.* Death of Erasmus. Marot: French translation of the Psalms.
1537	Rabelais visits Paris, then Montpellier, where he obtains his doctorate in medicine and lectures on Hippocrates.	
1539		Calvin: *Letter to Cardinal Sadoleto; Commentary on the Romans.*
1540		
1540–42	Rabelais spends much of this period in Turin and elsewhere in Piedmont assisting his patron Guillaume Du Bellay, seigneur de Langey, the governor of Piedmont.	
1541		
1542		
1543	Death of Guillaume Du Bellay, also of Geoffroy d'Estissac. The Sorbonne draws up a list of books to be censored, including *Gargantua* and *Pantagruel*.	
1544	The Sorbonne's list of censorable books is sent to the printers, but is not published until 1545.	Death of Marot.

HISTORICAL EVENTS

French negotiations with Protestant Princes resume; Guillaume Du Bellay in Germany. Execution of Sir Thomas More in England.

War between France and the Empire. Dissolution of the Monasteries begins in England.

Papal commission reports on need for reform in the Church, ('Consilium delectorum Cardinalium de emendanda Ecclesia'). Danish Church becomes Protestant.

François I issues Edict of Fontainebleau against heretics. Calvin settles permanently in Geneva. Society of Jesus authorized by papal bull.

First French edition of Calvin's *Institutes of the Christian Religion*. Copernicus publishes *De revolutionibus orbium coelestium*, putting forward the theory that the earth and planets revolve around the sun.
Bull *Licet initio* sets up a Roman Inquisition.

Confiscated copies of Calvin's *Institutes* publicly burnt. Peace of Crépy between France and the Empire.

DATE	AUTHOR'S LIFE	LITERARY CONTEXT
1545	Jean Du Bellay's secretary François Bribart is burned at the stake. François I grants a royal privilege for Rabelais's *Tiers Livre* (Third Book).	New French translation of Boccaccio's *Decameron* by Antoine Le Maçon.
1546	The *Tiers Livre* is printed several times, but is included in a new list of censorable books. Rabelais goes to Metz, perhaps to avoid condemnation.	
1547	Rabelais travels to Rome, where he remains, presumably with Jean Du Bellay, until 1549.	First published poem by Ronsard.
1548	The first (partial) version of the *Quart Livre* (Fourth Book) is printed twice.	Ignatius Loyola: *Spiritual Exercises*.
1549	Rabelais composes a *Sciomachie* ('Shadow Battle') describing the festivities arranged by Du Bellay in Rome for the birth of Henri II's second son. Rabelais returns to France.	Joachim Du Bellay: *Deffence et illustration de la langue françoyse* (programme for renewal of French poetry); *Olive* (cycle of love sonnets).
1550	Rabelais spends a few months at Saint-Maur. He obtains the protection of Cardinal Odet de Châtillon, and a royal privilege is granted for all his works.	Ronsard: four books of *Odes*.
1551	Rabelais obtains two benefices, one at Meudon, the other at Saint-Christophe-du-Jambet.	
1552	The *Quart Livre* is published in expanded form, but is condemned soon afterwards.	Ronsard: *Amours* (cycle of love sonnets).
1553	Rabelais resigns his benefices; he dies not long afterwards (early March?).	
1555		
1556		
1558		Marguerite de Navarre's *Heptameron* first printed posthumously.

CHRONOLOGY

Massacre of the Waldenses of Provence. Council of Trent assembles (further sessions, with many interruptions, until 1564).

Death of Luther. Etienne Dolet, leading French humanist and printer, burnt at stake. Execution of the 'Fourteen of Meaux', reformers who had established their own church.

Death of François I, accession of Henri II. Special criminal court created for the trial of heretics; condemns to death at least one hundred people in two years (becomes known as *La Chambre Ardente*). In England, death of Henry VIII and accession of Edward IV.
Betrothal of Mary Stuart to the Dauphin, François (married 1558). First Prayer Book of Edward IV.

Death of Marguerite de Navarre. War between France and England (to 1550). The anti-Lutheran *Consensus Tigurinus* of Calvin and Bullinger unites Protestant Switzerland.

Treaty of Chambord between Henri II and German Protestant Princes. French invasion of Lorraine and occupation of the bishoprics of Metz, Toul and Verdun.
Execution of the 'Five Scholars of Lausanne'. Accession of Mary Tudor in England.

First Protestant Church established in Paris, followed by many others throughout France (1555–8), largely under Calvin's supervision. Renewed persecution of Protestants. Religious Peace of Augsburg in Germany. In England, Bishops Cranmer, Latimer and Ridley burnt at the stake as heretics.
Abdication of Charles V.
Accession of Elizabeth I in England.

DATE	AUTHOR'S LIFE	LITERARY CONTEXT
1559		
1560		
1562		
1564	The Fifth Book, of uncertain authenticity, is published (chapters 1–8, a fragment known as 'The Ringing Island', date from 1562).	
1653	Sir Thomas Urquhart's translation of the First and Second Books appears.	
1693	Urquhart's translation of the Third Book.	
1694	Pierre Le Motteux's translation of the Fourth and Fifth Books.	

1

CHRONOLOGY

HISTORICAL EVENTS

First Protestant Synod at Paris. Treaty of Cateau-Cambrésis; Henri II
killed in tournament, accession of François II.
Death of François II, accession of Charles IX.
Beginning of French wars of religion.
Death of Calvin.

The Lives, Heroick Deeds,
and sayings of

GARGANTUA

and his son

PANTAGRUEL

CONTENTS

THE FIRST BOOK

CONTENTS

CONTENTS

5

CONTENTS

THE SECOND BOOK

CONTENTS

7

CONTENTS

THE THIRD BOOK

CONTENTS

CONTENTS

CONTENTS

THE FOURTH BOOK

CONTENTS

CONTENTS

13

CONTENTS

THE FIFTH BOOK

CONTENTS

15

CONTENTS

THE FIRST BOOK

THE INESTIMABLE LIFE OF THE GREAT GARGANTUA, FATHER OF PANTAGRUEL, HERETOFORE COMPOSED BY M. ALCOFRIBAS,* ABSTRACTOR OF THE QUINTESSENCE, A BOOK FULL OF PANTAGRUELISM

* *Alcofribas Nasier*, anagram of François Rabelais

THE AUTHORS PROLOGUE

MOST Noble and Illustrious Drinkers, and you thrice precious Pockified blades, (for to you, and none else do I dedicate my writings) *Alcibiades*, in that Dialogue of *Plato's*, which is entituled *The Banquet*, whil'st he was setting forth the praises of his Schoolmaster *Socrates* (without all question the Prince of Philosophers) amongst other discourses to that purpose said, that he resembled the *Silenes*. *Silenes* of old were little boxes, like those we now may see in the shops of Apothecaries, painted on the outside with wanton toyish figures, as *Harpyes, Satyrs, bridled Geese, horned Hares, saddled Ducks, flying Goats, Thiller Harts*, and other suchlike counterfeted pictures at discretion, to excite people unto laughter, as *Silenus* himself, who was the foster-father of good *Bacchus*, was wont to do; but within those capricious caskets were carefully preserved and kept many rich jewels, and fine drugs, such as *Balme, Ambergreece, Amamon, Musk, Civet*, with several kindes of precious stones, and other things of great price. Just such another thing was *Socrates*, for to have eyed his outside, and esteemed of him by his exterior appearance, you would not have given the peel of an Oinion for him, so deformed he was in body, and ridiculous in his gesture: he had a sharp pointed nose, with the look of a Bull, and countenance of a foole: he was in his carriage simple, boorish in his apparel, in fortune poore, unhappy in his wives, unfit for all offices in the Common-wealth, alwayes laughing, tipling, and merrily carousing to every one, with continual gybes and jeeres, the better by those meanes to conceale his divine knowledge: now opening this boxe you would have found within it a heavenly and inestimable drug, a more then humane understanding, an admirable vertue, matchlesse learning, invincible courage, unimitable sobriety, certaine contentment of minde, perfect assurance, and an incredible misregard of all that, for which men commonly do so much watch, run, saile, fight, travel, toyle and turmoile themselves.

Whereunto (in your opinion) doth this little flourish of a preamble tend? For so much as you, my good disciples, and some other jolly fooles of ease and leasure, reading the pleasant titles of some books of our invention, as *Gargantua, Pantagruel, Whippot*,* the dignity of Cod-peeces, of Peas and Bacon with a Commentary, etc., are too ready to judge, that there is nothing in them but jests, mockeries, lascivious discourse, and recreative lies; because the outside (which is the title) is usually (without any farther enquiry) entertained with scoffing and derision: but truly it is very unbeseeming to make so light account of the works of men, seeing your selves avouch that it is not the habit makes the Monk, many being Monasterially accoutred, who inwardly are nothing less then monachal, and that there are of those that weare *Spanish* caps, who have but little of the valour of *Spaniards* in them. Therefore is it, that you must open the book, and seriously consider of the matter treated in it, then shall you finde that it containeth things of farre higher value then the boxe did promise; that is to say, that the subject thereof is not so foolish, as by the Title at the first sight it would appear to be.

And put the case that in the literal sense, you meet with purposes merry and solacious enough, and consequently very correspondent to their inscriptions, yet must not you stop there as at the melody of the charming Syrens, but endeavour to interpret that in a sublimer sense, which possibly you intended to have spoken in the jollitie of your heart; did you ever pick the lock of a cupboard to steal a bottle of wine out of it? Tell me truly, and if you did call to minde the countenance which then you had? or, did you ever see a Dog with a marrow-bone in his mouth, (the beast of all other, saies *Plato, lib*. 2, *de Republica*, the most Philosophical). If you have seene him, you might have remarked with what devotion and circumspectnesse he wards and watcheth it; with what care he keeps it: how fervently he holds it: how prudently he gobbets it: with what affection he breaks it: and with what diligence he sucks it: To what end all this?

* Sessepinet.

what moveth him to take all these paines? what are the hopes of his labour? what doth he expect to reap thereby? nothing but a little marrow: True it is, that this little is more savoury and delicious than the great quantities of other sorts of meat, because the marrow (as Galen *testifieth*, 3. *facult. nat.* and II *de usu partium*) is a nourishment most perfectly elaboured by nature.

In imitation of this Dog, it becomes you to be wise, to smell, feele and have in estimation these faire goodly books, stuffed with high conceptions, which though seemingly easie in the pursuit, are in the cope and encounter somewhat difficult; and then like him you must, by a sedulous Lecture, and frequent meditation break the bone, and suck out the marrow; that is, my allegorical sense, or the things I to my self propose to be signified by these *Pythagorical* Symbols, with assured hope, that in so doing, you will at last attaine to be both well-advised and valiant by the reading of them: for in the perusal of this Treatise, you shall finde another kinde of taste, and a doctrine of a more profound and abstruse consideration, which will disclose unto you the most glorious Sacraments, and dreadful mysteries, as well in what concerneth your Religion, as matters of the publike State, and Life œconomical.

Do you beleeve upon your conscience, that *Homer* whil'st he was a couching his *Iliads* and *Odysses*, had any thought upon those Allegories, which *Plutarch, Heraclides, Ponticus, Fristatius, Cornutus* squeesed out of him, and which *Politian* filched againe from them: if you trust it, with neither hand nor foot do you come neare to my opinion, which judgeth them to have beene as little dreamed of by *Homer*, as the Gospel-sacraments were by *Ovid* in his *Metamorphosis*, though a certaine gulligut Fryer* and true bacon-picker would have undertaken to prove it, if perhaps he had met with as very fools as himself, (and as the Proverb saies) a lid worthy of such a kettle: if you give no credit thereto, why do not you the same in these jovial new chronicles of mine; albeit when I did dictate them, I thought upon no more then you, who possibly were drinking (the whil'st) as I was; for in the composing of this lordly book, I never lost nor bestowed any more, nor any other time then what was appointed to serve

---

* Frere lubin croq. lardon.

me for taking of my bodily refection, that is, whil'st I was eating
and drinking. And indeed that is the fittest, and most proper
hour, wherein to write these high matters and deep Sciences: as
Homer knew very well, the Paragon of all Philologues, and *Ennius*,
the father of the Latine Poets (as *Horace* calls him) although a
certain sneaking jobernol alledged that his Verses smelled more
of the wine then oile.

So saith a *Turlupin* or a new start-up grub of my books, but
a turd for him. The fragrant odour of the wine; O how much
more dainty, pleasant, laughing,* celestial and delicious it is,
then that smell of oile! And I will glory as much when it is said
of me, that I have spent more on wine then oile, as did *Demosthenes*, when it was told him, that his expense on oile was greater
than on wine; I truly hold it for an honour and praise to be called
and reputed a frolick *Gualter*, and a Robin goodfellow; for under
this name am I welcome in all choise companies of *Pantagruelists*: it was upbraided to *Demosthenes* by an envious surly knave,
that his Orations did smell like the sarpler or wrapper of a foul
and filthy oile-vessel; for this cause interpret you all my deeds
and sayings in the perfectest sense; reverence the cheese-like
brain that feeds you with these faire billevezees, and trifling
jollities, and do what lies in you to keep me alwayes merry. Be
frolick now my lads, cheer up your hearts, and joyfully read the
rest, with all the ease of your body and profit of your reines; but
hearken joltheads, you viedazes, or dickens take ye, remember
to drink a health to me for the like favour again, and I will
pledge you instantly, *Tout ares metys*.

* Riant, priant, friand.

RABELAIS
TO THE READER

Good friends, my Readers, who peruse this Book,
Be not offended, whil'st on it you look:
Denude your selves of all deprav'd affection,
For it containes no badnesse, nor infection:
'Tis true that it brings forth to you no birth
Of any value, but in point of mirth;
Thinking therefore how sorrow might your minde
Consume, I could no apter subject finde;
  One inch of joy surmounts of grief a span;
  Because to laugh, is proper to the man.

THE FIRST BOOK

CHAPTER I

Of the Genealogy and Antiquity of Gargantua.

I MUST referre you to the Great Chronicle of *Pantagruel* for the knowledge of that Genealogy, and Antiquity of race by which *Gargantua* is come unto us; in it you may understand more at large how the Giants were born in this world, and how from them by a direct line issued *Gargantua* the father of *Pantagruel*: and do not take it ill, if for this time I passe by it, although the subject be such, that the oftener it were remembered, the more it would please your worshipful *Seniorias*; according to which you have the authority of *Plato* in *Philebo* and *Gorgias*; and *Flaccus*, who saies that there are some kindes of purposes (such as these are without doubt) which the frequentlier they be repeated, still prove the more delectable.

Would to God every one had as certaine knowledge of his Genealogy since the time of the Arke of *Noah* untill this age. I think many are at this day Emperours, Kings, Dukes, Princes, and Popes on the earth, whose extraction is from some porters, and pardon-pedlars, as on the contrary, many are now poor wandring beggars, wretched and miserable, who are descended of the blood and lineage of great Kings and Emperours, occasioned (as I conceive it) by the transport and revolution of Kingdomes and Empires, from the *Assyrians* to the *Medes*, from the *Medes* to the *Persians*, from the *Persians* to the *Macedonians*, from the *Macedonians* to the *Romans*, from the *Romans* to the *Greeks*, from the *Greeks* to the *French*, & c.

And to give you some hint concerning my self, who speaks unto you, I cannot think but I am come of the race of some rich King or Prince in former times, for never yet saw you any man that had a greater desire to be a King, and to be rich, then I have, and that onely that I may make good chear, do nothing, nor care

RABELAIS

for any thing, and plentifully enrich my friends, and all honest and learned men: but herein do I comfort myself, that in the other world I shall be so, yea and greater too then at this present I dare wish: as for you, with the same or a better conceit consolate your selves in your distresses, and drink fresh if you can come by it.

To returne to our wethers, I say, that by the sovereign gift of heaven, the Antiquity and Genealogy of *Gargantua* hath been reserved for our use more full and perfect then any other except that of the *Messias*, whereof I mean not to speak; for it belongs not unto my purpose, and the Devils (that is to say) the false accusers, and dissembled gospellers will therein oppose me. This Genealogy was found by *John Andrew* in a meadow, which he had near the Pole-arch, under the Olive-tree, as you go to *Marsay*: where, as he was making cast up some ditches, the diggers with their mattocks struck against a great brazen tomb, and unmeasurably long, for they could never finde the end thereof, by reason that it entered too farre within the Sluces of *Vienne*; opening this Tomb in a certain place thereof, sealed on the top with the mark of a goblet, about which was written in *Hetrurian* letters HIC BIBITUR; They found nine Flaggons set in such order as they use to ranke their kyles in *Gasgonie*, of which that which was placed in the middle, had under it a big, fat, great, gray, pretty, small, mouldy, little pamphlet, smelling stronger, but no better than roses. In that book the said Genealogy was found written all at length, in a Chancery hand, not in paper, not in parchment, nor in wax, but in the bark of an elme-tree, yet so worne with the long tract of time, that hardly could three letters together be there perfectly discerned.

I (though unworthy) was sent for thither, and with much help of those Spectacles, whereby the art of reading dim writings, and letters that do not clearly appear to the sight, is practised, as *Aristotle* teacheth it, did translate the book as you may see in your *pantagruelising*, that is to say, in drinking stiffly to your own hearts desire; and reading the dreadful and horrifick acts of *Pantagruel*: at the end of the book there was a little Treatise entituled the *Antidoted Fanfreluches*, or a *Galimatia* of extravagant conceits. The rats and mothes or (that I may not lie) other wicked beasts, had nibled off the beginning, the rest I have hereto subjoyned, for the reverence I beare to antiquity.

CHAPTER II

*The Antidoted Fanfreluches: Or, A Galimatia of extravagant
conceits found in an ancient Monument.*

No sooner did the Cymbrians overcommer
Pass through the air to shun the dew of summer
But at his coming streight great tubs were fill'd
With pure fresh Butter down in showers distill'd,
Wherewith when water'd was his Grandam heigh.
Aloud he cryed, Fish it, Sir, I pray 'ye;
Because his beard is almost all beray'd,
Or that he would hold to 'm a scale he pray'd.

To lick his slipper, some told was much better,
Then to gaine pardons and the merit greater.
In th' interim a crafty chuff approaches,
From the depth issued, where they fish for Roches;
Who said, Good sirs, some of them let us save,
The Eele is here, and in this hollow cave
You'll finde, if that our looks on it demurre,
A great wast in the bottome of his furre.

To read this chapter when he did begin,
Nothing but a calves hornes were found therein;
I feel (quoth he) the Miter which doth hold
My head so chill, it makes my braines take cold.
Being with the perfume of a turnup warm'd,
To stay by chimney hearths himself he arm'd,
Provided that a new thill horse they made
Of every person of a hair-braind head.

They talked of the bunghole of Saint *Knowles*,
Of *Gilbathar* and thousand other holes;
If they might be reduc'd t' a scarry stuffe,
Such as might not be subject to the cough:
Since ev'ry man unseemly did it finde,
To see them gaping thus at ev'ry winde:
For, if perhaps they handsomely were clos'd,
For pledges they to men might be expos'd.

In this arrest by *Hercules* the Raven
Was flayd at her returne from *Lybia* haven.
Why am not I said *Minos* there invited,
Unlesse it be my self, not one's omitted:
And then it is their minde, I do no more
Of Frogs and Oysters send them any store;
In case they spare my life and prove but civil,
I give their sale of distaffs to the Devil.

To quell him comes *Q. B.* who limping frets
At the safe passe of trixie crackarets,
The boulter, the grand Cyclops cousin, those
Did massacre whil'st each one wip'd his nose:
Few ingles in this fallow ground are bred,
But on a tanners mill are winnowed:
Run thither all of you, th' alarmes sound clear,
You shall have more then you had the last year.

Short while thereafter was the bird of *Jove*
Resolv'd to speak, though dismal it should prove;
Yet was afraid, when he saw them in ire,
They should o'rthrow quite flat down dead th' empire
He rather chus'd the fire from heaven to steale,
To boats where were red Herrings put to sale;
Then to be calm 'gainst those who strive to brave us
And to the *Massorets* fond words enslave us.

All this at last concluded galantly,
In spight of *Ate* and Hern-like thigh,
Who sitting saw *Penthesilea* tane,
In her old age, for a cresse-selling quean;
Each one cry'd out, Thou filthy Collier toad,
Doth it become thee to be found abroad?
Thou has the *Roman* Standard filtch'd away,
Which they in rags of parchment did display.

Juno was borne who under the Rainbow,
Was a bird-catching with her Duck below:
When her with such a grievous trick they plyed,
That she had almost been bethwacked by it:

The bargain was that of that throatfull she
Should of *Proserpina* have two egges free;
And if that she thereafter should be found,
She to a Haw-thorn hill should be fast bound.

Seven moneths thereafter lacking twenty two,
He, that of old did *Carthage* town undo:
Did bravely midd'st them all himself advance,
Requiring of them his inheritance;
Although they justly made up the division,
According to the shoe-welt-lawes decision;
By distributing store of brews and beef,
To those poor fellows, that did pen the Brief.

But th' year will come signe of a Turkish Bowe,
Five spindles yarnd, and three pot-bottomes too,
Wherein of a discourteous King the dock
Shall pepper'd be under an Hermits frock,
Ah that for one she hypocrite you must
Permit so many acres to be lost:
Cease, cease, this vizard may become another,
Withdraw your selves unto the Serpents brother.

'Tis in times past, that he who is shall reigne
With his good friends in peace now and againe;
No rash nor heady Prince shall then rule crave,
Each good will its arbitrement shall have:
And the joy promised of old as doome
To the heavens guests, shall in its beacon come:
Then shall the breeding mares, that benumm'd were,
Like royall palfreys ride triumphant there.

And this continue shall from time to time,
Till *Mars* be fettred for an unknown crime.
Then shall one come who others will surpasse,
Delightful, pleasing, matchlesse, full of grace.
Chear up your hearts, approach to this repast,
All trusty friends of mine, for hee's deceast,
Who would not for a world return againe,
So highly shall time past be cri'd up then.

He who was made of waxe shall lodge each member
Close by the hinges of a block of timber:
We then no more shall *master master* whoot,
The swagger, who th' alarum bell holds out;
Could one seaze on the dagger which he bears,
Heads would be free from tingling in the eares,
To baffle the whole storehouse of abuses,
And thus farewell *Apollo* and the *Muses*.

CHAPTER III

*How Gargantua was carried
eleven moneths in his mothers belly.*

GRANGOUSIER was a good fellow in his time, and notable jester;
he loved to drink neat, as much as any man that then was in the
world, and would willingly eate salt meat: to this intent he was
ordinarily well furnished with gammons of Bacon, both of *Westphalia*, *Mayence* and *Bayone*; with store of dried Neats tongues,
plenty of Links, Chitterlings and Puddings in their season;
together with salt Beef and mustard, a good deale of hard rows
of powdered mullet called *Botargos*, great provision of Sauciges,
not of *Bolonia* (for he feared the Lombard boccone) but of *Bi-
gorre*, *Longaulnay*, *Brene*, and *Rouargue*. In the vigor of his age he
married *Gargamelle*, daughter to the King of the *Parpaillons*, a
jolly pug, and well mouthed wench. These two did often times
do the two backed beast together, joyfully rubbing & frotting
their Bacon 'gainst one another, insofarre, that at last she
became great with childe of a faire sonne, and went with him
unto the eleventh moneth, for so long, yea longer, may a woman
carry her great belly, especially when it is some master-piece of
nature, and a person predestinated to the performance, in his
due time, of great exploits; as *Homer* saies, that the childe,
which *Neptune* begot upon the *Nymph*, was borne a whole year
after the conception, that is, in the twelfth moneth; for, as *Aulus
Gellius* saith, *libr*. 3. this long time was suitable to the majesty
of *Neptune*, that in it the childe might receive his perfect forme:
for the like reason *Jupiter* made the night, wherein he lay with
Alcmena, last fourty eight houres, a shorter time not being

sufficient for the forging of *Hercules*, who cleansed the world of the Monstres and Tyrants, wherewith it was supprest. *My masters*, the ancient pantagruelists have confirmed that which I say, and withall declared it to be not onely possible, but also maintained the lawful birth and legitimation of the infant borne of a woman in the eleventh moneth after the decease of her husband. *Hypocrates, lib. de alimento. Plinius lib. 2. cap. 5. Plautus in his Cistellaria. Marcus Varo in his Satyr inscribed*, The Testament, alledging to this purpose the authority of *Aristotle. Censorinus lib. de die natali. Arist. lib. 2. cap. 3 & 4 de natura animalium. Gellius lib. 3. cap. 16. Servius* in his exposition upon this verse of *Virgils* Eclogues, *Matri longa decem, &c.* and a thousand other fooles whose number hath been increased by the Lawyers. *§. De suis et legit., l. Intestato, § fi., & in Autent., De restitut. et ea quæ parit in xj. mense*; moreover upon these grounds they have foysted in their *Robidilardick*, or *Lapiturolive* Law. *Gallus, §. De lib. et posthu., & l. septimo §. De stat. homi.* And some other Lawes, which at this time I dare not name; by means whereof the honest widows may without danger play at the close buttock game with might and maine, and as hard as they can for the space of the first two moneths after the decease of their husbands. I pray you, my good lusty springal lads, if you finde any of these females, that are worth the paines of untying the cod-peece-point, get up, ride upon them, and bring them to me; for if they happen within the third moneth to conceive, the childe shall be heire to the deceased, *if before he died he had no other children, and the mother shall passe for an honest woman*.

When she is known to have conceived, thrust forward boldly, spare her not, whatever betide you, seeing the paunch is full; as *Julia* the daughter of the Emperour *Octavian* never prostituted her self to her belly-bumpers, but when she found her self with childe, after the manner of Ships that receive not their steersman, till they have their ballast and lading; and if any blame them for this their rataconniculation, and reiterated lechery upon their pregnancy and big belledness, seeing beasts in the like exigent of their fullnesse, will never suffer the male-masculant to incroach them: their answer will be, that those are beasts, but they are women, very well skilled in the pretty vales, and small fees of the pleasant trade and mysteries of superfetation:

as *Populius* heretofore answered, according to the relation of *Macrobius lib*. 2. *Saturnal*. If the Devill would not have them to bagge, he must wring hard the spigot, and stop the bung-hole.

CHAPTER IV

How Gargamelle, being great with Gargantua,
did eate a huge deal of tripes.

THE occasion and manner how *Gargamelle* was brought to bed, and delivered of her childe, was thus: and, if you do not beleeve it, I wish your bum-gut fall out, and make an escapade. Her bum-gut, indeed, or fundament escaped her in an afternoone, on the third day of *February*, with having eaten at dinner too many *Godebillios*. *Godebillios* are the fat tripes of *coiros*, *coiros* are beeves fatned at the cratch in Oxe stalls, or in the fresh *guimo meadows*, *guimo meadows* are those, that for their fruitfulnesse may be mowed twice a yeare, and of those fat beeves they had killed three hundred sixty seven thousand and fourteen, to be salted at Shrovetide, that in the entring of the Spring they might have plenty of poudred beef, wherewith to season their mouths at the beginning of their meales, and to taste their wine the better.

They had abundance of tripes, as you have heard, and they were so delicious, that every one licked his fingers, but the mis-chiefe was this, that for all men could do, there was no poss-ibility to keep them long in that relish; for in a very short while they would have stunk, which had been an undecent thing: it was therefore concluded, that they should be all of them gulched up, without losing any thing; to this effect they invited all the Burguers of *Sainais*, of *Suille*, of the *Roche clermand*, of *Vau-gaudry*, without omitting the *Boudray*, *Monpensier*, the *Guedevede*, and other their neighbours, all stiffe drinkers, brave fellows, and good players at the kyles. The good man *Grangousier* took great pleasure in their company, and commanded there should be no want nor pinching for any thing: neverthelesse he bade his wife eate sparingly, because she was near her time, and that these tripes were no very commendable meat: they would faine (said he) be at the chewing of ordure, that would eat the case wherein it was.

Notwithstanding these admonitions, she did eate sixteen quarters, two bushels, three pecks and a pipkin full: O the fair fecality, wherewith she swelled by the ingrediency of such shitten stuffe; after dinner they all went out in a hurle, to the grove of the willows, where on the green grasse, to the sound of the merry Flutes and pleasant Bagpipes they danced so gallantly, that it was a sweet and heavenly sport to see them so frolick.

CHAPTER V

The discourse of the drinkers.

THEN did they fall upon the chat of victuals and some belly furniture to be snatched at in the very same place, which purpose was no sooner mentioned, but forthwith began flaggons to go, gammons to trot, goblets to fly, great bowles to ting, glasses to ring. Draw, reach, fill, mixe. Give it me without water, so my friend. So, whip me off this glasse neatly, bring me hither some claret, a full weeping glasse till it run over. A cessation and truce with thirst. Ha thou false Fever, wilt thou not be gone? By my figgins, god-mother, I cannot as yet enter in the humour of being merry, nor drink so currantly as I would. You have catch'd a cold, gamer. Yea forsooth Sir. By the belly of Sanct *Buf* let us talk of our drink. I never drink but at my hours, like the Popes Mule. And I never drink but in my breviary, like a faire father Gardien. Which was first, thirst or drinking? Thirst, for who in the time of innocence would have drunk without being athirst? Nay, Sir, it was drinking; for *privatio præsupponit habitum*. I am learned you see, *Fæcundi calices quem non fecere disertum?* We poor innocents drink but too much without thirst: not I truly, who am a sinner, for I never drink without thirst, either present or future, to prevent it, (as you know) I drink for the thirst to come; I drink eternally, this is to me an eternity of drinking, and drinking of eternity. Let us sing, let us drink, and tune up our round-lays. Where is my funnel? What, it seems I do not drink but by an Attourney? Do you wet your selves to dry, or do you dry to wet you? Pish, I understand not the Rhethorick (Theorick, I should say) but I help my self somewhat by the practice. *Baste* enough, I sup, I wet, I humect, I moisten my gullet, I drink, and all for fear of dying. Drink alwayes and you shall never die. If I drink not, I am a ground dry, gravelled and spent, I am stark dead without drink, and my soul ready to flie into some marish amongst Frogs; the soul never dwells in a dry place, drouth kills it. O you butlers, creators of new formes, make me of no drinker a drinker. A perennity and everlastingnesse of sprinkling, and bedewing me through these my parched and sinnewy bowels. He drinks in vaine that feels not the pleasure of it. This entereth into my veines, the pissing tooles and urinal vessels shall have nothing of it. I would willingly wash the tripes of the calf, which I apparelled this morning. I have pretty well now balasted my stomach, and stuft my paunch. If the papers of my bonds and bills could drink as well as I do, my creditors would not want for wine when they come to see me, or when they are to make any formal exhibition of their rights to what of me they can demand. This hand of yours spoyles your nose. O how many other such will enter here before this go out. What, drink so shallow, it is enough to break both girds and pettrel. This is called a cup of dissimulation, or flaggonal hypocrisie.

What difference is there between a bottle and a flaggon? Great difference, for the bottle is stopped and shut up with a stoppel, but the flaggon with a vice.* Bravely and well plaid apon the words. Our fathers drank lustily, and emptied their cans. Well cack'd, well sung; come let us drink. Will you send nothing to the river, here is one going to wash the tripes. I drink no more then a spunge. I drink like a Templer Knight. And I *tanquam sponsus*. And I *sicut terra sine aqua*. Give me a *synonymon* for a gammon of bacon? It is the compulsory of drinkers: it is a *pully*; by a *pully*-rope wine is let down into a *cellar*, and by a gammon into the stomach. Hei now boyes hither, some drink some drink, there is no trouble in it, *respice personam, pone pro duos, bus non est in usu*. If I could get up as well as I can swallow down, I had been long ere now very high in the aire.

Thus became *Tom tosse-pot* rich. Thus went in the Taylors stitch. Thus did *Bacchus* conquer th' inde. Thus Philosophy *Melinde*. A little raine allayes a great deale of winde: long tipling breaks the thunder. But if there came such liquor from my

* 'La bouteille est fermee à bouchon, et le flaccon à vis.'

ballock, would not you willingly thereafter suck the udder
whence it issued? Here, page, fill; I prethee, forget me not when
it comes to my turne, and I will enter the election I have made
of thee into the very register of my heart. Sup *Guillot*, and spare
not, there is yet somewhat in the pot. I appeale from thirst, and
disclaim its jurisdiction. *Page*, sue out my appeale in forme, this
remnant in the bottome of the glasse must follow its Leader. I
was wont heretofore to drink out all, but now I leave nothing.
Let us not make too much haste, it is requisite we carry all along
with us. Hey day, here are tripes fit for our sport, and in earnest
excellent *Godebillios* of the dun Oxe (you know) with the black
streak. O for Gods sake let us lash them soundly, yet thriftily.
Drink, or I will. No, no, drink, I beseech you. Sparrows will not
eate unlesse you bob them on the taile, nor can I drink if I be
not fairly spoke to. The concavities of my body are like another
Hell for their capacity. *Lagonædatera,** there is not a corner, nor
cunniborow in all my body where this wine doth not ferret out
my thirst. Ho, this will bang it soundly. But this shall banish it
utterly. Let us winde our hornes by the sound of flaggons and
bottles, and cry aloud, that whoever hath lost his thirst, come
not hither to seek it. Long clysters of drinking are to be voided
without doors. The great God made the *Planets*, and we make
the *platters* neat. I have the word of the Gospel in my mouth,
Sitio. The stone called *Asbestos*, is not more unquenchable, then
the thirst of my paternitie. Appetite comes with eating saies
Angeston, but the thirst goes away with drinking. I have a remedy against thirst, quite contrary to that which is good against the
biting of a mad dog. Keep running after a Dog, and he will never
bite you, drink alwayes before the thirst, & it wil never come
upon you. There I catch you, I awake you. *Argus* had a hundred
eyes for his sight, a butler should have (like *Briareus*) a hundred
hands wherewith to fill us wine indefatigably. Hey now lads, let
us moisten our selves, it will be time to dry hereafter. White
wine here, wine boyes, poure out all in the name of Lucifer, fill
here you, fill and fill (pescods on you) till it be full. My tongue
peels. *Lanstrinque*, to thee Countrèyman, I drink to thee good
fellow, camarade to thee, lustie, lively. Ha, la, la, that was drunk

* Λαγών, *lateris cavitas:* ἀίδης, *orcus:* and ἕτερος, *alter.*

35

to some purpose, and bravely gulped over. O *lachryma Christi*. It
is of the best grape; I, faith, pure *Greek*, *Greek*. O the fine white
wine, upon my conscience it is a kinde of taffatas wine. *Hin, hin*,
it is of one eare, well wrought, and of good wooll. Courage, camrade, up thy heart billy, we will not be beasted at this bout, for
I have got one trick. *Ex hoc in hoc*, there is no inchantment, nor
charme there, every one of you hath seene it, my prentiship is
out, I am a free man at this trade. I am prester mast,* (*Prish-Brun*
I should say) master past. O the drinkers, those that are a dry, O
poore thirsty souls. Good Page my friend, fill me here some, and
crowne the wine, I pray thee, like a Cardinal. *Natura abhorret
vacuum*. Would you say that a flie could drink in this? This is
after the fashion of *Swisserland*, cleare off, neat, *super-naculum*.
Come therefore blades to this divine liquor, and celestial juyce,
swill it over heartily, and spare not, it is a decoction of Nectar
and Ambrosia.

CHAPTER VI

How Gargantua was borne in a strange manner.

Whilest they were on this discourse, & pleasant tattle of
drinking, *Gargamelle* began to be a little unwell in her lower
parts; whereupon *Grangousier* arose from off the grasse, and fell
to comfort her very honestly and kindly, suspecting that she was
in travel, and told her that it was best for her to sit down upon
the grasse under the willows, because she was like very shortly
to see young feet, and that therefore it was convenient she
should pluck up her spirits, and take a good heart of new at the
fresh arrival of her baby, saying to her withal, that although the
paine was somewhat grievous to her, it would be but of short
continuance, and that the succeeding joy would quickly remove
that sorrow, in such sort that she should not so much as remember it. On with a sheeps courage (quoth he) dispatch this boy,
and we will speedily fall to work for the making of another. Ha
(said she) so well as you speak at your own ease, you that are
men; well then, in the name of God i 'le do my best, seeing you

* Prestre macé maistre passé.

will have it so, but would to God that it were cut off from you: what? (said *Grangousier*). Ha (said she) you are a good man indeed, you understand it well enough; what, my member? (said he) by the goats blood, if it please you that shall be done instantly, cause bring hither a knife; alas, (said she,) the Lord forbid, I pray Jesus to forgive me, I did not say it from my heart, therefore let it alone, and do not do it neither more nor lesse any kinde of harme for my speaking so to you; but I am like to have work enough to do to day, and all for your member, yet God blesse you and it.

Courage, courage, (said he) take you no care of the matter, let the four formost oxen do the work. I will yet go drink one whiffe more, and if in the meane time any thing befall you that may require my presence, I will be so near to you, that, at the first whistling in your fist, I shall be with you forthwith: a little while after she began to groane, lament and cry, then suddenly came the midwives from all quarters, who groping her below, found some *peloderies*, which was a certaine filthy stuffe, and of a taste truly bad enough; this they thought had been the childe, but it was her fundament, that was slipt out with the mollification of her *streight intrall*, which you call the *bum-gut*, and that meerly by eating of too many tripes, as we have shewed you before: whereupon an old ugly trot in the company, who had the repute of an expert she-Physician, and was come from *Brispaille* near to Saint *Gnou* three-score years before, made her so horrible a restrictive and binding medicine, and whereby all her *Larris*, arse-pipes and conduits were so opilated, stopped, obstructed, and contracted, that you could hardily have opened and enlarged them with your teeth, which is a terrible thing to think upon; seeing the Devill at the Masse at Saint *Martins* was puzled with the like task, when with his teeth he had lengthened out the parchment whereon he wrote the tittle tattle of two young mangy whoores; by this inconvenient the *cotyledons* of her matrix were presently loosed, through which the childe sprung up and leapt, and so entering into the hollow veine, did climbe by the diaphragm even above her shoulders, where that veine divides it self into two, and from thence taking his way towards the left side, issued forth at her left eare; as soone as he was borne, he cried not as other babes use to do, *miez, miez, miez,*

miez, but with a high, sturdy, and big voice shouted aloud, Some drink, some drink, some drink, as inviting all the world to drink with him; the noise hereof was so extreamly great, that it was heard in both the Countreys at once, of *Beauce* and *Bibarois*. I doubt me, that you do not throughly beleeve the truth of this strange nativity, though you beleeve it not, I care not much: but an honest man, and of good judgement beleeveth still what is told him, and that which he findes written.

Is this beyond our Law? or our faith? against reason or the holy Scripture? for my part, I finde nothing in the sacred Bible that is against it; but tell me, if it had been the will of God, would you say that he could not do it? Ha, for favour sake, (I beseech you) never *emberlucock* or *inpulregafize* your spirits with these vaine thoughts and idle conceits; for I tell you, it is not impossible with God, and if he pleased all women henceforth should bring forth their children at the eare; was not *Bacchus* engendred out of the very thigh of *Jupiter*? did not *Roquetaillade* come out at his mothers heel? and *Crocmoush* from the slipper of his nurse? was not *Minerva* born of the braine, even through the eare of *Jove*? *Adonis* of the bark of a Myrretree; and *Castor* and *Pollux* of the doupe of that Egge which was laid and hatched by *Leda*? But you would wonder more, and with farre greater amazement, if I should now present you with that chapter of *Plinius*, wherein he treateth of strange births, and contrary to nature, and yet am not I so impudent a lier as he was. Reade the seventh book of his Natural History, chapt. 4. and trouble not my head any more about this.

CHAPTER VII

After what manner Gargantua had his name given him, and how he tippled, bibbed, and curried the canne.

THE good man *Grangousier* drinking and making merry with the rest, heard the horrible noise which his sonne had made as he entered into the light of this world, when he cried out, Some drink, some drink, some drink; whereupon he said in French, *Que grand tu as et souple le gousier*, that is to say, *How great and nimble a throat thou hast*; which the company hearing said, that

verily the childe ought to be called *Gargantua*, because it was
the first word that after his birth his father had spoke, in imitation, and at the example, of the ancient *Hebrewes*; whereunto he
condescended, and his mother was very well pleased therewith;
in the mean while to quiete the childe, they gave him to drink
à tirelarigot, that is, till his throat was like to crack with it; then
was he carried to the Font, and there baptized, according to the
manner of good *Christians*.

Immediately thereafter were appointed for him seventeen
thousand, nine hundred, and thirteen Cowes of the towns
of *Pautille* and *Breemond* to furnish him with milk in ordinary,
for it was impossible to finde a Nurse sufficient for him in all
the Countrey, considering the great quantity of milk that was
requisite for his nourishment; although there were not wanting
some Doctors of the opinion of *Scotus*, who affirmed that his
own mother gave him suck, and that she could draw out of her
breasts one thousand, four hundred, two pipes, and nine pailes
of milk at every time.

Which indeed is not probable, and this point hath been found
duggishly scandalous and offensive to tender eares, for that it
savoured a little of Heresie. Thus was he handled for one yeare
and ten moneths, after which time by the advice of Physicians,
they began to carry him, and then was made for him a fine little
cart drawn with Oxen, of the invention of *Jan Denio*, wherein
they led him hither and thither with great joy, and he was worth
the seeing; for he was a fine boy, had a burly physnomie, and
almost ten chins; he cried very little, but beshit himself every
hour: for to speak truly of him, he was wonderfully flegmatick
in his posteriors, both by reason of his natural complexion, and
the accidental disposition which had befallen him by his too
much quaffing of the septembral juyce. Yet without a cause did
not he sup one drop; for if he happened to be vexed, angry,
displeased, or sorry; if he did fret, if he did weep, if he did cry,
and what grievous quarter soever he kept, in bringing him some
drink, he would be instantly pacified, reseated in his own temper, in a good humour againe, and as still and quiet as ever. One
of his governesses told me (swearing by her fig) how he was so
accustomed to this kinde of way, that, at the sound of pintes and
flaggons, he would on a sudden fall into an extasie, as if he had

then tasted of the joyes of Paradise: so that they upon consideration of this his divine complexion, would every morning, to cheare him up, play with a knife upon the glasses, on the bottles with their stopples, and on the pottlepots with their lids and covers, at the sound whereof he became gay, did leap for joy, would loll and rock himself in the cradle, then nod with his head, monocordising with his fingers, and barytonising with his taile.

CHAPTER VIII

How they apparelled Gargantua.

Being of this age, his father ordained to have clothes made to him in his owne livery, which was white and blew. To work then went the Tailors, and with great expedition were those clothes made, cut, and sewed, according to the fashion that was then in request. I finde by the ancient Records or Pancarts, to be seene in the chamber of accounts, or Court of the Exchequer at *Montforeo*, that he was accoutred in manner as followeth. To make him every shirt of his were taken up nine hundred ells of *Chatelero* linnen, and two hundred for the guissets, in manner of cushions, which they put under his arm-pits; his shirt was not gathered nor plaited, for the plaiting of shirts was not found out, till the Seamstresses (when the point of their needles was broken) began to work and occupie with the taile;* there were taken up for his doublet, eight hundred and thirteen ells of white Satin, and for his points fifteen hundred and nine dogs skins and a half. Then was it that men began to tie their breeches to their doublets, and not their doublets to their breeches: for it is against nature, as hath most amply been shewed by *Ockam* upon the exponibles of Master *Hautechaussade*.

For his breeches were taken up eleven hundred and five ells, and a third of white broad cloth; they were cut in forme of pillars, chamfered, channel'd and pinked behinde, that they might not over-heat his reines: and were within the panes, puffed out with the lining of as much blew damask as was needful: and

---

* *Besoigner du cul*, English'd, *The eye of the needle.*

remark, that he had very good Leg-harnish, proportionable to the rest of his stature.

For his Codpeece was used sixteen ells and a quarter of the same cloth, and it was fashioned on the top like unto a Triumphant Arch, most gallantly fastened with two enamell'd Clasps, in each of which was set a great Emerauld, as big as an Orange; for, as sayes *Orpheus lib. de lapidibus*, and *Plinius libr. ultimo*, it hath an erective vertue and comfortative of the natural member. The extiture, out-jecting or outstanding of his Codpiece, was of the length of a yard, jagged and pinked, and withal bagging, and strouting out with the blew damask lining, after the manner of his breeches; but had you seen the faire Embroyderie of the small needle-work purle, and the curiously interlaced knots, by the Goldsmiths Art, set out and trimmed with rich Diamonds, precious Rubies, fine Turquoises, costly Emeraulds, and *Persian* pearles; you would have compared it to a faire *Cornucopia*, or Horne of abundance, such as you see in Anticks, or as *Rhea* gave to the two Nymphs, *Amalthea* and *Ida*, the Nurses of *Jupiter*.

And like to that Horn of abundance, it was still gallant, succulent, droppie, sappie, pithie, lively, always flourishing, alwayes fructifying, full of juice, full of flower, full of fruit, and all manner of delight. I avow God, it would have done one good to have seen him, but I will tell you more of him in the book which I have made of the dignity of Codpieces. One thing I will tell you, that, as it was both long and large, so was it well furnished and victualled within, nothing like unto the hypocritical Codpieces of some fond Wooers, and Wench-courters, which are stuffed only with wind, to the great prejudice of the female sexe.

For his shoes, were taken up foure hundred and six elles of blew Crimson-velvet, and were very neatly cut by parallel lines, joyned in uniforme cylindres: for the soling of them were made use of eleven hundred Hides of brown Cowes, shapen like the taile of a Keeling.

For his coat were taken up eighteen hundred elles of blew velvet, died in grain, embroidered in its borders with faire Gilliflowers, in the middle decked with silver purle, intermixed with plates of gold, and store of pearles, hereby shewing, that in his time he would prove an especial good fellow, and singular whip-can.

His girdle was made of three hundred elles and a halfe of silken serge, halfe white and halfe blew, if I mistake it not. His sword was not of *Valentia*, nor his dagger of *Saragosa*, for his father could not endure these *hidalgos borrachos maranisados como diablos:* but he had a faire sword made of wood, and the dagger of boiled leather, as well painted and guilded as any man could wish.

His purse was made of the cod of an Elephant, which was given him by *Herre Præcontal*, Proconsul of *Lybia*.

For his Gown were employed nine thousand six hundred elles, wanting two thirds, of blew velvet, as before, all so diagonally purled, that by true perspective issued thence an unnamed colour, like that you see in the necks of Turtle-doves or Turkie-cocks, which wonderfully rejoyceth the eyes of the beholders. For his Bonnet or Cap were taken up three hundred two elles, and a quarter of white velvet, and the forme thereof was wide and round, of the bignesse of his Head; for his father said, that the Caps of the *Mirabaise* fashion, made like the Cover of a Pastie, would one time or other bring a mischief on those that wore them. For his Plume, he wore a faire great blew feather, plucked from an *Onocrotal* of the countrey of *Hircania* the wilde, very prettily hanging down over his right eare: for the Jewel or broach which in his Cap he carried, he had in a Cake of gold, weighing three score and eight marks, a faire piece enamell'd, wherein was portrayed a mans body with two heads, looking towards one another, foure armes, foure feet, two arses, such as *Plato in Symposio* sayes, was the mystical beginning of mans nature; and about it was written in Ionick letters, Ἀγάπη οὐ ζητεῖ τὰ ἑαυτῆς, or rather, Ἀνὴρ καὶ γυνὴ ζυγάδην ἄνθρωπος ἰδιαίτατα, that is, *Vir & Mulier junctim propriissimé homo*. To wear about his neck, he had a golden chaine, weighing twenty five thousand and sixty three marks of gold, the links thereof being made after the manner of great berries, amongst which were set in work green Jaspers ingraven, and cut Dragon-like, all invironed with beams and sparks, as king *Nicepsos* of old was wont to weare them, and it reached down to the very bust of the rising of his belly, whereby he reaped great benefit all his long life, as the

Greek Physicians knew well enough. For his Gloves were put in work sixteen Otters skins, and three of *lougarous* or men-eating wolves, for the bordering of them: and of this stuffe were they made, by the appointment of the Cabalists of *Sanlono*. As for the Rings which his father would have him to weare to renew the ancient mark of Nobility; He had on the forefinger of his left hand a Carbuncle as big as an Ostrige's Egge, inchased very daintily in gold of the finenesse of a *Turkie Seraph*. Upon the middle finger of the same hand, he had a Ring made of foure metals together, of the strangest fashion that ever was seen; so that the steel did not crash against the gold, nor the silver crush the copper. All this was made by Captain *Chappius*, and *Alcofribas* his good Agent. On the medical finger of his right hand, he had a Ring made Spire wayes, wherein was set a perfect baleu rubie, a pointed Diamond, and a Physon Emerald of an inestimable value; for *Hanscarvel* the King of *Melinda*'s Jeweller, esteemed them at the rate of threescore nine millions, eight hundred ninety foure thousand and eighteen French Crowns of *Berrie*, and at so much did the foucres of *Auspurg* prize them.

CHAPTER IX

The Colours and Liveries of Gargantua.

GARGANTUA'S colours were white and blew, as I have shewed you before, by which his father would give us to understand, that his sonne to him was a heavenly joy, for the white did signifie gladnesse, pleasure, delight, and rejoycing, and the blew, celestial things. I know well enough, that in reading this you laugh at the old drinker, and hold this exposition of colours to be very extravagant, and utterly disagreeable to reason, because white is said to signifie faith, and blew constancy. But without moving, vexing, heating or putting you in a chafe, (for the weather is dangerous) answer me if it please you; for no other compulsory way of arguing will I use towards you, or any else; only now and then I will mention a word or two of my bottle. What is it that induceth you? what stirs you up to believe, or who told you that white signifieth faith, and blew, constancy?

An old paultry book, say you, sold by the hawking Pedlars and Balladmongers, entituled *The Blason of Colours:* Who made it? whoever it was, he was wise in that he did not set his name to it; but besides, I know not what I should rather admire in him, his presumption or his sottishnesse: his presumption and over-weening, for that he should without reason, without cause, or without any appearance of truth, have dared to prescribe by his private authority, what things should be denotated and signi-fied by the colour: which is the custome of Tyrants, who will have their will to bear sway in stead of equity; and not of the wise and learned, who with the evidence of reason satisfie their Readers: His sottishnesse and want of spirit, in that he thought, that without any other demonstration or sufficient argument, the world would be pleased to make his blockish and ridiculous impositions, the rule of their devices. In effect, (according to the Proverb, *To a shitten taile failes never ordurre*,) he hath found (it seems) some simple Ninnie in those rude times of old, when the wearing of high round Bonnets was in fashion, who gave some trust to his writings, according to which they carved and ingraved their apophthegms and motto's, trapped and capari-soned their Mules and Sumpter-horses, apparelled their Pages, quartered their breeches, bordered their gloves, fring'd the courtains and vallens of their beds, painted their ensignes, com-posed songs, and which is worse, placed many deceitful juglings, and unworthy base tricks undiscoveredly, amongst the very chastest Matrons, and most reverend Sciences. In the like darknesse and mist of ignorance, are wrapped up these vain-glorious Courtiers, and name-transposers, who going about in their impresa's, to signifie *esperance*, (that is, hope) have por-trayed a sphere: birds pennes for peines: *Ancholie* (which is the flower colombine) for melancholy: A waning Moon or Cressant, to shew the increasing or rising of ones fortune; A bench rotten and broken, to signifie bankrout: *non* and a *corslet* for *non dur habit*, (otherwise *non durabit*, it shall not last) *un lit sanc ciel*, that is, a bed without a testerne, for *un licencié*, a graduated person, as Batchelour in Divinity, or utter Barrester at law; which are æquivocals so absurd and witlesse, so barbarous and clownish, that a foxes taile should be fastened to the neck-piece of, and a Vizard made of a Cowsheard, given to every one that henceforth should offer, after the restitution of learning, to make use of any such fopperies in *France*. By the same reasons (if reasons I should call them, and not ravings rather, and idle triflings about words,) might I cause paint a panier, to signifie that I am in peine: a Mustard-pot, that my heart tarries much for 't: one pissing upwards for a Bishop: the bottom of a paire of breeches for a vessel full of farthings: a Codpiece for the office of the Clerks of the sentences, decrees or judgements, or rather (as the *English* beares it,) for the taile of a Cod-fish; and a dogs turd, for the dainty turret, wherein lies the love of my sweet heart. Farre otherwise did heretofore the Sages of *Egypt*, when they wrote by letters, which they called Hieroglyphicks, which none understood who were not skilled in the vertue, propertie and nature of the things represented by them; of which *Orus Apollon* hath in Greek composed two books, and *Polyphilus* in his dream of love, set down more: In *France* you have a taste of them, in the device or impresa of my Lord Admiral, which was carried before that time by *Octavian Augustus*. But my little skiffe alongst these unpleasant gulphs and sholes, will saile no further, therefore must I return to the Port from whence I came: yet do I hope one day to write more at large of these things, and to shew both by Philosophical arguments and authorities, received and approved of by and from all antiquity, what, and how many colours there are in nature, and what may be signified by every one of them, if God save the mould of my Cap, which is my best Wine-pot, as my Grandame said.

CHAPTER X

Of that which is signified by the Colours, white and blew.

THE white therefore signifieth joy, solace and gladnesse, and that not at random, but upon just and very good grounds: which you may perceive to be true, if laying aside all prejudicate affections, you will but give eare to what presently I shall expound unto you.

Aristotle saith, that supposing two things contrary in their kinde, as good and evill, vertue and vice, heat and cold, white and black, pleasure and pain, joy and grief: And so of others, if

you couple them in such manner, that the contrary of one kinde
may agree in reason with the contrary of the other, it must follow by consequence, that the other contrary must answer to the
remanant opposite to that wherewith it is conferred; as for
example, vertue and vice are contrary in one kinde, so are good
and evil: if one of the contraries of the first kinde, be consonant
to one of those of the second, as vertue and goodnesse, for it
is clear that vertue is good, so shall the other two contraries,
(which are evil and vice) have the same connexion, for vice
is evil.

This Logical rule being understood, take these two contraries, joy and sadnesse: then these other two, white and black,
for they are Physically contrary; if so be, then, that black do
signifie grief, by good reason then should white import joy. Nor
is this signification instituted by humane imposition, but by the
universal consent of the world received, which Philosophers
call *Jus Gentium*, the Law of Nations, or an uncontrolable right
of force in all countreyes whatsover: for you know well enough,
that all people, and all languages and nations, (except the ancient
Syracusans, and certain *Argives*, who had crosse and thwarting
soules) when they mean outwardly to give evidence of their sorrow, go in black; and all mourning is done with black, which
general consent is not without some argument, and reason in
nature, the which every man may by himself very suddenly
comprehend, without the instruction of any; and this we call the
Law of nature: By vertue of the same natural instinct, we know
that by white all the world hath understood joy, gladnesse, mirth,
pleasure, and delight. In former times, the *Thracians* and *Cre-
cians* did mark their good, propitious, and fortunate dayes with
white stones: and their sad, dismal, and unfortunate ones
with black; is not the night mournful, sad and melancholick? it
is black and dark by the privation of light; doth not the light
comfort all the world? and it is more white then any thing else,
which to prove, I could direct you to the book of *Laurentius Valla*
against *Bartolus*; but an Evangelical testimony I hope will content you, *Matth.* 7. it is said, that at the transfiguration of our
Lord, *Vestimenta ejus facta sunt alba sicut lux*, his apparel was
made white like the light, by which lightsome whitenesse he
gave his three Apostles to understand the *Idea* and figure of the

eternal joyes; for by the light are all men comforted, according
to the word of the old woman, who although she had never a
tooth in her head, was wont to say, *Bona lux*: and *Tobit, chap.* 5.
after he had lost his sight, when *Raphael* saluted him, answered,
What joy can I have, that do not see the light of Heaven? In that colour
did the Angels testifie the joy of the whole world, at the Resur-
rection of our Saviour, *John* 20. and at his Ascension, *Acts* I. with
the like colour of vesture did St. *John* the Evangelist, *Apoc.* 4. 7.
see the faithful clothed in the heavenly and blissed *Jerusalem*.

Reade the ancient both *Greek* and *Latine* histories, and you
shall finde, that the towne of *Alba*, (the first patern of *Rome*,) was
founded, and so named by reason of a white sow that was seen
there: You shall likewise finde in those stories, that when any
man, after he had vanquished his enemies, was by decree of the
Senate to enter into *Rome* triumphantly, he usually rode in a
chariot drawn by white horses: which in the Ovation triumph
was also the custome; for by no signe or colour would they so
significantly expresse the joy of their coming, as by the white.
You shall there also finde, how *Pericles*, the General of the *Athenians*, would needs have that part of his Army, unto whose lot
befel the white beanes, to spend the whole day in mirth, pleasure and ease, whilest the rest were a fighting. A thousand other
examples and places could I alledge to this purpose, but that it
is not here where I should do it.

By understanding hereof, you may resolve one Problem,
which *Alexander Aphrodiseus* hath accounted unanswerable, why
the Lion, who with his only cry and roaring affrights all beasts,
dreads and feareth only a white cock? For (as *Proclus* saith, *libro
de Sacrificio & Magia*) it is because the presence of the vertue of
the Sunne, which is the Organ and Promptuarie of all terrestrial
and *syderial* light, doth more symbolize and agree with a white
cock, as well in regard of that colour, as of his property and specifical quality, then with a Lion. He saith furthermore, that Devils
have been often seen in the shape of Lions, which at the sight
of a white cock have presently vanished. This is the cause, why
Galli or *Gallices*, (so are the *Frenchmen* called, because they are
naturally white as milk, which the Greeks call *Gala*,) do willingly weare in their Caps white feathers, for by nature they are of
a candid disposition, merrie, kinde, gracious and well-beloved,

and for their cognizance and armes have the whitest flower of any, the *Flower de luce* or *Lilie*. If you demand, how, by white, nature would have us understand joy and gladnesse? I answer, that the analogy and uniformity is thus, for, as the white doth outwardly disperse and scatter the rayes of the sight, whereby the optick spirits are manifestly dissolved, according to the opinion of *Aristotle* in his Problemes and perspective Treatises; as you may likewise perceive by experience, when you passe over mountains covered with snow, how you will complain that you cannot see well: as *Xenophon* writes to have hapned to his men, and as *Galen* very largely declareth, *lib.* 10. *de usu partium*: Just so the heart with excessive joy is inwardly dilated, and suffereth a manifest resolution of the vital spirits, which may go so farre on, that it may thereby be deprived of its nourishment, and by consequence of life it self, by this *Pericharie* or extremity of gladnesse, as *Galen* saith, *lib.* 12. *method. lib.* 5. *de locis affectis, & lib.* 2. *de symptomatum causis*; and as it hath come to passe in former times, witnesse *Marcus Tullius lib.* 1. *quæst Tuscul., Verrius, Aristotle, Titus Livius* in his relation of the battel of *Cannas, Plinius lib.* 7. *cap.* 32 & 53, *A. Gellius lib.* 3. *c.* 15, and many other Writers, of *Diagoras* the *Rhodian, Chilon, Sophocles, Dionysius* the tyrant of *Sicilie, Philippides, Philemon, Polycrates, Philipion, M. Juventi*; and others who died with joy, and as *Avicen* speaketh, *in 2. canon. & lib. de virib. cordis*, of the Saffron, that it doth so rejoyce the heart, that, if you take of it excessively, it will by a superfluous resolution and dilatation deprive it altogether of life. Here peruse *Alex. Aphrodiseus lib.* I. *Probl. cap.* 19. and that for a cause. But what? it seems I am entred further into this point then I intended at the first; Here, therefore, will I strike saile, referring the rest to that book of mine, which handleth this matter to the full. Mean while, in a word I will tell you, that blew doth certainly signifie Heaven and heavenly things, by the same very tokens and *symbols*, that white signifieth joy and pleasure.

CHAPTER XI

Of the youthful age of Gargantua.

GARGANTUA from three yeares upwards unto five, was brought up and instructed in all convenient discipline, by the commandment of his father; and spent that time like the other little children of the countrey, that is, in drinking, eating and sleeping: in eating, sleeping and drinking: and in sleeping, drinking and eating: still he wallowed and rowled up and down himself in the mire and dirt: he blurred and sullied his nose with filth: he blotted and smutch't his face with any kinde of scurvie stuffe, he trode down his shoes in the heele: At the flies he did oftentimes yawn, and ran very heartily after the Butterflies, the Empire whereof belonged to his father. He pissed in his shoes, shit in his shirt, and wiped his nose on his sleeve: He did let his snot and snivel fall in his pottage, and dabled, padled and slabbered every where: He would drink in his slipper, and ordinarily rub his belly against a Panier: He sharpened his teeth with a top, washed his hands with his broth, and combed his head with a bole: He would sit down betwixt two stooles, and his arse to the ground, would cover himself with a wet sack, and drink in eating of his soupe: He did eate his Cake sometimes without bread, would bite in laughing, and laugh in biting; Oftentimes did he spit in the basin, and fart for fatnesse; pisse against the Sunne, and hide himself in the water for fear of raine. He would strike out of the cold iron, be often in the dumps, and frig and wriggle it. He would flay the Fox, say the Apes Paternoster, return to his sheep, and turn the Hogs to the Hay: He would beat the Dogs before the Lion, put the Plough before the Oxen, and claw where it did not itch: He would pump one to draw somewhat out of him, by griping all would hold fast nothing, and alwayes eat his white bread first. He shoo'd the Geese, kept a self-tickling to make himself laugh, and was very stedable in the Kitchin: made a mock at the gods, would cause sing *Magnificat* at *Matines*, and found it very convenient so to do; He would eat cabbage, and shite beets; knew flies in a dish of milk, and would make them lose their feet: He would scrape paper, blur parchment, then run away as hard as he could: He would pul at the Kids leather, or vomit up his dinner, then reckon without his Host: He would beat the bushes without catching the birds, thought the Moon was made of green cheese, and that bladders are lanternes: out of one sack he would take two moutures or fees for grinding; would act the Asses part to get some bran, and of his fist would make a Mallet: He took the cranes at the first leap, and would have the Mail-coats to be made link after link: He alwayes looked a given horse in the mouth, leaped from the cock to the asse, and put one ripe between two green: By robbing *Peter* he payed *Paul*, he kept the Moon from the wolves, and hoped to catch Larks if ever the Heavens should fall: He did make of necessity vertue, of such bread such pottage, and cared as little for the peeled as for the shaven: Every morning he did cast up his gorge, and his fathers little dogs eat out of the dish with him, and he with them: He would bite their eares, and they would scratch his nose: he would blow in their arses, and they would lick his chaps. But hearken, good fellows, the spigot ill betake you, and whirle round your braines, if you do not give eare: This little Lecher was alwayes groping his Nurses and Governesses, upside down, arsiversie, topsiturvie, *harri-bourriquet*, with a *Yacco haick, hyck gio*, handling them very rudely in jumbling and tumbling them to keep them going; for he had already begun to exercise the tooles, and put his Codpiece in practice; which Codpiece or *Braguette*, his Governesses did every day deck up and adorn with faire nosegayes, curious rubies, sweet flowers, and fine silken tufts, and very pleasantly would passe their time, in taking you know what between their fingers, and dandling it, till it did revive and creep up to the bulk and stiffenesse of a suppository, or *streat magdaleon*, which is a hard rowled up salve spread upon leather. Then did they burst out in laughing, when they saw it lift up its eares, as if the sport had liked them; one of them would call it her little dille, her staffe of love, her quillety, her faucetin, her dandilollie: Another, her peen, her jolly kyle, her bableret, her membretoon, her quickset Imp: Another again, her branch of coral, her female adamant, her placket-racket, her cyprian scepter, her jewel for Ladies: and some of the other women would give it these names, my bunguetee, my stopple too, my busherusher, my gallant wimble, my pretty boarer, my coney-borow ferret, my little piercer, my augretine, my dangling hangers, down right to it, stiffe and stout, in & to, my pusher, dresser, pouting stick, my hony pipe, my pretty pillicock, linkie pinkie, futilletie, my lustie andouille, and crimson chitterlin, my little couille bredouille, my pretty rogue, and so forth: It belongs to me, said one: it is mine, said the other: What, quoth a third, shall I have no share in it? by my faith, I will cut it then. Ha, to cut it, (said the other,) would hurt him; *Madam*, do you cut little childrens things? were his cut off, he would be then *Monsieur sans queue*, the curtail'd Master. And that he might play and sport himself after the manner of the other little children of the countrey, they made him a faire weather whirljack, of the wings of the windmil of *Myrebalais*.

CHAP. XII

Of Gargantua's wooden Horses.

AFTERWARDS, that he might be all his lifetime a good Rider, they made to him a faire great horse of wood, which he did make leap, curvete, yerk out behinde, and skip forward, all at a time: to pace, trot, rack, gallop, amble, to play the hobbie, the hackney-guelding: go the gate of the camel & of the wilde asse. He made him also change his colour of hair, as the Monks of *Coultibo*, (according to the variety of their holy-days) use to do their clothes, from bay, brown, to sorrel, daple-gray, mouse-dun, deer-colour, roan, cow-colour, gingioline, skued colour, pybal'd, and the colour of the savage elk.

Himself of an huge big post made a hunting nag; and another for daily service, of the beam of a Vinepresse: and of a great Oak made up a mule, with a footcloth, for his chamber. Besides this, he had ten or twelve spare horses, and seven horses for post; and all these were lodged in his own chamber, close by his bed-side. One day the Lord of *Breadinbag** came to visit his father in great bravery, and with a gallant traine: and at the same time, to see him came likewise the Duke of *Free-meale*,** and the Earle of *Wetgullet*.† The house truly for so many guests at once was

---

* Pain en sac. ** Franc repas. † mouille vent.

somewhat narrow, but especially the stables; whereupon the steward and harbinger of the said Lord *Breadinbag*, to know if there were any other empty stables in the house, came to *Gargantua*, a little young lad, and secretly asked him where the stables of the great horses were, thinking that children would be ready to tell all? Then he led them up along the stairs of the Castle, passing by the second Hall unto a broad great Gallery, by which they entred into a large Tower, and as they were going up at another paire of stairs, said the harbinger to the steward, This childe deceives us, for the stables are never on the top of the house: You may be mistaken (said the steward,) for I know some places at *Lyons*, at the *Basmette*, at *Chaunon*, and elsewhere, which have their stables at the very tops of the houses, so it may be, that behinde the house there is a way to come to this ascent, but I will question with him further. Then said he to *Gargantua*, My pretty little boy, whither do you lead us? To the stable (said he,) of my great horses, we are almost come to it, we have but these staires to go up at; then leading them alongst another great Hall, he brought them into his chamber, and opening the door said unto them, This is the stable that you ask for; this is my gennet, this is my gelding, this is my courser, and this is my hackney, and laid on them with a great Leaver: I will bestow upon you, (said he,) this *Frizeland* horse, I had him from *Francfort*, yet will I give him you; for he is a pretty little nagge, and will go very well, with a tessel of goose-hawk, halfe a dosen of spaniels, and a brace of greyhounds, thus are you King of the hares and partridges for all this winter. By St. *John* (said they,) now we are payed, he hath gleeked us to some purpose, bobbed we are now for ever; I deny it (said he) he was not here above three dayes. Judge you now, whether they had most cause, either to hide their heads for shame, or to laugh at the jest: as they were going down again thus amazed, he asked them, Will you have a *whim-wham*?* What is that, said they? It is (said he) five turds to make you a muzzel: To day (said the steward,) though we happen to be rosted, we shall not be burnt, for we are pretty well quipped and larded in my opinion. O my jolly daper boy, thou hast given us a gudgeon, I hope to see thee Pope before I die: I think so,

* Aubeliere.

(said he) my self; and then shall you be a *puppie*, and this gentle *popinjeay* a perfect *papelard*, that is, dissembler: Well, well, (said the harbinger,) But (said *Gargantua*,) guesse how many stitches there are in my mother's smock: Sixteen (quoth the harbinger,) You do not speak Gospel (said *Gargantua*,) for there is sent before, and sent behinde, and you did not reckon them ill, considering the *two under holes*. When (said the harbinger?) Even then (said *Gargantua*,) when they made a shovel of your nose to take up a quarter of dirt, and of your throat a funnel, wherewith to put it into another vessel, because the bottom of the old one was out. *Cocksbod* (said the steward) we have met with a Prater. Farewel (Master tatler) God keep you, so goodly are the words which you come out with, and so fresh in your mouth, that it had need to be salted.

Thus going down in great haste, under the arch of the staires, they let fall the great Leaver, which he had put upon their backs, whereupon *Gargantua* said, What a deedle, you are, (it seems,) but bad horsemen, that suffer your bilder to faile you, when you need him most, if you were to go from hence to *Chausas*, whether had you rather ride on a gesling, or lead a sow in a Leash? I had rather drink, (said the harbinger,) with this they entered into the lower Hall, where the company was, and relating to them this new story, they made them laugh like a swarm of flies.

CHAPTER XIII

How Gargantua's wonderful understanding, became known to his father Grangousier, by the invention of a Torchcul or Wipebreech.

ABOUT the end of the fifth yeare, *Grangousier* returning from the Conquest of the *Canarians*, went by the way to see his sonne *Gargantua*, there was he filled with joy, as such a father might be at the sight of such a childe of his: and whilest he kist him and embrac'd him, he asked many childish questions of him about divers matters, and drank very freely with him and with his governesses, of whom in great earnest, he asked amongst other things, whether they had been careful to keep him clean and sweet? To this *Gargantua* answered, that he had taken such

a course for that himself, that in al the country there was not to
be found a cleanlier boy then he. How is that (said *Grangousier*?)
I have (answered *Gargantua*) by a long and curious experience
found out a meanes to wipe my bum, the most lordly, the most
excellent, and the most convenient that ever was seen? What is
that, (said *Grangousier*,) how is it? I will tell you by and by (said
Gargantua,) once I did wipe me with a Gentlewomans Velvet-
mask, and found it to be good; for the softnesse of the silk was
very voluptuous and pleasant to my fundament. Another time
with one of their Hoods, and in like manner that was comfortable: At another time with a Ladies Neck-kerchief, and after
that I wiped me with some ear-pieces of hers made of Crimson
sattin, but there was such a number of golden spangles in them
(turdie round things, a pox take them) that they fetched away
all the skin of my taile with a vengeance. Now I wish St.
Anthonies fire burn the bum-gut of the Goldsmith that made
them, and of her that wore them: This hurt I cured by wiping
my self with a Pages cap, garnished with a feather after the
Suitsers fashion.

Afterwards, in dunging behinde a bush, I found a March-
Cat, and with it wiped my breech, but her clawes were so sharp
that they scratched and exulcerated all my perinee; Of this I
recovered the next morning thereafter, by wiping my self with
my mother's gloves, of a most excellent perfume and sent of the
Arabian Benin. After that I wiped me with sage, with fennil, with
anet, with marjoram, with roses, with gourd-leavs, with beets,
with colewort, with leaves of the vine-tree, with mallowes,
wool-blade, (which is a tail-scarlet,) with latice and with spinage
leaves. All this did very great good to my leg. Then with Mercurie, with pursley, with nettles, with comfrey, but that gave me
the bloody flux of *Lumbardie*, which I healed by wiping me with
my braguette; then I wiped my taile in the sheets, in the cover-
let, in the curtains, with a cushion, with Arras hangings, with a
green carpet, with a table-cloth, with a napkin, with a handkerchief, with a combing cloth, in all which I found more pleasure
then do the mangy dogs when you rub them. Yea, but (said
Grangousier,) which torchecul didst thou finde to be the best? I
was coming to it (said *Gargantua*) and by and by shall you heare
the *tu autem*, and know the whole mysterie and knot of the

matter: I wiped my self with hay, with straw, with thatch-rushes, with flax, with wooll, with paper, but

> *Who his foule taile with paper wipes,*
> *Shall at his ballocks leave some chips.*

What, (said *Grangousier*) my little rogue, hast thou been at the pot, that thou dost rime already? Yes, yes, my Lord the King (answered *Gargantua*,) I can rime gallantly, and rime till I become hoarse with *Rheum*; Heark, what our Privy sayes to the Skyters:

> Shittard
> Squirtard
> Crackard
>   Turdous.
> Thy bung
> Hath flung
> Some dung
>   on us:
> Filthard
> Cackard
> Stinkard:
>   St. *Antonie*'s fire seize on
>   thy toane,
> If thy
> Dirty
> Dounby
>   Thou do not wipe ere
>   thou be gone.

Will you have any more of it? Yes, yes, (answered *Grangousier*:) Then said *Gargantua*,

A ROUNDLAY

> In shiting yesday I did know
> The sesse I to my arse did owe:
> The smell was such came from that slunk,
> That I was with it all bestunk:
> O had but then some brave *Signor*
> Brought her to me I waited for,
>   in shiting:
> I would have cleft her watergap,
> And joyn'd it close to my flipflap,
> Whilest she had with her fingers guarded
> My foule Nockandrow, all bemerded
>   in shiting.

55

Now say that I can do nothing, by the *Merdi* they are not of my making, but I heard them of this good old grandam, that you see here, and ever since have retained them in the budget of my memory.

Let us return to our purpose (said *Grangousier*,) What (said *Gargantua*) to skite? No (said *Grangousier*) but to wipe our taile; But (said *Gargantua*) will not you be content to pay a punchion of Britton-wine, if I do not blank and gravel you in this matter, and put you to a *non-plus*? Yes truly (said *Grangousier*.)

There is no need of wiping ones taile (said *Gargantua*) but when it is foule; foule it cannot be unlesse one have been a skiting; skite then we must before we wipe our tailes. O my pretty little waggish boy (said *Grangousier*,) what an excellent wit thou hast? I will make thee very shortly proceed Doctor in the jovial quirks of gay learning, and that by G—, for thou hast more wit then age; now I prethie go on in this torcheculaife, or wipe-bummatory discourse, and by my beard I swear, for one puncheon thou shalt have threescore pipes, I mean of the good *Breton* wine, not that which grows in *Britain*, but in the good countrey of *Verron*. Afterwards I wiped my bum (said *Gargantua*,) with a kerchief, with a *pillow*, with a *pantoufle*, with a pouch, with a pannier, but that was a wicked and unpleasant torchecul; then with a hat, of hats note that some are shorne, and others shaggie, some velveted, others covered with taffities, and others with sattin, the best of all these is the shaggie hat, for it makes a very neat abstersion of the fecal matter.

Afterwards I wiped my taile with a hen, with a cock, with a pullet, with a calves skin, with a hare, with a pigeon, with a cormorant, with an Atturneyes bag, with a montero, with a coife, with a faulconers lure; but, to conclude, I say and maintain, that of all torcheculs, arsewisps, bumfodders, tail-napkins, bunghole cleansers and wipe-breeches, there is none in the world comparable to the neck of a goose, that is well douned, if you hold her head betwixt your legs; and beleeve me therein upon mine honour, for you will thereby feele in your nockhole a most wonderful pleasure, both in regard of the softnesse of the said doune, and of the temperate heat of the goose, which is easily communicated to the bum-gut, and the rest of the inwards, insofarre as to come even to the regions of the heart and braines;

And think not, that the felicity of the *heroes* and *demi-gods* in the *Elysian* fields consisteth either in their *Asphodele*, *Ambrosia*, or *Nectar*, as our old women here used to say; but in this, (according to my judgement) that they wipe their tailes with the neck of a goose, holding her head betwixt their legs, and such is the opinion of *Master John* of *Scotland*, aliàs *Scotus*.

CHAPTER XIV

How Gargantua was taught Latine by a Sophister.

THE good man *Grangousier*, having heard this discourse, was ravished with admiration, considering the high reach, and marvellous understanding of his sonne *Gargantua*, and said to his governesses, *Philip* King of *Macedon* knew the great wit of his sonne *Alexander*, by his skilful managing of a horse; for his horse *Bucephalus* was so fierce and unruly, that none durst adventure to ride him, after that he had given to his Riders such devillish falls, breaking the neck of this man, the other mans leg, braining one, and putting another out of his jawbone. This by *Alexander* being considered, one day in the *hippodrome*, (which was a place appointed for the breaking and managing of great horses,) he perceived that the fury of the horse proceeded meerly from the feare he had of his own shadow, whereupon getting on his back, he run him against the Sun, so that the shadow fell behinde, and by that meanes tamed the horse, and brought him to his hand; whereby his father, knowing the divine judgement that was in him, caused him most carefully to be instructed by *Aristotle*, who at that time was highly renowned above all the Philosophers of *Greece*: after the same manner I tell you, that by this only discourse, which now I have here had before you with my sonne *Gargantua*; I know that his understanding doth participate of some divinity, and that if he be well taught, and have that education which is fitting, he will attain to a supreme degree of wisdome. Therefore will I commit him to some learned man, to have him indoctrinated according to his capacity, and will spare no cost. Presently they appointed him a great Sophister-Doctor, called Master *Tubal Holophernes*, who taught him his A B C, so well, that he could say it by heart backwards; and about this he was five yeares and three moneths. Then read he to him *Donet*, *Facet*, *Theodolet*, and *Alanus in parabolis*: About this he was thirteen years, six moneths, and two weeks; but you must remark, that in the mean time he did learn to write in *Gottish* characters, and that he wrote all his books, for the Art of printing was not then in use, and did ordinarily carry a great pen and inkhorne, weighing above seven thousand quintals, (that is, 700000 pound weight,) the penner whereof was as big and as long, as the great pillars of *Enay*, and the horne was hanged to it in great iron chaines, it being of the widenesse of a tun of merchand ware. After that he read unto him the book *de modis significandi*, with the Commentaries of *Hurtbise*, of *Fasquin*, of *Tropifeu*, of *Gualhaut*, of *Jhon Calf*, of *Billonio*, of *Berlinguandus*, and a rabble of others, and herein he spent more then eighteen yeares and eleven monethes, and was so well versed in it, that to try masteries in School-disputes with his condisciples, he would recite it by heart backwards: and did sometimes prove on his fingers ends to his mother, *quod de modis significandi non erat scientia*. Then did he reade to him the compost, for knowing the age of the Moon, the seasons of the year, and tides of the sea, on which he spent sixteen yeares and two moneths, and that justly at the time that his said *Præceptor* died of the *French* Pox, which was in the yeare one thousand foure hundred and twenty. Afterwards he got an old coughing fellow to teach him, named Master *Jobelin Bride*, or muzled doult, who read unto him *Hugotio*, *Flebard*, *Grecisme*, the *doctrinal*, the *parts*, the *quid est*, the *supplementum*, *Marmotretus*, *de moribus in mensa servandis*, Seneca *de quatuor virtutibus cardinalibus*, Passavantus *cum commentar:* and *dormi securè* for the holy days, and some other of such like mealie stuffe, by reading whereof he became as wise as any we ever since baked in an Oven.

CHAPTER XV

How Gargantua was put under other Schoolmasters.

AT the last his father perceived, that indeed he studied hard, and that although he spent all his time in it, did neverthelesse profit nothing, but which is worse, grew thereby foolish, simple, doted and blockish, whereof making a heavie regret to *Don Philip* of *Marays*, Viceroy or deputie-King of *Papeligosse*, he found that it were better for him to learne nothing at all, then to be taught such like books, under such Schoolmasters, because their knowledge was nothing but brutishnesse, and their wisdome but blunt foppish toyes, serving only to bastardize good and noble spirits, and to corrupt all the flower of youth. That it is so, take (said he) any young boy of this time, who hath only studied two yeares, if he have not a better judgement, a better discourse, and that expressed in better termes then your sonne, with a compleater carriage and civility to all manner of persons, account me for ever hereafter a very clounch, and bacon-slicer of *Brene*. This pleased *Grangousier* very well, and he commanded that it should be done. At night at supper, the said *Des Marays* brought in a young page of his, of *Ville-gouges*, called *Eudemon*, so neat, so trim, so handsom in his apparel, so spruce, with his haire in so good order, and so sweet and comely in his behaviour, that he had the resemblance of a little Angel more then of a humane creature. Then he said to *Grangousier*, Do you see this young boy? he is not as yet full twelve yeares old; let us try, (if it please you,) what difference there is betwixt the knowledge of the doting *Mateologians* of old time, and the young lads that are now. The trial pleased *Grangousier*, and he commanded the Page to begin. Then *Eudemon*, asking leave of the Vice-King his Master so to do, with his cap in his hand, a clear and open countenance, beautiful and ruddie lips, his eyes steadie, and his looks fixed upon *Gargantua*, with a youthful modesty; standing up streight on his feet, began very gracefully to commend him; first for his vertue and good manners; secondly for his knowledge; thirdly for his nobility; fourthly for his bodily accomplishments: and, in the fifth place, most sweetly exhorted him to reverence his father with all due observancy, who was so careful to have him well brought up. In the end he prayed him, that he would vouchsafe to admit of him amongst the least of his servants; for other favour at that time desired he none of heaven, but that he might do him some grateful and acceptable service; all this was by him delivered with such proper gestures, such distinct pronunciation, so pleasant a delivery, in such exquisite fine termes, and so good *Latine*, that he seemed rather a *Gracchus*, a *Cicero*, an *Æmilius* of the time past, then a youth of this age: but all the countenance that *Gargantua* kept was, that he fell to crying like a Cow, and cast down his face, hiding it with his cap, nor could they possibly draw one word from him, no more then a fart from a dead Asse; whereat his father was so grievously vexed, that he would have killed Master *Jobelin*, but the said *Des Marays* withheld him from it by faire persuasions, so that at length he pacified his wrath. Then *Grangousier* commanded he should be payed his wages, that they should whittle him up soundly, like a Sophister with good drink, and then give him leave to go to all the devils in hell: at least (said he) to day, shall it not cost his hoste much, if by chance he should die as drunk as a *Suitser*. Master *Jobelin* being gone out of the house, *Grangousier* consulted with the *Viceroy* what Schoolmaster they should choose for him, and it was betwixt them resolved, that *Ponocrates* the Tutor of *Eudemon* should have the charge, and that they should go altogether to *Paris*, to know what was the study of the young men of *France* at that time.

CHAPTER XVI

How Gargantua was sent to Paris, and of the huge great Mare that he rode on; How she destroyed the Oxe-flies of the Beauce.

IN the same season *Fayoles*, the fourth King of *Numidia*, sent out of the countrey of *Africk* to *Grangousier*, the most hideously great Mare that ever was seen, and of the strangest forme, (for you know well enough how it is said, that *Africk* alwayes is productive of some new thing:) she was as big as six elephants, and had her feet cloven into fingers, like *Julius Cæsars* horse, with slouch-hanging eares, like the goats in *Languedoc*, and a little horne on her buttock; she was of a burnt sorel hue, with a little mixture of daple gray spots, but above all she had a horrible taile; for it was little more or lesse, then every whit as great as the Steeple-pillar of St. *Mark* beside *Langes*: and squared as that is, with tuffs and *ennicroches*, or haire-plaits wrought within one another, no otherwise then as the beards are upon the eares of corne.

If you wonder at this, wonder rather at the tails of the *Scy-thian* Rams, which weighed above thirty pounds each, and of the *Surian* sheep, who need (if *Tenaud* say true,) a little cart at their heeles to beare up their taile, it is so long and heavy. You female Lechers in the plaine countreys have no such tailes. And she was brought by sea in three Carricks and a Brigantine unto the harbour of *Olone* in *Thalmondois*. When *Grangousier* saw her, Here is (said he) what is fit to carry my sonne to *Paris*. So now, in the name of God, all will be well, he will in times coming be a great Scholar, if it were not (my masters) for the beasts, we should live like Clerks: The next morning (after they had drunk, you must understand) they took their journey; *Gargantua*, his Pedagogue *Ponocrates*, and his traine, and with them *Eudemon* the young Page, and because the weather was faire and temperate, his father caused to be made for him a paire of dun boots, *Babin* calls them buskins: Thus did they merrily passe their time in travelling on their high way, alwayes making good chear, and were very pleasant till they came a little above *Orleans*, in which place there was a forrest of five and thirty leagues long, and seventeen in breadth, or thereabouts. This forrest was most horribly fertile and copious in dorflies, hornets and wasps, so that it was a very Purgatory for the poor mares, asses and horses: But *Gargantua*'s mare did avenge herself handsomly of all the out-rages therein committed upon beasts of her kinde, and that by a trick whereof they had no suspicion; for assoon as ever they were entred into the said forest, and that the wasps had given the assault, she drew out and unsheathed her taile, and therewith skirmishing, did so sweep them, that she over-threw all the wood alongst and athwart, here and there, this way and that way, longwise and sidewise, over and under, and felled every where the wood with as much ease, as a mower doth the grasse, in such sort that never since hath ther been there, neither wood, nor *Dorflies*: for all the countrey was thereby reduced to a plain champian-field: which *Gargantua* took great pleasure to behold, and said to his company no more but this, *Je trouve beau ce*, I finde this pretty; whereupon that countrey hath been ever since that time called *Beauce*: but all the breakfast the mare got that day, was but a little yawning and gaping, in memory whereof the Gentlemen of *Beauce*, do as yet to this day break their fast with gaping, which they finde to be very good, and do spit the better for it; at last they came to *Paris*, where *Gargantua* refresh't himself two or three dayes, making very merry with his folks, and enquiring what men of learning there were then in the city, and what wine they drunk there.

CHAPTER XVII

How Gargantua payed his welcome to the Parisians, and how he took away the great Bells of our Ladies Church.

SOME few dayes after that they had refresh't themselves, he went to see the city, and was beheld of every body there with great admiration; for the People of *Paris* are so sottish, so badot, so foolish and fond by nature, that a jugler, a carrier of indulgences, a sumpter-horse, or mule with cymbals, or tinkling bells, a blinde fidler in the middle of a crosse lane, shall draw a greater confluence of people together, then an Evangelical Preacher: and they prest so hard upon him, that he was constrained to rest himself upon the towers of our Ladies Church; at which place, seeing so many about him, he said with a loud voice, I beleeve that these buzzards wil have me to pay them here my welcom hither, and my *Proficiat*: it is but good reason, I will now give them their wine, but it shall be only in sport; Then smiling, he untied his faire *Braguette*, and drawing out his *mentul* into the open aire, he so bitterly all-to-bepist them, that he drowned two hundred and sixty thousand, foure hundred and eighteen, besides the women and little children: some neverthelesse of the company escaped this piss-flood by meer speed of foot, who when they were at the higher end of the University, sweating, coughing, spitting, and out of breath, they began to swear and curse, some in good hot earnest, and others in jest, *Carimari, Carimara: Golynoly, Golynolo*: by my sweet Sanctesse, we are wash't in sport, a sport truly to laugh at, in *French Par ris*, for which that city hath been ever since called Paris, whose name formerly was *Leucotia*, (as *Strabo* testifieth, *lib. quarto*) from the Greek word λευκότης, whitenesse, because of the white thighs of the Ladies of that place. And forasmuch as at this imposition of a new name, all the people that were there, swore every one by the Sancts of his parish, the *Parisians*, which are patch'd up of all nations, and all pieces of countreyes, are by nature both good

Jurers, and good *Jurists*, and somewhat overweening; whereupon *Joanninus de Barrauco libro de copiositate reverentiarum*, thinks that they are called *Parisians*, from the *Greek* word παρρησία, which signifies boldnesse and liberty in speech. This done, he considered the great bells, which were in the said tours, and made them sound very harmoniously, which whilest he was doing, it came into his minde, that they would serve very well for *tingling Tantans*, and *ringing Campanels*, to hang about his mares neck, when she should be sent back to his father, (as he intended to do) loaded with *Brie* cheese, and fresh herring; and indeed he forthwith carried them to his lodging. In the mean while there came a master begar of the Fryers of S. *Anthonie*, to demand in his canting way the usual benevolence of some hoggish stuffe, who, that he might be heard afar off, and to make the bacon, he was in quest of, shake in the very chimneys, made account to filch them away privily. Neverthelesse, he left them behinde very honestly, not for that they were too hot, but that they were somewhat too heavy for his carriage. This was not he of *Bourg*, for he was too good a friend of mine. All the city was risen up in sedition, they being (as you know) upon any slight occasion, so ready to uproars and insurrections, that forreign nations wonder at the patience of the Kings of *France*, who do not by good justice restrain them from such tumultuous courses, seeing the manifold incoveniences which thence arise from day to day. Would to God I knew the shop, wherein are forged these divisions, and factious combinations, that I might bring them to light in the confraternities of my parish. Beleeve for a truth, that the place wherein the people gathered together, were thus sulfured, hopurymated, moiled and bepist, was called *Nesle*, where then was, (but now is no more) the Oracle of *Leucotia*: There was the case proposed, and the inconvenience shewed of the transporting of the bells: After they had well *ergoted pro* and *con*, they concluded in *Baralipton*, that they should send the oldest and most sufficient of the facultie unto *Gargantua*, to signifie unto him the great and horrible prejudice they sustain by the want of those bells; and notwithstanding the good reasons given in by some of the University, why this charge was fitter for an Oratour then a Sophister, there was chosen for this purpose our Master *Janotus de Bragmardo*.

CHAPTER XVIII

How Janotus de Bragmardo was sent to Gargantua,
to recover the great bells.

MASTER *Janotus*, with his haire cut round like a dish *a La cæsarine*, in his most antick accoustrement *Liripipionated* with a graduates hood, and, having sufficiently antidoted his stomack with Oven-*Marmalades*, that is, bread and holy water of the Cellar, transported himself to the lodging of *Gargantua*, driving before him three red muzled beadles, and dragging after him five or six artlesse masters, all throughly bedaggled with the mire of the streets. At their entry *Ponocrates* met them, who was afraid, seeing them so disguised, and thought they had been some maskers out of their wits, which moved him to enquire of one of the said artlesse masters of the company, what this mummery meant? it was answered him, that they desired to have their bells restored to them. Assoon as *Ponocrates* heard that, he ran in all haste to carry the newes unto *Gargantua*, that he might be ready to answer them, and speedily resolve what was to be done. *Gargantua* being advertised hereof, called apart his Schoolmaster *Ponocrates*, *Philotimus* Steward of his house, *Gymnastes* his Esquire, and *Eudemon*, and very summarily conferred with them, both of what he should do, and what answer he should give. They were all of opinion that they should bring them unto the goblet-office, which is the Buttery, and there make them drink like Roysters, and line their jackets soundly: and that this cougher might not be puft up with vain-glory, by thinking the bells were restored at his request, they sent (whilest he was chopining and plying the pot) for the Major of the City, the Rector of the facultie, and the Vicar of the Church, unto whom they resolved to deliver the bells, before the *Sophister* had propounded his commission; after that, in their hearing, he should pronounce his gallant Oration, which was done, and they being come, the Sophister was brought into a full hall, and began as followeth, in coughing.

CHAPTER XIX

*The Oration of Master Janotus de Bragmardo, for recovery of
the bells.*

HEM, hem, *Gudday* Sirs, *Gudday & vobis* my masters, it were but
reason that you should restore to us our bells; for we have great
need of them. *Hem, hem, aihfuhash*, we have often-times heretofore refused good money for them of those of *London* in *Cahors*,
yea and of those of *Bordeaux* in *Brie*, who would have bought
them for the substantifick quality of the elementary complexion, which is intronificated in the terrestreity of their quiddit-
ative nature, to extraneize the blasting mists, and whirlwindes
upon our Vines; indeed not ours, but these round about us; for
if we lose the *piot* and liquour of the grape, we lose all both
sense and law. If you restore them unto us at my request, I shall
gaine by it six basketfuls of sauciges, and a fine paire of
breeches, which will do my legs a great deal of good, or else they
will not keep their promise to me. Ho by gob *domine*, a paire of
breeches is good, *& vir sapiens non abhorrebit eam*. Ha, ha, a paire
of breeches is not so easily got, I have experience of it my self.
Consider, *Domine*, I have been these eighteen dayes in *metagra-
bolising* this brave speech, *Reddite quæ sunt Cæsaris, Cæsari, & quæ
sunt Dei, Deo. Ibi jacet lepus*, by my faith, *Domine*, if you will sup
with me in *cameris*, by cox body, *charitatis nos faciemus bonum
cherubin; ego occidit unum porcum, & ego habet bonum vino*: but of
good wine we cannot make bad Latine. Well, *de parte Dei datè
nobis bellas nostras*; Hold, I give you in the name of the facultie
a *Sermones de utino*, that *utinam* you would give us our bells. *Vul-
tis etiam pardonos? per diem vos habebitis, & nihil payabitis*. O Sir
Domine, Bellagivaminor nobis; verily, *est bonum vobis*. They are
useful to every body, if they fit your mare well, so do they do
our facultie; *quæ comparata est jumentis insipientibus, & similis
facta est eis, Psalmo nescio quo*; yet did I quote it in my note-book *&
est unum bonum* Achilles, a good defending argument, *hem, hem,
hem, haikhash*; for I prove unto you that you should give me
them. *Ego sic argumentor, Omnis bella bellabilis in Bellerio* bellan-
do, bellans bellative, *bellare facit, bellabiliter bellantes: parisius*

habet bellas; ergo gluc. Ha, ha, ha, this is spoken to some purpose; it is *in tertio primæ*, in *Darii*, or elsewhere. By my soul, I have seen the time that I could play the devil in arguing, but now I am much failed, and henceforward want nothing but a cup of good wine, a good bed, my back to the fire, my belly to the table, and a good deep dish. *Hei domine*, I beseech you, *in nomine Patris, Filii, & Spiritûs sancti*, Amen, to restore unto us our bells: and God keep you from evil, and our Lady from health; *qui vivit & regnat per omnia secula seculorum. Amen.* Hem, *hashchehhawksash, qzrchremhemhash, verùm enim vero, quandoquidem, dubio procul, ædepol, quoniam, ità certè, medius fidius*; A Town without bells is like a blinde man without a staffe, an Asse without a crupper, and a Cow without Cymbals; therefore be assured, until you have restored them unto us, we will never leave crying after you, like a blinde man that hath lost his staffe, braying like an Asse without a crupper, and making a noise like a Cow without Cymbals. A certain Latinisator, dwelling near the Hospital, said since, producing the authority of one *Taponnus*, I lie, it was *Pontanus* the secular Poet, who wish't those bells had been made of feathers, and the clapper of a foxtail, to the end they might have begot a chronicle in the bowels of his braine, when he was about the composing of his carminiformal lines: but, *Nac petet in petetac tic torche Lorgne*, or *Rot kipipur kipipot put pantse malf*, he was declared an Heretick; We make them as of wax. And no more said the deponent. *Valete & plaudite. Calepinus recensui.*

CHAPTER XX

How the Sophister carried away his cloth, and how he had a suite in law against the other Masters.

THE Sophister had no sooner ended, but *Ponocrates* and *Eudemon* burst out in a laughing so heartily, that they had almost split with it, and given up the ghost, in rendering their souls to God: even just as *Crassus* did, seeing a lubberly Asse eate thistles; and as *Philemon*, who, for seeing an Asse eate those figs which were provided for his own dinner, died with force of laughing; together with them Master *Janotus* fell a laughing too as fast as he could, in which mood of laughing they continued so long, that their eyes did water by the vehement concussion of the substance of the braine, by which these lachrymal humidities, being prest out, glided through the optick nerves, and so to the full represented *Democritus Heraclitising*, and *Heraclitus Democritising*. When they had done laughing, *Gargantua* consulted with the prime of his retinue, what should be done. There *Ponocrates* was of opinion, that they should make this faire Orator drink again, and seeing he had shewed them more pastime, and made them laugh more then a natural soule could have done, that they should give him ten baskets full of sauciges, mentioned in his pleasant speech, with a paire of hose, three hundred great billets of logwood, five and twenty hogsheads of wine, a good large down-bed, and a deep capacious dish, which he said were necessary for his old age. All this was done as they did appoint: only *Gargantua*, doubting that they could not quickly finde out breeches fit for his wearing, because he knew not what fashion would best become the said Orator, whether the martingal fashion of breeches, wherein is a spunghole with a draw-bridge, for the more easie caguing: or the fashion of the Marriners, for the greater solace and comfort of his kidneys: or that of the *Switsers*, which keeps warm the *bedondaine* or belly-tabret: or round breeches with streat cannions, having in the seat a piece like a Cods taile, for feare of over-heating his reines; all which considered he caused to be given him seven elles of white cloth for the linings. The wood was carried by the Porters, the Masters of Arts carried the sauciges and the dishes, and Master *Janotus* himself would carry the cloth. One of the said Masters, (called *Jesse Bandouille*,) shewed him that it was not seemly nor decent for one of his condition to do so, and that therefore he should deliver it to one of them: Ha, said *Janotus*, *Baudet*, *Baudet*, or, Blockhead, Blockhead, thou dost not conclude *in modo & figura;* for loe, to this end serve the suppositions, *& parva Logicalia: pannus, pro quo supponit? Confusè* (said *Bandouille) & distributivè.* I do not ask thee (said *Janotus*,) Blockhead, *quomodo supponit,* but *pro quo?* It is, *Blockhead, pro tibiis meis,* and therefore I will carry it, *Egomet, sicut suppositum portat appositum*; so did he carry it away very close and covertly, as *Patelin* the *Buffoon* did his cloth. The best was, that when this cougher in a full act or assembly held at the *Mathurins*, had with great confidence required his breeches and sauciges, and that they were flatly denied him, because he had them of *Gargantua*, according to the informations thereupon made, he shewed them that this was *gratìs* and out of his liberality, by which they were not in any sort quit of their promises. Notwithstanding this, it was answered him, that he should be content with reason, without expectation of any other bribe there. Reason: (said *Janotus*,) we use none of it here, unluckie traitors, you are not worth the hanging: the earth beareth not more arrant Villains then you are, I know it well enough; Halt not before the lame; I have practised wickednesse with you: By Gods rattle I will inform the King of the enormous abuses that are forged here, and carried underhand by you, and let me be a Leper, if he do not burn you alive like *Sodomites*, Traitors, Hereticks and Seducers, enemies to God and vertue. Upon these words they framed articles against him: he on the other side warned them to appear: In summe, the Processe was retained by the Court, and is there as yet. Hereupon the *Magisters* made a vow, never to *decrott* themselves in rubbing off the dirt of either their shoes or clothes: Master *Janotus* with his Adherents, vowed never to blow or snuffe their noses, until judgement were given by a definitive sentence; by these vows do they continue unto this time both dirty and snottie; for the Court hath not garbeled, sifted, and fully looked into all the pieces as yet. The judgement or decree shall be given out & pronounced at the next *Greek* Calends, that is, never: as you know that they do more then nature, and contrary to their own articles: the articles of *Paris* maintain, that to God alone belongs infinitie, and nature produceth nothing that is immortal; for she putteth an end and period to all things by her engendered, according to the saying, *Omnia orta cadunt, &c.* But these thick mist-swallowers make the suits in law depending before them both infinite and immortal; in doing whereof, they have given occasion to, and verified the saying of *Chilo* the *Lacedemonian*, consecrated to the Oracle at *Delphos*, that misery is the inseparable companion of law-debates: and that pleaders are miserable; for sooner shall they attain to the end of their lives, then to the final decision of their pretended rights.

THE FIRST BOOK

CHAPTER XXI

The Study of Gargantua, according to the discipline of his Schoolmasters the Sophisters.

THE first day being thus spent, and the bells put up again in their own place, the Citizens of *Paris*, in acknowledgement of this courtesie, offered to maintain and feed his Mare as long as he pleased, which *Gargantua* took in good part, and they sent her to graze in the forrest of *Biere*. I think she is not there now. This done, he with all his heart submitted his study to the discretion of *Ponocrates*: who for the beginning appointed that he should do as he was accustomed, to the end he might understand by what meanes, in so long time, his old Masters had made him so sottish and ignorant. He disposed therefore of his time in such fashion, that ordinarily he did awake betwixt eight and nine a clock, whether it was day or not, (for so had his ancient governours ordained,) alledging that which *David* saith, *Vanum est vobis ante lucem surgere.* Then did he tumble and tosse, wag his legs, and wallow in the bed sometime, the better to stirre up, and rouse his vital spirits, and apparelled himself according to the season: but willingly he would weare a great long gown of thick freeze, furred with fox-skins. Afterwards he combed his head with an *Alman* combe, which is the foure fingers and the thumb; for his *Præceptor* said, that to comb himself otherwayes, to wash and make himself neat, was to lose time in this world. Then he dung'd, pist, spued, belched, cracked, yawned, spitted, coughed, yexed, sneezed and snotted himself like an *Arch-deacon*: and, to suppresse the dew and bad aire, went to breakfast, having some good fried tripes, faire rashers on the coales, excellent gamons of bacon, store of fine minced meat, and a great deal of sippet brewis, made up of the fat of the beef-pot, laid upon bread, cheese, and chop't parsley strewed together. *Ponocrates* shewed him, that he ought not to eat so soon after rising out of his bed, unlesse he had performed some exercise beforehand: *Gargantua* answered, What have not I sufficiently well exercised my self? I have wallowed and rolled my self six or seven turnes in my bed, before I rose: is not that enough? Pope *Alexander* did

69

so, by the advice of a Jew his Physician, and lived till his dying day in despite of his enemies. My first Masters have used me to it, saying that to breakfast made a good memory, and therefore they drank first. I am very well after it, and dine but the better: and Master *Tubal*, (who was the first Licenciat at *Paris*,) told me, that it was not enough to run apace, but to set forth betimes; so doth not the total welfare of our humanity depend upon perpetual drinking in a rible rable, like ducks, but on drinking early in the morning: *unde versus*,

> To rise betimes is no good houre.
> To drink betimes is better sure.

After that he had throughly broke his fast, he went to Church, and they carried to him in a great basket, a huge *impantoufled* or thick-covered breviary, weighing what in grease, clasps, parchment and cover, little more or lesse then eleven hundred and six pounds. There he heard six and twenty or thirty Masses: This while, to the same place came his orison-mutterer *impaletocked*, or lap't up about the chin, like a tufted whoop, and his breath pretty well antidoted with store of the Vine-tree-sirrup: with him he mumbled all his *Kiriels*, and dunsical breborions, which he so curiously thumbed and fingered, that there fell not so much as one graine to the ground; as he went from the Church, they brought him upon a Dray drawn with oxen, a confused heap of *Patinotres* and *Aves* of *Sante Claude*, every one of them being of the bignesse of a hat-block; and thus walking through the cloysters, galleries or garden, he said more in turning them over, then sixteen Hermites would have done. Then did he study some paltry half-houre with his eyes fixed upon his book; but (as the Comick saith,) his minde was in the Kitchin. Pissing then a full Urinal, he sate down at table; and because he was naturally flegmatick, he began his meale with some dozens of gammons, dried neats tongues, hard rowes of mullet, called *Botargos*, *Andouilles* or sauciges, and such other forerunners of wine; in the mean while, foure of his folks did cast into his mouth one after another continually mustard by whole shovels full. Immediately after that, he drank a horrible draught of white-wine for the ease of his kidneys. When that was done, he ate according to the season meat agreeable to his appetite, and then left off eating when his belly began to strout, and was like to crack for fulnesse; as for his drinking, he had in that neither end nor rule; for he was wont to say, that the limits and bounds of drinking were, when the cork of the shoes of him that drinketh, swelleth up half a foot high.

CHAPTER XXII

The Games of Gargantua.

THEN blockishly mumbling with a set on countenance a piece of scurvie grace, he wash't his hands in fresh wine, pick't his teeth with the foot of a hog, and talked jovially with his Attendants: then the Carpet being spred, they brought plenty of cardes, many dice, with great store and abundance of checkers and chesse-boards.

There he played.

At Flusse.	At puffe, or let him speak that hath it.
At Primero.	At take nothing and throw out.
At the beast.	
At the rifle.	
At trump.	At the marriage.
At the prick and spare not.	At the frolick or jackdaw.
At the hundred.	At the opinion.
At the peenie.	At who doth the one, doth the other.
At the unfortunate woman.	
At the fib.	At the sequences.
At the passe ten.	At the ivory bundles.
At one and thirtie.	At the tarots.
At post and paire, or even and sequence.	At losing load him.
	At he's gulled and *esto*.
At three hundred.	At the torture.
At the unluckie man.	At the handruf.
At the last couple in hell.	At the click.
At the hock.	At honours.
At the surlie.	At love.
At the lanskenet.	At the chesse.
At the cukoe.	At *Reynold* the fox.

At the squares.
At the cowes.
At the lottery.
At the chance or mumchance.
At three dice or maniest bleaks.
At the tables.
At nivinivinack.
At the lurch.
At doublets or queens-game.
At the failie.
At the french tictac.
At the long tables or fer-keering.
At feldown.
At Todsbody.
At needs must.
At the dames or draughts.
At bob and mow.
At *primus secundus*.
At mark-knife.
At the keyes.
At span-counter.
At even or odd.
At crosse or pile.
At bal and huckle-bones.
At ivory balls.
At the billiards.
At bob and hit.
At the owle.
At the charming of the hare.
At pull yet a little.
At trudgepig.
At the magatapies.
At the horne.
At the flowerd or shrove-tide oxe.

At the madge-owlet.
At pinch without laughing.
At prickle me tickle me.
At the unshoing of the Asse.
At the cocksesse.
At hari hohi.
At I set me down.
At earle beardie.
At the old mode.
At draw the spit.
At put out.
At gossip lend me your sack.
At the ramcod ball.
At thrust out the harlot.
At marseil figs.
At nicknamrie.
At stick and hole.
At boke or him, or flaying the fox.
At the branching it.
At trill madam, or graple my Lady.
At the oat selling.
At blow the coale.
At the rewedding.
At the quick and dead judge.
At unoven the iron.
At the false clown.
At the flints, or at the nine stones.
At to the crutch hulch back.
At the Sanct is found.
At hinch, pinch and laugh not.
At the leek.
At Bumdockdousse.
At the loose gig.
At the hoop.

At the sow.
At belly to belly.
At the dales or straths.
At the twigs.
At the quoits.
At I'm for that.
At tilt at weekie.
At nine pins.
at the cock *quintin*.
at tip and hurle.
at the flat bowles.
at the veere and tourn.
at rogue and ruffian.
at bumbatch touch.
at the mysterious trough.
at the short bowles.
at the daple gray.
at cock and crank it.
at break-pot.
at my desire.
at twirlie whirlietrill.
at the rush bundles.
at the short staffe.
at the whirling gigge.
at hide and seek, or are you all hid.
at the picket.
at the blank.
at the pilfrers.
at the caveson.
at prison barres.
at have at the nuts.
at cherrie-pit.
at rub and rice.
at whip-top.
at the casting top.
at the hobgoblins.
at the O wonderful.
at the soilie smutchie.

at fast and loose.
at scutchbreech.
at the broom-beesome.
at St. *Cosme* I come to adore thee.
at the lustie brown boy.
at I take you napping.
at faire and softly passeth lent.
at the forked oak.
at trusse.
at the wolfes taile.
at bum to busse, or nose in breech.
at *Geordie* give me my lance.
at swaggie, waggie or shoggieshou.
at stook and rook, sheare, and threave.
at the birch.
at the musse.
at the dillie dilli darling.
at oxe moudie.
at purpose in purpose.
at nine lesse.
at blinde-man-buffe.
at the fallen bridges.
at bridled *nick*.
at the white at buts.
at thwack swinge him.
at apple, peare, plum.
at mumgi.
at the toad.
at cricket.
at the pounding stick.
at jack and the box.
at the queens.
at the trades.

at heads and points.

at the vine-tree hug.

at black be thy fall.

at ho the distaffe.

at Joane Thomson.

at the boulting cloth.

at the oats seed.

at greedie glutton.

at the morish dance.

at feebie.

at the whole frisk and gambole.

at battabum, or riding of the wilde mare.

at *Hinde* the Plowman.

at the good mawkin.

at the dead beast.

at climbe the ladder *Billie*.

at the dying hog.

at the salt doup.

at the pretty pigeon.

at barley break.

at the bavine.

at the bush leap.

at crossing.

at bo-peep.

at the hardit arsepursie.

at the harrowers nest.

at forward hey.

at the fig.

at gunshot crack.

at mustard peel.

at the gome.

at the relapse.

at jog breech, or prick him forward.

at knockpate.

at the Cornish cough.

at the crane-dance.

at slash and cut.

at bobbing, or the flirt on the nose.

at the larks.

at filipping.

After he had thus well played, reveled, past and spent his time, it was thought fit to drink a little, and that was eleven glassefuls the man, and immediately after making good cheer again, he would stretch himself upon a faire bench, or a good large bed, and there sleep two or three houres together, without thinking or speaking any hurt. After he was awakened he would shake his eares a little. In the mean time they brought him fresh wine, there he drank better then ever. *Ponocrates* shewed him, that it was an ill diet to drink so after sleeping. It is (answered *Gargantua*,) the very life of the Patriarchs and holy Fathers; for naturally I sleepe salt, and my sleep hath been to me in stead of so many gamons of bacon. Then began he to study a little, and out came the *patenotres* or rosary of beads; which the better and more formally to dispatch, he got up on an old mule, which had served nine Kings, and so mumbling with his mouth, nodding and dodling his head, would go see a coney ferretted or caught in a ginne; At his return he went into the Kitchin, to know what roste meat was on the spit, and what otherwayes was to be drest for supper: and supped very well upon my conscience: and commonly did invite some of his neighbours that were good drinkers, with whom carousing and drinking merrily, they told stories of all sorts from the old to the new. Amongst others, he had for domesticks the Lords of *Fou*, of *Gourville*, of *Griniot*, and of *Marigny*. After supper were brought in upon the place the faire wooden Gospels, and the books of the foure Kings, that is to say, many paires of tables and cardes: or the faire flusse, one, two, three: or at all to make short work: or else they went to see the wenches thereabouts, with little small banquets, intermixed with collations and reer-Suppers. Then did he sleep without unbrideling, until eight a clock in the next morning.

CHAPTER XXIII

How Gargantua was instructed by Ponocrates, and in such sort disciplinated, that he lost not one houre of the day.

WHEN *Ponocrates* knew *Gargantua*'s vicious manner of living, he resolved to bring him up in another kinde; but for a while he bore with him, considering that nature cannot endure a sudden change, without great violence. Therefore to begin his work the better, he requested a learned Physician of that time, called Master *Theodorus*, seriously to perpend (if it were possible,) how to bring *Gargantua* unto a better course; the said Physician purged him canonically with *Anticyrian ellebore*, by which medicine he cleansed all the alteration, and perverse habitude of his braine. By this meanes also *Ponocrates* made him forget all that he had learned under his ancient *Præceptors*, as *Timothie* did to his disciples, who had been instructed under other Musicians. To do this the better, they brought him into the company of learned men, which were there, in whose imitation he had a great desire and affection to study otherwayes, and to improve his parts. Afterwards he put himself into such a road and way of studying, that he lost not any one houre in the day, but employed all his time in learning, and honest knowledge. *Gargantua* awaked them about foure a clock in the morning: whilest

they were in rubbing of him, there was read unto him some
chapter of the holy Scripture aloud and clearly, with a pronunciation fit for the matter, and hereunto was appointed a young
page borne in *Basche*, named *Anagnostes*. According to the purpose and argument of that lesson, he oftentimes gave himself to
worship, adore, pray, and send up his supplications to that good
God, whose Word did shew his majesty and marvellous judgement. Then went he unto the secret places to make excretion
of his natural digestions: there his Master repeated what had
been read, expounding unto him the most obscure and difficult
points; in returning, they considered the face of the sky, if it was
such as they had observed it the night before, and into what
signes the Sun was entering, as also the Moon for that day. This
done, he was apparelled, combed, curled, trimmed and perfumed, during which time they repeated to him the lessons of
the day before: he himself said them by heart, and upon them
would ground some practical cases concerning the estate of man,
which he would prosecute sometimes two or three houres, but
ordinarily they ceased as soon as he was fully clothed. Then for
three good houres he had a lecture read unto him. This done,
they went forth, still conferring of the substance of the lecture,
either unto a field near the University called the *Brack*, or unto
the medowes where they played at the ball, the long-tennis,
and at the *Piletrigone*, (*which is a play wherein we throw a triangular
piece of iron at a ring, to passe it,*) most gallantly exercising their
bodies, as formerly they had done their mindes. All their play
was but in liberty, for they left off when they pleased, and that
was commonly when they did sweat over all their body, or were
otherwayes weary. Then were they very well wiped and
rubbed, shifted their shirts, and, walking soberly, went to see if
dinner was ready. Whilest they stayed for that, they did clearly
and eloquently pronounce some sentences that they had
retained of the lecture. In the mean time Master Appetite came,
and then very orderly sate they down at table; at the beginning
of the meale, there was read some pleasant history of the warlike actions of former times, until he had taken a glasse of wine.
Then, (if they thought good,) they continued reading, or began
to discourse merrily together; speaking first of the vertue, propriety, efficacy and nature of all that was served in at the table;

of bread, of wine, of water, of salt, of fleshes, fishes, fruits, herbs, roots, and of their dressing; by meanes whereof, he learned in a little time all the passages competent for this, that were to be found in *Plinie*, *Athenæus*, *Dioscorides*, *Julius Pollux*, *Galen*, *Porphirie*, *Oppian*, *Polybius*, *Heliodore*, *Aristotle*, *Elian*, and others. Whilest they talked of these things, many times to be the more certain, they caused the very books to be brought to the table, and so well and perfectly did he in his memory retain the things above-said, that in that time there was not a Physician that knew half so much as he did. Afterwards they conferred of the lessons read in the morning, and ending their repast with some conserve or marmelade of quinces: he pick't his teeth with mastick tooth-pickers; wash't his hands and eyes with faire fresh water, and gave thanks unto God in some fine Canticks, made in praise of the divine bounty and munificence. This done, they brought in cards, not to play, but to learn a thousand pretty tricks, and new inventions, which were all grounded upon *Arithmetick*: by this meanes he fell in love with that numerical science, and every day after dinner and supper he past his time in it as pleasantly, as he was wont to do at cardes and dice: so that at last he understood so well both the Theory and Practical part thereof; that *Tunstal* the *Englishman*, who had written very largely of that purpose, confessed that verily in comparison of him he had no skill at all. And not only in that, but in the other *Mathematical* Sciences, as *Geometrie*, *Astronomie*, *Musick*, &c. For in waiting on the concoction, and attending the digestion of his food, they made a thousand pretty instruments and *Geometrical* figures, & did in some measure practise the *Astronomical* canons.

After this they recreated themselves with singing *musically*, in foure or five parts, or upon a set theme or ground at random, as it best pleased them; in matter of *musical* instruments, he learned to play upon the Lute, the Virginals, the Harp, the Allman Flute with nine holes, the Viol, and the Sackbut. This houre thus spent, and digestion finished, he did purge his body of natural excrements, then betook himself to his principal study for three houres together, or more, as well to repeat his matutinal lectures, as to proceed in the book wherein he was, as also to write handsomly, to draw and forme the *Antick* and *Romane* letters. This being done, they went out of their house, and with them a young Gentleman of *Touraine*, named the Esquire *Gymnast*, who taught him the Art of riding; changing then his clothes, he rode a *Naples* courser, a *Dutch* roussin, a *Spanish* gennet, a barbed or trapped steed, then a light fleet horse, unto whom he gave a hundred carieres, made him go the high saults, bounding in the aire, free the ditch with a skip, leap over a stile or pale, turne short in a ring both to the right and left hand. There he broke not his lance; for it is the greatest foolery in the world, to say, I have broken ten lances at tilt or in fight, a Carpenter can do even as much; but it is a glorious and praise-worthy action, with one lance to break and overthrow ten enemies: therefore with a sharp, stiffe, strong and well-steeled lance, would he usually force up a door, pierce a harnesse, beat down a tree, carry away the ring, lift up a cuirasier saddle, with the male-coat and gantlet; all this he did in compleat armes from head to foot. As for the prancing flourishes, and smacking popismes, for the better cherishing of the horse, commonly used in riding, none did them better then he. The cavallerize of *Ferrara* was but as an Ape compared to him. He was singularly skilful in leaping nimbly from one horse to another, without putting foot to ground, and these horses were called *desultories*: he could likewise from either side, with a lance in his hand, leap on horseback without stirrups, and rule the horse at his pleasure without a bridle, for such things are useful in military engagements. Another day he exercised the battel-axe, which he so dextrously wielded, both in the nimble, strong and smooth management of that weapon, and that in all the feats practiseable by it, that he past Knight of Armes in the field, and at all Essayes. Then tost he the pike, played with the two-handed sword, with the backsword, with the spanish tuck, the dagger, poiniard, armed, unarmed, with a buckler, with a cloak, with a targuet. Then would he hunt the Hart, the Roe-buck, the Beare, the fallow Deer, the wilde Boare, the Hare, the Phesant, the Partridge and the Bustard. He played at the baloon, and made it bound in the aire, both with fist and foot. He wrestled, ran, jumped, not at three steps and a leap (*called the hops*,) nor at *clochepied*, (*called the Hares leap*,) nor yet at the *Almanes*; for (said *Gymnast*,) these jumps are for the warres altogether unprofitable, and of no use: but at one leap he would skip over a ditch, spring over a hedge, mount six paces upon a wall, ramp and grapple after this fashion up against a window, of the full height of a lance. He did swim in deep waters on his belly, on his back, sidewise, with all his body, with his feet only, with one hand in the air, wherein he held a book, crossing thus the bredth of the river of *Seine*, without wetting it, and dragged along his cloak with his teeth, as did *Julius Cæsar*; then with the help of one hand, he entred forcibly into a boat, from whence he cast himself again headlong into the water, sounded the depths, hollowed the rocks, and plunged into the pits and gulphs. Then turned he the boat about, governed it, led it swiftly or slowly with the stream and against the stream, stopped it in its course, guided it with one hand, and with the other laid hard about him with a huge great Oare, hoised the saile, hied up along the mast by the shrouds, ran upon the edge of the decks, set the compasse in order, tackled the boulins, and steer'd the helme. Coming out of the water, he ran furiously up against a hill, and with the same alacrity and swiftnesse ran down again; he climbed up at trees like a cat; and leaped from the one to the other like a squirrel: he did pull down the great boughes and branches, like another *Milo*; then with two sharp well-steeled daggers, and two tried bodkins, would he run up by the wall to the very top of a house like a cat; then suddenly came down from the top to the bottom, with such an even composition of members, that by the fall he would catch no harme.

He did cast the dart, throw the barre, put the stone, practise the javelin, the boar-spear or partisan, and the halbard; he broke the strongest bowes in drawing, bended against his breast the greatest crosse-bowes of steele, took his aime by the eye with the hand-gun, and shot well, traversed and planted the Canon, shot at but-marks, at the papgay from below upwards, *or to a height*; from above downwards, *or to a descent*, then before him, sidewise, and behinde him, like the *Parthians*. They tied a cable-rope to the top of a high Tower, by one end whereof hanging near the ground, he wrought himself with his hands to the very top: Then upon the same tract came down so sturdily and firme that you could not on a plaine meadow have run with more assurance. They set up a great pole fixed upon two trees, there would he hang by his hands, and with them alone, his feet touching at nothing, would go back and fore along the foresaid

rope with so great swiftnesse, that hardly could one overtake
him with running; and then to exercise his breast and lungs, he
would shout like all the Devils in hell. I heard him once call
Eudemon from St. *Victors* gate to *Monmartre: Stentor* had never
such a voyce at the siege of *Troy*. Then for the strengthening of
his nerves or sinewes, they made him two great sows of lead,
each of them weighing eight thousand and seven hundred kintals, which they called *Alteres*; those he took up from the ground,
in each hand one, then lifted them up over his head, and held
them so without stirring three quarters of an hour and more,
which was an inimitable force; he fought at Barriers with the
stoutest and most vigorous Champions; and when it came to the
cope, he stood so sturdily on his feet, that he abandoned himself
unto the strongest, in case they could remove him from his
place, as *Milo* was wont to do of old; in whose imitation likewise
he held a Pomgranat in his hand, to give it unto him that could
take it from him: The time being thus bestowed, and himself
rubbed, cleansed, wiped, and refresht with other clothes, he returned fair and softly; and passing through certain meadows,
or other grassie places, beheld the trees and plants, comparing
them with what is written of them in the books of the Ancients,
such as *Theophrast, Dioscorides, Marinus, Plinie, Nicander, Macer,*
and *Galen*, and carried home to the house great handfuls of
them, whereof a young Page called *Rizotomos* had charge;
together with little Mattocks, Pick-axes, Grubbing-hooks, Cab-
bies, Pruning-knives, and other instruments requisite for herborising. Being come to their lodging, whilest supper was
making ready, they repeated certain passages of that which hath
been read, and sate down at table. Here remark, that his dinner
was sober and thrifty, for he did then eat only to prevent the
gnawings of his stomack, but his supper was copious and large;
for he took then as much as was fit to maintaine and nourish
him; which indeed is the true diet prescribed by the Art of good
and sound *Physick*. Although a rabble of loggerheaded Physicians, nuzzeled in the brabling shop of *Sophisters*, counsel the
contrary; during that repast was continued the lesson read
at dinner as long as they thought good: the rest was spent in
good discourse, learned and profitable. After that they had
given thanks, he set himself to sing vocally, and play upon

harmonious instruments, or otherwayes passed his time at some
pretty sports, made with cards or dice; or in practising the feats of
Legerdemain, with cups and balls. There they stayed some nights
in frolicking thus, and making themselves merrie till it was time
to go to bed; and on other nights they would go make visits unto
learned men, or to such as had been travellers in strange and
remote countreys. When it was full night before they retired
themselves, they went unto the most open place of the house
to see the face of the sky, and there beheld the comets, if any-
where, as likewise the figures, situations, aspects, oppositions
and conjunctions of the both fixed starres and planets.

Then with his Master did he briefly recapitulate after the
manner of the *Pythagoreans*, that which he had read, seen,
learned, done and understood in the whole course of that day.

Then prayed they unto *God* the Creator, in falling down before him, and strengthening their faith towards him, and glor-
ifying him for his boundlesse bounty, and, giving thanks unto
him for the time that was past, they recommended themselves
to his divine clemency for the future, which being done, they
went to bed, and betook themselves to their repose and rest.

CHAPTER XXIV

How Gargantua spent his time in rainie weather.

IF it happened that the weather were any thing cloudie, foul &
rainie, all the forenoon was employed, as before specified,
according to custom, with this difference only, that they had a
good clear fire lighted, to correct the distempers of the aire: but
after dinner, instead of their wonted exercitations they did
abide within, and, by way of *Apotherapie*, (that is, *a making the
body healthful by exercise*,) did recreate themselves in botteling up
of hay, in cleaving and sawing of wood, and in threshing sheaves
of corn at the Barn. Then they studied the Art of painting or
carving; or brought into use the antick play of tables, as *Leonicus*
hath written of it, and as our good friend *Lascaris* playeth at it.
In playing they examined the passages of ancient Authors,
wherein the said play is mentioned, or any metaphore drawn
from it. They went likewise to see the drawing of mettals, or the

casting of great ordnance: how the Lapidaries did work, as also the Goldsmiths and Cutters of precious stones: nor did they omit to visit the Alchymists, moneycoiners, Upholsters, Weavers, Velvet-workers, Watchmakers, Looking-glasse-framers, Printers, Organists, and other such kinde of Artificers, and every where giving them somewhat to drink, did learne and consider the industry and invention of the trades. They went also to heare the publick lectures, the solemn commencements, the repetitions, the acclamations, the pleadings of the gentle Lawyers, and Sermons of Evangelical Preachers. He went through the Halls and places appointed for fencing, and there played against the Masters themselves at all weapons, and shewed them by experience that he knew as much in it as (yea more then) they. And in stead of herborising, they visited the shops of Druggists, Herbalists and Apothecaries, and diligently considered the fruits, roots, leaves, gums, seeds, the grease and ointments of some forreign parts, as also how they did adulterate them. He went to see the Juglers, Tumblers, Mountebanks and Quacksalvers, and considered their cunning, their shifts, their summer-saults and smooth tongue, especially of those of *Chauny* in *Picardie*, who are naturally great praters, and brave givers of fibs in matter of green apes. At their return they did eate more soberly at supper then at other times, and meats more desiccative and extenuating; to the end that the intemperate moisture of the aire, communicated to the body by a necessary confinitie, might by this means be corrected, and that they might not receive any prejudice for want of their ordinary bodily exercise. Thus was *Gargantua* governed, and kept on in this course of education, from day to day profiting, as you may understand such a young man of his age may of a pregnant judgement with good discipline well continued. Which although at the beginning it seemed difficult, became a little after so sweet, so easie, and so delightful, that it seemed rather the recreation of a King, then the study of a Scholar. Neverthelesse *Ponocrates*, to divert him from this vehement intension of the spirits, thought fit, once in a month, upon some fair and clear day to go out of the City betimes in the morning, either towards *Gentilly*, or *Boulogne*, or to *Montrouge*, or *Charantonbridge*, or to *Vanures*, or St. *Clou*, and there spent all the day long in making the greatest chear that could be devised, sporting, making merry, drinking healths, playing, singing, dancing, tumbling in some faire medow, unnestling of sparrowes, taking of quailes, and fishing for frogs and crabs; but although that day was past without books or lecture, yet was it not spent without profit; for in the said medowes they usually repeated certain pleasant verses of *Virgils* Agriculture, of *Hesiod* and of *Politians* husbandrie, would set a broach some wittie Latine Epigrams, then immediately turned them into roundlays and songs for dancing in the French language. In their feasting, they would sometimes separate the water from the wine that was therewith mixed, as *Cato* teacheth *de re rustica*, and *Plinie*, with an ivie cup: would wash the wine in a basin full of water, then take it out again with a funnel as pure as ever. They made the water go from one glasse to another, and contrived a thousand little *automaterie* Engines, that is to say, moving of themselves.

CHAPTER XXV

How there was great strife and debate, raised betwixt the Cake-bakers of Lerne, and those of Gargantua's countrey— whereupon were waged great warres.

AT that time, which was the season of Vintage, in the beginning of Harvest, when the countrey shepherds were set to keep the Vines, and hinder the Starlings from eating up the grapes; as some cake-bakers of *Lerne* happened to passe along in the broad high way, driving unto the City ten or twelve horses loaded with cakes, the said shepherds courteously intreated them to give them some for their money, as the price then ruled in the market; for here it is to be remarked, that it is a celestial food to eate for breakfast hot fresh cakes with grapes, especially the frail clusters, the great red grapes, the muscadine, the verjuice grape and the luskard, for those that are costive in their belly; because it will make them gush out, and squirt the length of a Hunters staffe, like the very tap of a barrel; and often-times thinking to let a squib, they did all-to-besquatter and conskite themselves, whereupon they are commonly called the Vintage-thinkers. The Bunsellers or Cake-makers were in nothing inclinable to

their request; but (which was worse) did injure them most outragiously, calling them pratling gablers, lickorous gluttons,
freckled bittors, mangie rascals, shiteabed scoundrels, drunken
roysters, slie knaves, drowsie loiterers, slapsauce fellows, slab-
berdegullion druggels, lubbardly lowts, cosening foxes, ruffian
rogues, paultrie customers, sycophant-varlets, drawlatch hoydons, flouting milksops, jeering companions, staring clowns, forlorn snakes, ninnie lobcocks, scurvie sneaksbies, fondling fops,
base lowns, sawcie coxcombs, idle lusks, *scoffing Braggards, noddie meacocks, blockish grutnols, doddi-pol-jolt-heads, jobernol goose-
caps, foolish loggerheads, slutch calf-lollies, grouthead gnat-snappers,
lob-dotterels, gaping changelings, codshead loobies, woodcock slangams,
ninnie-hammer flycatchers, noddiepeak simpletons*; Turdie gut, shitten shepherds, and other such like defamatory epithetes, saying
further, that it was not for them to eate of these dainty cakes,
but might very well content themselves with the course
unraunged bread, or to eat of the great brown houshold loaf.
To which provoking words, one amongst them, called *Forgier*,
(an honest fellow of his person, and a notable springal,) made
answer very calmly thus: How long is it since you have got hornes,
that you are become so proud? indeed formerly you were wont
to give us some freely, and will you not now let us have any for
our money? This is not the part of good neighbours, neither do
we serve you thus when you come hither to buy our good corn,
whereof you make your cakes and buns: besides that, we would
have given you to the bargain some of our grapes, but *by his
zounds*, you may chance to repent it, and possibly have need of
us at another time, when we shall use you after the like manner,
and therefore remember it. Then *Marquet*, a prime man in the
confraternity of the cake-bakers, said unto him, Yea Sir, thou art
pretty well crest-risen this morning, thou didst eat yesternight
too much millet and bolymong, come hither *Sirrah*, come
hither, I will give thee some cakes: whereupon *Forgier* dreading
no harm, in all simplicity went towards him, and drew a six-
pence out of his leather sachel, thinking that *Marquet* would
have sold him some of his cakes; but in stead of cakes, he gave
him with his whip such a rude lash overthwart the legs, that
the marks of the whipcord knots were apparent in them; then
would have fled away, but *Forgier* cried out as loud as he could,

O murther, murther, help, help, help, and in the mean time
threw a great cudgel after him, which he carried under his arme,
wherewith he hit him in the *coronal* joynt of his head, upon the
crotaphick arterie of the right side thereof, so forcibly, that *Marquet*
fell down from his mare, more like a dead then living man.
Mean-while the farmers and countrey-swaines, that were watching their walnuts near to that place, came running with their
great poles and long staves, and laid such load on these cake-
bakers, as if they had been to thresh upon green rie. The other
shepherds and shepherdesses hearing the lamentable shout of
Forgier, came with their slings and slackies following them, and
throwing great stones at them, as thick as if it had been haile.
At last they overtook them, and took from them about foure or
five dosen of their cakes; neverthelesse they payed for them the
ordinary price, and gave them over and above one hundred
egges, and three baskets full of mulberries. Then did the cake-
bakers help to get up to his mare *Marquet*, who was most shrewdly wounded, and forthwith returned to *Lerne*, changing the
resolution they had to go to *Pareille*, threatning very sharp and
boistrously the cowherds, shepherds, and farmers of *Sevile* and
Sinays. This done, the shepherds and shepherdesses made
merry with these cakes and fine grapes, and sported themselves
together at the sound of the pretty small pipe, scoffing and
laughing at those vain-glorious cake-bakers, who had that day
met with a mischief for want of crossing themselves with a good
hand in the morning. Nor did they forget to apply to *Forgiers* leg
some faire great red medicinal grapes, and so handsomly drest
it and bound it up, that he was quickly cured.

CHAPTER XXVI

How the inhabitants of Lerne, by the commandment of
Picrochole their King, assaulted the shepherds of Gargantua,
unexpectedly and on a sudden.

THE Cake-bakers, being returned to *Lerne*, went presently,
before they did either eat or drink, to the *Capitol*, and there before
their King called *Picrochole*, the third of that name; made their
complaint, shewing their paniers broken, their caps all crumpled,

their coats torn, their cakes taken away, but, above all *Marquet* most enormously wounded, saying, that all that mischief was done by the shepherds and herdsmen of *Grangousier*, near the broad high way beyond *Sevile*: *Picrochole* incontinent grew angry and furious; and without asking any further what, how, why or wherefore? commanded the *ban* and *arriere ban* to be sounded throughout all his countrey, that all his vassals of what condition soever, should upon paine of the halter come in the best armes they could, unto the great place before the Castle, at the houre of noone, and, the better to strengthen his designe, he caused the drum to be beat about the town. Himself, whilest his dinner was making ready, went to see his artillery mounted upon the carriage, to display his colours, and set up the great royal standard, and loaded waines with store of ammunition both for the field and the belly, armes and victuals: at dinner he dispatch't his commissions, and by his expresse Edict my Lord *Shagrag* was appointed to command the Vanguard, wherein were numbered sixteen thousand and fourteen harquebusiers or fire-locks, together with thirty thousand and eleven Voluntier-adventurers. The great *Touquedillion*, Master of the horse, had the charge of the Ordnance, wherein were reckoned nine hundred and fourteen brazen pieces, in cannons, double cannons, basilisks, *serpentines, culverins*, bombards or murtherers, falcons, *bases* or *passevolans, spiroles* and other sorts of great guns. The Reerguard was committed to the *Duke of Scrapegood*: In the maine battel was the King, and the Princes of his Kingdome. Thus being hastily furnished, before they would set forward, they sent three hundred light horsemen under the conduct of Captain *Swill-wind*, to discover the countrey, clear the avenues, and see whether there was any ambush laid for them: but after they had made diligent search, they found all the land round about in peace and quiet, without any meeting or convention at all; which *Picrochole* understanding, commanded that every one should march speedily under his colours: then immediately in all disorder, without keeping either rank or file, they took the fields one amongst another, wasting, spoiling, destroying and making havock of all whereever they went, not sparing poor nor rich, priviledged nor unpriviledged places, Church nor Laity, drove away oxen and cowes, bulls, calves, heifers, wethers,

ewes, lambs, goats, kids, hens, capons, chickens, geese, ganders, goslings, hogs, swine, pigs and such like. Beating down
the walnuts, plucking the grapes, tearing the hedges, shaking
the fruit-trees, and committing such incomparable abuses, that the
like abomination was never heard of. Neverthelesse, they met
with none to resist them, for every one submitted to their
mercy, beseeching them, that they might be dealt with courteously, in regard that they had alwayes carried themselves, as
became good and loving neighbours, and that they had never
been guilty of any wrong or outrage done upon them, to be thus
suddenly surprised, troubled and disquieted, and that if they
would not desist, God would punish them very shortly; to which
expostulations and remonstrances no other answer was made,
but that they would teach them to eat cakes.

CHAPTER XXVII

*How a Monk of Sevile saved the Closse of the Abbey from being
ransacked by the enemie.*

So much they did, and so farre they went pillaging and stealing,
that at last they came to *Sevile*, where they robbed both men and
women, and took all they could catch: nothing was either too
hot or too heavie for them. Although the plague was there in the
most part of all the houses, they neverthelesse entered every
where; then plundered and carried away all that was within; and
yet for all this not one of them took any hurt, which is a most
wonderful case. For the Curates, Vicars, Preachers, Physicians,
Chirurgions and Apothecaries, who went to visit, to dresse, to
cure, to heale, to preach unto, and admonish those that were
sick, were all dead of the infection; and these devillish robbers
and murtherers caught never any harme at all. Whence comes
this to passe, (my masters) I beseech you think upon it? The
town being thus pillaged, they went unto the Abbey with a horrible noise and tumult, but they found it shut and made fast
against them; whereupon the body of the army marched forward towards a passe or ford called the *Gue de Vede*, except seven
companies of foot, and two hundred lanciers, who staying there,
broke down the walls of the Closse, to waste, spoile and make

havock of all the Vines and Vintage within that place. The Monks (poor devils) knew not in that extremity to which of all their Sancts they should vow themselves; neverthelesse, at all adventures they rang the bells *ad capitulum capitulantes*: there it was decreed, that they should make a faire Procession, stuffed with good lectures, prayers and letanies, *contra hostium insidias*, and jollie responses *pro pace*.

There was then in the Abbey a claustral Monk, called *Freer Ihon* of the funnels and gobbets, in French *des entoumeures*, young, gallant, frisk, lustie, nimble, *quick, active*, bold, adventurous, resolute, tall, lean, wide-mouthed, long-nosed, a faire dispatcher of morning prayers, unbridler of masses, and runner over of vigils; and to conclude summarily in a word, a right Monk, if ever there was any, since the Monking world monked a Monkerie: for the rest a Clerk even to the teeth in matter of breviary. This Monk hearing the noise that the enemy made within the inclosure of the Vineyard, went out to see what they were doing; and perceiving that they were cutting and gathering the grapes, whereon was grounded the foundation of all their next yeares wine, returned unto the quire of the Church where the other Monks were, all amazed and astonished like so many Bell-melters, whom when he heard sing, *im, nim, pe, ne, ne, ne, ne, nene, tum, ne, num, num, ini, i mi, co, o, no, o, o, neno, ne, no, no, no, rum, nenum, num*. It is well shit, well sung, (said he) by the vertue of God, why do not you sing Paniers farewell, Vintage is done; The devil snatch me, if they be not already within the middle of our Closse, and cut so well both Vines and Grapes, that *by cods body* there will not be found for these four yeares to come so much as a gleaning in it. *By the belly of Sanct James*, what shall we (*poor devils*) drink the while? Lord God! *da mihi potum*. Then said the Prior of the Covent, What should this drunken fellow do here, let him be carried to prison for troubling the divine service: Nay, said the Monk, the wine service, let us behave our selves so, that it be not troubled; for you your self, *my Lord Prior*, love to drink of the best, and so doth every honest man. Never yet did a man of worth dislike good wine, it is a monastical apoph-thegme. But these responses that you chant here by G— are not in season; wherefore is it, that our devotions were instituted to be short in the time of Harvest and Vintage, and long in the

Advent, and all the winter? The late Friar, *Massepelosse* of good memory, a true zealous man, (or else I give my self to the devil,) of our religion, told me, and I remember it well, how the reason was, that in this season we might presse and make the wine, and in Winter whiffe it up. Heark you, my masters, you that love the wine, *Cops body*, follow me, for *Sanct Antonie* burn me as freely as a fagot, if they get leave to taste one drop of the liquour, that will not now come and fight for relief of the Vine. Hogs belly, the goods of the Church! Ha, no, no: what the devil, *Sanct Thomas of England* was well content to die for them; if I died in the same cause, should not I be a *Sanct* likewise? Yes: yet shall I not die there for all this, for it is I that must do it to others and send them a packing. As he spake this, he threw off his great Monks habit, and laid hold upon the staffe of the crosse, which was made of the heart of a sorbaple-tree, it being of the length of a lance, round, of a full gripe, and a little poudred with lilies called *flower de luce*, the workmanship whereof was almost all defaced and worn out. Thus went he out in a faire long-skirted jacket, putting his frock scarfewayes athwart his breast, and in this equipage, with his staffe, shaft or truncheon of the crosse, laid on so lustily, brisk and fiercely upon his enemies, who without any order, or ensigne, or trumpet, or drum, were busied in gathering the grapes of the Vineyard; for the Cornets, Guidons, and Ensigne-bearers, had laid down their standards, banners, and colours by the wallsides: the Drummers had knockt out the heads of their Drums on one end, to fill them with grapes: the Trumpeters were loaded with great bundles of bunches, and huge knots of clusters: In summe, every one of them was out of aray, and all in disorder. He hurried therefore upon them so rudely, without crying *gare* or beware, that he overthrew them like hogs, tumbled them over like swine, striking athwart and alongst, and by one means or other laid so about him, after the old fashion of fencing, that to some he beat out their braines, to others he crushed their armes, battered their legs, and bethwacked their sides till their ribs cracked with it; to others again he unjoynted the spondyles *or knuckles of the neck*, disfigured their chaps, gashed their faces, made their cheeks hang flapping on their chin, and so swinged and belammed them, that they fell down before him like hay before a Mower: to some others he spoiled the frame of their kidneys, marred their backs, broke their thigh-bones, pash't in their noses, poached out their eyes, cleft their mandibules, tore their jaws, dug in their teeth into their throat, shook asunder their omoplates or shoulder-blades, *sphacelated* their shins, mortified their shanks, inflamed their ankles, heaved off of the hinges their ishies, their *sciatica* or hip-gout, dislocated the joints of their knees, squattered into pieces the boughts or pestles of their thighs, and so thumped, mawled and belaboured them every where, that never was corne so thick and threefold thresh't upon by Plowmens flailes, as were the pitifully disjoynted members of their mangled bodies, under the mercilesse baton of the crosse. If any offered to hide himself amongst the thickest of the Vines, he laid him squat as a flounder, bruised the ridge of his back, and dash't his reines like a dog. If any thought by flight to escape, he made his head to flie in pieces by the *Lambdoidal commissure, which is a seame in the hinder part of the scull.* If any one did scramble up into a tree, thinking there to be safe, he rent up his perinee, and impaled him in at the fundament. If any of his old acquaintance happened to cry out, Ha *Fryar Ihon* my friend, *Fryar Ihon*, quarter, quarter, I yield my self to you, to you I render my self: So thou shalt (said he) and must whether thou wouldst or no, and withal render and yield up thy soul to all the devils in hell, then suddenly gave them *Dronos*, that is, so many knocks, thumps, raps, dints, thwacks and bangs, as sufficed to warne *Pluto* of their coming, and dispatch them a going: if any was so rash and full of temerity as to resist him to his face, then was it he did shew the strength of his muscles, for without more ado he did transpierce him by running him in at the breast, through the mediastine and the heart. Others, again, he so quashed and bebumped, that with a sound bounce under the hollow of their short ribs, he overturned their stomachs so that they died immediately: to some with a smart souse on the *Epigaster*, he would make their midrif swag; then redoubling the blow, gave them such a home-push on the navel, that he made their puddings to gush out. To others through their ballocks he pierced their bum-gut, and left not bowel, tripe nor intral in their body, that had not felt the impetuosity, fiercenesse and fury of his violence. Beleeve that it was the most horrible spectacle that

ever one saw: Some cried unto *Sanct Barbe*, others to *St. George*;
O the holy *Lady Nytouch*, said one, the good Sanctesse; *O our
Lady of Succours*, said another, help, help: others cried, Our Lady
of *Cunaut*, of *Loretta*, of good tidings on the other side of the
water St. *Mary over*; some vowed a pilgrimage to St. *James*, and
others to the holy handkerchief at *Chamberrie*, which three
moneths after that burnt so well in the fire, that they could not
get one thread of it saved: others sent up their vowes to St.
Cadouin, others to St. *Ihon d'Angelie*, and to St. *Eutropius* of *Xaintes*:
others again invoked St. *Mesmes* of *Chinon*, St. *Martin* of *Candes*,
S. *Clouod* of *Sinays*, the holy relicks of *Laurezay*, with a thousand
other jolly little Sancts and Santrels: Some died without speaking, others spoke without dying; some died in speaking, others
spoke in dying. Others shouted as loud as they could, Confession, Confession, *Confiteor, miserere, in manus*; so great was the
cry of the wounded, that the *Prior* of the Abbey with all his
Monks came forth, who when they saw these poor wretches so
slain amongst the Vines, and wounded to death, confessed
some of them: but whilest the Priests were busied in confessing
them, the little Monkies ran all to the place where *Friar Ihon*
was, and asked him, wherein he would be pleased to require
their assistance? To which he answered, that they should cut
the throats of those he had thrown down upon the ground. They
presently leaving their outer habits and cowles upon the railes,
began to throttle and make an end of those whom he had already crushed: Can you tell with what instruments they did it?
with faire *gullies*, which are little hulch-back't demi-knives,
the iron toole whereof is two inches long, and the wooden
handle one inch thick, and three inches in length, wherewith
the little boyes in our countrey cut ripe walnuts in two, (while
they are yet in the shell,) and pick out the kernel, and they
found them very fit for the expediting of that wezand-slitting
exploit. In the mean time *Friar Ihon* with his formidable baton
of the Crosse, got to the breach which the enemies had made,
and there stood to snatch up those that endeavoured to escape:
Some of the *Monkito's* carried the standards, banners, ensignes,
guidons and colours into their cells and chambers, to make garters
of them. But when those that had been shriven, would have
gone out at the gap of the said breach, the sturdy *Monk* quash't

and fell'd them down with blowes, saying, These men have had confession and are penitent soules, they have got their absolution, and gained the pardons: they go into Paradise as streight as a sickle, or as the way is to *Faye*, (*like Crooked-Lane at East-cheap*.) Thus by his prowesse and valour were discomfited all those of the army that entered into the Closse of the Abbey, unto the number of thirteen thousand, six hundred, twenty and two, besides the women and little children, which is alwayes to be understood. Never did *Maugis* the Hermite bear himself more valiantly with his *bourdon* or *Pilgrims* staffe against the Saracens, of whom is written in the Acts of the foure sons of *Haymon*, then did this *Monk* against his enemies with the staffe of the Crosse.

CHAPTER XXVIII

How Picrochole stormed and took by assault the Rock
Clermond, and of Grangousiers unwillingnesse and aversion
from the undertaking of warre.

WHILEST the Monk did thus skirmish, as we have said, against those which were entred within the Closse; *Picrochole* in great haste passed the ford of *Vede*, (a very especial passe) with all his souldierie, and set upon the rock *Clermond*, where there was made him no resistance at all: and because it was already night, he resolved to quarter himself and his army in that town, and to refresh himself of his pugnative choler. In the morning he stormed and took the Bulwarks and Castle, which afterwards he fortified with rampiers, and furnished with all ammunition requisite, intending to make his retreat there, if he should happen to be otherwise worsted; for it was a strong place, both by Art and Nature, in regard of the stance and situation of it. But let us leave them there, and return to our good *Gargantua*, who is at *Paris* very assiduous and earnest at the study of good letters, and athletical exercitations, and to the good old man *Grangousier* his father, who after supper warmeth his ballocks by a good, clear, great fire, and, waiting upon the broyling of some chestnuts, is very serious in drawing scratches on the hearth, with a stick burnt at the one end, wherewith they did stirre up the fire, telling to his wife and the rest of the family pleasant old stories and tales of former times. Whilest he was thus employed, one of the shepherds which did keep the Vines, (named *Pillot*) came towards him, and to the full related the enormous abuses which were committed, and the excessive spoil that was made by *Picrochole* King of *Lerne*, upon his lands and territories, and how he had pillaged, wasted and ransacked all the countrey, except the inclosure at *Sevile*, which Friar *Ihon des entoumeures* to his great honour had preserved: and that at the same present time the said King was in the rock *Clermond*: and there with great industry and circumspection, was strengthening himself and his whole army. *Halas, halas, alas*, (said *Grangousier*,) what is this, good people? do I dream, or is it true that they tell me? *Picrochole* my ancient friend of old time, of my own kinred and alliance, comes he to invade me? what moves him? what provokes him? what sets him on? what drives him to it? who hath given him this counsel? *Ho, ho, ho, ho, ho*, my God, my Saviour, help me, inspire me, and advise me what I shall do. I protest, I swear before thee, so be thou favourable to me, if ever I did him or his subjects any damage or displeasure, or committed any the least robbery in his countrey; but on the contrary I have succoured and supplied him with men, money, friendship and counsel upon any occasion, wherein I could be steadable for the improvement of his good; that he hath therefore at this nick of time so outraged and wronged me, it cannot be but by the malevolent and wicked spirit. Good God, thou knowest my courage, for nothing can be hidden from thee; if perhaps he be grown mad, and that thou hast sent him hither to me for the better recovery & re-establishment of his brain; grant me power and wisdome to bring him to the yoke of thy holy will by good discipline. *Ho, ho, ho, ho*, my good people, my friends and my faithful servants, must I hinder you from helping me? alas, my old age required henceforward nothing else but rest, and all the dayes of my life I have laboured for nothing so much as peace: but now I must (I see it well) load with armes my poor, weary and feeble shoulders; and take in my trembling hand the lance and horsemans mace, to succour and protect my honest subjects: reason will have it so; for by their labour am I entertained, and with their sweat am I nourished, I, my children and my family. This notwithstanding, I will not undertake warre, until I have first tried all the wayes and meanes of peace, that I resolve upon. Then assembled he his counsel, and proposed the matter as it was indeed, whereupon it was concluded, that they should send some discreet man unto *Picrochole*, to know wherefore he had thus suddenly broken the Peace, and invaded those lands unto which he had no right nor title. Furthermore, that they should send for *Gargantua*, and those under his command, for the preservation of the countrey, and defence thereof now at need. All this pleased *Grangousier* very well, and commanded that so it should be done. Presently therefore he sent the *Basque* his Lackey, to fetch *Gargantua* with all diligence, and wrote to him as followeth.

CHAPTER XXIX

The tenor of the letter which Grangousier wrote to his sonne
Gargantua.

THE fervency of thy studies did require, that I should not in a long time recall thee from that Philosophical rest thou now enjoyest; if the confidence reposed in our friends and ancient confederates had not at this present disappointed the assurance of my old age: But seeing such is my fatal destiny, that I should be now disquieted by those in whom I trusted most: I am forced to call thee back to help the people and goods, which by the right of nature belong unto thee; for even as armes are weak abroad if there be not counsel at home: so is that study vaine, and counsel unprofitable, which in a due and convenient time is not by vertue executed and put in effect. My deliberation is not to provoke, but to appease; not to assault, but to defend: not to conquer, but to preserve my faithful subjects and hereditary dominions: into which *Picrochole* is entred in a hostile manner without any ground or cause, and from day to day pursueth his furious enterprise with that height of insolence that is intolerable to free-born spirits. I have endeavoured to moderate his tyrannical *choler*, offering him all that which I thought might give him satisfaction: and oftentimes have I sent lovingly unto him, to understand wherein, by whom, and how he found himself to be wronged. But of him could I obtain no other answer, but a meer defiance, and that in my lands he did pretend only

94

to the right of a civil correspondency and good behaviour, whereby I knew that the eternal God hath left him to the disposure of his own free will and sensual appetite, which cannot chuse but be wicked, if by divine grace it be not continually guided: and to contain him within his duty, and bring him to know himself, hath sent him hither to me by a grievous token. Therefore, my beloved son, as soon as thou canst, upon sight of these letters, repaire hither with all diligence, to succour not me so much (which neverthelesse by natural Piety thou oughtest to do,) as thine own People, which by reason thou mayest save and preserve. The exploit shall be done with as little effusion of blood as may be; and if possible, by meanes far more expedient, such as military policy, devices and stratagems of warre; we shall save all the souls, and send them home as merry as crickets unto their own houses. My dearest Son, the peace of *Jesus Christ* our Redeemer be with thee; salute from me *Ponocrates, Gymnastes* and *Eudemon*; the twentieth of *September*.

Thy Father Grangousier.

CHAPTER XXX

How Ulrich Gallet was sent unto Picrochole.

THE letters being dictated, signed and sealed, *Grangousier* ordained that *Ulrich Gallet*, Master of the requests (a very wise and discreet man, of whose prudence and sound judgement he had made trial in several difficult and debateful manners) to go unto *Picrochole*, to shew what had been decreed amongst them. At the same houre departed the good man *Gallet*, and having past the ford, asked at the Miller that dwelt there, in what condition *Picrochole* was: who answered him, that his souldiers had left him neither cock nor hen, that they were retired and shut up into the rock *Clermond*, and that he would not advise him to go any further for feare of the Scouts, because they were enormously furious; which he easily beleeved, and therefore lodged that night with the Miller. The next morning he went with a Trumpeter to the gate of the Castle, and required the guards he might be admitted to speak with the King of somewhat that concerned him. These words being told unto the King, he would by no means consent that they should open the gate; but getting upon the top of the bulwark, said unto the Ambassadour, What is the newes? what have you to say? then the Ambassadour began to speak as followeth.

CHAPTER XXXI

The speech made by Gallet to Picrochole.

THERE cannot arise amongst men a juster cause of grief, then when they receive hurt and damage, where they may justly expect for favour and good will; and not without cause, (though without reason,) have many, after they had fallen into such a calamitous accident, esteemed this indignity lesse supportable then the losse of their own lives, in such sort, that if they have not been able by force of armes, nor any other means, by reach of wit or subtilty, to stop them in their course, and restrain their fury, they have fallen into desperation, and utterly deprived themselves of this light. It is therefore no wonder if King *Gran-gousier* my Master be full of high displeasure, and much disquieted in minde upon thy outragious and hostile coming: but truly it would be a marvel, if he were not sensible of, and moved with the incomparable abuses and injuries perpetrated by thee and thine upon those of his countrey, towards whom there hath been no example of inhumanity omitted; which in it self is to him so grievous for the cordial affection, wherewith he hath alwayes cherished his subjects, that more it cannot be to any mortal man; yet in this (above humane apprehension) is it to him the more grievous, that these wrongs and sad offences have been committed by thee and thine, who time out of minde from all antiquity, thou and thy Predecessors have been in a continual league and amity with him, and all his Ancestors; which, even until this time, you have as sacred together inviolably preserved, kept and entertained, so well, that not he and his only, but the very barbarous Nations of the *Poictevins, Bretons, Manceaux*, and those that dwell beyond the isles of the *Canaries*, and that of *Isabella*, have thought it as easie to pull down the firmament, and to set up the depths above the clouds, as to

THE FIRST BOOK

make a breach in your alliance; and have been so afraid of it in
their enterprises, that they have never dared to provoke, incense
or indamage the one for feare of the other. Nay, which is more,
this sacred league hath so filled the world, that there are few
Nations at this day inhabiting throughout all the continent and
isles of the Ocean, who have not ambitiously aspired to be received into it, upon your own covenants and conditions, holding
your joynt confederacie in as high esteem as their own territories and dominions, in such sort, that from the memory of
man, there hath not been either Prince or league so wilde and
proud, that durst have offered to invade, I say not your countreys, but not so much as those of your confederates: and if by
rash and headie counsel they have attempted any new designe
against them, assoon as they heard the name and title of your
alliance, they have suddenly desisted from their enterprises.
What rage and madnesse therefore doth now incite thee, all old
alliance infringed, all amity trod under foot, and all right viol-
ated, thus in a hostil manner to invade his countrey, without
having been by him or his in any thing prejudiced, wronged or
provoked? where is faith? where is law? where is reason? where
is humanity? where is the feare of God? dost thou think that
these atrocious abuses are hidden from the eternal spirits, and
the supreme God, who is the just rewarder of all our undertakings? if thou so think, thou deceivest thy self; for all things shall
come to passe, as in his incomprehensible judgement he hath
appointed. Is it thy fatal destiny, or influences of the stars that
would put an end to thy so long enjoyed ease and rest? for that
all things have their end and period, so as that when they are
come to the superlative point of their greatest height, they are in
a trice tumbled down again, as not being able to abide long
in that state. This is the conclusion and end of those who cannot
by reason and temperance moderate their fortunes and prosper-
ities. But if it be predestinated that thy happinesse and ease
must now come to an end, must it needs be by wronging my
King? him by whom thou wert established? If thy house must
come to ruine, should it therefore in its fall crush the heels of
him that set it up? The matter is so unreasonable, and so dis-
sonant from common sense, that hardly can it be conceived
by humane understanding, and altogether incredible unto

strangers, till by the certain and undoubted effects thereof it be made apparent, that nothing is either sacred or holy to those, who having emancipated themselves from God and reason, do meerly follow the perverse affections of their own depraved nature. If any wrong had been done by us to thy subjects and dominions: if we had favoured thy ill-willers: if we had not assisted thee in thy need: if thy name and reputation had been wounded by us: or (to speak more truly) if the calumniating spirit, tempting to induce thee to evil, had by false illusions and deceitful fantasies, put into thy conceit the impression of a thought, that we had done unto thee any thing unworthy of our ancient correspondence and friendship, thou oughtest first to have enquired out the truth, and afterwards by a seasonable warning to admonish us thereof; and we should have so satisfied thee, according to thine own hearts desire, that thou shouldest have had occasion to be contented. But, O eternal God, what is thy enterprise? wouldest thou like a perfidious tyrant, thus spoile and lay waste my Masters Kingdome? hast thou found him so silly and blockish, that he would not: or so destitute of men and money, of counsel and skill in military discipline, that he cannot withstand thy unjust invasion? March hence presently, and to morrow some time of the day retreat unto thine own countrey, without doing any kinde of violence or disorderly act by the way: and pay withal a thousand *besans of gold*, (which in *English* money, amounteth to five thousand pounds) for reparation of the damages thou hast done in his countrey: halfe thou shalt pay to morrow, and the other halfe at the *ides* of *May* next coming, leaving with us in the mean time for hostages, the Dukes of *Turnebank*, *Lowbuttock* and *Small-trash*: together with the Prince of *Itches*, and Viscount of *Snatch-bit*.*

* Tournemoule, Basdefesses, Menuail, Gratelles, Morpiaille.

CHAPTER XXXII

How Grangousier to buy Peace, caused the Cakes to be restored.

WITH that the good man *Gallet* held his peace, but *Picrochole* to
all his discourse answered nothing but Come and fetch them,
come and fetch them: they have ballocks faire and soft, they
will knead and provide some cakes for you. Then returned he to
Grangousier, whom he found upon his knees bareheaded, crouching in a little corner of his cabinet, and humbly praying unto
God, that he would vouchsafe to asswage the choler of *Picrochole,* and bring him to the rule of reason without proceeding by
force. When the good man came back, he asked him, Ha,
my friend, my friend, what newes do you bring me? There is
neither hope nor remedy, (said *Gallet*) the man is quite out of
his wits, and forsaken of God. Yea but (said *Grangousier,*) my
friend, what cause doth he pretend for his outrages? He did not
shew me any cause at all (said *Gallet,*) only that in a great anger,
he spoke some words of cakes. I cannot tell if they have done
any wrong to his Cake-bakers. I will know (said *Grangousier,*)
the matter throughly, before I resolve any more upon what is to
be done; then sent he to learn concerning that businesse, and
found by true information, that his men had taken violently
some cakes from *Picrocholes* people, and that *Marquets* head was
broken with a *slackie* or short cudgel: that neverthelesse all was
well paid, and that the said *Marquet* had first hurt *Forgier* with a
stroke of his whip athwart the legs; and it seemed good to his
whole counsel, that he should defend himself with all his might.
Notwithstanding all this (said *Grangousier,*) seeing the question
is but about a few cakes, I will labour to content him; for I am
very unwilling to wage warre against him. He enquired then
what quantity of cakes they had taken away, and understanding
that it was but some foure or five dozen, he commanded five
cartloads of them to be baked that same night: and that there
should be one full of cakes made with fine butter, fine yolks of
egges, fine saffron and fine spice, to be bestowed upon *Marquet,*
unto whom likewise he directed to be given seven hundred
thousand and three *Philips,* (that is, at three shillings the piece,

one hundred five thousand pounds and nine shillings of *English* money) for reparation of his losses and hinderances, and for satisfaction of the Chirurgion that had dressed his wound: and furthermore setled upon him and his for ever in freehold the Apple-Orchard called *La Pomardiere*; for the conveyance and passing of all which was sent *Gallet*, who by the way as they went made them gather near the willow-trees great store of boughs, canes and reeds, wherewith all the Cariers were injoyned to garnish and deck their carts, and each of them to carry one in his hand, as himself likewise did, thereby to give all men to understand that they demanded but Peace, and that they came to buy it.

Being come to the gate, they required to speak with *Picrochole* from *Grangousier*. *Picrochole* would not so much as let them in, nor go to speak with them, but sent them word that he was busie, and that they should deliver their minde to Captain *Touquedillon*, who was then planting a piece of Ordnance upon the wall. Then said the good man unto him, *My Lord*, to ease you of all this labour, and to take away all excuses why you may not return unto our former alliance, we do here presently restore unto you the Cakes upon which the quarrel arose; five dozen did our people take away, they were well payed for; we love Peace so well, that we restore unto you five cartloads, of which this cart shall be for *Marquet*, who doth most complain; besides, to content him entirely, here are seven hundred thousand and three *Philips*, which I deliver to him: and for the losses he may pretend to have sustained, I resigne for ever the farme of the *Pomardiere*, to be possessed in fee-simple by him and his for ever, without the payment of any duty, or acknowledgement of homage, fealtie, fine or service whatsoever: and here is the tenor of the deed, and for Gods sake let us live henceforward in Peace, and withdraw your selves merrily into your own countrey from within this place, unto which you have no right at all, as your selves must needs confesse, and let us be good friends as before. *Touquedillon* related all this to *Picrochole*, and more and more exasperated his courage, saying to him, These clowns are afraid to some purpose: by G— *Grangousier* conskites himself for feare; the poor drinker he is not skilled in warfare, nor hath he any stomach for it, he knows better how to empty the flaggons, that is his Art. I am of opinion that it is fit we send back the carts and the money; and for the rest, that very speedily we fortifie our selves here, then prosecute our fortune. But what do they think to have to do with a *ninnie-whoop*, to feed you thus with cakes? You may see what it is; the good usage, and great familiarity which you have had with them heretofore, hath made you contemptible in their eyes. *Anoint a villain, he will prick you: prick a villain, and he will anoint you:** Sa, sa, sa, (said *Picrochole*,) by St. *James* you have given a true character of them. One thing I will advise you (said *Touquedillon*,) we are here but badly victualled, and furnished with mouth-harnasse very slenderly: if *Grangousier* should come to besiege us, I would go presently, and pluck out of all your souldiers heads and mine own all the teeth except three to each of us, and with them alone we should make an end of our provision. But too soon we shall have (said *Picrochole*,) but too much sustenance and feeding-stuffe: came we hither to eat or to fight? To fight indeed (said *Touquedillon*,) yet from the panch comes the dance, and where famine rules force is exiled. Leave off your prating (said *Picrochole*,) and forthwith seize upon what they have brought. Then took they money and cakes, oxen and carts, and sent them away without speaking one word, only that they would come no more so near, for a reason that they would give them the morrow after. Thus without doing any thing, returned they to *Grangousier*, and related the whole matter unto him, subjoyning that there was no hope left to draw them to Peace, but by sharp and fierce warres.

CHAPTER XXXIII

How some Statesmen of Picrochole, by hairebrain'd counsel put him in extreme danger.

THE carts being unloaded, and the money and cakes secured, there came before *Picrochole*, the Duke of *Small-trash*, the Earle *Swash-buckler*, and Captain *Durtaille*,** who said unto him, *Sir*, this day we make you the happiest, the most warlike and chivalrous Prince that ever was since the death of *Alexander* of

---

* *Ungentem pungit, pungentem rusticus ungit.*
** Menuaille, Spadassin, Merdaile.

Macedonia. Be covered, be covered, (said *Picrochole*). Grammercie (said they) we do but our duty: The manner is thus, you shall leave some Captain here to have the charge of this Garrison, with a Party competent for keeping of the place, which besides its natural strength, is made stronger by the rampiers and fortresses of your devising. Your Army you are to divide into two parts, as you know very well how to do: one part thereof shall fall upon *Grangousier* and his forces, by it shall he be easily at the very first shock routed, and then shall you get money by heaps, for the *Clown* hath store of ready coine: *Clown* we call him, because a noble and generous Prince hath never a penny, and that to hoard up treasure is but a clownish trick. The other part of the Army in the mean time shall draw towards *Onys*, *Xaintonge*, *Angoulesme* and *Gascony*: then march to *Perigourt*, *Medos* and *Elanes*, taking whereever you come without resistance, townes, castles and forts: Afterwards to *Bayonne*, St. *Ihon de luz*, to *Fuentarabia*, where you shall seize upon all the ships, and coasting along *Galicia* and *Portugal*, shall pillage all the maritine places, even unto *Lisbone*, where you shall be supplied with all necessaries befitting a Conquerour. By copsodie *Spain* will yield, for they are but a race of *Loobies*: then are you to passe by the streights of *Gibraltar*, where you shall erect two pillars more stately then those of *Hercules*, to the perpetual memory of your name, and the narrow entrance there shall be called the *Picrocholinal* sea.

Having past the *Picrocholinal* sea, behold, *Barbarossa* yields himself your slave: I will (said *Picrochole*) give him faire quarter and spare his life. Yea (said they) so that he be content to be christened. And you shall conquer the Kingdomes of *Tunes*, of *Hippos*, *Argier*, *Bomine*, *Corode*, yea all *Barbary*. Furthermore, you shall take into your hands *Majorca*, *Minorca*, *Sardinia*, *Corsica*, with the other Islands of the *Ligustick* and *Balearian* seas. Going alongst on the left hand, you shall rule all *Gallia Narbonensis*, *Provence*, the *Allobrogians*, *Genua*, *Florence*, *Luca*, and then *God biwy Rome*; By my faith (said *Picrochole*,) I will not then kisse his pantuffle.

Italy being thus taken, behold, *Naples*, *Calabria*, *Apulia* and *Sicilie*, all ransacked, and *Malta* too. I wish the pleasant Knights of the *Rhodes* heretofore would but come to resist you, that we might see their urine. I would (said *Picrochole*) very willingly go to *Loretta*. No, no, (said they) that shall be at our return; from thence we will saile Eastwards, and take *Candia*, *Cyprus*, *Rhodes*, and the *Cyclade Islands*, and set upon *Morea*. It is ours by St. *Trenian*, the Lord preserve *Jerusalem*; for the great *Soldan* is not comparable to you in power: I will then (said he) cause *Solomon's* Temple to be built: No, (said they) not yet, have a little patience, stay a while, be never too sudden in your enterprises. Can you tell what *Octavian Augustus* said, *Festina lentè*; it is requisite that you first have the lesser *Asia*, *Caria*, *Lycia*, *Pamphilia*, *Cilicia*, *Lydia*, *Phrygia*, *Mysia*, *Bithynia*, *Carazia*, *Satalia*, *Samagaria*, *Castamena*, *Luga*, *Sanasta*, even unto *Euphrates*; Shall we see (said *Picrochole*,) *Babylon* and Mount *Sinai*? There is no need (said they) at this time; have we not hurried up and down, travelled and toyled enough, in having transfreted and past over the *Hircanian* sea, marched alongst the two *Armenias* and the three *Arabias*? By my faith (said he) we have played the fooles, and are undone: Ha, poor soules! What's the matter, said they? What shall we have (said he) to drink in these deserts? for *Julian Augustus*, with his whole Army died there for thirst, as they say. We have already (said they) given order for that. In the *Siriack* sea you have nine thousand and fourteen great ships laden with the best wines in the world: they arrived at *Port-Joppa*, there they found two and twenty thousand Camels, and sixteen hundred Elephants, which you shall have taken at one hunting about *Sigelmes*, when you entered into *Lybia*: and, besides this, you had all the *Mecca Caravane*. Did not they furnish you sufficiently with wine? Yes, but (said he) we did not drink it fresh: By the vertue (said they) not of a fish, a valiant man, a Conquerour, who pretends and aspires to the Monarchy of the world, cannot alwayes have his ease. God be thanked, that you and your men are come safe and sound unto the banks of the river *Tigris*; But (said he) what doth that part of our Army in the mean time, which overthrows that unworthy Swill-pot *Grangousier*? They are not idle (said they) we shall meet with them by and by, they shall have won you *Britany*, *Normandy*, *Flanders*, *Haynault*, *Brabant*, *Artois*, *Holland*, *Zealand*; they have past the *Rhine* over the bellies of the *Switsers* and *Lanskenets*, and a Party of these hath subdued *Luxemburg*, *Lorrain*, *Champaigne* and *Savoy*, even to *Lions*, in which place they have met with your forces, returning from the naval Conquests of the *Mediterranean* sea: and have rallied again in *Bohemia*, after they had plundered and sacked *Suevia*, *Wittemberg*, *Bavaria*, *Austria*, *Moravia* and *Styria*. Then they set fiercely together upon *Lubeck*, *Norway*, *Swedeland*, *Rie*, *Denmark*, *Gitland*, *Greenland*, the *Sterlins*, even unto the frozen sea; this done, they conquered the isles of *Orkney*, and subdued *Scotland*, *England* and *Ireland*. From thence sailing through the sandie sea, and by the *Sarmates*, they have vanquished and over-come *Prussia*, *Poland*, *Lituania*, *Russia*, *Walachia*, *Transilvania*, *Hungarie*, *Bulgaria*, *Turquieland*, and are now at *Constantinople*. Come (said *Picrochole*,) let us go joyn with them quickly, for I will be Emperour of *Trebezonde* also: shall we not kill all these dogs, *Turks* and *Mahumetans*? What a devil should we do else, said they: and you shall give their goods and lands to such as shall have served you honestly. Reason (said he) will have it so, that is but just, I give unto you the *Caramania*, *Surie*, and all the *Palestine*. Ha, Sir, (said they) it is out of your goodnesse; Grammercie, we thank you, God grant you may alwayes pros-per. There was there present at that time an old Gentleman well experienced in the warres, a sterne souldier, and who had been in many great hazards, named *Echephron*, who hearing this discourse, said, I do greatly doubt that all this enterprise will be like the tale or interlude of the pitcher full of milk, wherewith a Shoemaker made himself rich in conceit: but when the pitcher was broken, he had not whereupon to dine: what do you pre-tend by these large Conquests? what shall be the end of so many labours and crosses? Thus it shall be (said *Picrochole*) that when we are returned, we shall sit down, rest and be merry: But (said *Echephron*,) if by chance you should never come back, for the voyage is long and dangerous, were it not better for us to take our rest now, then unnecessarily to expose our selves to so many dangers? O (said *Swashbuckler*,) by G— here is a good dotard, come, let us go hide our selves in the corner of a chimney, and there spend the whole time of our life amongst Ladies, in threading of pearles, or spinning like *Sardanapalus*: He that nothing ventures, hath neither horse nor mule, (sayes *Salomon*:) He who adventureth too much (said *Echephron*) loseth both horse and mule, answered *Malchon*. Enough (said *Picrochole*,) go forward: I feare nothing, but that these devillish legions of

Grangousier, whilest we are in *Mesopotamia*, will come on our backs, and charge up our reer, what course shall we then take? what shall be our remedy? A very good one; (said *Durtaille*) a pretty little commission, which you must send unto the *Muscoviters*, shall bring you into the field in an instant foure hundred and fifty thousand choise men of warre; O that you would but make me your Lieutenant General, I should for the lightest faults of any inflict great punishments. I fret, I charge, I strike, I take, I kill, I slay, I play the devil. On, on (said *Picrochole*) make haste, my lads, and let him that loves me, follow me.

CHAPTER XXXIV

How Gargantua left the city of Paris, to succour his countrey, and how Gymnast encountered with the enemy.

IN this same very houre *Gargantua*, who was gone out of *Paris*, assoon as he had read his fathers letters, coming upon his great mare had already past the Nunnerie-bridge himself, *Ponocrates*, *Gymnast* and *Eudemon*, who all three, the better to inable them to go along with him, took Post-horses: the rest of his traine came after him by even journeys at a slower pace, bringing with them all his books and Philosophical instruments; as soon as he had alighted at *Parille*, he was informed by a farmer of *Gouget*, how *Picrochole* had fortified himself within the rock *Clermond*, and had sent Captain *Tripet* with a great army to set upon the wood of *Vede* and *Vaugaudry*, and that they had already plundered the whole countrey, not leaving cock nor hen, even as farre as to the wine-presse of *Billiard*. These strange and almost incredible newes of the enormous abuses, thus committed over all the land, so affrighted *Gargantua*, that he knew not what to say nor do: but *Ponocrates* counselled him to go unto the Lord of *Vauguyon*, who at all times had been their friend and confederate, and that by him they should be better advised in their businesse: which they did incontinently, and found him very willing, and fully resolved to assist them, and therefore was of opinion, that they should send some one of his company, to scout along and discover the countrey, to learn in what condition and posture the enemy was, that they might take counsel, and proceed

according to the present occasion. *Gymnast* offered himself to
go; whereupon it was concluded, that for his safety, and the better expedition, he should have with him some one that knew
the wayes, avenues, turnings, windings and rivers thereabout.
Then away went he and *Prelingot*, (the Querry or Gentleman of
Vauguyons horse,) who scouted and espied as narrowly as they
could upon all quarters without any feare. In the mean time
Gargantua took a little refreshment, ate somewhat himself, the
like did those who were with him, and caused to give to his
mare a *Picotine* of Oats, that is, threescore and fourteen quarters
and three bushels. *Gymnast* and his Camerade rode so long, that
at last they met with the enemies forces, all scattered and out of
order, plundering, stealing, robbing and pillaging all they could
lay their hands on: and as far off as they could perceive him,
they ran thronging upon the back of one another in all haste
towards him, to unload him of his money, and untrusse his Port-
mantles. Then cried he out unto them, (My Masters,) I am a
poor devil, I desire you to spare me, I have yet one Crown left,
come, we must drink it; for it is *aurum potabile*, and this horse
here shall be sold to pay my welcome: afterwards take me for
one of your own; for never yet was there any man that knew
better how to take, lard, rost and dresse, yea by G— to teare
asunder and devoure a hen, then I that am here: and for my
Proficiat I drink to all good fellowes. With that he unscrued his
Borracho, (which was a great *dutch* leathern bottle,) and without
putting in his nose drank very honestly: the *maroufle* Rogues
looked upon him, opening their throats a foot wide, and putting
out their tongues like Greyhounds, in hopes to drink after him:
but Captain *Tripet*, in the very nick of that their expectation,
came running to him to see who it was. To him *Gymnast* offered
his bottle, saying, Hold, Captain, drink boldly and spare not; I
have been thy taster, it is wine of *La fay monjau*. What? (said *Tripet*)
this fellow gybes and flowts us; Who art thou? (said *Tripet*) I am
(said *Gymnast*) a poor devil, (*pauvre diable:*) Ha, (said *Tripet*)
seeing thou art a poor devil, it is reason that thou shouldest be
permitted to go whithersoever thou wilt, for all poor devils
passe every where without toll or taxe; but it is not the custome
of poor devils to be so wel mounted, therefore, Sir devil, come
down, and let me have your horse, and if he do not carry me

well, you, Master devil, must do it: for I love a life that such a devil as you should carry me away.

CHAPTER XXXV

How Gymnast very souply and cunningly killed Captain
Tripet, and others of Picrocholes men.

WHEN they heard these words, some amongst them began to be afraid, and blest themselves with both hands, thinking indeed that he had been a devil disguised: insomuch that one of them, named *good Ihon*, Captain of the trained bands of the Countrey bumpkins, took his Psalter out of his Codpiece, and cried out aloud, *Hagios ho theos*. If thou be of God speak: if thou be of the other spirit avoid hence, and get thee going: yet he went not away; which words being heard by all the souldiers that were there, divers of them being a little inwardly terrified, departed from the place: all this did *Gymnast* very well remark and consider, and therefore making as if he would have alighted from off his horse, as he was poysing himself on the mounting side, he most nimbly (with his short sword by his thigh,) shifting his foot in the stirrup, performed the stirrup-leather feat, whereby after the inclining of his body downwards, he forthwith lanch't himself aloft in the aire, and placed both his feet together on the saddle, standing upright with his back turned towards the horses head; Now (said he) my case goes backward. Then suddenly in the same very posture wherein he was, he fetched a gambole upon one foot, and turning to the left hand, failed not to carry his body perfectly round, just into its former stance, without missing one jot. Ha (said *Tripet*,) I will not do that at this time, and not without cause. Well, (said *Gymnast*) I have failed, I will undo this leap: then with a marvellous strength and agility, turning towards the right hand he fetch't another frisking gambole, as before, which done, he set his right hand thumb upon the hinde bowe of the saddle, raised himself up, and sprung in the aire, poysing and upholding his whole body, upon the muscle and nerve of the said thumb: and so turned and whirled himself about three times: at the fourth reversing his body, and overturning it upside down, and foreside back, without touching any

thing he brought himself betwixt the horses two eares, springing with all his body into the aire, upon the thumb of his left
hand, and in that posture turning like a windmill, did most
actively do that trick which is called the Millers Passe. After
this, clapping his right hand flat upon the middle of the saddle,
he gave himself such a jerking swing, that he thereby seated
himself upon the crupper, after the manner of Gentlewomens
sitting on horseback: this done, he easily past his right leg over
the saddle, and placed himself like one that rides in croup: But,
said he, it were better for me to get into the saddle; then putting
the thumbs of both hands upon the crupper before him, and
thereupon leaning himself, as upon the only supporters of his
body, he incontinently turned heels over head in the aire, and
streight found himself betwixt the bowe of the saddle in a good
settlement. Then with a *summer-sault* springing into the aire again,
he fell to stand with both his feet close together upon the
saddle, and there made above a hundred frisks, turnes and demi-
pommads, with his armes held out acrosse, and in so doing,
cried out aloud, I rage, I rage, devils, I am stark mad; devils, I
am mad, hold me, devils, hold me, hold, devils, hold, hold.

Whilest he was thus vaulting, the Rogues in great astonishment said to one another, By cocks death he is a goblin or a devil
thus disguised, *Ab hoste maligno libera nos, Domine*, and ran away
in a ful flight, as if they had been routed, looking now and then
behinde them, like a dog that carrieth away a goose-wing in his
mouth. Then *Gymnast* spying his advantage, alighted from
his horse, drew his sword, & laid on great blows upon the thickest, and highest-crested amongst them and overthrew them in
great heaps, hurt, wounded and bruised, being resisted by
no body, they thinking he had been a starved devil, as well in
regard of his wonderful feats in vaulting, which they had seen,
as for the talk *Tripet* had with him, calling him poor devil: only
Tripet would have traiterously cleft his head with his horsemans
sword, or lanse-knight fauchion; but he was well armed, and felt
nothing of the blow, but the weight of the stroke; whereupon
turning suddenly about, he gave *Tripet* a home-thrust, and upon
the back of that, whilest he was about to ward his head from a
slash, he ran him in at the breast with a hit, which at once cut
his stomack, the fifth gut called the *Colon*, and the half of his

liver, wherewith he fell to the ground, and in falling gushed forth above foure pottles of pottage, and his soule mingled with the pottage.

This done, *Gymnast* withdrew himself, very wisely considering, that a case of great adventure and hazard, should not be pursued unto its utmost period, and that it becomes all Cavaliers modestly to use their good fortune, without troubling or stretching it too farre; wherefore getting to horse, he gave him the spurre, taking the right way unto *Vauguyon*, and *Prelingot* with him.

CHAPTER XXXVI

How Gargantua demolished the Castle at the Ford of Vede,
and how they past the Ford.

As soon as he came, he related the estate and condition wherein they had found the enemie, and the stratagem which he alone had used against all their multitude, affirming that they were but rascally rogues, plunderers, thieves and robbers, ignorant of all military discipline, and that they might boldly set forward unto the field; it being an easie matter to fell and strike them down like beasts. Then *Gargantua* mounted his great Mare, accompanied as we have said before, and finding in his way a high and great tree, (which commonly was called by the name of St. *Martins* tree, because heretofore St. *Martin* planted a Pilgrim's staffe there, which in tract of time grew to that height and greatnesse,) said, This is that which I lacked; this tree shall serve me both for a staffe and lance: with that he pulled it up easily, plucked off the boughs, and trimmed it at his pleasure: in the mean time his Mare pissed to ease her belly, but it was in such abundance, that it did overflow the countrey seven leagues, and all the pisse of that Urinal flood, ran glib away towards the Ford of *Vede*, wherewith the water was so swollen, that all the Forces the enemy had there, were with great horrour drowned, except some who had taken the way on the left hand towards the hills. *Gargantua* being come to the place of the wood of *Vede*, was informed by *Eudemon*, that there was some remainder of the enemy within the Castle, which to know, *Gargantua* cried out as loud as he was able, Are you there, or are you not there? if you be there, be there no more; and if you be not there, I have no more to say. But a ruffian gunner, whose charge was to attend the Portcullis over the gate, let flie a cannon-ball at him, and hit him with that shot most furiously on the right temple of his head, yet did him no more hurt, then if he had but cast a prune or kernel of a wine-grape at him: What is this? (said *Gargantua*) do you throw at us grape-kernels here? the Vintage shall cost you dear, thinking indeed that the bullet had been the kernel of a grape, or raisin-kernel.

Those who were within the Castle, being till then busie at the pillage, when they heard this noise, ran to the towers and fortresses, from whence they shot at him above nine thousand and five and twenty falcon-shot and harcabusades, aiming all at his head, and so thick did they shoot at him, that he cried out, *Ponocrates* my friend, these flies here are like to put out mine eyes, give me a branch of those willow-trees to drive them away, thinking that the bullets and stones shot out of the great ordnance had been but dunflies. *Ponocrates* looked and saw that there were no other flies, but great shot which they had shot from the Castle. Then was it that he rusht with his great tree against the Castle, and with mighty blowes overthrew both towers and fortresses, and laid all level with the ground, by which meanes all that were within were slaine and broken in pieces. Going from thence, they came to the bridge at the Mill, where they found all the Ford covered with dead bodies, so thick, that they had choaked up the Mill, and stopped the current of its water, and these were those that were destroyed in the Urinal deluge of the Mare. There they were at a stand, consulting how they might passe without hinderance by these dead carcasses. But *Gymnast* said, If the devils have past there, I will passe well enough. The devils have past there (said *Eudemon*,) to carry away the damned soules. By St. *Rhenian* (said *Ponocrates*,) then by necessary consequence he shall passe there: Yes, yes, (said *Gymnastes*) or I shall stick in the way: then setting spurs to his horse, he past through freely, his horse not fearing, nor being any thing affrighted at the sight of the dead bodies; for he had accustomed him (according to the doctrine of *Ælian*) not to feare armour, nor the carcasses of dead men; and that not by killing men as *Diomedes* did the *Thracians*, or as *Ulysses* did in throwing the Corpses of his enemies at his horses feet, as *Homer* saith, but by putting a Jack-a-lent amongst his hay, & making him go over it ordinarily, when he gave him his oates. The other three followed him very close, except *Eudemon* only, whose horses foreright or far forefoot, sank up to the knee in the paunch of a great fat chuffe, who lay there upon his back drowned, and could not get it out: there was he pestered, until *Gargantua* with the end of his staffe thrust down the rest of the Villains tripes into the water, whilest the horse pulled out his foot; and (which is a wonderful thing in *Hippiatrie*,) the said horse was throughly cured of a ringbone which he had in that foot, by this touch of the burst guts of that great loobie.

CHAPTER XXXVII

How Gargantua in combing his head, made the great
cannon-ball fall out of his haire.

BEING come out of the river of *Vede*, they came very shortly after to *Grangousiers* Castle, who waited for them with great longing; at their coming they were entertained with many congies, and cherished with embraces, never was seen a more joyful company, for *supplementum supplementi Chronicorum* saith that *Gargamelle* died there with joy; for my part, truly I cannot tell, neither do I care very much for her, nor for any body else. The truth was, that *Gargantua*, in shifting his clothes, and combing his head with a combe, (which was nine hundred foot long of the *Jewish* Canne-measure, and whereof the teeth were great tusks of Elephants, whole and entire,) he made fall at every rake above seven balls of bullets, *at a dozen the ball*, that stuck in his haire, at the razing of the Castle of the wood of *Vede*, which his father *Grangousier* seeing, thought they had been lice, and said unto him, What, my dear sonne, hast thou brought us thus farre some short-winged hawkes of the Colledge of *Mountague*? I did not mean that thou shouldest reside there; Then answered *Ponocrates*, my soveraign Lord, think not that I have placed him in that lowsie Colledge, which they call *Montague*; I had rather have put him amongst the grave-diggers of *Sanct Innocent*, so

enormous is the cruelty and villany that I have known there; for
the Galley-slaves are far better used amongst the *Moors* and
Tartars, the murtherers in the criminal dungeons, yea the very
dogs in your house, then are the poor wretched Students in the
aforesaid Colledge; and if I were King of *Paris*, the devil take
me if I would not set it on fire, and burne both Principal and
Regents, for suffering this inhumanity to be exercised before
their eyes: then taking up one of these bullets, he said, These
are cannon-shot, which your sonne *Gargantua* hath lately received
by the treachery of your enemies, as he was passing before the
Wood of *Vede*.

But they have been so rewarded, that they are all destroyed
in the ruine of the Castle, as were the *Philistines* by the policy of
Samson, and those whom the tower of *Silohim* slew, as it is written in the thirteenth of *Luke*; My opinion is, that we pursue
them whilest the luck is on our side, for occasion hath all her
haire on her forehead, when she is past, you may not recal her,
she hath no tuft whereby you can lay hold on her, for she is bald
in the hind-part of her head, and never returneth again. Truly
(said *Grangousier*,) it shall not be at this time; for I will make you
a feast this night, and bid you welcome.

This said, they made ready supper, and of extraordinary
besides his daily fare, were rosted sixteen oxen three heifers
two and thirty calves, threescore and three *fat kids*, fourscore
and fifteen *wethers*, three hundred *barrow-pigs* or *sheats* sowced
in sweet wine or must, elevenscore *partridges*, seven hundred
snites and *woodcocks*, foure hundred *Loudon* and *Cornwal-capons*,
six thousand *pullets*, and as many *pigeons*, six hundred *crammed
hens*, fourteen hundred *leverets*, or young *hares* and *rabbets*, three
hundred and three *buzzards*, and one thousand and seven hundred *cockrels*. For *venison*, they could not so suddenly come by
it, only eleven *wilde bores*, which the Abbot of *Turpenay* sent, and
eighteen fallow deer which the Lord of *Gramount* bestowed;
together with sevenscore *phesants*, which were sent by the Lord
of *Essars*; and some dozens of *queests*, *coushots*, *ringdoves*, and
woodculvers; River-fowle, *teales* and *awteales*, *bittorns*, *courtes*,
plovers, *francolins*, *briganders*, *tyrasons*, *young lapwings*, *tame ducks*,
shovelers, *woodlanders*, *herons*, *moore-hens*, *criels*, *storks*, *canepetiers*,
oronges, *flamans*, which are *phænicopters*, or crimson-winged

sea-fowles, *terrigoles, turkies, arbens, coots, solingeese, curlews, terma-gants* and *water-wagtails*, with a great deal of *cream, curds* and *fresh cheese*, and store of *soupe, pottages*, and *brewis* with variety. With-out doubt there was meat enough, and it was handsomly drest by *Snapsauce, Hotchpot* and *Brayverjuice, Grangousiers* Cooks. *Jenkin, Trudg-apace* and *Clean-glasse* were very careful to fill them drink.

CHAPTER XXXVIII

How Gargantua did eate up six Pilgrims in a sallet.

THE story requireth, that we relate that which happened unto six Pilgrims, who came from *Sebastian* near to *Nantes*: and who for shelter that night, being afraid of the enemy, had hid them-selves in the garden upon the chichling pease, among the cab-bages and lettices. *Gargantua* finding himself somewhat dry, asked whether they could get any lettice to make him a sallet; and hearing that there were the greatest and fairest in the countrey (for they were as great plum-trees, or as walnut-trees,) he would go thither himself, and brought thence in his hand what he thought good, and withal carried away the six Pilgrims, who were in so great feare, that they did not dare to speak nor cough.

Washing them therefore first at the fountain, the Pilgrims said one to another softly, What shall we do? we are almost drowned here amongst these lettice, shall we speak? but if we speak, he will kill us for spies: and, as they were thus deliber-ating what to do, *Gargantua* put them with the lettice into a plat-ter of the house, as large as the huge tun of the *white Friars* of the *Cistertian* order, which done, with oile, vineger and salt he ate them up, to refresh himself a little before supper: and had already swallowed up five of the Pilgrims, the six being in the platter, totally hid under a lettice, except his *bourdon* or *staffe* that appeared, and nothing else. Which *Grangousier* seeing, said to *Gargantua*, I think that is the horne of a shell-snail, do not eat it. Why not, (said *Gargantua*) they are good all this moneth, which he no sooner said, but drawing up the staffe, and therewith taking up the Pilgrim, he ate him very well, then drank a terrible draught of excellent white wine. The Pilgrims thus devoured, made shift to save themselves as wel as they could,

by withdrawing their bodies out of the reach of the grinders of
his teeth, but could not escape from thinking they had been put
in the lowest dungeon of a prison. And when *Gargantua* whiffed
the great draught, they thought to have been drowned in his
mouth, and the flood of wine had almost carried them away into
the gulf of his stomack. Neverthelesse skipping with their bour-
dons, as St. *Michaels* Palmers use to do, they sheltered themselves from the danger of that inundation, under the banks of
his teeth. But one of them by chance, groping or sounding the
countrey with his staffe, to try whether they were in safety or
no, struck hard against the cleft of a hollow tooth, and hit the
mandibulary sinew, or nerve of the jaw, which put *Gargantua* to
very great pain, so that he began to cry for the rage that he felt;
to ease himself therefore of his smarting ache, he called for his
tooth-picker, and rubbing towards a young walnut-tree, where
they lay skulking, unnestled you my Gentlemen Pilgrims.

For he caught one by the legs, another by the scrip, another
by the pocket, another by the scarf, another by the band of the
breeches, and the poor fellow that had hurt him with the bourdon, him he hooked to him by the Codpiece, which snatch
neverthelesse did him a great deal of good, for it pierced unto
him a pockie botch he had in the groine, which grievously tormented him ever since they were past *Ancenis*. The Pilgrims
thus dislodged ran away athwart the Plain a pretty fast pace, and
the paine ceased, even just at the time when by *Eudemon* he was
called to supper, for all was ready. I will go then (said he) and
pisse away my misfortune; which he did do in such a copious
measure, that the urine, taking away the feet from the Pilgrims,
they were carried along with the stream unto the bank of a tuft
of trees: upon which, assoon as they had taken footing, and that
for their self-preservation they had run a little out of the road,
they on a sudden fell all six, except *Fourniller*, into a trap that
had been made to take wolves by a train: out of which neverthelesse they escaped by the industry of the said *Fourniller*, who
broke all the snares and ropes. Being gone from thence, they lay
all the rest of that night in a lodge near unto *Coudry*, where they
were comforted in their miseries, by the gracious words of one
of their company, called *Sweertogo*, who shewed them that this
adventure had been foretold by the Prophet *David, Psalm.*

Quum exurgerent homines in nos, fortè vivos deglutissent nos; when we were eaten in the sallet, with salt, oile and vineger, *Quum irasceretur furor eorum in nos, forsitan aqua absorbuisset nos*; when he drank the great draught, *Torrentem pertransivit anima nostra*; when the stream of his water carried us to the thicket, *Forsitan pertransisset anima nostra aquam intolerabilem*; that is, the water of his Urine, the flood whereof cutting our way, took our feet from us. *Benedictus Dominus qui non dedit nos in captionem dentibus eorum: anima nostra sicut passer erepta est de laqueo venantium*; when we fell in the trap, *Laqueus contritus est*, by *Fourniller, Et nos liberati sumus, adjutorium nostrum, & c.*

CHAPTER XXXIX

How the Monk was feasted by Gargantua, and of the jovial discourse they had at supper.

WHEN *Gargantua* was set down at table, after all of them had somewhat stayed their stomacks by a snatch or two of the first bits eaten heartily; *Grangousier* began to relate the source and cause of the warre, raised between him and *Picrochole*: and came to tell how *Friar Ihon* of the *Funnels*, had trimphed at the defence of the close of the Abbey, and extolled him for his valour above *Camillus, Scipio, Pompey, Cæsar* and *Themistocles*. Then *Gargantua* desired that he might be presently sent for, to the end that with him they might consult of what was to be done; whereupon by a joynt consent his steward went for him, and brought him along merrily, with his staffe of the Crosse, upon *Grangousiers* Mule: when he was come, a thousand huggings, a thousand embracements, a thousand good dayes given: Ha Friar *Ihon* my friend, Friar *Ihon* my brave cousin, Friar *Ihon* from the devil: let me clip thee (my heart) about the neck, to me an armesful; I must gripe thee (my ballock) till thy back crack with it. Come (my cod,) let me coll thee till I kill thee; and Friar *Ihon* the gladdest man in the world, never was man made welcomer, never was any more courteously and graciously received then Friar *Ihon*. Come, come, (said *Gargantua*,) a stool here close by me at this end: I am content, (said the Monk) seeing you will have it so. Some water (Page) fill, my boy fill, it is to refresh my liver;

give me some (*childe*) to gargle my throat withal. *Depositâ cappâ*, (said *Gymnast*) let us pull off this frock. Ho, by G— Gentleman (said the Monk) there is a chapter *in statutis ordinis*, which opposeth my laying of it down; Pish (said *Gymnast*) a fig for your chapter, this frock breaks both your shoulders, put it off. My friend (said the Monk) let me alone with it; for by G— I'le drink the better that it is on: it makes all my body jocund; if I should lay it aside, the waggish Pages would cut to themselves garters out of it, as I was once served at *Coulaines*: and which is worse, I should lose my appetite: but if in this habit I sit down at table, I will drink by G— both to thee and to thy horse, and so courage, frolick, God save the company: I have already sup't, yet will I eat never a whit the lesse for that; for I have a paved stomack, as hollow as a But of malvoisie, or St. *Benedictus* boot, and alwayes open like a Lawyers pouch. Of all fishes, but the tench, take the wing of a Partridge, or the thigh of a Nunne; Doth not he die like a good fellow that dies with a stiffe *Catso*? Our *Prior* loves exceedingly the white of a capon: In that (said *Gymnast*) he doth not resemble the foxes; for of the capons, hens and pullets which they carry away, they never eat the white: Why? (said the Monk) Because (said *Gymnast*) they have no Cooks to dresse them; and if they be not competently made ready, they remaine red and not white, the rednesse of meats being a token that they have not got enough of the fire, whether by boyling, rosting or otherwise, except the shrimps, lobsters, crabs and crayfishes, which are *cardinalised* with boyling: by Gods feast-gazers (said the Monk) the Porter of our Abbey then hath not his head wellboyled, for his eyes are as red as a mazer made of an alder-tree. The thigh of this leveret, is good for those that have the gout. To the purpose of the truel, what is the reason that the thighs of a Gentlewoman are alwayes fresh and coole: This Probleme (said *Gargantua*) is neither in *Aristotle*, in *Alexander Aphrodiseus*, nor in *Plutarch*. There are three causes (said the Monk) by which that place is naturally refreshed. *Primò*, because the water runs all along by it. *Secundò*, because it is a shadie place, obscure and dark, upon which the Sun never shines. And thirdly, because it is continually flabbell'd, blown upon and aired by the northwindes of the *hole arstick*, the fan of the *smock*, and *flipflap* of the Codpiece. And lustie my lads, some bousing liquour,

Page; so: *Crack, crack, crack*. O how good is God that gives us of this excellent juice! I call him to witnesse, if I had been in the time of *Jesus Christ*, I would have kept him from being taken by the *Jewes* in the garden of *Olivet*: and the devil faile me, if I should have failed to cut off the hams of these Gentlemen Apostles, who ran away so basely after they had well supped, and left their good Master in the lurch. I hate that man worse then poison that offers to run away, when he should fight and lay stoutly about him. Oh that I were but King of *France* for fourescore or a hundred years! by G— I should whip like curtail-dogs these runawayes of *Pavie*: A plague take them, why did not they chuse rather to die there, then to leave their good Prince in that pinch and necessity? Is it not better and more honourable to perish in fighting valiantly, then to live in disgrace by a cowardly running away? We are like to eate no great store of goslings this yeare, therefore, friend, reach me some of that rosted pig there.

Diavolo, is there no more must? no more sweet wine? *Germinavit radix Jesse, je renie ma vie, j'enrage de soif*; I renounce my life, I rage for thirst, this wine is none of the worst; what wine drink you at *Paris*? I give my self to the devil, if I did not once keep open house at *Paris* for all commers six moneths together; Do you know *Friar Claud* of the *high kildrekins*: Oh the good fellow that he is, but I do not know what flie hath stung him of late, he is become so hard a student; for my part, I study not at all. In our Abbey we never study for feare of the mumps, (which disease in horses is called the mourning in the chine;) Our late Abbot was wont to say, that it is a monstrous thing to see a learned Monk. By G—, Master, my friend, *Magìs magnos clericos non sunt magìs magnos sapientes*. You never saw so many hares as there are this year. I could not any where come by a gossehawk, nor tassel of falcon: my Lord *Beloniere* promised me a *Lanner*, but he wrote to me not long ago, that he was become pursie. The Partridges will so multiply henceforth, that they will go near to eat up our eares: I take no delight in the stalking-horse; for I catch such cold, that I am like to founder my self at that sport; if I do not run, toile, travel and trot about, I am not well at ease. True it is, that in leaping over hedges and bushes, my frock leaves alwayes some of its wooll behinde it. I have recovered a dainty greyhound; I give him to the devil if he suffer a hare to escape him. A groom was leading him to my Lord *Hunt-little*, and I robbed him of him; did I ill? No, *Friar Ihon*, (said *Gymnast*,) no, by all the devils that are, no: So (said the Monk) do I attest these same devils so long as they last, or rather vertue G—, what could that gowtie Limpard have done with so fine a dog? by the body of G— he is better pleased, when one presents him with a good yoke of oxen. How now? (said *Ponocrates*) you swear, *Friar Ihon*; It is only (said the Monk) but to grace and adorn my speech; they are colours of a *Ciceronian* Rhetorick.

CHAPTER XL

Why Monks are the out-casts of the world? and wherefore some have bigger noses than others?

BY the faith of a *Christian* (said *Eudemon*) I do wonderfully dote, and enter in a great extasie, when I consider the honesty and good fellowship of this Monk; for he makes us here all merry. How is it then that they exclude the *Monks* from all good companies? calling them feast-troublers, marrers of mirth, and disturbers of all civil conversation, as the bees drive away the drones from their hives; *Ignavum fucos pecus* (said *Maro*) *à præsepibus arcent*. Hereunto answered *Gargantua*, There is nothing so true, as that the frock and cowle draw unto it self the opprobries, injuries and maledictions of the world, just as the winde called *Cecias* attracts the clouds: the peremptory reason is, because they eat the ordure and excrements of the world, that is to say, the sins of the people, and like dung-chewers and excrementitious eaters, they are cast into the privies and secessive places; that is, the Covents and Abbeys separated from Political conversation, as the jakes and retreats of a house are: but if you conceive how an Ape in a family is always mocked, and provokingly incensed, you shall easily apprehend how Monks are shunned of all men, both young and old. The Ape keeps not the house as a dog doth: He drawes not in the plow as the oxe: He yields neither milk nor wooll as the sheep: He carrieth no burthen as a horse doth; that which he doth, is only to conskite, spoil and defile all, which is the cause wherefore he hath of all men mocks, frumperies and bastonadoes.

After the same manner a Monk (I mean those lither, idle, lazie Monks) doth not labour and work, as do the Peasant and Artificer: doth not ward and defend the countrey, as doth the man of warre: cureth not the sick and diseased, as the Physician doth: doth neither preach nor teach, as do the Evangelical Doctors and Schoolmasters: doth not import commodities and things necessary for the Common-wealth, as the Merchant doth: therefore is it, that by and of all men they are hooted at, hated and abhorred. Yea, but (said *Grangousier*,) they pray to God for us. Nothing lesse, (answered *Gargantua*.) True it is, that with a tingle tangle jangling of bells they trouble and disquiet all their neighbours about them: Right, (said the Monk,) a masse, a matine, a vespre well rung are half said. They mumble out great store of Legends and Psalmes, by them not at all understood: they say many *patenotres*, interlarded with *ave-maries*, without thinking upon, or apprehending the meaning of what it is they say, which truly I call mocking of God, and not prayers. But so help them God, as they pray for us, and not for being afraid to lose their victuals, their manchots, and good fat pottage. All true *Christians*, of all estates and conditions, in all places and at all times send up their prayers to God, and the Mediatour prayeth and intercedeth for them, and God is gracious to them. Now such a one is our good *Friar Ihon*, therefore every man desireth to have him in his company, he is no *bigot* or hypocrite, he is not torne and divided betwixt reality and appearance, no wretch of a rugged and peevish disposition, but honest, jovial, resolute and a good fellow: he travels, he labours, he defends the oppressed, comforts the afflicted, helps the needie, and keeps the close of the Abbey: Nay (said the Monk) I do a great deal more then that; for whilest we are in dispatching our matines and anniversaries in the quire, I make withal some crossebowe-strings, polish glasse-bottles and boults; I twist lines and weave purse-nets, wherein to catch coneys; I am never idle; but now hither come, some drink, some drink here, bring the fruit. These chestnuts are of the wood of *Estrox*, and with good new wine are able to make you a fine cracker and composer of bum-sonnets. You are not as yet (it seems) well moistened in this house with the sweet wine and must, by G— I drink to all men freely, and at all Fords like a Proctor or Promoters horse. *Friar Ihon*, (said

Gymnast) take away the snot that hangs at your nose. Ha, ha, (said the Monk), am not I in danger of drowning, seeing I am in water even to the nose? No, no, *quare? quia*, though some water come out from thence, there never goes in any; for it is well antidoted with pot-proof-armour, and sirrup of the Vine-leaf.

O my friend, he that hath winter-boots made of such leather, may boldly fish for oysters, for they will never take water. What is the cause (said *Gargantua*) that *Friar Ihon* hath such a faire nose? Because (said *Grangousier*) that God would have it so, who frameth us in such forme, and for such end, as is most agreeable with his divine Will, even as a Potter fashioneth his vessels. Because (said *Ponocrates*) he came with the first to the faire of noses, and therefore made choice of the fairest and the greatest. Pish, (said the Monk) that is not the reason of it, but, according to the true Monastical Philosophy, it is because my Nurse had soft teats, by virtue whereof, whilest she gave me suck, my nose did sink in as in so much butter. The hard breasts of Nurses make children short-nosed. But *hey gay, Ad formam nasi cognoscitur ad te levavi.* I never eat any confections, *Page*, whilest I am at the bibbery; *Item*, bring me rather some tosts.

CHAPTER XLI

How the Monk made Gargantua sleep, and of his houres and breviaries.

SUPPER being ended, they consulted of the businesse in hand, and concluded that about midnight they should fall unawares upon the enemie, to know what manner of watch and ward they kept, and that in the mean while they should take a little rest, the better to refresh themselves. But *Gargantua* could not sleep by any meanes, on which side soever he turned himself. Whereupon the Monk said to him, I never sleep soundly, but when I am at Sermon or Prayers; Let us therefore begin, you and I, the seven penitential *Psalmes*, to try whether you shall not quickly fall asleep. The conceit pleased *Gargantua* very well, and, beginning the first of these *Psalmes*, assoon as they came to the words *Beati quorum*, they fell asleep both the one and the other. But the Monk for his being formerly accustomed to the houre

of Claustral matines, failed not to awake a little before midnight, and being up himself awaked all the rest, in singing
aloud, and with a full clear voice, the song,

> *Awake, O Reinian; Ho, awake;*
> *Awake, O Reinian, Ho:*
> *Get up, you no more sleep must take,*
> *Get up; for we must go.*

When they were all rowsed and up, he said, *My Masters*, it is a
usual saying, that we begin matines with coughing, and supper
with drinking; let us now (in doing clean contrarily) begin our
matines with drinking, and at night before supper we shall
cough as hard as we can. What? (said *Gargantua*) to drink so soon
after sleep, this is not to live according to the diet and prescript
rule of the Physicians, for you ought first to scoure and cleanse
your stomack of all its superfluities and excrements. O well
physicked, (said the *Monk*) a hundred devils leap into my body,
if there be not more old drunkards, then old Physicians: I have
made this paction and convenant with my appetite, that it alwayes lieth down, and goes to bed with my self, (for to that I
every day give very good order,) then the next morning it also
riseth with me, and gets up when I am awake. Minde you your
charges, (Gentlemen) or tend your cures as much as you will; I
will get me to my *Drawer*, (in termes of falconrie, my *tiring*.)
What *drawer* or *tiring* do you mean? (said *Gargantua*.) My breviary (said the Monk,) for just as the Falconers, before they feed
their hawks, do make them draw at a hens leg, to purge their
braines of flegme, and sharpen them to a good appetite: so by
taking this merry little breviary, in the morning I scoure all my
lungs, and am presently ready to drink.

After what manner (said *Gargantua*) do you say these faire
houres and prayers of yours? After the manner of *Whipfield*,*
said the Monk, by three Psalmes, and three Lessons, or nothing
at all, he that will: I never tie my self to houres, prayers and
sacraments: for they are made for the man, and not the man for
them; therefore is it that I make my Prayers in fashion of stirrup-
leathers; I shorten or lengthen them when I think good. *Brevis*

* Fessecamp *and corruptly* Fecan.

oratio penetrat cælos, & longa potatio evacuat Scyphos: where is
that written? by my faith (said *Ponocrates*,) I cannot tell (my
Pillicock,) but thou art more worth then gold: Therein (said the
Monk) I am like you: but, *venite, apotemus*. Then made they ready
store of *Carbonadoes*, or rashers on the coales, and good fat *soupes*,
or brewis with sippets; and the *Monk* drank what he pleased. Some
kept him company, and the rest did forbear, *for their stomachs
were not as yet opened*. Afterwards every man began to arme and
befit himself for the field; and they armed the *Monk* against his
will; for he desired no other armour for back and breast, but
his frock, nor any other weapon in his hand, but the staffe of
the Crosse: yet at their pleasure was he completely armed
cap-a-pe, and mounted upon one of the best horses in the Kingdome, with a good slashing shable by his side, together with
Gargantua, Ponocrates, Gymnast, Eudemon, and five and twenty
more of the most resolute and adventurous of *Grangousiers*
house, all armed at proof with their lances in their hands,
mounted like St. *George*, and every one of them having a harque-
busier behinde him.

CHAPTER XLII

*How the Monk encouraged his fellow-champions, and how he
hanged upon a tree.*

THUS went out those valiant champions on their adventure, in
full resolution, to know what enterprise they should undertake,
and what to take heed of, and look well to, in the day of the great
and horrible battel. And the *Monk* encouraged them, saying, My
children, do not feare nor doubt, I will conduct you safely; God
and Sanct *Benedict* be with us. If I had strength answerable to
my courage, *by Sdeath* I would plume them for you like ducks. I
feare nothing but the great ordnance; yet I know of a charm by
way of Prayer, which the sub-sexton of our Abbey taught me,
that will preserve a man from the violence of guns, and all manner of fire-weapons and engines, but it will do me no good, because I do not believe it. Neverthelesse, I hope my staffe of the
crosse shall this day play devillish pranks amongst them; by G—
whoever of our Party shall offer to play the duck, and shrink

when blowes are a dealing, I give myself to the devil, if I do not make a Monk of him in my stead, and hamper him within my frock, which is a sovereign cure against cowardise. Did you never heare of my Lord *Meurles* his grey-hound, which was not worth a straw in the fields; he put a frock about his neck; by the body of G— there was neither hare nor fox that could escape him, and which is more, he lined all the bitches in the countrey, though before that he was feeble-reined, and *ex frigidis & maleficiatis*. The Monk uttering these words in choler, as he past under a walnut-tree, in his way towards the Causey, he broached the vizor of his helmet on the stump of a great branch of the said tree: neverthelesse, he set his spurres so fiercely to the horse, who was full of mettal, and quick on the spurre, that he bounded forwards, and the Monk going about to ungrapple his vizor, let go his hold of the bridle, and so hanged by his hand upon the bough, whilest his horse stole away from under him. By this meanes was the Monk left, hanging on the walnut-tree, and crying for help, murther, murther, swearing also that he was betrayed: *Eudemon* perceived him first, and calling *Gargantua* said, *Sir*, come and see *Absalom* hanging. *Gargantua* being come, considered the countenance of the Monk, and in what posture he hanged; wherefore he said to *Eudemon*, You were mistaken in comparing him to *Absalom*; for *Absalom* hung by his haire, but this shaveling Monk hangeth by the eares. Help me (said the Monk) in the devils name, is this a time for you to prate? you seem to me to be like the decretalist Preachers, who say, that whosoever shall see his neighbour in the danger of death, ought upon paine of trisulk excommunication, rather choose to admonish him to make his Confession to a Priest, and put his conscience in the state of Peace, then otherwise to help and relieve him.

And therefore when I shall see them fallen into a river, and ready to be drowned, I shall make them a faire long sermon *de contemptu mundi, & fuga seculi*; and when they are stark dead, shall then go to their aid and succour in fishing after them: Be quiet (said *Gymnast*,) and stirre not my minion; I am now coming to unhang thee, and to set thee at freedome, for thou art a pretty little gentle *Monachus; Monachus in claustro non valet ova duo; sed quando est extra bene valet triginta*: I have seen above five hundred hanged, but I never saw any have a better countenance in his dangling and *pendilatory* swagging; truly if I had so good a one, I would willingly hang thus all my life-time; What? (said the Monk) have you almost done preaching: help me in the name of God, seeing you will not in the name of the other spirit, or by the habit which I wear you shall repent it, *tempore & loco prælibatis*.

Then *Gymnast* alighted from his horse, and climbing up the walnut-tree, lifted up the *Monk* with one hand, by the gushets of his armour under the arm-pits, and with the other undid his vizor from the stump of the broken branch, which done, he let him fall to the ground and himself after. Assoon as the *Monk* was down, he put off all his armour, and threw away one piece after another about the field, & taking to him again his staffe of the Crosse, remounted up to his horse, which *Eudemon* had caught in his running away. Then went they on merrily, riding along on the high way.

CHAPTER XLIII

How the Scouts and fore-party of Picrochole were met with by Gargantua, and how the Monk slew captain Draw-forth,* and then was taken prisoner by his enemies.

PICROCHOLE at the relation of those who had escaped out of the broile and defeat, wherein *Tripet* was untriped, grew very angry that the devils should have so run upon his men, and held all that night a counsel of warre, at which *Rashcalf*** and *Touchfaucet*† concluded his power to be such, that he was able to defeat all the devils of hell, if they should come to justle with his forces. This *Picrochole* did not fully beleeve, though he doubted not much of it: Therefore sent he under the command and conduct of the Count *Draw-forth*, for discovering of the countrey, the number of sixteen hundred horsemen, all well-mounted upon light horses for skirmish, and throughly besprinkled with holy water; and every one for their field-mark or cognizance had the signe of a starre in his scarf, to serve at all adventures, in case

---

* Tireavant. ** Hastueau. † Touquedillon.

they should happen to incounter with devils; that by the vertue, as well of that *Gregorian* water, as of the starres which they wore, they might make them disappear and evanish.

In this equipage, they made an excursion upon the countrey, till they came near to the *Vauguyon*, (*which is the valley of* Guyon) and to the spittle, but could never finde any body to speak unto; whereupon they returned a little back, and took occasion to passe above the aforesaid hospital, to try what intelligence they could come by in those parts, in which resolution riding on, and by chance in a pastoral lodge, or shepherds cottage near to *Coudray*, hitting upon the six Pilgrims, they carried them way-bound and manacled, as if they had been spies, for all the exclamations, adjurations and requests that they could make. Being come down from thence towards *Seville*, they were heard by *Gargantua*, who said then unto those that were with him, Camerades and fellow souldiers, we have here met with an encounter, and they are ten times in number more then we: shall we charge them or no? What a devil (said the *Monk*) shall we do else? Do you esteem men by their number, rather then by their valour and prowes? With this he cried out, Charge, *devils*, charge; which when the enemies heard, they thought certainly that they had been very devils, and therefore even then began all of them to run away as hard as they could drive, *Draw-forth* only excepted, who immediately setled his lance on its rest, and therewith hit the *Monk* with all his force on the very middle of his breast, but, coming against his horrifick frock, the point of the iron, being with the blow either broke off or blunted, it was in matter of execution, as if you had struck against an Anvil with a little wax-candle.

Then did the *Monk* with his staffe of the Crosse, give him such a sturdie thump and whirret betwixt his neck and shoulders, upon the *Acromion* bone, that he made him lose both sense and motion, and fall down stone dead at his horses feet; and, seeing the signe of the starre which he wore scarfwayes, he said unto *Gargantua*, these men are but Priests, which is but the beginning of a Monk; by St. *Ihon* I am a perfect Monk, I will kill them to you like flies: Then ran he after them at a swift and full gallop, till he overtook the reere, and felled them down like tree-leaves, striking athwart and alongst and every way. *Gymnast* presently asked *Gargantua* if they should pursue them? To whom *Gargantua* answered, by no means; for, according to right military discipline, you must never drive your enemy unto despair, for that such a strait doth multiply his force, and increase his courage, which was before broken and cast down; neither is there any better help, or outgate of relief for men that are amazed, out of heart, toiled and spent, then to hope for no favour at all. How many victories have been taken out of the hands of the Victors by the vanquished, when they would not rest satisfied with reason, but attempt to put all to the sword, and totally to destroy their enemies, without leaving so much as one to carry home newes of the defeat of his fellowes? Open therefore unto your enemies all the gates and wayes, and make to them a bridge of silver rather then faile, that you may be rid of them. Yea, but (said *Gymnast*) they have the *Monk*: Have they the *Monk?* (said *Gargantua*). Upon mine honour then it will prove to their cost: but to prevent all dangers, let us not yet retreat, but halt here quietly, as in an ambush; for I think I do already understand the policie and judgement of our enemies, they are truly more directed by chance and meer fortune, then by good advice and counsel. In the mean while, whilest these made a stop under the walnut-trees, the *Monk* pursued on the chase, charging all he overtook, and giving quarter to none, until he met with a trouper, who carried behinde him one of the poor Pilgrims, and there would have rifled him. The Pilgrim, in hope of relief at the sight of the *Monk*, cried out, Ha, my Lord *Prior*, my good friend, my Lord *Prior*, save me, I beseech you, save me; which words being heard by those that rode in the van, they instantly faced about, and seeing there was no body but the *Monk* that made this great havock & slaughter among them, they loded him with blows as thick as they use to do an Asse with wood: but of all this he felt nothing, especially when they struck upon his frock, his skin was so hard. Then they committed him to two of the Marshals men to keep, and looking about, saw no body coming against them, whereupon they thought that *Gargantua* and his Party were fled: then was it that they rode as hard as they could towards the walnut-trees to meet with them, and left the *Monk* there all alone, with his two foresaid men to guard him. *Gargantua* heard the noise and neighing of the

horses, and said to his men, *Camerades*, I hear the track and beating of the enemies horse-feet, and withall perceive that some of
them come in a troupe and full body against us; let us rallie and
close here, then set forward in order, and by this means we shall
be able to receive their charge, to their losse and our honour.

CHAPTER XLIV

How the Monk rid himself of his Keepers, and how Picrocholes
forlorne hope was defeated.

THE Monk seeing them break off thus without order, conjec-
tured that they were to set upon *Gargantua* and those that were
with him, and was wonderfully grieved that he could not succour
them; then considered he the countenance of the two keepers
in whose custody he was, who would have willingly runne after
the troops to get some booty and plunder, and were always looking towards the valley unto which they were going; farther, he
syllogized, saying, These men are but badly skilled in matters
of warre, for they have not required my paroll, neither have they
taken my sword from me; suddenly hereafter he drew his brackmard or horsemans sword, wherewith he gave the keeper which
held him, on the right side such a sound slash, that he cut clean
thorough the *jugularie* veins, and the *sphagitid* or transparent arteries of the neck, with the fore-part of the throat called the
gargareon, even unto the two *Adenes*, which are throat-kernels;
and redoubling the blow, he opened the *spinal* marrow betwixt
the second and third verteber; there fell down that keeper stark
dead to the ground. Then the *Monk*, reining his horse to the left,
ranne upon the other, who seeing his fellow dead, and the *Monk*
to have the advantage of him, cried with a loud voice, Ha, my
Lord *Prior*, quarter, I yeeld, my Lord *Prior*, quarter, quarter,
my good friend, my Lord *Prior*: and the *Monk* cried likewise, my
Lord *Posterior*, my friend, my Lord *Posterior*, you shall have it
upon your *posteriorums*: Ha, said the keeper, my Lord *Prior*, my
Minion, my Gentile, Lord *Prior*, I pray God make you an *Abbot*;
By the habit (said the *Monk*) which I weare, I will here make you
a Cardinal; what do you use to pay ransomes to religious men?
you shall therefore have by and by a red hat of my giving: and

the fellow cried, Ha, my Lord *Prior*, my Lord *Prior*, my Lord *Abbot* that shall be, my Lord *Cardinal*, my Lord all, *ha, ha, hes*, no my Lord *Prior*, my good little Lord the *Prior*, I yeeld, render and deliver my self up to you: and I deliver thee (said the *Monk*) to all the Devils in hell; then at one stroak he struck off his head, cutting his *scalp* upon the *temple*-bones, and lifting up in the upper part of the *scul* the two triangularie bones called *sincipital*, or the two bones *bregmatis*, together with the *sagittal* commissure or dart-like seame which distinguisheth the right side of the head from the left, as also a great part of the coronal or forehead-bone, by which terrible blow likewise he cut the two meninges or filmes which inwrap the braine, and made a deep wound in the braines two posterior ventricles, and the *cranium* or *skull* abode hanging upon his shoulders, by the skin of the *pericranium* behinde, in forme of a Doctors bonnet, black without and red within. Thus fell he down also to the ground stark dead.

And presently the Monk gave his horse the spurre, and kept the way that the enemy held, who had met with *Gargantua* and his companions in the broad highway, and were so diminished of their number, for the enormous slaughter that *Gargantua* had made with his great tree amongst them, as also *Gymnast*, *Ponocrates*, *Eudemon*, and the rest, that they began to retreat disorderly and in great haste, as men altogether affrighted and troubled in both sense and understanding; and, as if they had seen the very proper *species* and forme of death before their eyes; or rather as when you see an Asse with a *brizze* or gad-bee under his taile, or flie that stings him, run hither and thither without keeping any path or way, throwing down his load to the ground, breaking his bridle and reines, and taking no breath nor rest, and no man can tell what ailes him, for they see not any thing touch him: so fled these people destitute of wit, without knowing any cause of flying, only pursued by a *panick* terror, which in their mindes they had conceived. The *Monk* perceiving that their whole intent was to betake themselves to their heels, alighted from his horse, and got upon a big large rock, which was in the way, and with his great *Brackmard* sword laid such load upon those runawayes, and with maine strength fetching a compasse with his arme without feigning or sparing, slew and overthrew so many, that his sword broke in two peces, then thought he within himself that he had slaine and killed sufficiently, and that the rest should escape to carry newes; therefore he took up a battle-axe of those that lay there dead, and got upon the rock againe, passing his time to see the enemy thus flying, and to tumble himself amongst the dead bodies, only that he suffered none to carry Pike, Sword, Lance nor Gun with him, and those who carried the Pilgrims bound, he made to alight, and gave their horses unto the said Pilgrims, keeping them there with him under the hedge, and also *Touchefaucet*, who was then his prisoner.

CHAPTER XLV

How the Monk carried along with him the Pilgrims, and of the good words that Grangousier gave them.

THIS skirmish being ended, *Gargantua* retreated with his men, excepting the *Monk*, and about the dawning of the day they came unto *Grangousier*, who in his bed was praying unto God for their safety and victory: and seeing them all safe and sound, he embraced them lovingly, and asked what was become of the *Monk?* *Gargantua* answered him, that without doubt the enemies had the *Monk*. Then have they mischief and ill luck (said *Grangousier*) which was very true. Therefore is it a common proverb to this day, *to give a man the Monk* (or as in French, *luy bailler le moine*), when they would expresse the doing unto one a mischief; then commanded he a good breakfast to be provided for their refreshment: when all was ready, they called *Gargantua*, but he was so agrieved that the *Monk* was not to be heard of, that he would neither eate nor drink: in the meane while the *Monk* comes, and from the gate of the outer Court cries out aloud, *Fresh wine, fresh wine Gymnast* my friend. *Gymnast* went out and saw that it was Frier *Jhon*, who brought along with him six pilgrims and *Touch-faucet* prisoners; whereupon *Gargantua* likewise went forth to meet him, and all of them made him the best welcome that possibly they could, and brought him before *Grangousier*, who asked him of all his adventures: the *Monk* told him all, both how he was taken, how he rid himself of his keepers, of the slaughter he had made by the way, and how he had rescued the Pilgrims, and brought along with him Captaine *Touch-faucet*.

Then did they altogether fall to banqueting most merrily; in the meane time *Grangousier* asked the Pilgrims what countreymen they were, whence they came, and whither they went? *Sweertogo* in the name of the rest answered, My Sovereign Lord, I am of Saint *Genou* in *Berrie*, this man is of *Patvau*, this other is of *Onzay*, this of *Argy*, this of St. *Nazarand*, and this man of *Villebrenin*; we come from Saint *Sebastian* near *Nantes*, and are now returning, as we best may, by easie journeys; Yea, but said *Grangousier*, what went you to do at Saint *Sebastian*? We went (said *Sweertogo*) to offer up unto that Sanct our vowes against the Plague. Ah poor men (said *Grangousier*) do you think that the Plague comes from Saint *Sebastian*? Yes truly, (answered *Sweertogo*) our Preachers tell us so indeed. But is it so? (said *Grangousier*) do the false Prophets teach you such abuses? do they thus blaspheme the Sancts and holy men of God, as to make them like unto the Devils, who do nothing but hurt unto mankinde, as *Homer* writeth, that the Plague was sent into the camp of the *Greeks* by *Apollo*, and as the Poets feign a great rabble of *Vejoves* and mischievous gods. So did a certaine *Cafard* or dissembling religionarie preach at *Sinay*, that Saint *Antonie* sent the fire into mens legs, that Saint *Eutropius* made men hydropick; Saint *Clidas*, fooles; and that Saint *Genou* made them goutish: but I punished him so exemplarily, though he called me Heretick for it, that since that time no such hypocritical rogue durst set his foot within my territories; and truly I wonder that your King should suffer them in their sermons to publish such scandalous doctrine in his dominions; for they deserve to be chastised with greater severity then those who by magical art, or any other device have brought the pestilence into a countrey; the pest killeth but the bodies, but such abominable Impostors empoyson our very souls. As he spake these words, in came the *Monk* very resolute, and asked them, whence are you, you poor wretches? of Saint *Genou* (said they;) And how (said the *Monk*) doth the Abbot *Gulligut* the good drinker, and the Monks, what cheere make they? by G— body they'll have a fling at your wives, and breast them to some purpose whilest you are upon your roaming rant and gadding Pilgrimage: *Hin, hen* (said *Sweertogo*) I am not afraid of mine; for he that shall see her by day, will never break his neck to come to her in the night-time: Yea mary (said the *Monk*) now

THE FIRST BOOK

you have hit it, let her be as ugly as ever was *Proserpina*, she will
once by the Lord G— be over-turned, and get her skin-coat
shaken, if there dwell any Monks near to her, for a good Carpenter will make use of any kinde of timber: let me be pepper'd
with the pox, if you finde not all your wives with childe at your
returne; for the very shadow of the steeple of an *Abbey* is fruitful:
It is (said *Gargantua*) like the water of *Nilus* in *Egypt*, if you
beleeve *Strabo* and *Plinie, lib.* 7. *cap.* 3. What vertue will there
be then (said the *Monk*) in their bullets of concupiscence, their
habits and their bodies?

Then (said *Grangousier,*) Go your wayes, poor men in the
name of God the Creatour, to whom I pray to guide you perpetually, and henceforward be not so ready to undertake these
idle and unprofitable journeys; Look to your families, labour
every man in his vocation, instruct your children, and live as the
good Apostle St. *Paul* directeth you: in doing whereof, God, his
Angels and Sancts, will guard and protect you, and no evil or
plague at any time shall befal you. Then *Gargantua* led them
into the hall to take their refection: but the Pilgrims did nothing
but sigh, and said to *Gargantua*, O how happy is that land which
hath such a man for their Lord! we have been more edified and
instructed by the talk which he hath had with us, then by all the
Sermons that ever were preached in our town. That is (said
Gargantua) that which *Plato* saith, *lib.* 5. *de republ.* That *those
Commonwealths are happy, whose Rulers philosophate, and whose
Philosophers rule.* Then caused he their wallets to be filled with
victuals, and their bottles with wine, and gave unto each of
them a horse to ease them upon the way, together with some
pence to live by.

CHAPTER XLVI

*How Grangousier did very kindly entertain Touchefaucet his
Prisoner.*

TOUCHEFAUCET was presented unto *Grangousier*, and by him
examined upon the enterprise and attempt of *Picrochole*, what it
was he could pretend to, or aim at, by the rustling stirre, and
tumultuary coyle of this his sudden invasion: whereunto he

answered, that his end and purpose was to conquer all the countrey, if he could, for the injury done to his cake-bakers: It is too
great an undertaking (said *Grangousier*;) and (as the Proverb is)
He that gripes too much, holds fast but little: the time is not
now as formerly, to conquer the Kingdomes of our neighbour
Princes, and to build up our own greatnesse upon the losse
of our nearest Christian brother: this imitation of the ancient
Herculeses, Alexanders, Hannibals, Scipios, Cæsars, and other such
heroes is quite contrary to the Profession of the Gospel of Christ,
by the which we are commanded to preserve, keep, rule, and
govern every man his own countrey and lands, and not in a hostile manner to invade others, and that which heretofore the *Bar-
bars* and *Saracens* called prowesse and valour, we do now call
robbing, theevery and wickednes; It would have been more commendable in him to have contained himself within the bounds
of his own territories, royally governing them, then to insult and
domineer in mine, pillaging and plundering every where like a
most unmerciful enemy; for by ruling his own with discretion,
he might have increas't his greatnesse, but by robbing me he
cannot escape destruction; Go your wayes in the name of God,
prosecute good enterprises, shew your King what is amisse, and
never counsel him with regard unto your own particular profit,
for the publick losse will swallow up the private benefit. As for
your ransome, I do freely remit it to you, and will that your
armes and horse be restored to you; so should good neighbours
do, and ancient friends; seeing this our difference is not properly
warre, as *Plato, lib.* 5. *de repub.* would not have it called warre but
sedition, when the *Greeks* took up armes against one another,
and that therefore when such combustions should arise
amongst them, his advice was to behave themselves in the managing of them, with all discretion and modesty. Although you
call it warre, it is but superficial, it entereth not into the closet
and inmost cabinet of our hearts; for neither of us hath been
wronged in his honour, nor is there any question betwixt us in
the main, but only how to redresse by the by some petty faults
committed by our men; I mean, both yours and ours, which
although you knew you ought to let passe; for these quarrel-
some persons deserve rather to be contemned then mentioned,
especially seeing I offered them satisfaction according to the

wrong. God shall be the just Judge of our variances, whom I beseech by death rather to take me out of this life, and to permit my goods to perish and be destroyed before mine eyes, then that by me or mine he should in any sort be wronged. These words uttered, he called the *Monk*, and before them all spoke thus unto him: Friar *Ihon*, my good friend, is it you that took prisoner the Captain *Touchfaucet* here present? Sir (said the Monk) seeing himself is here, and that he is of the yeares of discretion, I had rather you should know it by his confession then by any words of mine. Then said *Touchfaucet*, My sovereign Lord, it is he indeed that took me, and I do therefore most freely yield my self his prisoner. Have you put him to any ransom? said *Grangousier* to the *Monk*. No, (said the *Monk*,) of that I take no care: How much would you have for having taken him? nothing, nothing, (said the *Monk*,) I am not swayed by that, nor do I regard it; Then *Grangousier* commanded, that in presence of *Touchefaucet*, should be delivered to the Monk for taking him, the summe of threescore and two thousands saluts (*in* English *money, fifteen thousand and five hundred pounds*) which was done, whilest they made a collation or little banquet to the said *Touchfaucet*, of whom *Grangousier* asked, if he would stay with him, or if he loved rather to return to his King? *Touchfaucet* answered, that he was content to take whatever course he would advise him to; Then (said *Grangousier*) return unto your King, and God be with you.

Then he gave him an excellent sword of a *Vienne* blade, with a golden scabbard wrought with Vine-branch-like flourishes, of faire Goldsmiths work, and a coller or neck-chain of gold, weighing seven hundred and two thousand marks (*at eight ounces each,*) garnished with precious stones of the finest sort, esteemed at a hundred and sixty thousand ducats, and ten thousand crownes more, as an honourable donative, by way of present.

After this talk, *Touchefaucet* got to his horse, and *Gargantua* for his safety allowed him the guard of thirty men at armes, and six score archers to attend him under the conduct of *Gymnast*, to bring him even unto the gate of the rock *Clermond*, if there were need. Assoon as he was gone, the *Monk* restored unto *Grangousier* the three-score and two thousand saluts, which he had received, saying, Sir, it is not as yet the time for you to give such

133

gifts, stay till this warre be at an end, for none can tell what accidents may occurre, and war begun without good provision of money before-hand for going through with it, is but as a breathing of strength, and blast that will quickly passe away; coine is the sinews of warre. Well then (said *Grangousier*) at the end I will content you by some honest recompence, as also all those who shall do me good service.

CHAPTER XLVII

How Grangousier sent for his legions, and how Touchefaucet slew Rashcalf, and was afterwards executed by the command of Picrochole.

ABOUT this same time those of *Besse*, of the *old Market*, of St. *James* bourg, of the draggage of *Parille*, of the *Rivers*, of the rocks St. *Pol*, of the *Vaubreton*, of *Pautille*, of the *Brahemont*, of *Clainbridge*, of *Cravant*, of *Grammont*, of the town at the *Badger-holes*, of *Huymes*, of *Serge*, of *Husse*, of St. *Lovant*, of *Panzoust*, of the *Coldraux*, of *Vernon*, of *Coulaines*, of *Chose*, of *Varenes*, of *Bourgueil*, of the *Bouchard Claud*, of the *Croulay*, of *Narsie*, of *Cand*, of *Monsoreau*, and other bordering places, sent Ambassadours unto *Grangousier*, to tell him that they were advised of the great wrongs which *Picrochole* had done him, and in regard of their ancient confederacy, offered him what assistance they could afford, both in money, victuals and ammunition, and other necessaries for warre; The money, which by the joynt agreement of them all was sent unto him, amounted to sixscore and fourteen millions, two crowns and a half of pure gold. The forces wherewith they did assist him, did consist in fifteen thousand cuirasiers, two and thirty thousand light horsemen, fourscore and nine thousand dragoons, and a hundred and fourty thousand voluntier adventurers. These had with them eleven thousand and two hundred cannons, double cannons, long pieces of Artillery called *Basilisks*, and smaller sized ones, known by the name of *spirols, besides the mortar-pieces and granadoes*. Of pioneers they had seven and fourty thousand, all victualled and payed for six moneths and foure dayes of advance: which offer *Gargantua* did not altogether refuse, nor wholly accept of: but giving them hearty thanks, said that he would compose and order the warre by such a device, that there should not be found great need to put so many honest men to trouble in the managing of it; And therefore was content at that time to give order only for bringing along the legions, which he maintained in his ordinary Garison-townes of the *Deviniere*, of *Chavignie*, of *Gravot*, and of *Quinquenais*, amounting to the number of two thousand cuirasiers, threescore and six thousand foot-souldiers, six and twenty thousand dragoons, attended by two hundred pieces of great ordnance, two and twenty thousand Pioneers, and six thousand light horsemen, all drawn up in troupes, so well befitted and accommodated with their commissaries, sutlers, ferriers, harnasse-makers, and other such like necessary members in a military camp; so fully instructed in the Art of warfare, so perfectly knowing and following their colours, so ready to hear and obey their Captains, so nimble to run, so strong at their charging, so prudent in their adventures, and every day so well disciplined, that they seemed rather to be a consort of organ-pipes, or mutual concord of the wheels of a clock, then an infantry and cavalry, or army of souldiers.

Touchefaucet immediately after his return, presented himself before *Picrochole*, and related unto him at large all that he had done and seen, and at last endeavoured to perswade him with strong and forcible arguments, to capitulate and make an agreement with *Grangousier*, whom he found to be the honestest man in the world, saying further, that it was neither right nor reason thus to trouble his neighbours, of whom they had never received any thing but good: and in regard of the main point, that they should never be able to go through stitch with that warre, but to their great damage and mischief: for the forces of *Picrochole* were not so considerable, but that *Grangousier* could easily overthrow them.

He had not well done speaking, when *Rashcalf* said out aloud, Unhappy is that Prince, which is by such men served, who are so easily corrupted, as I know *Touchefaucet* is; for I see his courage so changed, that he had willingly joyned with our enemies to fight against us and betray us, if they would have received him; but as vertue is of all, both friends and foes, praised and esteemed, so is wickednes soon known and suspected, and although it happen the enemies to make use thereof for their profit, yet have they alwayes the wicked, and the traitors in abomination.

Touchefaucet being at these words very impatient, drew out his sword, and therewith ran *Rashcalf* through the body, a little under the nipple of his left side, whereof he died presently, and pulling back his sword out of his body, said boldly, *So let him perish, that shall a faithful servant blame. Picrochole* incontinently grew furious, and seeing *Touchefaucets* new sword and his scabbard so richly diapred with flourishes of most excellent workmanship, said, Did they give thee this weapon, so felloniously therewith to kill before my face my so good friend *Rashcalf?* then immediately commanded he his guard to hew him in pieces, which was instantly done, and that so cruelly, that the chamber was all died with blood: Afterwards he appointed the corps of *Rashcalf* to be honourably buried, and that of *Touchefaucet*, to be cast over the walls into the ditches.

The newes of these excessive violences were quickly spread through all the Army; whereupon many began to murmure against *Picrochole*, insofarre that *Pinchpennie* said to him, My sovereign Lord, I know not what the issue of this enterprise will be; I see your men much dejected, and not well resolved in their mindes, by considering that we are here very ill provided of victuall, and that our number is already much diminished by three or foure sallies. Furthermore, great supplies and recruits come daily in to your enemies: but we so moulder away, that, if we be once besieged, I do not see how we can escape a total destruction; *Tush, pish,* (said *Picrochole*) you are like the *Melun* eeles, you cry before they come to you; Let them come, *let them come,* if they dare.

CHAPTER XLVIII

How Gargantua set upon Picrochole, within the rock Clermond, and utterly defeated the Army of the said Picrochole.

GARGANTUA had the charge of the whole Army, and his father *Grangousier* stayed in his Castle, who encouraging them with good words, promised great rewards unto those that should do any notable service. Having thus set forward, assoon as they had

gained the Passe at the Ford of *Vede*, with boats and bridges
speedily made, they past over in a trice, then considering the
situation of the town, which was on a high and advantageous
place, *Gargantua* thought fit to call his counsel, and passe that
night in deliberation upon what was to be done: But *Gymnast*
said unto him, My sovereign Lord, such is the nature and complexion of the *frenches*, that they are worth nothing, but at the
first push, then are they more fierce then devils; but if they
linger a little, and be wearied with delays, they'l prove more
faint and remisse then women: my opinion is therefore, that
now presently after your men have taken breath, and some
small refection, you give order for a resolute assault, and that we
storme them instantly. His advice was found very good, and for
effectuating thereof, he brought forth his army into the plain
field, and placed the reserves on the skirt or rising of a little hill.
The *Monk* took along with him six companies of foot, and two
hundred horsemen well armed, and with great diligence
crossed the marish, and valiantly got up on the top of the green
hillock, even unto the high-way which leads to *Loudin*. Whilest
the assault was thus begun, *Picrocholes* men could not tell well
what was best, to issue out and receive the Assailants, or keep
within the town and not to stirre: Himself in the mean time,
without deliberation, sallied forth in a rage with the cavalry of
his guard, who were forthwith received, and royally entertained
with great cannon-shot, that fell upon them like haile from the
high grounds, on which the Artillery was planted; whereupon
the *Gargantuists* betook themselves unto the valleys, to give the
ordnance leave to play, and range with the larger scope.

Those of the town defended themselves as well as they
could, but their shot past over us, without doing us any hurt at
all: Some of *Picrocholes* men that had escaped our Artillery, set
most fiercely upon our souldiers, but prevailed little; for they
were all let in betwixt the files, and there knock't down to
the ground, which their fellow-souldiers seeing, they would
have retreated, but the *Monk* having seised upon the Passe, by
the which they were to return, they run away and fled in all the
disorder and confusion that could be imagined.

Some would have pursued after them, and followed the chase,
but the *Monk* withheld them, apprehending that in their pursuit

the Pursuers might lose their ranks, and so give occasion to the besieged to sallie out of the town upon them. Then staying there some space, and none coming against him, he sent the Duke *Phrontist*, to advise *Gargantua* to advance towards the hill up on the left hand, to hinder *Picrocholes* retreat at that gate, which *Gargantua* did with all expedition, and sent thither foure brigades under the conduct of *Sebast*, which had no sooner reach't the top of the hill, but they met *Picrochole* in the teeth, and those that were with him scattered.

Then charged they upon them stoutly, yet were they much indamaged by those that were upon the walles, who galled them with all manner of shot, both from the great ordnance, small guns and bowes. Which *Gargantua* perceiving, he went with a strong Partie to their relief, and with his Artillery began to thunder so terribly upon that canton of the wall, and so long, that all the strength within the town, to maintain and fill up the breach, was drawn thither. The *Monk* seeing that quarter which he kept besieged, void of men and competent guards, and in a manner altogether naked and abandoned, did most magnanimously on a sudden lead up his men towards the Fort, and never left it till he had got up upon it, knowing that such as come to the reserve in a conflict, bring with them alwayes more feare and terrour, then those that deal about them with their hands in the fight.

Neverthelesse he gave no alarm till all his souldiers had got within the wall, except the two hundred horsemen, whom he left without to secure his entry. Then did he give a most horrible shout, so did all these who were with him, and immediately thereafter without resistance, putting to the edge of the sword the guard that was at that gate, they opened it to the horsemen, with whom most furiously they altogether ran towards the East-gate, where all the hurlie burlie was, and coming close upon them in the reer, overthrew all their forces. The besieged seeing that the *Gargantuists* had won the town upon them, and that they were like to be secure in no corner of it, submitted themselves unto the mercy of the *Monk*, and asked for quarter, which the *Monk* very nobly granted to them, yet made them lay down their armes; then shutting them up within Churches, gave order to seise upon all the staves of the Crosses, and placed men at the doores to keep them from coming forth; then opening that East-gate, he issued out to succour and assist *Gargantua*: but *Picrochole*, thinking it had been some relief coming to him from the towne, adventured more forwardly then before, and was upon the giving of a most desperate home-charge, when *Gargantua* cried out, Ha, Friar *Ihon*, my friend, Friar *Ihon*, you are come in a good houre; which unexpected accident so affrighted *Picrochole* and his men, that giving all for lost, they betook themselves to their heels, and fled on all hands. *Gargantua* chased them till they came near to *Vaugaudry*, killing and slaying all the way, and then sounded the retreat.

CHAPTER XLIX

How Picrochole in his flight fell into great misfortunes, and what Gargantua did after the battel.

PICROCHOLE thus in despaire, fled towards the *Bouchard Island*, and in the way to *Rivere* his horse stumbled and fell down, whereat he on a sudden was so incensed, that he with his sword without more ado killed him in his choler; then not finding any that would remount him, he was about to have taken an Asse at the Mill that was thereby: but the Millers men did so baste his bones, and so soundly bethwack him, that they made him both black and blew with strokes; then, stripping him of all his clothes, gave him a scurvie old canvas jacket wherewith to cover his nakednesse. Thus went along this poor cholerik wretch, who passing the water at *Porthuaux*, and relating his misadventurous disasters, was foretold by an old *Lourpidon* hag, that his Kingdome should be restored to him at the coming of the *Cocklicranes*, which she called *Coquecigrues*. What is become of him since we cannot certainly tell, yet was I told that he is now a porter at *Lyons*, as testie and pettish in humour as ever he was before, and would be alwayes with great lamentation enquiring at all strangers of the coming of the *Cocklicranes*, expecting assuredly, (according to the old womans prophecie,) that at their coming he shall be re-established in his Kingdom. The first thing *Gargantua* did after his return into the town was to call the Muster-roll of his men, which when he had done, he found

that there were very few either killed or wounded, only some
few foot of Captain *Tolmeres* company, and *Ponocrates* who was
shot with a musket-ball through the doublet. Then he caused
them all at and in their several posts and divisions to take a little
refreshment, which was very plenteously provided for them in
the best drink and victuals that could be had for money, and
gave order to the Treasurers and Commissaries of the Army,
to pay for and defray that repast, and that there should be no
outrage at all, nor abuse committed in the town, seeing it was
his own. And furthermore commanded, that immediately after
the souldiers had done with eating and drinking for that time
sufficiently, and to their own hearts desire, a gathering should
be beaten for bringing them altogether, to be drawn up on the
Piazza before the Castle, there to receive six moneths pay compleatly, all which was done. After this by his direction, were
brought before him in the said place, all those that remained
of *Picrocholes* Party; unto whom in the presence of the Princes,
Nobles, and Officers of his Court and Army, he spoke as followeth.

CHAPTER L

Gargantua's speech to the vanquished.

OUR forefathers and Ancestors of all times, have been of this
nature and disposition, that, upon the winning of a battel, they
have chosen rather for a signe and memorial of their triumphs
and victories, to erect trophies and monuments in the hearts of
the vanquished by clemencie, then by architecture in the lands
which they had conquered; for they did hold in greater estimation, the lively remembrance of men purchased by liberality,
then the dumb inscription of arches, pillars and pyramides, subject to the injury of stormes and tempests, and to the envie of
every one. You may very well remember of the courtesie, which
by them was used towards the *Bretons*, in the battel of St. *Aubin*
of *Cormier*, and at the demolishing of *Partenay*. You have heard,
and hearing admire their gentle comportment towards those at
the barreers of *Spaniola*, who had plundered, wasted and ransacked the maritime borders of *Olone* and *Talmondois*. All this

hemisphere of the world was filled with the praises and congratulations, which your selves and your fathers made, when *Alpharbal* King of *Canarre*, not satisfied with his own fortunes, did most furiously invade the land of *Onyx*, and with cruel Piracies molest all the *Armorick* islands, and confine regions of *Britanie*; yet was he in a set naval fight justly taken and vanquished by my father, whom God preserve and protect. But what? whereas other Kings and Emperours, yea those who entitle themselves Catholiques, would have dealt roughly with him, kept him a close prisoner, and put him to an extream high ransom: he intreated him very courteously, lodged him kindly with himself in his own Palace, and out of his incredible mildnesse and gentle disposition sent him back with a safe conduct, loaden with gifts, loaden with favours, loaden with all offices of friendship: what fell out upon it? Being returned into his countrey, he called a Parliament, where all the Princes and States of his Kingdom being assembled, he shewed them the humanity which he had found in us, and therefore wished them to take such course by way of compensation therin, as that the whole world might be edified by the example, as well of their honest graciousness to us, as of our gracious honesty towards them. The result hereof was, that it was voted and decreed by an unanimous consent, that they should offer up entirely their Lands, Dominions and Kingdomes, to be disposed of by us according to our pleasure.

Alpharbal in his own person, presently returned with nine thousand and thirty eight great ships of burden, bringing with him the treasures, not only of his house and royal linage, but almost of all the countrey besides; for he imbarking himself, to set saile with a *West-North-East* winde, every one in heaps did cast into the ship gold, silver, rings, jewels, spices, drugs, and aromatical parfumes, parrets, pelicans, monkies, civet-cats, black-spotted weesils, porcupines, &c. He was accounted no good Mothers son, that did not cast in all the rare and precious things he had.

Being safely arrived, he came to my said father, and would have kist his feet: that action was found too submissively low, and therefore was not permitted, but in exchange he was most cordially embraced: he offered his presents, they were not received, because they were too excessive: he yielded himself voluntarily a servant and vassal, and was content his whole posterity should be liable to the same bondage; this was not accepted of, because it seemed not equitable: he surrendered by vertue of the decree of his great Parliamentarie councel, his whole Countreys and Kingdomes to him, offering the Deed and Conveyance, signed, sealed and ratified by all those that were concerned in it; this was altogether refused, and the parchments cast into the fire. In end, this free good will, and simple meaning of the *Canarriens* wrought such tendernesse in my fathers heart, that he could not abstain from shedding teares, and wept most profusely: then by choise words very congruously adapted, strove in what he could to diminish the estimation of the good offices which he had done them, saying, that any courtesie he had conferred upon them, was not worth a rush, and what favour so ever he had shewed them, he was bound to do it. But so much the more did *Alpharbal* augment the repute thereof. What was the issue? whereas for his ransom in the greatest extremity of rigour, and most tyrannical dealing, could not have been exacted above twenty times a hundred thousand crownes, and his eldest sons detained as hostages, till that summe had been payed, they made themselves perpetual tributaries, and obliged to give us every year two millions of gold at foure and twenty carats fine: The first year we received the whole sum of two millions: the second yeare of their own accord they payed freely to us three and twenty hundred thousand crowns: the third year six and twenty hundred thousand: the fourth year, three millions, and do so increase it alwayes out of their own good will, that we shall be constrained to forbid them to bring us any more. This is the nature of gratitude and true thankfulnesse. For time which gnawes and diminisheth all things else, augments and increaseth benefits; because a noble action of liberality, done to a man of reason, doth grow continually, by his generous thinking of it, and remembring it.

Being unwilling therefore any way to degenerate from the hereditary mildnesse and clemency of my Parents; I do now forgive you, deliver you from all fines and imprisonments, fully release you, set you at liberty, and every way make you as frank and free as ever you were before. Moreover, at your going out of the gate, you shall have every one of you three moneths pay to bring you home into your houses and families, and shall have a safe convoy of six hundred cuirasiers and eight thousand foot under the conduct of *Alexander*, Esquire of my body, that the Clubmen of the Countrey may not do you any injury. *God be with you.* I am sorry from my heart that *Picrochole* is not here; for I would have given him to understand, that this warre was undertaken against my will, and without any hope to increase either my goods or renown: but seeing he is lost, and that no man can tell where nor how he went away, it is my will that his Kingdome remain entire to his sonne; who, because he is too young, (he not being yet full five yeares old) shall be brought up and instructed by the ancient Princes, and learned men of the Kingdom. And because a Realm thus desolate, may easily come to ruine; if the covetousnesse and avarice of those, who by their places are obliged to administer justice in it, be not curbed and restrained: I ordain and will have it so, that *Ponocrates* be overseer & superintendent above all his governours, with whatever power and authority is requisite thereto, & that he be continually with the childe, until he finde him able & capable to rule and govern by himself.

Now I must tell you, that you are to understand how a too feeble and dissolute facility in pardoning evil-doers, giveth them occasion to commit wickednesse afterwards more readily, upon this pernicious confidence of receiving favour; I consider, that *Moses*, the meekest man that was in his time upon the earth, did severely punish the mutinous and seditious people of *Israel*: I consider likewise, that *Julius Cæsar*, who was so gracious an Emperour, that *Cicero* said of him, that his fortune had nothing more excellent then that he could; and his vertue nothing better, then that he would always save and pardon every man: He notwithstanding all this, did in certain places most rigorously punish the authors of rebellion; After the example of these good men, it is my will and pleasure, that you deliver over unto me, before you depart hence, first, that fine fellow *Marquet*, who was the prime cause, origin and ground-work of this warre, by his vain presumption and overweening: secondly, his fellow cake-bakers, who were neglective in checking and reprehending his idle haire-brain'd humour in the instant time: and lastly, all the Councillors, Captains, Officers and Domesticks of *Picrochole*,

who had been incendiaries or fomenters of the warre, by provoking, praising or counselling him to come out of his limits
thus to trouble us.

CHAPTER LI

*How the victorious Gargantuists were recompensed
after the battel.*

WHEN *Gargantua* had finished his speech, the seditious men
whom he required, were delivered up unto him, except *Swash-
buckler*, *Durtaille* and *Smaltrash*, who ran away sixe houres before
the battel, one of them as farre as to *Lainielneck* at one course,
another to the valley of *Vire*, and the third even unto *Logroine*,
without looking back, or taking breath by the way; and two of
the Cake-bakers who were slaine in the fight. *Gargantua* did
them no other hurt, but that he appointed them to pull at the
Presses of his Printing-house, which he had newly set up; then
those who died there he caused to be honourably buried in
Black-soile-valley, and *Burn-hag-field*, and gave order that the
wounded should be drest and had care of in his great Hospital
or *Nosocome*. After this, considering the great prejudice done to
the towne and its inhabitants, he re-imbursed their charges, and
repaired all the losses that by their confession upon oath could
appear they had sustained: and for their better defence and
security in times coming against all sudden uproars and invasions,
commanded a strong citadel to be built there with a competent
Garison to maintaine it; at his departure he did very graciously
thank all the souldiers of the brigades that had been at this overthrow, and sent them back to their winter-quarters in their several stations and Garisons; the *Decumane Legion* onely excepted,
whom in the field on that day he saw do some great exploit, and
their Captains also, whom he brought along with himself unto
Grangousier.

At the sight and coming of them, the good man was so joyful,
that it is not possible fully to describe it; he made them a feast
the most magnificent, plentiful, and delicious that ever was
seen since the time of the King *Assuerus*; at the taking up of the
table he distributed among them his whole cupboard of plate,

which weighed eight hundred thousand & fourteen *Besants** of gold, in great antick vessels, huge pots, large basins, big tasses, cups, goblets, candlesticks, comfit-boxes, and other such plate, all of pure massie gold besides the precious stones, enameling and workmanship, which by all mens estimation was more worth then the matter of the gold; then unto every one of them out of his coffers caused he to be given the summe of twelve hundred thousand crownes ready money: and further he gave to each of them for ever and in perpetuity (unlesse he should happen to decease without heires) such Castles and neighbouring lands of his as were most commodious for them: to *Ponocrates* he gave the rock *Clermond;* to *Gymnast*, the *Coudray;* to *Eudemon, Monpensier; Rinan* to *Tolmere;* to *Itchibolle, Montsaureau;* to *Acamas, Cande; Varenes*, to *Chironacte; Gravot to Sebast; Quinquenais* to *Alexander; Ligre* to *Sophrone;* and so of his other places.

CHAPTER LII

How Gargantua caused to be built for the Monk the Abbey of Theleme

THERE was left onely the Monk to provide for, whom *Gargantua* would have made Abbot of *Seville*, but he refused it; he would have given him the Abby of *Bourgueil*, or of Sanct *Florent* which was better, or both, if it pleased him; but the Monk gave him a very peremptory answer, that he would never take upon him the charge nor government of Monks; For how shall I be able (said he) to rule over others, that have not full power and command of my self: if you think I have done you, or may hereafter do any acceptable service, give me leave to found an Abby after my owne minde and fancie; the motion pleased *Gargantua* very well, who thereupon offered him all the Countrey of *Thelem* by the river of *Loire*, till within two leagues of the great forrest of *Port-huaut*: the *Monk* then requested *Gargantua* to institute his religious order contrary to all others. First then (said *Gargantua*) you must not build a wall about your convent, for all other

---

* Each *Besant* is worth five pounds English money.

Abbies are strongly walled and mured about: See (said the *Monk*) and not without cause (*seeing wall and mure signifie but one and the same thing*;) where there is *Mur* before, and *Mur* behinde, there is store of *Murmur*, envie, and mutual conspiracie. More-over, seeing there are certaine convents in the world, whereof the custome is, if any woman come in (I mean chaste and honest women) they immediately sweep the ground which they have trod upon; therefore was it ordained that if any man or woman entered into religious orders, should by chance come within this new Abbey, all the roomes should be throughly washed and cleansed through which they had passed; and because in all other Monasteries and Nunneries all is compassed, limited, and regulated by houres, it was decreed that in this new structure there should be neither Clock nor Dial, but that according to the opportunities, and incident occasions, all their hours should be disposed of; for (said *Gargantua*) The greatest losse of time that I know, is to count the hours, what good comes of it? now can there be any greater dotage in the world, then for one to guide and direct his courses by the sound of a Bell, and not by his owne judgement and discretion.

Item, Because at that time they put no women into Nunneries, but such as were either purblinde, blinkards, lame, crooked, ill-favoured, mis-shapen, fooles, senselesse, spoyled or corrupt; nor encloystered any men, but those that were either sickly, subject to defluxions, ill-bred lowts, simple sots, or peevish trouble-houses: but to the purpose; (said the *Monk*) A woman that is neither faire nor good, to what use serves she? To make a Nunne of, said *Gargantua:* Yea (said the *Monk*) and to make shirts and smocks; therefore was it ordained that into this religious order should be admitted no women that were not faire, well featur'd, and of a sweet disposition; nor men that were not comely, personable and well conditioned.

Item, Because in the convents of women men come not but under-hand, privily, and by stealth, it was therefore enacted that in this house there shall be no women in case there be not men, nor men in case there be not women.

Item, Because both men and women that are received into religious orders after the expiring of their noviciat or probation-year, were constrained and forced perpetually to stay there all the days of their life; it was therefore ordered, that all whatever, men or women, admitted within this Abbey, should have full leave to depart with peace and contentment, whensoever it should seem good to them so to do.

Item, for that the religious men and women did ordinarily make three Vows, to wit, those of chastity, poverty & obedience, it was therefore constituted and appointed, that in this Convent they might be honourably married, that they might be rich, and live at liberty. In regard of the legitimat time of the persons to be initiated, and years under and above, which they were not capable of reception, the women were to be admitted from ten till fifteen, and the men from twelve til eighteen.

CHAPTER LIII

How the Abbey of the Thelemites was built and endowed.

For the fabrick and furniture of the Abbey, *Gargantua* caused to be delivered out in ready money seven and twenty hundred thousand, eight hundred and one and thirty of those golden rams of *Berrie*, which have a sheep stamped on the one side, and a flowred crosse on the other; and for every yeare, until the whole work were compleated, he allotted threescore nine thousand crowns of the Sunne, and as many of the seven starres, to be charged all upon the receipt of the custom. For the foundation and maintenance thereof for ever, he setled a perpetual fee-farm-rent of three and twenty hundred, threescore and nine thousand, five hundred and fourteen rose nobles, exempted from all homage, fealty, service or burden whatsoever, and payable every yeare at the gate of the Abbey; and of this by letters pattent passed a very good grant. The Architecture was in a figure hexagonal, and in such a fashion, that in every one of the six corners there was built a great round tower of threescore foot in diameter, and were all of a like forme and bignesse. Upon the north-side ran along the river of *Loire*, on the bank whereof was situated the tower called *Arctick*: going towards the East, there was another called *Calaer*, the next following *Anatole*; the next *Mesembrine*: the next *Hesperia*, and the last *Criere*. Every tower was distant from other the space of three hundred and twelve paces. The whole Ædifice was every where six stories high, reckoning the Cellars under ground for one; the second was arched after the fashion of a basket-handle; the rest were seeled with pure wainscot, flourished with *Flanders* fret-work, in the forme of the foot of a lamp: and covered above with fine slates, with an indorsement of lead, carrying the antick figures of little puppets, and animals of all sorts, notably well suited to one another, and guilt, together with the gutters, which, jetting without the walls, from betwixt the crosse barres in a diagonal figure, painted with gold and azur, reach'd to the very ground, where they ended into great conduit-pipes, which carried all away unto the river from under the house.

This same building was a hundred times more sumptuous and magnificent then ever was *Bonnivet, Chambourg* or *Chantillie*; for there were in it nine thousand, three hundred and two and thirty chambers, every one whereof had a withdrawing room, a handsom closet, a wardrobe, an oratory, and neat passage, leading into a great and spacious hall. Between every tower, in the midst of the said body of building, there was a paire of winding (*such as we now call lantern*) staires, whereof the steps were part of Porphyrie, (*which is a dark red marble, spotted with white,*) part of *Numidian* stone, (*which is a kinde of yellowishly streaked marble upon various colours,*) and part of *Serpentine* marble, (*with light spots on a dark green ground*) each of those steps being two and twenty foot in length, and three fingers thick, and the just number of twelve betwixt every rest, or, (as we now terme it) landing place. In every resting place were two faire antick arches where the light came in: and by those they went into a Cabinet, made even with and of the bredth of the said winding, and the re-ascending above the roofs of the house, ended *conically* in a pavillion: By that vize or winding, they entered on every side into a great hall, and from the halls into the chambers; from the *Arctick* tower unto the *Criere*, were the faire great libraries in *Greek, Latine, Hebrew, French, Italian* and *Spanish*, respectively distributed in their several cantons, according to the diversity of these languages. In the midst there was a wonderful scalier or winding-staire, the entry whereof was without the house, in a vault or arch six fathom broad. It was made in such symmetrie and largenesse, that six men at armes with their lances in their rests, might together in a breast ride all up to the very top of all the Palace; from the tower *Anatole* to the *Mesembrine* were faire spacious galleries, all coloured over and painted with the ancient prowesses, histories and descriptions of the world. In the midst therof there was likewise such another ascent and gate, as we said there was on the river-side. Upon that gate was written in great antick letters, that which followeth.

CHAPTER LIV

The Inscription set upon the great gate of Theleme.

HERE enter not vile bigots, hypocrites,
Externally devoted Apes, base snites,
Puft up, wry-necked beasts, worse then the *Huns*
Or *Ostrogots*, forerunners of baboons:
Curst snakes, dissembled varlets, seeming Sancts,
Slipshod caffards, beggers pretending wants,
Fat chuffcats, smell-feast knockers, doltish gulls,
Out-strouting cluster-fists, contentious bulls,
Fomenters of divisions and debates,
Elsewhere, not here, make sale of your deceits.

> Your filthy trumperies
> Stuff't with pernicious lies,
> (Not worth a bubble)
> Would do but trouble,
> Our earthly Paradise,
> Your filthy trumperies.

HERE enter not Atturneys, Barresters,
Nor bridle-champing law-Practitioners:
Clerks, Commissaries, Scribes nor Pharisees,
Wilful disturbers of the Peoples ease:
Judges, destroyers, with an unjust breath,
Of honest men, like dogs, ev'n unto death.
Your salarie is at the gibet-foot:
Go drink there; for we do not here fly out
On those excessive courses, which may draw
A waiting on your courts by suits in law.

Law-suits, debates and wrangling
Hence are exil'd, and jangling.
  Here we are very
  Frolick and merry,
And free from all intangling,
Law-suits, debates and wrangling.

HERE enter not base pinching Usurers,
Pelf-lickers, everlasting gatherers.
Gold-graspers, coine-gripers, gulpers of mists:
Niggish deformed sots, who, though your chests
Vast summes of money should to you affoard,
Would ne'rthelesse adde more unto that hoard,
And yet not be content, you cluntchfist dastards,
Insatiable fiends, and *Plutoes* bastards.
Greedie devourers, chichie sneakbil rogues,
Hell-mastiffs gnaw your bones, you rav'nous dogs.

  You beastly looking fellowes,
  Reason doth plainly tell us,
    That we should not
    To you allot
  Roome here, but at the Gallowes,
  You beastly looking fellowes.

HERE enter not, fond makers of demurres
In love adventures, peevish, jealous curres.
Sad pensive dotards, raisers of garboyles,
Hags, goblins, ghosts, firebrands of household broyls.
Nor drunkards, liars, cowards, cheaters, clowns,
Theeves, cannibals, faces o'recast with frowns.
Nor lazie slugs, envious, covetous:
Nor blockish, cruel, nor too credulous.
Here mangie, pockie folks shall have no place,
No ugly lusks, nor persons of disgrace.

  Grace, honour, praise, delight,
  Here sojourn day and night.
    Sound bodies lin'd
    With a good minde,
  Do here pursue with might
  Grace, honour, praise, delight.

HERE enter you, and welcom from our hearts,
All noble sparks, endow'd with gallant parts.
This is the glorious place, which bravely shall
Afford wherewith to entertain you all.
Were you a thousand, here you shall not want
For any thing; for what you'l ask, we'l grant.
Stay here you lively, jovial, handsom, brisk,
Gay, witty, frolick, chearful merry, frisk,
Spruce, jocund, courteous, furtherers of trades,
And in a word, all worthy gentile blades.

> Blades of heroick breasts
> Shall taste here of the feasts,
>   Both privily
>   And civilly
> Of the celestial guests,
> Blades of heroick breasts.

HERE enter you, pure, honest, faithful, true,
Expounders of the Scriptures old and new.
Whose glosses do not blind our reason, but
Make it to see the clearer, and who shut
Its passages from hatred, avarice,
Pride, factious cov'nants, and all sort of vice.
Come, settle here a charitable faith,
Which neighbourly affection nourisheth.
And whose light chaseth all corrupters hence,
Of the blist Word, from the aforesaid sense.

> The Holy Sacred Word
> May it alwayes afford
>   T' us all in common
>   Both man and woman
> A sp'ritual shield and sword,
> The holy sacred Word.

HERE enter you all Ladies of high birth,
Delicious, stately, charming, full of mirth,
Ingenious, lovely, miniard, proper, faire,
Magnetick, graceful, splendid, pleasant, rare,
Obliging, sprightly, vertuous, young, solacious,

Kinde, neat, quick, feat, bright, compt, ripe, choise, dear,
  precious.
Alluring, courtly, comely, fine, compleat,
Wise, personable, ravishing and sweet.
Come joyes enjoy, the Lord celestial
Hath giv'n enough, wherewith to please us all.

> Gold give us, God forgive us,
> And from all woes relieve us.
>   That we the treasure
>   May reap of pleasure.
> And shun what e'er is grievous.
> Gold give us, God forgive us.

CHAPTER LV

What manner of dwelling the Thelemites had.

In the middle of the lower Court there was a stately fountain of
faire Alabaster; upon the top thereof stood the three Graces,
with their *cornucopias*, or hornes of abundance, and did jert out
the water at their breasts, mouth, eares, eyes, and other open
passages of the body; the inside of the buildings in this lower
Court stood upon great pillars of *Cassydonie* stone, and *Porphyrie*
marble, made arch-wayes after a goodly antick fashion. Within
those were spacious galleries, long and large, adorned with curious pictures, the hornes of Bucks and Unicornes: with *Rhino-
ceroses*, water-horses called *Hippopotames*, the teeth and tusks of
Elephants, and other things well worth the beholding. The lodging of the Ladies (*for so we may call those gallant women*) took up
all from the tower *Arctick* unto the gate *Mesembrine*: the men possessed the rest. Before the said lodging of the Ladies, that they
might have their recreation, between the two first towers, on
the out-side, were placed the tilt-yard, the barriers or lists for
turnements, the *hippodrome* or riding Court, the *theater* or publike play-house, and *Natatorie* or place to swim in, with most
admirable bathes in three stages, situated above one another,
well furnished with all necessary accommodation, and store of
myrtle-water. By the river-side was the faire garden of pleasure:
and in the midst of that the glorious labyrinth. Between the two

other towers were the Courts for the tennis and the baloon. Towards the tower *Criere* stood the Orchard full of all fruit-trees, set and ranged in a *quincuncial* order. At the end of that was the great Park, abounding with all sort of Venison. Betwixt the third couple of towers were the buts and marks for shooting with a snap-work gun, an ordinary bowe for common archery, or with a Crosse-bowe. The office-houses were without the tower *Hesperie*, of one story high. The stables were beyond the offices, and before them stood the falconrie, managed by Ostridge-keepers and Falconers, very expert in the Art, and it was yearly supplied and furnished by the *Candians, Venetians, Sarmates* (now called *Moscoviters*) with all sorts of most excellent hawks, *eagles, gerfalcons, gosehawkes, sacres, lanners, falcons, sparhawks, Marlins*, and other kindes of them, so gentle and perfectly well manned, that flying of themselves sometimes from the Castle for their own disport, they would not faile to catch whatever they encountred. The Venerie where the Beagles and Hounds were kept, was a little farther off drawing towards the Park.

All the halls, chambers, and closets or cabinets, were richly hung with tapestrie, and hangings of divers sorts, according to the variety of the seasons of the year. All the pavements and floors were covered with green cloth: the beds were all embroidered: in every back-chamber or withdrawing room there was a looking-glasse of pure crystal set in a frame of fine gold, garnished all about with pearles, and was of such greatnesse, that it would represent to the full the whole lineaments and proportion of the person that stood before it. At the going out of the halls, which belong to the Ladies lodgings, were the perfumers and trimmers, through whose hands the gallants past when they were to visit the Ladies; those sweet Artificers did every morning furnish the Ladies chambers with the spirit of roses, orange-flower-water and *Angelica*; and to each of them gave a little precious casket vapouring forth the most odoriferous exhalations of the choicest aromatical sents.

CHAPTER LVI

*How the men and women of the religious order of Theleme
were apparelled.*

THE Ladies at the foundation of this order, were apparelled
after their own pleasure and liking: but since that of their own
accord and free will they have reformed themselves, their accoutrement is in manner as followeth. They wore stockins of
scarlet crimson, or ingrained purple die, which reached just three
inches above the knee, having a list beautified with exquisite
embroideries, and rare incisions of the Cutters Art. Their garters were of the colour of their bracelets, and circled the knee a
little, both over and under. Their shoes, pumps and slippers
were either of red, violet, or crimson-velvet, pinked and jagged
like Lobster wadles.

Next to their smock they put on the pretty kirtle or vasquin
of pure silk chamlet: above that went the taffatie or tabie vardingale, of white, red, tawnie, gray, or any other colour; Above
this taffatie petticoat they had another of cloth of tissue or bro-
cado, embroidered with fine gold, and interlaced with needle-
work, or as they thought good, and according to the temperature
and disposition of the weather, had their upper coats of sattin,
damask or velvet, and those either orange, tawnie, green, ash-
coloured, blew, yelow, bright red, crimson or white, and so
forth; or had them of cloth of gold, cloth of silver, or some other
choise stuffe, inriched with purle, or embroidered according to
the dignity of the festival dayes and times wherein they wore
them.

Their gownes being still correspondent to the season, were
either of cloth of gold frizled with a silver-raised work; of red
sattin, covered with gold purle: of tabie, or taffatie, white, blew,
black, tawnie, &c., of silk serge, silk chamlot, velvet, cloth of
silver, silver tissue, cloth of gold, gold wire, figured velvet,
or figured sattin tinselled and overcast with golden threads, in
divers variously purfled draughts.

In the summer some dayes in stead of gowns they wore light
handsome mantles, made either of the stuffe of the aforesaid

attire, or like *Moresco* rugs, of violet velvet frizled, with a raised work of gold upon silver purle: or with a knotted cord-work of gold embroiderie, every where garnished with little *Indian* pearles. They alwayes carried a faire *Pannache*, or plume of feathers, of the colour of their muffe, bravely adorned and tricked out with glistering spangles of gold. In the winter-time they had their taffatie gownes of all colours, as above-named: and those lined with the rich furrings of hinde-wolves, or speckled linxes, black-spotted weesils, martlet-skins of *Calabria*, sables, and other costly furres of an inestimable value. Their beads, rings, brace-lets, collars, carcanets and neck-chaines were all of precious stones, such as carbuncles, rubies, baleus, diamonds, saphirs, emeralds, turkoises, garnets, agates, berilles, and excellent mar-garits. Their head-dressing also varied with the season of the yeare, according to which they decked themselves. In winter it was of the *French* fashion, in the spring of the *Spanish*: in sum-mer of the fashion of *Tuscanie*, except only upon the holy dayes and Sundayes, at which times they were accoutred in the *French* mode, because they accounted it more honourable, and better befitting the garb of a matronal pudicity.

The men were apparelled after their fashion: their stockins were of tamine or of cloth-serge, of white, black, scarlet, or some other ingrained colour: their breeches were of velvet, of the same colour with their stockins, or very near, embroidered and cut according to their fancy; their doublet was of cloth of gold, of cloth of silver, of velvet, sattin, damask, taffaties, &c. of the same colours, cut, embroidered, and suitably trimmed up in perfection: the points were of silk of the same colours; the tags were of gold well enameled: their coats and jerkins were of cloth of gold, cloth of silver, gold, tissue or velvet embroidered; as they thought fit: their gownes were every whit as costly as those of the Ladies: their girdles were of silk, of the colour of their doublets; every one had a gallant sword by his side, the hilt and handle whereof were gilt, and the scabbard of velvet, of the col-our of his breeches, with a chape of gold, and pure Goldsmiths work: the dagger was of the same: their caps or bonnets were of black velvet, adorned with jewels and buttons of gold: upon that they wore a white plume, most prettily and minion-like parted by so many rowes of gold spangles, at the end whereof hung dangling in a more sparkling resplendencie faire rubies, emeralds, diamonds, &c. But there was such a sympathy betwixt the gallants & the Ladies, that every day they were apparelled in the same livery: and that they might not misse, there were certain Gentlemen appointed to tell the youths every morning what vestments the Ladies would on that day weare; for all was done according to the pleasure of the Ladies. In these so handsome clothes, and abiliaments so rich, think not that either one or other of either sex did waste any time at all; for the Masters of the wardrobes had all their raiment and apparel so ready for every morning, and the chamber-Ladies so well skilled, that in a trice they would be dressed, and compleatly in their clothes from head to foot. And to have those accoutrements with the more conveniency; there was about the wood of *Teleme* a row of houses of the extent of half a league, very neat and cleanly, wherein dwelt the Goldsmiths, Lapidaries, Jewellers, Embroiderers, Tailors, Gold-drawers, Velvet-weavers, Tapestrie-makers and Upholsters, who wrought there every one in his own trade, and all for the aforesaid jollie Friars and Nuns of the new stamp; they were furnished with matter and stuffe from the hands of the Lord *Nausiclete*, who every year brought them seven ships from the *Perlas & Cannibal*-islands, laden with ingots of gold, with raw silk, with pearles and precious stones. And if any *margarites* (called *unions*) began to grow old, and lose somewhat of their natural whitenesse and lustre, those with their Art they did renew, by tendering them to eat to some pretty cocks, as they use to give casting unto hawkes.

CHAPTER LVII

*How the Thelemites were governed, and of their
manner of living.*

ALL their life was spent not in lawes, statutes or rules, but according to their own free will and pleasure. They rose out of their beds, when they thought good: they did eat, drink, labour, sleep, when they had a minde to it, and were disposed for it. None did awake them, none did offer to constrain them to eat, drink, nor to do any other thing; for so had *Gargantua* established it. In all their rule, and strictest tie of their order, there was but this one clause to be observed.

Do what thou wilt.

Because men that are free, well-borne, well-bred, and conversant in honest companies, have naturally an instinct and spurre that prompteth them unto vertuous actions, and withdraws them from vice, which is called *honour*. Those same men, when by base subjection and constraint they are brought under and kept down, turn aside from that noble disposition, by which they formerly were inclined to vertue, to shake off and break that bond of servitude, wherein they are so tyrannously inslaved; for it is agreeable with the nature of man to long after things forbidden, and to desire what is denied us.

By this liberty they entered into a very laudable emulation, to do all of them what they saw did please one; if any of the gallants or Ladies should say, *Let us drink*, they would all drink: if any one of them said, *Let us play*, they all played; if one said, *Let us go a walking into the fields*, they went all: if it were to go a hawking or a hunting, the Ladies mounted upon dainty well-paced nags, seated in a stately palfrey saddle, carried on their lovely fists, miniardly begloved every one of them, either a Sparhawk, or a Laneret, or a Marlin, and the young gallants carried the other kinds of Hawkes: so nobly were they taught, that there was neither he nor she amongst them, but could read, write, sing, play upon several musical instruments, speak five or sixe several languages, and compose in them all very quaintly, both in Verse and Prose: never were seene so valiant Knights, so noble and worthy, so dextrous and skilful both on foot and a horseback, more brisk and lively, more nimble and quick, or better handling all manner of weapons then were there. Never were seene Ladies so proper and handsome, so miniard and dainty, lesse froward, or more ready with their hand, and with their needle, in every honest and free action belonging to that sexe then were there; for this reason when the time came, that any man of the said Abbey, either at the request of his parents, or for some other cause, had a minde to go out of it, he carried along with him one of the Ladies, namely her whom he had before that chosen for his Mistris, and were married together:

and if they had formerly in *Theleme* lived in good devotion and amity, they did continue therein and increase it to a greater height in their state of matrimony: and did entertaine that mutual love till the very last day of their life, in no lesse vigour and fervency, then at the very day of their wedding: here must not I forget to set down unto you a riddle, which was found under the ground, as they were laying the foundation of the Abbey, ingraven in a copper plate; and it was thus as followeth.

CHAPTER LVIII

A Propheticall Riddle.

POOR mortals, who wait for a happy day,
Cheer up your hearts, and hear what I shall say:
If it be lawful firmly to beleeve,
That the celestial bodies can us give
Wisdom to judge of things that are not yet:
Or if from Heav'n such wisdom we may get,
As may with confidence make us discourse
Of years to come, their destinie and course;
I to my hearers give to understand,
That this next Winter, though it be at hand,
Yea and before, there shall appear a race
Of men, who loth to sit still in one place
Shall boldly go before all peoples eyes,
Suborning men of divers qualities,
To draw them into covenants and sides,
In such a manner, that whate're betides,
They 'l move you, if you give them eare (no doubt)
With both your friends and kinred to fall out.
They 'l make a vassal to gain-stand his Lord,
And children their own Parents, in a Word,
All reverence shall then be banished:
No true respect to other shall be had:
They 'l say that every man shall have his turn,
Both in his going forth, and his return;
And hereupon there shall arise such woes,
Such jarrings, and confused toos and froes,

That never were in history such coyles
Set down as yet, such tumults and garboyles.
Then shall you many gallant men see by
Valour stirr'd up, and youthful fervencie,
Who trusting too much in their hopeful time,
Live but a while, and perish in their prime.
Neither shall any who this course shall run,
Leave off the race which he hath once begun,
Till they the heavens with noise by their contention
Have fill'd, and with their steps the earths dimension.
Then those shall have no lesse authority,
That have no faith, then those that will not lie;
For all shall be governed by a rude,
Base, ignorant, and foolish multitude;
The veriest lowt of all shall be their Judge,
O horrible, and dangerous deluge!
Deluge I call it, and that for good reason,
For this shall be omitted in no season;
Nor shall the earth of this foule stirre be free,
Till suddenly you in great store shall see
The waters issue out, with whose streams the
Most moderate of all shall moist'ned be,
And justly too; because they did not spare
The flocks of beasts that innocentest are,
But did their sinews, and their bowels take,
Not to the gods a sacrifice to make,
But usually to serve themselves for sport;
And now consider, I do you exhort,
In such commotions so continual,
What rest can take the globe terrestrial?
Most happy then are they, that can it hold,
And use it carefully as precious gold,
By keeping it in Goale, whence it shall have
No help but him, who being to it gave.
And to increase his mournful accident,
The Sunne, before it set in th' occident
Shall cease to dart upon it any light,
More then in an eclipse, or in the night.
So that at once its favour shall be gone,

And liberty with it be left alone.
And yet, before it come to ruine thus,
Its quaking shall be as impetuous
As *Ætna*'s was, when *Titan*'s sons lay under,
And yeeld, when lost, a fearful sound like thunder.
Inarime did not more quickly move,
When *Typheûs* did the vast huge hills remove,
And for despite into the sea them threw.
   Thus shall it then be lost by wayes not few,
And changed suddenly, when those that have it
To other men that after come shall leave it.
Then shall it be high time to cease from this
So long, so great, so tedious exercise;
For the great waters told you now by me,
Will make each think where his retreat shall be;
And yet before that they be clean disperst,
You may behold in th' aire where nought was erst,
The burning heat of a great flame to rise,
Lick up the water, and the enterprise.
   It resteth after those things to declare,
That those shall sit content, who chosen are,
With all good things, and with celestial *man*,
And richly recompensed every man:
The others at the last all strip't shall be,
That after this great work all men may see
How each shall have his due, this is their lot;
O he is worthy-praise that shrinketh not.

No sooner was this ænigmatical monument read over, but *Gargantua* fetching a very deep sigh, said unto those that stood by, It is not now only (I perceive) that People called to the faith of the Gospel, and convinced with the certainty of Evangelical truths are persecuted; but happy is that man that shall not be scandalized, but shall alwayes continue to the end, in aiming at that mark, which God by his dear Son hath set before us, without being distracted or diverted by his carnal affections and depraved nature.

The *Monk* then said, What do you think in your conscience is meant and signified by this riddle? What? (said *Gargantua*) the progresse and carrying on of the divine truth. By St. *Goderan* (said the *Monk*) that is not my exposition; it is the stile of the Prophet *Merlin*: make upon it as many grave allegories and glosses as you will, and dote upon it you and the rest of the world as long as you please: for my part, I can conceive no other meaning in it, but a description of a set at tennis in dark and obscure termes. The suborners of men are the Makers of matches, which are commonly friends. After the two chases are made, he that was in the upper end of the tennis-court goeth out, and the other cometh in. They beleeve the first, that saith the ball was over or under the line. The waters are the heats that the players take till they sweat again. The cords of the rackets are made of the guts of sheep or goats. The Globe terrestrial is the tennis-ball. After playing, when the game is done, they refresh themselves before a clear fire, and change their shirts: and very willingly they make all good cheer, but most merrily those that have gained; And so farewel.

FINIS

THE SECOND BOOK

PANTAGRUEL, KING OF THE DIPSODES
WITH HIS HEROIC ACTS AND PROWESSES,
COMPOSED BY M. ALCOFRIBAS

THE AUTHORS PROLOGUE

Most Illustrious and thrice valourous Champions, Gentlemen and others, who willingly apply your mindes to the entertainment of pretty conceits, and honest harmlesse knacks of wit: You have not long ago seen, read and understood the great and inestimable Chronicle of the huge and mighty Gyant *Gargantua*, and like upright Faithfullists, have firmly beleeved all to be true that is contained in them, and have very often passed your time with them amongst Honourable Ladies and Gentlewomen, telling them faire long stories, when you were out of all other talk, for which you are worthy of great praise and sempiternal memory: and I do heartily wish that every man would lay aside his own businesse, meddle no more with his Profession nor Trade, and throw all affaires concerning himself behinde his back, to attend this wholly, without distracting or troubling his minde with any thing else, until he have learned them without book; that if by chance the Art of printing should cease, or in case that in time to come all books should perish, every man might truly teach them unto his children, and deliver them over to his successors and survivors from hand to hand, as a religious *Cabal*: for there is in it more profit, then a rabble of great pockie Loggerheads are able to discern, who surely understand far lesse in these little merriments, then the foole *Raclet* did in the institutions of *Justinian*.

I have known great and mighty Lords, and of those not a few, who going a Deer-hunting, or a hawking after wilde Ducks, when the chase had not encountred with the blinks, that were cast in her way to retard her course, or that the Hawk did but *plaine* and smoothly fly without moving her wings, perceiving the prey by force of flight to have gained bounds of her, have been much chafed and vexed, as you understand well anough; but the comfort unto which they had refuge, and that they might not take cold, was to relate the inestimable deeds of the said *Gargantua*. There are others in the world, (These are no flimflam stories, nor tales of a tub) who being much troubled with the toothache, after they had spent their goods upon Physicians, without receiving at all any ease of their pain, have found no more ready remedy, then to put the said *Chronicles* betwixt two pieces of linnen cloth made somewhat hot, and so apply them to the place that smarteth, synapising them with a little powder of projection, otherwayes called *doribus*.

But what shall I say of those poor men, that are plagued with the Pox and the Gowt? O how often have we seen them, even immediately after they were anointed and throughly greased, till their faces did glister like the Key-hole of a powdering tub, their teeth dance like the jacks of a paire of little Organs or Virginals, when they are played upon, and that they foamed from their very throats like a boare, which the Mongrel Mastiffe-hounds have driven in, and overthrown among the foyles: what did they then? All their consolation was to have some page of the said jollie book read unto them: and we have seen those who have given themselves to a hundred punchions of old devils, in case that they did not feele a manifest ease and asswagement of paine, at the hearing of the said book read, even when they were kept in a purgatory of torment; no more nor lesse then women in travel use to finde their sorrow abated, when the life of St. *Margarite* is read unto them: is this nothing? finde me a book in any language, in any faculty or science what-soever, that hath such vertues, properties and prerogatives, and I will be content to pay you a quart of tripes. No, my Masters, no, it is peerlesse, incomparable, and not to be matched; and this am I resolved for ever to maintaine even unto the fire *exclu-sivè*. And those that will pertinaciously hold the contrary opi-nion, let them be accounted Abusers, Predestinators, Impostors and Seducers of the People. It is very true, that there are found in some gallant and stately books, worthy of high estimation, certain occult and hid properties; in the number of which are reckoned *Whippot, Orlando furioso, Robert the devil, Fierabras, William without feare, Huon* of *Bourdeaux, Monteville*, and *Mata-brune*: but they are not comparable to that which we speak of; and the world hath well known by infallible experience, the great emolument and utility, which it hath received by this

Gargantuine Chronicle; for the Printers have sold more of them in two moneths time, then there will be bought of Bibles in nine years.

I therefore (your humble slave) being very willing to increase your solace and recreation yet a little more, do offer you for a Present another book of the same stamp, only that it is a little more reasonable and worthy of credit then the other was; for think not, (unlesse you wilfully will erre against your knowledge) that I speak of it as the *Jewes* do of the Law; I was not born under such a Planet, neither did it ever befall me to lie, or affirme a thing for true that was not: I speak of it like a lustie frolick *Onocrotarie,** I should say *Crotenotarie*** of the martyrised lovers and *Croquenotarie* of love: *Quod vidimus, testamur*. It is of the horrible and dreadful feats and prowesses of *Pantagruel*, whose menial servant I have been ever since I was a page till this houre, that by his leave I am permitted to visit my Cow-countrey, and to know if any of my Kindred there be alive.

And therefore to make an end of this Prologue, even as I give my selfe to an hundred Pannier-fulls of faire devils, body and soule, tripes and guts, in case that I lie so much as one single word in this whole History: After the like manner, St. *Anthonies* fire burne you; *Mahooms* disease whirle you; the squinance with a stitch in your side, and the *Wolfe* in your stomack trusse you, the bloody flux seize you, the curst sharp inflammations of wilde fire, as slender and thin as Cowes haire, strengthened with quick silver, enter into your fundament, and like those of *Sodom* and *Gomorrha*, may you fall into sulphur, fire and bottomlesse pits, in case you do not firmly beleeve all that I shall relate unto you in this present *Chronicle*.

---

* *Onocratal* is a bird not much unlike a Swan, which sings like an Asses braying.

** *Crotenotaire* or *notaire crotté*, *croquenotaire* or *notaire croqué* are but allusions in derision of *Protonotaire*, which signifieth a *Pregnotarie*.

THE SECOND BOOK

CHAPTER I

Of the Original and Antiquity of the great Pantagruel.

IT will not be an idle nor unprofitable thing, seeing we are at
leasure, to put you in minde of the Fountain and Original
Source, whence is derived unto us the good *Pantagruel*; for I see
that all good Historiographers have thus handled their *Chronicle*;
not only the *Arabians*, *Barbarians* and *Latines*, but also the gentle
Greeks, who were eternal drinkers. You must therefore remark,
that at the beginning of the world, (I speak of a long time, it is
above fourty *quarantaines*, or fourty times fourty nights, according to the supputation of the ancient *Druids*) a little after that
Abel was killed by his brother *Cain*, the earth, imbrued with the
blood of the just, was one year so exceeding fertil in all those
fruits which it usually produceth to us, and especially in *Med-*
lars, that ever since, throughout all ages it hath been called the
yeare of the great *medlars*, for three of them did fill a bushel: in
it the *Calends* were found by the *Grecian* Almanacks, there was
that yeare nothing of the moneth of *March* in the time of *Lent*,
and the middle of *August* was in *May*: in the moneth of *October*,
as I take it, or at least *September*, (that I may not erre; for I will
carefully take heed of that) was the week so famous in the
Annals, which they call the week of the three *Thursdayes*; for it
had three of them by meanes of the irregular Leap-yeares,
(called *Bissextils*) occasioned by the Sunnes having tripped and
stumbled a little towards the left hand, like a debtor afraid of
Serjeants coming right upon him to arrest him: and the Moon
varied from her course about five fathom, and there was manifestly seen the motion of trepidation in the firmament of the
fixed starres, called *Aplanes*, so that the middle *Pleiade* leaving
her fellowes, declined towards the *Equinoctial*, and the starre
named *Spica*, left the constellation of the *Virgin* to withdraw her

self towards the balance known by the name of *Libra*, which are cases very terrible, and matters so hard and difficult, that *Astrologians* cannot set their teeth in them; and indeed their teeth had been pretty long if they could have reached thither.

However account you it for a truth, that every body then did most heartily eat of those medlars, for they were faire to the eye, and in taste delicious: but even as *Noah* that holy man, (to whom we are so much beholding, bound and obliged, for that he planted to us the Vine, from whence we have that nectarian, delicious, precious, heavenly, joyful and deifick liquour, which they call the *piot* or *tiplage*) was deceived in the drinking of it, for he was ignorant of the great vertue and power thereof: so likewise the men and women of that time did delight much in the eating of that faire great fruit, but divers and very different accidents did ensue thereupon; for there fell upon them all in their bodies a most terrible swelling, but not upon all in the same place, for some were swollen in the belly, and their belly strouted out big like a great tun, of whom it is written *ventrem omnipotentem*, who were all very honest men, and merry blades: and of this race came St. *Fatgulch** and *Shrove-tuesday;*** Others did swell at the shoulders, who in that place were so crump and knobbie, that they were therefore called *Montifers*, (which is as much to say as *Hill-carriers*,) of whom you see some yet in the world of divers sexes and degrees: of this race came *Æsop*, some of whose excellent words and deeds you have in writing: some other *puffes* did swell in length by the member, which they call the Labourer of nature, in such sort that it grew marvellous long, fat, great, lustie, stirring and Crest-risen, in the Antick fashion, so that they made use of it as of a girdle, winding it five or six times about their waste: but if it happened the foresaid member to be in good case, spooming with a full saile, bunt faire before the winde, then to have seen those strouting Champions, you would have taken them for men that had their lances setled on their Rest, to run at the ring or tilting *whintam*: of these beleeve me the race is utterly lost and quite extinct, as the women say; for they do lament continually, that there are none extant now of those great, &c. you know the rest of the song. Others did

* Pansart.   ** Mardigras.

grow in matter of ballocks so enormously, that three of them would well fill a sack, able to contain five quarters of wheat, from them are descended the ballocks of *Lorraine*, which never dwell in Codpieces, but fall down to the bottome of the breeches. Others grew in the legs, and to see them, you would have said they had been Cranes, or the reddish-long-bill'd-stork-lik't-scrank-legged sea-fowles, called *Flamans*, or else men walking upon stilts or scatches: the little Grammar school-boyes (known by the name of *Grimos*,) called those leg-grown slan-gams *Jambus*, in allusion to the *French* word *Jambe*, which signi-fieth a leg. In others, their nose did grow so, that it seemed to be the beak of a *Limbeck*, in every part thereof most variously diapred with the twinkling sparkles of Crimson-blisters bud-ding forth, and purpled with pimples all enameled with thick-set wheales of a sanguine colour, bordered with *Queules*, and such have you seen the *Chanon* or Prebend *Panzoul*, and *Woodenfoot* the Physician of *Angiers*: of which race there were few that liked the *Ptisane*, but all of them were perfect lovers of the pure sep-tembral juice; *Naso* and *Ovid* had their extraction from thence, and all those of whom it is written, *Ne reminiscaris*. Others grew in eares, which they had so big, that out of one would have been stuffe enough got, to make a doublet, a paire of breeches and a jacket, whilest with the other they might have covered them-selves as with a *Spanish* Cloak: and they say, that in Bourbonois this race remaineth yet. Others grew in length of body, and of those came the *Giants*, and of them *Pantagruel*.

And the first was *Chalbroth*

who begat *Sarabroth*

who begat *Faribroth*

who begat *Hurtali*, that was a brave eater of pottage, and reigned in the time of the flood.

who begat *Nembroth*

who begat *Atlas*, that with his shoulders kept the sky from fall-ing.

who begat *Goliah*

who begat *Erix*, that invented the *Hocus pocus* playes of *Leger-demain*.

who begat *Titius*

who begat *Eryon*

who begat *Polyphemus*

who begat *Cacos*

who begat *Etion*, the first man that ever had the pox, for not drinking fresh in Summer, as *Bartachin* witnesseth.

who begat *Enceladus*

who begat *Ceus*

who begat *Tiphœus*

who begat *Alœus*

who begat *Othus*

who begat *Ægeon*

who begat *Briareus* that had a hundred hands.

who begat *Porphyrio*

who begat *Adamastor*

who begat *Anteus*

who begat *Agatho*

who begat *Porus*, against whom fought *Alexander* the great.

who begat *Aranthas*

who begat *Gabbara*, that was the first inventor of the drinking of healths.

who begat *Goliah* of *Secondille*

who begat *Offot*, that was terribly well nosed for drinking at the barrel-head.

who begat *Artachæus*

who begat *Oromedon*

who begat *Gemmagog*, the first inventor of *Poulan* shoes, which are open on the foot, and tied over the instep with a latchet.

who begat *Sisyphus*

who begat the *Titans*, of whom *Hercules* was born.

who begat *Enay*, the most skilful man that ever was, in matter of taking the little wormes (called *Cirons*) out of the hands.

who begat *Fierabras*, that was vanquished by *Oliver* Peer of *France*, and *Rowlands* Camrade.

who begat *Morgan*, the first in the world that played at dice with spectacles.

who begat *Fracassus*, of whom *Merlin Coccaius* hath written, and of him was borne *Ferragus*.

who begat *Hapmouche*, the first that ever invented the drying of neats tongues in the Chimney; for before that, people salted them, as they do now gammons of bacon.

who begat *Bolivorax*

who begat *Longis*

who begat *Gayoffo*, whose ballocks were of *poplar*, and his pr. . . of
the *servise* or *sorb-apple*-tree.

who begat *Maschefain*

who begat *Bruslefer*

who begat *Angoulevent*

who begat *Galehaut* the inventor of flaggons.

who begat *Mirelangaut*

who begat *Gallaffre*

who begat *Salourdin*

who begat *Roboast*

who begat *Sortibrant* of *Conimbres*.

who begat *Brusbant* of *Mommiere*

who begat *Bruyer* that was overcome by *Ogier* the *Dane* Peer of
France.

who begat *Mabrun*

who begat *Foutasnon*

who begat *Haquelebas*

who begat *Vitdegrain*

who begat *Grangousier*

who begat *Gargantua*

who begat the noble *Pantagruel* my Master.

I know that reading this passage, you will make a doubt within your selves, and that grounded upon very good reason: which
is this, how it is possible that this relation can be true, seeing at
the time of the flood all the world was destroyed, except *Noah*,
and seven persons more with him in the Ark, into whose number
Hurtali is not admitted; doubtlesse the demand is well made,
and very apparent, but the answer shall satisfie you, or my wit
is not rightly caulked: and because I was not at that time to tell
you any thing of my own fancie, I will bring unto you the authority of the *Massorets*, good honest fellows, true *ballokeering*
blades, and exact *Hebraical* bag-pipers, who affirm that verily
the said *Hurtali* was not within the Ark of *Noah*, (neither could
he get in, for he was too big) but he sate astride upon it, with
one leg on the one side, and another on the other, as little children use to do upon their wooden horses: or as the great Bull of

Berne, which was killed at *Marinian*, did ride for his Hackney the great murthering piece called the *Canon-pevier*, a pretty beast of a faire and pleasant amble without all question.

In that posture, he after God, saved the said Ark from danger, for with his legs he gave it the brangle that was needful, and with his foot turned it whither he pleased, as a ship answereth her rudder. Those that were within sent him up victuals in abundance by a Chimney, as people very thankfully acknowledging the good that he did them; And sometimes they did talk together as *Icaromenippus* did to *Jupiter*, according to the report of *Lucian*. Have you understood all this well? drink then one good draught without water; for if you beleeve it not: no truly do I not, quoth she.

CHAPTER II

Of the Nativity of the most dread and redoubted Pantagruel.

GARGANTUA at the age of foure hundred, fourescore fourty, and foure yeares begat his sonne *Pantagruel*, upon his wife named *Badebec*, daughter to the King of the *Amaurots* in *Utopia*, who died in childe-birth, for he was so wonderfully great and lumpish, that he could not possibly come forth into the light of the world, without thus suffocating his mother. But that we may fully understand the cause and reason of the name of *Pantagruel*, which at his Baptism was given him, you are to remark, that in that yeare there was so great drought over all the countrey of *Affrick*, that there past thirty and six moneths, three weeks, foure dayes, thirteen houres, and a little more without raine, but with a heat so vehement, that the whole earth was parched and withered by it: neither was it more scorched and dried up with heat in the dayes of *Eliah*, then it was at that time; for there was not a tree to be seen, that had either leafe or bloom upon it: the grasse was without verdure or greennesse, the rivers were drained, the fountaines dried up, the poore fishes abandoned and forsaken by their proper element, wandring and crying upon the ground most horribly: the birds did fall down from the aire for want of moisture and dew, wherewith to refresh them: the wolves, foxes, harts, wild-boares, fallow-deer, hares, coneys, weesils, brocks, badgers, and other such beasts were found dead in the fields with their mouthes open; in respect of men, there was the pity, you should have seen them lay out their tongues like hares that have been run six houres: many did throw themselves into the wells: others entred within a Cowes belly to be in the shade; those *Homer* calls *Alibants*: all the Countrey was idle, and could do no vertue: it was a most lamentable case to have seen the labour of mortals in defending themselves from the vehemencie of this horrifick drought; for they had work enough to do to save the holy water in the Churches from being wasted; but there was such order taken by the counsel of my Lords the Cardinals, and of our holy Father, that none did dare to take above one lick: yet when any one came into the Church, you should have seen above twenty poor thirsty fellows hang upon him that was the distributer of the water, and that with a wide open throat, gaping for some little drop, (like the rich glutton in *Luke*,) that might fall by, lest any thing should be lost. O how happy was he in that yeare, who had a coole Cellar under ground, well plenished with fresh wine!

The Philosopher reports in moving the question, wherefore it is that the sea-water is salt? that at the time when *Phœbus* gave the government of his resplendent chariot to his sonne *Phaeton*, the said *Phaeton*, unskilful in the Art, and not knowing how to keep the ecliptick line betwixt the two tropicks of the latitude of the Sunnes course, strayed out of his way, and came so near the earth, that he dried up all the Countreys that were under it, burning a great part of the Heavens, which the *Philosophers* call *via lactea*, and the *Huffsnuffs*, St. *James* his way, although the most coped, lofty, and high-crested Poets affirme that to be the place where *Juno's* milk fell, when she gave suck to *Hercules*.

The earth at that time was so excessively heated, that it fell into an enormous sweat, yea such a one as made it sweat out the sea, which is therefore salt, because all sweat is salt; and this you cannot but confesse to be true, if you will taste of your own, or of those that have the pox, when they are put into a sweating, it is all one to me. Just such another case fell out this same yeare: for on a certain *Friday*, when the whole people were bent upon their devotions, and had made goodly Processions, with store of Letanies, and faire preachings, and beseechings of God

Almighty, to look down with his eye of mercy upon their miserable and disconsolate condition, there was even then visibly
seen issue out of the ground great drops of water, such as fall
from a puff-bagg'd man in a top sweat; and the poore Hoydons
began to rejoyce, as if it had been a thing very profitable unto
them; for some said that there was not one drop of moisture in
the aire, whence they might have any rain, and that the earth
did supply the default of that. Other learned men said, that it
was a showre of the *Antipodes*, as *Seneca* saith in his fourth book
Quæstionum naturalium, speaking of the source and spring of
Nilus: but they were deceived, for the Procession being ended,
when every one went about to gather of this dew, and to drink
of it with full bowles, they found that it was nothing but pickle,
and the very brine of salt, more brackish in taste then the saltest
water of the sea: and because in that very day *Pantagruel* was
borne, his father gave him that name; for *panta* in *Greek* is as
much to say as *all*, and *Gruel* in the *Hagarene* language doth signifie *thirsty*; inferring hereby, that at his birth the whole world
was a dry and thirstie, as likewise foreseeing that he would be
some day Suprem Lord, & Sovereign of the *thirstie Ethrappels*,
which was shewn to him at that very same hour by a more evident signe; for when his mother *Badebec* was in the bringing of
him forth, and that the Midwives did wait to receive him: there
came first out of her belly three-score and eight *Tregeneers* (that
is, Salt-sellers,) every one of them leading in a Halter a Mule
heavy loaden with salt: after whom issued forth nine Dromedaries, with great loads of gammons of bacon, and dried neats
tongues on their backs: then followed seven Camels loaded with
links and chitterlins, hogs puddings and salciges: after them
came out five great waines, full of leeks, garlick, onions and
chibols, drawn with five and thirty strong Cart-horses, which
was six for every one, besides the *Thiller*. At the sight hereof the
said Midwives were much amazed; yet some of them said, Lo,
here is good provision, and indeed we need it; for we drink but
lazily, as if our tongues walked on crutches, and not lustily like
Lansman dutches: truly this is a good signe, there is nothing here
but what is fit for us, these are the spurres of wine that set it a
going. As they were tatling thus together after their own manner
of chat, behold, out comes *Pantagruel* all hairie like a Beare,

whereupon one of them inspired with a prophetical Spirit, said, This will be a terrible fellow, he is borne with all his haire, he is undoubtedly to do wonderful things, and, if he live, he shall have age.

CHAPTER III

Of the grief wherewith Gargantua was moved at the decease of his wife Badebec.

WHEN *Pantagruel* was borne, there was none more astonished and perplexed then was his father *Gargantua*; for of the one side, seeing his wife *Badebec* dead, and on the other side his sonne *Pantagruel* born, so faire and so great, he knew not what to say nor what to do: and the doubt that troubled his braine, was to know whether he should cry for the death of his wife, or laugh for the joy of his sonne: he was *hinc indè* choked with sophistical arguments, for he framed them very well *in modo & figura*, but he could not resolve them, remaining pestered and entangled by this means, like a mouse catch't in a trap, or kite snared in a ginne: Shall I weep (said he?) Yes, for why? my so good wife is dead, who was the most *this*, the most *that*, that ever was in the world: never shall I see her, never shall I recover such another, it is unto me an inestimable losse! O my good God, what had I done that thou shouldest thus punish me? why didst thou not take me away before her? seeing for me to live without her is but to languish. Ah *Badebec, Badebec*, my minion, my dear heart, my sugar, my sweeting, my honey, my little C . . . (yet it had in circumference full six acres, three rods, five poles, foure yards, two foot, one inche and a half of good woodland measure) my tender peggie, my Codpiece darling, my bob and hit, my slip-shoelovie, never shall I see thee! Ah, poor *Pantagruel*, thou has lost thy good mother, thy sweet nurse, thy well-beloved Lady! O false death, how injurious and despightful hast thou been to me? how malicious and outragious have I found thee? in taking her from me, my well-beloved wife, to whom immortality did of right belong. With these words he did cry like a Cow, but on a sudden fell a laughing like a Calfe, when *Pantagruel* came into his minde: Ha, my little sonne, (said he) my childilollie, fedlifondie, dandlichuckie, my ballockie, my pretty rogue; O how jollie thou art, and how much am I bound to my gracious God, that hath been pleased to bestow on me a sonne, so faire, so spriteful, so lively, so smiling, so pleasant, and so gentle. *Ho, ho, ho, ho*, how glad I am? Let us drink, *ho*, and put away melancholy: bring of the best; rense the glasses, lay the cloth, drive out these dogs, blow this fire, light candles, shut that door there, cut this bread in sippets for brewis, send away these poore folks in giving them what they ask, hold my gown, I will strip my self into my doublet, (*én cuerpo*) to make the Gossips merry, and keep them company.

As he spake this, he heard the Letanies and the *memento's* of the Priests that carried his wife to be buried, upon which he left the good purpose he was in, and was suddenly ravished another way, saying, Lord God, must I again contrist my self? this grieves me; I am no longer young, I grow old, the weather is dangerous; I may perhaps take an ague, then shall I be foiled, if not quite undone; by the faith of a Gentleman, it were better to cry lesse, and drink more.

My wife is dead, well, by G—, (*da jurandi*) I shall not raise her again by my crying: she is well, she is in Paradise at least, if she be no higher: she prayeth to God for us, she is happy, she is above the sense of our miseries, nor can our calamities reach her: what though she be dead, must not we also die? The same debt which she hath paid, hangs over our heads; nature will require it of us, and we must all of us some day taste of the same sauce: let her passe then, and the Lord preserve the Survivors; for I must now cast about how to get another wife. But I will tell you what you shall do, (said he) to the Midwives in *France* called *wise women* (Where be they, good folks? I cannot see them,) go you to my wife's interrement, and I will the while rock my sonne: for I finde my self somewhat altered and distempered, and should otherwayes be in danger of falling sick: but drink one good draught first, you will be the better for it; and beleeve me upon mine honour. They at his request went to her burial and funeral obsequies: in the mean while, poor *Gargantua* staying at home, and willing to have somewhat in remembrance of her to be engraven upon her tomb, made this *Epitaph* in the manner as followeth.

Dead is the noble Badebec,
Who had a face like a Rebeck;
A Spanish body, and a belly
Of Swisserland, *she dy'd, I tell ye,*
In childe-birth: pray to God, that her
He pardon wherein she did erre.
Here lies her body, which did live
Free from all vice, as I beleeve:
And did decease at my bed-side,
The yeare and day in which she dy'd.

CHAPTER IV

Of the Infancie of Pantagruel.

I FINDE by the ancient Historiographers and Poets, that divers have been borne in this world, after very strange manners, which would be too long to repeat; reade therefore the seventh chapter of *Pliny*, if you have so much leisure: yet have you never heard of any so wonderful as that of *Pantagruel*; for it is a very difficult matter to beleeve, how in the little time he was in his mothers belly, he grew both in body and strength. That which *Hercules* did was nothing, when in his Cradle he slew two serpents; for those serpents were but little and weak: but *Pantagruel*, being yet in the Cradle, did farre more admirable things, and more to be amazed at. I passe by here the relation of how at every one of his meales he supped up the milk of foure thousand and six hundred Cowes: and how to make him a skellet to boil his milk in, there were set a work all the Brasiers of *Somure* in *Anjou*, of *Villedieu* in *Normandy*, and of *Bramont* in *Lorraine*: and they served in this whitepot-meat to him in a huge great Bell, which is yet to be seen in the city of *Bourge* in *Berrie*, near the Palace; but his teeth were already so well grown, and so strengthened in vigour, that of the said Bell he bit off a great morsel, as very plainly doth appeare till this houre.

One day in the morning, when they would have made him suck one of his Cows, (for he never had any other Nurse, as the History tell us) he got one of his armes loose from the swadling bands, wherewith he was kept fast in the Cradle, laid hold on the said Cow under the left fore hamme, and grasping her to him, ate up her udder and half of her paunch, with the liver and the kidneys, and had devoured all up, if she had not cried out most horribly, as if the wolves had held her by the legs, at which noise company came in, and took away the said cow from *Pantagruel*; yet could they not so well do it, but that the quarter whereby he caught her was left in his hand, of which quarter he gulp't up the flesh in a trice, even with as much ease as you would eate a salcige; and that so greedily with desire of more, that when they would have taken away the bone from him, he swallowed it down whole, as a Cormorant would do a little fish; and afterwards began fumblingly to say, *Good, good, good*, for he could not yet speak plaine; giving them to understand thereby, that he had found it very good, and that he did lack but so much more; which when they saw that attended him, they bound him with great cable-ropes, like those that are made at *Tain*, for the carriage of salt to *Lyons*; or such as those are, whereby the great *French* ship rides at Anchor, in the Road of *Newhaven* in *Normandie*. But on a certain time, a great Beare which his father had bred, got loose, came towards him, began to lick his face, for his Nurses had not throughly wiped his chaps, at which unexpected approach being on a sudden offended, he as lightly rid himself of those great cables, as *Samson* did of the haulser ropes wherewith the *Philistines* had tied him, and by your leave, takes me up my Lord the Beare, and teares him to you in pieces like a pullet, which served him for a gorge-ful or good warme bit for that meale.

Whereupon *Gargantua* fearing lest the childe should hurt himself, caused foure great chaines of iron to be made to binde him, and so many strong wooden arches unto his Cradle, most firmely stocked and mortaised in huge frames: of those chaines you have one at *Rochel*, which they draw up at night betwixt the two great towers of the Haven: Another is at *Lyons*: A third at *Angiers*: And the fourth was carried away by the devils to binde *Lucifer*, who broke his chaines in those dayes, by reason of a cholick that did extraordinarily torment him, taken with eating a Serjeants soule fried for his breakfast, and therefore you may beleeve that which *Nicholas de Lyra* saith upon that place of the *Psalter*, where it is written, *Et Og regem Basan*, that the said *Og*, being yet little, was so strong and robustious, that they were

faine to binde him with chaines of iron in his Cradle; thus continued *Pantagruel* for a while very calme and quiet, for he was
not able so easily to break those chaines, especially having no
room in the Cradle to give a swing with his armes. But see what
happened, once upon a great Holiday, that his father *Gargantua*
made a sumptuous banquet to all the Princes of his Court: I am
apt to beleeve, that the menial officers of the house were so
imbusied in waiting each on his proper service at the feast, that
nobody took care of poor *Pantagruel*, who was left *a reculorum*,
behinde-hand all alone, and as forsaken. What did he? Heark
what he did, good people: he strove and essayed to break the
chaines of the Cradle with his armes, but coold not, for they
were too strong for him: then did he keep with his feet such a
stamping stirre, and so long, that at last he beat out the lower
end of his Cradle, which notwithstanding was made of a great
post five foot in square: and, as soon as he had gotten out his
feet, he slid down as well as he could, till he had got his soales
to the ground; and then with a mighty force he rose up, carrying
his Cradle upon his back, bound to him like a Tortoise that
crawles up against a wall; and to have seen him, you would have
thought it had been a great *Carrick* of five hundred tunne upon
one end. In this manner he entred into the great Hall were they
were banquetting, and that very boldly, which did much affright
the companie; yet because his armes were tied in, he could not
reach any thing to eate, but with great pain stooped now and
then a little, to take with the whole flat of his tongue some lick,
good bit, or morsel.

Which when his father saw, he knew well enough that they
had left him without giving him any thing to eate, and therefore
commanded that he should be loosed from the said chaines, by
the counsel of the Princes and Lords there present: besides
that, also the Physicians of *Gargantua* said, that if they did thus
keep him in the Cradle, he would be all his life-time subject to
the stone. When he was unchained they made him to sit down,
where after he had fed very well, he took his Cradle, and broke
it into more then five hundred thousand pieces with one blow
of his fist, that he struck in the midst of it, swearing that he
would never come into it again.

CHAPTER V

Of the Acts of the noble Pantagruel in his youthful age.

THUS grew *Pantagruel* from day to day, and to every ones eye waxed more and more in all his dimensions, which made his father to rejoyce by a natural affection: therefore caused he to be made for him, whilest he was yet little, a pretty Crossebowe, wherewith to shoot at small birds, which now they call the great Crossebowe at *Chantelle*. Then he sent him to the school to learn, and to spend his youth in vertue: in the prosecution of which designe he came first to *Poictiers*, where, as he studied and profited very much, he saw that the Scholars were often-times at leisure, and knew not how to bestow their time, which moved him to take such compassion on them, that one day he took from a long ledge of rocks (called there *Passelourdin*), a huge great stone, of about twelve fathom square, and fourteen handfuls thick, and with great ease set it upon foure pillars in the midst of a field, to no other end, but that the said Scholars, when they had nothing else to do, might passe their time in getting up on that stone, and feast it with store of gammons, pasties and flaggons, and carve their names upon it with a knife, in token of which deed till this houre the stone is called the lifted stone: and in remembrance hereof there is none entered into the Register and matricular Book of the said University, or accounted capable of taking any degree therein, till he have first drunk in the *Caballine* fountain of *Croustelles*, passed at *Passelourdin* and got up upon the *lifted stone*.

Afterwards, reading the delectable Chronicles of his Ancestors, he found that *Jafrey* of *Lusinian*, called *Jafrey* with the great tooth, Grandfather to the Cousin in law of the eldest Sister of the Aunt of the Son in law of the Uncle of the good daughter of his Stepmother, was interred at *Maillezais*; therefore one day he took *campos*, (which is a little vacation from study to play a while,) that he might give him a visit as unto an honest man: and going from *Poictiers* with some of his companions, they passed by the *Guge*, visiting the noble Abbot *Ardillon*: then by *Lusinian*, by *Sansay*, by *Celles*, by *Coalonges*, by *Fontenay* the *Conte*, saluting the learned *Tiraqueau*, and from thence arrived at *Maillezais*, where he went to see the Sepulchre of the said *Jafrey* with the great tooth; which made him somewhat afraid, looking upon the picture, whose lively draughts did set him forth in the representation of a man in an extreme fury, drawing his great *Malchus* faulchion half way out of his scabbard: when the reason hereof was demanded, the Chanons of the said place told him, that there was no other cause of it, but that *Pictoribus atque Poetis, &c.* that is to say, that Painters and Poets have liberty to paint and devise what they list after their own fancie: but he was not satisfied with their answer, and said, He is not thus painted without a cause; and I suspect that at his death there was some wrong done him, whereof he requireth his Kinred to take revenge: I will enquire further into it, and then do what shall be reasonable; then he returned not to *Poictiers*, but would take a view of the other Universities of *France:* therefore going to *Rochel*, he took shipping and arrived at *Bourdeaux*, where he found no great exercise, only now and then he would see some Marriners and Lightermen a wrestling on the key or strand by the riverside: From thence he came to *Tholouse*, where he learned to dance very well, and to play with the *two-handed sword*, as the fashion of the Scholars of the said University is to bestir themselves in *games*, whereof they may have their *hands full*: but he stayed not long there, when he saw that they did cause burne their *Regents* alive like red herring, saying, Now God forbid that I should die this death; for I am by nature sufficiently dry already, without heating my self any further.

He went then to *Montpellier*, where he met with the good wines of *Mirevaux*, and good jovial company withal, and thought to have set himself to the study of Physick; but he considered that that calling was too troublesome and melancholick; and that Physicians did smell of glisters like old devils. Therefore he resolved he would studie the lawes; but seeing that there were but three scauld, and one bald-pated Legist in that place, he departed from thence, and in his way made the bridge of *Gard*, and the *Amphitheater* of *Neems* in lesse then three houres, which neverthelesse seems to be a more divine then humane work. After that he came to *Avignon*, where he was not above three dayes before he fell in love; for the women there take great delight in playing at the close buttock-game, because it is Papal ground; which his Tutor and Pedagogue *Epistemon* perceiving, he drew him out of that place, and brought him to *Valence* in the *Dauphinee*, where he saw no great matter of recreation, only that the Lubbards of the Town did beat the Scholars, which so incensed him with anger, that when upon a certain very faire Sunday, the people being at their publick dancing in the streets, and one of the Scholars offering to put himself into the ring to partake of that sport, the foresaid lubbardy fellowes would not permit him the admittance into their society; He taking the Scholars part, so belaboured them with blowes, and laid such load upon them, that he drove them all before him, even to the brink of the river *Rhosne*, and would have there drowned them, but that they did squat to the ground, and they lay a close full halfe league under the river. The hole is to be seen there yet.

After that he departed from thence, and in three strides and one leap came to *Angiers*, where he found himself very well, and would have continued there some space, but that the plague drove them away. So from thence he came to *Bourges*, where he studied a good long time, and profited very much in the faculty of the Lawes, and would sometimes say, that the books of the Civil Law, were like unto a wonderfully precious, royal and triumphant robe of cloth of gold, edged with dirt; for in the world are no goodlier books to be seen, more ornate, nor more eloquent then the texts of the Pandects; but the bordering of them, that is to say, the glosse of *Accursius*, is so scurvie, vile, base, and unsavourie, that it is nothing but filthinesse and villany.

Going from *Bourges*, he came to *Orleans*, where he found store of swaggering Scholars that made him great entertainment at his coming, and with whom he learned to play at tennis so well, that he was a Master at that game; for the Students of the said place make a prime exercise of it; and sometimes they carried him unto *Cupids* houses of commerce (in that City termed *Islands*, because of their being most ordinarily environed with other houses, and not contiguous to any,) there to recreate his person at the sport of *Poussavant*, which the wenches of *London* call the *Ferkers in and in*. As for breaking his head with overmuch study he had an especial care not to do it in any case, for feare of spoiling his eyes; while he the rather observed, for that it was told him by one of his Teachers, (there called Regents,) that the paine of the eyes was the most hurtful thing of any to the sight: for this cause when he one day was made a *Licentiate*, or Graduate in law, one of the Scholars of his acquaintance, who of learning had not much more then his burthen, though in stead of that he could dance very well, and play at tennis, made the blason and device of the *Licentiates* in the said University, saying,

> So you have in your hand a racket,
> A tennis-ball in your Cod-placket,
> A *Pandect* law in your Caps tippet,
> And that you have the skill to trip it
> In a low dance, you will b' allow'd
> The grant of the *Licentiates* hood.

CHAPTER VI

How Pantagruel met with a Limousin, who too affectedly did counterfeit the French language.

UPON a certain day, I know not when, *Pantagruel* walking after supper with some of his fellow-Students without that gate of the City, through which we enter on the rode to *Paris*, encountered with a young spruce-like Scholar that was coming upon the same very way; and after they had saluted one another, asked him thus; My friend, from whence comest thou now? the *Scholar* answered him: From the alme, inclyte and celebrate Academie, which is *vocitated Lutetia. What is the meaning of this* (said *Pantagruel*) *to one of his men*? It is (answered he) from *Paris*. Thou comest from *Paris* then (said *Pantagruel*,) and how do you spend your time there, you my Masters the Students of *Paris*? the *Scholar* answered, We transfretate the *Sequan* at the *dilucul* and *crepuscul*, we deambulate by the compites and quadrives by the Urb: we despumate the *Latial* verbocination: and like verisimilarie amorabons, we captat the benevolence of the omnijugal, omniform, and omnigenal fœminine sexe: upon certain diecules we invisat the Lupanares, and in a *venerian* extase inculcate our veretres into the penitissime recesses of the

pudends of these amicabilissim meretricules: then do we cau-
ponisate in the meritory taberns of the *pineapple*, the *castle*, the
magdalene, and the *mule*, goodly vervecine spatules perforami-
nated with petrocile; and if by fortune there be rarity, or penury
of pecune in our marsupies, and that they be exhausted of fer-
ruginean mettal, for the shot we dimit our codices, and
oppugnerat our vestiments, whilest we prestolate the coming of
the Tabellaries from the Penates and patriotick Lares: to which
Pantagruel answered, *What devillish language is this?* by the Lord,
I think thou are some kind of Heretick: My Lord, no, said the
Scholar, for libentissimally, assoon as it illucesceth any minutle
slice of the day, I demigrate into one of these so well architected
minsters, and there irrorating my self with faire lustral water,
I mumble off little parcels of some missick precation of our
sacrificuls: and submurmurating my horarie precules, I elevate
and absterge my anime from its noctural inquinations: I revere
the Olympicols: I latrially venere the supernal Astripotent: I dilige
and redame my proxims: I observe the decalogical precepts; and
according to the facultatule of my vires, I do not discede from
them one late unguicule; neverthelesse it is veriforme, that
because *Mammona* doth not supergurgitate any thing in my loculs,
that I am somewhat rare and lent to supererogate the elemo-
synes to those egents, that hostially queritate their stipe.

    Prut, tut, (said *Pantagruel*,) what doth this foole meane to say?
I think he is upon the forging of some diabolical tongue, and
that inchanter-like he would charme us; to whom one of his
men said, Without doubt (Sir) this fellow would counterfeit the
Language of the *Parisians*, but he doth only flay the *Latine*, im-
agining by so doing that he doth highly *Pindarize* it in most eloquent termes, and strongly conceiteth himself to be therefore a
great Oratour in the *French*, because he disdaineth the common
manner of speaking; to which *Pantagruel* said, *Is it true?* The
Scholar answered, My worshipful Lord, my *genie* is not apt nate
to that which this flagitious Nebulon saith, to excoriate the
cutule of our vernacular Gallick, but viceversally I gnave opere
and by veles and rames enite to locupletate it, with the Latini-
come redundance. By G— (*said Pantagruel*), I will teach you to
speak, but first come hither, and tell me whence thou art? To
this the Scholar answered: The primeval origin of my aves and

ataves was indigenarie of the *Lemovick* regions, where requies-
ceth the corpor of the hagiotat St. *Martial*. I understand thee
very well (said *Pantagruel*), when all comes to all, thou art a
Limousin, and thou wilt here by thy affected speech counterfeit
the *Parisiens*: well now, come hither, I must shew thee a new
trick, and handsomely give thee the *combfeat*: with this he took
him by the throat, saying to him, Thou flayest the Latine: by
St. *John*, I will make thee flay the foxe, for I will now flay thee
alive: Then began the poor *Limousin* to cry; Haw, *gwid* Maaster,
haw, Laord, *my halp and St*. Marshaw, haw, *I'm worried*: Haw, *my
thropple, the bean of my cragg is bruck*! Haw, *for* gauads *seck, lawt
my lean*, Mawster; *waw, waw, waw*. Now (said *Pantagruel*) thou
speakest naturally, and so let him go, for the poor *Limousin* had
totally berayed, and throughly conshit his breeches, which were
not deep and large enough, but round streat caniond gregs, having in the seat a piece like a keelings taile; and therefore in
French called *de chausses à queüe de merlus*. Then (said *Pantagruel*)
St. *Alipantin*, what civette! *fi* to the devil with this Turnepeater,
as he stinks, and so let him go: but this hug of *Pantagruels* was
such a terrour to him all the dayes of his life, and took such deep
impression in his fancie, that very often, distracted with sudden
affrightments, he would startle and say that *Pantagruel* held him
by the neck; besides that it procured him a continual drought
and desire to drink, so that after some few years he died of
the death *Roland*, in plain *English* called thirst, a work of divine
vengeance, shewing us that which saith the Philosopher and
Aulus Gellius, that it becometh us to speak according to the common language: and that we should, (as said *Octavian Augustus*)
strive to shun all strange and unknown termes with as much
heedfulnesse and circumspection as Pilots of ships use to avoid
the rocks and banks in the sea.

CHAPTER VII

*How Pantagruel came to Paris, and of the choise Books of the
Library of St. Victor.*

AFTER that *Pantagruel* had studied very well at *Orleans*, he
resolved to see the great University at *Paris*; but before his

departure, he was informed that there was a huge big bell at St. *Anian* in the said town of *Orleans*, under the ground, which had been there above two hundred and fourteen years; for it was so great that they could not by any device get it so much as above the ground, although they used all the meanes that are found in *Vitruvius de Architectura*, *Albertus de re ædificatoria*, *Euclid*, *Theon*, *Archimedes*, and *Hero de ingeniis*: for all that was to no purpose, wherefore condescending heartily to the humble request of the Citizens and Inhabitants of the said Town, he determined to remove it to the tower that was erected for it: with that he came to the place where it was, and lifted it out of the ground with his little finger, as easily as you would have done a Hawks bell, or Bell-wethers tingle tangle; but before he would carry it to the foresaid tower or steeple appointed for it, he would needs make some Musick with it about the Town, and ring it alongst all the streets, as he carried it in his hand, wherewith all the people were very glad; but there happened one great inconveniency, for with carrying it so, and ringing it about the streets, all the good *Orleans* wine turned instantly, waxed flat, and was spoiled, which no body there did perceive till the night following; for every man found himself so altered, and a-dry with drinking these flat wines, that they did nothing but spit, and that as white as *Maltha* cotton, saying; We have of the *Pantagruel*, and our very throats are salted. This done, he came to *Paris* with his retinue, and at his entry every one came out to see him, (as you know well enough, that the people of *Paris* is sottish by *nature*, by *B. flat*, and *B. sharp*), and beheld him with great astonishment, mixed with no lesse feare, that he would carry away the Palace into some other countrey, *à remotis*, and farre from them, as his father formerly had done the great peal of Bells at our *Ladies* Church, to tie about his Mares neck. Now after he had stayed there a pretty space and studied very well in all the seven liberal Arts, he said it was a good towne to live in, but not to die; for that the grave-digging rogues of *St. Innocent* used in frostie nights to warme their bums with dead mens bones. In his abode there he found the Library of *St. Victor*, a very stately and magnifick one, especially in some books which were there, of which followeth the Repertory and Catalogue, *Et primò*,

The for Godsake of salvation.

The Codpiece of the Law.

The Slipshoe of the Decretals.

The Pomegranate of vice.

The Clew-bottom of Theologie.

The Duster or Foxtail-flap of Preachers, composed by *Turlupin*.

The Churning Ballock of the Valiant:

The Henbane of the Bishops.

Marmotretus *de baboonis & apis*, cum Commento Dorbellis.

Decretum Universitatis Parisiensis *super gorgiasitate muliercularum ad placitum.*

The Apparition of *Sancte Geltrud*, to a Nun of *Poissie*, being in travel, at the bringing forth of a childe.

Ars honestè fartandi *in societate*, per Marcum Corvinum.

The mustard-pot of Penance.

The Gamashes, *aliàs* the boots of patience.

Formicarium artium.

De brodiorum usu, & honestate quartandi per Sylvestrem prioratem Jacobinum.

The coosened, or gulled in Court.

The Fraile of the Scriveners.

The Marriage-packet.

The cruizie or crucible of Contemplation.

The Flimflams of the Law.

The Prickle of Wine.

The Spurre of Cheese.

Ruboffatorium scolarium.

Tartaretus de modo cacandi.

The Bravades of *Rome*.

Bricot de differentis Browsarum.

The tail-piece-cushion, or close-breech of Discipline.

The cobled Shoe of Humility.

The Trevet of good thoughts.

The Kettle of Magnanimity.

The cavilling intanglements of Confessors.

The Snatchfare of the Curats.

Reverendi patris fratris Lubini, *provincialis* Bavardiæ, de *gulpendis lardslicionibus libri tres.*

Pasquilli *doctoris marmorei, de capreolis cum artichoket a co-medendis, tempore Papali ab Ecclesia interdicto.*

The Invention of the Holy Crosse, personated by six wilie Priests.

The Spectacles of Pilgrims bound for *Rome.*

Majoris *de modo faciendi Puddinos.*

The Bagpipe of the Prelates.

Beda *de optimitate triparum.*

The complaint of the Barresters upon the reformation of Confites.

The Furred Cat of the Sollicitors and Atturneys.

Of Pease and Bacon, *cum Commento.*

The small vales or drinking money of the Indulgences.

Præclarissimi juris utriusque Doctoris Maistre pilloti, &c.

Scrapfarthingi *de botchandis gloss accursianæ Triflis repetitio enucidiluculissima.*

Stratagemata francharchæri de Baniolet.

Carlbumpkinus *de re militari cum figuris* Tevoti.

De usu & utilitate flayandi equos & equas, authore Magistro nostro de quebecu.

The sawcinesse of Countrey-Stuarts.

M. N. Rostocostojan Bedanesse *de mustarda post prandium servienda, libri quatuor decim, apostillati per* M. Vaurillonis.

The *covillage* or wench-tribute of Promooters.

Quæstio subtilissima, utrum Chimæra in vacuo bombinans posset comedere secundas intentiones, & fuit debatuta per decem hebdomadas in Consilio Constantiensi.

The bridle-champer of the Advocates.

Smutchudlamenta Scoti.

The rasping and hard-scraping of the Cardinals.

De calcaribus removendis Decades undecim per M. Albericum *de* rosata.

Ejusdem de castramentandis criminibus libri tres.

The entrance of *Antonie de leve* into the territories of *Brasil.*

Marforii, bacalarii cubantis Romæ, De peelandis aut unskinnandis blurrandisque Cardinalium mulis.

The said Authors Apologie against those who alledge that the Popes mule doth eat but at set times.

Prognosticatio quæ incipit Silvitriquebillobalata per M. N., the deep dreaming gull *Sion*.

Boudarini *Episcopi de emulgentiarum profectibus* Æneades *novem, cum privilegio Papali ad triennium & postea non.*

The shitabranna of the maids.

The bald arse or peel'd breech of the widows.

The cowle or capouch of the Monks.

The mumbling devotion of the *Cœlestine* Fryars.

The passage-toll of beggarlinesse.

The teeth-chatter or gum-didder of lubberly lusks.

The paring-shovel of the Theologues.

The drench-horne of the Masters of Arts.

The scullions of *Olcam* the uninitiated Clerk.

Magistri N. lickdishetis de garbellisiftationibus horarum canonicarum, libri quadriginta.

Arsiversitatorium confratriarum, incerto authore.

The gulsgoatonie or rasher of Cormorants and ravenous feeders.

The Rammishnesse of the *Spaniards* supergivure gondigaded by Fryar *Inigo*.

The muttring of pitiful wretches.

Dastardismus rerum Italicarum, authore Magistro Burnegad.

R. Lullius de batisfolagiis Principum.

Calibistratorium Caffardiæ, authore M. Jacobo *hocstraten hereticometrâ.*

Codtickler *de magistro nostrandorum magistro nostratorumque beneventi libri octo galantissimi.*

The Crackarades of balists or stone-throwing Engines, contrepate Clerks, Scriveners, Brief-writers, Rapporters, and Papal Bull-dispatchers lately compiled by *Regis*.

A perpetual Almanack for those that have the gowt and the pox.

Manera sweepandi fornacellos per Mag. Eccium.

The shable or cimeterre of Merchants.

The pleasures of the Monachal life.

The hotchpot of Hypocrites.

The history of the Hobgoblins.

The ragamuffianisme of the pensionary maimed souldiers.

The gulling fibs and counterfeit shewes of Commissaries.

The litter of Treasurers.

The juglingatorium of Sophisters.

Antipericatametanaparbeugedamphisistationes toordicantium.

The periwinkle of ballad-makers.

The push-forward of the Alchimists.

The niddie noddie of the sachel-loaded seekers, by Friar *Bindfastatis.*

The shackles of Religion.

The racket of swag-waggers.

The leaning-stock of old age.

The muzzle of Nobility.

The Apes *pater noster.*

The Crickets and Hawks bells of Devotion.

The pot of the Emberweeks.

The mortar of the politick life.

The flap of the Hermites.

The riding-hood or *Montero* of the Penitentiaries.

The trictrac of the knocking Friars.

Blockheadodus *de vita & honestate bragadochiorum.*

Lyrippii Sorbonici *moralisationes per* M. Lupoldum.

The Carrier-horse-bells of Travellers.

The bibbings of the tipling Bishops.

Dolloporediones Doctorum Coloniensium *adversus* Reuclin.

The Cymbals of Ladies.

The Dungers martingale.

Whirlingfriskorum Chasemarkerorum per fratrem Crackwood-loguetis.

The clouted patches of a stout heart.

The mummerie of the racket-keeping Robin-good-fellows.

Gerson *de auferibilitate Papæ ab Ecclesia.*

The Catalogue of the nominated and graduated persons.

Jo. Dytebrodii *de terribilitate excommunicationis libellus acephalos.*

Ingeniositas invocandi diabolos & diabolas, per M. Guingolphum.

The hotchpotch or gallimafree of the perpetually begging Friars.

The *morrish*-dance of the Hereticks.

The whinings of *Cajetan.*

Muddisnowt *Doctoris cherubici de origine roughfootedarum & wryneckedorum ritibus libri septem.*

Sixty nine fat breviaries.

The night-Mare of the five orders of Beggars.

The skinnery of the new start-ups extracted out of the fallow
butt, incornifistibulated and plodded upon in the Ange-
lick summe.

The raver and idle talker in cases of conscience.

The fat belly of the Presidents.

The bafling flowter of the Abbots.

Sutoris *adversus eum qui vocaverat eum Slabsauceatorem, &
quod Slabsauceatores non sunt damnati ab Ecclesia.*

Cacatorium medicorum.

The chimney-sweeper of Astrologie.

Campi clysteriorum per paragraph C.

The bumsquibcracker of Apothecaries.

The kissebreech of Chirurgerie.

Justinianus de Whiteleperotis tollendis.

Antidotarium animæ.

Merlinus Coccaius *de patria diabolorum.*

The Practice of iniquity by Cleuraunes sadden.

The Mirrour of basenesse by Radnecu Waldenses.

The ingrained rogue by Dwarsencas Eldenu.

The mercilesse Cormorant by Hoxinidno the Jew.

Of which library some books are already printed, and the rest
are now at the Presse, in this noble City of *Tubinge.*

CHAPTER VIII

*How Pantagruel being at Paris received letters from his father
Gargantua, and the Copy of them.*

PANTAGRUEL studied very hard, as you may well conceive, and
profited accordingly; for he had an excellent understanding,
and notable wit, together with a capacity in memory, equal to
the measure of twelve oyle budgets, or butts of Olives. And as
he was there abiding one day, he received a letter from his
father in manner as followeth.

Most dear sonne, amongst the gifts, graces and prerogatives,
with which the Soveraign *Plasmator* God Almighty, hath endowed
and adorned humane Nature at the beginning, that seems to me

most singular and excellent, by which we may in a mortal estate attain to a kinde of immortality, and in the course of this transitory life perpetuate our name and seed, which is done by a progeny issued from us in the lawful bonds of Matrimony: whereby that in some measure is restored unto us, which was taken from us by the sin of our first Parents, to whom it was said, that because they had not obeyed the Commandment of God their Creator, they should die, and by death should be brought to nought that so stately frame and *Plasmature*, wherein the man at first had been created.

But by this meanes of seminal propagation, there continueth in the children what was lost in the Parents, and in the grand-children that which perished in their fathers, and so successively until the day of the last judgement, when *Jesus Christ* shall have rendered up to God the Father his Kingdom in a peace-able condition, out of all danger and contamination of sin; for then shall cease all generations and corruptions, and the ele-ments leave off their continual transmutations; seeing the so much desired peace shall be attained unto and enjoyed, and that all things shall be brought to their end and period; and therefore not without just and reasonable cause do I give thanks to God my Saviour and Preserver, for that he hath inabled me to see my bald old age reflourish in thy youth: for when at his good pleasure, who rules and governs all things, my soul shall leave this mortal habitation; I shall not account my self wholly to die, but to passe from one place unto another: considering that, in and by that, I continue in my visible image living in the world, visiting and conversing with people of honour, and other my good friends, as I was wont to do: which conversation of mine, although it was not without sin, (because we are all of us trespassers, and there-fore ought continually to beseech his divine Majesty, to blot our transgressions out of his memory) yet was it by the help and grace of God, without all manner of reproach before men.

Wherefore if those qualities of the minde but shine in thee, wherewith I am endowed, as in thee remaineth the perfect image of my body, thou wilt be esteemed by all men to be the perfect guardian and treasure of the immortality of our name: but if otherwise, I shall truly take but small pleasure to see it, considering that the lesser part of me, which is the body, would abide in thee: and the best, to wit, that which is the soule, and by which our name continues blessed amongst men, would be degenerate and abastardised: This I do not speak out of any distrust that I have of thy vertue, which I have heretofore already tried, but to encourage thee yet more earnestly to proceed from good to better: and that which I now write unto thee is not so much that thou shouldest live in this vertuous course, as that thou shouldest rejoyce in so living and having lived, and cheer up thy self with the like resolution in time to come; to the prosecution and accomplishment of which enterprise and generous undertaking thou mayest easily remember how that I have spared nothing, but have so helped thee, as if I had had no other treasure in this world, but to see thee once in my life, compleatly well bred and accomplished, as well in vertue, honesty and valour, as in all liberal knowledge and civility: and so to leave thee after my death as a mirrour, representing the person of me thy father, and if not so excellent, and such *indeed* as I do wish thee, yet such in my *desire*.

But although my deceased father of happy memory *Grangousier*, had bent his best endeavours to make me profit in all perfection and Political knowledge, and that my labour and study was fully correspondent to, yea, went beyond his desire: neverthelesse, as thou mayest well understand, the time then was not so proper and fit for learning as it is at present, neither had I plenty of good Masters such as thou hast had; for that time was darksome, obscured with clouds of ignorance, and savouring a little of the infelicity and calamity of the *Gothes*, who had, wherever they set footing, destroyed all good literature, which in my age hath by the divine goodnesse been restored unto its former light and dignity, and that with such amendment and increase of the knowledge, that now hardly should I be admitted unto the first forme of the little Grammar-school-boyes: I say, I, who in my youthful dayes was, (and that justly) reputed the most learned of that age; which I do not speak in vain boasting, although I might lawfully do it in writing unto thee, in verification whereof thou hast the authority of *Marcus Tullius* in his book of old age, and the sentence of *Plutarch*, in the book intituled, how a man may praise himself without envie: but to give thee an emulous encouragement to strive yet further.

Now is it that the mindes of men are qualified with all manner of discipline, and the old sciences revived, which for many ages were extinct: now it is, that the learned languages are to their pristine purity restored, *viz. Greek*, (without which a man may be ashamed to account himself a scholar,) *Hebrew, Arabick, Chaldæan* and *Latine*. Printing likewise is now in use, so elegant, and so correct, that better cannot be imagined, although it was found out but in my time by divine inspiration, as by a diabolical suggestion on the other side was the invention of Ordnance. All the world is full of knowing men, of most learned Schoolmasters, and vast Libraries: and it appears to me as a truth, that neither in *Plato's* time, nor *Cicero's*, nor *Papinian's*, there was ever such conveniency for studying, as we see at this day there is: nor must any adventure henceforward to come in publick, or present himself in company, that hath not been pretty well polished in the shop of *Minerva*: I see robbers, hangmen, freebooters, tapsters, ostlers, and such like, of the very rubbish of the people, more learned now, then the Doctors and Preachers were in my time.

What shall I say? the very women and children have aspired to this praise and celestial Manna of good learning: yet so it is, that in the age I am now of, I have been constrained to learn the *Greek* tongue, which I contemned not like *Cato*, but had not the leasure in my younger years to attend the study of it: and take much delight in the reading of *Plutarchs* Morals, the pleasant Dialogues of *Plato*, the Monuments of *Pausanias*, and the Antiquities of *Athenæus*, in waiting on the houre wherein God my Creator shall call me, and command me to depart from this earth and transitory pilgrimage. Wherefore (my sonne) I admonish thee, to imploy thy youth to profit as well as thou canst, both in thy studies and in vertue. Thou art at *Paris*, where the laudable examples of many brave men may stirre up thy minde to gallant actions, and hast likewise for thy Tutor and *Pædagogue* the learned *Epistemon*, who by his lively and vocal documents may instruct thee in the Arts and Sciences.

I intend, and will have it so, that thou learn the Languages perfectly: first of all, the *Greek*, as *Quintilian* will have it: secondly, the *Latine*; and then the *Hebrew*, for the holy Scripture-sake: and then the *Chaldee* and *Arabick* likewise, and that thou frame thy stile in *Greek* in imitation of *Plato*, and, for the *Latine*, after *Cicero*. Let there be no history which thou shalt not have ready in thy memory; unto the prosecuting of which designe, books of *Cosmographie* will be very conducible, and help thee much. Of the liberal Arts of *Geometry*, *Arithmetick*, and *Musick*, I gave thee some taste when thou wert yet little, and not above five or six yeares old; proceed further in them, & learn the remainder if thou canst. As for *Astronomy*, study all the rules thereof, let passe neverthelesse the divining and judicial *Astrology* and the Art of *Lullius*, as being nothing else but plain abuses and vanities. As for the *Civil Law*, of that I would have thee to know the texts by heart, and then to conferre them with *Philosophie*.

Now in matter of the knowledge of the works of Nature, I would have thee to study that exactly, and that so there be no sea, river nor fountain, of which thou doest not know the fishes, all the fowles of the aire, all the several kindes of shrubs and trees, whether in forrests or orchards: all the sorts of herbes and flowers that grow upon the ground: all the various mettals that are hid within the bowels of the earth: together with all the diversity of precious stones, that are to be seen in the Orient & South-parts of the world, let nothing of all these be hidden from thee. Then faile not most carefully to peruse the books of the *Greek*, *Arabian*, and *Latine* Physicians, not despising the *Talmudists* and *Cabalists*; and by frequent Anatomies get thee the perfect knowledge of the other world, called the Microcosme, which is man: and at some houres of the day apply thy minde to the study of the holy Scriptures: first in *Greek*, the New Testament, with the Epistles of the Apostles; and then the Old Testament in *Hebrew*. In brief, let me see thee an Abysse, and bottomlesse pit of knowledge: for from hence forward, as thou growest great and becomest a man, thou must part from this tranquillity and rest of study, thou must learn chivalrie, warfare, and the exercises of the field, the better thereby to defend my house and our friends, and to succour and protect them at all their needs against the invasion and assaults of evil doers.

Furthermore, I will that very shortly thou try how much thou hast profited, which thou canst not better do, then by maintaining publickly *Theses* and Conclusions in all Arts, against all persons whatsoever, and by haunting the company of learned men, both at *Paris* and otherwhere. But because as the wise man *Solomon* saith, *Wisdome entereth not into a malicious minde*; and that knowledge without conscience is but the ruine of the soule, it behooveth thee to serve, to love, to feare God, and on him to cast all thy thoughts and all thy hope, and by faith formed in charity to cleave unto him, so that thou mayest never be separated from him by thy sins. Suspect the abuses of the world: set not thy heart upon vanity; for this life is transitory, but the Word of the Lord endureth for ever. Be serviceable to all thy neighbours, and love them as thy self: reverence thy Præceptors: shun the conversation of those whom thou desirest not to resemble, and receive not in vaine the graces which God hath bestowed upon thee: and when thou shalt see that thou hast attained to all the knowledge that is to be acquired in that part, return unto me, that I may see thee, and give thee my blessing before I die. *My sonne*, the peace and grace of our Lord be with thee. *Amen*.

From Utopia the 17. day of the
      moneth of March
                                        Thy father Gargantua.

These letters being received and read, *Pantagruel* pluck't up his heart, took a fresh courage to him, and was inflamed with a desire to profit in his studies more then ever, so that if you had seen him, how he took paines, and how he advanced in learning, you would have said that the vivacity of his spirit amidst the books, was like a great fire amongst dry wood, so active it was, vigorous and indefatigable.

CHAPTER IX

How Pantagruel found Panurge, whom he loved all his life-time.

ONE day as *Pantagruel* was taking a walk without the City, towards *St. Antonies* Abbey, discoursing and philosophating with his own servants and some other Scholars, he met with a young man of very comely stature, and surpassing handsome in all the lineaments of his body, but in several parts thereof most pitifully wounded; in such bad equipage in matter of his apparel, which was but tatters and rags, and every way so far out of order, that he seemed to have been a fighting with mastiffe-dogs, from whose fury he had made an escape, or, to say better, he looked in the condition wherein he then was, like an Apple-gatherer of the countrey of *Perche.*

As farre off as *Pantagruel* saw him, he said to those that stood by: Do you see that man there, who is a coming hither upon the road from *Charanton*-bridge? by my faith, he is only poor in fortune; for I may assure you, that by his *Physiognomie* it appeareth, that nature hath extracted him from some rich and noble race, and that too much curiosity hath thrown him upon adventures, which possibly have reduced him to this indigence, want and penurie. Now as he was just amongst them, *Pantagruel* said unto him, Let me intreat you, (*friend*) that you may be pleased to stop here a little, and answer me to that which I shall ask you, and I am confident you will not think your time ill-bestowed; for I have an extream desire (according to my ability), to give you some supply in this distresse, wherein I see you are; because I do very much commiserate your case, which truly moves me to great pity; Therefore (my friend) tell me, who you are? Whence you come? whither you go? what you desire? and what your name is? the companion answered him in the *Dutch* tongue, thus.

Juncker, Gott geb euch glück unnd hail. Zuvor, lieber Juncker, ich las euch wissen das da ir mich von fragt, ist ein arm unnd erbarmglich ding, unnd wer vil darvon zu sagen, welches euch verdruslich zu hœren, unnd mir zu erzelen wer, wievol die Poeten unnd Orators vor-zeiten haben gesagt in irem Sprüchen unnd Sentenzen, das die Gedecht-nus des Ellends unnd Armuot vorlangs erlitten ist ain grosser Lust. My friend (said *Pantagruel,*) I have no skill in that gibberish of yours; therefore, if you would have us to understand you, speak to us in some other language; then did the drole answer him thus.

Al barildim gotfano dech min brin alabo dordin falbroth ringuam albaras. Nin porth zadikim almucathin milko prin al elmim enthoth dal heben ensouim; kuthim al dum alkatim nim broth dechoth porth min michais im endoth; pruch dal maisoulum hol moth dansrilrim lupaldas im voldemoth. Nin hur diavosth mnarbotim dal gousch

*palfrapin duch im scoth pruch galeth dal Chinon min foulchrich al
conin butathen doth dal prim.* Do you understand none of this,
said *Pantagruel* to the company? I beleeve (said *Epistemon*,) that
this is the language of the *Antipodes*, and such a hard one that
the devil himself knowes not what to make of it. Then, said
Pantagruel, Gossip, I know not if the walls do comprehend the
meaning of your words, but none of us here doth so much as
understand one syllable of them; then said *my blade* again.—

*Signor mio, voi videte per exemplo che la cornamusa non suona
mai, s'ela non a il ventre pieno; cosi io parimente non vi saprei contare
le mie fortune, se prima il tribulato ventre non a la solita refectione, al
quale è adviso che le mani et li dente abbui perso il loro ordine naturale
et del tuto annichillati.* To which *Epistemon* answered as much of
the one as of the other, and nothing of either. Then said *Panurge.*

*Lard, ghest tholb be sua virtuis be intelligence ass yi body schal biss
be naturall relvth, tholb suld of me pety have; for natur hass ulss egualy
maide; bot fortune sum exaltit hess and oyis deprevit. Non ye less viois
mou virtius deprevit and virtiuss men discrivis, for anen ye lad end iss
non gud.* Yet lesse said *Pantagruel;* then said my jollie *Panurge.*

*Jona andie, guaussa goussyetan behar da erremedio, beharde, ver-
sela ysser lan da. Anbates, otoyyes nausu, eyn essassu gourr ay prop-
osian ordine den. Non yssena bayta fascheria egabe, genherassy badia
sadassu noura assia. Aran hondovan gualde eydassu nay dassuna.
Estou oussyc eguinan soury hin, er darstura eguy harm, Genicoa pla-
sar vadu.* Are you there (said *Eudemon?*) *Genicoa*, to this (said
Carpalin) St. *Trinian*'s rammer unstitch your bum, for I had almost understood it. Then answered *Panurge.*

*Prug frest strinst sorgdmand strochdt drhds pag brledand Gravot
Chavigny Pomardiere rusth pkallhdracg Deviniere pres Nays, Bcuille
kalmuch monach drupp delmeupplistrincq dlrnd dodelb up drent loch
minc stzrinquald de vins ders cordelis hur jocststzampenards.* Do you
speak Christian (said *Epistemon*) or the *Buffoon* language, otherwise called *patelinois*? Nay, it is the *puzlatory* tongue (said another) which some call *Lanternois*. Then said *Panurge.*

*Herre, ie en spreke anders gheen taele dan kersten taele; my dunct
nochtans, al en seg ie v niet een wordt, myuen noot v claert ghenonch
wat ie beglere; gheest my unyt bermherticheyt yet waer un ie ghevoet
mach zunch.* To which answered *Pantagruel*, as much of that:
then said *Panurge.*

Señor, de tanto hablar yo soy cansado. Por que supplico a Vostra Reverentia que mire a los preceptos evangeliquos, para que ellos movant Vostra Reverentia a lo qu'es de conscientia, y, sy ellos non bastarent para mover Vostra Reverentia a piedad, supplico que mire a la piedad natural, la qual yo creo que le movra, como es de razon, y con esto non digo mas. Truly (my friend), I doubt not but you can speak divers languages, but tell us that which you would have us to do for you in some tongue, which you conceive we may understand? then said the companion.

Myn Herre, endog jig med inghen tunge talede, lygesom boeen, ocg uskvvlig creatner! myne kleebon, och myne legoms magerhed uudviser allygue klalig huvad tyng meg meest behoff girereb, som aer sandeligh mad och drycke: hwarfor forbarme teg omsyder offvermeg, och bef ael at gyffuc meg nogeth, aff huylket jig kand styre myne groeendes maghe, lygeruss son mand Cerbero en soppe forsetthr. Soa shal tue loeffve lenge och lyksalight: I think really (said *Eusthenes*) that the *Gothes* spoke thus of old, and that, if it pleased God, we would all of us speak so with our tailes. Then again said *Panurge*.

Adoni, scolom lecha. Im ischar harob hal habdeca, bemeherah thithen li kikar lehem, chancathub: 'Laah al Adonai chonen ral'. To which answered *Epistemon*, at this time have I understood him very well; for it is the *Hebrew* tongue most Rhetorically pronounced: Then again said the *Gallant*.

Despota ti nyn panagathe, dioti sy mi uc artodotis? Horas gar limo analiscomenon eme athlios. Ce en to metaxy eme uc eleis udamos, zetis de par emu ha u chre, ce homos philologi pamdes homologusi tote logus te ce rhemata peritta hyparchin, opote pragma afto pasi delon esti. Entha gar anancei monon logi isin, hina pragmata, hon peri amphibetumen, me phosphorus epiphenete. What? (said *Carpalim*, *Pantagruels* footman), it is *Greek*, I have understood him: and how? hast thou dwelt any while in *Greece*? Then said the *drole* again.

Agonou dont oussys vou denaguez algarou, nou den farou zamist vous mariston ulbrou, fousquez vou brol, tam bredaguez moupreton den goul houst, daguez daguez nou croupys fost bardounnoflist nou grou. Agou paston tol nalprissys hourton los ecbatonous prou dhouquys brol panygou den bascrou noudous caguous goulfren goul oust troppassou. Me thinks I understand him (said *Pantagruel*) for either it is the language of my countrey of *Utopia*, or sounds very like it: and as he was about to have begun some purpose, the companion said,

Jam toties vos per sacra, perque deos deásque omnis obtestatus sum, ut si qua vos pietas permovet, egestatem meam solaremini nec hilum proficio clamans & ejulans: sinite, quæso, sinite, viri impii, quo me fatavocant abire; nec ultrà vanis vestris interpellationibus obtundatis, memores veteris illius adagii quo venter famelicus auriculis carere dicitur. Well, my friend, (said *Pantagruel*) but cannot you speak *French*? That I can do (*Sir*) very well, (said the companion) God be thanked: it is my natural language and mother-tongue, for I was borne and bred in my younger yeares in the garden of *France*, to wit, *Touraine:* Then (*said Pantagruel*) tell us what is your name, and from whence you are come; for by my faith, I have already stamped in my minde such a deep impression of love towards you, that if you will condescend unto my will, you shall not depart out of my company, and you and I shall make up another couple of friends, such as *Æneas* and *Achates* were; Sir (said the companion) my true and proper *christen* name is *Panurge*, and now I come out of *Turkie*, to which countrey I was carried away prisoner at that time, when they went to *Metelin* with a mischief: and willingly would I relate unto you my fortunes, which are more wonderful than those of *Ulysses* were: but seeing that it pleaseth you to retain me with you, I most heartily accept of the offer, protesting never to leave you, should you go to all the devils in hell; we shall have therefore more leisure at another time, and a fitter opportunity wherein to report them; for at this present I am in a very urgent necessity to feed, my teeth are sharp, my belly empty, my throat dry, and my stomack fierce and burning: all is ready, if you will but set me to work, it will be as good as a *balsamum* for sore eyes, to see me gulch and raven it, for Gods sake give order for it. Then *Pantagruel* commanded that they should carry him home, and provide him good store of victuals, which being done, he ate very well that evening, and (capon-like) went early to bed, then slept until dinner-time the next day, so that he made but three steps and one leap from the bed to the board.

CHAPTER X

How Pantagruel judged so equitably of a Controversie, which was wonderfully obscure and difficult; that by reason of his just decree therein, he was reputed to have a most admirable judgement.

PANTAGRUEL, very well remembring his fathers letter and admonitions, would one day make trial of his knowledge. Thereupon in all the *Carrefours*, that is, throughout all the foure quarters, streets and corners of the City, he set up Conclusions to the number of nine thousand seven hundred sixty and foure, in all manner of learning, touching in them the hardest doubts that are in any science. And first of all, in the *fodder-street* he held dispute against all the *Regents* or Fellowes of Colledges, *Artists* or Masters of Arts, and Oratours, and did so gallantly, that he overthrew them, and set them all upon their tailes. He went afterwards to the *Sorbone*, where he maintained argument against all the *Theologians* or Divines, for the space of six weeks, from foure a clock in the morning, until six in the evening, except an interval of two houres to refresh themselves, and take their repast: and at this were present the greatest part of the Lords of the Court, the Masters of Requests, Presidents, Counsellors, those of the Accompts, Secretaries, Advocates and others: as also the Sheriffes of the said town, with the Physicians and Professors of the canon-law; amongst which it is to be remarked, that the greatest part were stubborn jades, and in their opinions obstinate; but he took such course with them, that for all their *Ergo's* and fallacies, he put their backs to the wall, gravelled them in the deepest questions, and made it visibly appear to the world, that compared to him, they were but monkies, and a knot of mufled calves: Whereupon every body began to keep a bustling noise, and talk of his so marvellous knowledge, through all degrees of persons in both sexes, even to the very Laundresses, Brokers, Rostmeat-sellers, Penknife-makers and others, who, when he past along in the street, would say, This is he; in which he took delight, as *Demosthenes* the prince of *Greek* Oratours did, when an old crouching wife, pointing at him with her fingers said, That is the man.

Now at this same very time there was a processe or suit in law, depending in Court between two great Lords, of which one was called my Lord *Kissebreech*, Plaintiffe of one side, and the other my Lord *Suckfist*, Defendant of the other; whose Controversie was so high and difficult in Law, that the Court of Parliament could make nothing of it. And therefore by the Commandment of the King there were assembled foure of the greatest and most learned of all the Parliaments of *France*, together with the great Councel, and all the principal Regents of the Universities, not only of *France*, but of *England* also and *Italy*, such as *Jason*, *Philippus-Decius*, *Petrus de Petronibus*, and a rabble of other old *Rabbinists*: who being thus met together, after they had thereupon consulted for the space of six and fourty weeks, finding that they could not fasten their teeth in it, nor with such clearnesse understand the case, as that they might in any manner of way be able to right it, or take up the difference betwixt the two aforesaid Parties, it did so grievously vex them, that they most villanously conshit themselves for shame. In this great extremity, one amongst them named *Du Douhet*, the learnedst of all, and more expert and prudent then any of the rest, whilest one day they were thus at their wits end, all-to-be-dunced and *philogrobolized* in their braines, said unto them: We have been here (my Masters,) a good long space without doing any thing else, then trifle away both our time and money, and can neverthelesse finde neither brim nor bottome in this matter; for the more we study about it, the lesse we understand therein, which is a great shame and disgrace to us, and a heavy burthen to our consciences; yea such, that in my opinion we shall not rid our selves of it without dishonour, unlesse we take some other course, for we do nothing but doat in our consultations.

See therefore what I have thought upon: you have heard much talking of that worthy personage named Master *Pantagruel*, who hath been found to be learned above the capacity of this present age, by the proofs he gave in those great disputations, which he held publickly against all men: my opinion is, that we send for him, to conferre with him about this businesse; for never any man will encompasse the bringing of it to an end, if he do it not.

THE SECOND BOOK

Hereunto all the Counsellors and Doctors willingly agreed, and according to that their result having instantly sent for him, they intreated him to be pleased to canvass the processe, and sift it throughly, that after a deep search and narrow examination of all the points thereof, he might forthwith make the report unto them, such as he shall think good in true and legal knowledge: to this effect they delivered into his hands the bags wherein were the Writs and Pancarts concerning that suit, which for bulk and weight were almost enough to lade foure great *couillard* or stoned Asses; but *Pantagruel* said unto them, Are the two Lords, between whom this debate and processe is, yet living? it was answered him, Yes: To what a devil then (said he,) serve so many paultry heapes, and bundles of papers and copies which you give me? is it not better to heare their Controversie from their own mouthes, whilest they are face to face before us, then to reade these vile fopperies, which are nothing but trumperies, deceits, diabolical cosenages of *Cepola*, pernicious slights and subversions of equity? for I am sure, that you, and all those thorough whose hands this processe hath past, have by your devices added what you could to it *pro & contra* in such sort, that although their difference perhaps was clear and easie enough to determine at first, you have obscured it, and made it more intricate, by the frivolous, sottish, unreasonable and foolish reasons and opinions of *Accursius, Baldus, Bartolus, de castro, de imola, Hippolytus, Panormo, Bertachin, Alexander, Curtius*, and those other old Mastiffs, who never understood the least law of the Pandects, they being but meer blockheads & great tithe-calvs, ignorant of all that which was needful for the understanding of the lawes; for (as it is most certain) they had not the knowledge either of the *Greek* or *Latine* tongue, but only of the *Gothick* and *Barbarian*; the lawes neverthelesse were first taken from the *Greeks*, according to the testimony of *Ulpian. l. poster. de origine juris*, which we likewise may perceive by that all the lawes are full of *Greek* words and sentences: and then we finde that they are reduced into a *Latine* stile, the most elegant and ornate, that whole language is able to afford, without excepting that of any that ever wrote therein; nay, not of *Salust, Varo, Cicero, Seneca, Titus Livius*, nor *Quintilian*; how then could these old dotards be able to understand aright the text of the lawes,

who never in their time had looked upon a good *Latine* book, as
doth evidently enough appear by the rudenesse of their stile,
which is fitter for a Chimney-sweeper, or for a Cook or a Scullion,
then for a Juris-consult and Doctor in the Lawes?

Furthermore, seeing the Lawes are excerpted out of the
middle of moral and natural Philosophie, how should these fooles
have understood it, that have, by G—, studied lesse in Philosophie
then my Mule? in respect of humane learning, and the knowledge of Antiquities and History, they were truly laden with
those faculties as a toad is with feathers: and yet of all this the
Lawes are so full, that without it they cannot be understood, as
I intend more fully to shew unto you in a peculiar Treatise,
which on that purpose I am about to publish. Therefore if you
will that I take any medling in this processe; first, cause all these
papers to be burnt: secondly, make the two Gentlemen come
personally before me; and afterwards, when I shall have heard
them, I will tell you my opinion freely without any feignednes
or dissimulation whatsoever.

Some amongst them did contradict this motion, as you know
that in all companies there are more fooles then wise men, and
that the greater part alwayes surmounts the better, as saith *Titus
Livius*, in speaking of the *Carthaginians*: but the foresaid *Du Douet*
held the contrary opinion, maintaining that *Pantagruel* had said
well, and what was right, in affirming that these records, bills of
inquest, replies, rejoinders, exceptions, depositions, and other
such diableries of truth-intangling Writs, were but Engines
wherewith to overthrow justice, and unnecessarily to prolong
such suits as did depend before them; and that therefore the
devil would carry them all away to hell, if they did not take
another course, and proceeded not in times coming according
to the Prescripts of Evangelical and Philosophical equity. In fine,
all the papers were burnt, and the two Gentlemen summoned
and personally convented; at whose appearance before the
Court, *Pantagruel* said unto them, Are you they, that have this
great difference betwixt you? Yes (my Lord) said they: Which
of you (said *Pantagruel*,) is the Plaintiffe? It is I, said *my Lord
Kissebreech*: Go to then, my friend, (said he) and relate your matter unto me from point to point, according to the real truth, or
else (by cocks body), if I finde you to lie so much as in one word,

I will make you shorter by the head, and take it from off your shoulders, to shew others by your example, that in justice and judgement men ought to speak nothing but the truth; therefore take heed you do not adde nor impare any thing in the Narration of your case. *Begin*.

CHAPTER XI

How the Lords of Kissebreech and Suckfist did plead before Pantagruel without an Atturney.

THEN began *Kissebreech* in manner as followeth; *My Lord*, it is true, that a good woman of my house, carried egges to the market to sell: Be covered, *Kissebreech*, said *Pantagruel*: Thanks to you, *my Lord*, said the Lord *Kissebreech*; but to the purpose, there passed betwixt the two tropicks, the summe of three pence towards the zenith and a halfpeny, forasmuch as the *Riphæan* mountaines had been that yeare opprest with a great sterility of counterfeit gudgions, and shewes without substance, by meanes of the babling tattle, and fond fibs, seditiously raised between the gibble-gablers, and *Accursian* gibberish-mongers, for the rebellion of the *Swissers*, who had assembled themselves to the full number of the bum-bees, and myrmidons, to go a handsel-getting on the first day of the new yeare, at that very time when they gave brewis to the oxen, and deliver the key of the coales to the Countrey-girles, for serving in of the oates to the dogs. All the night long they did nothing else (keeping their hands still upon the pot) but dispatch both on foot and horseback, leaden-sealed Writs or letters, (to wit Papal Commissions commonly called Bulls,) to stop the boats: for the Tailors and Seamsters would have made of the stollen shreds and clippings a goodly sagbut to cover the face of the Ocean, which then was great with childe of a potfull of cabbidge, according to the opinion of the hay-bundlemakers: but the physicians said, that by the Urine they could discern no manifest signe of the Bustards pace, nor how to eat double-tongued mattocks with mustard, unless the Lords and Gentlemen of the Court should be pleased to give by *B.mol* expresse command to the pox, not to run about any longer, in gleaning up of Coppersmiths and

Tinkers; for the Jobernolls had already a pretty good beginning in their dance of the British gig, called the *estrindore*, to a perfect *diapason*, with one foot in the fire, and their head in the middle, as good man Ragot was wont to say.

Ha (*my Masters*,) God moderates all things, and disposeth of them at his pleasure, so that against unluckie fortune a Carter broke his frisking whip, which was all the winde-instrument he had: this was done at his return from the little paultry town, even then when Master *Antitus of Cresseplots* was licentiated, and had past his degrees in all dullerie and blockishnesse, according to this sentence of the Canonists, *Beati Dunces, quoniam ipsi stumblaverunt*. But that which makes lent to be so high, by St. *Fiacre* of *Bry*, is for nothing else, but that the *Pentecost* never comes, but to my cost; yet *on afore there hoe*, a little rain stills a great winde, and we must think so, seeing that the Serjeant hath propounded the matter so farre above my reach, that the Clerks and Secondaries could not with the benefit thereof lick their fingers feathered with gaunders, so orbicularly as they were wont in other things to do. And we do manifestly see, that every one acknowledgeth himself to be in the errour, wherewith another hath been charged, reserving only those cases whereby we are obliged to take an ocular inspection in a perspective glasse of these things, towards the place in the Chimney, where hangeth the signe of the wine of fourty girths, which have been alwayes accounted very necessary for the number of twenty pannels and pack-saddles of the bankrupt Protectionaries of five yeares respit; howsoever at least he that would not let flie the fowle before the Cheesecakes, ought in law to have discovered his reason why not, for the memory is often lost with a wayward shooing: Well, God keep *Theobald Mitain* from all danger. Then said *Pantagruel*, Hold there: Ho, *my friend*, soft and faire, speak at leisure, and soberly without putting your self in choler; I understand the case, go on. Now then (*my Lord*) said *Kissebreech*, the foresaid good woman, saying her *gaudez and audinos*, could not cover her selfe with a treacherous backblow, ascending by the wounds and passions of the priviledges of the Universitie, unlesse by the vertue of a warming-pan she had Angelically fomented every part of her body, in covering them with a hedge of garden-beds: then giving in a swift unavoidable thrust very near to the place where they sell the old rags, whereof the Painters of *Flanders* make great use, when they are about neatly to clap on shoes on grashoppers, locusts, *cigals*, and such like flie-fowles, so strange to us, that I am wonderfully astonished why the world doth not lay, seeing it is so good to hatch.

Here the Lord of *Suckfist* would have interrupted him and spoken somewhat, whereupon *Pantagruel* said unto him, *St*, by St. *Antonies* belly, doth it become thee to speak without command? I sweat here with the extremity of labour and exceeding toile I take to understand the proceeding of your mutual difference, and yet thou comest to trouble and disquiet me: peace, in the devils name, peace, thou shalt be permitted to speak thy belly full, when this man hath done, and no sooner. Go on, (said he) to *Kissebreech*, speak calmly, and do not over-heat your self with too much haste.

I perceiving then (said *Kissebreech*,) that the pragmatical sanction did make no mention of it, and that the holy Pope to every one gave liberty to fart at his own ease, if that the blankets had no streaks, wherein the liars were to be crossed with a ruffian-like crue: & the rain-bow being newly sharpned at *Milan* to bring forth larks, gave his full consent that the good woman should tread down the heel of the hipgut-pangs, by vertue of a solemn protestation put in by the little testiculated or codsted fishes, which to tell the truth, were at that time very necessary for understanding the syntax and construction of old boots. Therefore *John Calfe*, her Cosen gervais once removed with a log from the woodstack, very seriously advised her not to put her selfe into the hazard of quagswagging in the Lee, to be scowred with a buck of linnen clothes, till first she had kindled the paper: this counsel she laid hold on, because he desired her to take nothing, and throw out, for *Non de ponte vadit, qui cum sapientia cadit*: matters thus standing, seeing the Masters of the chamber of Accompts, or members of that Committee, did not fully agree amongst themselves in casting up the number of the *Almanie* whistles, whereof were framed those spectacles for Princes, which have been lately printed at *Antwerp*, I must needs think that it makes a bad return of the Writ, and that the adverse Party is not to be beleeved, *in sacer verbo dotis*; for that having a great desire to obey the pleasure of the King, I armed my self from toe to top with belly furniture, of the soles of good venison-pasties, to go see how my grape-gatherers and vintagers had pinked and cut full of small holes their high coped-caps, to lecher it the better, and play at *in and in*. And indeed the time was very dangerous in coming from the Faire, in so farre that many trained bowe-men were cast at the muster, and quite rejected, although the chimney-tops were high enough, according to the proportion of the *windgalls* in the legs of horses, or of the *Malaunders*, which in the esteem of expert Farriers is no better disease, or else the story of *Ronypatifam*, or *Lamibaudichon*, interpreted by some to be the tale of a tub, or of a roasted horse, savours of *Apocrypha*, and is not an authentick history; and by this means there was that yeare great abundance throughout all the countrey of *Artois*, of tawny buzzing beetles, to the no small profit of the Gentlemen-great-stick-faggot-carriers, when they did eate without disdaining the *cocklicranes*, till their belly was like to crack with it again: as for my own part, such is my Christian charity towards my neighbours, that I could wish from my heart every one had as good a voice, it would make us play the better at the tennis and the baloon. And truly (*my Lord*) to expresse the real truth without dissimulation, I cannot but say, that those petty subtile devices, which are found out in the etymologizing of patins, would descend more easily into the river of *Seine*, to serve for ever at the Millars bridge upon the said water, as it was heretofore decreed by the King of the *Canarrians*, according to the sentence or judgement given thereupon, which is to be seen in the Registry and Records within the Clerks office of this house.

And therefore (my Lord) I do most humbly require, that by your Lordship there may be said and declared upon the case what is reasonable, with costs, damages, and interests. Then said *Pantagruel*, My friend, is this all you have to say? *Kissebreech* answered, Yes, (my Lord) for I have told all the *tu-autem*, and have not varied at all upon mine honour in so much as one single word. You then, (said *Pantagruel*) my Lord of *Suckfist*, say what you will, and be brief, without omitting neverthelesse any thing that may serve to the purpose.

CHAPTER XII

How the Lord of Suckfist pleaded before Pantagruel.

THEN began the Lord *Suckfist* in manner as followeth: *My Lord*, and you *my masters*, if the iniquity of men were as easily seene in categoricall judgement, as we can discerne flies in a milk-pot, the worlds four Oxen had not beene so eaten up with Rats, nor had so many eares upon the earth beene nibled away so scurvily; for although all that my adversary hath spoken be of a very soft and downy truth, in so much as concernes the Letter and History of the *factum*: yet neverthelesse the crafty slights, cunning subtilties, slie cosenages, and little troubling intanglements are hid under the Rose-pot, the common cloak and cover of all fraudulent deceits.

Should I endure, that, when I am eating my pottage equall with the best, and that without either thinking or speaking any manner of ill, they rudely come to vexe, trouble, and perplex my braines with that antick Proverb, which saith,

> *Who in his pottage-eating drinks will not*
> *When he is dead and buri'd, see one jot.*

and good Lady, how many great Captaines have we seen in the day of battel, when in open field the Sacrament was distributed in lunchions of the sanctified bread of the Confraternity, the more honestly to nod their heads, play on the lute, and crack with their tailes, to make pretty little platforme leaps, in keeping level by the ground: but now the world is unshackled from the corners of the packs of *Leycester*. One flies out lewdly and becomes debauch't, another likewise five, four and two, and that at such randome, that if the Court take not some course therein, it will make as bad a season in matter of gleaning this yeare, as ever it made, or it will make goblets. If any poor creature go to the stoves to illuminate his muzzle with a Cowshard, or to buy winter-boots, and that the Serjeants passing by, or those of the watch happen to receive the decoction of a clystere, or the fecal matter of a close-stool, upon their rustling-wrangling-clutter-keeping-masterships, should any because of that make bold to clip the shillings and testers, and fry the wooden dishes? sometimes, when we think one thing, God does another; and when the Sunne is wholly set, all beasts are in the shade: let me. never be beleeved again, if I do not gallantly prove it by several people that have seen the light of the day.

In the yeare thirty and six, buying a *Dutch* curtail, which was a middle sized horse, both high and short, of a wool good enough, and died in graine, as the Goldsmiths assured me, although the Notarie put an &c. in it; I told really, that I was not a Clerk of so much learning as to snatch at the Moon with my teeth; but as for the Butter-firkin, where *Vulcanian* deeds and evidences were sealed, the rumour was, and the report thereof went currant, that salt-beefe will make one finde the way to the wine without a candle, though it were hid in the bottom of a Colliers sack, and that with his drawers on he were mounted on a barbed horse furnished with a fronstal, and such armes, thighs and leg-pieces as are requisite for the well frying and broyling of a swaggering sawcinesse. Here is a sheeps head, and it is well they make a proverb of this, that it is good to see black Cowes in burnt wood, when one attains to the enjoyment of his love. I had a consultation upon this point with my Masters the Clerks, who for resolution concluded in *frisesomorum*, that there is nothing like to mowing in the summer, and sweeping clean away in water, well garnished with paper, ink, pens and penknives of *Lyons* upon the river of *Rosne; dolopym dolopof, tarabin tarabas, tut, prut, pish*: for incontinently after that armour begins to smell of garlick, the rust will go near to eat the liver, not of him that weares it, and then do they nothing else but withstand others courses, and wry-neckedly set up their bristles 'gainst one another, in lightly passing over their afternoons sleep, and this is that which maketh salt so dear. My Lords, beleeve not, when the said good woman had with bird-lime caught the shovelar fowle, the better before a Serjeants witnesse, to deliver the younger sons portion to him, that the sheeps pluck, or hogs haslet, did dodge and shrink back in the Usurers purses, or that there could be any thing better to preserve one from the Cannibals, then to make a rope of onions, knit with three hundred turneps, and a little of a Calves Chaldern of the best allay that the Alchymists have: provided, that they daub and do over with clay, as also calcinate and burne to dust these pantoffles, muf in muf out; *Mouflin mouflard*, with the fine sauce of the juice of the rabble rout, whilest they hide themselves in some petty mold-warphole, saving alwayes the little slices of bacon. Now if the dice will not favour you with any other throw but ambesace, and the chance of three at the great end, mark well the ace, then take me your dame, settle her in a corner of the bed, and whisk me her up drilletrille there there, *tourelouralala*, which when you have done, take a hearty draught of the best, *despicando grenovillibus*, in despight of the frogs; whose faire course be-buskined stockins shall be set apart for the little green geese, or mued goslings, which, fatned in a coope, take delight to sport themselves at the wagtaile game, waiting for the beating of the mettal, and heating of the waxe by the slavering drivellers of consolation.

Very true it is, that the foure oxen which are in debate, and whereof mention was made, were somewhat short in memory: neverthelesse, to understand the *gamme* aright, they feared neither the Cormorant nor Mallard of *Savoy*, which put the good people of my countrey in great hope, that their children some-time should become very skilful in *Algorisme*; therefore is it, that by a law rubrick and special sentence thereof, that we cannot faile to take the wolfe, if we make our hedges higher then the wind-mill, whereof somewhat was spoken by the Plaintiffe. But the great Devil did envie it, and by that means put the high *Dutches* farre behinde, who played the devils in swilling down and tipling at the good liquour, *trink meen herr, trink*, trink, by two of my table men in the corner-point I have gained the lurch; for it is not probable, nor is there any appearance of truth in this saying, that at *Paris* upon a little bridge the hen is proportion-able: and were they as copped and high-crested as marish whoops, if veritably they did not sacrifice the Printers pumpet-balls at *Moreb*, with a new edge set upon them by text letters, or those of a swift-writing hand, it is all one to me, so that the headband of the book breed not moths or wormes in it. And put the case, that at the coupling together of the buck-hounds, the little puppies should have waxed proud before the Notarie could have given an account of the serving of his Writ by the Cabalistick Art, it will necessarily follow (under correction of

213

the better judgement of the Court,) that six acres of medow ground of the greatest breadth, will make three butts of fine ink, without paying ready money; considering that at the Funeral of King *Charles*, we might have had the fathom in open market for one and two, that is, *deuce ace*: this I may affirm with a safe conscience, upon my oath of wooll.

And I see ordinarily in all good bagpipes, that when they go to the counterfeiting of the chirping of small birds, by swinging a broom three times about a chimney, and putting his name upon record, they do nothing but bend a Crossebowe backward, and winde a horne, if perhaps it be too hot, and that by making it fast to a rope he was to draw, immediately after the sight of the letters, the Cowes were restored to him. Such another sentence after the homeliest manner was pronounced in the seventeenth yeare, because of the bad government of *Louzefougarouse*, whereunto it may please the Court to have regard. I desire to be rightly understood; for truly I say not, but that in all equity, and with an upright conscience, those may very well be dispossest, who drink holy water, as one would do a weavers shuttle, whereof suppositories are made to those that will not resigne, but on the termes of ell and tell, and giving of one thing for another. *Tunc* (my Lords) *quid juris pro minoribus?* for the common custom of the *Salick* law is such, that the first incendiarie or fire-brand of sedition, that flayes the Cow, and wipes his nose in a full consort of musick, without blowing in the Coblers stitches, should in the time of the night-mare sublimate the penury of his member by mosse gathered when people are like to foundre themselves at the messe at midnight, to give the estrapade to these white-wines of *Anjou*, that do the feat of the leg in lifting it (by horsemen called the *Gambetta*,) and that neck to neck, after the fashion of *Britanie*, (concluding as before with costs, damages and interests).

After that the Lord of *Suckfist* had ended, *Pantagruel* said to the Lord of *Kissebreech*, My friend, have you a minde to make any reply to what is said? No, (my Lord) answered *Kissebreech*; for I have spoke all I intended, and nothing but the truth, therefore put an end for Gods sake to our difference, for we are here at great charge.

CHAPTER XIII

How Pantagruel gave judgement upon the difference of the two Lords.

THEN *Pantagruel* rising up, assembled all the Presidents, Counsellors and Doctors that were there, and said unto them: Come now (my Masters) you have heard (*vivæ vocis oraculo*) the Controversie that is in question; what do you think of it? They answered him, We have indeed heard it, but have not understood the devil so much as one circumstance of the case; and therefore we beseech you, *unâ voce*, and in courtesie request you, that you would give sentence as you think good, and *ex nunc prout ex tunc*, we are satisfied with it, and do ratifie it with our full consents: Well, my Masters (*said Pantagruel*) seeing you are so well pleased, I will do it: but I do not truly finde the case so difficult as you make it: your paragraph *Caton*: the law *Frater*, the law *Gallus*, the law *Quinque pedum*, the law *Vinum*, the law *Si Dominus*, the law *Mater*, the law *Mulier bona*, the law *Si quis*, the law *Pomponius*, the law *Fundi*, the law *Emptor*, the law *Prætor*, the law *Venditor*, and a great many others, are farre more intricate in my opinion. After he had spoke this, he walked a turn or two about the hall, plodding very profoundly, as one may think; for he did groan like an Asse, whilest they girth him too hard, with the very intensiveness of considering how he was bound in conscience to do right to both parties, without varying or accepting of persons. Then he returned, sate down, and began to pronounce sentence as followeth.

Having seen, heard, calculated and well considered of the difference between the Lords of *Kissebreech* and *Suckfist*; the Court saith unto them, that in regard of the sudden quaking, shivering and hoarinesse of the flickermouse, bravely declining from the estival soltice, to attempt by private means the surprisal of toyish trifles in those, who are a little unwell for having taken a draught too much, through the lewd demeanour and vexation of the beetles, that inhabit the *Diarodal* climate of an hyprocritical Ape on horseback, bending a Crossebow backwards, the Plaintiffe truly had just cause to calfet, or with *Ockam*, to

stop the chinks of the gallion, which the good woman blew up
with winde, having one foot shod and the other bare, reimburs-
ing and restoring to him low and stiffe in his conscience, as
many bladder-nuts and wilde pistaches as there is of haire in
eighteen Cowes, with as much for the embroiderer, and so
much for that. He is likewise declared innocent of the case priviledged from the *Knapdardies*, into the danger whereof it was
thought he had incurred; because he could not jocundly and
with fulnesse of freedom untrusse and dung, by the decision of
a paire of gloves perfumed with the sent of bum-gunshot, at the
walnut-tree taper, as is usual in his countrey of *Mirobalois*.
Slacking therefore the top-saile, and letting go the boulin with
the brazen bullets, where with the Mariners did by way of protestation bake in paste-meat, great store of pulse, interquilted
with the dormouse, whose hawks bells were made with a *punti-
naria*, after the manner of *Hungary* or *Flanders* lace, and which
his brother in law carried in a Panier, lying near to *three chevrons
or bordered gueules*, whilest he was clean out of heart, drooping
and crest-fallen by the too narrow sifting, canvassing, and curious examining of the matter, in the angularly doghole of nastie
scoundrels, from whence we shoot at the vermiformal popingay,
with the flap made of a foxtaile.

But in that he chargeth the Defendant, that he was a
botcher, cheese-eater, and trimmer of mans flesh imbalmed,
which in the arsiversie swagfall tumble was not found true, as
by the Defendant was very well discussed;

The Court therefore doth condemn and amerce him in three
porringers of curds, well cemented and closed together, shining
like pearles, and Codpieced after the fashion of the Countrey,
to be payed unto the said Defendant about the middle of *August*
in *May*: but, on the other part the Defendant shall be bound to
furnish him with hay and stubble, for stopping the caltrops of
his throat, troubled and impulregafized, with gabardines garbeled shufflingly, and friends as before, without costs, and for
cause.

Which sentence being pronounced, the two Parties departed
both contented with the decree, which was a thing almost incredible; for it never came to passe since the great rain, nor shall
the like occur in thirteen jubilees hereafter, that two Parties,

contradictorily contending in judgment, be equally satisfied and well pleased with the definitive sentence. As for the Counsellors, and other Doctors in the law, that were there present, they were all so ravished with admiration at the more then humane wisdom of *Pantagruel*, which they did most clearly perceive to be in him, by his so accurate decision of this so difficult and thornie cause, that their spirits, with the extremity of the rapture, being elevated above the pitch of actuating the organs of the body, they fell into a trance and sudden extasie, wherein they stayed for the space of three long houres, and had been so as yet in that condition, had not some good people fetched store of vineger and rosewater, to bring them again unto their former sense and understanding, for the which God be praised every where; And so be it.

CHAPTER XIV

How Panurge related the manner how he escaped out of the hands of the Turks.

THE great wit and judgement of *Pantagruel*, was immediately after this made known unto all the world, by setting forth his praises in print, and putting upon record this late wonderful proof he hath given thereof amongst the Rolls of the Crown, and Registers of the Palace, in such sort, that every body began to say, that *Solomon*, who by a probable guesse only, without any further certainty, caused the childe to be delivered to its own mother, shewed never in his time such a Masterpiece of wisdom, as the good *Pantagruel* hath done; happy are we therefore that have him in our Countrey. And indeed they would have made him thereupon Master of the Requests, and President in the Court: but he refused all, very graciously thanking them for their offer, for (said he) there is too much slavery in these offices, and very hardly can they be saved that do exercise them, considering the great corruption that is amongst men: which makes me beleeve, if the empty seats of Angels be not fil'd with other kind of people then those, we shall not have the final judgement these seven thousand sixty and seven jubilees yet to come; and so *Cusanus* will be deceived in his conjecture:

Remember that I have told you of it, and given you faire advertisement in time and place convenient.

But if you have any hogsheads of good wine, I willingly will
accept of a present of that, which they very heartily did do, in
sending him of the best that was in the City, and he drank
reasonably well, but poor *Panurge* bibbed and bowsed of it most
villainously, for he was as dry as a red-herring, as lean as a rake,
and like a poor, lank, slender cat, walked gingerly as if he had
trod upon egges: so that by some one being admonished, in the
midst of his draught of a large deep bowle, full of excellent
Claret, with these words, Faire and softly, *Gossip*, you suck up
as if you were mad; I give thee to the devil, (said he) thou hast
not found here thy little tipling sippers of *Paris*, that drink no
more then the little bird called a *spink* or *chaffinch*, and never
take in their beak ful of liquour, till they be bobbed on the tailes
after the manner of the sparrows. O companion, if I could
mount up as well as I can get down, I had been long ere this
above the sphere of the Moon with *Empedocles*. But I cannot tell
what a devil this meanes. This wine is so good and delicious,
that the more I drink thereof, the more I am athirst; I beleeve
that the shadow of my Master *Pantagruel*, engendereth the
altered and thirsty men, as the Moon doth the catarres and
defluxions; at which word the company began to laugh: which
Pantagruel perceiving, said, *Panurge*, What is that which moves
you to laugh so? Sir, said he, I was telling them that these devillish *Turks* are very unhappy, in that they never drink one drop
of wine, and that though there were no other harme in all
Mahomets Alcoran, yet for this one base point of abstinence from
wine, which therein is commanded, I would not submit my self
unto their law. But now tell me, (said *Pantagruel*) how you
escaped out of their hands. By G— Sir, (said *Panurge*) I will not
lie to you in one word.

The rascally *Turks* had broached me upon a spit all larded
like a rabbet, (for I was so dry and meagre, that otherwise of my
flesh they would have made but very bad meat) and in this manner began to rost me alive. As they were thus roasting me, I
recommended my self unto the divine grace, having in my
minde the good St. *Lawrence*, and alwayes hoped in God that he
would deliver me out of this torment, which came to passe, and

218

that very strangely; for as I did commit my self with all my heart unto God, crying, Lord God, help me, Lord God, save me, Lord God, take me out of this paine and hellish torture, wherein these traiterous dogs detain me for my sincerity in the maintenance of thy law: the roster or turn-spit fell asleep by the divine will, or else by the vertue of some good *Mercury*, who cunningly brought *Argus* into a sleep for all his hundred eyes: when I saw that he did no longer turne me in roasting, I looked upon him, and perceived that he was fast asleep, then took I up in my teeth a firebrand by the end where it was not burnt, and cast it into the lap of my roaster, and another did I throw as well as I could under a field-couche, that was placed near to the chimney, wherein was the straw-bed of my Master turnspit; presently the fire took hold in the straw, and from the straw to the bed, and from the bed to the loft, which was planked and seeled with firre, after the fashion of the foot of a lamp: but the best was, that the fire which I had cast into the lap of my paultry roaster, burnt all his groine, and was beginning to seize upon his cullions, when he became sensible of the danger, for his smelling was not so bad, but that he felt it sooner then he could have seen daylight: then suddenly getting up, and in a great amazement running to the window, he cried out to the streets as high as he could, *dalbaroth, dalbaroth, dalbaroth*, which is as much to say as, *Fire, fire, fire*: incontinently turning about, he came streight towards me, to throw me quite into the fire, and to that effect had already cut the ropes, wherewith my hands were tied, and was undoing the cords from off my feet; when the Master of the house hearing him cry, Fire, and smelling the smoke from the very street where he was walking with some other *Baashaws and Mustaphaes*, ran with all the speed he had to save what he could, and to carry away his Jewels; yet such was his rage (before he could well resolve how to go about it,) that he caught the broach whereon I was spitted, and therewith killed my roaster stark dead, of which wound he died there for want of government or otherwise; for he ran him in with the spit a little above the navel, towards the right flank, till he pierced the third lappet of his liver, and, the blow slanting upwards from the midriffe or *diaphragme*, through which it had made penetration, the spit passed athwart the *pericardium*, or capsule of his heart, and came out above at his shoulders, betwixt the *spondyls* or turning joints of the chine of the back, and the left *homoplat*, which we call the shoulder-blade.

True it is, (for I will not lie,) that, in drawing the spit out of my body, I fell to the ground near unto the Andirons, and so by the fall took some hurt, which indeed had been greater, but that the *lardons*, or little slices of bacon, wherewith I was stuck, kept off the blow. My *Baashaw* then seeing the case to be desperate, his house burnt without remission, and all his goods lost, gave himselfe over unto all the devils in hell, calling upon some of them by their names, *Gringoth, Astaroth, Rappalus*, and *Gribouillis*, nine several times, which when I saw, I had above six pence worth of feare, dreading that the devils would come even then to carry away this foole, and seeing me so near him would perhaps snatch me up too: I am already (thought I) halfe rosted, and my lardons, will be the cause of my mischief; for these devils are very lickorous of lardons, according to the authority which you have of the Philosopher *Jamblicus*, and *Murmault*, in the Apology of *Bossutis*, adulterated *pro magistros nostros*: but for my better security I made the signe of the Crosse; crying *Hagios, athanatos, ho theos*, and none came: at which my rogue *Baashaw* being very much aggrieved, would in transpiercing his heart with my spit have killed himself; and to that purpose had set it against his breast, but it could not enter, because it was not sharp enough; whereupon I perceiving that he was not like to work upon his body the effect which he intended, although he did not spare all the force he had to thrust it forward, came up to him and said, Master *Bugrino*, thou dost here but trifle away thy time, or rashly lose it, for thou wilt never kill thy self as thou doest: well thou mayest hurt or bruise somewhat within thee, so as to make thee languish all thy lifetime most pitifully amongst the hands of the Chirurgions; but if thou wilt be counselled by me, I will kill thee clear out-right, so that thou shalt not so much as feel it, and trust me, for I have killed a great many others, who have found themselves very well after it: Ha, my friend, said he, I prethee do so, and for thy paines I will give thee my Codpiece; take, here it is, there are six hundred Seraphs in it, and some fine Diamonds, and most excellent Rubies. And, where are they (said *Epistemon*?) By St. *John* (said *Panurge*) they are a good way hence, if they alwayes keep going: but where is the last yeares snow? this was the greatest care that *Villon* the *Parisien* Poet took. Make an end (said *Pantagruel*) that we may know how thou didst dresse thy *Baashaw*: By the faith of an honest man (said *Panurge*) I do not lie in one word. I swadled him in a scurvie swathel-binding, which I found lying there half burnt, and with my cords tied him royster-like both hand and foot, in such sort that he was not able to winse; then past my spit thorough his throat, and hanged him thereon, fastening the end thereof at two great hooks or cramp-irons, upon which they did hang their Halberds; and then kindling a faire fire under him, did flame you up my *Milourt*, as they use to do dry herrings in a chimney: with this, taking his budget, and a little javelin that was upon the foresaid hooks, I ran away a faire gallop-rake, and God he knows how I did smell my shoulder of mutton.

When I was come down into the street, I found every body come to put out the fire with store of water, and seeing me so halfe-roasted, they did naturally pity my case, and threw all their water upon me, which by a most joyful refreshing of me, did me very much good: then did they present me with some victuals, but I could not eat much, because they gave me nothing to drink but water after their fashion. Other hurt they did me none, only one little villainous *Turkie* knobbreasted rogue, came thiefteously to snatch away some of my lardons, but I gave him such a sturdie thump and sound rap on the fingers, with all the weight of my javelin, that he came no more the second time. Shortly after this, there came towards me a pretty young *Corinthian* wench, who brought me a box full of Conserves, of round *Mirabolan* plums, called *Emblicks*, and looked upon my poor *Robin* with an eye of great compassion, as it was flea-bitten and pinked with the sparkles of the fire from whence it came, for it reached no further in length, (beleeve me) then my knees; but note, that this roasting cured me entirely of a Sciatick, whereunto I had been subject about seven yeares before, upon that side, which my roaster, by falling asleep, suffered to be burnt.

Now whilest they were thus busie about me, the fire triumphed, never ask, How? for it took hold on above two thousand houses, which one of them espying cried out, saying,

By *Mahooms* belly all the City is on fire, and we do neverthelesse stand gazing here, without offering to make any relief: upon this every one ran to save his own; for my part, I took my way towards the gate. When I was got upon the knap of a little hillock, not farre off, I turned me about as did *Lots* wife, and looking back, saw all the City burning in a faire fire, whereat I was so glad, that I had almost beshit my selfe for joy: but God punished me well for it: How? said *Pantagruel*: Thus, said *Panurge*; for when with pleasure I beheld this jolly fire, jesting with my self, and saying, Ha poor flies, ha poor mice, you will have a bad winter of it this yeare, the fire is in your reeks, it is in your bed-straw,—out came more then six, yea more than thirteen hundred and eleven dogs great and small, altogether out of the town, flying away from the fire; at the first approach they ran all upon me, being carried on by the sent of my leacherous half-roasted flesh, and had even then devoured me in a trice, if my good Angel had not well inspired me with the instruction of a remedy, very sovereign against the tooth-ache. And wherefore (said *Pantagruel*) wert thou afraid of the toothache, or paine of the teeth? wert thou not cured of thy Rheumes? By Palme-sunday, (said *Panurge*) is there any greater pain of the teeth, then when the dogs have you by the legs? but on a sudden, (as my good Angel directed me) I thought upon my lardons, and threw them into the midst of the field amongst them: then did the dogs run, and fight with one another at faire teeth, which should have the lardons: by this means they left me, and I left them also bustling with, and hairing one another. Thus did I escape frolick and lively, grammercie roastmeat and cookery.

CHAPTER XV

How Panurge shewed a very new way to build the walls of Paris.

PANTAGRUEL one day to refresh himself of his study, went a walking towards St. *Marcels* suburbs, to see the extravagancie of the *Gobeline* building, and to taste of their spiced bread. *Panurge* was with him, having alwayes a flaggon under his gown, and a good slice of a gammon of bacon; for without this he never went, saying, that it was as a Yeoman of the guard to him, to preserve his body from harme, other sword carried he none: and when *Pantagruel* would have given him one, he answered, that he needed none, for that it would but heat his milt. Yea, but (said *Epistemon*) if thou shouldest be set upon, how wouldest thou defend thy self? With great *buskinades* or brodkin blowes, answered he, provided thursts were forbidden. At their return, *Panurge* considered the walls of the City of *Paris*, and in derision said to *Pantagruel*, See what faire walls here are! O how strong they are, and well fitted to keep geese in a mue or coop to fatten them! by my beard they are competently scurvie for such a City as this is; for a Cow with one fart would go near to overthrow above six fathoms of them. O my friend (said *Pantagruel*) doest thou know what *Agesilaus* said, when he was asked, Why the great City of *Lacedemon* was not inclosed with walls? Lo here (said he) the walls of the City, in shewing them the inhabitants and Citizens thereof, so strong, so well armed, and so expert in military discipline; signifying thereby, that there is no wall but of bones, and that Towns and Cities cannot have a surer wall, nor better fortification, then the prowesse and vertue of the Citizens and Inhabitants; so is this City so strong, by the great number of warlike people that are in it, that they care not for making any other walls. Besides, whosoever would go about to wall it, as *Strasbourg*, *Orleans*, or *Ferrara*, would finde it almost impossible, the cost and charges would be so excessive. Yea, but (said *Panurge*) it is good neverthelesse to have an out-side of stone, when we are invaded by our enemies, were it but to ask, Who is below there? As for the enormous expence, which you say would be needful for undertaking the great work of walling this City about, if the Gentlemen of the Town will be pleased to give me a good rough cup of wine, I will shew them a pretty, strange and new way, how they may build them good cheap. How (said *Pantagruel*?) Do not speak of it then (answered *Panurge*,) and I will tell it you. I see that the *sine quo nons*, *killibistris*, or *contrapunctums* of the women of this Countrey, are better cheap then stones: of them should the walls be built, ranging them in good symmetrie by the rules of Architecture, and plac-ing the largest the first ranks, then sloping downwards ridge-wayes, like the back of an Asse, the middle sized ones must be ranked next, and last of all the least and smallest. This done, there must be a fine little interlacing of them, like points of Diamonds, as is to be seen in the great Tower of *Bourges*, with a like number of the *nudinnudo's, nilnisistando's*, and stiffe *bracmards*, that dwell in amongst the claustral Codpieces. What devil were able to overthrow such walls? there is no metal like it to resist blowes, in so farre that if Culverin-shot should come to grease upon it, you would incontinently see distill from thence the blessed fruit of the great pox, as small as raine: beware in the name of the devils, and hold off; furthermore, no thunderbolt or lightning would fall upon it, for why? they are all either blest or consecrated: I see but one inconveniency in it ho: ho, ha, ha, ha! (said *Pantagruel*,) and what is that? It is that the flies would be so lickorish of them, that you would wonder, and would quickly gather there together, and there leave their ordure and excretions, and so all the work would be spoiled. But see how that might be remedied, they must be wiped and made rid of the flies with faire fox-tailes, or good great *viedazes* (which are Asse-pizzles) of *Provence*. And to this purpose I will tell you (as we go to supper,) a brave example set down by *Frater Lubinus libro de compotationibus mendicantium*; in the time that the beasts did speak, which is not yet three dayes since.

A poor Lion, walking through the forrest of *Bieure*, and saying his own little private devotions, past under a tree, where there was a roguish Collier gotten up to cut down wood, who seeing the Lion, cast his hatchet at him, and wounded him enormously in one of his legs, whereupon the Lion halting, he so long toiled and turmoiled himself in roaming up and down the forrest to finde helpe, that at last he met with a Carpenter, who willingly look't upon his wound, cleansed it as well as he could, and filled it with mosse, telling him that he must wipe his wound well, that the flies might not do their excrements in it, whilest he should go search for some yarrow or millefoile, commonly called the Carpenters herbe. The Lion, being thus healed, walked along in the forrest, at what time a sempiternous Crone and old Hag, was picking up and gathering some sticks in the said forrest, who seeing the Lion coming towards her, for feare fell down backwards, in such sort, that the winde blew up her gown, coats and smock, even as farre as above her shoulders;

which the Lion perceiving, for pity ran to see whether she had taken any hurt by the fall, and thereupon considering her *how do you call it* said, O poor woman, who hath thus wounded thee? which words when he had spoken, he espied a fox, whom he called to come to him, saying, *Gossip Renard*, hau, hither, hither, and for cause: when the fox was come, he said unto him, My gossip and friend, they have hurt this good woman here between the legs most villainously, and there is a manifest solution of continuity, see how a great wound it is, even from the taile up to the navel, in measure foure, nay full five handfulls and a half; this is the blow of an hatchet, I doubt me it is an old wound, and therefore that the flies may not get into it, wipe it lustily well and hard; I prethy, both within and without; thou hast a good taile and long, wipe, my friend, wipe, I beseech thee, and in the mean while I will go get some mosse to put into it; for thus ought we to succour and help one another, wipe it hard, thus, my friend, wipe it well, for this wound must be often wiped, otherwise the Party cannot be at ease: go to, wipe well, my little gossip, wipe, God hath furnished thee with a taile, thou hast a long one, and of a bignesse proportionable, wipe hard, and be not weary. A good *wiper*, who, in *wiping* continually *wipeth* with his *wipard*, by wasps shall never be wounded: wipe, my pretty minion, wipe, my little bullie, I will not stay long. Then went he to get store of mosse; and, when he was a little way off, he cried out in speaking to the fox thus, Wipe well still, gossip, wipe, and let it never grieve thee to wipe well, my little gossip, I will put thee into service to be wiper to *Don Pedro de Castille*, wipe, only wipe, and no more: the poor fox wiped as hard as he could, here and there, within and without; but the false old trot did so fizzle and fist, that she stunk like a hundred devils, which put the poor fox to a great deal of ill ease, for he knew not to what side to turn himself, to escape the unsavoury perfume of this old womans postern blasts, and whilest to that effect he was shifting hither and thither, without knowing how to shun the annoyance of those unwholesom gusts, he saw that behinde there was yet another hole, not so great as that which he did wipe out of which came this filthy and infectious aire. The Lion at last returned, bringing with him of mosse more then eighteen packs would hold, and began to put into the wound,

225

with a staffe that which he had provided for that purpose, and
had already put in full sixteen packs and a half, at which he was
amazed: What a devil? (said he) this wound is very deep, it
would hold above two cart-loads of mosse. The fox perceiving
this, said unto the Lion, O gossip Lion, my friend, I pray thee,
do not put in all thy mosse there, keep somewhat, for there is yet
here another little hole, that stinks like five hundred devils; I
am almost choaked with the smell thereof, it is so pestiferous
and impoisoning.

Thus must these walls be kept from the flies, and wages
allowed to some for wiping of them. Then said *Pantagruel*, How
dost thou know that the privy parts of women are at such cheap
rate? for in this City there are many vertuous, honest and chaste
women besides the maids: *Et ubi prenus*, said *Panurge*? I will give
you my opinion of it, and that upon certain and assured knowledge. I do not brag that I have bumbasted four hundred and
seventeen, since I came into this City, though it be but nine
dayes ago: but this very morning I met with a good fellow, who
in a wallet, such as *Æsops* was, carried two little girles of two or
three yeares old at the most, one before, and the other behinde:
he demanded almes of me, but I made him answer, that I had
more cods then pence; afterwards I asked him, *Good man*, these
two girles are they maids? Brother, said he, I have carried them
thus these two yeares, and in regard of her that is before, whom
I see continually, in my opinion she is a Virgin, neverthelesse I
will not put my finger in the fire for it; as for her that is behinde,
doubtlesse I can say nothing. Indeed (said *Pantagruel*) thou art
a gentile companion, I will have thee to be apparelled in my
livery, and therefore caused him to be clothed most gallantly
according to the fashion that then was, only that *Panurge* would
have the Codpiece of his breeches three foot long, and in shape
square, not round, which was done and was well worth the
seeing. Oftentimes was he wont to say, that the world had not
yet known the emolument and utility that is in wearing great
Codpieces; but time would one day teach it them, as all things
have been invented in time. God keep from hurt (said he) the
good fellow whose long Codpiece or Braguet hath saved his life:
God keep from hurt him, whose long Braguet hath been worth
to him in one day, one hundred three-score thousand and nine

Crowns! God keep from hurt him, who by his long Braguet hath saved a whole City from dying by famine. And by G— I will make a book of the commodity of long Braguets, when I shall have more leasure. And indeed he composed a faire great book with figures, but it is not printed as yet that I know of.

CHAPTER XVI

Of the qualities and conditions of Panurge.

PANURGE was of a middle stature, not too high, not too low, and had somewhat an Aquiline nose, made like the handle of a rasor: he was at that time five and thirty years old or there-abouts, fine to gild like a leaden dagger; for he was a notable cheater and cony-catcher, he was a very gallant and proper man of his person, only that he was a little leacherous, and naturally subject to a kinde of disease, which at that time they called lack of money: it is an incomparable grief, yet notwithstanding he had threescore and three tricks to come by it at his need, of which the most honourable and most ordinary was in manner of thieving, secret purloining and filching; for he was a wicked lewd rogue, a cosener, drinker, royster, rover, and a very dissolute and debautch'd fellow, if there were any in *Paris*; otherwise, and in all matters else, the best and most vertuous man in the world: and he was still contriving some plot, and devising mischief against the Serjeants and the watch.

At one time he assembled three or four especial good hacksters and roaring boyes, made them in the evening drink like *Templers*, afterwards led them till they came under St. *Genevieve*, or about the Colledge of *Navarre*, and at the houre that the watch was coming up that way, which he knew by putting his sword upon the pavement, and his eare by it, and, when he heard his sword shake, it was an infallible signe that the watch was near at that instant: then he and his companions took a tumbrel or dung-cart, and gave it the brangle, hurling it with all their force down the hill, and so overthrew all the poor watchmen like pigs, and then ran away upon the other side; for in lesse then two dayes, he knew all the streets, lanes and turning in *Paris*, as well as his *Deus det*.

At another time he made in some faire place, where the said watch was to passe, a traine of gun-powder, and, at the very instant, that they went along, set fire to it, and then made himself sport to see what good grace they had in running away, thinking that St. *Antonies* fire had caught them by the legs. As for the poor Masters of Arts, he did persecute them above all others: when he encountered with any of them upon the street, he would not never faile to put some trick or other upon them, sometimes putting the bit of a fried turd in their graduate hoods: At other times pinning on little fox-tails, or hares-eares behind them, or some such other roguish prank. One day that they were appointed all to meet in the *fodder-street*, he made a *Borbonesa* tart, or filthy and slovenly compound, made of store of garlick, of *Assa fœtida*, of *Castoreum*, of dogs turds very warm, which he steeped, temper'd and liquifi'd in the corrupt matter of pockie biles, and pestiferous botches, and, very early in the morning, therewith anointed all the pavement, in such sort, that the devil could not have endured it, which made all these good people, there to lay up their gorges and vomit what was upon their stomacks before all the world, as if they had flayed the fox; and ten or twelve of them died of the plague, fourteen became lepers, eighteen grew lousie, and above seven and twenty had the pox, but he did not care a button for it. He commonly carried a whip under his gowne wherewith he whipt without remission the pages, whom he found carrying wine to their Masters, to make them mend their pace. In his coat he had above six and twenty little fabs and pockets alwayes full, one with some lead-water, and a little knife as sharp as a glovers needle, wherewith he used to cut purses: Another with some kinde of bitter stuffe, which he threw into the eyes of those he met: another with clotburrs, penned with little geese or capons feathers, which he cast upon the gowns and caps of honest people, and often made them faire hornes, which they wore about all the City, sometimes all their life. Very often also upon the womens *French* hoods would he stick in the hind-part somewhat made in the shape of a mans member. In another he had a great many little hornes full of fleas and lice, which he borrowed from the beggars of St. *Innocent*, and cast them with small canes or quills to write with, into the necks of the daintiest Gentlewomen that he could finde, yea even in the Church, for he never seated himself above in the quire, but alwayes sate in the body of the Church amongst the women, both at Masse, at Vespres, and at Sermon. In another, he used to have good store of hooks and buckles, wherewith he would couple men and women together, that sate in company close to one another, but especially those that wore gownes of crimson taffaties, that when they were about to go away, they might rent all their gownes. In another, he had a squib furnished with tinder, matches, stones to strike fire, and all other tackling necessary for it: in another, two or three burning glasses, wherewith he made both men and women sometimes mad, and in the Church put them quite out of countenance; for he said that there was but an *Antistrophe*, or little more difference then of a literal inversion between a woman, *folle a la messe*, and *molle a la fesse*; that is, *foolish at the Masse*, and *of a plaint buttock*.

In another he had a good deal of needles and thread, wherewith he did a thousand little devillish pranks. One time at the entry of the Palace unto the great Hall, where a certain gray Friar or *Cordelier* was to say Masse to the Counsellors: He did help to apparel him, and put on his vestments, but in the accoutring of him, he sowed on his alb, surplice or stole to his gowne and shirt, and then withdrew himself, when the said Lords of the Court, or Counsellors came to heare the said Masse; but when it came to the *Ite missa est*, that the poor *Frater* would have laid by his *stole* or surplice (as the fashion then was) he plucked off withal both his frock and shirt which were well sowed together, and thereby stripping himself up to the very shoulders, shewed his *bel vedere* to all the world, together with his *Don Cypriano*, which was no small one, as you may imagine: and the Friar still kept haling, but so much the more did he discover himself, and lay open his back-parts, till one of the Lords of the Court said, How now, what's the matter? will this faire Father make us here an offering of his taile to kisse it? nay, St. *Antonies* fire kisse it for us. From thenceforth it was ordained that the poor fathers should never disrobe themselves any more before the world, but in their vestry-room, or sextry, as they call it; especially in the presence of women, lest it should tempt them to the sin of longing, and disordinate desire. The people then asked, why it was the Friars had so long and large genitories? the said *Panurge* resolved the *Probleme* very neatly, saying, That which makes Asses to have such great eares is that their dams did put no biggins on their heads, as *Alliaco* mentioneth in his *suppositions*: by the like reason, that which makes the genitories or generation-tooles of those so faire Fraters so long is, for that they ware no bottomed breeches, and therefore their jolly member, having no impediment, hangeth dangling at liberty, as farre as it can reach, with a wigle-wagle down to their knees, as women carry their *patinotre* beads: and the cause wherefore they have it so correspondently great is, that in this constant wig-wagging, the humours of the body descend into the said member, for, according to the *Legists*, Agitation and continual motion is cause of attraction.

Item, he had another pocket full of itching powder, called *stone-allum*, whereof he would cast some into the backs of those women, whom he judged to be most beautiful and stately, which did so ticklishly gall them, that some would strip themselves in the open view of the world, and others dance like a cock upon hot embers, or a drumstick on a taber: others again ran about the streets, and he would run after them: to such as were in the stripping veine, he would very civilly come to offer his attendance, and cover them with his cloak, like a courteous and very gracious man.

Item, in another he had a little leather bottle full of old oile, wherewith, when he saw any man or woman in a rich new handsome suit, he would grease, smutch and spoile all the best parts of it under colour and pretence of touching them, saying, This is good cloth, this is good sattin, good taffaties: *Madam*, God give you all that your noble heart desireth; you have a new suit, *pretty Sir*; and you a new gown, *sweet Mistris*, God give you joy of it, and maintain you in all prosperity! and with this would lay his hand upon their shoulder, at which touch such a villainous spot was left behind, so enormously engraven to perpetuity in the very soule, body and reputation, that the devil himself could never have taken it away: Then upon his departing, he would say, *Madam*, take heed you do not fall, for there is a filthy great hole before you, whereinto if you put your foot, you will quite spoile your selfe. Another he had all full of *Euphorbium*,

very finely pulverised, in that powder did he lay a faire handkerchief curiously wrought, which he had stollen from a pretty
Seamstresse of the Palace, in taking away a lowse from off her
bosome, which he had put there himself: and when he came
into the company of some good Ladies, he would trifle them
into a discourse of some fine workmanship of bone-lace, then
immediately put his hand into their bosome asking them, and
this work, is it of *Flanders*, or of *Hainault*? and then drew out his
handkerchief, and said, Hold, hold, look what work here is, it is
of *Foutiaman* or of *Fontarabia*, and shaking it hard at their nose,
made them sneeze foure houres without ceasing: in the mean
while he would fart like a horse, and the women would laugh
and say, How now, do you fart, *Panurge?* No, no, *Madam* (said
he,) I do but tune my taile to the plain song of the Musick,
which you make with your nose. In another he had a picklock,
a pellican, a crampiron, a crook, and some other iron tooles,
wherewith there was no door nor coffer which he would not pick
open. He had another full of little cups, wherewith he played
very artificially, for he had his fingers made to his hand, like
those of *Minerva* or *Arachne*, and had heretofore cried *Triacle*.
And when he changed a teston, cardecu, or any other piece of
money, the changer had been more subtil then a fox, if *Panurge*
had not at every time made five or six sols (that is some six or
seven pence) vanish away invisibly, openly and manifestly,
without making any hurt or lesion, whereof the changer should
have felt nothing but the winde.

CHAPTER XVII

How Panurge gained the pardons, and married the old women,
and of the suit in law which he had at Paris.

ONE day I found *Panurge* very much out of countenance, melancholick and silent, which made me suspect that he had no
money; whereupon I said unto him, *Panurge*, you are sick, as I
do very well perceive by your physiognomie, and I know the
disease, you have a flux in your purse; but take no care. I have
yet seven pence half penny, that never saw father nor mother,
which shall not be wanting, no more than the pox in your

necessity: whereunto he answered me, Well, well, for money one day I shall have but too much; for I have a Philosophers stone, which attracts money out of mens purses, as the adamant doth iron; but will you go with me to gaine the pardons, said he? By my faith (said he) I am no great pardon-taker in this world; if I shall be any such in the other, I cannot tell; yet let us go in Gods name, it is but one farthing more or lesse. But (said he) lend me then a farthing upon interest. No, no, (said I) I will give it to you freely, and from my heart. *Grates vobis dominos*, said he.

So we went along, beginning at St. *Gervase*, and I got the pardons at the first boxe only, for in those matters very little contenteth me: then did I say my small suffrages, and the prayers of St. *Brigid*, but he gained them at all the boxes, and alwayes gave money to every one of the Pardoners; from thence we went to our *Ladies* Church, to St. *Johns*, to St. *Antonies*, and so to the other Churches, where there was a banquet of pardons. For my part, I gained no more of them: but he at all the boxes kissed the relicks, and gave at every one: to be brief, when we were returned, he brought me to drink at the Castle-tavern, and there shewed me ten or twelve of his little bags full of money, at which I blest my self, and made the signe of the Crosse, saying, Where have you recovered so much money in so little time? unto which he answered me, that he had taken it out of the basins of the pardons; For in giving them the first farthing (said he) I put it in with such slight of hand, and so dexterously, that it appeared to be a three-pence; thus with one hand I took three-pence, nine-pence, or six-pence at the least, and with the other as much, and so thorough all the Churches where we have been. Yea, but (said I) you damn your selfe like a snake, and art withal a thief and sacrilegious person. True (said he) in your opinion, but I am not of that minde; for the Pardoners do give me it, when they say unto me in presenting the relicks to kisse, *Centuplum accipies*, that is, that for one penny I should take a hundred; for *accipies* is spoken according to the manner of the Hebrewes, who use the future tense in stead of the imperative, as you have in the law, *Diliges Dominum*, that is, *dilige*: even so when the Pardon-bearer sayes to me, *Centuplum accipies*, his meaning is, *Centuplum accipe*; and so doth *Rabbi Kimy*, and *Rabbi Aben Ezra* expound it, and all the *Massorets*, & *ibi Bartholus*.

Moreover, Pope *Sixtus* gave me fifteen hundred francks of year-ly pension (which in *English* money is a hundred and fifty pounds) upon his Ecclesiastical revenues and treasure, for hav-ing cured him of a canckrous botch, which did so torment him, that he thought to have been a cripple by it all his life. Thus I do pay my self at my owne hand (for otherwise I get nothing) upon the said Ecclesiastical treasure. Ho, my friend (said he) if thou didst know what advantage I made, and how well I feathered my nest, by the Popes bull of the Croisade, thou wouldest wonder exceedingly. It was worth to me above six thousand *florins* (in *English* coine six hundred pounds), and what a devil is become of them? (said I) for of that money thou hast not one half penny. They returned from whence they came (said he) they did no more but change their Master.

But I employed at least three thousand of them (that is, three hundred pounds *English*,) in marrying (not young Virgins; for they finde but too many husbands) but great old sempiternous trots, which had not so much as one tooth in their heads; and that out of the consideration I had, that these good old women had very well spent the time of their youth in playing at the close-buttock-game to all commers, serving the foremost first, till no man would have any more dealing with them. And by G—, I will have their skin-coat shaken once yet before they die; by this means, to one I gave a hundred florins, to another six score, to another three hundred, according to that they were infamous, detestable and abominable; for, by how much the more horrible and execrable they were, so much the more must I needs have given them, otherwayes the devil would not have jum'd them. Presently I went to some great and fat woodporters, or such like, and did my selfe make the match, but before I did shew him the old Hags, I made a faire muster to him of the Crownes saying, Good fellow, see what I will give thee, if thou wilt but condescend to dufle, dinfredaille, or lecher it one good time: then began the poor rogues to gape like old mules, and I caused to be provided for them a banquet, with drink of the best, and store of spiceries, to put the old women in rut and heat of lust. To be short, they occupied all, like good soules; only to those that were horribly ugly and ill-favoured, I caused their head to be put within a bag, to hide their face.

233

Besides all this, I have lost a good deal in suits of law: And what lawsuits couldest thou have? (said I) thou hast neither house nor lands. My friend, (said he) the Gentlewomen of this City had found out, by the instigation of the devil of hell, a manner of high-mounted bands, and neckerchiefs for women, which so closely cover their bosomes, that men could no more put their hands under; for they had put the slit behinde, and those neckcloths were wholly shut before, whereat the poor sad comtemplative lovers were much discontented. Upon a faire *Tuesday*, I presented a Petition to the Court, making my self a Party against the said Gentlewomen, and shewing the great interest that I pretended therein, protesting that by the same reason, I would cause the Codpeece of my breeches to be sowed behinde, if the Court would not take order for it. In summe, the Gentlewomen put in their defences, shewed the grounds they went upon, and constituted their Atturney for the prosecuting of the cause, but I pursued them so vigorously, that by a sentence of the Court it was decreed, those high neckclothes should be no longer worne, if they were not a little cleft and open before, but it cost me a good summe of money. I had another very filthy and beastly processe against the dung-farmer (called master *Fifi*) and his Deputies, that they should no more reade privily the pipe, punchon, nor quart of sentences, but in faire full day, and that in the fodder schools, in face of the *Arrian* Sophisters, where I was ordained to pay the charges, by reason of some clause mistaken in the relation of the Serjeant. Another time I framed a complaint to the Court against the mules of the Presidents, Counsellors and others, tending to this purpose, that when in the lower Court of the Palace they left them to champ on their bridles, some bibs were made for them, that with their drivelling they might not spoile the pavement, to the end, that the Pages of the Palace might play upon it with their dice, or at the game of coxbody, at their own ease, without spoiling their breeches at the knees; and for this I had a faire decree, but it cost me deare. Now reckon up what expence I was at in little banquets, which from day to day I made to the Pages of the Palace, and to what end, said I? My friend (said he) thou hast no passe-time at all in this world. I have more then the King, and if thou wilt joyne thy self with me, we will do the devil together. No, no, (said I) by St. *Adauras*, that will I not, for thou wilt be hanged one time or another. And thou (said he) wilt be interred sometime or other; now which is most honourable, the aire or the earth? Ho, grosse pecore, whilest the Pages are at their banqueting, I keep their mules, and to some one I cut the stirrup-leather of the mounting side, till it hang but by a thin strap or thread, that when the great puffeguts of the Counsellor or some other hath taken his swing to get up, he may fall flat on his side like a pork, and so furnish the Spectators with more then a hundred francks worth of laughter. But I laugh yet further, to think how at his home-coming the Master-page is to be whipt like green rie, which makes me not to repent what I have bestowed in feasting them. In brief, he had (as I said before) threescore and three wayes to acquire mony, but he had two hundred and fourteen to spend it, besides his drinking.

CHAPTER XVIII

How a great Scholar of England would have argued against Pantagruel, and was overcome by Panurge.

IN that same time, a certain learned man, named *Thaumast*, hearing the fame and renown of *Pantagruels* incomparable knowledge, came out of his own countrey of *England*, with an intent only to see him, to try thereby, and prove, whether his knowledge in effect was so great as it was reported to be. In this resolution, being arrived at *Paris*, he went forthwith unto the house of the said *Pantagruel*, who was lodged in the Palace of St. *Denys*, and was then walking in the garden thereof with *Panurge*, philosophizing after the fashion of the Peripateticks. At his first entrance he startled, and was almost out of his wits for feare, seeing him so great and so tall, then did he salute him courteously as the manner is, and said unto him, Very true it is, (saith *Plato* the Prince of Philosophers,) that if the image and knowledge of wisdom were corporeal and visible to the eyes of mortals, it would stirre up all the world to admire her: which we may the rather beleeve, that the very bare report thereof, scattered in the air, if it happen to be received into the eares of men, who for being studious, and lovers of vertuous things, are called

Philosophers, doth not suffer them to sleep nor rest in quiet, but
so pricketh them up, and sets them on fire, to run unto the place
where the person is, in whom the said knowledge is said to have
built her Temple, and uttered her Oracles, as it was manifestly
shewn unto us in the Queen of *Sheba*, who came from the
utmost borders of the East and Persian sea, to see the order of
Solomons house, and to heare his wisdom; in *Anacharsis*, who
came out of *Scythia*, even unto *Athens*, to see *Solon*; in *Pythagoras*,
who travelled farre to visit the *Memphitical* Vaticinators; in
Platon, who went a great way off to see the *Magicians* of *Egypt*,
and *Architas* of *Tarentum*; in *Apollonius Tianeus*, who went as farre
as unto Mount *Caucasus*, passed along the *Scythians*, the *Mas-
sagetes*, the *Indians*, and sailed over the great river *Phison*, even
to the *Brachmans* to see *Hiarchas*; as likewise unto *Babylon*, *Chaldea*,
Media, *Assyria*, *Parthia*, *Syria*, *Phœnicia*, *Arabia*, *Palestina* and *Alexandria*, even unto *Æthiopia*, to see the *Gymnosophists*: the like
example have we of *Titus Livius*, whom to see and heare, divers
studious persons came to *Rome*, from the Confines of *France* and
Spaine; I dare not reckon my self in the number of those so
excellent persons, but well would be called studious, and a
lover, not only of learning, but of learned men also: and indeed,
having heard the report of your so inestimable knowledge, I
have left my countrey, my friends, my kindred and my house,
and am come thus farre, valuing at nothing the length of the
way, the tediousnesse of the sea, nor strangenesse of the land,
and that only to see you, and to conferre with you about some
passages in Philosophy, of *Geomancie*, and of the Cabalistick Art;
whereof I am doubtful, and cannot satisfie my minde; which if
you can resolve, I yield my self unto you for a slave henceforward, together with all my posterity; for other gift have I
none, that I can esteem a recompence sufficient for so great a
favour: I will reduce them into writing, and to morrow publish
them to all the learned men in the City, that we may dispute
publickly before them.

But see in what manner, I mean that we shall dispute: I will
not argue *pro & contra*, as do the sottish *Sophisters* of this town,
and other places: likewise I will not dispute after the manner of
the *Academicks* by declamation: nor yet by numbers, as *Pythagoras* was wont to do, and as *Picus de la Mirandula* did of late at

Rome: but I will dispute by signes only without speaking, for the matters are so abstruse, hard and arduous, that words proceeding from the mouth of man, will never be sufficient for unfolding of them to my liking. May it therefore please your Magnificence to be there, it shall be at the great Hall of *Navarre* at seven a clock in the morning. When he had spoke these words, *Pantagruel* very honourably said unto him, Sir, of the graces that God hath bestowed upon me, I would not deny to communicate unto any man to my power; for whatever comes from him is good, and his pleasure is, that it should be increased, when we come amongst men worthy and fit to receive this celestial Manna of honest literature: in which number, because that in this time (as I do already very plainly perceive,) thou holdest the first rank, I give thee notice, that at all houres thou shalt finde me ready to condescend to every one of thy requests, according to my poor ability: although I ought rather to learn of thee, then thou of me, but, as thou hast protested, we will conferre of these doubts together, and will seek out the resolution, even unto the bottom of that undrainable Well, where *Heraclitus* sayes the truth lies hidden: and I do highly commend the manner of arguing which thou hast proposed, to wit, by signes without speaking; for by this means thou and I shall understand one another well enough, and yet shall be free from this clapping of hands, which these blockish Sophisters make, when any of the Arguers hath gotten the better of the Argument: Now to morrow I will not faile to meet thee at the place and houre that thou hast appointed, but let me intreat thee that there be not any strife or uproare between us, and that we seek not the honour and applause of men, but the truth only: to which *Thaumast* answered, The Lord God maintain you in his favour and grace, and instead of my thankfulnesse to you, poure down his blessings upon you, for that your Highnesse and magnificent greatnesse, hath not disdained to descend to the grant of the request of my poor basenesse, so farewel till to-morrow! Farewel, said *Pantagruel*. Gentlemen, you that read this present discourse, think not that ever men were more elevated and transported in their thoughts, then all this night were both *Thaumast* and *Pantagruel*; for the said *Thaumast* said to the Keeper of the house of *Cluny*, where he was lodged, that in all his life he had never known himself so dry, as he was that night. I think (said he) that *Pantagruel* held me by the throat; Give order, I pray you, that we may have some drink, and see that some fresh water be brought to us, to gargle my palat: on the other side, *Pantagruel* stretched his wits as high as he could, entring into very deep and serious meditations, and did nothing all that night but dote upon, and turn over the book of *Beda, de numeris & signis*: *Plotins* book, *de inenarrabilibus*; the book of *Proclus, de magia*; the book of *Artemidorus*, περὶ ὀνειροκριτικῶν; of *Anaxagoras*, περὶ σημείων *Dinatius*, περὶ ἀφάτων; the books of *Philistion*: *Hipponax*, περὶ ἀνεκφωνήτων and a rabble of others, so long, that *Panurge* said unto him,

My Lord, leave all these thoughts and go to bed; for I perceive your spirits to be so troubled by a too intensive bending of them, that you may easily fall into some Quotidian fever with this so excessive thinking and plodding: but, having first drunk five and twenty or thirty good draughts, retire your self and sleep your fill: for in the morning I will argue against, and answer my master the *Englishman*; and if I drive him not *ad metam non loqui*, then call me Knave: Yea, but (said he) my friend *Panurge*, he is marvellously learned, how wilt thou be able to answer him? Very well, (answered *Panurge*) I pray you talk no more of it, but let me alone; is any man so learned as the devils are? No, indeed (said *Pantagruel*,) without Gods especial grace: Yet for all that (said *Panurge*) I have argued against them, gravelled and blanked them in disputation, and laid them so squat upon their tailes, that I have made them look like Monkies; therefore be assured, that to morrow I will make this vain-glorious *Englishman* to skite vineger before all the world. So *Panurge* spent the night with tipling amongst the Pages, and played away all the points of his breeches at *primus secundus*, and at peck point, in *French* called *Lavergette*. Yet when the condescended on time was come, he failed not to conduct his Master *Pantagruel* to the appointed place, unto which (beleeve me) there was neither great nor small in *Paris* but came, thinking with themselves that this devillish *Pantagruel*, who had overthrown and vanquished in dispute all these doting fresh-water Sophisters, would now get full payment and be tickled to some purpose; for this *Englishman* is a terrible bustler and horrible coyle-keeper, we will see who will be Conquerour, for he never met with his match before.

Thus all being assembled, *Thaumast* stayed for them, and then when *Pantagruel* and *Panurge* came into the Hall, all the School-boyes, Professors of Arts, Senior-Sophisters, and Batchelors began to clap their hands, as their scurvie custome is. But *Pantagruel* cried out with a loud voice, as if it had been the sound of a double cannon, saying, Peace, with a devil to you, peace: by G— you rogues, if you trouble me here, I will cut off the heads of every one of you: at which words they remained all daunted and astonished, like so many ducks, and durst not do so much as cough, although they had swallowed fifteen pounds of feathers: withal they grew so dry with this only voice, that they laid out their tongues a full half foot beyond their mouthes, as if *Pantagruel* had salted all their throats. Then began *Panurge* to speak, saying to the *Englishman*, Sir, are you come hither to dispute contentiously in those Propositions you have set down, or, otherwayes but to learn and know the truth? To which answered *Thaumast*, Sir, no other thing brought me hither but the great desire I had to learn, and to know that of which I have doubted all my life long, and have neither found book nor man able to content me in the resolution of those doubts which I have proposed: and as for disputing contentiously, I will not do it, for it is too base a thing, and therefore leave it to those sottish *Sophisters*, who in their disputes do not search for the truth, but for contradiction only and debate. Then said *Panurge*, if I who am but a mean and inconsiderable disciple of my Master my Lord *Pantagruel*, content and satisfie you in all and every thing, it were a thing below my said Master, wherewith to trouble him: therefore is it fitter that he be Chair-man, and sit as a Judge and Moderator of our discourse and purpose, and give you satisfaction in many things, wherein perhaps I shall be wanting to your expectation. Truly (said *Thaumast*) it is very well said: begin then. Now you must note that *Panurge* had set at the end of his long Codpiece a pretty tuft of red silk, as also of white, green and blew, and within it had put a faire orange.

CHAPTER XIX

*How Panurge put to a Non-plus the Englishman, that argued
by signes.*

EVERY body then taking heed, and hearkening with great
silence, the *Englishman* lift up on high into the aire his two
hands severally, clunching in all the tops of his fingers together
after the manner which (*a la chinonnese*) they call the hens arse,
and struck the one hand on the other by the nailes foure several
times: then he opening them, struck the one with the flat of the
other, till it yielded a clashing noise, and that only once: again
in joyning them as before he struck twice, and afterwards foure
times in opening them; then did he lay them joyned, and
extended the one towards the other, as if he had been devoutly
to send up his prayers unto God. *Panurge* suddenly lifted up in
the aire his right hand, and put the thumb thereof into the nostril
of the same side, holding his foure fingers streight out, and
closed orderly in a parallel line to the point of his nose, shutting
the left eye wholly, and making the other wink with a profound
depression of the eye-brows and eye-lids. Then lifted he up his
left hand, with hard wringing and stretching forth his foure fingers, and elevating his thumb, which he held in a line directly
correspondent to the situation of his right hand, with the distance of a cubit and a halfe between them. This done, in the
same forme he abased towards the ground, both the one and the
other hand; Lastly, he held them in the midst, as aiming right
at the *English* mans nose: And if *Mercurie*, said the *English* man:
there *Panurge* interrupted him, and said, You have spoken,
Mask.

Then made the *English* man this signe, his left hand all open
he lifted up into the aire, then instantly shut into his fist the
foure fingers thereof, and his thumb extended at length he
placed upon the gristle of his nose; Presently after, he lifted up
his right hand all open, and all open abased and bent it downwards, putting the thumb thereof in the very place where the
little finger of the left hand did close in the fist, and the foure
right hand fingers he softly moved in the aire: then contrarily he

did with the right hand what he had done with the left, and with the left what he had done with the right.

Panurge, being not a whit amazed at this, drew out into the aire his *Trismegist* Codpiece with the left hand, and with his right drew forth a trunchion of a white oxe-rib, and two pieces of wood of a like forme, one of black eben, and the other of incarnation brasil, and put them betwixt the fingers of that hand in good symmetrie; then knocking them together, made such a noise as the Lepers of *Britanie* use to do with their clappering clickets, yet better resounding, and farre more harmonious; and with his tongue contracted in his mouth, did very merrily warble it, alwayes looking fixedly upon the *English* man. The Divines, Physicians and Chirurgions, that were there, thought that by this signe he would have inferred that the *English* man was a Leper: the Counsellors, Lawyers and Decretalists conceived, that by doing this he would have concluded some kinde of mortal felicity to consist in Leprosie, as the Lord maintained heretofore.

The *English* man for all this was nothing daunted, but holding up his two hands in the aire, kept them in such forme, that he closed the three master-fingers in his fist, and passing his thumbs through his indical, or foremost and middle fingers, his auricularie or little fingers remained extended and stretched out, and so presented he them to *Panurge*; then joyned he them so, that the right thumb touched the left, and the left little finger touched the right. Hereat *Panurge*, without speaking one word, lift up his hands and made this signe.

He put the naile of the forefinger of his left hand, to the naile of the thumb of the same, making in the middle of the distance as it were a buckle, and of his right hand shut up all the fingers into his fist, except the forefinger, which he often thrust in and out through the said two others of the left hand: then stretched he out the forefinger, and middle finger or medical of his right hand, holding them asunder as much as he could, and thrusting them towards *Thaumast*. Then did he put the thumb of his left hand upon the corner of his left eye, stretching out all his hand like the wing of a bird or the finne of a fish, and moving it very daintily this way and that way, he did as much with his right hand upon the corner of his right eye. *Thaumast* began then to waxe somewhat pale, and to tremble, and made him this signe.

With the middle finger of his right hand, he struck against the muscle of the palme or pulp, which is under the thumb: then put he the forefinger of the right hand in the like buckle of the left, but he put it under and not over, as *Panurge* did. Then *Panurge* knocked one hand against another, and blowed in his palme, and put again the forefinger of his right hand into the overture or mouth of the left, pulling it often in and out; then held he out his chinne, most intentively looking upon *Thaumast*. The people there which understood nothing in the other signes, knew very well what therein he demanded (without speaking a word to *Thaumast*,) What do you mean by that? In effect, *Thaumast* then began to sweat great drops, and seemed to all the Spectators a man strangely ravished in high contemplation. Then he bethought himself, and put all the nailes of his left hand against those of his right, opening his fingers as if they had been semicircles, and with this signe lift up his hands as high as he could. Whereupon *Panurge* presently put the thumb of his right hand under his jawes, and the little finger thereof in the mouth of the left hand, and in this posture made his teeth to sound very melodiously, the upper against the lower. With this *Thaumast*, with great toile and vexation of spirit rose up, but in rising let a great bakers fart, for the bran came after, and, pissing withal very strong vineger, stunk like all the devils in hell: the company began to stop their noses; for he had conskited himself with meer anguish and perplexity. Then lifted he up his right hand, clunching it in such sort, that he brought the ends of all his fingers to meet together, and his left hand he laid flat upon his breast: whereat *Panurge* drew out his long Codpiece with his tuffe, and stretched it forth a cubit and a half, holding it in the aire with his right hand, and with his left took out his orange, and, casting it up into the aire seven times, at the eight he hid it in the fist of his right hand, holding it steadily up on high, and then began to shake his faire Codpiece, shewing it to *Thaumast*.

After that *Thaumast* began to puffe up his two cheeks like a player on a bagpipe, and blew as if he had been to puffe up a pigs bladder; whereupon *Panurge* put one finger of his left hand in his nockandrow, by some called St. *Patricks* hole, and with his mouth suck't in the aire, in such a manner as when one eats oysters in the shell, or when we sup up our broth; this done, he opened his mouth somewhat, and struck his right hand flat upon it, making therewith a great and a deep sound, as if it came from the superficies of the midriffe through the *trachiartere* or pipe of the lungs, and this he did for sixteen times; but *Thaumast* did alwayes keep blowing like a goose. Then *Panurge* put the forefinger of his right hand into his mouth, pressing it very hard to the muscles thereof; then he drew it out, and withal made a great noise, as when little boyes shoot pellets out of the potcanons made of the hollow sticks of the branch of an auldertree, and he did it nine times.

Then *Thaumast* cried out, Ha, my Masters, a great secret; with this he put in his hand up to the elbow; then drew out a dagger that he had, holding it by the point downwards; whereat *Panurge* took his long Codpiece, and shook it as hard as he could against his thighes; then put his two hands intwined in manner of a combe upon his head, laying out his tongue as farre as he was able, and turning his eyes in his head, like a goat that is ready to die. Ha, I understand (said *Thaumast*) but what? making such a signe, that he put the haft of his dagger against his breast, and upon the point thereof the flat of his hand, turning in a little the ends of his fingers; whereat *Panurge* held down his head on the left side, and put his middle finger into his right eare, holding up his thumb bolt upright; then he crost his two armes upon his breast, and coughed five times, and at the fifth time he struck his right foot against the ground: then he lift up his left arme, and closing all his fingers into his fist, held his thumbe against his forehead, striking with his right hand six times against his breast. But *Thaumast*, as not content therewith, put the thumb of his left hand upon the top of his nose, shutting the rest of his said hand, whereupon *Panurge* set his two Masterfingers upon each side of his mouth, drawing it as much as he was able, and widening it so, that he shewed all his teeth: and with his two thumbs pluck't down his two eye-lids very low, making therewith a very ill-favour'd countenance, as it seemed to the company.

CHAPTER XX

How Thaumast relateth the vertues, and knowledge of Panurge.

THEN *Thaumast* rose up, and putting off his cap, did very kindly
thank the said *Panurge*, and with a loud voice said unto all the
people that were there, My Lords, Gentlemen and others, at
this time may I to some good purpose speak that Evangelical
word, *Et ecce plus quàm Salomon hîc*: You have here in your
presence an incomparable treasure, that is, my Lord *Pantagruel*,
whose great renown hath brought me hither, out of the very
heart of *England*, to conferre with him about the insoluble
problemes, both in *Magick*, *Alchymie*, the *Caballe*, *Geomancie*,
Astrologie and *Philosophie*, which I had in my minde: but at present
I am angry, even with fame it self, which I think was envious to
him, for that it did not declare the thousandth part of the worth
that indeed is in him: You have seen how his disciple only hath
satisfied me, and hath told me more than I asked of him:
besides, he hath opened unto me, and resolved other inestimable doubts, wherein I can assure you he hath to me discovered
the very true Well, Fountain, and Abysse of the *Encyclopedeia* of
learning; yea in such a sort, that I did not think I should ever
have found a man that could have made his skill appear, in so
much as the first elements of that concerning which we disputed by signes, without speaking either word or half word. But
in fine, I will reduce into writing that which we have said and
concluded, that the world may not take them to be fooleries,
and will thereafter cause them to be printed, that every one may
learne as I have done. Judge then what the Master had been
able to say, seeing the disciple hath done so valiantly; for, *Non
est discipulus super Magistrum*. Howsoever God be praised, and I
do very humbly thank you, for the honour that you have done
us at this Act: God reward you for it eternally: the like thanks
gave *Pantagruel* to all the company, and going from thence, he
carried *Thaumast* to dinner with him, and beleeve that they
drank as much as their skins could hold, or, as the phrase is, with
unbuttoned bellies, (for in that age they made fast their bellies
with buttons, as we do now the colars of our doublets or jerkins,)

THE SECOND BOOK

even till they neither knew where they were, nor whence they came. Blessed Lady, how they did carouse it, and pluck (as we say) at the Kids leather: and flaggons to trot, and they to toote, Draw, give (page) some wine here, reach hither, fill with a devil, so! There was not one but did drink five and twenty or thirty pipes, can you tell how? even *Sicut terra sine aqua*; for the weather was hot, and besides, that they were very dry. In matter of the exposition of the Propositions set down by *Thaumast*: and the signification of the signes which they used in their disputation, I would have set them down for you according to their own relation: but I have been told that *Thaumast* made a great book of it imprinted at *London*, wherein he hath set down all without omitting any thing, and therefore at this time I do passe by it.

CHAPTER XXI

How Panurge was in love with a Lady of Paris.

PANURGE began to be in great reputation in the City of *Paris*, by means of this disputation, wherein he prevailed against the *English* man, and from thenceforth made his Codpiece to be very useful to him, to which effect he had it pinked with pretty little Embroideries after the *Romanesca* fashion; And the world did praise him publickly, in so farre that there was a song made of him, which little children did use to sing, when they went to fetch mustard: he was withal made welcome in all companies of Ladies and Gentlewomen, so that at last he became presumptuous, and went about to bring to his lure one of the greatest Ladies in the City: and indeed leaving a rabble of long prologues and protestations, which ordinarily these dolent contemplative Lent-lovers make, who never meddle with the flesh; one day he said unto her, *Madam*, it would be a very great benefit to the Common-wealth, delightful to you, honourable to your progeny, and necessary for me, that I cover you for the propagating of my race, and beleeve it, for experience will teach it you: the Lady at this word thrust him back above a hundred leagues, saying, You mischievous foole, is it for you to talk thus unto me? whom do you think you have in hand? be gone, never to come in my sight again; for if one thing were not, I would have your

245

legs and armes cut off. Well, (said he) that were all one to me, to want both legs and armes, provided you and I had but one merry bout together, at the brangle buttock-game; for here within is (in shewing her his long Codpiece) Master *John Thursday*, who will play you such an *Antick*, that you shall feel the sweetnesse thereof even to the very marrow of your bones: He is a gallant, and doth so well know how to finde out all the corners, creeks and ingrained inmates in your carnal trap, that after him there needs no broom, he 'l sweep so well before, and leave nothing to his followers to work upon: whereunto the Lady answered, Go, villain, go, if you speak to me one such word more, I will cry out, and make you to be knocked down with blowes. Ha, (said he), you are not so bad as you say, no, or else I am deceived in your physiognomie, for sooner shall the earth mount up unto the Heavens, and the highest Heavens descend unto the Hells, and all the course of nature be quite perverted, then that in so great beauty and neatnesse as in you is, there should be one drop of gall or malice: they say indeed, that hardly shall a man ever see a faire woman that is not also stubborn: yet that is spoke only of those vulgar beauties, but yours is so excellent, so singular, and so heavenly, that I beleeve nature hath given it you as a paragon, and master-piece of her Art, to make us know what she can do, when she will imploy all her skill, and all her power. There is nothing in you but honey, but sugar, but a sweet and celestial Manna: to you it was, to whom *Paris* ought to have adjudged the golden Apple, not to *Venus*, no, nor to *Juno*, nor to *Minerva*; for never was there so much magnificence in *Juno*, so much wisdom in *Minerva*, nor so much comelinesse in *Venus*, as there is in you. O heavenly *gods* and *goddesses*! how happy shall that man be to whom you will grant the favour to embrace her, to kisse her, and to rub his bacon with hers? by G— that shall be I, I know it well; for she loves me already her belly full, I am sure of it, and so was I predestinated to it by the *Fairies*: and therefore that we lose no time, put on, thrust out your gamons, and would have embraced her, but she made as if she would put out her head at the window, to call her neighbours for help. Then *Panurge* on a sudden ran out, and, in his running away, said, *Madam*, stay here till I come again, I will go call them my self, do not you take so much paines: thus went he away not much caring for the repulse he had got, nor made he any whit the worse cheer for it. The next day he came to the Church, at the time that she went to Masse, at the door he gave her some of the holy water, bowing himself very low before her, afterwards he kneeled down by her very familiarly, and said unto her, *Madam*, know that I am so amorous of you, that I can neither pisse nor dung for love: I do not know (*Lady*,) what you mean, but if I should take any hurt by it, how much would you be to blame? Go, said she, go, I do not care, let me alone to say my prayers. I but (said he) equivocate upon this; *a Beaumon le viconte* or to faire mount the priccunts: I cannot, said she: It is, said he, *a beau con le vit monte* or to faire C. the pr.: and, upon this pray to God to give you that which your noble heart desireth, and I pray you give me these patenotres. Take them (said she) & trouble me no longer: this done, she would have taken off her patenotres, which were made of a kinde of yellow stone called *Cestrin*, and adorned with great spots of gold, but *Panurge* nimbly drew out one of his knives, wherewith he cut them off very handsomly, and whilest he was going away to carry them to the Brokers, he said to her, Will you have my knife? No, no, said she: But (said he) to the purpose, I am at your commandment, body and goods, tripes and bowels.

In the mean time, the Lady was not very well content with the want of her patinotres, for they were one of her implements to keep her countenance by in the Church: then thought with her self, this bold flowting Royster, is some giddy, fantastical, light-headed foole of a strange countrey; I shall never recover my patenotres again, what will my husband say, he will no doubt be angry with me; but I will tell him, that a thief hath cut them off from my hands in the Church, which he will easily beleeve, seeing the end of the riban left at my girdle. After dinner *Panurge* went to see her carrying in his sleeve a great purse full of Palace-crowns, called counters,—and began to say unto her, Which of us two loveth other best, you me, or I you? whereunto she answered, As for me, I do not hate you; for as God commands, I love all the world: But to the purpose, (said he) are not you in love with me? I have (said she) told you so many times already, that you should talk so no more to me, and if you speak of it again, I will teach you, that I am not one to be talked unto dishonestly: get you hence packing, and deliver me my pate-notres, that my husband may not ask me for them.

How now, (*Madame*) said he, your patenotres? nay, by mine oath I will not do so, but I will give you others; had you rather have them of gold well enameled in great round knobs, or after the manner of love-knots, or otherwise all massive, like great *ingots*, or if you had rather have them of *Ebene*, of *Jacinth*, or of *grained* gold, with the marks of fine *Turkoises*, or of faire *Topazes*, marked with fine *Saphirs*, or of *baleu Rubies*, with great marks of *Diamonds* of eight and twenty squares? No, no, all this is too little; I know a faire bracelet of fine *Emeraulds*, marked with spotted *Ambergris*, and at the buckle a *Persian pearle* as big as an Orange: it will not cost above five and twenty thousand ducates, I will make you a present of it, for I have ready coine enough, and withal he made a noise with his counters as if they had been *French* crownes.

Will you have a piece of velvet, either of the violet colour, or of crimson died in graine: or a piece of broached or crimson sat-tin? will you have chaines, gold, tablets, rings? You need no more but say, Yes, so farre as fifty thousand ducates may reach, it is but as nothing to me; by the vertue of which words he made the water come in her mouth: but she said unto him, No, I thank you, I will have nothing of you. By G—, said he, but I will have somewhat of you; yet shall it be that which shall cost you noth-ing, neither shall you have a jot the lesse, when you have given it, hold, (shewing his long Codpiece) this is Master *John Good-fellow*, that askes for lodging, and with that would have em-braced her; but she began to cry out, yet not very loud. Then *Panurge* put off his counterfeit garb, changed his false visage, and said unto her, You will not then otherwayes let me do a little, a turd for you, you do not deserve so much good, nor so much honour: but by G—, I will make the dogs ride you, and with this he ran away as fast as he could, for feare of blowes, whereof he was naturally fearful.

CHAPTER XXII

*How Panurge served a Parisian Lady a trick that pleased her
not very well.*

Now you must note that the next day was the great festival of
Corpus Christi, called the *Sacre*, wherein all women put on their
best apparel, and on that day the said Lady was cloathed in a
rich gown of crimson-sattin, under which she wore a very costly
white velvet petticoat.

The day of the Eve (called the vigile) *Panurge* searched so
long of one side and another, that he found a hot or salt bitch,
which when he had tied her with his girdle, he led to his chamber, and fed her very well all that day and night; in the morning
thereafter he killed her, and took that part of her which the
Greek Geomanciers know, and cut it into several pieces as small
as he could; then carrying it away as close as might be, he went
to the place where the Lady was to come along, to follow the
Procession, as the custome is upon the said holy day; and when
she came in, *Panurge* sprinkled some holy water on her, saluting
her very courteously: then a little while after she had said her
petty devotions, he sate down close by her upon the same bench,
and gave her this roundlay in writing, in manner as followeth.

A Roundlay

For this one time, that I to you my love
Discovered, you did too cruel prove
To send me packing, hopelesse, and so soon,
Who never any wrong to you had done
In any kinde of action, word or thought:
So that if my suit lik'd you not, you ought
T' have spoke more civilly, and to this sense,
My friend, be pleased to depart from hence,
     For this one time.

What hurt do I to wish you to remark
With favour and compassion how a spark
Of your great beauty hath inflam'd my heart
With deep affection, and that for my part,
I only ask that you with me would dance

The brangle gay in feats of dalliance,
For this one time.

And as she was opening this paper to see what it was, *Panurge* very promptly and lightly scattered the drug that he had, upon her in divers places, but especially in the plaits of her sleeves, and of her gowne: then said he unto her, Madam, the poor lovers are not alwayes at ease: as for me, I hope that those heavy nights, those paines and troubles, which I suffer for love of you, shall be a deduction to me of so much paine in Purgatory: yet at the least pray to God to give me patience in my misery. *Panurge* had no sooner spoke this, but all the dogs that were in the Church came running to this Lady with the smell of the drugs that he had strowed upon her, both small and great, big and little, all came, laying out their member; smelling to her, and pissing every where upon her, it was the greatest villainy in the world. *Panurge* made the fashion of driving them away; then took his leave of her, and withdrew himself into some Chappel or Oratory of the said Church, to see the sport; for these villain-ous dogs did compisse all her habiliaments, and left none of her attire unbesprinkled with their staling, in so much that a tall grey-hound pist upon her head, others in her sleeves, others on her crupper-piece, and the little ones pissed upon her pataines; so that all the women that were round about her had much ado to save her. Whereat *Panurge* very heartily laughing, he said to one of the Lords of the City, I beleeve that same Lady is hot, or else that some grey-hound hath covered her lately. And when he saw that all the dogs were flocking about her, yarring at the retardment of their accesse to her and every way keeping such a coyle with her, as they are wont to do about a proud or salt bitch, he forthwith departed from thence, and went to call *Pan-tagruel*: not forgetting in his way alongst the streets, thorough which he went, where he found any dogs to give them a bang with his foot, saying, Will you not go with your fellowes to the wedding? Away, hence, avant, avant, with a devil avant! And being come home, he said to *Pantagruel*, Master, I pray you come and see all the dogs of the countrey, how they are assembled about a Lady, the fairest in the City, and would dufle and line her: whereunto *Pantagruel* willingly condescended, and saw the mystery, which he found very pretty and strange: But the best was at the Procession, in which were seen above six hundred thousand and fourteen dogs about her, which did very much trouble and molest her, and whithersoever she past, those dogs that came afresh, tracing her footsteps, followed her at the heeles, and pist in the way where her gown had touched. All the world stood gazing at this spectacle, considering the countenance of those dogs, who leaping up got about her neck, and spoiled all her gorgeous accoutrements, for the which she could finde no remedy, but to retire unto her house, which was a Palace. Thither she went, and the dogs after her; she ran to hide her self, but the Chamber-maids could not abstaine from laughing. When she was entered into the house, and had shut the door upon her self, all the dogs came running, of half a league round, and did so well bepisse the gate of her house, that there they made a stream with their urine, wherein a duck might have very well swimmed, and it is the same current that now runs at St. *Victor*, in which *Gobelin* dieth scarlet, for the specifical vertue of these pisse-dogs, as our master *Doribus* did heretofore preach publickly. So may God help you: a Mill would have ground corne with it; yet not so much as those of *Basacle* at *Toulouse*.

CHAPTER XXIII

How Pantagruel departed from Paris, hearing newes, that the Dipsodes had invaded the Land of the Amaurots: and the cause wherefore the leagues are so short in France.

A LITTLE while after *Pantagruel* heard newes that his father *Gargantua* had been translated into the land of the Fairies by *Morgue*, as heretofore were *Oger* and *Arthur* together, and that the report of his translation being spread abroad, the *Dipsodes* had issued out beyond their borders, with inrodes had wasted a great part of *Utopia*, and at that very time had beseiged the great City of the *Amaurots*: whereupon departing from *Paris*, without bidding any man farewel, for the businesse required diligence, he came to *Rowen*.

Now *Pantagruel* in his journey, seeing that the leagues of that little territory about *Paris* called *France* were very short in

regard of those of other Countreys, demanded the cause and
reason of it from *Panurge*, who told him a story which *Marotus*
set down of the *lac Monachus*, in the acts of the Kings of *Canarre*,
saying, that in old times Countreys were not distinguished into
leagues, miles, furlongs, nor parasanges, until that King *Phara-
mond* divided them, which was done in manner as followeth.
The said King chose at *Paris* a hundred faire, gallant, lustie,
briske young men, all resolute and bold adventurers in *Cupids*
duels, together with a hundred comely, pretty, handsome, lovely
and well-complexioned wenches of *Picardie*, all which he caused
to be well entertained, and highly fed for the space of eight
dayes; then, having called for them, he delivered to every one
of the young men his wench, with store of money to defray their
charges, and this injunction besides, to go unto divers places
here and there, and wheresoever they should biscot and thrum
their wenches, that they setting a stone there, it should be
accounted for a league; thus went away those brave fellowes
and sprightly blades most merrily, and because they were fresh,
and had been at rest, they very often jum'd and fanfreluched
almost at every fields end, and this is the cause why the leagues
about *Paris* are so short; but when they had gone a great way,
and were now as weary as poor devils, all the oile in their lamps
being almost spent, they did not chinke and dufle so often, but
contented themselves, (I mean for the mens part,) with one
scurvie paultry bout in a day, and this is that which makes the
leagues in *Britany*, *Delanes*, *Germany*, and other more remote
Countreys so long: other men give other reasons for it, but this
seems to me of all other the best. To which *Pantagruel* willingly
adhered. Parting from *Rowen*, they arrived at *Honfleur*, where
they took shipping, *Pantagruel*, *Panurge*, *Epistemon*, *Eusthenes*
and *Carpalim*.

   In which place, waiting for a favourable winde, and caulking
their ship, he received from a Lady of *Paris* (which he had formerly kept, and entertained a good long time,) a letter directed
on the out-side thus, *To the best beloved of the faire women, and least
loyal of the valiant men*,

PNTGRL.

252

CHAPTER XXIV

A Letter which a messenger brought to Pantagruel from a Lady of Paris, together with the exposition of a Posie, written in a gold Ring.

WHEN *Pantagruel* had read the superscription, he was much amazed, and therefore demanded of the said messenger the name of her that had sent it: then opened he the letter, and found nothing written in it, nor otherwayes inclosed, but only a gold ring, with a square table-diamond. Wondering at this, he called *Panurge* to him, and shewed him the case; whereupon *Panurge* told him, that the leafe of paper was written upon, but with such cunning and artifice, that no man could see the writing at the first sight, therefore to finde it out he set it by the fire, to see if it was made with *Sal Armoniack* soaked in water; then put he it into the water, to see if the letter was written with the juice of *Tithymalle*: after that he held it up against the candle, to see if it was written with the juice of white onions.

Then he rubbed one part of it with oile of nuts, to see if it were not written with the lee of a fig-tree: and another part of it with the milk of a woman giving suck to her eldest daughter, to see if it was written with the blood of red toads, or green earth-frogs: Afterwards he rubbed one corner with the ashes of a Swallowes nest, to see if it were not written with the dew that is found within the herb *Alcakengie*, called the winter-cherry. He rubbed after that one end with eare-waxe, to see if it were not written with the gall of a Raven: then did he dip it into vineger, to try if it was not written with the juice of the garden *Spurge*: After that he greased it with the fat of a bat or flitter-mouse, to see if it was not written with the sperm of a whale, which some call ambergris: Then put it very fairly into a basin full of fresh water, and forthwith took it out, to see whether it were written with stone-allum: But after all experiments, when he perceived that he could finde out nothing, he called the messenger, and asked him, Good fellow, the lady that sent thee hither, did she not give thee a staffe to bring with thee? thinking that it had been according to the conceit, whereof *Aulus Gellius*

maketh mention, and the messenger answered him, *No, Sir.*
Then *Panurge* would have caused his head to be shaven, to see
whether the Lady had written upon his bald pate, with the hard
lie whereof sope is made, that which she meant; but perceiving
that his hair was very long, he forbore, considering that it could
not have grown to so great a length in so short a time.

Then he said to *Pantagruel,* Master, by the vertue of G— I
cannot tell what to do nor say in it; for to know whether there
be any thing written upon this or no, I have made use of a good
part of that which Master *Francisco di Nianto,* the *Tuscan* sets
down, who hath written the manner of reading letters that do
not appear; that which *Zoroastes* published, *peri grammaton acri-
ton*; and *Calphurnius Bassus de literis illegibilibus*: but I can see
nothing, nor do I beleeve that there is any thing else in it then
the Ring: let us therefore look upon it. Which when they had
done, they found this in *Hebrew* written within, *Lamach sabatha-
ni*; whereupon they called *Epistemon,* and asked him what that
meant? to which he answered, that they were Hebrew words,
signifying, *Wherefore hast thou forsaken me*? upon that *Panurge*
suddenly replied: I know the mystery, do you see this diamond?
it is a false one; this, then is the exposition of that which the
Lady meanes, *Diamant faux,* that is, false lover, why hast thou
forsaken me? which interpretation *Pantagruel* presently understood, and withal remembering, that at his departure he had not
bid the Lady farewel, he was very sorry, and would faine have
returned to *Paris,* to make his peace with her; but *Epistemon* put
him in minde of *Æneas*'s departure from *Dido,* and the saying of
Heraclitus of *Tarentum,* That the ship being at anchor when need
requireth, we must cut the cable rather then lose time about
untying of it, and that he should lay aside all other thoughts, to
succour the City of his Nativity, which was then in danger; and
indeed within an houre after that, the winde arose at the north-
north-west, wherewith they hoised saile, and put out, even into
the maine sea, so that within few dayes, passing by *Porto Sancto,*
and by the *Maderas,* they went ashore in the *Canarie* islands;
parting from thence, they passed by *Capobianco,* by *Senege,* by
Capoverde, by *Gambre,* by *Sagres,* by *Melli,* by the *Cap di buona
Speranza,* and set ashore againe in the Kingdom of *Melinda*;
parting from thence, they sailed away with a tramontan or

northerly winde, passing by *Meden*, by *Uti*, by *Uden*, by *Gelasim*, by the isles of the Fairies, and alongst the Kingdom of *Achorie*, till at last they arrived at the port of *Utopia*, distant from the city of the *Amaurots* three leagues and somewhat more.

When they were ashore, and pretty well refreshed, *Panta-gruel* said, Gentlemen, the City is not farre from hence, therefore were it not amisse, before we set forward, to advise well what is to be done, that we be not like the *Athenians*, who never took counsel until after the fact: Are you resolved to live and die with me? Yes, Sir, said they all, and be as confident of us, as of your own fingers. Well (said he) there is but one thing that keeps my minde in great doubt and suspense, which is this, that I know not in what order nor of what number the enemie is, that layeth siege to the City; for if I were certain of that, I should go forward, and set on with the better assurance. Let us therefore consult together, and bethink our selves by what meanes we may come to this intelligence: whereunto they all said, Let us go thither and see, and stay you here for us, for this very day, without further respite do we make account to bring you a certain report thereof.

My self (said *Panurge*) will undertake to enter into their camp, within the very midst of their guards, unespied by their watch, and merrily feast and lecher it at their cost, without being known of any, to see the Artillery and the Tents of all the Captaines, and thrust my self in with a grave and magnifick carriage, amongst all their troopes and companies, without being discovered; the devill would not be able to peck me out with all his circumventions: for I am of the race of *Zopyrus*.

And I (said *Epistemon*) know all the plots and stratagems of the valiant Captaines, and warlike Champions of former ages, together with all the tricks and subtilties of the Art of warre; I will go, and though I be detected and revealed, I will escape, by making them beleeve of you whatever I please, for I am of the race of *Sinon*.

I (said *Eusthenes*) will enter and set upon them in their trenches, in spight of their Centries, and all their guards; for I will tread upon their bellies, and break their legs and armes, yea, though they were every whit as strong as the devil himself; for I am of the race of *Hercules*.

And I (said *Carpalin*) will get in there, if the birds can enter, for I am so nimble of body, and light withal, that I shall have leaped over their trenches, and ran clean through all their camp, before that they perceive me, neither do I feare shot, nor arrow, nor horse, how swift soever, were he the *Pegasus* of *Persee* or *Pacolet*, being assured that I shall be able to make a safe and sound escape before them all, without any hurt: I will undertake to walk upon the eares of corne, or grasse in the meddows, without making either of them do so much as bow under me; for I am of the race of *Camilla* the *Amazone*.

CHAPTER XXV

How Panurge, Carpalin, Eusthenes, and Epistemon (the Gentlemen Attendants of Pantagruel) vanquished and discomfitted six hundred and threescore horsemen very cunningly.

As he was speaking this, they perceived six hundred and threescore light horsemen, gallantly mounted, who made an outrode thither, to see what ship it was that was newly arrived in the harbour, and came in a full gallop to take them if they had been able: Then said *Pantagruel*, My Lads, retire your selves unto the ship, here are some of our enemies coming apace, but I will kill them here before you like beasts, although they were ten times so many, in the meane time withdraw your selves, and take your sport at it. Then answered *Panurge*, No, Sir, there is no reason that you should do so, but on the contrary retire you unto the ship, both you and the rest; for I alone will here discomfit them, but we must not linger, come, set forward; whereunto the others said, It is well advised Sir, withdraw your self and we will help *Panurge* here, so shall you know what we are able to do; Then said *Pantagruel*, Well, I am content, but if that you be too weak, I will not faile to come to your assistance. With this *Panurge* took two great cables of the ship, and tied them to the kemstock or capstane which was on the deck towards the hatches, and fastened them in the ground, making a long circuit, the one further off, the other within that. Then said he to *Epistemon*, Go aboard the ship, and, when I give you a call, turn about the capstane upon the orlop diligently, drawing unto you the two cable-ropes: and said to *Eusthenes*, and to *Carpalin*, *My Bullies*, stay you here, and offer your selves freely to your enemies, do as they bid you, and make as if you would yield unto them: but take heed you come not within the compasse of the ropes, be sure to keep your selves free of them; and presently he went aboard the ship, and took a bundle of straw, and a barrel of gun-powder, strowed it round about the compasse of the cordes, and stood by with a brand of fire or match lighted in his hand. Presently came the horsemen with great fury, and the foremost ran almost home to the ship, and by reason of the slipperinesse of the bank, they fell they and their horses, to the number of foure and fourty, which the rest seeing, came on, thinking that resistance had been made them at their arrival. But *Panurge* said unto them, My Masters, I beleeve that you have hurt your selves, I pray you pardon us, for it is not our fault, but the slipperinesse of the sea-water that is alwayes flowing; we submit our selves to your good pleasure; so said likewise his two other fellowes, and *Epistemon* that was upon the deck; in the mean time *Panurge* withdrew himselfe, and seeing that they were all within the compasse of the cables, and that his two companions were retired, making room for all those horses which came in a croud, thronging upon the neck of one another to see the ship and such as were in it, cried out on a sudden to *Epistemon*, Draw, draw: then began *Epistemon* to winde about the capstane, by doing whereof the two cables so intangled and impestered the legs of the horses, that they were all of them thrown down to the ground easily, together with their Riders: but they seeing that, drew their swords, and would have cut them: whereupon *Panurge* set fire to the traine, and there burnt them up all like damned souls, both men and horses, not one escaping save one alone, who being mounted on a fleet *Turkie* courser, by meere speed in flight got himself out of the circle of the ropes; but when *Carpalin* perceived him, he ran after him with such nimblenesse and celerity, that he overtook him in lesse than a hundred paces; then leaping close behinde him upon the crupper of his horse, clasped him in his armes, and brought him back to the ship.

The exploit being ended, *Pantagruel* was very jovial, and wondrously commended the industry of these Gentlemen, whom he called his fellow-souldiers, and made them refresh themselves, and feed well and merrily upon the sea-shore, and drink heartily with their bellies upon the ground, and their prisoner with them, whom they admitted to that familiarity: only that the poor devil was somewhat afraid that *Pantagruel* would have eaten him up whole, which, considering the widenesse of his mouth, and capacity of his throat, was no great matter for him to have done; for he could have done it, as easily as you would eate a small comfit, he shewing no more in his throat, then would a graine of millet-seed in the mouth of an Asse.

CHAPTER XXVI

How Pantagruel and his company were weary in eating still salt meats: and how Carpalin went a hunting to have some Venison.

THUS as they talked & chatted together, *Carpalin* said, And by the belly of St. *Quenet*, shal we never eat any venison? this salt meat makes me horribly dry, I will go fetch you a quarter of one of those horses which we have burnt, it is well roasted already: as he was rising to go about it, he perceived under the side of a wood a fair great roe-buck, which was come out of his Fort (as I conceive) at the sight of *Panurge*'s fire: him did he pursue and run after with as much vigour and swiftnesse, as if it had been a bolt out of a Crossebowe, and caught him in a moment; and whilest he was in his course, he with his hands took in the aire foure great bustards, seven bitterns, six and twenty gray partridges, two and thirty red legged ones, sixteen pheasants, nine woodcocks, nineteen herons, two and thirty coushots and ringdoves; and with his feet killed ten or twelve hares and rabbets, which were then at relief, and pretty big withal, eighteen rayles in a knot together, with fifteen young wilde boares, two little Bevers, and three great foxes: so striking the kid with his fauchion athwart the head he killed him, and bearing him on his back, he in his return took up his hares, rayls, and young wilde boares, and as far off as he could be heard, cried out, & said, *Panurge* my friend, vineger, vineger: then the good *Pantagruel*, thinking he had fainted, commanded them to provide him some vineger; but *Panurge* knew well that there was some good prey in hands, and forthwith shewed unto noble *Pantagruel*, how he was bearing upon his back a faire roe-buck, and all his girdle bordered with hares; then immediately did *Epistemon* make in the name of the nine Muses, nine antick wooden spits: *Eusthenes* did help to flay, and *Panurge* placed two great cuirasier saddles, in such sort that they served for Andirons and making their prisoner to be their Cook, they roasted their venison by the fire, wherein the horsemen were burnt: and making great chear with a good deal of vineger, the devil a one of them did forbear from his victuals, it was a triumphant and incomparable spectacle to see how they ravened and devoured. Then said *Pantagruel*, Would to God, every one of you had two paires of little *Anthem* or *Sacring* bells hanging at your chin, and that I had at mine the great clocks of *Renes*, of *Poitiers*, of *Tours*, and of *Cambray*, to see what a peale they would wring with the wagging of our chaps; But, said *Panurge*, it were better we thought a little upon our businesse, and by what meanes we might get the upper hand of our enemies: That is well remembered, said *Pantagruel*; therefore spoke he thus to the prisoner, My friend, tell us here the truth, and do not lie to us at all if thou wouldest not be flayed alive, for it is I that eat the little children: relate unto us at full the order, the number and the strength of the Army: to which the prisoner answered, Sir, know for a truth that in the army there are three hundred giants all armed with armour of proof, and wonderful great: neverthelesse, not fully so great as you, except one that is their head, named *Loupgarou*, who is armed from head to foot with *Cyclopical* annuils; furthermore, one hundred threescore and three thousand foot, all armed with the skins of hobgoblins, strong and valiant men: eleven thousand foure hundred men at armes or cuirasiers: three thousand six hundred double cannons, and harquebusiers without number; fourscore and fourteen thousand Pioneers; one hundred and fifty thousand whores, faire like goddesses, (that is for me, said *Panurge*,) whereof some are *Amazons*, some *Lionnoises*, others *Parisiennes*, *Taurangelles*, *Angevines*, *Poictevines*, *Normandes*, and high *dutch*, there are of them of all Countreys, and all languages.

Yea, but (said *Pantagruel*) is the King there? Yes Sir, (said the prisoner) he is there in person, and we call him *Anarchus*, King of the *Dipsodes*, which is as much to say as thirsty people, for you never saw men more thirsty, nor more willing to drink, and his tent is guarded by the Giants: It is enough (said *Pantagruel*) come brave boyes, are you resolved to go with me? To which *Panurge* answered, God counfound him that leaves you: I have already bethought myself how I will kill them all like pigs, and so the devil one leg of them shall escape; but I am somewhat troubled about one thing: And what is that? said *Pantagruel*: It is, (said *Panurge*) how I shall be able to set forward to the jusling and bragmardising of all the whores that be there this afternoon, in such sort, that there escape not one unbumped by me, breasted and jum'd after the ordinary fashion of man and woman, in the Venetian conflict. Ha, ha, ha, ha, said *Pantagruel*.

And *Carpalin* said; The Devil take these sink-holes, if by G— I do not bumbast some one of them: Then said *Eusthenes*, What shall not I have any, whose paces since we came from *Rowen*, were never so well winded up, as that my needle could mount to ten or eleven a clock till now, that I have it hard, stiffe and strong, like a hundred devils? Truly, (said *Panurge*,) thou shalt have of the fattest, and of those that are most plump, and in the best case.

How now? (said *Epistemon*), every one shall ride, and I must lead the Asse, the devil take him that will do so, and will make use of the right of warre, *Qui potest capere, capiat*: No, no, said *Panurge*, but tie thine Asse to a crook, and ride as the world doth: And the good *Pantagruel* laughed at all this, and said unto them, You reckon without your host; I am much afraid, that before it be night, I shall see you in such taking, that you will have no great stomach to ride, but more like to be rode upon, with sound blowes of pike and lance: *Baste*, (said *Epistemon*), enough of that, I will not faile to bring them to you, either to roste or boile, to fry or put in paste; they are not so many in number, as were in the army of *Xerxes*, for he had thirty hundred thousand fighting men, if you will beleeve *Herodotus* and *Trogus Pompeius*: and yet *Themistocles* with a few men overthrew them all: for Gods sake take you no care for that. *Cobsminnie, Cobsminnie*, (said *Panurge*) my Codpiece alone shall suffice to overthrow all the men: and my St. *Sweep-hole*, that dwells within it, shall lay all the women squat upon their backs. Up then my lads (said *Pantagruel*) and let us march along.

CHAPTER XXVII

How Pantagruel set up one Trophee in memorial of their
valour, and Panurge another in remembrance of the hares:
how Pantagruel likewise with his farts begat little men, and
with his fisgs little women: and how Panurge broke a great
staffe over two Glasses.

BEFORE we depart hence, (said *Pantagruel*) in remembrance of
the exploit that you have now performed, I will in this place
erect a faire *Trophee*: then every man amongst them with great
joy, and fine little Countrey-songs, set up a huge big post,
whereunto they hanged a great cuirasier saddle, the fronstal of
a barbed horse, bridle bosses, pullie-pieces for the knees, stir-
rup-leathers, spurres, stirrups, a coat of male, a corslet tempered
with steel, a battel-axe, a strong, short, and sharp horsemans
sword, a gantlet, a horsemans mace, gushet-armour for the arme-
pits, leg-harnesse, and a gorget, with all other furniture needful
for the decorement of a triumphant arch, in signe of a *Trophee*.
And then *Pantagruel*, for an eternal memorial, wrote this victor-
ial *Ditton*, as followeth.

> Here was the prowesse made apparent of
> Foure brave and valiant champions of proof,
> Who without any arms but wit, at once
> (Like *Fabius*, or the two *Scipions*)
> Burn't in a fire six hundred and threescore,
> Crablice, strong rogues ne'er vanquished before.
> By this each *King* may learn, *rock, pawn, and Knight*,
> That slight is much more prevalent then might.

> For victory,
> (As all men see)
> Hangs on the Dittie
> Of that Committie,
> Where the great God
> Hath his abode:

> Nor doth he it to strong and great men give,
> But to his elect, as we must beleeve;
> Therefore shall he obtain wealth and esteem,
> Who thorough faith doth put his trust in him.

RABELAIS

Whilest *Pantagruel* was writing these foresaid verses, *Panurge* halved and fixed upon a great stake the hornes of a roe-buck, together with the skin, and the right forefoot thereof, the eares of three levrets, the chine of a coney, the jawes of a hare, the wings of two bustards, the feet of foure queest-doves, a bottle or *borracho* full of vineger, a horne wherein to put salt, a wooden spit, a larding stick, a scurvie kettle full of holes, a dripping pan to make sauce in, an earthen salt-cellar, and a goblet of *Beauvais*. Then in imitation of *Pantagruels* verses and Trophee, wrote that which followeth:

> Here was it that foure jovial blades sate down
> To a profound carowsing, and to crown
> Their banquet with those wines, which please best great
> *Bacchus*, the Monarch of their drinking state:
> Then were the reines and furch of a young hare,
> With salt and vineger, displayed there,
> Of which to snatch a bit or two at once
> They all fell on like hungry scorpions:

>> For th' Inventories
>> Of Defensories
>> Say that in heat
>> We must drink neat
>> All out, and of
>> The choicest stuffe;

> But it is bad to eat of young hares flesh,
> Unlesse with vineger we it refresh:
> Receive this tenet then without controll,
> That vineger of that meat is the soul.

Then (said *Pantagruel*,) Come, my lads, let us be gone, we have stayed here too long about our victuals; for very seldom doth it fall out, that the greatest eaters do the most martial exploits, there is no *shadow* like that of flying colours, no *smoke* like that of horses, no *clattering* like that of armour: at this *Epistemon* began to smile, and said, There is no *shadow* like that of the kitchin, no *smoke* like that of the pasties, and no *clattering* like that of goblets: unto which answered *Panurge*, There is no *shadow* like that of courtaines, no *smoke* like that of womens breasts, and no *clattering* like that of ballocks: then forthwith rising up he

262

gave a fart, a leap, and a whistle, and most joyfully cried out aloud, Ever live *Pantagruel*: when *Pantagruel* saw that, he would have done as much; but with the fart that he let, the earth trembled nine leagues about, wherewith and with the corrupted aire, he begot about three and fifty thousand little men, ill favoured dwarfes, and with one fisg that he let, he made as many little women, crouching down, as you shall see in divers places, which never grow but like Cowes tailes downwards, or like the *Limosin* radishes, round. How now (said *Panurge*) are your farts so fertile and fruitful? by G— here be brave farted men, and fisgued women, let them be married together, they will beget fine hornets and dorflies; so did *Pantagruel*, and called them Pygmies; those he sent to live in an island thereby, where since that time they are increased mightily: but the cranes make warre with them continually, against which they do most couragiously defend themselves; for these little ends of men and dandiprats (whom in *Scotland* they call whiphandles, and knots of a tarre-barrel) are commonly very teastie and cholerick: the Physical reason whereof is, because their heart is near their spleen.

At this same time, *Panurge* took two drinking glasses that were there, both of one bignesse, and filled them with water up to the brim, and set one of them upon one stool, and the other upon another, placing them about five foot from one another: then he took the staffe of a javelin, about five foot and a half long, and put it upon the two glasses, so that the two ends of the staffe did come just to the brims of the glasses: This done, he took a great stake or billet of wood, and said to *Pantagruel*, and to the rest: *My Masters*, behold, how easily we shall have the victory over our enemies; for just as I shall break this staffe here upon these glasses, without either breaking or crazing of them, nay, which is more, without spilling one drop of the water that is within them, even so shall we break the heads of our *Dipsodes*, without receiving any of us any wound or losse in our person or goods: but that you may not think there is any *witchcraft* in this, hold (said he to *Eusthenes*) strike upon the midst as hard as thou canst with this log: *Eusthenes* did so, and the staffe broke in two pieces, and not one drop of the water fell out of the glasses: Then said he, I know a great many such other tricks, let us now therefore march boldly, and with assurance.

CHAPTER XXVIII

How Pantagruel got the victory very strangely over the
Dipsodes and the Giants.

AFTER all this talk, *Pantagruel* took the prisoner to him, and sent
him away, saying, Go thou unto thy King in his Camp, and tell
him tidings of what thou hast seen, and let him resolve to feast
me to morrow about noon; for assoon as my galleys shall come,
which will be to-morrow at furthest; I will prove unto him by
eighteen hundred thousand fighting men, and seven thousand
Giants, all of them greater than I am; that he hath done foolishly
and against reason, thus to invade my countrey, wherein *Panta-*
gruel feigned that he had an army at sea; but the Prisoner
answered, that he would yield himself to be his slave, and that
he was content never to return to his own people, but rather
with *Pantagruel* to fight against them, and for Gods sake besought him, that he might be permitted so to do: whereunto
Pantagruel would not give consent, but commanded him to depart thence speedily, and be gone as he had told him, and to that
effect gave him a box full of *Euphorbium*, together with some
grains of the black *chameleon thistle*, steeped into *aqua vitæ*, and
made up into the condiment of a wet sucket, commanding him
to carry it to his King, and to say unto him, that if he were able
to eate one ounce of that without drinking after it, he might
then be able to resist him, without any feare or apprehension of
danger.

The Prisoner then besought him with joynt hands, that in
the houre of the battel he would have compassion upon him:
whereat *Pantagruel* said unto him, After that thou hast delivered
all unto the King, put thy whole confidence in God, and he will
not forsake thee; because, although for my part I be mighty, as
thou mayest see, and have an infinite number of men in armes,
I do neverthelesse trust neither in my force nor in mine industry, but all my confidence is in God my Protectour, who doth
never forsake those that in him do put their trust and confidence. This done, the Prisoner requested him that he would
afford him some reasonable composition for his ransome: to which

Pantagruel answered, that his end was not to rob nor ransom men, but to enrich them, and reduce them to total liberty; Go thy way (said he) in the peace of the living God, and never follow evil company, lest some mischief befall thee. The Prisoner being gone, *Pantagruel* said to his men, Gentlemen, I have made this Prisoner believe that we have an army at sea, as also that we will not assault them till to-morrow at noon, to the end, that they doubting of the great arrival of our men, may spend this night in providing and strengthening themselves, but in the mean time my intention is, that we charge them about the houre of the first sleep.

Let us leave *Pantagruel* here with his Apostles, and speak of King *Anarchus* and his army. When the Prisoner was come, he went unto the King, and told him how there was a great Giant come, called *Pantagruel*, who had overthrown, and made to be cruelly roasted all the six hundred and nine and fifty horsemen, and he alone escaped to bring the news: besides that, he was charged by the said Giant to tell him, that the next day about noon he must make a dinner ready for him, for at that houre he was resolved to set upon him: then did he give him that boxe wherein were those confitures: but as soon as he had swallowed down one spoonful of them, he was taken with such a heat in the throat, together with an ulceration in the flap of the top of the winde-pipe, that his tongue peel'd with it, in such sort that for all they could do unto him, he found no ease at all, but by drinking only without cessation; for as soon as ever he took the goblet from his head, his tongue was on a fire, and therefore they did nothing but still poure in wine into his throat with a funnel, which when his Captains, *Bashawes* and guard of his body did see, they tasted of the same drugs, to try whether they were so thirst-procuring and alterative or no: but it so befell them as it had done their King, and they plied the flaggon so well, that the noise ran throughout all the Camp, how the Prisoner was returned, that the next day they were to have an assault, that the King and his Captains did already prepare themselves for it, together with his guards, and that with carowsing lustily, and quaffing as hard as they could, every man therefore in the army began to tipple, ply the pot, swill and guzzle it as fast as they could. In summe, they drunk so much, and so long, that they fell asleep like pigs, all out of order throughout the whole camp.

Let us now return to the good *Pantagruel*, and relate how he carried himself in this businesse, departing from the place of the *Trophies*: he took the mast of their ship in his hand like a Pilgrims staffe, and put within the top of it two hundred and seven and thirty poinsons of white wine of *Anjou*, the rest was of *Rowen*, and tied up to his girdle the bark all full of salt, as easily as the *Lanskennets* carry their little panniers, and so set onward on his way with his fellow-souldiers. When he was come near to the enemies Camp, *Panurge* said unto him, *Sir*, if you would do well, let down this white wine of *Anjou* from the scuttle of the mast of the ship, that we may all drink thereof, like *Britains*.

Hereunto *Pantagruel* very willingly consented, and they drank so neat, that there was not so much as one poor drop left, of two hundred and seven and thirty punchons, except one *Boracho* or leathern bottle of *Tours*, which *Panurge* filled for himself, (for he called that his *vade mecum*,) and some scurvie lees of wine in the bottom, which served him instead of vineger. After they had whitled and curried the canne pretty handsomely, *Panurge* gave *Pantagruel* to eate some devillish drugs, compounded of *Lithotripton*, (which is a stone-dissolving ingredient,) *nephro-catarticon*, (that purgeth the reines) the marmalade of Quinces, (called *Codiniac*) a confection of *Cantharides*, (which are green flies breeding on the tops of olive-trees) and other kindes of *diuretick* or pisse-procuring simples. This done, *Pantagruel* said to *Carpalin*, Go into the city, scrambling like a cat up against the wall, as you can well do, and tell them, that now presently they come out, and charge their enemies as rudely as they can, and having said so, come down taking a lighted torch with you, wherewith you shall set on fire all the tents and pavillions in the Camp, then cry as loud as you are able with your great voice, and then come away from thence. Yea, but, said *Carpalin*, were it not good to cloy all their ordnance? No, no, (said *Pantagruel*,) only blow up all their powder. *Carpalin* obeying him, departed suddenly, and did as he was appointed by *Pantagruel*, and all the Combatants came forth that were in the City, and, when he had set fire in the tents and pavillions, he past so lightly through them, and so highly and profoundly did they snort and sleep, that they never perceived him. He came to the place where their Artillery was, and set their munition on fire: but here was the danger, the fire was so sudden, that poor *Carpalin* had almost been burnt; and had it not been for his wonderful agility, he had been fried like a roasting pig: but he departed away so speedily, that a bolt or arrow out of a Crossebowe could not have had a swifter motion. When he was clear of their trenches he shouted aloud, and cried out so dreadfully, and with such amazement to the hearers, that it seemed all the devils of hell had been let loose: at which noise the enemies awaked, but can you tell how? even no lesse astonished then are *Monks*, at the ringing of the first peale to *Matins*, which in *Lusonnois* is called *Rubbalock*.

In the meantime *Pantagruel* began to sowe the salt that he had in his bark, and, because they slept with an open gaping mouth, he filled all their throats with it, so that those poor wretches were by it made to cough like foxes. Ha, *Pantagruel*, how thou addest greater heat to the firebrand that is in us. Suddenly *Pantagruel* had will to pisse, by meanes of the drugs which *Panurge* had given him, and pist amidst the camp so well and so copiously, that he drowned them all, and there was a particular deluge, ten leagues round about, of such considerable depth, that the history saith, if his fathers great mare had been there, and pist likewise, it would undoubtedly have been a more enormous deluge than that of *Deucalion*; for she did never pisse, but she made a river, greater then is either the *Rhosne*, or the *Danow*; which those that were come out of the City seeing, said, They are all cruelly slain, see how the blood runs along; but they were deceived in thinking *Pantagruels* urine had been the blood of their enemies; for they could not see but by the light of the fire of the pavillions, and some small light of the Moon.

The enemies after that they were awaked, seeing on one side the fire in the Camp, and on the other the inundation of the urinal deluge, could not tell what to say, nor what to think; some said, that it was the end of the world, and the final judgement, which ought to be by fire: Others again thought that the sea-gods, *Neptune, Protheus, Triton*, and the rest of them, did persecute them, for that indeed they found it to be like sea-water and salt.

O who were able now condignely to relate, how *Pantagruel* did demean himself against the three hundred Giants; O my

Muse, my *Calliope*, my *Thalia*, inspire me at this time, restore unto me my spirits; for this is the *Logical* bridge of asses! here is the pitfall, here is the difficultie, to have ability enough to expresse the horrible battel that was fought; Ah, would to God that I had now a bottle of the best wine, that ever those drank, who shall read this so veridical history.

CHAPTER XXIX

How Pantagruel discomfitted the three hundred giants armed with free stone, and Loupgarou their Captain.

THE Giants, seeing all their Camp drowned, carried away their King *Anarchus* upon their backs, as well as they could, out of the Fort, as *Æneas* did to his father *Anchises*, in the time of the conflagration of *Troy*. When *Panurge* perceived them, he said to *Pantagruel*, Sir, yonder are the Giants coming forth against you, lay on them with your mast gallantly like an old Fencer: for now is the time that you must shew your self a brave man and an honest. And for our part we will not faile you; I my self will kill to you a good many boldly enough; for why, *David* killed *Goliath* very easily, and then this great lecher *Eusthenes*, who is stronger then foure oxen, will not spare himself. Be of good courage therefore, and valiant, charge amongst them with point and edge, and by all manner of meanes. Well (said *Pantagruel*,) of courage I have more then for fifty francks, but let us be wise, for *Hercules* first never undertook against two; that is well cack'd, well scummered, (said *Panurge*) do you compare your self with *Hercules*? You have by G— more strength in your teeth, and more sent in your bum than ever *Hercules* had in all his body and soule: so much is a man worth as he esteems himself. Whilest they spake those words behold, *Loupgarou* was come with all his Giants, who seeing *Pantagruel* in a manner alone, was carried away with temerity and presumption, for hopes that he had to kill the good man; whereupon he said to his companions the Giants, You Wenchers of the low countrey, by *Mahoom*, if any of you undertake to fight against these men here, I will put you cruelly to death: it is my will that you let me fight single, in the mean time you shall have good sport to look upon us: then all the other

Giants retired with their King, to the place where the flaggons
stood, and *Panurge* and his *Camerades* with them, who counter-
feited those that have had the pox, for he wreathed about his
mouth, shrunk up his fingers, and with a harsh and hoarse voice
said unto them, I forsake -od, (fellow souldiers) if I would have
it to be beleeved, that we make any warre at all; Give us somewhat to eat with you, whilest our Masters fight against one another; to this the King and Giants joyntly condescended, and
accordingly made them to banquet with them. In the meantime
Panurge told them the follies of *Turpin*, the examples of St.
Nicholas, and the tale of a tub. *Loupgarou* then set forward towards *Pantagruel*, with a mace all of steel, and that of the best sort,
weighing nine thousand seven hundred kintals, and two quar-
terons, at the end whereof were thirteen pointed diamonds, the
least whereof was as big as the greatest bell of our *Ladies* Church
at *Paris*, there might want perhaps the thicknesse of a naile, or
at most, that I may not lie, of the back of those knives which
they call cut-lugs or eare-cutters, but for a little off or on, more
or lesse, it is no matter, and it was inchanted in such sort, that it
could never break, but contrarily all that it did touch, did break
immediately. Thus then as he approached with great fiercenesse
and pride of heart: *Pantagruel*, casting up his eyes to heaven,
recommended himself to God with all his soule, making such a
Vow as followeth.

O thou Lord God, who hast alwayes been my Protectour, and
my Saviour, thou seest the distresse wherein I am at this time:
nothing brings me hither but a natural zeale, which thou hast
permitted unto mortals, to keep and defend themselves, their
wives and children, countrey and family, in case thy own proper
cause were not in question, which is the faith; for in such a businesse thou wilt have no coadjutors, only a Catholick Confession
and service of thy Word, and hast forbidden us all arming and
defence; for thou art the Almighty, who in thine owne cause,
and where thine own businesse is taken to heart, canst defend
it far beyond all that we can conceive, thou who hast thousand
thousands of hundreds of millions of legions of Angels, the least
of which is able to kill all mortal men, and turn about the Heavens
and earth at his pleasure, as heretofore it very plainly appeared
in the army of *Sennacherib*, if it may please thee therefore at this

time to assist me, as my whole trust and confidence is in thee alone: I vow unto thee, that in all Countreys whatsoever, wherein I shall have any power or authority, whether in this of *Utopia*, or elsewhere, I will cause thy holy Gospel to be purely, simply and entirely preached, so that the abuses of a rabble of hypocrites and false prophets, who by humane constitutions, and depraved inventions, have impoisoned all the world, shall be quite exterminated from about me. This Vow was no sooner made, but there was heard a voice from heaven, saying, *Hoc fac, & vinces:* that is to say, *Do this, and thou shalt overcome.*

Then *Pantagruel*, seeing that *Loupgarou* with his mouth wide open was drawing near to him, went against him boldly, and cried out as loud as he was able, Thou diest, villain, thou diest, purposing by his horrible cry to make him afraid, according to the discipline of the *Lacedemonians*. Withal, he immediately cast at him out of his bark which he wore at his girdle, eighteen cags, and foure bushels of salt, wherewith he filled both his mouth, throat, nose and eyes: at this *Loupgarou* was so highly incensed, that most fiercely setting upon him, he thought even then with a blow of his mace to have beat out his braines: but *Pantagruel* was very nimble, and had alwayes a quick foot, and a quick eye, and therefore with his left foot did he step back one pace, yet not so nimbly, but that the blow falling upon the bark, broke it in foure thousand, fourescore and six pieces, and threw all the rest of the salt about the ground: *Pantagruel*, seeing that, most gallantly displayed the vigour of his armes, and, according to the Art of the axe, gave him with the great end of his mast a homethrust a little above the breast; then bringing along the blow to the left side, with a slash struck him between the neck and shoulders: After that, advancing his right foot, he gave him a push upon the couillons, with the upper end of his said mast, wherewith breaking the scuttle on the top thereof he spilt three or foure punchions of wine that were left therein.

Upon that *Loupgarou* thought that he had pierced his bladder, and that the wine that came forth had been his urine: *Pantagruel*, being not content with this, would have doubled it by a side-blow; but *Loupgarou*, lifting up his mace, advanced one step upon him, and with all his force would have dash't it upon *Pantagruel*, wherein (to speak the truth) he so sprightly carried himself, that if God had not succoured the good *Pantagruel*, he had been cloven from the top of his head to the bottom of his milt, but the blow glanced to the right side, by the brisk nimble-nesse of *Pantagruel*, and his mace sank into the ground above threescore and thirteen foot, through a huge rock, out of which the fire did issue greater than nine thousand and six tuns. *Pantagruel* seeing him busie about plucking out his mace, which stuck in the ground between the rocks, ran upon him, and would have clean cut off his head, if by mischance his mast had not touched a little against the stock of *Loupgarous* mace, which was inchanted, as we have said before: by this meanes his mast broke off about three handfuls above his hand, whereat he stood amazed like a Bell-Founder, and cried out, Ah *Panurge*, where art thou? *Panurge* seeing that, said to the King and the Giants, By G— they will hurt one another, if they be not parted; but the Giants were as merry as if they had been at a wedding: then *Carpalin* would have risen from thence to help his Master; but one of the Giants said unto him, By *Golfarin* the Nephew of *Mahoon*, if thou stir hence I will put thee in the bottom of my breeches, in stead of a Suppository, which cannot chuse but do me good; for in my belly I am very costive, and cannot well *cagar* without gnashing my teeth, and making many filthy faces. Then *Pantagruel*, thus destitute of a staffe, took up the end of his mast, striking athwart and alongst upon the Giant, but he did him no more hurt then you would do with a filip upon a Smiths Anvil. In the time *Loupgarou* was drawing his mace out of the ground, and having already plucked it out, was ready therewith to have struck *Pantagruel*, who being very quick in turning, avoided all his blowes in taking only the defensive part in hand, until on a sudden he saw, that *Loupgarou* did threaten him with these words, saying, Now, villain, will not I faile to chop thee as small as minced meat, and keep thee henceforth from ever making any more poor men athirst; for then without any more ado, *Pantagruel* struck him such a blow with his foot against the belly, that he made him fall backwards, his heels over his head, and dragged him thus along at flay-buttock above a flight-shot. Then *Loupgarou* cried out, bleeding at the throat, *Mahoon, Mahoon, Mahoon*, at which noise all the Giants arose to succour him: but *Panurge* said unto them, Gentlemen, do not go,

271

if you will beleeve me, for our Master is mad, and strikes athwart and alongst, he cares not where, he will do you a mischief; but the Giants made no account of it, seeing that *Pantagruel* had never a staffe.

And when *Pantagruel* saw those Giants approach very near unto him, he took *Loupgarou* by the two feet, and lift up his body like a pike in the aire, wherewith (it being harnished with Anvils) he laid such heavy load amongst those Giants armed with free stone, that striking them down as a mason doth little knobs of stones, there was not one of them that stood before him, whom he threw not flat to the ground, and by the breaking of this stony armour there was made such a horrible rumble, as put me in minde of the fall of the butter-tower of St. *Stephens* at *Bourge*, when it melted before the Sunne. *Panurge*, with *Carpalin* and *Eusthenes*, did cut in the mean time the throats of those that were struck down; in such sort that there escaped not one. *Pantagruel* to any mans sight was like a Mower, who with his sithe (which was *Loupgarou*,) cut down the meddow grasse (to wit the Giants,) but with this fencing of *Pantagruels*, *Loupgarou* lost his head, which happened when *Pantagruel* struck down one whose name was *Riflandouille* or pudding-plunderer, who was armed *capape* with grison stones, one chip whereof splintring abroad cut off *Epistemons* neck clean and faire: for otherwise the most part of them were but lightly armed with a kinde of sandie brittle stone, and the rest with slaits: at last when he saw that they were all dead, he threw the body of *Loupgarou*, as hard as he could against the City, where falling like a frog upon his belly, in the great *piazza* thereof, he with the said fall killed a singed he-cat, a wet she-cat, a farting duck, and a brideled goose.

CHAPTER XXX

How Epistemon, who had his head cut off, was finely healed by Panurge, and of the newes which he brought from the devils, and of the damned people in hell.

THIS Gigantal victory being ended, *Pantagruel* withdrew himself to the place of the flaggons, and called for *Panurge* and the rest, who came unto him safe and sound, except *Eusthenes*, (whom one of the Giants had scratched a little in the face, whilest he was about the cutting of his throat), & *Epistemon*, who appeared not at all: whereat *Pantagruel* was so aggrieved, that he would have killed himself; but *Panurge* said unto him, Nay, Sir, stay a while, and we will search for him amongst the dead, and finde out the truth of all: thus as they went seeking after him, they found him stark dead, with his head between his armes all bloody. Then *Eusthenes* cried out, Ah cruel death! hast thou taken from me the perfectest amongst men? At which words *Pantagruel* rose up with the greatest grief that ever any man did see, and said to *Panurge*, Ha, my friend, the prophecy of your two glasses, and the javelin staffe, was a great deal too deceitful, but *Panurge* answered, My dear bullies all, weep not one drop more, for he being yet all hot, I will make him as sound as ever he was; in saying this, he took the head, and held it warme fore-gainst his Codpiece, that the winde might not enter into it, *Eusthenes* and *Carpalin* carried the body to the place where they had banqueted, not out of any hope that ever he would recover, but that *Pantagruel* might see it.

Neverthelesse *Panurge* gave him very good comfort, saying, If I do not heale him, I will be content to lose my head (which is a fooles wager), leave off therefore crying, and help me. Then cleansed he his neck very well with pure white wine, and after that, took his head, and into it *synapised* some powder of diamerdis, which he alwayes carried about him in one of his bags. Afterwards, he anointed it with I know not what ointment, and set it on very just, veine against veine, sinew against sinew, and spondyle against spondyle, that he might not be wry-necked, (for such people he mortally hated) this done, he gave it round about some fifteen or sixteen stitches with a needle, that it might not fall off again, then on all sides, and every where he put a little ointment on it, which he called *resuscitative*.

Suddenly *Epistemon* began to breath, then opened his eyes, yawned, sneezed, and afterwards let a great houshold fart; whereupon *Panurge* said, Now certainly he is healed, and therefore gave him to drink a large full glasse of strong white wine, with a sugred toast. In this fashion was *Epistemon* finely healed, only that he was somewhat hoarse for above three weeks

together, and had a dry cough of which he could not be rid, but
by the force of continual drinking: and now he began to speak,
and said, that he had seen the divel, had spoken with *Lucifer*
familiarly, and had been very merry in hell, and in the *Elysian*
fields, affirming very seriously before them all, that the devils
were boone companions, and merry fellowes: but in respect of
the damned, he said he was very sorry that *Panurge* had so
soon called him back into this world again; for (said he) I took
wonderful delight to see them: How so? said *Pantagruel*: because
they do not use them there (said *Epistemon*) so badly as you
think they do: their estate and condition of living is but only
changed after a very strange manner; for I saw *Alexander* the
great there, amending and patching on clowts upon old
breeches and stockins, whereby he got but a very poor living.

Xerxes was a Cryer of mustard.
Romulus, a Salter and patcher of patines.
Numa, a nailsmith.
Tarquin, a Porter.
Piso, a clownish swaine.
Sylla, a Ferrie-man.
Cyrus, a Cowheard.
Themistocles, a glasse-maker.
Epaminondas, a maker of Mirrours or Looking-glasses.
Brutus and *Cassius*, Surveyors or Measurers of land.
Demosthenes, a Vine-dresser.
Cicero, a fire-kindler.
Fabius, a threader of beads.
Artaxerxes, a rope-maker.
Æneas, a Miller.
Achilles was a scauld-pated maker of hay-bundles.
Agamemnon, a lick-box.
Ulysses, a hay-mower.
Nestor, a Deer-keeper or Forrester.
Darius, a Gold-finder, or Jakes-farmer.
Ancus Martius, a ship-trimmer.
Camillus, a foot-post.
Marcellus, a sheller of beans.
Drusus, a taker of money at the doors of play-houses.

Scipio Africanus, a Crier of Lee in a wooden slipper.

Asdrubal, a Lanterne-maker.

Hannibal, a Kettlemaker and seller of eggeshels.

Priamus, a seller of old clouts.

Lancelot of the lake was a flayer of dead horses.

All the Knights of the round Table were poore day-labourers, employed to rowe over the rivers of *Cocytus, Phlegeton, Styx, Acheron* and *Lethe*, when my Lords, the devils had a minde to recreate themselves upon the water, as in the like occasion are hired the boatmen at *Lions*, the *gondeleers* of *Venice*, and oares at *London*; but with this difference, that these poor Knights have only for their fare a bob or flirt on the nose, and in the evening a morsel of course mouldie bread.

Trajan was a fisher of frogs.

Antoninus, a Lackey.

Commodus, a Jeat-maker.

Pertinax, a peeler of wall-nuts.

Lucullus, a maker of rattles and Hawks bells.

Justinian, a Pedlar.

Hector, a Snap-sauce Scullion.

Paris was a poore beggar.

Cambyses, a Mule-driver.

Nero, a base blinde fidler, or player on that instrument which is called a windbroach: *Fierabras* was his serving-man, who did him a thousand mischievous tricks, and would make him eat of the brown bread, and drink of the turned wine, when himself did both eate and drink of the best.

Julius Cæsar and *Pompey* were boat-wrights and tighters of ships.

Valentine and *Orson* did serve in the stoves of hell, and were sweat-rubbers in hot houses.

Giglan and *Govian* were poor Swine-herds.

Jafrey with the great tooth was a tinder-maker and seller of matches.

Godfrey de bullion, a Hood-maker.

Jason was a Bracelet-maker.

Don Pietro de Castille, a Carrier of Indulgences.

Morgan, a beer-Brewer.

Huon of *Bourdeaux*, a Hooper of barrels.

Pyrrhus, a Kitchin-Scullion.

Antiochus, a Chimney-sweeper.

Octavian, a Scraper of parchment.

Nerva, a Mariner.

Pope Julius was a Crier of pudding pyes, but he left off wearing there his great buggerly beard.

John of *Paris* was a greaser of boots.

Arthur of Britain, an ungreaser of caps.

Pierce Forrest, a Carrier of fagots.

Pope Boniface the eighth, a Scummer of pots.

Pope *Nicholas* the third, a Maker of paper.

Pope *Alexander*, a rat-catcher.

Pope *Sixtus*, an Anointer of those that have the pox.

What, (said *Pantagruel*) have they the pox there too? Surely (said *Epistemon*) I never saw so many: there are there, I think, above a hundred millions; for beleeve, that those who have not had the pox in this world, must have it in the other.

Cotsbody (said *Panurge*) then I am free; for I have been as farre as the hole of *Gibraltar*, reached unto the outmost bounds of *Hercules*, and gathered of the ripest.

Ogier the *Dane* was a Furbisher of armour.

The King *Tigranes*, a mender of thatched houses.

Galien Restored, a taker of Moldwarps.

The foure sons of *Aymon* were all tooth-drawers.

Pope *Calixtus* was a barber of a womans *Sine quo non*.

Pope *Urban*, a bacon-pecker.

Melusina was a Kitchin drudge-wench.

Mattabrune, a Laundresse.

Cleopatra, a Crier of onions.

Helene, a broker for Chamber-maids.

Semiramis, the Beggars lice-killer.

Dido did sell mushrooms.

Pentasilea sold cresses.

Lucretia was an Ale-house-keeper.

Hortensia, a Spinstresse.

Livia, a grater of verdigreece.

After this manner, those that had been great Lords and Ladies here, got but a poor scurvie wretched living there below. And on the contrary, the Philosophers and others, who in this

world had been altogether indigent and wanting, were great
lords there in their turne. I saw *Diogenes* there strout it out most
pompously, and in great magnificence, with a rich purple gown
on him, and a golden Scepter in his right hand. And which is
more, he would now and then make *Alexander* the great mad, so
enormously would he abuse him, when he had not well patched
his breeches; for he used to pay his skin with sound bastonadoes; I saw *Epictetus* there most gallantly apparelled after the
French fashion, sitting under a pleasant Arbour, with store of handsom Gentlewomen, frolicking, drinking, dancing, and making
good cheare, with abundance of Crowns of the Sunne. Above
the lattice were written these verses for his device:

> *To leap and dance, to sport and play,*
> *And drink good wine both white and brown:*
> *Or nothing else do all the day,*
> *But tell bags full of many a Crown.*

When he saw me, he invited me to drink with him very
courteously, and I being willing to be entreated, we tipled and
chopined together most theologically. In the mean time came
Cyrus to beg one farthing of him for the honour of *Mercurie*,
therewith to buy a few onions for his supper? No, no, said *Epictetus*, I do not use in my almes-giving to bestow farthings, hold
thou Varlet, there's a crown for thee, be an honest man: *Cyrus*
was exceeding glad to have met with such a bootie; but the
other poor rogues, the Kings that are there below, as *Alexander*,
Darius, and others stole it away from him by night. I saw *Pathelin*
the Treasurer of *Rhadamantus*, who in cheapening the pudding-
pyes that Pope *Julius* cried, asked him, How much a dozen?
Three blanks (said the Pope:) Nay (said *Pathelin*) three blowes
with a cudgel, lay them down here you rascal and go fetch more:
the poor Pope went away weeping, who when he came to his
Master the Pye-maker, told him that they had taken away his
pudding-pyes; whereupon his Master gave him such a sound
lash with an eele-skin, that his own would have been worth
nothing to make bag-pipe-bags of. I saw master *John le maire*
there personate the Pope in such fashion, that he made all the
poor Kings and Popes of this world kisse his feet, and taking
great state upon him, gave them his benediction, saying, Get

the pardons, rogues, get the pardons, they are good cheap: I absolve you of bread and pottage, and dispense with you to be never good for anything: then, calling *Caillet* and *Triboulet*, to him, he spoke these words, My Lords the Cardinals, dispatch their bulls, to wit, to each of them a blow with a Cudgel upon the reines, which accordingly was forthwith performed.

I heard Master *Francis Villon* ask *Xerxes*, How much the messe of mustard? A farthing, said *Xerxes*: to which the said *Villon* answered, The pox take thee for a villain: as much of square-ear'd wheat is not worth half that price, and now thou offerest to inhance the price of victuals: with this he pist in his pot as the mustard-makers of *Paris* used to do. I saw the trained bowe-man of the bathing tub, (known by the name of the *Francarcher de baignolet*) who being one of the trustees of the Inquisition, when he saw *Pierce Forrest* making water against a wall, in which was painted the fire of St. *Antonie*, declared him heretick, and would have caused him to be burnt alive, had it not been for *Morgant*, who for his *Proficiat* and other small fees gave him nine tuns of beer. Well (said *Pantagruel*,) reserve all these faire stories for another time, only tell us how the Usurers are there handled: I saw them (said *Epistemon*) all very busily employed in seeking of rustie pins, and old nailes in the kennels of the streets, as you see poor wretched rogues do in this world; but the *quintal*, or hundred weight of this old iron ware, is there valued but at the price of a cantle of bread, and yet they have but a very bad dispatch and riddance in the sale of it: thus the poor Misers are sometimes three whole weeks, without eating one morsel or crumb of bread, and yet work both day and night, looking for the faire to come: neverthelesse, of all this labour, toile and misery, they reckon nothing, so cursedly active they are in the prosecution of that their base calling, in hopes at the end of the yeare, to earne some scurvie penny by it.

Come, (said *Pantagruel*) let us now make our selves merry one bout, and drink (my Lads) I beseech you, for it is very good drinking all this moneth: then did they uncase their flaggons by heaps and dozens, and with their leaguer-provision made excellent good chear: but the poor King *Anarchus* could not all this while settle himselfe towards any fit of mirth; whereupon *Panurge* said, Of what trade shall we make my Lord the King here, that he may be skilful in the Art, when he goes thither to sojourn amongst all the devils of hell? Indeed (said *Pantagruel*) that was well advised of thee, do with him what thou wilt: I give him to thee: Grammercie (said *Panurge*) the present is not to be refused, and I love it from you.

CHAPTER XXXI

How Pantagruel entered into the City of the Amaurots, and
how Panurge married King Anarchus to an old
Lantern-carrying Hag, and made him a Cryer of green sauce.

AFTER this wonderful victory, *Pantagruel* sent *Carpalin* unto the City of the *Amaurots*, to declare and signifie unto them how the King *Anarchus* was taken prisoner, and all the enemies of the City overthrown, which news when they heard, all the inhabitants of the City came forth to meet him in good order, and with a great triumphant pomp, conducting him with a heavenly joy into the City, where innumerable bonefires were set on, thorough all the parts thereof, and faire round tables which were furnished with store of good victuals, set out in the middle of the streets; this was a renewing of the golden age in the time of *Saturn*, so good was the cheere which then they made.

But *Pantagruel* having assembled the whole Senate, and Common Councel-men of the town, said (My Masters) we must now strike the iron whilest it is hot; it is therefore my will, that before we frolick it any longer, we advise how to assault and take the whole Kingdom of the *Dipsodes*: to which effect let those that will go with me provide themselves against to-morrow after drinking; for then will I begin to march, not that I need any more men then I have to help me to conquer it; for I could make it as sure that way as if I had it already, but I see this City is so full of inhabitants, that they scarce can turn in the streets; I will, therefore, carry them as a Colonie into *Dipsodie*, and will give them all that Countrey, which is fair, healthie, fruitful and pleasant, above all other Countreys in the world, as many of you can tell who have been there heretofore, every one of you, therefore that will go along, let him provide himself as I have said. This counsel and resolution being published in the City, the next morning there assembled in the *piazza*, before the Palace, to the number of eighteen hundred fifty six thousand and eleven, besides women and little children: thus began they to march straight into *Dipsodie*, in such good order as did the people of *Israel*, when they departed out of *Egypt*, to passe over the red-sea.

But before we proceed any further in this purpose, I will tell you how *Panurge* handled his prisoner the King *Anarchus*; for having remembered that which *Epistemon* had related, how the Kings and rich men in this world were used in the *Elysian* fields, and how they got their living there by base and ignoble trades; he therefore one day apparelled his King in a pretty little can-vass doublet, all jagged and pinked like the tippet of a light horsemans cap, together with a paire of large Mariners breeches, and stockins without shoes; For (said he) they would but spoile his sight; and a little peach-coloured bonnet, with a great capons feather in it: I lie, for I think he had two: and a very handsome girdle of a sky-colour and green, (in *French* called *pers et vert*) saying, that such a livery did become him well, for that he had alwayes been *perverse*, and in this plight bringing him before *Pantagruel*, said unto him, Do you know this royster? No, indeed, said *Pantagruel*: It is (said *Panurge*) my Lord the King of the three batches, or thread-bare sovereign: I intend to make him an honest man. These devillish Kings which we have here are but as so many calves, they know nothing, and are good for nothing, but to do a thousand mischiefs to their poor subjects, and to trouble all the world with warre for their unjust and detestable pleasure: I will put him to a trade, and make him a Crier of green sauce. Go to, begin and cry: *Do you lack any green sauce*? and the poor wretch cried: That is too low (said *Panurge*,) then took him by the eare, saying, Sing higher in *Gesolreut*: So, so (poor wretch) thou hast a good throat: thou wert never so happy as to be no longer King: and *Pantagruel* made himself merry with all this; for I dare boldly say, that he was the best little gaffer that was to be seen between this and the end of a staffe. Thus was *Anarchus* made a good Crier of green sauce, two dayes thereafter *Panurge* married him with an old Lanterne-carrying Hag, and he himselfe made the wedding with fine sheeps-heads, brave haslets with mustard, gallant salligots with garlick, of which he sent five horse-loads unto *Pantagruel*, which he ate up all, he found them so appetizing: and for their drink, they had a kinde of small well-watered wine, and some sorbapple-cider: and, to make them dance, he hired a blinde man, that made musick to them with a windbroach.

After dinner he led them to the Palace, and shewed them to *Pantagruel*, and said, pointing to the married woman, You need not feare that she will *crack*. Why? said *Pantagruel*: Because, said *Panurge*, she is well slit and broke up already; What do you mean by that? said *Pantagruel*: Do not you see? said *Panurge*, that the chestnuts which are roasted in the fire, if they be whole, they *crack* as if they were mad; and, to keep them from *cracking*, they make an incision in them, and slit them; so this new Bride is in her lower parts well slit before, and therefore will not crack behinde.

Pantagruel gave them a little lodge near the lower street, and a mortar of stone wherein to bray and pound their sauce, and in this manner did they do their little businesse, he being as pretty a Crier of green sauce, as ever was seene in the Countrey of *Utopia*. But I have been told since, that his wife doth beat him like plaister, and the poor sot dare not defend himself, he is so simple.

CHAPTER XXXII

How Pantagruel with his tongue covered a whole Army, and what the Author saw in his mouth.

THUS as *Pantagruel* with all his Army had entered into the Countrey of the *Dipsodes*, every one was glad of it, and incontinently rendred themselves unto him, bringing him out of their own good wills the Keyes of all the Cities where he went, the *Almirods* only excepted, who being resolved to hold out against him, made answer to his Heraulds, that they would not yield but upon very honourable and good conditions.

What? (said *Pantagruel*) do they ask any better terms, then the hand at the pot, and the glasse in their fist? Come, let us go sack them, and put them all to the sword: then did they put themselves in good order as being fully determined to give an assault, but by the way passing through a large field, they were

overtaken with a great shower of raine, whereat they began to
shiver and tremble, to croud, presse and thrust close to one another. When *Pantagruel* saw that, he made their Captains tell
them, that it was nothing, and that he saw well above the
clouds, that it would be nothing but a little dew; but howsoever,
that they should put themselves in order, and he would cover
them: then did they put themselves in a close order, and stood
as near to other as they could: and *Pantagruel* drew out his
tongue only half-wayes and covered them all, as a hen doth her
chickens. In the mean time I, who relate to you these so veritable stories, hid myself under a burdock-leafe, which was not
much lesse in largenesse then the arch of the bridge of *Mon-
trible*, but when I saw them thus covered, I went towards them
to shelter my self likewise; which I could not do; for that they
were so (as the saying is) *At the yards end there is no cloth left*. Then
as well as I could, I got upon it, and went along full two leagues
upon his tongue, and so long marched, that at last I came into
his mouth: but, oh gods and goddesses, what did I see there?
Jupiter confound me with his trisulk lightning if I lie: I walked
there as they do in *Sophie* and *Constantinople*, and saw there great
rocks, like the mountains in *Denmark*, I beleeve that those were
his teeth. I saw also faire meddows, large forrests, great and
strong Cities, not a jot lesse then *Lyons* or *Poictiers*, the first man
I met with there, was a good honest fellow planting coleworts,
whereat being very much amazed, I asked him, My friend, what
dost thou make here? I plant coleworts, said he; but how, and
wherewith, said I? Ha, Sir, said he, every one cannot have his
ballocks as heavy as a mortar, neither can we be all rich: thus do
I get my poor living, and carry them to the market to sell in the
City which is here behinde. Jesus! (said I) is there here a new
world? Sure (said he) it is never a jot new, but it is commonly
reported, that without this there is an earth, whereof the inhabitants enjoy the light of a Sunne and a Moone, and that it is full
of, and replenished with very good commodities; but yet this is
more ancient than that: Yea, but (said I) my friend, what is the
name of that City, whither thou carriest thy Coleworts to sell?
It is called *Aspharage*, (said he) and all the indwellers are Christians, very honest men, and will make you good chear. To be
brief, I resolved to go thither. Now in my way, I met with a

fellow that was lying in wait to catch pigeons, of whom I asked, (My friend) from whence come these pigeons? Sir, (said he) they come from the other world: then I thought, that when *Panta-gruel* yawned, the pigeons went into his mouth in whole flocks, thinking that it had been a pigeon-house.

Then I went into the City, which I found faire, very strong, and seated in a good aire; but at my entry the guard demanded of me my passe or ticket: whereat I was much astonished, and asked them, (My Masters) is there any danger of the plague here? O Lord, (said they) they die hard by here so fast, that the cart runs about the streets; Good God! (said I) and where? whereun-to they answered that it was in *Larinx* and *Phærinx*, which are two great Cities, such as *Rowen* and *Nants*, rich and of great trad-ing: and the cause of the plague was by a stinking and infectious exhalation, which lately vapoured out of the abismes, whereof there have died above two and twenty hundred and three-score thousand and sixteen persons within this sevennight; then I considered, calculated and found, that it was a rank and un-savoury breathing, which came out of *Pantagruels* stomack, when he did eat so much garlick, as we have aforesaid.

Parting from thence, I past amongst the rocks, which were his teeth, and never left walking, till I got up on one of them; and there I found the pleasantest places in the world, great large tennis-Courts, faire galleries, sweet meddows, store of Vines, and an infinite number of banqueting summer out-houses in the fields, after the *Italian* fashion, full of pleasure and delight, where I stayed full foure moneths, and never made better cheer in my life as then. After that I went down by the hinder teeth to come to the chaps; but in the way I was robbed by thieves in a great forrest, that is in the territory towards the eares: then (after a little further travelling) I fell upon a pretty petty village, (truly I have forgot the name of it) where I was yet merrier than ever, and got some certain money to live by, can you tell how? by sleeping; for there they hire men by the day to sleep, and they get by it sixpence a day, but they that can snort hard get at least nine pence. How I had been robbed in the valley I in-formed the Senators, who told me that, in very truth the people of that side were bad livers, and naturally theevish, whereby I perceived well, that as we have with us the Countreys *cisalpin and transalpine*, that is, behither and beyond the mountains, so have they there the Countreys *cidentine* and *tradentine*, that is, behither and beyond the teeth: but it is farre better living on this side, and the aire is purer. There I began to think, that it is very true which is commonly said, that the one half of the world knoweth not how the other half liveth; seeing none before my self had ever written of that Countrey, wherein are above five and twenty Kingdoms inhabited, besides deserts, and a great arme of the sea: concerning which purpose, I have composed a great book intituled *The History of the* Throttias, because they dwell in the throat of my Master *Pantagruel*.

At last I was willing to return, and passing by his beard, I cast my self upon his shoulders, and from thence slid down to the ground, and fell before him: assoon as I was perceived by him, he asked me, Whence comest thou, *Alcofribas*? I answered him, Out of your mouth, *my Lord*: and how long hast thou been there? said he. Since the time (said I) that you went against the *Almirods*; That is, about six moneths ago, said he: and wherewith didst thou live? what didst thou drink? I answered, My Lord, of the same that you did, and of the daintest morsels that past through your throat I took toll: Yea, but, said he, where didst thou shite? In your throat (my lord) said I. Ha ha, thou art a merry fellow, said he. We have with the help of God conquered all the land of the *Dipsodes*; I will give thee the *Chastelleine* or Lairdship of *Salmigondin*. Grammercy, my Lord, said I, you gratifie me beyond all that I have deserved of you.

CHAPTER XXXIII

How Pantagruel became sick, and the manner how he was recovered.

A WHILE after this the good *Pantagruel* fell sick, and had such an obstruction in his stomack, that he could neither eate nor drink: and because mischief seldome comes alone, a hot pisse seised on him, which tormented him more then you would beleeve: His Physicians neverthelesse helped him very well, and with store of lenitives and diuretick drugs made him pisse away his paine: his urine was so hot, that since that time it is not yet cold,

and you have of it in divers places of *France*, according to the
course that it took, and they are called the hot baths, as

> At *Coderets*.
> At *Limous*.
> At *Dast*.
> At *Ballervie*.
> At *Nerie*.
> At *Bourbonansie*, and elsewhere in *Italie*.
> At *Mongros*.
> At *Appone*.
> At *Sancto Petro de Adua*.
> At *St. Helen*.
> At *Casa Nuova*.
> At St. *Bartolomee*, in the County of *Boulogne*.
> At the *Lorrette*, and a thousand other places.

And I wonder much at a rabble of foolish Philosophers and
Physicians, who spend their time in disputing, whence the heat
of the said waters cometh, whether it be by reason of *Borax*, or
sulphur, or allum, or salt-peter that is within the mine; for they
do nothing but dote, and better were it for them, to rub their
arse against a thistle, then to waste away their time thus in disputing of that, whereof they know not the original; for the resolution is easie, neither need we to enquire any further, then that
the said baths came by a hot pisse of the good *Pantagruel*.

Now to tell you after what manner he was cured of his principal disease; I let passe how for a *minorative*, or gentle potion,
he took foure hundred pound weight of *Colophoniack Scammonee*,
six score and eighteen cartloads of *Cassia*: an eleven thousand
and nine hundred pound weight of *Rubarb*, besides other confused jumblings of sundry drugs: You must understand, that by
the advice of the *Physicians* it was ordained, that what did offend
his stomach should be taken away; and therefore they made
seventeen great balls of copper, each whereof was bigger then
that which is to be seen on the top of St. *Peters* needle at *Rome*,
and in such sort, that they did open in the midst, and shut with
a spring. Into one of them entered one of his men, carrying a
Lanterne and a torch lighted, and so *Pantagruel* swallowed him
down like a little pill: into seven others went seven Countrey-
fellows, having every one of them a shovel on his neck: into

nine others entred nine wood-carriers, having each of them a basket hung at his neck, and so were they swallowed down like pills: when they were in his stomack, every one undid his spring, and came out of their cabins: the first whereof was he that carried the Lantern, and so they fell more than half a league into a most horrible gulph, more stinking and infectious than ever was *Mephitis*, or the marishes of *Camerina*, or the abominably unsavoury lake of *Sorbona*, whereof *Strabo* maketh mention. And had it not been, that they had very well antidoted their stomach, heart and winepot, which is called the noddle, they had been altogether suffocated and choaked with these detestable vapours. O what a perfume! O what an evaporation wherewith to bewray the mask or muflers of young mangie queans: after that with groping and smelling they came near to the fecal matter and the corrupted humours; finally, they found a *montjoy* or heap of ordure and filth: then fell the Pioneers to work to dig it up, and the rest with their shovels filled the baskets; and when all was cleansed, every one retired himself into his ball.

This done, *Pantagruel* enforcing himself to a vomit, very easily brought them out, and they made no more shew in his mouth, than a fart in yours: but when they came merrily out of their pills, I thought upon the *Grecians* coming out of the *Trojan* horse: by this meanes was he healed, and brought unto his former state and convalescence; and of these brazen pilles, or rather copper-balls, you have one at *Orleans*, upon the steeple of the Holy Crosse Church.

CHAPTER XXXIV

The Conclusion of this present Book, and the excuse of the Author.

NOW (my masters) you have heard a beginning of the horrifick history of my Lord and Master *Pantagruel*: Here will I make an end of the first book: My head akes a little, and I perceive that the Registers of my braine are somewhat jumbled and disordered with this septembral juice. You shall have the rest of the history at *Franckfort mart* next coming, and there shall you see

how *Panurge* was married and made a Cuckold within a moneth
after his wedding: how *Pantagruel* found out the Philosophers
stone, the manner how he found it, and the way how to use it:
how he past over the *Caspian* mountaines, and how he sailed
through the *Atlantick* sea, defeated the *Cannibals*, and conquered the isles of *Perles*, how he married the daughter of the
King of *India*, called *Prestian*, how he fought against the devil,
and burnt up five chambers of hell, ransacked the great black
chamber, threw *Proserpina* into the fire, broke five teeth to
Lucifer, and the horne that was in his arse. How he visited the
regions of the Moon, to know whether indeed the Moon were
not entire and whole, or if the women had three quarters of it in
their heads, and a thousand other little merriments all veritable.
These are brave things truly; Good night, Gentlemen, *Perdonate
mi*, and think not so much upon my faults, that you forget your
own. If you say to me, (Master) it would seem that you were not
very wise in writing to us these flimflam stories, and pleasant
fooleries:

    I answer you, that you are not much wiser to spend your time
in reading them: neverthelesse, if you read them to make your
selves merry, as in manner of pastime I wrote them, you and I
both are farre more worthy of pardon, then a great rabble of
squint-minded fellowes, dissembling and counterfeit Saints,
demure lookers, hypocrites, pretended zealots, tough Fryars,
buskin-Monks, and other such sects of men, who disguise
themselves like Maskers to deceive the world, for, whilest they
give the common people to understand, that they are busied
about nothing but contemplation and devotion in fastings, and
maceration of their sensuality; and that only to sustain and
aliment the small frailty of their humanity: It is so far otherwise,
that on the contrary (God knows) what cheer they make, *Et
Curios simulant, sed bacchanalia vivunt*. You may read it in great
letters, in the colouring of their red snowts, and gulching bellies
as big as a tun, unlesse it be when they perfume themselves
with sulphur; as for their study, it is wholly taken up in reading of
Pantagruelin books, not so much to passe the time merrily, as to
hurt some one or other mischievously, to wit, in *articling, sole-
articling, wry-neckifying, buttock-stirring, ballocking*, and *diablicula-
ting*, that is, culumniating; wherein they are like unto the poor

rogues of a village, that are busie in stirring up and scraping in the ordure and filth of little children, in the season of cherries and guinds, and that only to find the kernels, that they may sell them to the druggists, to make thereof pomander-oile. Fly from these men, abhorre and hate them as much as I do, and upon my faith you will finde your selves the better for it. And if you desire to be good *Pantagruelists* (that is to say, to live in peace, joy, health, making your selves alwayes merry) never trust those men that alwayes peep out at one hole.

The End of the Second
Book of RABELAIS.

THE THIRD BOOK

OF THE WORKS OF
MR. FRANCIS RABELAIS,
DOCTOR IN PHYSICK

CONTAINING THE HEROICK DEEDS OF
PANTAGRUEL, THE SON OF GARGANTUA

FRANCIS RABELAIS TO THE SOUL OF THE DECEASED QUEEN OF NAVARRE

ABSTRACTED *Soul, ravish'd with extasies,*
Gone back, and now familiar in the Skies.
Thy former Host, thy Body, leaving quite,
Which to obey thee always took delight;
Obsequious, ready. Now from motion free,
Senseless, and as it were, in Apathy.
Wouldst thou not issue forth, for a short space,
From that Divine, Eternal, Heavenly place,
To see the third part, in this earthly Cell,
Of the brave Acts of good Pantagruel.

THE AUTHORS PROLOGUE

GOOD People, most Illustrious Drinkers, and you thrice precious gouty Gentlemen. Did you ever *see Diogenes* the *Cynick* Philosopher, if you have *seen* him, you then had your Eyes in your Head, or I am very much out of my Understanding and Logical Sense. It is a gallant thing to see the clearness of (Wine, Gold) the Sun. I'll be judged by the blind-born, so renowned in the Sacred Scriptures; who having at his choice to ask whatever he would from Him who is Almighty, and whose Word in an Instant is effectually performed, asked nothing else but that he might *see. Item* you are not young, which is a competent Quality for you to Philosophat more than Physically in *Wine* (not in vain) and henceforwards to be of the *Bacchick* Council; to the end that *opining* there, you may give your *Opinion* faithfully of the Substance, Colour, excellent Odour, Eminency, Propriety, Faculty, Vertue, and effectual Dignity of the said blessed and desired Liquor.

If you have not *seen* him (as I am easily induced to believe that you have not) at least you have heard some talk of him. For through the Air, and the whole extent of this Hemisphere of the Heavens, hath his Report and Fame, even until this present time, remained very memorable and renowned. Then all of you are derived from the *Phrygian* Blood (if I be not deceived). If you have not so many Crowns as *Midas* had, yet have you something (I know not what) of him, which the *Persians* of old esteemed more of in all their *Otacusts*, and which was more desired by the Emperor *Antonine*; and gave occasion thereafter to the *Basilisco* at *Rohan* to be Surnamed *Goodly ears*. If you have not heard of him, I will presently tell you a Story to make your Wine relish: Drink then, so, to the purpose; hearken now whilst I give you notice (to the end that you may not, like Infidels be by your simplicity abused) that in his time he was a rare Philosopher, and the chearfullest of a thousand: If he had some Imperfection,

291

so have you, so have we; for there is nothing (but God) that is perfect: Yet so it was, that by *Alexander* the Great (altho' he had *Aristotle* for his Instructor and Domestick) was he held in such Estimation, that he wish'd, if *he had not been* Alexander, *to have been* Diogenes *the* Sinopian.

When *Philip* King of *Macedon* enterprised the Siege and Ruine of *Corinth*, the *Corinthians* having received certain Intelligence by their Spies, that he with a numerous Army in Battle Rank was coming against them, were all of them (not without cause) most terribly afraid; and therefore were not neglective of their Duty, in doing their best Endeavours to put themselves in a fit posture to resist his Hostile Approach, and defend their own City.

Some from the Fields brought into the Fortify'd Places their Movables, Bestial, Corn, Wine, Fruit, Victuals, and other necessary Provision.

Others did fortifie and rampire their Walls, set up little Fortresses, Bastions, squared Ravelins, digged Trenches, cleansed Countermines, fenced themselves with *Gabions*, contrived Platforms, emptied *Casemates*, barricado'd the false *Brayes*, erected the *Cavalliers*, repaired the Contrescarfes, plaister'd the *Courtines*, lengthned *Ravelins*, stopt *Parapets*, mortaised *Barbacans*, assured the *Port-culleys*, fasten'd the *Herses, Sarasinesks* and *Cataracks*, placed their Centries, and doubled their *Patrouille*.

Every one did watch and ward, and not one was exempted from carrying the Basket.

Some polish'd Corselets, varnish'd Backs and Breasts, clean'd the Head-pices, Mail-Coats, *Brigandins, Salads*, Helmets, Murrions, Jacks, Gushets, *Gorgets, Hoguines, Brassars* and *Cuissars, Corseletts, Haubergeons*, Shields, Bucklers, Targuets, *Greves*, Gantlets and Spurs.

Others made ready Bows, Slings, Cross-bows, Pellets, *Catapults, Migrames* or Fire-balls, Firebrands, *Balists*, Scorpions, and other such Warlike Engines *expugnatorie*, and destructive to the *Hellepolists*.

They sharpned and prepared Spears, Staves, Pikes, Brown Bills, Halberts, Long Hooks, Lances, *Zagages*, Quarterstaves, Eelspears, Partisans, Troutstaves, Clubs, Battle-axes, Maces, Darts, Dartlets, Glaves, Javelins, Javelots, and Trunchions.

They set Edges upon Cimeters, Cutlasses, *Badelans*, Back-swords, Tucks, Rapiers, Bayonets, Arrow-heads, Dags, Daggers, *Mandousians*, Poigniards, Whinyards, Knives, Skenes, Sables, Chipping Knives, and *Raillons*.

Every Man exercis'd his Weapon, every Man scowr'd off the Rust from his natural Hanger: Nor was there a Woman amongst them (tho' never so reserv'd or old) who made not her Harnish to be well furbish'd; as you know the *Corinthian* Women of old were reputed very couragious Combatants.

Diogenes seeing them all so warm at work, and himself not employed by the Magistrates in any business whatsoever, he did very seriously (for many days together, without speaking one Word) consider, and contemplate the Countenance of his Fellow-Citizens.

Then on a sudden, as if he had been roused up and inspired by a Martial Spirit, he girded his Cloak, scarf-ways, about his Left Arm, tucked up his Sleeves to the Elbow, trussed himself like a Clown gathering Apples, and giving to one of his old Acquaintance his Wallet, Books, and *Opistographs*, away went he out of Town towards a little Hill or Promontory of *Corinth* called *Cranie*; and there on the Strand, a pretty level place, did he roul his Jolly Tub, which serv'd him for an House to shelter him from the Injuries of the Weather: There, I say, in a great Vehemency of Spirit, did he turn it, veer it, wheel it, whirl it, frisk it, jumble it, shuffle it, huddle it, tumble it, hurry it, joult it, justle it, overthrow it, evert it, invert it, subvert it, overturn it, beat it, thwack it, bump it, batter it, knock it, thrust it, push it, jerk it, shock it, shake it, toss it, throw it, overthrow it up-side down, topsiturvy, arsiturvy, tread it, trample it, stamp it, tap it, ting it, ring it, tingle it, towl it, sound it, resound it, stop it, shut it, unbung it, close it, unstopple it. And then again in a mighty bustle he bandy'd it, slubber'd it, hack'd it, whitled it, way'd it, darted it, hurled it, stagger'd it, reel'd it, swindg'd it, brangled it, totter'd it, lifted it, heav'd it, transformed it, transfigur'd it, transpos'd it, transplaced it, reared it, raised it, hoised it, washed it, dighted it, cleansed it, rinsed it, nailed it, setled it, fastned it, shackled it, fetter'd it, level'd it, block'd it, tugg'd it, tew'd it, carry'd it, bedash'd it, beray'd it, parch'd it, mounted it, broach'd it, nick'd it, notch'd it, bespatter'd it, deck'd it, adorn'd it, trimmed it, garnished it, gaged it, furnish'd it, boar'd it, pierc'd it, trap'd it, rumbled it, slid it down the Hill, and precipitated it from the very height of the *Cranie*; then from the foot to the top (like another *Sisyphus* with his Stone) bore it up again, and every way so bang'd it and belabour'd it, that it was ten thousand to one he had not struck the bottom of it out.

Which when one of his Friends had seen, and asked him why he did so toil his Body, perplex his Spirit, and torment his Tub? The Philosopher's Answer was, That not being employed in any other Charge by the *Republick*, he thought it expedient to thunder and storm it so tempestuously upon his *Tub*, that amongst a People so fervently busie, and earnest at work, he alone might not seem a loytering Slug and lasie Fellow. To the same Purpose may I say of my self,

Tho' I be rid from Fear,
I am not void of Care.

For perceiving no Account to be made of me towards the Discharge of a Trust of any great Concernment, and considering that through all the parts of this most noble Kingdom of *France*, both on this and the other side of the *Mountains*, every one is most diligently exercised and busied; some in the fortifying of their own Native Country, for its Defence; others, in the repulsing of their Enemies by an Offensive War; and all this with a Policy so excellent, and such admirable Order, so manifestly profitable for the future, whereby *France* shall have its Frontiers most *magnifically* enlarged, and the *Frenches* assured of a long and well-grounded Peace, that very little withholds me from the Opinion of good *Heraclitus*, which affirmeth *War to be the Father of all good things*; and therefore do I believe that *War* is in Latin called *Bellum*, not by *Antiphrasis*, as some Patchers of old rusty Latin would have us to think; because in War there is little *Beauty* to be seen, but absolutely and simply; for that in *War* appeareth all that is *good* and graceful, and that by the *Wars* is purged out all manner of Wickedness and Deformity. For Proof whereof, the wise and pacifick *Solomon* could no better represent the unspeakable Perfection of the Divine Wisdom, than by comparing it to the due Disposure and Ranking of *an Army in Battle Array, well provided and ordered.*

Therefore by reason of my Weakness and Inability, being reputed by my Compatriots unfit for the *Offensive* part of Warfare; and on the other side, being no way employed in matter of the *Defensive*, although it had been but to carry Burthens, fill Ditches, or break Clods, either whereof had been to me indifferent, I held it not a little disgraceful to be only an *Idle Spectator* of so many valorous, eloquent and warlike Persons, who in the view and sight of all *Europe* act this notable *Interlude* or *Tragicomedy*, and not make some Effort towards the Performance of this, *nothing at all* remains for me to be done. In my Opinion, little Honour is due to such as are meer *Lookers on*, liberal of their Eyes, and of their Purse parsimonious; who conceal their Crowns, and hide their Silver, scratching their Head with one Finger like grumbling Puppies, gaping at the Flies like *Tithe Calves*; clapping down their Ears like *Arcadian* Asses at the Melody of Musicians, who with their very Countenances in the depth of silence express their Consent to the *Prosopopeie*.

Having made this Choice and Election, it seem'd to me that my Exercise therein would be neither unprofitable nor troublesom to any, whilst I should thus set a-going my *Diogenical* Tub, which is all that is left me safe from the Shipwrack of my former Misfortunes.

At this dingle dangle wagging of my Tub, what would you have me to do? By the *Virgin* that tucks up her Sleeve, I know not as yet: Stay a little till I suck up a Draught of this Bottle; it is my true and only *Helicon*; it is my *Caballine* Fountain; it is my sole *Entousiasm*. Drinking thus I meditate, discourse, resolve and conclude. After that the *Epilogue* is made, I laugh, I write, I compose, and drink again. *Ennius* drinking wrote, and writing, drank. *Æschylus* (if *Plutarch* in his *Symposiaes* merit any Faith) drank composing, and drinking, composed. *Homer* never wrote fasting, and *Cato* never wrote till after he had drunk. These Passages I have brought before you, to the end you may not say that I live without the Example of Men well praised, and better prised. It is good and fresh enough, even (as if you would say) it is entring upon the Second Degree. God, the good God *Sabaoth* (that is to say, the *God of Armies*) be praised for it eternally. If you after the same manner would take one great Draught, or two little ones, whilst you have your Gown about you, I truly find no kind of Inconveniency in it, provided you send up to God for all some small scantling of Thanks.

Since then my Luck or Destiny is such as you have heard, for it is not for every body to go to *Corinth*, I am fully resolved to be so little idle and unprofitable, that I will set my self to serve the one and the other sort of People, amongst the *Diggers*, Pioniers, and Rampire-builders, I will do as did *Neptune* and *Apollo* at *Troy* under *Laomedon*, or as did *Renault* of *Mountauban* in his latter days: I will serve the Masons, I'll set on the Pot to boyl for the Bricklayers; and whilst the minced Meat is making ready at the sound of my small Pipe, I'll measure the muzzle of the musing Dotards. Thus did *Amphion*, with the Melody of his Harp, found, build, and finish the great and renowned City of *Thebes*.

For the Use of the *Warriours* I am about to broach off new my Barrel to give them a taste, (which by two former Volumes of mine, if by the deceitfulness and falshood of Printers they had not been jumbled, marred and spoiled, you would have very well relished) and draw unto them of the growth of our own trippery Pastimes, a gallant third-part of a Gallon, and consequently a jolly chearful Quart of *Pantagruelick* Sentences, which you may lawfully call (if you please) *Diogenical*; and shall have me (seeing I cannot be their *Fellow-Soldier*) for their faithful *Butler*, refreshing and cheering, according to my little power, their return from the Alarms of the Enemy; as also, for an indefatigable *Extoller* of their Martial Exploits and Glorious Atchievements. I shall not fail therein *par lapathium acutum de dieu*, if Mars fail not in *Lent*, which the cunning Lecher (I warrant you) will be loth to do.

I remember nevertheless to have read, that *Ptolemee* the Son of *Lagus* one day, among the many Spoils and Booties, which by his Victories he had acquired, presenting to the *Egyptians*, in the open view of the People, a *Bactrian* Camel all black, and a partycolour'd *Slave*, in such sort, as that the one half of his Body was black, and the other white, not in partition of breadth by the *Diaphragma*, as was that Woman consecrated to the *Indian Venus*, whom the *Tyanean* Philosopher did see between the River *Hydaspes*, and Mount *Caucasus*, but in a perpendicular Dimension of Altitude; which were things never before that seen in *Egypt*.

He expected by the show of these Novelties, to win the Love of the People. But what hapned thereupon? At the production of the *Camel* they were all affrighted, and offended at the sight of the party-coloured Man: Some scoffed at him, as a detestible Monster brought forth by the Errour of Nature. In a word, of the hope which he had to please these *Egyptians*, and by such means to encrease the Affection which they naturally bore him, he was altogether frustrate and disappointed; understanding fully by their Deportments, that they took more pleasure and delight in things that were proper, handsom and perfect, than in mishapen, monstrous and ridiculous Creatures; since which time he had both the *Slave* and the *Camel* in such dislike, that very shortly thereafter, either through Negligence, or for want of ordinary Sustenance, they did exchange their Life with Death.

This Example, My Cake will be Dough, and for my *Venus* I shall have but some deformed Puppy, putteth me in a suspence between hope and fear, misdoubting that for the Contentment which I aim at, I will but reap what shall be most distastful to me; instead of serving them, I shall but vex them, and offend them whom I purpose to exhilirate; resembling in this dubious adventure *Euclion*'s Cock, so renowned by *Plautus* in his *Pot*; and by *Ausonius* in his *Griphon*, and by divers others; which Cock, for having by his scraping discover'd a Treasure, had his Hide well curry'd. Put the case I get no Anger by it, though formerly such things fell out, and the like may occur again: Yet, by *Hercules*, it will not. So I perceive in them all one, and the same specifical Form, and the like individual Proprieties, which our Ancestors call'd *Pantagruelism*; by vertue whereof, they will bear with any thing that floweth from a good, free, and loyal Heart. I have seen them ordinarily take *good will in part of payment*, and remain satisfied therewith, when one was not able to do better. Having dispatched this point, I return to my *Barrel*.

Up my Lads, to this Wine spare it not; drink, Boys, and trowl it off at full Bowls; If you do not think it good, let it alone. I am not like those officious and importunate Sots, who by Force, Outrage and Violence constrain an easie good-natur'd Fellow to whiffle, quaff, carouse, and what is worse. All honest Tiplers, all honest gouty Men, all such as are a-dry, coming to this little Barrel of mine, need not drink thereof, if it please them not: But if they have a mind to it, and that the Wine prove agreeable to the Tastes of their worshipful Worships, let them drink frankly, freely and boldly, without paying any thing, and welcome. This is my Decree, my Statute and Ordinance; And let none fear there shall be any want of Wine as at the Marriage of *Cana* in *Galilee*; for how much soever you shall draw forth at the *Faucet*, so much shall I tun in at the Bung. Thus shall the *Barrel* remain inexhaustible; it hath a lively Spring, and perpetual Current. Such was the Beverage contained within the Cup of *Tantalus*, which was figuratively represented amongst the *Bracman* Sages. Such was in *Iberia* the *Mountain of Salt*, so highly written of by *Cato*. Such was the *Branch of Gold* consecrated to the *subterranean* Goddess, which *Virgil* treats of so sublimely. It is a true *Cornu-copia* of Merriment and *Railery*. If at any time it seem to you to be emptied to the very Lees, yet shall it not, for all that, be drawn wholly dry: good Hope remains there at the bottom, as in *Pandora*'s Bottle; and not despair, as in the Punction of the *Danaids*. Remark well what I have said, and what manner of People they be whom I do invite; for to the end that none be deceived, I (in imitation of *Lucilius*, who did protest that he wrote only to his own *Tarentias* and *Consentius*) have not pierced this Vessel for any else, but you honest Men, who are Drinkers of the *First Edition*, and gouty Blades of the highest degree. The great *Dorophages*, Bribe-mongers, have (on their hands) Occupation enough, and enough on the hooks, for their *Venison*. There may they follow their Prey; here is no Garbage for them. You Pettifoggers, *Garbellers*, and Masters of *Chicanery*, speak not to me, I beseech you, in the name of, and for the Reverence you bear to the *Four Hips* that ingendred you, and to the *Quickning Peg* which at that time conjoined them. As for *Hypocrites*, much less; although they were all of them unsound in Body, pockify'd, scurfie, furnish'd with unquenchable Thirst, and insatiable Eating; because indeed they are not *of good*, but *of evil*, and of that *evil* from which we daily pray to God to *deliver us*. And albeit we see them sometimes counterfeit Devotion, yet never did Old Age make pretty Moppet. Hence Mastiffs, Dogs in a Doublet; get you behind, aloof Villains, out of my Sunshine; Curs, to the Devil. Do you jog hither, wagging your Tails, to pant at my Wine, and bepiss my Barrel? Look here is the *Cudgel*, which *Diogines*, in his last Will, ordained to be set by him after his Death, for beating away, crushing the Reins, and breaking the Backs of these *Bustuary Hobgoblins*, and *Cerberian Hell-hounds*. Pack you hence therefore, you *Hypocrites*, to your Sheep-dogs, Get you gone, you Dissemblers to the Devil. Hay! What, are you there yet? I renounce my part of *Papimanie* if I snatch you, Grr, Grrr, Grrrrrr. Avant, Avant, will you not be gone? May you never shit till you be soundly lash'd with *Stirrup-Leather*, never piss but by the *Strapado*, nor be otherways warmed, than by the *Bastinado*.

THE THIRD BOOK

CHAPTER I

How Pantagruel transported a Colony of Utopians into Dypsodie.

PANTAGRUEL having wholly subdued the Land of *Dypsodie*, transported thereunto a Colony of *Utopians*, to the number of 9876543210 Men, besides the Women and little Children, Artificers of all Trades, and Professors of all Sciences; to people, cultivate and improve that Country, which otherways was ill inhabited, and in the greatest part thereof but a meer Desert and Wilderness; and did transport them not so much for the excessive multitude of Men and Women which were in *Utopia* multiplied (for number) like Grashoppers upon the face of the Land. You understand well enough, nor is it needful further to explain it to you, that the *Utopian* Men had so rank and fruitful Genetories, and that the *Utopian* Women carried Matrixes so ample, so glutonous, so tenaciously retentive, and so *Architectonically cellulated*, that at the end of every Ninth Month, Seven Children at the least (what Male what Female) were brought forth by every married Woman, in imitation of the People of *Israel* in *Egypt*, if *Anthony de Lira* be to be trusted. Nor yet was this Transplantation made so much for the Fertility of the Soil, the Wholesomness of the Air, or Commodity of the Country of *Dypsodie*, as to retain that Rebellious People within the Bounds of their Duty and Obedience, by this new Transport of his ancient and most faithful Subjects, who from all time out of mind, never knew, acknowledged, owned or served any other *Sovereign Lord* but him; and who likewise from the very instant of their Birth, as soon as they were entred into this World, had, with the *Milk* of their Mothers and Nurses, sucked in the Sweetness, Humanity and Mildness of his Government, to which they were all of them so nourished and habituated, that there was nothing surer, than

that they would sooner abandon their Lives, than swerve from
this singular and primitive Obedience *naturally* due to their
Prince, whithersoever they should be dispersed or removed.

And not only should they, and their Children successively
descending from their Blood, be such, but also would keep and
maintain in this same *Fealty*, and obsequious Observance, all the
Nations lately annexed to his Empire; which so truly came to pass,
that therein he was not disappointed of his intent. For if the *Utopians* were before their Transplantation thither dutiful and faithful
Subjects, the *Dypsodes*, after some few days conversing with them,
were every whit as (if not more) *loyal* than they; and that by vertue
of I know not what *natural* Fervency incident to all Humane Creatures at the beginning of any labour wherein they took delight;
solemnly attesting the *Heavens*, and Supreme *Intelligences*, of their
being only sorry, that no sooner unto their knowledge had arrived
the great Renown of the good *Pantagruel*.

Remark therefore here (honest Drinkers) that the manner of
preserving and retaining Countries newly Conquered in Obedience, is not (as hath been the Erronieous Opinion of some
Tyrannical Spirits to their own Detriment and Dishonour) to pillage, plunder, force, spoil, trouble, oppress, vex, disquiet, ruine
and destroy the People, ruling, governing, and keeping them in
awe with *Rods of Iron*; and (in a word) *eating* and *devouring* them,
after the fashion that *Homer* calls an unjust and wicked King,
δημόβορον, that is to say, *a Devourer of his People*.

I will not bring you to this purpose the Testimony of Ancient
Writers; it shall suffice to put you in mind of what your Fathers
have seen thereof, and your selves too, if you be not very Babes.
New-born, they must be given suck to, rocked in a Cradle, and
dandled. Trees newly planted must be supported, underpropped,
strengthned and defended against all Tempests, Mischiefs, Injuries and Calamities. And one lately saved from a long and dangerous Sickness, and new upon his Recovery, must be forborn,
spared and cherished, in such sort, that they may harbour in their
own Breasts this Opinion, That there is not in the World a *King or
a Prince, who does not desire fewer Enemies, and more Friends*.

Thus *Osiris* the great King of the *Egyptians*, conquered almost the whole Earth, not so much by Force of Arms, as by
easing the People of their Troubles, teaching them how to *live well*

and honestly giving them good *Laws*, and using them with all possible Affability, Courtesy, Gentleness and Liberality: Therefore was he by all Men deservedly Entituled, The Great King *Evergetes* (that is to say *Benefactor*), which style he obtained by vertue of the Command of *Jupiter* to *Pamyla*.

And in effect, *Hesiod*, in his *Hierarchy*, placed the *good Demons* (call them *Angels* if you will, or *Geniuses*) as *Intercessors* and *Mediators* betwixt the Gods and Men, they being of a degree inferiour to the Gods, but superiour to Men; and for that through their Hands the Riches and Benefits we get from Heaven are dealt to us; and that they are *continually doing us good*, and still *protecting us from evil*, he saith, that they exercise the Offices of *Kings*; because to *do always good* and *never ill*, is an Act most *singularly Royal*.

Just such another was the Emperor of the Universe, *Alexander* the *Macedonian*. After this manner was *Hercules* Sovereign Possessor of the whole Continent, relieving Men from monstrous Oppressions, Exactions and Tyrannies; governing them with Discretion, maintaining them in Equity and Justice, instructing them with seasonable Policies and wholsom Laws, convenient for, and suitable to the Soil, Climate and Disposition of the Country, supplying where was wanting, abating what was superfluous, and pardoning all that was past, with a sempiternal forgetfulness of all preceding Offences, as was the *Amnestie* of the *Athenians*, when by the Prowess, Valour and Industry of *Thrasybulus* the Tyrants were exterminated; afterwards at *Rome* by *Cicero* exposed, and renewed under the Emperor *Aurelian*. These are the Philtres, Allurements, *Jynges*, Inveiglements, Baits and Enticements of *Love*, by the means whereof that may be peaceably revived, which was painfully acquired. Nor can a Conqueror reign more happily, whether he be a Monarch, Emperor, King, Prince or Philosopher, than by making his Justice to second his Valour. His *Valour* shows it self in Victory and Conquest; his *Justice* will appear in the good Will and Affection of the People, when he maketh Laws, publisheth Ordinances, establisheth Religion, and doth what is right to every one, as the noble Poet *Virgil* writes of *Octavian Augustus*.

Victorque volentes
Per populos dat jura.

Therefore it is that *Homer*, in his *Iliads* calleth a good Prince and great King, κοσμήτορα λαων, that is, *The Ornament of the People*.

Such was the Consideration of *Numa Pompilius* the Second King of the *Romans*, a just Politician and wise Philosopher, when he ordained that to God *Terminus*, on the Day of his Festival called *Terminales*, nothing should be sacrificed that had *died*; teaching us thereby, that the Bounds, Limits and Frontiers of Kingdoms should be guarded, and preserved in Peace, Amity and Meekness, without polluting our Hands with Blood and Robbery: Who doth otherways, shall not only lose what he hath gained, but also be loaded with this Scandal and Reproach, That he is an *unjust* and wicked Purchaser, and his Acquests perish with him, *Juxta illud, male parta, male dilabuntur*. And although during his whole Life-time, he should have peaceable Possession thereof; yet if what hath been so acquired moulder away in the Hands of his Heirs, the same Opproby, Scandal and Imputation will be charged upon the Defunct, and his Memory remain accursed, for his unjust and unwarrantable Conquest; *Juxta illud, de male quæsitis vix gaudet tertius hæres*.

Remark likewise, Gentlemen, you Gouty Feoffees, in this main Point worthy of your Observation, how, by these means, *Pantagruel* of one *Angel* made two, which was a Contingency opposite to the Council of *Charlemaine*, who made *two Devils of one, when he transplanted the* Saxons *into* Flanders, *and the* Flemins *into* Saxony. For not being able to keep in such Subjection the *Saxons*, whose Dominion he had joyned to the Empire, but that ever and anon they would break forth into open Rebellion, if he should casually be drawn into *Spain*, or other remote Kingdoms: He caused them to be brought unto his own Country of *Flanders*, the Inhabitants whereof did naturally obey him; and transported the *Haynaults* and *Flemens*, his ancient loving Subjects, into *Saxony*, not mistrusting their *Loyalty*, now that they were transplanted into a strange Land. But it hapned that the *Saxons* persisted in their Rebellion and primitive Obstinacy; and the *Flemins* dwelling in *Saxony* did imbibe the stubborn Manners and Conditions of the *Saxons*.

CHAPTER II

*How Panurge was made Laird of Salmygoudin in Dypsodie,
and did waste his Revenue before it came in.*

WHILST *Pantagruel* was giving Order for the Government of all
Dypsodie, he assigned to *Panurge* the *Lairdship* of *Salmygondin*,
which was yearly worth 6789106789 Ryals of certain Rent,
besides the uncertain Revenue of the *Locusts* and *Periwinkles*,
amounting one year with another to the value of 2435768, or
2435769 *French* Crowns of *Berry*. Sometimes it did amount to
1234554321 Seraphs when it was a good Year, and that Locusts
and Periwinkles were in request; but that was not every Year.

Now his Worship, the new *Laird*, husbanded this his Estate
so providently well and prudently, that in less than fourteen
days he wasted and dilapidated all the certain and uncertain
Revenue of his Lairdship for three whole Years: Yet did not he
properly dilapidate it, as you might say, in founding of Monasteries, building of Churches, erecting of Colleges, and setting
up of Hospitals, or casting his Bacon-Flitches to the Dogs; but
spent it in a thousand little Banquets and jolly Collations, keeping open House for all Comers and Goers; yea, to all good Fellows, young Girls, and pretty Wenches; felling Timber, burning
the great Logs for the sale of the Ashes, borrowing Money
before-hand, buying dear, selling cheap, and eating his Corn (as
it were) whilst it was but Grass.

Pantagruel being advertised of this his Lavishness, was in
good sooth no way offended at the matter, angry nor sorry; for I
once told you, and again tell it you, that he was the best, little,
great Good-man that ever girded a Sword to his Side; he took
all things in good part, and interpreted every Action to the best
Sence: He never vexed nor disquieted himself with the least
pretence of Dislike to any thing; because he knew that he must
have most grosly abandoned the Divine Mansion of Reason, if
he had permitted his Mind to be never so little grieved, afflicted
or altered at any occasion whatsoever. For all the Goods that the
Heaven covereth, and that the *Earth* containeth in all their
Dimensions and Height, Depth, Breadth, and Length, are not

of so much worth, as that we should for them disturb or disorder our Affections, trouble or perplex our Senses or Spirits.

He drew only *Panurge* aside, and then making to him a sweet Remonstrance and mild Admonition, very gently represented before him in strong Arguments, That if he should continue in such an unthrifty course of living, and not become a better *Mesnagier*, it would prove altogether impossible for him, or at least hugely difficult at any time to make him rich. Rich! answered *Panurge*, Have you fixed your Thoughts there? Have you undertaken the Task to enrich me in this World? Set your Mind to live merrily in the Name of God and good Folks, let no other Cark nor Care be harboured within the *Sacro sanctified Domicile* of your Celestial Brain. May the Calmness and Tranquility thereof be never incommodated with, or evershadowed by any frowning Clouds of sullen Imaginations and displeasing Annoyance. For if you live joyful, merry, jocund and glad, I cannot be but rich enough. Every body cries up *thrift, thrift*, and good Husbandry; but many speak of *Robin Hood* that never shot in his Bow; and talk of that Vertue of *Mesnagery*, who know not what belong to it. It is by me that they must be advised. From me therefore take this Advertisement and Information, that what is imputed to me for a Vice, hath been done in imitation of the *University* and Parliament of *Paris*, places in which is to be found the true Spring and *Source* of the lively *Idea* of *Pantheology*, and all manner of Justice. Let him be counted an *Heretick* that doubteth thereof, and doth not firmly believe it: Yet they in one day eat up their *Bishop*, or the Revenue of the Bishoprick (is it not all one) for a whole year; yea, sometimes for two. This is done on the day he makes his Entry, and is *installed*: Nor is there any place for an Excuse; for he cannot avoid it, unless he would be houted at and stoned for his Parsimony.

It hath been also esteemed an act flowing from the Habit of the Four *Cardinal* Vertues. Of *Prudence* in borrowing Money before-hand; for none knows what may fall out; who is able to tell if the World shall last yet three years? But although it should continue longer, is there any Man so foolish, as to have the Confidence to promise himself three years?

What fool so confident to say
That he shall live one other day?

Of *Commutative Justice*, in buying dear (I say upon trust) and selling goods cheap, (that is, for ready Money) what says *Cato* in his Book of *Husbandry* to this purpose? The *Father of a Family* (says he) *must be a perpetual Seller*; by which means it is impossible but that at last he shall become rich, if he have of vendible Ware enough still ready for Sale.

Of *Distributive Justice* it doth partake, in giving Entertainment to good (remark good) and gentle Fellows, whom fortune had Shipwrack'd (like *Ulysses*) upon the Rock of a hungry Stomach without provision of Sustenance: And likewise to the good (remark the good) and young Wenches: For according to the Sentence of *Hippocrates*, Youth is impatient of Hunger, chiefly if it be vigorous, lively, frolick, brisk, stirring and bouncing; which wanton Lasses willingly, and heartily devote themselves to the pleasure of Honest Men; and are in so far both *Platonick* and *Ciceronian*, that they do acknowledge their being *born* into this World, not to be *for themselves alone*, but that in their proper Persons their Acquaintance may claim one share, and their Friends another.

The Vertue of *Fortitude* appears therein by the cutting down and overthrowing of the great Trees, like a second *Milo* making Havock of the dark Forests, which did serve only to furnish Dens, Caves, and shelter to Wolves, wild Boars and Foxes; and afford Receptacles, withdrawing Corners and Refuges to Robbers; Thieves and Murtherers; lurking holes and sculking places for Cut-throat Assassinators; secret obscure Shops for Coiners of False Money, and safe Retreats for *Hereticks*, laying them even and level with the plain Champion Fields and pleasant Heathy Ground, at the sound of the Haubois and Bagpipes playing reeks with the high and stately Timber, and preparing Seats and Benches for the Eve of the dreadful day of Judgment.

I gave thereby proof of my *Temperance* in eating my Corn whilst it was but Grass, like an *Hermit* feeding upon Sallets and Roots, that so affranchising my self from the Yoak of sensual Appetites to the utter disclaiming of their Sovereignty, I might the better reserve somewhat in store, for the relief of the lame, blind, cripple, maimed, needy, poor and wanting Wretches.

In taking this course I save the Expence of the *Weedgrubbers*, who gain Money; of the *Reapers* in Harvest-time, who drink lustily, and without water; of *Gleaners*, who will expect their Cakes and Bannocks; of *Threshers*, who leave no Garlick, Scallions, Leeks nor Onyons in our Gardens, (by the Authority of *Thestilis* in *Virgil*) and of the *Millers*, who are generally Thieves; and of the *Bakers*, who are little better; is this small Saving or Frugality? besides the mischief and damage of the *Field-mice*, the decay of *Barns*, and the destruction usually made by *Weevils* and other Vermin.

Of *Corn* in the Blade you may make good Greensauce of a light Concoction, and easie Digestion, which recreates the Brain, and exhilerates the Animal Spirits, rejoyceth the Sight, openeth the Appetite, delighteth the Taste, comforteth the Heart, tickleth the Tongue, cheareth the Countenance, striking a fresh and lively Colour, strengthening the Muscles, tempers the Blood, disburthens the Midrif, refresheth the Liver, disobstructs the Spleen, easeth the Kidneys, suppleth the Reins, quickens the Joynts of the Back, cleanseth the Urine-Conduits, dilates the Spermatick Vessels, shortens the *Cremasters*, purgeth the Bladder, puffeth up the Genitories, correcteth the prepuce, hardens the Nut, and rectifies that Member. It will make you have a current Belly to trot, fart, dung, piss, sneeze, cough, spit, belch, spew, yawn, snuff, blow, breath, snort, sweat, and set taunt your *Robin*, with a thousand other rare advantages. I understand you very well (says *Pantagruel*) you would thereby infer, that those of a mean Spirit and shallow Capacity, have not the *skill to spend much in a short time*: You are not the first in whose conceit that *Heresie* hath entred: *Nero* maintained it, and above all Mortals admired most his Unkle *Caius Caligula*, for having in few days, by a most wonderful pregnant Invention, totally spent all the Goods and Patrimony which *Tiberius* had left him.

But instead of observing the *Sumptuous Supper-curbing* Laws of the *Romans*, to wit, the *Orchia*, the *Fannia*, the *Didia*, the *Licinia*, the *Cornelia*, the *Lepidiana*, the *Antia*, and of the *Corinthians*; by the which they were inhibited, under pain of great punishment, not to spend more in one year, than their annual Revenue did amount to, you have offered up the Oblation of *Protervia*, which was with the *Romans* such a Sacrifice as the *Paschal Lamb* was amongst the *Jews*, wherein all that was eatable was to be eaten, and the remainder to be thrown into the Fire, without reserving any thing for the next day. I may very justly say of you, as *Cato* did of *Albidius*, who after that he had by a most extravagant Expence wasted all the Means and Possessions he had to one only House, he fairly set it on Fire, that he might the better say, *Consummatum est*. Even just as since his time St. *Thomas Aquinas* did, when he had eaten up the whole Lamprey, although there was no necessity in it.

CHAPTER III

How Panurge praiseth the Debtors and Borrowers.

BUT, quoth *Pantagruel*, when will you be out of Debt? At the next ensuing term of the *Greek Calends*, answered *Panurge*, when all the World shall be content, and that it be your Fate to become your own Heir. The Lord forbid that I should be out of Debt, as if, indeed, I could not be trusted. *Who leaves not some Leaven over night, will hardly have paste the next morning.*

Be still indebted to some body or other, that there may be some body always to pray for you that the Giver of all good things may grant unto you a blessed, long, and prosperous Life; fearing if Fortune should deal crosly with you, that it might be his chance to come short of being paid by you, he will always speak good of you in every Company, ever and anon purchase new Creditors unto you, to the end that through their means you may make a shift by borrowing from *Peter* to pay *Paul*, and with other Folks Earth fill up his Ditch. When of old in the Region of the *Gauls*, by the Institution of the *Druids*, the Servants, Slaves and Bondmen were burnt quick at the Funerals and Obsequies of their Lords and Masters; had not they fear enough, think you, that their Lords and Masters should die? For *per force*, they were to die with them for Company. Did not they uncessantly send up their Supplications to their great God *Mercury*, as likewise unto *Dis* the Father of Wealth, to lengthen out their days, and preserve them long in health? Were not they very careful to entertain them well, punctually to look unto them, and to attend them faithfully and circumspectly? For by those means were they to live together at least until the hour of Death. Believe me your Creditors with a more fervent Devotion

will beseech Almighty God to prolong your Life, they being of
nothing more afraid than that you should die; for that they are
more concerned for the Sleeve than the Arm, and love Silver
better than their own Lives; as it evidently appeareth by the
Usurers of *Landerousse*, who not long since hanged themselves,
because the price of the Corn and Wines was fallen, by the
return of a gracious Season.

To this *Pantagruel* answering nothing, *Panurge* went on in his
Discourse, saying, Truly, and in good sooth (Sir,) when I ponder
my Destiny aright, and think well upon it, you put me shrewdly
to my Plunges, and have me at a Bay in twitting me with the
Reproach of my Debts and Creditors: And yet did I, in this only
respect and consideration of being a *Debtor*, esteem my self worshipful, reverend and formidable. For against the Opinion of
most Philosophers, that of *nothing ariseth nothing*; yet, without
having bottomed on so much as that which is called the *First
Matter*, did I out of *nothing* become such *Maker* and *Creator*, that
I have created—what? a gay number of fair and jolly *Creditors*.
Nay, *Creditors* (I will maintain it, even to the very *Fire* it self
exclusively) are fair and *goodly Creatures*. Who lendeth nothing
is an ugly and *wicked Creature*, and an accursed *Imp* of the Infernal *Old Nick*. And there is made, what? *Debts*: A thing most
precious and dainty, of great Use and Antiquity. *Debts*, (I say)
surmounting the number of Syllables which may result from the
Combinations of all the Consonants, with each of the Vowels
heretofore projected, reckoned and calculated by the Noble
Xenocrates. To judge of the perfection of *Debtors* by the Numer-
osity of their *Creditors*, is the readiest way for entring into the
Mysteries of *Practical Arithmetick*.

You can hardly imagine how glad I am, when every Morning
I perceive my self environed and surrounded with Brigades of
Creditors; humble, fawning, and full of their Reverences: And
whilst I remark, that as I look more favourably upon, and give a
chearfuller Countenance to one than to another, the Fellow thereupon buildeth a Conceit that he shall be the first Dispatched,
and the foremost in the Date of Payment; and he valueth my
Smiles at the rate of ready Money. It seemeth unto me, that I
then act and personate the *God of the Passion of* Saumure, accompanied with his Angels and Cherubims.

THE THIRD BOOK

These are my Flatterers, my Soothers, my Claw backs, my Smoothers, my Parasites, my Saluters, my Givers of good Morrows, and perpetual Orators; which makes me verily think, that the supreamest height of *Heroick* Vertue, described by *Hesiode*, consisteth in being a *Debtor*, wherein I held the first *degree* in my *Commencement*. Which Dignity though all Humane Creatures seem to aim at, and aspire thereto, few nevertheless, because of the difficulties in the way, and incumbrances of hard Passages are able to reach it, as is easily perceivable by the ardent desire and vehement longing harboured in the Breast of every one, to be still creating more *Debts*, and new *Creditors*.

Yet doth it not lie in the power of every one to be a *Debtor*. To acquire *Creditors* is not at the Disposure of each Man's Arbitriment. You nevertheless would deprive me of this sublime Felicity. You ask me when I will be out of Debt. Well, to go yet further on, and possibly worse in your Conceit, may *Sanct Bablin*, the good Sanct, snatch me, if I have not all my Lifetime held *Debt* to be as an Union or Conjunction of the Heavens with the Earth, and the whole Cement whereby the Race of Mankind is kept together; yea, of such Vertue and Efficacy, that, I say, the whole Progeny of *Adam* would very suddenly perish without it. Therefore, perhaps, I do not think amiss, when I repute it to be the great Soul of the *Universe*, which (according to the Opinion of the *Academicks*) vivifyeth all manner of things. In Confirmation whereof, that you may the better believe it to be so, represent unto your self, without any prejudicacy of Spirit, in a clear and serene Fancy, the *Idea* and Form of some other World than this; take if you please, and lay hold on the *thirtieth* of those which the Philosopher *Methrodorus* did enumerate, wherein it is to be supposed there is no *Debtor* or *Creditor*, that is to say, a World without *Debts*.

There amongst the Planets will be no regular Course, all will be in Disorder. *Jupiter* reckoning himself to be nothing indebted unto *Saturn*, will go near to detrude him out of his Sphere, and with the *Homerick* Chain will be like to hang up the *Intelligences*, Gods, Heavens, Demons, Heroes, Devils, Earth and Sea together with the other Elements. *Saturn* no doubt combining with *Mars* will reduce that so disturbed World into a Chaos of Confusion.

311

Mercury then would be no more subjected to the other Planets; he would scorn to be any longer their *Camillus*, as he was of old termed in the *Hetrurian* Tongue; for it is to be imagined that he is no way a Debtor to them.

Venus will be no more Venerable, because she shall have *lent* nothing. The *Moon* will remain bloody and obscure: For to what end should the *Sun* impart unto her any of his Light? He owed her nothing. Nor yet will the Sun shine upon the Earth, nor the Stars send down any good Influence, because the Terrestrial Globe hath desisted from sending up their wonted Nourishment by Vapours and Exhalations, wherewith *Heraclitus* said the Stoicks proved *Cicero* maintained they were cherished and *alimented*. There would likeways be in such a World no manner of *Symbolization*, *Alteration*, nor Transmutation amongst the Elements; for the one will not esteem it self obliged to the other, as having borrowed nothing at all from it. Earth then will not become Water, Water will not be changed into Air, of Air will be made no Fire, and Fire will afford no Heat unto the Earth; the Earth will produce nothing but Monsters, Titans, Giants; no Rain will descend upon it, nor Light shine thereon; no Wind will blow there, nor will there be in it any Summer or Harvest. *Lucifer* will break loose, and issuing forth of the depth of Hell, accompanied with his Furies, Fiends and Horned Devils, will go about to unnestle and drive out of Heaven all the Gods, as well of the greater as of the *lesser Nations*. Such a World without *lending*, will be no better than a Dog-kennel, a place of Contention and Wrangling, more unruly and irregular than that of the Rector of *Paris*; a Devil of an Hurly-burly, and more disordered Confusion, than that of the Plagues of *Douay*. Men will not then salute one another; it will be but lost labour to expect Aid or Succour from any, or to cry, *Fire*, *Water*, *Murther*, for none will put to their helping Hand. Why? He lent no *Money*, there is nothing due to him. No body is concerned in his Burning, in his Shipwrack, in his Ruine, or in his Death; and that because he hitherto had *lent* nothing, and would never thereafter have *lent* any thing. In short, *Faith*, *Hope* and *Charity* would be quite banish'd from such a World; for Men are *born to relieve and assist one another*; and in their stead should succeed and be introduced *Defiance*, *Disdain* and *Rancour*, with the most execrable Troop of all Evils, all

Imprecations and all Miseries. Whereupon you will think, and that not amiss, that *Pandora* had there spilt her unlucky Bottle. Men unto Men will be Wolves, Hobthrushers and Goblins, (as were *Lycaon*, *Bellorophon*, *Nebuchodonosor*), Plunderers, High-way Robbers, Cut-throats, Rapperees, Murtherers, Payloners, Assassin-ators, lewd, wicked, malevolent, pernicious Haters, set against every body, like to *Ismael*, *Metabus*, or *Timon* the *Athenian*, who for that cause was named *Misanthropos*; in such sort, that it would prove much more easie in Nature to have Fish enter-tained in the Air, and Bullocks fed in the bottom of the Ocean, than to support or tolerate a rascally Rabble of People that will not *Lend*. These Fellows (I vow) do I hate with a perfect Hatred; and if conform to the pattern of this grievous, peevish and per-verse *World* which *lendeth* nothing, you figure and liken the little *World*, which is Man, you will find in him a terrible justling Coyle and Clutter: The Head will not lend the sight of his Eyes to guide the Feet and Hands; the Legs will refuse to bear up the Body; the Hands will leave off working any more for the rest of the Members; the Heart will be weary of its continual Motion for the beating of the Pulse, and will no longer *lend* his Assist-ance; the Lungs will withdraw the use of their Bellows; the Liver will desist from conveying any more Blood through the Veins for the good of the whole; the Bladder will not be indebted to the Kidneys, so that the Urine thereby will be totally stopped. The Brains, in the interim, considering this unnatural course, will fall into a raving Dotage, and with-hold all feeling from the Sinews, and Motion from the Muscles: Briefly, in such a *World* without Order and Array, *owing* nothing, *lending* nothing, and *borrowing* nothing, you would see a more dangerous Conspira-tion than that which *Esope* exposed in his *Apologue*. Such a World will perish undoubtedly; and not only perish, but perish very quickly. Were it *Asculapius* himself, his Body would imme-diately rot, and the chafing Soul full of Indignation takes its flight to all the Devils of Hell after my Money.

CHAPTER IV

*Panurge continueth his Discourse in the praise of Borrowers
and Lenders.*

ON the contrary, be pleased to represent unto your Fancy another World, wherein every one lendeth, and every one oweth,
all are Debtors, and all Creditors. O how great will that Harmony be, which shall thereby result from the regular Motions
of the Heavens! Methinks I hear it every whit as well as ever
Plato did. What Sympathy will there be amongst the Elements!
O how delectable then unto Nature will be her own Works and
Productions? Whilst *Ceres* appeareth loaden with Corn, *Bacchus*
with Wines, *Flora* with Flowers, *Pomona* with Fruits, and *Juno*
fair in a clear Air, wholsom and pleasant: I lose my self in this
high Contemplation.

Then will among the Race of Mankind Peace, Love, Bene-
volence, Fidelity, Tranquility, Rest, Banquets, Feastings, Joy,
Gladness, Gold, Silver, single Money, Chains, Rings, with other
Ware, and Chaffer of that nature be found to trot from hand to
hand; no Suits at Law, no Wars, no Strife, Debate, nor Wrangling; none will be there a Usurer, none will be there a Pinch-
penny, a Scrape-good Wretch, or churlish hard-hearted Refuser.
Good God! Will not this be the Golden Age in the Reign of
Saturn? The true Idea of the Olympick Regions, wherein all
Vertues cease; Charity alone ruleth, governeth, domineereth and
triumpheth? All will be fair and goodly People there, all just
and vertuous.

O happy World! O People of that World most happy! Yea,
thrice and four times blessed is that People! I think in very deed
that I am amongst them, and swear to you, by my good Forsooth, that if this glorious aforesaid World had a Pope, abounding with Cardinals, that so he might have the Association of a
Sacred Colledge, in the space of very few years you should be
sure to see the Sancts much thicker in the Roll, more numerous,
wonder-working and mirifick, more Services, more Vows,
more Staves and Wax-Candles than are all those in the Nine
Bishopricks of *Britany*, St. *Yves* only excepted. Consider (Sir) I

pray you, how the noble *Patelin*, having a mind to Deify, and extol even to the Third Heavens the Father of *William Josseaume*, said no more but this, *And he did lend his Goods to those who were desirous of them*.

O the fine Saying! Now let our *Microcosm* be fancied conform to this Model in all its Members; *lending, borrowing* and *owing*, (that is to say) according to its own Nature: For Nature hath not to any other end created Man, but to *owe, borrow* and *lend*; no greater is the Harmony amongst the Heavenly Spheres, than that which shall be found in its well-ordered Policy. The Intention of the Founder of this Microcosm is, to have a Soul therein to be entertained, which is lodged there, as a Guest with its Host, it may live there for a while. Life consisteth in Blood, Blood is the Seat of the Soul; therefore the chiefest Work of the Microcosm is, to be making Blood continually.

At this Forge are exercised all the Members of the Body; none is exempted from Labour, each operates apart, and doth its proper Office. And such is their Hierarchy, that perpetually the one *borrows* from the other, the one *lends* the other, and the one is the others *Debtor*. The stuff and matter convenient which Nature giveth to be turned into Blood is *Bread* and *Wine*. All kind of nourishing Victuals is understood to be comprehended in these two, and from hence in the *Gothish* Tongue is called *Companage*. To find out this Meat and Drink, to prepare and boil it, the Hands are put to Work, the Feet do walk and bear up the whole Bulk of the Corporal Mass; the Eyes guide and conduct all; the Appetite in the Orifice of the Stomach, by means of little sowrish black Humour (called Melancholy) which is transmitted thereto from the Milt, giving warning to shut in the Food. The Tongue doth make the first Essay, and tastes it; the Teeth do chaw it, and the Stomach doth receive, digest and chylifie it; the Mesaraick Veins suck out of it what is good and fit, leaving behind the Excrements, which are, through special Conduits for that purpose, voided by an expulsive Faculty; thereafter it is carried to the Liver, where it being changed again, it by the vertue of the new Transmutation becomes *Blood*. What Joy, conjecture you, will then be found amongst those Officers, when they see this *Rivolet of Gold*, which is their sole *Restorative*? No greater is the Joy of Alchimists, when after long Travel, Toil and Expence, they see in their Furnaces the Transmutation: Then is it that every Member doth prepare it self, and strive a-new to purifie and to refine this Treasure. The Kidneys through the emulgent Veins draw that Aquosity from thence which you call Urine, and there send it away through the Ureters to be slipt downwards; where, in a lower Receptacle, and proper for it, (to wit, the Bladder) it is kept, and stayeth there until an opportunity to void it out in his due time. The Spleen draweth from the *Blood* its Terrestrial part, *viz.* The Grounds, Lees or thick Substance setled in the bottom thereof, which you term *Melancholy*: The Bottle of the Gall subtracts from thence all the superfluous *Choler*; whence it is brought to another Shop or Work-house to be yet better purified and fined, that is, the Heart, which by its agitation of *Diastolick* and *Systolick* Motions so neatly subtilizeth and inflames it, that in the *right side* Ventricle it is brought to perfection, and through the Veins is sent to all the Members; each parcel of the Body draws it then unto its self, and after its own fashion is cherished and alimented by it: Feet, Hands, Thighs, Arms, Eyes, Ears, Back, Breast, yea, all; and then it is, that who before were *Lenders*, now become *Debtors*. The Heart doth in its *left side* Ventricle so thinnifie the Blood, that it thereby obtains the Name of *Spiritual*; which being sent through the *Arteries* to all the Members of the Body, serveth to warm and winnow the other Blood which runneth through the Veins: The Lights never cease with its Lappets and Bellows to cool and refresh it; in acknowledgment of which good the Heart through the Arterial Vein imparts unto it the choicest of its Blood: At last it is made so fine and subtle within the *Rete Mirabilis*, that thereafter those *Animal Spirits* are framed and composed of it; by means whereof the Imagination, Discourse, Judgment, Resolution, Deliberation, Ratiocination and Memory have their Rise, Actings and Operations.

Cops body, I sink, I drown, I perish, I wander astray, and quite fly out of my self, when I enter into the Consideration of the profound Abyss of this World, thus *lending*, thus *owing*. Believe me, it is a Divine thing to *lend*, to owe an Heroick Vertue. Yet is not this all; this little world thus *lending*, *owing* and *borrowing*, is so good and charitable, that no sooner is the above-specified Alimentation finished, but that it forthwith projecteth, and hath already forecast, how it shall *lend* to those who are not as yet born, and by that Loan endeavour, what it may, to eternize it self, and multiply in Images like the Pattern, that is, Children. To this end every Member doth of the choicest and most precious of its Nourishment, pare and cut off a Portion, then instantly dispatcheth it downwards to that place, where Nature hath prepared for it very fit Vessels and Receptacles, through which descending to the Genitories by long Ambages, Circuits and Flexuosities, it receiveth a Competent Form, and Rooms apt enough both in the Man and Woman for the future Conservation and perpetuating of Humane Kind. All this is done by *Loans* and *Debts* of the one unto the other; and hence have we this word, the *Debt of Marriage*. Nature doth reckon Pain to the Refuser, with a most grievous Vexation to his Members, and an outragious Fury amidst his Senses. But on the other part, to the *Lender* a set Reward, accompanied with Pleasure, Joy, Solace, Mirth, and merry Glee.

CHAPTER V

How Pantagruel altogether abhorreth the Debtors and Borrowers.

I UNDERSTAND you very well, (quoth *Pantagruel*) and take you to be very good at Topicks, and throughly affectioned to your own Cause: But preach it up, and patrocinate it; prattle on it, and defend it as much as you will, even from hence to the next *Whitsuntide*, if you please so to do, yet in the end will you be astonish'd to find how you shall have gained no ground at all upon me, nor perswaded me by your fair Speeches and smooth Talk to enter never so little into the Thraldom of *Debt*. You *shall owe to none* (saith the Holy Apostle) *any thing save Love*, Friendship, and a mutual Benevolence.

You serve me here, I confess, with fine *Graphides* and *Diatyposes*, Descriptions and Figures, which truly please me very well: But let me tell you, if you will represent unto your Fancy an impudent blustering Bully and an importunate Borrower, entring afresh and newly into a Town already advertised of his Manners, you shall find that at his Ingress the Citizens will be more hideously affrighted and amazed, and in a greater terror and fear, dread and trembling, than if the Pest it self should step into it in the very same Garb and Accoutrement wherein the *Tyanæan* Philosopher found it within the City of *Ephesus*. And I am fully confirmed in the Opinion, that the *Persians* erred not, when they said, That *the second Vice was to Lie*, the *first* being that of *owing Money*. For in very truth, *Debts* and *Lying* are ordinarily joyned together. I will nevertheless not from hence infer, that none must *owe* any thing, or *lend* any thing. For who so rich can be, that sometimes may not *owe*; or who can be so poor, that sometimes may not *lend*?

Let the Occasion notwithstanding in that case (as *Plato* very wisely sayeth, and ordaineth in his Laws) be such, that none be permitted to draw any Water out of his Neighbour's Well, until first, they by continual digging and delving into their own proper Ground, shall have hit upon a kind of Potter's Earth, which is called *Ceramite*, and there had found no source or drop of Water; for that sort of Earth, by reason of its Substance, which is fat, strong, firm and close, so retaineth its Humidity, that it doth not easily evaporate it by any outward excursion or evaporation.

In good sooth, it is a great shame to choose rather to be still *borrowing* in all places from every one, than to work and win. Then only in my Judgment, should one *lend*, when the diligent, toiling and industrious Person is no longer able by his labour to make any Purchase unto himself, or otherwise, when by mischance he hath suddenly fallen into an unexpected loss of his Goods.

Howsoever, let us leave this Discourse, and from henceforwards do not hang upon *Creditors*, nor tie your self to them; I make account for the time past, to rid you freely of them, and from their Bondage to deliver you. The least I should in this Point, (quoth *Panurge*) is to thank you, though it be the most I can do: And if Gratitude and Thanksgiving be to be estimated and prized by the Affection of the Benefactor, that is to be done infinitely and sempiternally; for the love which you bear me of your own accord and free Grace, without any merit of mine, goeth far beyond the reach of any price or value; it transcends all weight, all number, all measure, it is endless and everlasting;

therefore should I offer to commensurate and adjust it, either to the size and proportion of your own noble and gracious Deeds, or yet to the Contentment and Delight of the obliged Receivers, I would come off but very faintly and flaggingly. You have verily done me a great deal of good, and multiplied your Favours on me more frequently than was fitting to one of my condition. You have been more bountiful towards me than I have deserved, and your Courtesies have by far surpassed the extent of my merits, I must needs confess it. But it is not, as you suppose, in the proposed matter: For there it is not where I itch, it is not there where it fretteth, hurts or vexeth me; for henceforth being *quit* and out of *Debt*, what Countenance will I be able to keep? You may imagine that it will become me very ill, for the first Month, because I have never hitherto been brought up or accustomed to it, I am very much afraid of it. Furthermore, there shall not one hereafter, Native of the Country of *Salmigondy*, but he shall level the Shot towards my Nose; all the back-cracking Fellows of the World, in discharging of their Postern Petarades, use commonly to say, *Voila pour les quitters*; that is, *For the quit*. My Life will be of very short continuance, I do foresee it, I recommend to you the making of my Epitaph; for I perceive I will die confected in the very stinch of Farts. If at any time to come, by way of restorative to such good Women as shall happen to be troubled with the grievous Pain of the Wind-Cholick, the ordinary Medicaments prove nothing effectual, the Mummy of all my befarted Body will streight be as a present Remedy appointed by the Physicians; whereof they taking any small *Modicum*, it will incontinently for their Ease afford them a Rattle or Bum-shot, like a Sal of Muskets.

Therefore would I beseech you to leave me some few Centuries of *Debts*: as King Louis the Eleventh, exempting from Suits in Law the Reverend *Milles d'Illiers* Bishop of *Chartre*, was by the said Bishop most earnestly sollicited to leave him some few for the Exercise of his mind. I had rather give them all my Revenue of the *Periwinkles*, together with the other Incomes of the *Locusts*, albeit I should not thereby have any parcel abated from off the principal Sums which I owe. Let us wave this matter (quoth *Pantagruel*) I have told it you over again.

CHAPTER VI

Why new Married Men were privileged from going to the Wars.

BUT, in the Interim, asked *Panurge*, by what Law was it constituted, ordained and established, that such as should plant a new Vineyard, those that should build a new House, and the new married Men should be exempted and discharged from the Duty of Warfare for the first year? By the Law, (answered *Pantagruel*) of *Moyses*. Why (replyed *Panurge*) the lately married? As for the Vine-Planters, I am now to old to reflect on them; my Condition, at this present, induceth me to remain satisfied with the Care of Vintage, finishing and turning the Grapes into Wine: Nor are these pretty new Builders of *Dead Stones* written or pricked down in my Book of Life; it is all with Live Stones that I set up, and erect the Fabricks of my Architecture, to wit, *Men*. It was (according to my Opinion, quoth *Pantagruel*) to the end, First, That the fresh married Folks should for the first Year reap a full and compleat Fruition of their Pleasures in their mutual exercise of the act of Love, in such sort, that in waiting more at leisure on the Production of Posterity, and propagating of their Progeny, they might the better encrease their Race, and make Provision of new Heirs. That if in the Years thereafter the Men should, upon their undergoing of some Military Adventure, happen to be killed, their Names and Coats of Arms might continue with their Children in the same Families: And next that, the Wives thereby, coming to know whether they were barren or fruitful (for one years Trial, in regard of the maturity of Age, wherein of old, they married, was held sufficient for the Discovery) they might pitch the more suitably, in case of their first Husbands Decease, upon a *Second Match*. The fertile Women to be wedded to those who desire to multiply their Issue; and the steril ones to such other Mates, as misregarding the storing of their own Lineage, chuse them only for their Vertues, Learning, Genteel Behaviour, Domestick Consolation, Management of the House, and Matrimonial Conveniences and Comforts, and such like. The Preachers of *Varennes* (saith *Panurge*) detest and abhor the *Second Marriages*, as altogether foolish and dishonest.

THE THIRD BOOK

Foolish and dishonest, (quoth *Pantagruel*) a plague take such Preachers! Yea, but (quoth *Panurge*) the like Mischief also befal the Friar, *Charmer*, who in a full Auditory, making a Sermon at *Perille*, and therein abominating the Reiteration of Marriage, and the entring again in the Bonds of a Nuptial Tie, did swear and heartily give himself to the swiftest Devil in Hell, if he had not rather choose, and would much more willingly undertake the *unmaidning* or *depucelating* of a hundred Virgins, than the simple Drudgery of one Widow. Truly, I find your Reason in that Point right good, and strongly grounded.

But what would you think, if the Cause why this Exemption or Immunity was granted, had no other Foundation, but that, during the whole space of the said first Year, they so lustily bobbed it with their Female Consorts, (as both Reason and Equity require they should do) that they had drained and evacuated their Spermatick Vessels; and were become thereby altogether feeble, weak, emasculated, drooping and flaggingly pithless; yea, in such sort, that they in the day of Battel, like Ducks which plunge over Head and Ears, would sooner hide themselves behind the Baggage than in the Company of valiant Fighters and daring Military Combatants, appear where stern *Bellona* deals her Blows, and moves a bustling Noise of Thwacks and Thumps. Nor is it to be thought that under the Standard of *Mars* they will so much as once strike a faire Stroke, because their most considerable Knocks have been already jerked and whirrited within the Curtines of his Sweet-heart *Venus*.

In confirmation whereof, amongst other Relicks and Monuments of Antiquity, we now as yet often see, that in all great Houses, after the expiring of some few days, these young married Blades are readily sent away to visit their *Uncles*, that in the absence of their Wives, reposing themselves a little, they may recover their decayed Strength by the recruit of a fresh Supply, the more vigorous to return again, and face about to renew the dueling Shock and Conflict of an amorous Dalliance: Albeit (for the greater part) they have neither *Uncle* nor *Aunt* to go to.

Just so did the King *Crackart*, after the Battle of the Cornets, not cashier us, (speaking properly) I mean me and the *Quaile-caller*, but for our Refreshment remanded us to our Houses; and he is as yet seeking after his own. My Grandfather's Godmother was wont to say to me when I was a Boy,

> *Patenostres & Oraisons*
> *Sont pour ceux-la qui les retiennent.*
> *Un fiffre en fenaisons*
> *Est plus que deux qui en viennent.*

> Not Orisons nor Patrenotres
>   Shall ever disorder my Brain:
> One Cadet, to the Field as he flutters,
>   Is worth two when they end the Campaign.

That which prompteth me to that Opinion, is, that the Vine-Planters did seldom eat of the Grapes, or drink of the Wine of their Labour, till the first Year was wholly elapsed: During all which time also the Builders did hardly inhabit their new structured Dwelling places, for fear of dying suffocated through want of Respiration; as *Galen* hath most learnedly remarked, in the Second Book of the *Difficulty of Breathing*. Under favour, Sir, I have not asked this Question without Cause causing, and *Reason* truly very ratiocinant. Be not offended I pray you.

CHAPTER VII

How Panurge had a Flea in his Ear, and forbore to wear any longer his magnificent Codpiece.

PANURGE, the day thereafter, caused pierce his Right Ear, after the *Jewish* Fashion, and thereto clasped a little Gold Ring, of a Fearny-like kind of Workmanship, in the Beazil or Collet whereof was set and enchased a *Flea*; and to the end you may be rid of all Doubts, you are to know that the Flea was black. O what a brave thing it is, in every case and circumstance of a matter, to be throughly well informed! The Sum of the Expence hereof, being cast up, brought in, and laid down upon his Council-board Carpet, was found to amount to no more quarterly than the Charge of the Nuptials of a *Hircanian* Tigress; even as you would say 600000 *Maravedis*. At these vast Costs and excessive Disbursements, as soon as he perceived himself to be out of Debt, he fretted much; and afterwards, as Tyrants and

Lawyers use to do, he nourish'd and fed her with the Sweat and Blood of his Subjects and Clients.

He then took four *French* Ells of a coarse brown Russet Cloth, and therin apparelling himself, as with a long, plain-seamed and single-stitch'd Gown, left off the wearing of his Breeches, and tied a pair of Spectacles to his Cap. In this Equipage did he present himself before *Pantagruel*; to whom this Disguise appeared the more strange, that he did not, as before, see that goodly fair and stately Codpiece, which was the sole Anchor of Hope, wherein he was wonted to rely, and last Refuge he had 'midst all the Waves and boisterous Billows, which a stormy Cloud in a cross Fortune would raise up against him. Honest *Pantagruel*, not understanding the Mystery, asked him, by way of interrogatory, what he did intend to personate in that new-fangled *Prosopopeia*? I have (answered *Panurge*) *a Flea in mine Ear*, and have a mind to marry. In good time (quoth *Pantagruel*) you have told me joyful Tidings; yet would not I hold a red hot Iron in my Hand for all the Gladness of them. But it is not the fashion of Lovers to be accoutred in such dangling Vestments, so as to have their Shirts flagging down over their Knees, without Breeches, and with a long Robe of a dark-brown mingled Hue, which is a Colour never used in *Talarian* Garments amongst any Persons of Honour, Quality or Vertue. If some *Heretical* Persons and Schismatical Sectaries have at any time formerly been so arrayed and cloathed (though many have imputed such a kind of Dress to Cosenage, Cheat, Imposture, and an Affectation of Tyranny upon credulous Minds of the rude Multitude) I will nevertheless not blame them for it, nor in that point judge rashly or sinistrously of them; every one overflowingly aboundeth in his own Sense and Fancy: Yea, in Things of a Foreign Consideration, altogether extrinsical and indifferent, which in and of themselves are neither commendable nor bad, because they proceed not from the Interior of the Thoughts and Heart, which is the Shop of all Good and Evil: Of Goodness, if it be upright, and that its Affections be regulated by the pure and clean Spirit of Righteousness; and on the other side, of Wickedness, if its Inclinations, straying beyond the Bounds of Equity be corrupted and depraved by the Malice and Suggestions of the Devil. It is only the novelty and Newfangledness thereof which I dislike, together with the Contempt of common Custom, and the Fashion which is in use.

The Colour (answered *Panurge*) is convenient, for it is conform to that of my Council-Board Carpet, therefore will I henceforth hold me with it, and more narrowly and circumspectly than ever hitherto I have done, look to my Affairs and Business. Seeing I am once out of *Debt*, you never yet saw Man more unpleasing then I will be, if God help me not. Lo, here be my Spectacles. To see me afar off, you would readily say, that it were Fryar *Burgess*. I believe certainly, that in the next ensuing Year, I shall once more preach the *Croisade, Bounce Buckram*. Do you see this Russet? doubt not but there lurketh under it some hid Property and occult Vertue, known to very few in the World. I did not take it on before this Morning; and nevertheless, am already in a rage of Lust, mad after a Wife, and vehemently hot upon untying the Codpiece-point, I itch, I tingle, I wriggle, and long exceedingly to be married; that without the danger of Cudgel blows, I may labour my Female Copes-mate with the hard push of a Bull-horned Devil. O the provident and thrifty Husband that I then will be! After my Death, with all Honour and Respect due to my Frugality, will they burn the Sacred Bulk of my Body, of purpose to preserve the Ashes thereof, in memory of the choicest Pattern that ever was, of a perfectly wary, and compleat Housholder. Copsbody, this is not the Carpet whereon my Treasurer shall be allowed to play false in his Accompts with me, by setting down an X for an V, or an L for an S; for in that case, should I make a hail of Fisti-cuffs to fly into his face. Look upon me (Sir) both before and behind, it is made after the manner of a Toge, which was the ancient fashion of the *Romans* in time of Peace. I took the Mode, Shape and Form thereof in *Trajan*'s Column at *Rome*, as also in the Triumphant Arch of *Septimus Severus*. I am tired of the Wars, weary of wearing Buffcoats, Cassocks, and Hoquetons. My Shoulders are pitifully worn and bruised with the carrying of Harness; let Armour cease, and the Long-Robe bear sway; at least it must be so for the whole space of the succeeding Years. If I be married as yesterday, by the *Mosaick* Law, you evidenced, in what concerneth the Breeches: my Great-Aunt *Laurence* did long ago tell me, that the Breeches were only ordained for the Use of the Codpiece, and to no other end; which I, upon a no less forcible Consequence, give Credit to every whit as well, as to the Saying of the fine Fellow *Galen*, who in his Ninth Book *Of the Use*, and *Employment of our Members*, alledgeth, That the *Head was made for the Eyes*: for Nature might have placed our Heads in our Knees or Elbows; but having before-hand determined that the Eyes should serve to discover things from afar, she, for the better enabling them to execute their designed Office, fixed them in the Head (as on the top of a long Pole) in the most eminent Part of all the Body: no otherwise than we see the *Phares*, or High Towers erected in the Mouths of Havens, that Navigators may the further off perceive with ease the Lights of the nightly Fires and Lanterns. And because I would gladly, for some short while (a Year at least) take a little Rest and breathing-time from the toylsom Labour of the Military Profession; that is to say, be married; I have desisted from wearing any more a Codpiece, and consequently have laid aside my Breeches: for the Codpiece is the principal and most especial Piece of Armour that a Warriour doth carry; and therefore do I maintain even to the Fire (exclusively, understand you me) that no *Turks* can properly be said to be armed Men, in regard that Codpieces are by their Law forbidden to be worn.

CHAPTER VIII

Why the Codpiece is held to be the chief piece of Armour amongst Warriours.

WILL you maintain (quoth *Pantagruel*) that the Codpiece is the chief piece of a Military Harness? It is a new kind of Doctrine very Paradoxical: For we say at Spurs begins the arming of a Man. Sir, I maintain it, (answered *Panurge*) and not wrongfully do I maintain it. Behold how Nature having a fervent desire after its Production of Plants, Trees, Shrubs, Herbs, Sponges and plant Animals, to eternize, and continue them unto all Succession of Ages (in their several Kinds, or Sorts at least, although the Individuals perish) unruinable, and in an everlasting Being, hath most curiously armed and fenced their Buds, Sprouts, Shutes, and Seeds, wherein the above-mentioned perpetuity consisteth, by strengthning, covering, guarding, and fortifying them with an admirable industry, with Husks, Cases, Scurfs, and Swads, Hulls, Cods, Stones, Films, Cartels, Shells, Ears, Rinds, Barks, Skins, Ridges, and Prickles, which serve them instead of strong, fair, and *natural Codpieces*: As is manifestly apparent in Pease, Beans, Fasels, Pomegranates, Peaches, Cottons, Gourds, Pumpions, Melons, Corn, Lemons, Almonds, Walnuts, Filberts, and Chestnuts; as likewise in all Plants, Slips, or Sets whatsoever, wherein it is plainly and evidently seen, that the Sperm and *Semenæ* is more closely veiled, overshadowed, corroborated, and throughly harnessed than any other part, portion, or parcel of the whole.

Nature nevertheless did not after that manner provide for the sempiternizing of Human Race: but on the contrary created Man naked, tender, and frail, without either offensive or defensive Arms; and that in the Estate of Innocence, in the first Age of all, which was the Golden Season; not as a Plant, but living Creature, born for Peace, not War, and brought forth into the World with an unquestionable Right and Title to the plenary fruition and enjoyment of all Fruits and Vegetables; as also to a certain calm and gentle Rule and Dominion over all kinds of Beasts, Fowls, Fishes, Reptils, and Insects. Yet afterwards it hapning in the time of the Iron Age, under the Reign of *Jupiter*, when to the multiplication of mischievous Actions, wickedness and malice began to take root and footing within the then perverted Hearts of Men, that the Earth began to bring forth Nettles, Thistles, Thorns, Bryars, and such other stubborn and rebellious Vegetables to the Nature of Man; nor scarce was there any Animal, which by a fatal disposition did not then revolt from him, and tacitly conspire, and covenant with one another to serve him no longer, (nor in case of their ability to resist) to do him any manner of Obedience, but rather (to the uttermost of their Power) to annoy him with all the hurt and harm they could. The Man then, that he might maintain his primitive Right and Prerogative, and continue his Sway and Dominion over all, both Vegetable and Sensitive Creatures; and knowing of a truth, that he could not be well accommodated as he ought, without the servitude and subjection of several Animals, bethought himself, that of necessity he must needs put on Arms, and make

THE THIRD BOOK

provision of Harness against Wars and Violence. By the holy Saint *Babingoose*, (cried out *Pantagruel*) you are become, since the last Rain, a great *Lifre lofre, Philosopher*, I should say. Take notice, Sir, (quoth *Panurge*) when Dame Nature had prompted him to his own Arming, what part of the Body it was, where, by her Inspiration, he clapped on the first Harness: It was forsooth by the double pluck of my little Dog the *Ballock*, and good *Senor Don Priapos Stabo-stando*, which done, he was content, and sought no more. This is certified by the Testimony of the great *Hebrew* Captain Philosopher *Moyses*, who affirmeth, That he fenced that Member with a brave and gallant Codpiece, most exquisitely framed, and by right curious Devices of a notably pregnant Invention, made up and composed of Fig-tree-leaves, which by reason of their solid stiffness, incisory notches, curled frisling, sleeked smoothness, large ampleness, together with their colour, smell, vertue, and faculty, were exceeding proper, and fit for the covering and arming of the Sachels of Generation, the hideously big Lorrain Cullions being from thence only excepted; which swaggring down to the lowermost bottom of the Breeches, cannot abide (for being quite out of all order and method) the stately fashion of the high and lofty Codpiece; as is manifest, by the Noble *Valentin Viardiere*, whom I found at *Nancie*, on the first Day of *May* (the more flauntingly to gallantrize it afterwards) rubbing his Ballocks spread out upon a Table after the manner of a *Spanish* Cloak. Wherefore it is, that none should henceforth say, who would not speak improperly, when any Country-Bumpkin hyeth to the Wars, *Have a care* (my Royster) *of the Wine-pot*, that is the Scull, but *have a care* (my Royster) *of the Milk-pot*; that is, the Testicles. By the whole Rabble of the horned Fiends of Hell, the Head being cut off, that single Person only thereby dieth: but if the Ballocks be marred, the whole Race of Humane Kind would forthwith perish, and be lost for ever.

This was the motive which incited the goodly Writer *Galen, Lib.* I. *De Spermate*, to aver with boldness, *That it were better* (that is to say, a less evil) *to have no Heart at all, than to be quite destitute of Genitories*: for there is laid up, conserved, and put in store, as in a Seccessive Repository, and Sacred Warehouse, the *Semenæ*, and Original Source of the whole Off-spring of Mankind.

Therefore would I be apt to believe, for less than a hundred Franks, that those are the very same Stones, by means whereof *Deucalion* and *Pyrrha* restored the Humane Race, in peopling with Men and Women the World, which a little before that, had been drowned in the overflowing Waves of a Poetical Deluge. This stirred up the valiant *Justinian*, L. I. 4. *De Cagotis tollendis*, to collocate his *Summum Bonum, in Braguibus, et Braguetis*. For this, and other Causes, the Lord *Humphry de Merville*, following of his King to a certain warlike Expedition, whilst he was in trying upon his own Person a new suit of Armour, for of his old rusty Harness he could make no more use, by reason that some few Years since, the Skin of his Belly was a great way removed from his Kidneys, his Lady thereupon in the profound musing of a contemplative Spirit, very maturely considering that he had but small care of the Staff of Love, and Packet of Marriage, seeing he did no otherwise arm that part of the Body, then with Links of Mail, advised him to shield, fence, and gabionate it with a big tilting Helmet, which she had lying in her Closet, to her otherways utterly unprofitable. On this Lady was penned these subsequent Verses; which are extant in the Third Book of the *Shitbrana* of paultry Wenches.

> *When* Yoland *saw her Spouse, equipt for Fight,*
> *And, save the* Codpiece, *all in Armour dight,*
> *My Dear, she cry'd, Why, pray, of all the rest*
> *Is that expos'd, you know I love the best?*
> *Was she to blame for an ill-manag'd fear?*
> *Or rather pious, conscionable Care:*
> *Wise Lady, She! in hurly-burly Fight,*
> *Can any tell where random Blows may hit?*

Leave off then (Sir) from being astonished, and wonder no more at this new manner of decking and trimming up of my self as you now see me.

CHAPTER IX

How Panurge asketh Counsel of Pantagruel whether he should marry, Yea or No.

To this *Pantagruel* replying nothing, *Panurge* prosecuted the Discourse he had already broached, and therewithal fetching, as far from the bottom of his Heart, a very deep sigh, said, My Lord and Master, you have heard the Design I am upon, which is to marry, if by some disastrous mischance, all the Holes in the World be not shut up, stopped, closed, and bush'd. I humbly beseech you for the Affection which of a long time you have born me, to give me your best Advice therein. Then (answered *Pantagruel*) seeing you have so decreed, taken deliberation thereon, and that the matter is fully determined, what need is there of any further Talk thereof, but forthwith to put it into execution what you have resolved. Yea but (quoth *Panurge*) I would be loath to act anything therein without your Counsel had thereto. It is my Judgment also (quoth *Pantagruel*) and I advise you to it. Nevertheless (quoth *Panurge*) if I understood aright that it were much better for me to remain a Batchelor as I am, than to run headlong upon new hair-brain'd Undertakings of Conjugal Adventure, I would rather choose not to marry. Quoth *Pantagruel*, Then do not marry. Yea, but (quoth *Panurge*) would you have me so solitarily drive out the whole Course of my Life without the Comfort of a Matrimonial Consort? You know it is written, *Væ soli*, and a single Person is never seen to reap the Joy and Solace that is found with married Folks. Then marry, in the Name of God, quoth *Pantagruel*. But if (quoth *Panurge*) my Wife should make me a Cuckold; as it is not unknown unto you, how this hath been a very plentiful Year in the production of that kind of Cattel; I would fly out, and grow impatient, beyond all measure and mean. I love Cuckolds with my Heart, for they seem unto me to be of a right honest Conversation, and I, truly, do very willingly frequent their Company: but should I die for it, I would not be one of their number, that is a Point for me of a two-sore prickling Point. Then do not marry (quoth *Pantagruel*) for without all controversie, this Sentence of

Seneca is infallibly true, *What thou to others shalt have done, others will do the like to thee.* Do you (quoth *Panurge*) aver that without all exceptions? Yes, truly, (quoth *Pantagruel*) without all exception. Ho, ho (says *Panurge*) by the Wrath of a little Devil, his meaning is, either *in this World*, or in *the other*, which *is to come*. Yet seeing I can no more want a Wife, then a blind Man his Staff, the Funnel must be in agitation, without which manner of Occupation I cannot live, were it not a great deal better for me to apply and associate my self to some one honest, lovely, and vertuous Woman, then (as I do) by a new change of Females every Day, run a hazard of being Bastinadoed, or (which is worse) of the Great Pox, if not of both together: For never (be it spoken, by their Husbands leave and favour) had I enjoyment yet of an honest Woman. Marry then in God's Name, quoth *Pantagruel*. But if (quoth *Panurge*) it were the Will of God, and that my Destiny did unluckily lead me to marry an honest Woman who should beat me, I would be stor'd with more than two third parts of the Patience of *Job*, if I were not stark mad by it, and quite destracted with such rugged Dealings: for it hath been told me, that those exceeding honest Women have ordinarily very wicked Head-pieces; therefore it is that their Family lacketh not for good Vinegar. Yet in that case should it go worse with me, if I did not then in such sort bang her Back and Breast, so thumpingly bethwack her Giblets, to wit, her Arms, Legs, Head, Lights, Liver, and Milt, with her other Intrails, and mangle, jag, and slash her Coats, so after the Cross billet fashion, that the greatest Devil of Hell should wait at the Gate for the reception of her damned Soul. I could make a shift for this Year to wave such molestation and disquiet, and be content to lay aside that trouble, and not to be engaged in it.

Do not marry then, answered *Pantagruel*. Yea, but (quoth *Panurge*) considering the Condition wherein I now am, out of Debt and Unmarried; mark what I say, free from all Debt, in an ill hour, (for were I deeply on the Score, my Creditors would be but too careful of my Paternity) but being quit, and not married, no Body will be so regardful of me, or carry towards me a Love like that which is said to be in a Conjugal Affection. And if by some mishap I should fall sick, I would be lookt to very way-wardly. The wise Man saith, *Where there is no Woman* (I mean the

Mother of a Family, and Wife in the Union of a lawful Wedlock) *the Crazy and Diseased are in danger of being ill used, and of having much brabling and strife about them*: as by clear Experience hath been made apparent in the Persons of Popes, Legates, Cardinals, Bishops, Abbots, Priors, Priests, and Monks: but there, assure your self, you shall not find me. Marry then in the Name of God, answered *Pantagruel*. But if (quoth *Panurge*) being ill at ease, and possibly thro' that Distemper, made unable to discharge the Matrimonial Duty that is incumbent to an active Husband, my Wife, impatient of that drooping Sickness, and faint Fits, of a pining Languishment, should abandon and prostitute herself to the embraces of another Man, and not only then not help and assist me in my extremity and need, but withal flout at, and make sport of that my grievous Distress and Calamity; or peradventure, (which is worse) imbezzle my goods and steal from me, as I have seen it oftentimes befal unto the lot of many other Men, it were enough to undo me utterly, to fill brimful the Cup of my Misfortune, and make me play the Mad-pate Reeks of *Bedlam*. Do not marry then (quoth *Pantagruel*). Yea, but (saith *Panurge*) I shall never by any other means come to have lawful Sons and Daughters, in whom I may harbour some hope of perpetuating my Name and Arms, and to whom also I may leave and bequeath my Inheritances and purchased Goods, (of which latter sort you need not doubt, but that in some one or other of these Mornings, I will make a fair and goodly show) that so I may chear up and make merry, when otherways I should be plunged into a pievish sullen Mood of pensive sullenness, as I do perceive daily by the gentle and loving Carriage of your kind and gracious Father towards you; as all honest Folks use to do at their own Homes, and private Dwelling-Houses. For being free from Debt, and yet not married, if casually I should fret and be angry, although the cause of my Grief and Displeasure were never so just, I am afraid instead of Consolation, that I should meet with nothing else but Scoffs, Frumps, Gibes, and Mocks at my disastrous Fortune. Marry then in the Name of God, quoth *Pantagruel*.

CHAPTER X

*How Pantagruel representeth unto Panurge the difficulty of
giving Advice in the matter of Marriage; and to that purpose
mentioneth somewhat of the Homerick and Virgilian Lotteries.*

YOUR Counsel (quoth *Panurge*) under your Correction and
Favour, seemeth unto me not unlike to the Song of Gammer *Yea-
bynay*; it is full of Sarcasms, Mockqueries, bitter Taunts, nipping
Bobs, derisive Quips, biting Jerks, and contradictory Iterations,
the one part destroying the other. I know not (quoth *Pantagruel*)
which of all my Answers to lay hold on; for your Proposals are so
full of *ifs* and *buts*, that I can ground nothing on them, nor pitch
upon any solid and positive Determination satisfactory to what
is demanded by them. Are not you assured within your self of
what you have a mind to? the chief and main point of the whole
matter lieth there; all the rest is merely casual, and totally
dependeth upon the fatal Disposition of the Heavens.

We see some so happy in the fortune of this Nuptial Encounter, that their Family shineth (as it were) with the radiant
Effulgency of an Idea, Model or Representation of the Joys of
Paradice; and perceive others again to be so unluckily match'd
in the Conjugal Yoak, that those very basest of Devils, which
tempt the Hermits that inhabit the Deserts of *Thebaida* and
Montserrat, are not more miserable than they. It is therefore expedient, seeing you are resolved for once to take a trial of the
state of Marriage, that, with shut Eyes, bowing your Head, and
kissing the Ground, you put the business to a Venture, and give
it a fair hazard in recommending the success of the residue to
the disposure of Almighty God. It lieth not in my Power to give
you any other manner of Assurance, or otherways to certifie you
of what shall ensue on this your Undertaking. Nevertheless (if
it please you) this you may do, Bring hither *Virgil*'s Poems, that
after having opened the Book, and with our Fingers sever'd the
Leaves thereof three several times, we may, according to the
number agreed upon betwixt our selves, explore the future Hap
of your intended Marriage: For frequently, by a *Homerick* Lottery, have many hit upon their Destinies; as is testified in the

Person of *Socrates*, who, whilst he was in Prison, hearing the
Recitation of this Verse of *Homer*, said of *Achilles*, in the Ninth
of the *Iliads*,

> Ἤματί κεν τριτάτῳ Φθίην ἐρίβωλον ἱκοίμην.
> *We, the third day, to fertile* Phthia *came.*

Thereby foresaw that on the third subsequent day he was to
die: Of the truth whereof he assured *Æschines*, as *Plato*, in *Cri-
tone*; *Cicero, in primo de Divinatione; Diogenes Laertius*, and others,
have to the full recorded in their Works. The like is also wit-
nessed by *Opilius Macrinus*, to whom, being desirous to know if
he should be the *Roman* Emperor, befell, by chance of Lot, this
Sentence in the Eighth of the *Iliads*,

> Ὦ γέρον, ἦ μάλα δή σε νέοι τείρουσι μαχηταί,
> Σῆ δὲ βίη λέλυται, χαλεπὸν δέ σε γῆρας ὀπάζει.
> *Dotard, new Warriours urge thee to be gone,*
> *Thy Life decays, and old Age weighs thee down.*

In Fact, he being then somewhat Ancient, had hardly enjoyed the Sovereignty of the Empire for the space of Fourteen
Months, when by *Heliogabalus* (then both young and strong) he
was dispossess'd thereof, thrust out of all, and killed. *Brutus* also
doth bear witness of another Experiment of this nature, who
willing, through this exploratory way by Lot, to learn what the
Event and Issue should be of the *Pharsalian* Battle, wherein he
perished, he casually encountred on this Verse, said of *Patroclus*
in the Sixteenth of the *Iliads*,

> Ἀλλά με Μοῖρ' ὀλοὴ, καὶ Λητοῦς ἔκτανεν υἱός.
> *Fate, and* Latona's *Son have shot me dead.*

And accordingly *Apollo* was the Field-word in the dreadful
Day of that Fight. Divers notable things of old have like-ways
been foretold and known by casting of *Virgilian* Lots; yea, in
matters of no less importance than the obtaining of the *Roman*
Empire, as it happened to *Alexander Severus*, who trying his Fortune at the same kind of Lottery, did hit upon this Verse written
in the Sixth of the *Æneids*,

Tu regere imperio populos, Romane, memento.
Know, Roman, *that thy business is to Reign.*

He within very few Years thereafter was effectually and in good earnest created and installed *Roman* Emperor. A semblable Story thereto is related of *Adrian*, who being hugely perplexed within himself, out of a longing Humour to know in what Accompt he was with the Emperor *Trajan*, and how large the measure of that Affection was which he did bear unto him, had recourse after the manner above specified, to the *Maronian* Lottery, which by hap-hazard tender'd him these Lines out of the Sixth of the *Æneids*,

> *Quis procul ille autem ramis insignis olivæ*
> *Sacra ferens? nosco crines incanaque menta*
> *Regis Romani.*
> *But who is he, conspicuous from afar,*
> *With Olive Boughs, that doth his Offerings bear?*
> *By the white Hair and Beard I know him plain,*
> *The* Roman *King.*

Shortly thereafter was he adopted by *Trajan*, and succeeded to him in the Empire. Moreover to the Lot of the praise-worthy Emperor *Claudius* befel this Line of *Virgil* written in the Sixth of his *Æneids*,

> *Tertia dum Latio regnantem viderit æstas,*
> *Whilst the third Summer saw him Reign, a King*
> *In* Latium.

And in effect he did not Reign above two years. To the said *Claudian* also, enquiring concerning his Brother *Quintilius*, whom he proposed as a Colleague with himself in the Empire, hapned the Responce following in the sixth of the *Æneids*,

> *Ostendent terris hunc tantum fata.*
> *—Whom Fate let us see,*
> *And would no longer suffer him to be.*

And it so fell out; for he was killed on the Seventeenth day after he had attained unto the management of the Emperial Charge. The very same Lot also, with the like misluck, did betide the Emperor *Gordian* the younger. To *Claudius Albinus*, being very sollicitous to understand somewhat of his future Adventures, did occur this Saying, which is written in the Sixth of the *Æneids*,

Hic rem Romanam magno turbante tumultu
Sistet Eques, etc.
The Romans boyling with tumultuous rage,
This Warriour shall the dangerous Storm asswage:
With Victories he the Carthaginian mawls,
And with strong hand shall crush the Rebel Gauls.

Likeways when the Emperor *D. Claudius*, *Aurelian*'s Predecessor, did with great eagerness research after the Fate to come of his Posterity, his hap was to alight on this Verse in the first of the *Æneids*.

His ego nec metas rerum, nec tempora pono.
No bounds are to be set, no limits here.

Which was fulfilled by the goodly Genealogical Row of his Race. When Mr. *Peter Amy* did in like manner explore and make trial, if he should escape the Ambush of the *Hobgoblins*, who lay in wait all to bemawl him, he fell upon this Verse in the Third of the *Æneids*,

Heu! fuge crudeles terras, fuge litus avarum
Oh flee the bloody Land, the wicked Shoar!

Which Counsel he obeying, safe and sound forthwith avoided all these Ambuscades.

Were it not to shun Prolixity, I could enumerate a thousand such like Adventures, which conform to the Dictate and Verdict of the Verse, have by that manner of Lot-casting encounter befallen to the curious Researchers of them. Do not you nevertheless imagine, lest you should be deluded, that I would upon this kind of Fortune flinging Proof infer an uncontrolable, and not to be gainsaid Infallibility of Truth.

CHAPTER XI

How Pantagruel sheweth the Trial of ones Fortune by the
throwing of Dice to be unlawful.

I T would be sooner done (quoth *Panurge*) and more expeditely, if we should trie the matter at the chance of three fair Dice. (Quoth *Pantagruel*) that sort of *Lottery* is deceitful, abusive, illicitous, and exceedingly scandalous; never trust in it; the accursed Book of the *Recreation of Dice* was a great while ago excogitated in *Achaia* near *Bourre*, by that ancient Enemy to Mankind, the Infernal Calumniator, who before the Statue or Massive Image of the *Bourraick Hercules*, did of old, and doth in several places of the World as yet, make many simple Souls to err and fall into his Snares. You know how my Father *Gargantua* hath forbidden it over all his Kingdoms and Dominions; how he hath caused burn the Moulds and Draughts thereof, and altogether suppressed, abolished, driven forth and cast it out of the Land, as a most dangerous Plague and Infection to any well-polished State or Commonwealth. What I have told you of *Dice*, I say the same of the Play at *Cockall*. It is a Lottery of the like Guile and Deceitfulness; and therefore do not for convincing of me, alledge in opposition to this my Opinion, or bring in the Example of the fortunate Cast of *Tiberius*, within the Fountain of *Appona*, at the Oracle of *Gerion*. These are the baited Hooks by which the Devil attracts and draweth unto him the foolish Souls of silly People into eternal Perdition. Nevertheless to satisfie your Humour in some measure, I am content you throw three *Dice* upon this Table, that according to the number of the Blots which shall happen to be cast up, we may hit upon a Verse of that Page, which in the setting open of the Book you shall have pitched upon.

Have you any Dice in your Pocket? A whole Bag full, answered *Panurge*, that is Provision against the Devil, as is ex-pounded by *Merlin Coccajus*, Lib. 2. *De Patria Diabolorum*; the Devil would be sure to take me napping, and very much at un-awares, if he should find me without Dice. With this the three Dice being taken out, produced and thrown, they fell so pat upon the lower Points, that the Cast was *Five, Six*, and *Five*. These are (quoth *Panurge*) *Sixteen* in all. Let us take the Six-teenth Line of the Page, the number pleaseth me very well; I hope we shall have a prosperous and happy Chance. May I be thrown amidst all the Devils of Hell, even as a great Bowl cast athwart at a Set of Nine Pins, or Cannon-ball shot among a Bat-talion of Foot, in case so many times I do not boult my future Wife the first Night of our Marriage. Of that, forsooth, I make no doubt at all: (quoth *Pantagruel*). You needed not to have rapped forth such a horrid Imprecation, the sooner to procure Credit for the Performance of so small a business, seeing possibly the first Bout will be *amiss*, and that you know is usually at Tennis called *Fifteen*. At the next justling Turn you may readily amend the Fault, and so compleat your Reckoning of *Sixteen*. Is it so (quoth *Panurge*) that you understand the matter? and must my words be thus interpreted? Nay, believe me, never yet was any *Solecism* committed by that valiant Champion, who often hath for me in *Belly-dale* stood Centry at the *Hypogastrian* Crany. Did you ever hitherto find me in the Confraternity of the Faulty? Never I trow; never, nor ever shall, for ever and a day. I do the Feat like a goodly Friar, or Father Confessor without Default: And therein am I willing to be judged by the Players. He had no sooner spoke these Words, than the Works of *Virgil* were brought in: But before the Book was laid open, *Panurge* said to *Pantagruel*, My Heart, like the Furch of a Hart in Rut, doth beat within my Breast. Be pleased to feel and grope my Pulse a little on this Artery of my Left Arm; at its frequent Rise and Fall you would say that they swinge and belabour me after the manner of a Probationer posed, and put to a peremptory Trial in the Examination of his Sufficiency for the Discharge of the Learned Duty of Graduate in some Eminent Degree in the Colledge of the *Sorbonists*.

But would not you hold it expedient, before we proceed any further, that we should invocate *Hercules* and the *Tenitian* Goddesses, who in the Chamber of Lots are said to Rule, sit in Judgment, and bear a Presidential Sway? Neither him nor them, (answered *Pantagruel*) only open up the Leaves of the Book with your Fingers, and set your Nails awork.

CHAPTER XII

*How Pantagruel doth explore by the Virgilian Lottery what
Fortune Panurge shall have in his Marriage.*

THEN at the opening of the Book in the Sixteenth Row of the Lines of the disclosed Page, did *Panurge* encounter upon this following Verse:

> *Nec Deus hunc mensa, Dea nec dignata cubili est.*
> *The God him from his Table banished,*
> *Nor would the Goddess have him in her Bed.*

This Response (quoth *Pantagruel*) maketh not very much for your benefit or advantage: for it plainly signifies and denoteth, that your Wife shall be a Strumpet, and your self by consequence a *Cuckold*; the Goddess, whom you shall not find propitious nor favourable unto you, is *Minerva*, a most redoubtable and dreadful Virgin, a powerful and fulminating Goddess, an Enemy to Cuckolds, and effeminate Youngsters, to Cuckold-makers and Adulterers: the God is *Jupiter*, a terrible and Thunder-striking God from Heaven; and withal, it is to be remarked, that conform to the Doctrine of the ancient *Hetrurians*, the *Manubes* (for so did they call the darting Hurls, or slinging Casts of the *Vulcanian Thunderbolts*) did only appertain to her, and to *Jupiter* her Father Capital. This was verified in the Conflagration of the Ship of *Ajax Oileus*, nor doth this fulminating Power belong to any other of the Olympick Gods; Men therefore stand not in such fear of them. Moreover, I will tell you, and you may take it as extracted out of the profoundest Mysteries of Mythology, that when the Giants had enterprized the waging of a War against the Power of the Cœlestial Orbs, the Gods at first did laugh at those attempts, and scorn'd such despicable Enemies, who were in their conceit, not strong enough to cope in Feats of Warfare with their Pages: but when they saw by the Gigantine labour the high Hill *Pelion* set on lofty *Ossa*, and that the Mount *Olympus* was made shake to be erected on the top of both.

Then was it that *Jupiter* held a Parliament, or General Convention, wherein it was unanimously resolved upon, and condescended to by all the Gods, that they should worthily and valiantly stand to their Defence. And because they had often seen Battles lost by the cumbersome Letts and disturbing incumbrances of Women, confusedly hudled in amongst Armies, it was at that time Decreed and Enacted, That they should expel and drive out of Heaven into *Ægypt*, and the Confines of *Nile*, that whole Crue of Goddesses disguised in the shapes of Weezils, Polcats, Bats, Shrew-Mice, Ferrets, Fulmarts, and other such like odd Transformations; only *Minerva* was reserved to participate with *Jupiter* in the horrifick fulminating Power; as being the Goddess both of War and Learning, of Arts and Arms, of Counsel and Dispatch, a Goddess arm'd from her Birth, a Goddess dreaded in Heaven, in the Air, by Sea and Land. By the *Belly of Saint Buff* (quoth *Panurge*) should I be *Vulcan*, whom the Poet blazons! Nay, I am neither a Cripple, Coyner of False Money, nor Smith as he was.

My Wife possibly will be as comely and handsome as ever was his *Venus*, but not a Whore like her, nor I a Cuckold like him.

The crook-leg'd slovenly Slave, made himself to be declared a Cuckold, by a definitive Sentence, and Judgment, in the open view of all the Gods: For this cause ought you to interpret the aforementioned Verse quite contrary to what you have said. This Lot importeth, that my Wife will be honest, virtuous, chast, loyal, and faithful; not armed, surly, waiward, cross, giddy, humorous, heady, hair-brain'd, or extracted out of the Brains, as was the Goddess *Pallas*: nor shall this fair jolly *Jupiter* be my Corrival, he shall never dip his Bread in my Broath, though we should sit together at one Table.

Consider his Exploits and gallant Actions, he was the manifest Ruffian, Wencher, Whoremonger, and most infamous Cuckold-maker that ever breathed: he did always lecher it like a Boar, and no wonder, for he was foster'd by a Sow in the Isle of *Candia*, (if *Agathocles* the *Babylonian* be not a Lyar) and more rammishly lascivious then a Buck, whence it is that he is said by others, to have been suckled and fed with the Milk of the *Amalthæan* Goat. By the vertue of *Acheron*, he jusled, bulled and lastauriated in one day the third part of the World, Beasts and People, Floods and Mountains, that was *Europa*.

For this grand subagitatory Atchievement, the *Ammonians* caused, draw, delineate, and paint him in the figure and shape of a *Ram*, ramming, and horned Ram. But I know well enough how to shield and preserve my self from that horned Champion: He will not, trust me, have to deal in my Person, with a sottish, dunsical *Amphytrion*; nor with a silly witless *Argus*, for all his hundred Spectacles; nor yet with the cowardly Meacock *Acrisius*; the simple Goosecap *Lyrus* of *Thebes*; the doating Blockhead *Agenor*; the flegmatick Pea-Goose *Æsop*; rough-footed *Lycaon*; the luskish mishapen *Corytus* of *Tuscany*; nor with the large-back'd and strong reined *Atlas*: let him alter, change, transform, and metamorphose himself into a hundred various shapes and figures; into a Swan, a Bull, a Satyr, a Showre of Gold, or into a Cuckow, as he did when he unmaiden'd his Sister *Juno*;

into an Eagle, Ram, or Dove, as when he was enamour'd of the Virgin *Phthia*, who then dwelt in the *Ægean* Territory; into Fire, a Serpent; yea, even into a Flea, into *Epicurian* and *Democratical Atomes*, or more *Magistronostralistically*, into those sly Intentions of the Mind, which in the Schools are called *Second Notions*, I'll catch him in the nick, and take him napping.

And would you know what I would do unto him, even that which to his Father *Cœlum*, *Saturn* did, (*Seneca* foretold it of me, and *Lactantius* hath confirmed it) what the Goddess *Rhea* did to *Athis*; I would make him two Stone lighter, rid him of his *Cyprian* Cimbals, and cut so close and neatly by the Breech, that there should not remain thereof so much as one ——, so cleanly would I shave him; and disable him for ever from being Pope; for *Testiculos non habet*. Hold there, said *Pantagruel*; *Hoc*, soft and fair (my Lad) enough of that, cast up, turn over the Leaves, and try your Fortune for the second time. Then did he fall upon this ensuing Verse.

> *Membra quatit, gelidusque coit formidine sanguis.*
> *His Joynts and Members quake, he becomes pale,*
> *And sudden Fear doth his cold Blood congeal.*

This importeth (quoth *Pantagruel*) that she will soundly bang your Back and Belly. Clean and quite contrary (answered *Panurge*) it is of me that he prognosticates, in saying that I will beat her like a Tyger, if she vex me. Sir *Martin Wagstaff* will perform that Office, and in default of a Cudgel, the Devil gulp him, if I shou'd not eat her up quick, as *Candaul* the *Lydian* King did his Wife, whom he ravened and devoured.

You are very stout, says *Pantagruel*, and couragious, *Hercules* himself durst hardly adventure to scuffle with you in this your raging Fury: Nor is it strange; for the *Jan* is worth two, and two in fight against *Hercules* are too too strong. Am I a *Jan*? quoth *Panurge*. No, no, (answer'd *Pantagruel*) my mind was only running upon the lurch and tricktrack. Thereafter did he hit, at the third opening of the Book, upon this Verse:

> *Fœmineo prædæ, & spoliorum ardebat amore.*
> *After the Spoil and Pillage (as in Fire)*
> *He burnt with a strong Feminine Desire.*

This portendeth (quoth *Pantagruel*) that she will steal your Goods, and rob you. Hence this, according to these three drawn Lots, will be your future Destiny, (I clearly see it) you will be a Cuckold, you will be beaten, and you will be robbed. Nay, it is quite otherways, (quoth *Panurge*) for it is certain that this Verse Presageth, that she will love me with a Perfect liking: nor did the Satyr-writing Poet lye in proof hereof, when he affirmed, That *a Woman burning with extream Affection, takes sometimes pleasure to steal from her Sweetheart*. And what I pray you? a Glove, a Point, or some such trifling Toy of no importance, to make him keep a gentle kind of stirring in the research and quest thereof: in like manner, these small scolding Debates, and pretty brabling Contentions, which frequently we see spring up, and for a certain space boil very hot betwixt a couple of high-spirited Lovers, are nothing else but recreative Diversions for their refreshment, spurs to, and incentives of a more fervent Amity than ever. As for example: We do sometimes see Cutlers with Hammers mawl their finest Whetstones, therewith to sharpen their Iron Tools the better.

And therefore do I think, that these three Lots make much for my advantage; which if not, I from their Sentence totally *appeal*. There is no *appellation* (quoth *Pantagruel*) from the Decrees of Fate or Destiny, of Lot or Chance: as is recorded by our ancient Lawyers, witness *Baldus, Lib. ult. Cap. de Leg.* The reason hereof is, Fortune doth not acknowledge a Superiour, to whom an Appeal may be made from her, or any of her Substitutes. And in this case, the *Pupil* cannot be restored to his Right in full, as openly by the said Author is alledged in *L. Ait prætor, § ult. ff. H. de minor.*

CHAPTER XIII

How Pantagruel adviseth Panurge to try the future good or bad luck of his Marriage, by Dreams.

Now seeing we cannot agree together in the manner of expounding or interpreting the Sense of the *Virgilian* Lots, let us bend our course another way, and try a new sort of *Divination*. Of what kind? (asked *Panurge*.) Of a good Ancient and Authentick

Fashion, (answered *Pantagruel*) it is by *Dreams*: For in Dreaming, such Circumstances and Conditions being thereto adhibited, as are clearly enough described by *Hippocrates* in *Lib.* Περὶ ἐνυπνίων, by *Plato, Plotin, Iamblicus, Sinesius, Aristotle, Xenophon, Galene, Plutarch, Artemidorus Valdianus, Herophilus, Q. Calaber, Theocritus, Pliny, Athenæus*, and others, the Soul doth often times foresee what is to come.

How true this is, you may conceive by a very vulgar and familiar Example; as when you see that at such a time as Suckling Babes, well nourished, fed and foster'd with good Milk, sleep soundly and profoundly, the Nurses in the interim get leave to sport themselves, and are licentiated to recreate their Fancies at what Range to them shall seem most fitting and expedient; their Presence, Sedulity and Attendance on the Cradle, being, during all that space, held unnecessary.

Even just so, when our Body is at Rest, that the Concoction is every where accomplished, and that, till it awake, it lacks for nothing, our Soul delighteth to disport it self, and is well-pleased in that Frolick to take a Review of its Native Country, which is the Heavens, where it receiveth a most notable Participation of its first beginning, with an Imbuement from its Divine Source, and in Contemplation of that Infinite and Intellectual Sphere, whereof the Center is every where, and the Circumference in no place of the universal World, to wit, God, according to the Doctrine of *Hermes Trismegistus*, to whom no new thing hapneth, whom nothing that is past escapeth, and unto whom all things are alike present, remarketh not only what is *preterit*, and gone in the inferiour Course and Agitation of sublunary matters, but withal taketh notice what is to come; then bringing a Relation of those future Events unto the Body by the outward Senses and exterior Organs, it is divulged abroad unto the hearing of others. Whereupon the Owner of that Soul deserveth to be termed a *Vaticinator*, or Prophet.

Nevertheless the truth is, that the Soul is seldom able to report those things in such Sincerity as it hath seen them, by reason of the Imperfection and Frailty of the Corporeal Senses, which obstruct the effectuating of that Office; even as the Moon doth not communicate unto this Earth of ours that Light which she receiveth from the Sun with so much Splendour, Heat, Vigour,

Purity and Liveliness as it was given her. Hence it is requisite
for the better reading, explaining and unfolding of these
Somniatory Vaticinations and Predictions of that nature, that a
dexterous, learned, skilful, wise, industrious, expert, rational and
peremptory Expounder or Interpreter be pitched upon, such a
one as by the *Greeks* is called *Onirocrit*, or *Oniropolist*.

For this cause *Heraclitus* was wont to say, that nothing is by
Dreams revealed to us, that nothing is by Dreams concealed
from us, and that only we thereby have a mystical Signification
and secret Evidence of Things to come, either for our prosperous or unlucky Fortune, or for the favourable or disasterous
Success of another. The Sacred Scriptures testify no less, and
profane Histories assure us of it, in both which are exposed to
our view a thousand several kinds of strange Adventures, which
have befallen pat according to the nature of the Dream, and that
as well to the Party Dreamer, as to others. The *Atlantick* People,
and those that inhabit the Land of *Thasos* (one of the *Cyclades*)
are of this grand Commodity deprived; for in their Countries
none yet ever dreamed. Of this sort, *Cleon* of *Daulia*, *Thrasy-
medes*; and in our days the learned Frenchman *Villanovanus*,
neither of all which knew what Dreaming was.

Fail not therefore to morrow, when the jolly and fair *Aurora*,
with her rosie Fingers draweth aside the Curtains of the Night,
to drive away the sable Shades of Darkness, to bend your Spirits
wholly to the task of sleeping sound, and thereto apply your
self. In the mean while you must denude your Mind of every
Human Passion or Affection, such as are Love and Hatred, Fear
and Hope; for as of old the great Vaticinator, most famous and
renowned Prophet *Proteus*, was not able in his Disguise or
Transformation into Fire, Water, a Tyger, a Dragon, and other
such like uncouth Shapes and Visors to presage any thing that
was to come, till he was restored to his own first natural and
kindly Form. Just so doth Man; for at his reception of the Art
of Divination, and Faculty of prognosticating future things,
that part in him which is the most Divine, (to wit, the νῆς, or
Mens) must be calm, peaceable, untroubled, quiet, still, husht,
and not imbusied or distracted with Foreign, Soul-disturbing
Preturbations. I am content, (quoth *Panurge*,) But I pray you,
Sir, must I this Evening, e're I go to Bed, eat much or little? I

do not ask this without Cause: For if I sup not well, large, round and amply, my sleeping is not worth a forked Turnep; all the Night long I then but dose and rave, and in my slumbering Fits talk idle Nonsence, my Thoughts being in a dull brown Study, and as deep in their Dumps as is my Belly hollow.

Not to sup (answered *Pantagruel*) were best for you, considering the state of your Complexion, and healthy Constitution of your Body. A certain very ancient Prophet named *Amphiaraus*, wished such as had a mind by Dreams to be imbued with any Oracles, for Four and Twenty Hours to taste no Victuals, and to abstain from Wine three days together; yet shall not you be put to such a sharp, hard, rigorous and extream sparing Diet.

I am truly right apt to believe, that a Man whose Stomach is repleat with various Cheer, and in a manner surfeited with drinking, is hardly able to conceive aright of Spiritual things; yet am not I of the Opinion of those, who after long and pertinacious Fastings, think by such means to enter more profoundly into the Speculation of Celestial Mysteries. You may very well remember how my Father *Gargantua*, (whom here for Honour sake I name) hath often told us, That the Writings of abstinent, abstemious, and long-fasting *Hermits*, were every whit as saltless, dry, jejune and insipid, as were *their* Bodies when they did compose them. It is a most difficult thing for the Spirits to be in a good plight, serene and lively, when there is nothing in the Body but a kind of Voidness and Inanity: Seeing the Philosophers with the Physicians jointly affirm, that the Spirits which are styled *Animal*, spring from, and have their constant practice in and through the *Arterial Blood*, refin'd and purify'd to the Life within the *admirable* Net, which, wonderfully framed, lieth under the *Ventricles* and Tunnels of the Brain. He gave us also the Example of the Philosopher, who, when he thought most seriously to have withdrawn himself unto a solitary Privacy; far from the rusling clutterments of the tumultuous and confused World, the better to improve his *Theory*, to contrive, comment and ratiocinate, was, notwithstanding his uttermost endeavours to free himself from all untoward noises, surrounded and environ'd about so with the barking of Currs, bawling of Mastiffs, bleating of Sheep, prating of Parrets, tatling of Jackdaws, grunting of Swine, girning of Boars, yelping of Foxes, mewing of Cats, cheeping of Mice, squeaking of Weasils, croaking of Frogs, crowing of Cocks, kekling of Hens, calling of Partridges, chanting of Swans, chattering of Jays, peeping of Chickens, singing of Larks, creaking of Geese, chirping of Swallows, clucking of Moorfowls, cucking of Cuckows, bumbling of Bees, rammage of Hawks, chirming of Linots, croaking of Ravens, screeching of Owls, whicking of Pigs, gushing of Hogs, curring of Pigeons, grumbling of Cushet-doves, howling of Panthers, curkling of Quails, chirping of Sparrows, crackling of Crows, nuzzing of Camels, wheening of Whelps, buzzing of Dromedaries, mumbling of Rabets, cricking of Ferrets, humming of Wasps, mioling of Tygers, bruzzing of Bears, sussing of Kitnings, clamring of Scarfes, whimpring of Fullmarts, boing of Buffalos, warbling of Nightingales, quavering of Meavises, drintling of Turkies, coniating of Storks, frantling of Peacocks, clattering of Magpyes, murmuring of Stock-doves, crouting of Cormorants, cigling of Locusts, charming of Beagles, gnarring of Puppies, snarling of Messens, rantling of Rats, guerieting of Apes, snuttering of Monkies, pioling of Pelicanes, quecking of Ducks, yelling of Wolves, roaring of Lions, neighing of Horses, crying of Elephants, hissing of Serpents, and wailing of Turtles, that he was much more troubled, than if he had been in the middle of the Crowd at the Fair of *Fontenoy* or *Niort*.

Just so it is with those who are tormented with the grievous pangs of Hunger; the Stomach begins to gnaw, (and bark as it were) the Eyes to look dim, and the Veins, by greedily sucking some Refection to themselves from the proper Substance of all the Members of a Fleshy Consistence: violently pull down and draw back that vagrant roaming Spirit, careless and neglecting of his Nurse and natural Host, which is the Body. As when a Hawk upon the Fist, willing to take her Flight by a soaring aloft into the open spacious Air, is on a sudden drawn back by a Leash tied to her Feet.

To this purpose also did he alledge unto us the Authority of *Homer*, the Father of all Philosophy, who said, that the Grecians did not put an end to their mournful mood for the Death of *Patroclus*, the most intimate Friend of *Achilles*, till Hunger in a rage declared her self, and their Bellies protested to furnish no more Tears unto their Grief. For from Bodies emptied and macerated by long Fasting, there could not be such supply of Moisture and brackish Drops, as might be proper on that Occasion.

Mediocrity at all times is commendable; nor in this case are you to abandon it. You may take a little Supper, but thereat must you not eat of a Hare, nor of any other Flesh: You are likewise to abstain from Beans, from the *Preak*, (by some called the *Polyp*) as also from Coleworts, Cabbidge, and all other such like windy Victuals, which may endanger the troubling of your Brains, and the dimming or casting a kind of Mist over your Animal Spirits: For as a Looking-glass cannot exhibit the Semblance or Representation of the Object set before it, and exposed, to have its Image to the life expressed, if that the polish'd sleekedness thereof be darken'd by gross Breathings, dampish Vapours, and foggy, thick, infectious Exhalations; even so the Fancy cannot well receive the impression of the likeness of those things, which *Divination* doth afford by Dreams, if any way the Body be annoyed or troubled with the fumish Steam of Meat, which it had taken in a while before; because betwixt these two there still hath been a mutual Sympathy and Fellow-feeling, of an indissolubly knit Affection. You shall eat good *Eusebian* and Bergamot-Pears, one Apple of the short-shank Pepin-kind, a parcel of the little Plums of *Tours*, and some few Cherries of the growth of my Orchard: Nor shall you need to fear, that thereupon will ensue doubtful Dreams, fallacious, uncertain, and not to be trusted to, as by some *Peripatetick* Philosophers hath been related; for that, say they, Men do more copiously in the Season of Harvest feed on Fruitages, than at any other time. The same is mystically taught us by the ancient Prophets and Poets, who alledge, *That all vain and deceitful Dreams lie hid and in covert, under the Leaves which are spread on the ground*: by reason that the Leaves fall from the Trees, in the Autumnal Quarter: for the natural fervour, which abounding in ripe, fresh, recent Fruits, cometh by the quickness of its ebullition, to be with ease evaporated into the Animal parts of the dreaming Person (the Experiment is obvious in *must*) is a pretty while before it be expired, dissolved, and evanished. As for your Drink, you are to have it of the fair, pure Water of my Fountain.

The Condition (quoth *Panurge*) is very hard: nevertheless, cost what price it will, or whatsoever come of it, I heartily condescend thereto; protesting that I shall to morrow break my Fast betimes, after my somniatory Exercitations; furthermore, I recommend my self to *Homer*'s two Gates, to *Morpheus*, to *Iselon*, to *Phantasus*, and unto *Phobetor*. If they in this my great need succour me, and grant me that assistance which is fitting, I will, in honour of them all, erect a jolly, gentiel Altar, composed of the softest Down. If I were now in *Laconia*, in the Temple of *Juno*, betwixt *Oetile* and *Thalamis*, she suddenly would disintangle my Perplexity, resolve me of my Doubts, and chear me up with fair and jovial Dreams in a deep Sleep. Then did he say thus unto *Pantagruel*: Sir, were it not expedient for my purpose, to put a Branch or two of curious *Laurel* betwixt the Quilt and Bolster of my Bed, under the Pillow on which my Head must lean? There is no need at all of that (quoth *Pantagruel*) for besides that it is a thing very Superstitious, the Cheat thereof hath been at large discovered unto us, in the Writings of *Serapion Ascalonites*, *Antiphon*, *Philochorus*, *Artemon*, and *Fulgentius Placiades*. I could say as much to you of the Left Shoulder of a Crocodile, as also of a Camelion, without prejudice be it spoken to the Credit which is due to the Opinion of old *Democritus*; and likewise of the Stone of the *Bactrians*, called *Eumerites*, and of the *Hammonian Horn*: for so by the *Æthiopians* is termed a certain precious Stone, coloured like Gold, and in the fashion, shape, form, and proportion of a Ram's Horn, as the Horn of *Jupiter Hammon* is reported to have been: they over and above assuredly affirming, that the Dreams of those who carry it about them are no less veritable and infallible, than the Truth of the Divine Oracles. Nor is this much unlike to what *Homer* and *Virgil* wrote of these two *Gates of Sleep*: to which you have been pleased to recommend the management of what you have in hand. The one is of *Ivory*, which setteth in confused, doubtful, and uncertain Dreams; for thro' *Ivory*, how small and slender it soever be, we can see nothing, the density, opacity, and close compactedness of its material parts, hindring the penetration of the visual Rays, and the reception of the Speciesses of such things as are visible: The other is of *Horn*, at which an entry is made to sure and certain Dreams, even as through *Horn*, by reason of the diaphanous splendour, and bright transparency thereof, the Species of all Objects of the sight distinctly pass, and so without confusion appear, that they are clearly seen. Your meaning is, and you would thereby infer (quoth Fryar *John*) that the Dreams of all horned Cuckolds (of which number *Panurge*, by the help of God, and his future Wife, is without controversie to be one) are always true and infallible.

CHAPTER XIV

Panurge's Dream, with the Interpretation thereof.

At Seven a Clock of the next following Morning, Panurge did not fail to present himself before *Pantagruel*, in whose Chamber were at that time *Epistemon*, Fryar *John of the Funnels*, *Ponocrates*, *Eudemon*, *Carpalin*, and others, to whom, at the entry of *Panurge*, *Pantagruel* said, *Lo, here cometh our Dreamer*. That word (quoth *Epistemon*) in ancient times cost very much, and was dearly sold to the Children of *Jacob*. Then, said *Panurge*, I have been plunged into my dumps so deeply, as if I had been lodged with Gaffer *Noddycap*: dreamed indeed I have, and that right lustily; but I could take along with me no more thereof, that I did goodly understand, save only, that I in my Vision had a pretty, fair, young, gallant, handsome Woman, who no less lovingly and kindly treated and entertained me, hugg'd, cherish'd, cocker'd, dandled, and made much of me, as if I had been another neat dillidarling Minion, like *Adonis*: never was Man more glad than I was then, my Joy at that time was incomparable; she flattered me, tickled me, stroaked me, groped me, frizled me, curled me, kissed me, embraced me, laid her Hands about my Neck, and now and then made jestingly, pretty little Horns above my Forehead: I told her in the like disport, as I did play the Fool with her, that she should rather place and fix them in a little below mine Eyes, that I might see the better what I should stick at, with them: for being so situated, *Momus* then would find no fault therewith, as he did once with the position of the Horns of Bulls. The wanton, toying Girl, notwithstanding any remonstrance of mine to the contrary, did always drive and thrust them further in: yet thereby (which to me seemed wonderful) she did not do me any hurt at all. A little after, though I know not how, I thought I was transformed into a *Tabor*, and she into a *Chough*.

My sleeping there being interrupted, I awaked in a start, angry, displeased, perplexed, chafing, and very wroth. There have you a large Platter-ful of Dreams, make thereupon good Chear, and, if you please, spare not to interpret them according to the Understanding which you may have in them. Come *Carpalin*, let us to Breakfast. To my sence and meaning, (quoth *Pantagruel*) if I have skill or knowledge in the Art of Divination by Dreams, your Wife will not really, and to the outward appearance of the World, plant, or set Horns, and stick them fast in your Forehead, after a visible manner, as Satyrs use to wear and carry them; but she will be so far from preserving herself Loyal in the discharge and observance of a Conjugal Duty, that on the contrary she will violate her plighted Faith, break her Marriage-Oath, infringe all Matrimonial Tyes, prostitute her Body to the Dalliance of other Men, and so make you a Cuckold. This point is clearly and manifestly explained and expounded by *Artemidorus*, just as I have related it. Nor will there be any metamorphosis, or transmutation made of you into a *Drum*, or *Tabor*, but you will surely be as soundly beaten as e're was *Tabor* at a merry Wedding: nor yet will she be changed into a *Chough*, but will steal from you, chiefly in the Night, as is the nature of that thievish Bird. Hereby may you perceive your *Dreams* to be in every jot conform and agreeable to the *Virgilian* Lots: A Cuckold you will be, beaten and robbed. Then cryed out Father *John* with a loud Voice: He tells the truth; upon my Conscience, thou wilt be a Cuckold, an honest one, I warrant thee; O the brave Horns that will be born by thee! Ha, ha, ha. Our good Master *De Cornibus*, God save thee, and shield thee; wilt thou be pleased to preach but two words of a Sermon to us, and I will go through the Parish Church to gather up Alms for the Poor.

You are (quoth *Panurge*) very far mistaken in your Interpretation; for the matter is quite contrary to your sence thereof: my Dream presageth, that I shall by Marriage be stared with plenty of all manner of Goods, the hornifying of me shewing, that I will possess a *Cornucopia*, that *Amalthæan* Horn, which is called, *The Horn of Abundance*, whereof the fruition did still portend the Wealth of the Enjoyer. You possibly will say, that they are rather like to be Satyrs Horns; for you of these did make some mention. *Amen, Amen, Fiat, fiat, ad differentiam papæ*. Thus shall I have my *Touch-her-home* still ready; my *Staff of Love* sempiternally in a good case, will, Satyr-like, be never toyled out; a thing which all Men wish for, and send up their Prayers to that purpose, but such a thing as nevertheless is granted but to a few; hence doth it follow by a consequence as clear as the Sun-beams, that I will never be in the danger of being made a Cuckold, for the defect hereof is, *Causa sine qua non*; yea, the sole cause (as many think) of making Husbands Cuckolds. What makes poor scoundrel Rogues to beg (I pray you)? Is it not because they have not enough at home, wherewith to fill their Bellies, and their Poaks. What is it makes the Wolves to leave the Woods? Is it not the want of Flesh Meat? What maketh Women Whores? you understand me well enough. And herein may I very well submit my Opinion to the Judgment of learned Lawyers, Presidents, Counsellors, Advocates, Procurers, Attorneys, and other Glossers and Commentators on the venerable Rubrick, *De Frigidis, & maleficiatis*. You are in truth, Sir, as it seems to me (excuse my boldness if I have transgressed) in a most palpable and absurd Error, to attribute my Horns to Cuckoldry: *Diana* wears them on her Head after the manner of a *Cressant*, is she a *Cucquean* for that? How the Devil can she be cuckolded, who never yet was married? Speak somewhat more correctly, I beseech you, least she being offended, furnish you with a pair of Horns, shapen by the Pattern of those which she made for *Actæon*. The goodly *Bacchus* also carries Horns; *Pan, Jupiter Hammon*, with a great many others, are they all Cuckolds? If *Jove* be a Cuckold, *Juno* is a Whore: this follows by the Figure *Metalepsis*. As to call a Child in the presence of his Father and Mother, a Bastard, or Whore's Son, is tacitly and under-board, no less than if he had said openly, the Father is a Cuckold, and his Wife a Punk. Let our Discourse come nearer to the purpose: The Horns that my Wife did make me are Horns of Abundance, planted and grafted in my Head for the increase and shooting up of all good things: this will I affirm for truth, upon my Word, and pawn my Faith and Credit both upon it; as for the rest, I will be no less joyful, frolick, glad, cheerful, merry, jolly, and gamesome than a well-bended *Tabor* in the Hands of a good Drummer, at a Nuptial Feast, still making a noise, still rowling, still buzzing and cracking. Believe me, Sir, in that consisteth none of my least good Fortunes. And my

Wife will be jocund, feat, compt, neat, quaint, dainty, trim, trick'd up, brisk, smirk and smug, even as a pretty little *Cornish Chough*: who will not believe this, let *Hell* or the *Gallows* be the Burden of his *Christmas* Carol.

I remark (quoth *Pantagruel*) the last point or particle which you did speak of, and having seriously conferred it with the first, find that at the beginning you were delighted with the sweetness of your Dream; but in the end and final closure of it, you startingly awaked, and on a sudden were forthwith vexed in choler, and annoyed. Yea, (quoth *Panurge*) the reason of that was, because I had fasted too long. Flatter not your self (quoth *Pantagruel*) all will go to ruine: know for a certain truth, that every Sleep that endeth with a starting, and leaves the Person irksome, grieved, and fretting, doth either signifie a present evil, or otherways presageth, and portendeth a future imminent mishap. To signifie an Evil, that is to say, to shew some Sickness hardly curable, a kind of pestilentious, or malignant Bile, Botch, or Sore, lying and lurking, hid, occult, and latent within the very Center of the Body, which many times doth by the means of Sleep (whose Nature is to reinforce, and strengthen the Faculty and Vertue of Concoction) begin according to the Theorems of Physick to declare itself, and moves toward the outward Superficies. At this sad stirring in the Sleeper's rest and ease disturbed and broken, whereof the first feeling and stinging smart admonisheth, that he must patiently endure great pain and trouble, and thereunto provide some Remedy: as when we say proverbially to incense Hornets, to move a stinking Puddle, and to awake a sleeping Lyon, instead of these more usual expressions, and of a more familiar and plain meaning, to provoke angry Persons, to make a thing the worse by medling with it, and to irritate a testy cholerick Man when he is at quiet. On the other part, to presage or fore-tell an Evil, especially in what concerneth the Exploits of the Soul, in matter of *Somnial Divinations*, is as much to say, as that it giveth us to understand, that some dismal Fortune or Mischance is destinated and prepared for us, which shortly will not fail to come to pass. A clear and evident example hereof is to be found in the Dream, and dreadful awaking of *Hecuba*, as likewise in that of *Euridice*, the Wife of *Orpheus*, neither of which was sooner finished, (saith *Ennius*) but that

incontinently thereafter they waked in a start, and were affrighted horribly; thereupon these Accidents ensued, *Hecuba*
had her Husband *Priamus*, together with her Children, slain before her eyes, and saw then the Destruction of her Country; and
Euridice died speedily thereafter, in a most miserable manner.
Æneas dreaming that he spoke to *Hector* a little after his Decease, did on a sudden in a great start awake, and was afraid:
now hereupon did follow this event; *Troy* that same night was
spoil'd, sack'd, and burnt. At another time the same *Æneas*, dreaming that he saw his familiar *Geniuses* and *Penates*, in a ghastly
fright and astonishment waked, of which terrour and amazement the issue was, that the very next day subsequent, by a
most horrible Tempest on the Sea, he was like to have perished,
and been cast-away. Moreover, *Turnus* being prompted, insti-
gated, and stirred up, by the fantastick Vision of an infernal
Fury, to enter into a bloody War against *Æneas*, awaked in a start
much troubled and disquieted in Spirit, in sequel whereof, after
many notable and famous Routs, Defeats and Discomfitures in
open Field, he came at last to be killed in a single Combat, by
the said *Æneas*. A thousand other instances I could afford, if it
were needful, of this matter. Whilst I relate these Stories of *Æneas*,
remark the saying of *Fabius Pictor*, who faithfully averred, That
nothing had at any time befallen unto, was done, or enterprized
by him, whereof he *preallably* had not Notice, and before-hand
fore-seen it to the full, by sure Predictions, altogether founded
on the Oracles of *Somnial Divination*. To this there is no want of
pregnant Reasons, no more then of Examples: For if Repose
and Rest in sleeping be a special Gift and Favour of the Gods,
as is maintained by the Philosophers, and by the Poet attested
in these Lines:

> *Then Sleep, that heavenly Gift, came to refresh,*
> *Of humane Labourers, the wearied Flesh.*

Such a Gift or Benefit can never finish or terminate in wrath and
indignation without portending some unlucky Fate, and most disastrous Fortune to ensue; otherways it were a Molestation, and
not an Ease; a Scourge and not a Gift, at least, proceeding from
the Gods above, but from the infernal Devils our Enemies, according to the common vulgar saying.

Suppose the Lord, Father, or Master of a Family, sitting at a very sumptuous Dinner, furnished with all manner of good Cheer, and having at his entry to the Table his Appetite sharp set upon his Victuals, whereof there was great plenty, should be seen to rise in a start, and on a sudden fling out of his Chair, abandoning his Meat, frighted, appalled, and in a horrid terrour, who should not know the cause hereof would wonder, and be astonished exceedingly: But what? he heard his Male Servants cry, *Fire, fire, fire, fire*; his Serving Maids and Woman yell, *Stop Thief, stop Thief*; and all his Children shout as loud as ever they could, *Murther, O Murther, Murther*. Then was it not high time for him to leave his Banqueting, for application of a Remedy in hast, and to give speedy Order for succouring of his distressed Houshold. Truly, I remember, that the *Cabalists* and *Massorats*, Interpreters of the Sacred Scriptures, in treating how with verity one might judge of Evangelical Apparitions (because oftentimes the *Angel* of *Satan* is disguized and transfigured into an Angel of Light) said, That the difference of these two mainly did consist in this: the favourable and comforting *Angel* useth in his appearing unto Man at first to terrifie and hugely affright him; but in the end he bringeth Consolation, leaveth the Person who hath seen him, joyful, well-pleased, fully content, and satisfied: on the other side, the *Angel* of Perdition, that wicked, devilish, and malignant Spirit, at his appearance unto any Person, in the beginning cheareth up the Heart of his Beholder, but at last forsakes him, and leaves him troubled, angry, and perplexed.

CHAPTER XV

Panurge's Excuse and Exposition of the Monastick Mystery concerning Pouder'd Beef.

THE Lord save those who see, and do not hear, (quoth *Panurge*) I see you well enough, but know not what it is that you have said: The Hunger-starved Belly wanteth Ears: For lack of Victuals, before God, I roar, bray, yell and fume as in a furious Madness. I have performed too hard a Task to day, an extraordinary Work indeed: He shall be craftier, and do far greater Wonders than ever did Mr. *Mush*, who shall be able any more this year to bring me on the Stage of Preparation for a dreaming Verdict. Fy; not to sup at all, that is the Devil. Pox take that Fashion. Come Friar *John*, let us go break our Fast; for if I hit on such a round Refection in the Morning, as will serve throughly to fill the Mill-hopper and Hogshide of my Stomach, and furnish it with Meat and Drink sufficient, then at a pinch, as in the case of some extream necessity which presseth, I could make a shift that day to forbear Dining. But not to Sup: A Plague rot that base Custom, which is an Error offensive to Nature. That *Lady* made the Day for Exercise, to travel, work, wait on and labour in each his Negotiation and Employment; and that we may with the more Fervency and Ardour prosecute our business, she sets before us a clear burning Candle, to wit, the Suns Resplendency: And at Night, when she begins to take the Light from us, she thereby tacitly implies no less, than if she would have spoken thus unto us: *My Lads and Lasses*, all of you are good and honest Folks, you have wrought well to day, toiled and turmoiled enough, the Night approacheth, therefore cast off these moiling Cares of yours, desist from all your swinking painful Labours, and set your Minds how to refresh your Bodies in the renewing of their Vigour with good Bread, choice Wine, and store of wholsom Meats; then may you take some Sport and Recreation, and after that lie down and rest your selves, that you may strongly, nimbly, lustily, and with the more Alacrity to morrow attend on your Affairs as formerly.

Falconers in like manner, when they have fed their Hawks, will not suffer them to fly on a full Gorge, but let them on a Pearch abide a little, that they may rouse, bait, tour and soar the better. That good *Pope*, who was the first Instituter of Fasting, understood this well enough; for he ordained that our *Fast* should reach but to the hour of *Noon*; all the remainder of that day was at our disposure, freely to eat and feed at any time thereon. In ancient times there were but few that dined, as you would say, some Church men, Monks and Canons; for they have little other Occupation; each day is a Festival unto them; who diligently heed the Claustral Proverb, *De missa ad mensam*. They do not use to linger and defer their sitting down and placing of themselves at Table, only so long as they have a mind in waiting for the coming of the Abbot; so they fell to without Ceremony, Terms or Conditions; and every body supped, unless it were some vain, conceited, dreaming Dotard. Hence was a Supper called *Cæna*, which sheweth that it is *common* to all sorts of People. Thou knowest it well, Friar *John*. Come let us go, my dear Friend, in the name of all the Devils of the Infernal Regions, let us go: The Gnawings of my Stomach, in this rage of Hunger, are so taring, that they make it bark like a Mastiff. Let us throw some Bread and Beef into his Throat to pacifie him, as once the *Sibyl* did to *Cerberus*. Thou likest best *Monastical Browess*, the prime, the flower of the Pot. I am for the solid, principal Verb that comes after: The good brown Loaf, always accompany'd with a round slice of the *Nine-lecture-poudred Labourer*. I know thy meaning, (answered Friar *John*) this Metaphor is extracted out of the *Claustral Kettle*; the *Labourer* is the Ox, that hath wrought and done the Labour; after the fashion of *Nine Lectures*, that is to say, most exquisitely well and throughly boil'd. These holy Religious Fathers, by a certain Cabalistick Institution of the Ancients, not written, but carefully by *Tradition* conveyed from hand to hand, rising betimes to go to Morning Prayers, were wont to flourish that their matutinal Devotion with some certain notable Preambles before their entry into the Church, *viz.* They dunged in the Dungeries, pissed in the Pisseries, spit in the Spitteries, melodiously coughed in the Cougheries, and doted in their Doteries, that to the Divine Service they might not bring any thing that was unclean or foul.

These things thus done, they very zealously made their repair to the *Holy Chapel*, (for so was, in their canting Language, termed the *Covent Kitchin*) where they with no small earnestness, had Care that the *Beef Pot* should be put on the Crook for the Breakfast of the Religious *Brothers* of our Lord and Saviour; and the Fire they would kindle under the Pot themselves. Now the *Matines* consisting of *Nine Lessons*, was so incumbent on them, that they must have risen the rather for the more expedite dispatching of them all. The sooner that they rose, the sharper was their Appetite, and the Barking of their Stomachs, and the Gnawings increase in the like proportion, and consequently made these Godly Men thrice more a hungred and a-thirst, than when their *Matines* were *hem'd* over only with three Lessons.

The more betimes they rose by the said Cabal, the sooner was the *Beef Pot* put on; the longer that the Beef was on the Fire, the better it was boiled; the more it boiled, it was the tenderer; the tenderer that it was, the less it troubled the Teeth, delighted more the Palats, less charged the Stomach, and nourished our good *Religious* Men the more substantially; which is the only end and prime intention of the first *Founders*, as appears by this, That *they eat not to live*, but *live to eat*, and in this World have nothing but their Life. Let us go, *Panurge*.

Now have I understood thee, (quoth *Panurge*) my Plushcod Friar, my Caballine and Claustral Ballock. I freely quit the Costs, Interest and Charges, seeing you have so egregiously commented upon the most especial Chapter of the *Culinary* and *Monastick Cabal*. Come along, my *Carpalin*, and you Friar *John*, my Leather-dresser: Good morrow to you all, my good Lords: I have dreamed too much to have so little. Let us go. *Panurge* had no sooner done speaking, than *Epistemon* with a loud Voice said these Words: It is a very ordinary and common thing amongst Men to conceive, foresee, know and presage the misfortune, bad luck or disaster of another; but to have the understanding, providence, knowledge and prediction of a Man's own mishap is very scarce and rare to be found any where. This is exceeding judiciously and prudently deciphered by *Esop* in his Apologues, who there affirmeth, That every Man in the World carrieth about his Neck a Wallet, in the Fore-bag whereof were contained the Faults and Mischances of others, always exposed to his view and knowledge; and in the other Scrip thereof, which hangs behind, are kept the Bearers proper Transgressions, and inauspicious Adventures, at no time seen by him, nor thought upon, unless he be a Person that hath a favourable Aspect from the Heavens.

CHAPTER XVI

How Pantagruel adviseth Panurge to consult with the Sibyl of Panzoust.

A LITTLE while thereafter *Pantagruel* sent for *Panurge*, and said unto him, The Affection which I bear you being now inveterate, and setled in my Mind by a long continuance of time, prompteth me to the serious consideration of your Welfare and Profit; in order whereto remark what I have thought thereon: It hath been told me that at *Panzoust* near *Crouly*, dwelleth a very famous *Sibyl*, who is endowed with the skill of foretelling all things to come. Take *Epistemon* in your Company, repair towards her, and hear what she will say unto you. She is possibly (quoth *Epistemon*) she is some *Canidia*, *Sagane* or *Pythonisse*, either whereof with us is vulgarly called a Witch. I being the more easily induced to give Credit to the truth of this Character of her, that the place of her Abode is vilely stained with the abominable repute of abounding more with *Sorcerers* and *Witches*, than ever did the Plains of *Thessaly*. I should not, to my thinking, go thither willingly, for that it seems to me a thing unwarrantable, and altogether forbidden in the Law of *Moyses*. We are not *Jews*, (quoth *Pantagruel*) nor is it a matter judiciously confess'd by her, nor authentically proved by others that she is a *Witch*. Let us for the present suspend our Judgment, and defer till after your return from thence, the sifting and garbeling of those Niceties. Do we know but that she may be an Eleventh *Sibyl*, or a Second *Cassandra*? But although she were neither, and she did not merit the Name or Title of any of these Renowned Prophetesses, what Hazard, in the Name of God, do you run, by offering to talk and confer with her of the instant Perplexity and Perturbation of your Thoughts? Seeing especially (and which is most of all) she is in the Estimation of those that are acquainted with her, held to know more, and to be of a deeper reach of Understanding, than is either customary to the Country wherein she liveth, or to the Sex whereof she is. What hindrance, hurt or harm doth the laudable desire of Knowledge bring to any Man, were it from a Sot, a Pot, a Fool, a Stool, a Winter Mittam, a Truckle for a Pully, the Lid of a Goldsmiths Crucible, an Oil Bottle, or old Slipper? You may remember to have read, or heard at least, that *Alexander* the Great, immediately after his having obtained a glorious Victory over the King *Darius* in *Arbeles*, refused in the Presence of the splendid and illustrious Courtiers that were about him, to give Audience to a poor certain despicable-like Fellow, who through the Solicitations and Mediation of some of his Royal Attendants was admitted humbly to beg that

Grace and Favour of him: But sore did he repent, although in vain, a thousand and ten thousand times thereafter, the surly State which he then took upon him to the Denial of so just a Suit, the Grant whereof would have been worth unto him the value of a Brace of potent Cities. He was indeed Victorious in *Persia*, but withal so far distant from *Macedonia*, his Hereditary Kingdom, that the Joy of the one did not expel the extream Grief, which through occasion of the other he had inwardly conceived; for not being able with all his Power to find or invent a convenient Mean and Expedient, how to get or come by the certainty of any News from thence; both by reason of the huge remoteness of the places from one to another, as also because of the impeditive Interposition of many great Rivers, the interjacent Obstacle of divers wild Deserts, and obstructive Interjection of sundry almost inaccessible Mountains. Whilst he was in this sad quandary and solicitous pensiveness, which, you may suppose, could not be of a small Vexation to him; considering that it was a matter of no great difficulty to run over his whole Native Soil, possess his Country, seize on his Kingdom, install a new King in the Throne, and plant thereon Foreign Colonies, long before he could come to have any Advertisement of it. For obviating the Jeopardy of so dreadful Inconveniency, and putting a fit Remedy thereto, a certain *Sydonian* Merchant of a low Stature, but high Fancy, very poor in shew, and to the outward appearance of little or no Account, having presented himself before him, went about to affirm and declare, that he had excogitated and hit upon a ready mean and way, by the which those of his Territories at home should come to the certain notice of his *Indian* Victories, and himself be perfectly informed of the state and condition of *Egypt* and *Macedonia* within less than five days. Whereupon the said *Alexander*, plunged into a sullen Animadvertency of Mind, through his rash Opinion of the Improbability of performing a so strange and impossible-like Undertaking, dismissed the Merchant without giving ear to what he had to say, and villify'd him. What could it have cost him to hearken unto what the honest Man had invented and contrived for his good? What Detriment, Annoyance, Damage or Loss could he have undergone to listen to the Discovery of that Secret, which the good Fellow would have most willingly revealed unto him? Nature, I am perswaded, did not without a cause frame our Ears open, putting thereto no Gate at all, nor shutting them up with any manner of Inclosures, as she hath done unto the Tongue, the Eyes, and other such out-jetting parts of the Body: The Cause, as I imagine, is, to the end that every Day and every Night, and that continually, we may be ready to hear, and by a perpetual hearing apt to learn: For of all the Senses, it is the fittest for the reception of the knowledge of Arts, Sciences and Disciplines; and it may be, that Man was an Angel, (that is to say, a Messenger sent from God) as *Raphael* was to *Toby*. Too suddenly did he contemn, despise and mis-regard him; but too long thereafter, by an untimely and too late Repentance did he do Pennance for it. You say very well, (answered *Epistemon*) yet shall you never for all that induce me to believe, that it can tend any way to the Advantage or Com-modity of a Man, to take Advice and Counsel of a *Woman*, namely, of such a Woman, and the Woman of such a *Country*. Truly I have found (quoth *Panurge*) a great deal of good in the Counsel of *Women*, chiefly in that of the Old Wives amongst them; who for every time I consult with them, I readily get a Stool or two extraordinary, to the great Solace of my Bum-gut passage. They are as Sloth-hounds in the Infallibility of their Scent, and in their Sayings no less Sententious than the Rubricks of the Law. Therefore in my Conceit it is not an improper kind of Speech to call them *Sage* or *Wise Women*. In confirmation of which Opinion of mine, the customary style of my Language alloweth them the Denomination of *Presage Women*. The Epithet of *Sage* is due unto them, because they are surpassing dextrous in the knowledge of most things. And I give them the Title of Presage, for that they *Divinely* foresee, and certainly *foretel* future Contingencies, and Events of things to come. Some-times I call them not *Maunettes*, but *Monettes*, from their whol-som Monitions. Whether it be so, ask *Pythagoras, Socrates, Empedocles*, and our Master *Ortuinus*. I furthermore praise and commend above the Skies the ancient memorable Institution of the pristine *Germans*, who ordained the Responses and Docu-ments of *Old Women* to be highly extolled, most cordially rev-erenced, and prised at a rate, in nothing inferiour to the weight, test and standeard of the Sanctuary: And as they were respectfully

prudent in receiving of these sound Advices, so by honouring
and following them did they prove no less fortunate in the
happy Success of all their Endeavours. Witness the old Wife
Antinia, and the good Mother *Villed*, in the days of *Vespasian*. You
need not any way doubt, but that Feminine Old Age is always
fructifying in Qualities *Sublime*, I would have said *Sibylline*.
Let us go, by the help; let us go, by the Vertue. God, let us go.
Farewel, *Friar John*, I recommend the care of my *Codpiece* to
you. Well, (quoth *Epistemon*) I will follow you, with this protestation nevertheless, that if I happen to get a sure Information,
or otherways find that she doth use any kind of Charm or
Enchantment in her Responses, it may not be imputed to me
for a blame to leave you at the Gate of her House, without accompanying you any further in.

CHAPTER XVII

How Panurge spoke to the Sibyl of Panzoust.

THEIR Voyage was three days Journeying, on the third whereof
was shewn unto them the House of the *Vaticinatress* standing on
the knap or top of a Hill, under a large and spacious Walnut-
Tree. Without great difficulty they entered into that straw-
thatch'd Cottage, scurvily built, naughtily movabled, and all
besmoaked. It matters not, (quoth *Epistemon*) *Heraclitus* the
grand *Scotist*, and tenebrous darksome Philosopher, was nothing
astonish'd at his Introit into such a coarse and paultry Habitation; for he did usually shew forth unto his Sectators and Disciples, *That the Gods made as cheerfully their Residence in these mean
homely Mansions as in sumptuous, magnifick Palaces*, replenished
with all manner of delight, pomp, and pleasure. I withal do
really believe, that the Dwelling-place of the so famous and
renowned *Hecale*, was just such another pretty Cell as this
is, when she made a Feast therein to the valiant *Theseus*. And
that of no other better Structure was the Coat or Cabin of *Hyre-
us*, or *Oenopion*, wherein *Jupiter*, *Neptune*, and *Mercury* were not
ashamed, all three together, to harbour and sojourn a whole
Night, and there to take a full and hearty Repast; for the payment of the Shot they thankfully pissed Orion.

They finding the ancient Woman, at a corner of her own Chimney, *Epistemon* said, She is indeed a true *Sibyl*, and the lively Pourtraict of one represented by the τῇ καμνοῖ of *Homer*. The old Hag was in a pitiful bad plight and condition, in matter of the outward state and complexion of her Body, the ragged and tottred Equipage of her Person, in the point of Accoutrement, and beggarly poor Provision of Fare for her Diet and Entertainment; for she was ill apparelled, worse nourished, Toothless, Blear-ey'd, Crook-shoulder'd, snotty, her Nose still dropping, and her self still drooping, faint, and pithless. Whilst in this wofully wretched case she was making ready for her Dinner, Porridge of wrinkled green Colworts, with a bit skin of yellow Bacon, mixed with a twice before cooked sort of watrish, unsavoury Broath, extracted out of bare and hollow Bones. *Epistemon* said, By the Cross of a Groat, we are to blame, nor shall we get from her any Responce at all, for we have not brought along with us the *Branch of Gold*. I have (quoth *Panurge*) provided pretty well for that, for here I have it within my Bag, in the substance of a Gold Ring, accompanied with some fair Pieces of small Money. No sooner were these Words spoken, when *Panurge* coming up towards her, after the Ceremonial performance of a profound and humble Salutation, presented her with six Neats-Tongues dried in the Smoke, a great Butter-pot full of fresh Cheese, a Boracho furnished with good Beverage, and a Rams Cod stored with Single Pence newly coyned: At last he, with a low Curtsie, put on her *Medical* Finger a pretty handsom Golden-Ring, whereinto was right artificially inchased a precious Toadstone of Beausse. This done, in few words, and very succinctly did he set open and expose unto her the motive Reason of his coming, most civilly and courteously entreating her, that she might be pleased to vouchsafe to give him an ample and plenary Intelligence, concerning the future good luck of his intended Marriage.

The Old Trot for a while remained silent, pensive and girning like a Dog, then, after she had set her withered Breech upon the bottom of a Bushel, she took into her Hands three old Spindles, which when she had turned and whirled betwixt her Fingers very diversly, and after several fashions, she pryed more narrowly into, by the tryal of their points; the sharpest whereof she retained in her hand, and threw the other two under a Stone Trough; after this, she took a pair of Yarn Windles, which she nine times unintermittedly veered, and frisked about, then at the ninth revolution or turn, without touching them any more, maturely perpending the manner of their motion, she very demurely waited on their repose and cessation from any farther stirring. In sequel whereof, she pull'd off one of her wooden Pattens, put her Apron over her Head, as a Priest uses to do his *Amice*, when he is going to sing *Mass*, and with a kind of antick, gaudy, party-colour'd String, knit it under her Neck. Being thus covered and muffled, she whiffed off a lusty good Draught out of the Borache, took three several Pence forth of the Ram Cod Fob, put them into so many Walnut-shells, which she set down upon the bottom of a Featherpot; and then, after she had given them three Whisks of a Broom Besom a-thwart the Chimney, casting into the Fire half a Bevin of long Heather, together with a Branch of dry Laurel, she observed with a very hush, and coy silence, in what form they did burn, and saw, that although they were in a flame, they made no kind of noise, or crackling din, hereupon she gave a most hideous and horribly dreadful shout, muttering betwixt her Teeth some few barbarous words, of a strange termination.

This so terrified *Panurge*, that he forthwith said to *Epistemon*, The Devil mince me into a *Gally-mafry*, if I do not tremble for fear. I do not think but that I am now inchanted; for *she uttereth not her Voice in the terms of any Christian Language*. O look, I pray you, how she seemeth unto me, to be by three full spans higher than she was, when she began to hood her self with her Apron.

What meaneth this restless wagging of her slouchy Chaps? What can be the signification of the uneven shrugging of her hulchy Shoulders? To what end doth she quaver with her Lips, like a Monkey in the dismembring of a Lobster? My Ears through horrour glow; ah! how they tingle. I think I hear the skreaking of *Proserpina*; the Devils are breaking loose to be all here. O the foul, ugly, and deformed Beasts! Let us run away! By the Hook of God, I am like to die for fear! I do not love the Devils; they vex me, and are unpleasant Fellows. Now let us fly, and betake us to our heels. Farewell, *Gammer*; Thanks and Grammercy for your Goods. I will not marry, no, believe me, I will not; I fairly quit my Interest therein, and totally abandon and renounce it, from this time forward, even as much as at present. With this, as he endeavoured to make an escape out of the room, the *old Crone* did anticipate his flight, and make him stop; The way how she prevented him was this: whilst in her hand she held the Spindle, she flung out to a Back-yard close by her Lodge, where after she had peeled off the Barks of an old Sycamore three several times, she very summarily, upon eight Leaves which dropt from thence, wrote with the spindle-point some curt, and briefly couched Verses, which she threw into the Air, then said unto them, Search after them if you will; find them if you can; the fatal Destinies of your Marriage written in them.

No sooner had she done thus speaking, when she did withdraw her self unto her lurking Hole, where, on the upper Seat of the Porch, she tucked up her Gown, her Coats and Smock, as high as her Arm-pits, and gave them a full inspection of the *Nockandroe*: which being perceived by *Panurge*, he said to *Epistemon*, Gods Bodekins, I see the *Sibyl's Hole*. She suddenly then bolted the Gate behind her, and was never since seen any more. They jointly ran in hast after the fallen and dispersed Leaves, and gathered them at last, though not without great labour and toyl, for the Wind had scattered them amongst the Thornbushes of the Valley. When they had ranged them each after other in their due Places, they found out their Sentence, as it is metrified in this Ocstatick:

> Thy Fame upheld,
> Even so, so:
> And she with Child
> Of thee: No.
> Thy Good End
> Suck she shall,
> And flay thee, Friend
> But not all.

CHAPTER XVIII

How Pantagruel, and Panurge did diversly Expound the
Verses of the Sibyl of Panzoust.

THE Leaves being thus collected, and orderly disposed, *Epistemon* and *Panurge* returned to *Pantagruel*'s Court, partly well pleased, and other part discontented: glad for their being come back, and vexed for the trouble they had sustained by the way, which they found to be craggy, rugged, stony, rough, and ill adjusted. They made an ample and full Relation of their Voyage, unto *Pantagruel*; as likewise of the Estate and Condition of the *Sibyl*. Then having presented to him the Leaves of the *Sycamore*, they shew him the short and twattle Verses that were written in them. *Pantagruel* having read and considered the whole sum and substance of the Matter, fetch'd from his Heart a deep and heavy Sigh, then said to *Panurge*: You are now, forsooth, in a good taking, and have brought your Hogs to a fine Market: the Prophesie of the *Sibyl* doth explain and lay out before us, the same very Predictions which have been denotated, foretold, and presaged to us by the Decree of the *Virgilian Lots*, and the Verdict of your own proper *Dreams*; to wit, that you shall be very much disgraced, shamed, and discredited by your Wife: for that she will make you a *Cuckold* in prostituting her self to others, being big with Child by another than you; will steal from you a great deal of your Goods, and will beat you, scratch, and bruise you, even from plucking the Skin in apart from off you; will leave the Print of her Blows in some Member of your Body. You understand as much (answered *Panurge*) in the veritable Interpretation, and Expounding of recent Prophesies, as a Sow in the Matter of Spicery. Be not offended (Sir, I beseech you) that I speak thus boldly; for I find my self a little in Choler, and that not without cause, seeing it is the contrary that is true; take heed, and give attentive ear unto my words: The old Wife said, that as the Bean is not seen till first it be unhuskt, and that its swad or hull be shaled, and *pilled* from off it: so is it that my Vertue and transcendent worth will never come by the *Mouth of Fame*, to be blazed abroad proportionable to the height, extent, and measure of the excellency thereof, until *preallably* I get a Wife, and make the full half of a married Couple. How many times have I heard you say, that the Function of a Magistrate, or Office of Dignity, discovereth the Merits, Parts and Endowments of the Person so advanced and promoted, and what is in him; that is to say, we are then best able to judge aright of the Deservings of a Man, when he is called to the Management of Affairs: for when before he lived in a private Condition, we could have no more certain knowledge of him, than of a *Bean* with-in his *Husk*. And thus stands the first Article explained: other-ways could you imagine, that the good Fame, Repute, and Estimation of an Honest Man, should depend upon the Tayl of a Whore?

Now to the meaning of the Second Article: My Wife will be *with Child* (here lies the prime Felicity of Marriage) but not of me. Copsbody, that I do believe indeed: It will be of a pretty little Infant: O how heartily I shall love it! I do already dote upon it: for it will be my dainty Fedle-darling, my gentiel Dilliminion. From thenceforth no Vexation, Care, or Grief, shall take such deep impression in my Heart, how hugely great or vehement soever it otherways appear; but that it shall evanish forthwith, at the sight of that my future Babe; and at the hearing of the Chat and Prating of its Childish Gibbrish: And blessed be the Old Wife. By my truly, I have a mind to settle some good Revenue or Pension upon her, out of the readiest Increase of the Lands of my *Salmigondinois*; not an inconstant, and uncertain Rent-seek, like that of witless, giddy-headed *Batchellors*, but sure and fixed, of the nature of the well-payed Incomes of *Regenting Doctors*.

If this Interpretation doth not please you, think you my Wife will *bear* me in her Flanks: Conceive with me, and be of me delivered, as Women use in Childbed to bring forth their Young ones; so as that it may be said, *Panurge* is a second *Bacchus*, he hath been twice born, he is re-born, as was *Hipolytus*; as was *Proteus*, one time of *Thetis*; and secondly, of the Mother of the Philosopher *Apollonius*: as were the two *Palices*, near the Flood *Symethos* in Sicily; his Wife was big of Child with him. In him is renewed and begun again the *Palintocy* of the *Megariens*, and the *Palingenesie* of *Democritus*. Fie upon such Errors, to hear stuff of that nature, rends my Ears.

The words of the third Article are: *She will suck me at my best End*. Why not? that pleaseth me right well. You know the thing, I need not tell you, that it is my intercrural Pudding with one end. I swear and promise, that in what I can, I will preserve it sappy, full of juyce, and as well victualled for her use as may be; she shall not *suck* me, I believe, in vain, nor be destitute of her allowance; there shall her *justum* both in Peck and Lippy be furnish'd to the full eternally. You expound this passage allegorically, and interpret it to Theft and Larceny. I love the Exposition, and the Allegory pleaseth me; but not according to the Sense whereto you stretch it. It may be that the Sincerity of the Affection which you bear me, moveth you to harbour in your Breast those refractory Thoughts concerning me, with a Suspition of my Adversity to come. We have this Saying from the Learned, *That a marvelously fearful thing is Love*, and that *true Love is never without fear*. But (Sir) according to my Judgment, you do understand both of and by your self, that here *Stealth* signifieth nothing else, no more than in a thousand other places of Greek and Latin, Old and Modern Writings, but the sweet fruits of amorous Dalliance, which *Venus* liketh best, when reap'd in secret, and cull'd by fervent Lovers filchingly.

Why so? I prithee tell: Because when the Feat of the Loose-Coat Skirmish happeneth to be done underhand and privily, between two well-disposed, athwart the Steps of a Pair of Stairs, lurkingly, and in covert, behind a Suit of Hangings, or close hid and trussed upon an unbound Faggot, it is more pleasing to the *Cyprian* Goddess, (and to me also, I speak this without prejudice to any better, or more sound Opinion) than to perform that Culbusting Art, after the *Cynick* manner, in the view of the clear Sun-shine, or in a rich Tent, under a precious stately Canopy, within a glorious and sublime Pavilion, or yet on a soft Couch betwixt rich Curtains of Cloth of Gold, without affrightment, at long intermediate Respits, enjoying of Pleasures and Delights a Belly-ful, all at great ease, with a huge fly-flap Fan of Crimson Sattin, and a Bunch of Feathers of some *East-Indian* Ostrich, serving to give chase unto the Flyes all round about: whilst, in the Interim, the Female picks her Teeth with a stiff-Straw, pick'd even then from out of the bottom of the Bed she lies on.

If you be not content with this my Exposition, are you of the mind that my Wife will *suck* and sup me up, as People use to gulp and swallow Oysters out of the shell? Or as the *Cilician* Women, according to the Testimony of *Dioscorides*, were wont to do the Grain of *Alkermes*? Assuredly that is an Error. Who seizeth on it, doth neither gulch up, nor swill down; but takes away what hath been packed up, catcheth, snatcheth, and plies the Play of *Hey pass, Repass*.

The Fourth Article doth imply, That my Wife will *flay* me, but *not all*. O the fine Word! You interpret this to beating Strokes and Blows. Speak wisely: Will you eat a Pudding? Sir, I beseech you to raise up your Spirits above the low-sized pitch of earthly Thoughts, unto that height of sublime Contemplation, which reacheth to the Apprehension of the Mysteries and Wonders of Dame Nature. And here be pleased to condemn your self, by a renouncing of those Errors which you have committed very grosly, and somewhat perversly, in expounding the Prophetick Sayings of the Holy *Sibyl*. You put the case (albeit I yield not to it) that by the Instigation of the Devil, my Wife should go about to wrong me, make me a Cuckold downwards to the very Breech, disgrace me otherways, steal my Goods from me, yea, and lay violently her Hands upon me; she nevertheless should fail of her Attempts, and not attain to the proposed end of her unreasonable Undertakings.

The Reason which induceth me hereto, is grounded totally on this last Point, which is extracted from the profoundest Privacies of a Monastick Pantheology, as good Friar *Arthur Wagtaile* told me once upon a *Monday* morning; as we were (if I have not forgot) eating a Bushel of Trotter-pies; and I remember well it rained hard: God give him the good Morrow.

The Women at the beginning of the World, or a little after, conspired to *flay* the Men quick, because they found the Spirit of Mankind inclined to domineer it, and bear rule over them upon the face of the whole Earth; and in pursuit of this their Resolution, promised, confirmed, sworn and covenanted amongst them all, by the pure Faith they owe to the nocturnal Sanct *Rogero*. But O the vain Enterprises of Women! O the great Fragility of that Sex Feminine! They did begin to *flay* the Man, or *pill* him, (as says *Catullus*) at that Member which of all the Body they loved best; to wit, the nervous and cavernous Cane; and that above five thousand years ago; yet have they not of that small part alone flayed any more till this hour but the Head: In meer despite whereof the *Jews* snip off that parcel of the Skin in Circumcision, choosing far rather to be called Clipyards, Raskals, than to be *flayed* by Women, as are other Nations. My Wife, according to this Female Covenant, will *flay* it to me, if it be not so already. I heartily grant my consent thereto, but will not give her leave to *flay* it all: Nay, truly will I not, my noble King. Yea, but (quoth *Epistemon*) you say nothing of her most dreadful Cries and Exclamations, when she and we both saw the Lawrel-bough burn without yielding any noise or crackling. You know it is a very dismal Omen, an inauspicious sign, unlucky judice, and token formidable, bad, disastrous, and most unhappy, as is certified by *Propertius, Tibullus*, the quick Philosopher *Porphyrius, Eustachius* on the *Iliads* of *Homer*, and by many others.

Verily, verily, (quoth *Panurge*) brave are the Allegations which you bring me, and Testimonies of two footed Calves. These Men were Fools, as they were Poets; and Dotards, as they were Philosophers; full of Folly, as they were of Philosophy.

CHAPTER XIX

How Pantagruel praiseth the Counsel of Dumb Men.

PANTAGRUEL, when this Discourse was ended, held for a pretty while his Peace, seeming to be exceeding sad and pensive, then said to *Panurge*, the malignant Spirit misleads, beguileth and seduceth you. I have read that in times past the surest and most veritable Oracles were not those which either were delivered in Writing, or utter'd by word of Mouth in speaking: For many times, in their Interpretation, right witty, learned and ingenious Men have been deceived thro' Amphibologies, Equivoks, and Obscurity of Words, no less than by the brevity of their Sentences. For which cause *Apollo*, the God of Vaticination, was surnamed λοξίας. Those which were represented then by Signs and outward Gestures were accounted the truest and the most infallible. Such was the Opinion of *Heraclitus*: And *Jupiter* did himself in this manner give forth in *Amon* frequently Predictions: Nor was he single in this Practice; for *Apollo* did the like amongst the *Assyrians*. His prophesying thus unto those People, moved them to paint him with a large long Beard, and Cloaths beseeming an old setled Person, of a most posed, stayed and grave Behaviour; not naked, young and beardless, as he was pourtrayed most usually amongst the *Græcians*. Let us make trial of this kind of Fatidicency; and go you take Advice of some dumb Person without any speaking. I am content, (quoth *Panurge*).

But, says *Pantagruel*, it were requisite that the Dumb you consult with be such as have been deaf from the hour of their Nativity, and consequently dumb; for none can be so lively, natural, and kindly dumb, as he who never heard.

How is it, (quoth *Panurge*) that you conceive this matter? If you apprehend it so, that never any spoke, who had not before heard the Speech of others, I will from that Antecedent bring you to infer very logically a most absurd and paradoxical Conclusion. But let it pass; I will not insist on it. You do not then believe what *Herodotus* wrote of two Children, who at the special Command and Appointment of *Psammetichus* King of *Egypt*, having been kept in a pretty Country Cottage, where they were nourished and entertained in a perpetual silence, did at last, after a certain long space of time, pronounce this word *Bec*, which in the *Phrygian* Language signifieth *Bread*. Nothing less (quoth *Pantagruel*) do I believe, than that it is a meer abusing of our Understandings to give Credit to the words of those, who say that there is any such thing as a Natural Language. All Speeches have had their primary Origin from the Arbitrary Institutions, Accords and Agreements of Nations in their respective Condescendments to what should be noted and betokened by them. An Articulate Voice (according to the Dialecticians) hath naturally no signification at all; for that the sence and meaning thereof did totally depend upon the good will and pleasure of the first Deviser and Imposer of it. I do not tell you this without a cause; for *Bartholus, Lib. 5. de Verb. Oblig.* very seriously reporteth, that even in his time there was in *Cugubia* one named *Sir Nello de Gabrielis*, who although he by a sad mischance became altogether deaf, understood nevertheless every one that talked in the *Italian* Dialect howsoever he expressed himself; and that only by looking on his external Gestures, and casting an attentive Eye upon the divers motions of his Lips and Chaps. I have read, I remember also, in a very literate and eloquent Author, that *Turidates* King of *Armenia*, in the days of *Nero*, made a Voyage to *Rome*, where he was received with great Honour and Solemnity, and with all manner of Pomp and Magnificence: Yea, to the end there might be a sempiternal Amity and Correspondence preserved betwixt him and the Roman Senate; there was no remarkable thing in the whole City which was not shown unto him.

At his Departure the Emperor bestowed upon him many ample
Donatives of an inestimable Value: And besides, the more entirely to testifie his Affection towards him, heartily intrusted
him to be pleased to make choice of any whatsoever thing in
Rome was most agreeable to his Fancy; with a Promise jurament-
ally confirmed, That he should not be refused of his Demand.
Thereupon, after a suitable Return of Thanks for a so gracious
Offer, he required a certain *Jack-pudding*, whom he had seen
to act his part most egregiously upon the Stage, and whose
meaning (albeit he knew not what it was he had spoken) he
understood perfectly enough by the Signs and Gesticulations
which he had made. And for this Suit of his, in that he asked
nothing else, he gave this Reason, That in the several wide and
spacious Dominions, which were reduced under the Sway and
Authority of his Sovereign Government, there were sundry
Countries and Nations much differing from one another in Language, with whom, whether he was to speak unto them, or give
any Answer to their Requests, he was always necessitated to
make use of divers sorts of *Truchmen* and Interpreters: Now with
this Man alone, sufficient for supplying all their places, will that
great Inconveniency hereafter be totally removed; seeing he is
such a fine Gesticulator, and in the Practice of *Chirology* an Artist so compleat, expert and dextrous, that with his very Fingers
he doth speak. Howsoever you are to pitch upon such a dumb
Bone as is deaf by Nature, and from his Birth; to the end that his
Gestures and Signs may be the more vively and truly Prophetick,
and not counterfeit by the intermixture of some adulterate
Lustre and Affectation. Yet whether this dumb Person shall be
of the Male or Female Sex is in your Option, lieth at your Discretion, and altogether dependeth on your own Election.

I would more willingly (quoth *Panurge*) consult with and be
advised by a dumb Woman, were it not that I am afraid of two
things. The first is, That the greater part of Women, whatever
it be that they see, do always represent unto their Fancies, think
and imagine, that it hath some relation to the sugred entring of
the goodly *Ithyphallos*, and graffing in the Cleft of the over-
turned Tree, the quick-set Imp of the Pin of Copulation. Whatever Signs, Shews or Gestures we shall make, or whatever our
Behaviour, Carriage or Demeanour shall happen to be in their

370

view and Presence, they will interpret the whole in reference to the act of *Androgynation*, and the culbatizing Exercise, by which means we shall be abusively disappointed of our Designs, in regard that she will take all our Signs for nothing else but Tokens and Representations of our Desire to entice her unto the Lists of a *Cyprian* Combat, or Catsenconny Skirmish.

Do you remember what hapned at *Rome* two hundred and threescore Years after the Foundation thereof? A young *Roman* Gentleman encountring by chance at the Foot of Mount *Celion* with a beautiful *Latin* Lady named *Verona*, who from her very Cradle upwards had always been both deaf and dumb, very civilly asked her, (not without a Chironomatick Italianising of his Demand, with various Jectigation of his Fingers, and other Gesticulations, as yet customary amongst the Speakers of that Country) what Senators in her Descent from the top of the Hill she had met with going up thither. For you are to conceive, that he knowing no more of her Deafness than Dumbness, was ignorant of both. She in the mean time, who neither heard nor understood so much as one word of what he had said, streight imagin'd, by all that she could apprehend in the lovely Gesture of his manual Signs, that what he then required of her was, what her self had a great mind to, even that which a Young Man doth naturally desire of a Woman. Then was it, that by Signs (which in all occurrences of Venerial Love are incomparably more attractive, valid and efficacious than Words) she beckned to him to come along with her to her House; which when he had done, she drew him aside to a privy Room, and then made a most lively alluring Sign unto him, to shew that the Game did please her. Whereupon, without any more Advertisement, or so much as the uttering of one Word on either side, they fell to, and bringuardised it lustily.

The other Cause of my being averse from consulting with dumb Women is, that to our Signs they would make no answer at all, but suddenly fall backwards in a divarication posture, to intimate thereby unto us the reality of their consent to the supposed motion of our tacit Demands. Or if they should chance to make any contre-signs responsory to our Propositions, they would prove so foolish, impertinent, and ridiculous, that by them our selves should easily judge their thoughts to have no excursion beyond the duffling Academy. You know very well how at *Cro-quiniole*, when the religious Nun, sister *Fatbum*, was made big with Child by the young *Stifly-Stantor*, her Pregnancy came to be known, and she cited by the *Abbess*, and in a full Convention of the Convent, accused of Incest. Her excuse was, That she did not consent thereto, but that it was done by the violence and impetuous force of the Friar *Stifly-stand-to't*. *Hereto* the Abbess very austerely replying, Thou naughty wicked Girl, why didst thou not cry, a Rape, a Rape, then should all of us have run to thy Succour. Her answer was, That the Rape was committed in the *Dorter*, where she durst not cry, because it was a place of sempiternal Silence. But (quoth the Abbess) thou roguish Wench, why didst not thou then make some sign to those that were in the next Chamber beside thee? To this she answered, That with her Buttocks she made a sign unto them, as vigorous-ly as she could, yet never one of them did so much as offer to come to her help and assistance. But (quoth the Abbess) thou scurvy Baggage, why didst thou not tell it me immediately after the perpetration of the Fact, that so we might orderly, regularly, and canonically have accused him? I would have done so, had the case been mine, for the clearer manifestation of mine In-nocency. I truly, Madam, would have done the like with all my heart and soul, (quoth Sister *Fatbum*) but that fearing I should remain in Sin, and in the hazard of Eternal Damnation, if prevented by a sudden Death, I did confess my self to the Father Fryar before he went out of the Room, who for my Pen-ance, enjoyned me not to tell it, or reveal the matter unto any. It were a most enormous and horrid Offence, detestable before God and the Angels, to reveal a Confession: such an abominable Wickedness would have possibly brought down fire from Heaven, wherewith to have burnt the whole Nunnery, and sent us all headlong to the bottomless Pit, to bear company with *Corah*, *Dathan*, and *Abiram*. You will not (quoth *Pantagruel*) with all your Jesting make me laugh; I know that all Monks, Fryars, and Nuns had rather violate and infringe the highest of the Commandments of God, than break the least of their Provincial Statutes.

Take you therefore *Goatsnose*, a Man very fit for your present purpose; for he is, and hath been, both dumb and deaf from the very remotest Infancy of his Childhood.

CHAPTER XX

*How Goatsnose by signs maketh answer to
Panurge.*

GOATSNOSE being sent for, came the day thereafter to *Pantagruel*'s Court; at his arrival to which *Panurge* gave him a fat Calf,
the half of a Hog, two Punchions of Wine, one Load of Corn,
and thirty Franks of small Money: Then having brought him
before *Pantagruel*, in presence of the Gentlemen of the Bed-
chamber, he made this sign unto him. He yawned a long time,
and in yawning made without his mouth with the thumb of his
right hand the figure of the Greek Letter *Tau* by frequent re-
iterations. Afterwards he lifted up his Eyes to Heavenwards,
then turned them in his Head like a Shee-goat in the painful fit
of an absolute Birth, in doing whereof he did cough and sigh
exceeding heavily: This done, after that he had made demonstration of the want of his Codpiece, he from under his shirt
took his Placket-racket in a full gripe, making it therewithal
clack very melodiously betwixt his Thighs: then no sooner had
he with his Body stooped a little forwards, and bowed his left
Knee, but that immediately thereupon holding both his Arms
on his Breast, in a loose faintlike Posture, the one over the
other, he paused a-while. *Goatsnose* looked wistly upon him, and
having heedfully enough viewed him all over, he lifted up into
the Air his left Hand, the whole fingers whereof he retained fist-
ways closed together, except the Thumb and the Fore-finger,
whose Nails he softly joyned and coupled to one another. I
understand (quoth *Pantagruel*) what he meaneth by that sign: It
denotes *marriage*, and withal the number *thirty*, according to the
Profession of *Pythagorians*; you will be *married*. Thanks to you
(quoth *Panurge*) in turning himself towards *Goatsnose*, my little
Sewer, pretty Masters-mate, dainty Baily, curious Sergeant-
Marshal, and jolly Catchpole-leader. Then did he lift higher up
than before his said left Hand, stretching out all the five Fingers
thereof, and severing them as wide from one another as he possibly could get done. Here (says *Pantagruel*) doth he more amply
and fully insinuate unto us, by the Token which he sheweth

373

forth of the *Quinary number*, that you shall be *married*. Yea, that you shall not only be affianced, betrothed, wedded, and *married*, but that you shall furthermore cohabit, and live jollily and merrily with your Wife; for *Pythagoras* called *five* the *Nuptial Number*, which together with *marriage*, signifieth the *Consummation* of Matrimony, because it is composed of a *ternary*, the first of the odd, and *binary*, the first of the even Numbers, as of a Male and Female knit and united together. In very deed it was the fashion of old in the City of *Rome* at Marriage Festivals to light *five* wax Tapers, nor was it permitted to kindle any more at the magnifick Nuptials of the most Potent and Wealthy; nor yet any fewer at the penurious Weddings of the Poorest and most Abject of the World. Moreover in times past, the Heathen or *Paynims* implored the Assistance of *five* Deities, or of one helpful (at least) in *five* several good Offices to those that were to be married: Of this sort were the Nuptial *Jove*, *Juno*, President of the Feast, the fair *Venus*, *Pitho* the Goddess of Eloquence and Perswasion, and *Diana*, whose aid and succour was required to the labour of Child-bearing. Then shouted *Panurge*, O the gentile *Goatsnose*, I will give him a Farm near *Gnais*, and a Windmill hard by *Mirebalais*. Hereupon the dumb Fellow sneezeth with an impetuous vehemency, and huge concussion of the Spirits of the whole Body, withdrawing himself in so doing with a jerting turn towards the left hand. By the Body of a Fox new slain (quoth *Pantagruel*) what is that? this maketh nothing for your advantage; for he betokeneth thereby that your *marriage* will be inauspicious and unfortunate. This sneezing (according to the Doctrine of *Terpsion*) is the *Socratick* Demon; if done towards the right side, it imports and portendeth, that boldly, and with all assurance, one may go whither he will, and do what he listeth, according to what deliberation he shall be pleased to have thereupon taken: his entries in the beginning, progress in his proceedings, and success in the events and issues will be all lucky, good, and happy. The quite contrary thereto is thereby implied and presaged, if it be done towards the left. You (quoth *Panurge*) do take always the matter at the worst, and continually, like another *Davus*, casteth in new disturbances and obstructions; nor ever yet did I know this old paultry *Terpsion* worthy of citation, but in points only of Cosenage and Imposture.

Nevertheless (quoth *Pantagruel*) *Cicero* hath written I know not what to the same purpose in his *Second Book of Divination*.

Panurge then turning himself towards *Goatsnose* made this sign unto him. He inverted his Eye-lids upwards, wrinched his Jaws from the right to the left side, and drew forth his Tongue half out of his Mouth; this done, he posited his left Hand wholly open (the mid-finger wholly excepted, which was perpendicularly placed upon the Palm thereof) and set it just in the room where his Codpiece had been. Then did he keep his right Hand altogether shut up in a fist, save only the Thumb, which he streight turned backwards directly under the right Arm-pit, and setled it afterwards on that most eminent part of the Buttocks which the *Arabs* call the *Alkatim*. Suddenly thereafter he made this interchange, he held his right Hand after the manner of the left, and posited it on the place wherein his Codpiece sometime was, and retaining his left Hand in the form and fashion of the right, he placed it upon his *Alkatim*: this altering of Hands did he reiterate nine several times; at the last whereof, he reseated his Eyelids into their own first natural position. Then doing the like also with his Jaws and Tongue, he did cast a squinting look upon *Goatsnose*, diddering and shivering his Chaps, as Apes use to do now-a-days, and Rabbets, whilst almost starved with Hunger, they are eating Oats in the Sheaf.

Then was it that *Goatsnose* lifting up into the Air his right Hand wholly open and displayed, put the Thumb thereof, even close unto its first Articulation, between the two third Joints of the middle and ring Fingers, pressing about the said Thumb thereof very hard with them both, and whilst the remanent Joints were contracted and shrunk in towards the Wrist, he stretched forth with as much straitness as he could, the fore and little fingers. That Hand thus framed and disposed of, he laid and posited upon *Panurge*'s Navel, moving withal continually the aforesaid Thumb, and bearing up, supporting, or under-propping that Hand upon the above specified, and fore and little Fingers, as upon two Leggs. Thereafter did he make in this posture his Hand by little and little, and by degrees and pauses, successively to mount from athwart the Belly to the Stomach, from whence he made it to ascend to the Breast, even upwards to *Panurge*'s Neck, still gaining ground, till having reached his Chin he had put within the concave of his Mouth his aforementioned Thumb: then fiercely brandishing the whole Hand, which he made to rub and grate against his Nose, he heaved it further up, and made the fashion, as if with the Thumb thereof he would have put out his Eyes. With this *Panurge* grew a little angry, and went about to withdraw, and rid himself from this ruggedly untoward dumb Devil. But *Goatsnose* in the mean time prosecuting the intended purpose of his *Prognosticatory Response*, touched very rudely with the above-mentioned shaking Thumb, now his Eyes, then his Forehead, and after that, the borders and corners of his Cap. At last *Panurge* cried out, saying, Before God, Master-Fool, if you do not let me alone, or that you will presume to vex me any more, you shall receive from the best hand I have a Mask, wherewith to cover your rascally scoundred Face, you paultry shitten Varlet. Then said Fryar *Jhon*, He is deaf, and doth not understand what thou sayest unto him. *Bulliballock*, make sign to him of a hail of Fisticuffs upon the Muzzle.

What the Devil (quoth *Panurge*) means this busie restless Fellow? What is it that this Polypragmonetick Ardeloine to all the Fiends of Hell doth aim at? he hath almost thrust out mine Eyes, as if he had been to potch them in a Skillet with Butter and Eggs, by God, *da Jurandi*, I will feast you with flirts and raps on the Snout, interlarded with a double row of bobs and finger filipings? Then did he leave him in giving him by way of *Salve* a Volley of Farts for his Farewel. *Goatsnose* perceiving *Panurge* thus to slip away from him, got before him, and by meer strength enforcing him to stand, made this sign unto him. He let fall his right Arm towards his Knee on the same side as low as he could, and raising all the fingers of that Hand into a close fist past his dexterer Thumb betwixt the foremost and midfingers thereto belonging. Then scrubbing and swindging a little with his left Hand alongst, and upon the uppermost in the very bought of the Elbow of the said dexter Arm, the whole Cubit thereof by leisure fair, and softly, at these thumpatory warnings, did raise and elevate it self even to the Elbow, and above it, on a suddain did he then let it fall down as low as before: and after that, at certain intervals and such spaces of time, raising and abasing it, he made a shew thereof to *Panurge*. This so incensed *Panurge*, that he forthwith lifted his Hand to have strucken him the dumb Royster, and given him a sound whirret on the Ear, but that the respect and reverence which he carried to the Presence of *Pantagruel* restrained his Choler, and kept his Fury within bounds and limits. Then said *Pantagruel*, If the bare signs now vex and trouble you, how much more grievously will you be perplexed and disquieted with the real things, which by them are represented and signified? All Truths agree, and are consonant with one another; this dumb Fellow Prophesieth and Foretelleth that you will be *married*, *cuckolded*, *beaten* and *robbed*. As for the marriage (quoth *Panurge*) I yield thereto, and acknowledge the verity of that point of his Prediction; as for the rest I utterly abjure and deny it: and believe Sir, I beseech you, if it may please you so to do, that *in the matter of Wives and Horses, never any Man was predestinated to a better Fortune than I.*

CHAPTER XXI

How Panurge consulteth with an old French Poet, named Raminagrobis.

I NEVER thought (said *Pantagruel*) to have encountred with any Man so headstrong in his Apprehensions, or in his Opinions so wilful, as I have found you to be, and see you are. Nevertheless, the better to clear and extricate your Doubts, let us try all courses, and leave no stone unturn'd, nor wind unsailed by. Take good heed to what I am to say unto you, the *Swans*, which are Fouls consecrated to *Apollo*, never chant but in the hour of their approaching Death, especially in the *Meander* Flood, which is a River that runneth along some of the Territories of *Phrygia*. This I say, because *Elianus* and *Alexander Myndius* write, that they had seen several Swans in other Places die, but never heard any of them sing, or chant before their Death. However, it passeth for current, that the imminent death of a Swan is presaged by his foregoing Song, and that no *Swan* dieth until preallably he have Sung.

After the same manner *Poets*, who are under the Protection of *Apollo*, when they are drawing near their latter end, do ordinarily become Prophets, and by the inspiration of that God sing sweetly, in vaticinating things which are to come. It hath been

likewise told me frequently, That old decrepit Men upon the
Brinks of *Charon*'s Banks, do usher their Disease with a disclos-
ure, all at ease (to those that are desirous of such Informations)
of the determinate and assured truth of future Accidents and
Contingencies. I remember also, that *Aristophanes*, in a certain
Comedy of his, calleth Folks *Sibyls*, Ὁ δὲ γερων σιβυλλιᾷ, for as
when being upon a Peer by the Shore, we see afar off Mariners,
Seafaring Men, and other Travellers alongst the curled Waves
of *Azure Thetis* within their Ships, we then consider them in
silence only, and seldom proceed any further than to wish them
a happy and prosperous Arrival: but when they do approach
near to the Haven, and come to wet their Keels within their
Harbour, then both with words and gestures we salute them,
and heartily congratulate their Access safe to the Port wherein
we are our selves. Just so the Angels, Heroes, and good Demons
(according to the Doctrin of *Platonicks*) when they see Mortals
drawing near unto the Harbour of the Grave, as the most sure
and calmest Port of any, full of Repose, Ease, Rest, Tranquility;
free from the Troubles and Sollicitudes of this tumultuous and
tempestuous World; then is it that they with alacrity hale and
salute them, Cherish and Comfort them, and speaking to them
lovingly, begin even then to bless them with Illuminations, and
to communicate unto them the abstrusest Mysteries of Divination. I will not offer here to confound your Memory by quoting
antick Examples of *Isaac*, of *Jacob*, of *Patroclus* towards *Hector*,
of *Hector* towards *Achilles*, of *Polymnester* towards *Agamemnon*, of
Hecuba, *of the Rhodian* renowned by *Possidonius*, of *Calanus* the
Indian towards *Alexander* the Great, of *Orodes* towards *Mezentius*,
and of many others; it shall suffice for the present, that I commemorate unto you the learned and valiant Knight and Cavalier
William of *Ballay*, late Lord of *Langey*, who died on the Hill of
Tarara, the Tenth of *January*, in the *Climacterick* Year of his
Age, and of our Supputation 1543. according to the *Roman*
Account. The last three or four hours of his Life he did employ
in the serious utterance of a very pithy Discourse, whilst with a
clear Judgment and Spirit void of all Trouble, he did foretel
several important Things, whereof a great deal is come to pass,
and the rest we wait for. Howbeit, his *Prophesies* did at that time
seem unto us somewhat strange, absurd, and unlikely; because

there did not then appear any sign of efficacy enough to engage our Faith to the Belief of what he did prognosticate.

We have here, near to the Town of *Villomer*, a Man that is both *Old* and a *Poet*, to wit *Raminagrobis*, who to his Second Wife espoused my Lady *Broadsow*, on whom he begot the fair *Basoche*; it hath been told me, he is a dying, and so near unto his latter end, that he is almost upon the very last moment, point, and article thereof; repair thither as fast as you can, and be ready to give an attentive Ear to what he shall *chant* unto you: it may be, that you shall obtain from him what you desire, and that *Apollo* will be pleased, by his means, to clear your scruples. I am content (quoth *Panurge*) let us go thither *Epistemon*, and that both instantly and in all hast, lest otherways his Death prevent our coming. Wilt thou come along with us, Fryar *Jhon*? Yes, that I will, (quoth Fryar *Jhon*) right heartily to do thee a Courtesie, my Billy-ballocks; for I love thee with the best of my Milt and Liver. Thereupon, incontinently, without any further lingring to the way, they all three went, and quickly thereafter (for they made good speed) arriving at the Poetical Habitation, they found the jolly Old Man, albeit in the Agony of his Departure from this World, looking chearfully, with an open Countenance, splendid Aspect, and Behaviour full of Alacrity. After that *Panurge* had very civilly saluted him, he in a free Gift did present him with a Gold Ring, which he even then put upon the Medical Finger of his Left-Hand, in the Collet or Bezle whereof was inchased an Oriental Saphire, very fair and large. Then, in imitation of *Socrates*, did he make an Oblation unto him of a fair *White Cock*; which was no sooner set upon the Tester of his Bed, than that with a high raised Head and Crest, lustily shaking his Feather-Coat, he crowed *Stentoriphonically* loud. This done, *Panurge* very courteously required of him, that he would vouchsafe to favour him with the Grant and Report of his Sence and Judgment, touching the future Destiny of his intended *Marriage*. For answer hereto, when the honest Old Man had forthwith commanded Pen, Paper and Ink to be brought unto him, and that he was at the same Call conveniently served with all the three, he wrote these following Verses:

Take, or not take her,
Off, or on:

RABELAIS

Handy-dandy is your Lot,
When her Name you write, you blot.
'Tis undone, when all is done,
Ended e're it was begun:
Hardly Gallop, if you Trot,
Set not forward when you Run,
Nor be single, tho' alone,
    Take, or not take her.

Before you Eat, begin to Fast;
For what shall be was never past.
Say, unsay, gainsay, save your Breath:
Then wish at once her Life and Death.
    Take, or not take her.

These Lines he gave out of his own Hands unto them, saying unto them, *Go my Lads, in Peace, the Great God of the highest Heavens be your Guardian and Preserver; and do not offer any more to trouble or disquiet me with this or any other Business whatsoever. I have this same very day (which is the last both of May and of me) with a great deal of labour, toyl and difficulty, chased out of my House a rabble of filthy, unclean, and plaguily pestilentious Rake-hells, black Beasts, dusk, dun, white, ash-colour'd, speckled, and a foul Vermine of other hues, whose obtrusive importunity would not permit me to die at mine own ease: for by fraudulent and deceitful pricklings, ravenous, Harpy-like graspings, waspish stingings, and such-like unwelcome Approaches, forged in the Shop of I know not what kind of Insatiabilities; they went about to withdraw, and call me out of those sweet Thoughts, wherein I was already beginning to repose myself, and acquiesce in the Contemplation and Vision; yea, almost in the very touch and tast of the Happiness and Felicity which the good God hath prepared for his faithful Saints and Elect in the other Life, and State of Immortality. Turn out of their Courses, and eschew them, step forth of their ways, and do not resemble them; mean while, let me be no more troubled by you, but leave me now in silence, I beseech you.*

380

CHAPTER XXII

How Panurge Patrocinates and Defendeth the Order of the Begging Fryars.

PANURGE, at his issuing forth of *Raminagrobis*'s Chamber, said, as if he had been horribly affrighted, By the Vertue of God, I believe that he is an *Heretick*, the Devil take me, if I do not; he doth so villanously rail at the *Mendicant* Fryars, and *Jacobins*; who are the two Hemispheres of the Christian World; by whose Gyronomonick Circumbilvaginations, as by two Celivagous Filopendulums, all the Autonomatick Metagrobolism of the *Romish* Church, when tottering and emblustricated with the Gibble gabble Gibbrish of this odious Error and Heresie, is homocentrically poised. But what harm, in the Devil's Name, have these poor Devils the *Capucins* and *Minims* done unto him? Are not these beggarly Devils sufficiently wretched already? Who can imagine that these poor Snakes, the very Extracts of *Ichthyophagy*, are not throughly enough besmoaked and besmeared with Misery, Distress, and Calamity? Dost thou think, Fryar *Jhon*, by thy Faith, that he is in the State of Salvation? He goeth, before God, as surely damn'd to Thirty thousand Baskets-full of Devils, as a Pruning-Bill to the lopping of a Vine-Branch.

To *revile* with opprobrious Speeches the good and couragious *Props* and *Pillars of the Church*, is that to be called a *Poetical Fury*? I cannot rest satisfied with him, he sinneth grosly, and blasphemeth against the true Religion. I am very much offended at his scandalizing Words, and contumelious Obloquy. I do not care a straw (quoth Fryar *Jhon*) for what he hath said; for altho' everybody should twit and jerk them, it were but a just Retaliation, seeing all Persons are served by them with the like Sauce: therefore do I pretend no interest therein. Let us see nevertheless what he hath written. *Panurge* very attentively read the Paper which the Old Man had penned, then said to his two Fellow-Travellers, *The poor Drinker doteth*: howsoever, I excuse him; for that I believe he is now drawing near to the end, and final closure of his Life: Let us go make his *Epitaph*.

By the Answer which he hath given us, I am not, I protest, one jot wiser than I was. Hearken here, *Epistemon*, my little Bully, doth thou not hold him to be very resolute in his *Responsory* Verdicts? He is a witty, quick and subtle Sophister: I will lay an even Wager, that he is a miscreant Apostate. By the Belly of a stalled Oxe, how careful he is not to be mistaken in his Words.

He answer'd but by *Disjunctives*, therefore can it not be true which he saith; for the verity of such-like Propositions is inherent only in one of its two Members. O the cozening Pratler that he is! I wonder if *Santiago of Bressure* be one of these cogging Shirks. Such was of old (quoth *Epistemon*) the Custom of the grand Vaticinator and Prophet *Teresias*, who used always (by way of a Preface) to say openly and plainly, at the beginning of his Divinations and Predictions, that *what he was to tell, would either come to pass, or not*: And such is truly the Style of all prudently presaging Prognosticators. He was, nevertheless (quoth *Panurge*) so unfortunately misadventrous in the Lot of his own Destiny, that *Juno* thrust out both his eyes.

Yes, (answer'd *Epistemon*) and that meerly out of a spight and spleen, for having pronounced his award more veritably than she, upon the Question which was merrily proposed by *Jupiter*. But (quoth *Panurge*) what Arch-Devil is it that hath possest this Master *Raminagrobis*, that so unreasonably, and without any occasion, he should have so snappishly and bitterly inveighed against these poor honest Father *Jacobins*, *Minors*, and *Minims*? It vexeth me grievously, I assure you; nor am I able to conceal my indignation. He hath transgressed most enormously; his Soul goeth infallibly to thirty thousand Panniers-full of Devils.

I understand you not (quoth *Epistemon*) and it disliketh me very much, that you should so absurdly and perversely interpret that of the Fryar *Mendicants*, which by the harmless *Poet* was spoken of black Beasts, dun, and other sorts of other coloured Animals. He is not in my opinion, guilty of such a sophistical and fantastick Allegory, as by that Phrase of his to have meant the *Begging Brothers*; he in down right Terms speaketh absolutely and properly of Fleas, Punies, Handworms, Flyes, Gnats, and other such-like scurvy Vermine, whereof some are black, some dun, some ash-coloured, some tawny, and some brown and dusky,

all noysome, molesting, tyrannous, cumbersome, and unpleasing Creatures, not only to sick and diseased Folks, but to those
also who are of a sound, vigorous, and healthful Temperament
and Constitution. It is not unlike, that he may have the *Ascarids*,
and the *Lumbricks* and Worms within the Intrails of his Body.
Possibly doth he suffer (as is frequent and usual amongst the
Ægyptians, together with all those who inhabit the *Erythræan*
Confines, and dwell along the Shores and Coasts of the Red
Sea) some sour prickings, and smart stingings in his Arms and
Legs of those little speckled Dragons, which the *Arabians*
call *Meden*. You are to blame for offering to expound his Words
otherways, and wrong the ingenuous *Poet*, and outragiously
abuse and miscall the said Fraters, by an imputation of baseness
undeservedly laid to their charge. We still should in such-like
Discourses of fatiloquent Soothsayers, interpret all things to the
best. Will you teach me (quoth *Panurge*) how to discern Flies
among Milk, or shew your Father the way how to beget Children: He is, by the Vertue of God, an *arrant Heretick, a resolute
formal Heretick*; I say, a *rooted combustible Heretick*, one as fit to
burn as the *little wooden Clock* at *Rochel*. His Soul goeth to Thirty
thousand Carts-full of Devils. Would you know whither?
Cocksbody, my Friend, streight under *Proserpina*'s Close-stool,
to the very middle of the self-same infernal Pan, within which
she, by an excrementitious evacuation, voideth the fecal stuff
of her stinking Clysters, and that just upon the left side of the
great Cauldron of three fathom height, hard by the Claws and
Talons of *Lucifer*, in the very darkest of the passage which leadeth
towards the Black Chamber of *Demigorgon*. Oh the Villain!

CHAPTER XXIII

How Panurge maketh the motion of a Return to Raminagrobis.

LET us return, quoth *Panurge*, not ceasing, to the uttermost of
our Abilities, to ply him with wholsome Admonitions, for the
furtherance of his Salvation. Let us go back for God's sake, let
us go, in the Name of God: it will be a very meritorious Work,
and of great Charity in us to deal so in the matter, and provide
so well for him, that albeit he come to lose both Body and Life,

he may at least escape the risk and danger of the eternal Damnation of his Soul. We will by our holy perswasions, bring him to a sence and feeling of his Escapes, induce him to acknowledge his Faults, move him to a cordial Repentance of his Errors, and stir up in him such a sincere Contrition of Heart for his Offences, as will prompt him with all earnestness to cry Mercy, and to beg Pardon at the Hands of the good *Fathers*, as well of the absent, as of such as are present: Whereupon we will take Instrument formally and authentically extended, to the end he be not, after his Decease, declared an *Heretick*, and condemned, as were *the Hobgoblins of the Provost's Wife of* Orleans, to the undergoing of such Punishments, Pains and Tortures, as are due to, and inflicted on those that inhabit the horrid Cells of the infernal Regions; and withal encline, instigate, and perswade him to bequeath and leave in Legacy (by way of an amends and satisfaction for the outrage and injury done) to those good *Religious Fathers*, throughout all the Convents, Cloysters and Monastries of this Province, *many Bribes*, a great deal of *Mass-singing*, store of *Obits*, and that sempiternally, on the Anniversary Day of his Decease, every one of them all be furnished with a quintuple Allowance: and that the great Borrachoe, replenished with the best Liquor, trudge apace along the Tables, as well of the young Duckling Monkito's, Lay-Brothers, and lowermost degree of the Abbey-Lubbards as of the Learned Priests, and Reverend Clerks. The very meanest of the Novices, and Initiants unto the Order being equally admitted to the benefit of those Funerary and Obsequial Festivals, with the aged Rectors, and professed Fathers; this is the surest ordinary means, whereby from God he may obtain forgiveness.

Ho, ho, I am quite mistaken, I digress from the purpose, and fly out of my Discourse, as if my Spirits were a wool-gathering. The Devil take me, if I go thither. Vertue, God, the Chamber is already full of Devils. O what a swindging, thwacking Noise is now amongst them! O the terrible Coyl that they keep! Hearken, do you not hear the rustling thumping bustle of their Stroaks and Blows, as they scuffle with one another, like true Devils indeed, who shall gulp up the *Raminagrobis* Soul, and be the first Bringer of it, whilst it is hot, to Monsieur *Lucifer*. Beware, and get you hence: For my part, I will not go thither; the Devil roast me if I go. Who knows but that these hundred mad Devils may in the hast of their rage and fury of their impatience, take a *quid* for a *quo*, and instead of *Raminagrobis* snatch up poor *Panurge* frank and free? Though formerly, when I was deep in Debt, they always failed. Get you hence: I will not go thither. Before God, the very bare apprehension thereof is like to kill me. To be in the place where there are greedy, famished, and hunger-starved Devils; amongst factious Devils: amidst trading and trafficking Devils: O the Lord preserve me! Get you hence, I dare pawn my Credit on it, that no *Jacobin, Cordelier, Carme, Capucin, Theatin,* or *Minim,* will bestow any personal Presence at his Interment. The wiser they, because he hath ordained nothing for them in his latter Will and Testament.

The Devil take me, if I go thither; if he be damned, to his own loss and hindrance be it. What the Deuce moved him to be so snappish and depravedly bent against the good Fathers of the true Religion? Why did he cast them off, reject them, and drive them quite out of his Chamber, even in that very nick of time when he stood in greatest need of the aid, suffrage, and assistance of their devout Prayers, and holy Admonitions? Why did not he by Testament leave them, at least, some jolly Lumps and Cantles of substantial Meat, a parcel of Cheek-puffing Victuals, and a little Belly-Timber, and Provision for the Guts of these poor Folks, who have *nothing but their Life in this World.*

Let him go thither, who will; the Devil take me, if I go; for if I should, the Devil would not fail to snatch me up. *Cancro*: Ho, the Pox! Get you hence, Fryar *Ihon*; Art thou content that Thirty thousand Waineload of Devils should get away with thee at this same very instant? If thou be, at my Request, do these Three things: *First,* Give me thy Purse; for besides, that thy Money is marked with Crosses, and the Cross is an Enemy to Charms, the same may befall to thee, which not long ago happened to *Ihon Dodin,* Collector of the Excise of *Coudray,* at the Ford of *Vede,* when the Soldiers broak the Planks. This money'd Fellow meeting at the very Brink of the Bank of the Ford, with Fryar *Adam Crankcod,* a *Franciscan Observantin* of *Mirebeau,* promised him a new Frock, provided, that in the transporting of him over the Water, he would bear him upon his Neck and

Shoulders, after the manner of carrying dead Goats: for he was a lusty, strong-limb'd, sturdy Rogue.

The Condition being agreed upon, Friar *Crankcod* trusseth himself up to his very Ballocks, and layeth upon his Back like a fair little Saint *Christopher*, the load of the said Supplicant *Dodin*, and so carry'd him gayly and with a good Will; as *Æneas* bore his Father *Anchises* through the Conflagration of *Troy*, singing in the mean while a prety *Ave maris Stella*. When they were in the very deepest place of all the Foord, a little above the Master-wheel of the Water-Mill, he asked if he had any Coin about him. Yes, (quoth *Dodin*) a whole Bag full; and that he needed not to mistrust his Ability in the performance of the Promise, which he had made unto him concerning a new Frock. How! (quoth Friar *Crankcod*) thou knowest well enough, that by the express Rules, Canons and Injunctions of our Order, we are forbidden to carry on us any kind of Money: Thou art truly unhappy, for having made me in this point to commit a heinous Trespass. Why didst thou not leave thy Purse with the Miller? Without fail thou shalt presently receive thy Reward for it; and if ever hereafter I may but lay hold upon thee within the Limits of our Chancel at *Mirebeau*, thou shalt have the *Miserere* even to the *Vitulos*. With this suddenly discharging himself of his Burthen, he throws me down your *Dodin* headlong.

Take Example by this *Dodin*, my dear Friend Friar *John*, to the end that the Devils may the better carry thee away at thine own ease. Give me thy Purse. Carry no manner of Cross upon thee. Therein lieth an evident and manifestly apparent Danger: For if you have any Silver coined with a Cross upon it, they will cast thee down headlong upon some Rocks; as the Eagles use to do with the Tortoises for the breaking of their Shells, as the bald Pate of the Poet *Eschilus* can sufficiently bear witness. Such a Fall would hurt thee very sore my Sweet Bully, and I would be sorry for it; or otherways they will let thee fall, and tumble down into the high swollen Waves of some capacious Sea, I know not where; but I warrant thee far enough hence, (as *Icarus* fell) which from thy Name would afterwards get the Denomination of the *Funnelian* Sea.

Secondly, Out of Debt: For the Devils carry a great liking to those that are out of Debt. I have sore felt the experience thereof in mine own particular; for now the lecherous Varlets are always wooing me, courting me, and making much of me, which they never did when I was all to pieces. The Soul of one in Debt is insipid, dry, and heretical altogether.

Thirdly, With the Cowl and *Domino de Grobis*, return to *Raminagrobis*, and in case, being thus qualify'd, Thirty Thousand Boats full of Devils forthwith come not to carry thee quite away, I shall be content to be at the charge of paying for the Pinte and Fagot. Now if for the more Security thou wouldst have some Associate to bear thee Company, let not me be the Comrade thou searchest for, think not to get a Fellow-Traveller of me; nay, do not, I advise thee for the best. Get you hence; I will not go thither; the Devil take me if I go. Notwithstanding all the Fright that you are in, (quoth Friar *Jhon*) I would not care so much, as might possibly be expected I should, if I once had but my Sword in my Hand. Thou hast verily hit the Nail on the Head, (quoth *Panurge*) and speakest like a Learned Doctor, subtile, and well skilled in the Art of Devilry.

At the time when I was a Student in the University of *Tolouse*, that same Reverend Father in the Devil, *Picarris*, Rector of the Diabological Faculty, was wont to tell us, that the Devils did naturally fear the bright glancing of Swords, as much as the Splendour and Light of the Sun. In confirmation of the Verity whereof he related this Story, That *Hercules* at his Descent into Hell to all the Devils of those Regions, did not by half so much terrifie them with his *Club* and *Lion's Skin*, as afterwards *Æneas* did with his clear shining Armour upon him, and his Sword in his Hand well furbished and unrusted, by the Aid, Counsel, and Assistance of the *Sybilla Cumana*. That was perhaps the reason why the Senior *Jhon Jacomo di Trivulcio*, whilst he was a dying at *Chartres* called for his Cutlass, and died with a Drawn Sword in his Hand, laying about him alongst and athwart around the Bed, and every where within his reach, like a stout, doughty, valorous and Knight-like Cavaleer: By which resolute manner of Fence he scared away and put to flight all the Devils that were then lying in wait for his Soul at the passage of his Death. When the *Massorets* and *Cabalists* are asked, Why it is that none of all the Devils do at any time enter into the Terestrial Paradice? Their Answer hath been, is, and will be still, That there is a

Cherubin standing at the Gate thereof with a Flame-like glistering Sword in his hand. Although to speak in the true *Diabological* Sence or Phrase of *Toledo*, I must needs confess and acknowledge, that veritably the Devils cannot be killed, or die by the stroke of a Sword. I do nevertheless avow and maintain, according to the Doctrine of the said *Diabology*, that they may suffer a Solution of Continuity (as if with thy Shable thou shouldst cut athwart the Flamme of a burning Fire, or the gross opacous Exhalations of a thick and obscure Smoak) and cry out, like very Devils, at their Sense and Feeling of this Dissolution, which in real deed I must averr and affirm is devilishly painful, smarting and dolorous.

When thou seest the impetuous Shock of two Armies, and vehement Violence of the Push in their horrid Encounter with one another; dost thou think, *Balockasso*, that so horrible a noise as is heard there proceedeth from the Voice and Shouts of Men? The dashing and joulting of Harnish? The clattering and clashing of Armies? The hacking and slashing of Battle-Axes? The justling and crashing of Pikes? The bustling and breaking of Lances? The clamour and Shrieks of the Wounded? The sound and din of Drums? The Clangour and Shrilness of Trumpets? The neighing and rushing in of Horses? With the fearful Claps and thundering of all sorts of Guns, from the Double Canon to the Pocket Pistol inclusively? I cannot, Goodly, deny, but that in these various things which I have rehearsed, there may be somewhat occasionative of the huge Yell and Tintamarre of the two engaged Bodies.

But the most fearful and tumultuous Coil and Stir, the terriblest and most boisterous Garboil and Hurry, the chiefest rustling *Black Santus* of all, and most principal Hurly Burly, springeth from the grievously plangorous howling and lowing of Devils, who Pell-mell, in a hand-over-head Confusion, waiting for the poor Souls of the maimed and hurt Soldiery, receive unawares some Stroaks with Swords, and so by those means suffering a Solution of, and Division in the Continuity of their Aerial and Invisible Substances: As if some Lackey, snatching at the Lardslices, stuck in a piece of Roast-meat on the Spit, should get from Mr. *Greazyfist* a good rap on the Knuckles with a Cudgel, they cry out and shout like Devils. Even as *Mars* did, when he was hurt by *Diomedes* at the Siege of *Troy*, who (as *Homer* testifieth of him) did then raise his Voice more horrifically loud, and sonoriferously high, than ten thousand Men together would have been able to do. What maketh all this for our present purpose? I have been speaking here of well-furbished Armour and bright Shining Swords. But so is it not (Friar *Ihon*) with thy Weapon; for by a long discontinuance of Work, cessation from Labour, desisting from making it officiate, and putting it into practice wherein it had been formerly accustomed; and in a word, for want of occupation, it is, upon my Faith, become more rusty than the Key-hole of an old Poudering-Tub. Therefore it is expedient that you do one of these two, either furbish your Weapon bravely, and as it ought to be, or otherwise have a care that in the rusty case it is in, you do not presume to return to the House of *Raminagrobis*. For my part, I vow I will not go thither, the Devil take me if I go.

CHAPTER XXIV

How Panurge consulteth with Epistemon.

HAVING left the Town of *Villomere*, as they were upon their return towards *Pantagruel*, *Panurge* in addressing his Discourse to *Epistemon*, spoke thus: My most ancient Friend and Gossip, thou seest the perplexity of my Thoughts, and knowest many Remedies for the removal thereof; art thou not able to help and succour me? *Epistemon* thereupon taking the Speech in hand, represented unto *Panurge*, how the open Voice and common Fame of the whole Country did run upon no other Discourse, but the derision and mockery of his new Disguise; wherefore his Counsel unto him was that he would in the first place be pleased to make use of a little *Hellebore*, for the purging of his Brain of that peccant humour, which thro' that extravagant and fantastick Mummery of his had furnished the People with a too just occasion of flouting and gibing, jeering and scoffing him; and that next he would resume his ordinary Fashion of Accoutrement, and go apparelled as he was wont to do. I am (quoth *Panurge*) my dear Gossip *Epistemon*, of a mind and resolution to Marry, but am afraid of being a Cuckold, and to be unfortunate in my Wedlock: For this cause have I made a Vow to young St. *Francis*, (who at *Plessiletours* is much reverenced of all Women, earnestly cried unto by them, and with great Devotion; for he was the First Founder of the Confraternity of good Men, whom they naturally covet, affect and long for) *to wear Spectacles in my Cap*, and *to carry no Codpiece in my Breeches*, until the present Inquietude and Perturbation of my Spirits be fully setled.

Truly (quoth *Epistemon*) that is a pretty jolly *Vow*, of Thirteen to a Dozen: It is a shame to you, and I wonder much at it, that you do not return unto your self, and recall your Senses from this their wild swarving, and straying abroad to that rest and stilness which becomes a vertuous Man. This whimsical Conceit of yours brings me to the remembrance of a solemn Promise made by the *Shaghaired Argives*, who having in their Controversie against the *Lacedemonians* for the Terretory of *Tyree* lost the Battle, which they hoped should have decided it for their Advantage, *vowed* to carry never any hair on their Heads, till preallably they had recovered the loss of both their Honour and Lands: As likewise to the memory of the *Vow* of a pleasant *Spaniard* called *Michel Doris*, who *vowed* to carry in his Hat a piece of the Shin of his Leg, till he should be revenged of him who had struck it off. Yet do not I know which of these two deserveth most to wear a Green and Yellow Hood with a Hares Ear tied to it, either the aforesaid vain-glorious *Champion*, or that Enguerrant, who having forgot the art and manner of writing Histories, set down by the *Samosatian* Philosopher, maketh a most tediously long Narrative and Relation thereof: For at the first reading of such a profuse Discourse, one would think it had been broached for the introducing of a Story of great importance and moment concerning the waging of some formidable War, or the notable change and mutation of potent States and Kingdoms; but in conclusion, the World laugheth at the capricious Champion, at the *English-man* who had affronted him, as also at their Scribler *Enguerrant*, more driveling at the Mouth than a Mustard-pot. The Jest and Scorn thereof is not unlike to that of the Mountain of *Horace*, which by the Poet was made to cry out and lament most enormously as a Woman in the Pangs and Labour of Child-birth, at which deplorable and exorbitant Cries and Lamentations the whole Neighbourhood being assembled in expectation to see some marvellous monstrous Production, could at last perceive no other but the paultry ridiculous Mouse.

Your mousing (quoth *Panurge*) will not make me leave my musing why Folks should be so frumpishly disposed, seeing I am certainly perswaded that some flout, who merit to be flouted at; yet as my *Vow* imports so will I do. It is now a long time since, by *Jupiter Philos*, we did swear Faith and Amity to one another: Give me your Advice, and tell me your Opinion freely, Should I marry or no? Truly (quoth *Epistemon*) the case is hazardous, and the danger so eminently apparent, that I find myself too weak and insufficient to give you a punctual and peremptory resolution therein; and if ever it was true, the *Judgment is difficult* in matters of the *Medicinal* Art, what was said by *Hippocrates* of *Lango*, it is certainly so in this case. True it is, that in my Brain there are some rowling Fancies, by means whereof somewhat may be pitched upon of a seeming efficacy to the disintangling your mind of those dubious Apprehensions wherewith it is perplexed; but they do not thoroughly satisfie me. Some of the *Platonick* Sect affirm, that whosoever is able to see his proper *Genius*, may know his own Destiny. I understand not their Doctrine; nor do I think that you adhere to them; there is a palpable Abuse. I have seen the experience of it in a very curious Gentleman of the Country of *Estrangowre*. This is one of the Points. There is yet another not much better. If there were any Authority now in the Oracles of *Jupiter Ammon*; of *Apollo* in *Lebadia*, *Delphos*, *Delos*, *Cyrra*, *Patara*, *Tegires*, *Preneste*, *Lycia*, *Colophon*, or in the *Castalian* Fountain near *Antiochia* in *Syria*; between the *Branchidians*; of *Bacchus* in *Dodona*; of *Mercure* in *Phares* near *Partras*; of *Apis* in *Egypt*; of *Serapis* in *Canorie*; of *Faunus* in *Menalia* and *Albunes* near *Tivoly*; of *Tiresias* in *Orchomenie*; of *Mosus* in *Silicia*; of *Orpheus* in *Lisbos*; and of *Trophonius* in *Lucadia*. I would in that case advise you, and possibly not, to go thither for their Judgment concerning the Design and Enterprize you have in hand. But you know that they are all of them become as dumb as so many Fishes, since the *Advent* of that *Saviour King*, whose coming to this World hath made all Oracles and Prophecies to cease; as the approach of the Suns radiant Beams expelleth Goblins, Bugbears, Hobthrushes, Broams, Schriech Owl-Mates, Nightwalking Spirits, and Tenebrions. These now are gone; but although they were as yet in continuance, and in the same Power, Rule and Request that formerly they were, yet would not I counsel you to be too credulous in putting any Trust in their Responses: Too many Folks have been deceived thereby. It stands furthermore upon Record, how *Agrippina* did charge the fair *Lollia* with the Crime of having interrogated the Oracle of *Apollo Clarius*, to understand if she should be at any time married to the Emperor *Claudius*; for which Cause she was first banished, and thereafter put to a shameful and ignominious Death.

But (saith *Panurge*) let us do better; the *Ogygian* Islands are not far distant from the Haven of *Sammalo*: Let us, after that we shall have spoken to our King, make a Voyage thither. In one of these four *Isles*, to wit, that which hath its primest Aspect towards the Sun setting, it is reported, (and I have read in good Antick and Authentick Authors) that there reside many Soothsayers, Fortune-tellers, Vaticinators, Prophets, and Diviners of things to come; that *Saturn* inhabiteth that place, bound with fair Chains of Gold, and within the Concavity of a Golden Rock, being nourished with Divine *Ambrosie* and *Nectar*, which are daily in great store and abundance transmitted to him from the Heavens by I do not know well what kind of Fowls (it may be that they are the same Ravens, which in the Deserts are said to have fed St. *Paul*, the first Hermit) he very clearly foretelleth unto every one, who is desirous to be certified of the condition of his Lot, what his Destiny will be, and what future Chance the Fates have ordained for him: For the *Parques*, or *Weerd Sisters* do not twist, spin, or draw out a Thread; nor yet doth *Jupiter* perpend, project, or deliberate any thing, which the good old Cœlestial Father knoweth not to the full, even whilst he is a sleep: This will be a very summary Abbreviation of our Labour, if we but hearken unto him a little upon the serious debate and canvassing of this my perplexity. That is (answered *Epistemon*) a Gullery too evident, a plain Abuse and Fib too fabulous. I will not go, not I, I will not go.

CHAPTER XXV

How Panurge consulteth with Her Trippa.

NEVERTHELESS, (quoth *Epistemon*, continuing his Discourse) I will tell you what you may do, if you will believe me, before we return to our King: Hard by here, in the *Brown-wheat-Island*, dwelleth *Her Trippa*; you know how by the Arts of Astrology, Geomancy, Chiromancy, Metopomancy, and others of a like stuff and nature, he foretelleth all things to come: Let us talk a little, and confer with him about your Business. Of that (answered *Panurge*) I know nothing: But of this much concerning him I am assured, that one day, and that not long since, whilst he was prating to the Great King, of Cœlestial, Sublime, and Transcendent Things, the Lackqueys and Footboys of the Court, upon the upper Steps of Stairs between two Doors, jumbled, one after another, as often as they listed, his Wife; who is passable fair, and a pretty snug Hussie. Thus he who seemed very clearly to see all Heavenly and Terrestrial Things without Spectacles, who discoursed boldly of Adventures past, with great confidence opened up present Cases and Accidents, and stoutly professed the presaging of all future Events and Contingencies, and was not able with all the Skill and Cunning that he had, to perceive the Bumbasting of his Wife, whom he reputed to be very chast; and hath not till this hour, got Notice of any thing to the contrary. Yet let us go to him, seeing you will have it so: for surely we can never learn too much. They on the very next ensuing Day, came to *Her Trippa*'s Lodging. *Panurge*, by way of Donative, presented him with a long Gown lined all thorough with Wolves-skins, with a short Sword mounted with a gilded Hilt, and covered with a Velvet Scabbard, and with fifty good single Angels: then in a familiar and friendly way did he ask of him his Opinion touching the Affair. At the very first *Her Trippa* looking on him very wistly in the face, said unto him: Thou hast the Metoposcopy, and Physiognomy of a Cuckold; I say, of a notorious and infamous Cuckold. With this casting an eye upon *Panurge*'s right Hand in all the parts thereof, he said, This rugged Draught which I see here, just under the Mount of

Jove, was never yet but in the Hand of a Cuckold. Afterwards, he with a White Lead Pen, swiftly, and hastily drew a certain Number of diverse kinds of Points, which by Rules of Geomancy he coupled and joyned together, then said, Truth it self is not truer, than that it is certain, thou wilt be a Cuckold, a little after thy Marriage. That being done, he asked of *Panurge* the Horoscope of his Nativity; which was no sooner by *Panurge* tendred unto him, than that, erecting a Figure, he very promptly and speedily formed and fashion'd a compleat Fabrick of the Houses of Heaven, in all their parts, whereof when he had considered the Situation and the Aspects in their Triplicities, he fetched a deep sigh, and said: I have clearly enough already discovered unto you the Fate of your Cuckoldry, which is unavoidable, you cannot escape it; and here have I got of new a further assurance thereof, so that I may now hardily pronounce, and affirm without any scruple or hesitation at all, that thou wilt be a cuckold; that furthermore, thou wilt be beaten by thine own Wife, and that she will purloyn, filch, and steal of thy Goods from thee; for I find the *Seventh House*, in all its Aspects, of a malignant Influence, and every one of the Planets threatning thee with Disgrace, according as they stand seated towards one another, in relation to the Horned Signs of *Aries*, *Taurus*, and *Capricorn*: In the *Fourth House* I find *Jupiter* in a Decadence, as also in a Tetragonal Aspect to *Saturn*, associated with *Mercury*. Thou wilt be soundly pepper'd, my good honest Fellow, I warrant thee. I will be: (answered *Panurge*) a Plague rot thee, thou old Fool, and doating Sot, how graceless and unpleasant thou art.

When all Cuckolds shall be at a General Rendezvous, thou shouldst be their Standard-bearer. But whence comes this Cironworm betwixt these two Fingers? This *Panurge* said, putting the Fore-finger of his Left-hand, betwixt the Fore and Mid-finger of the Right, which he thrust out towards *Her Trippa*, holding them open after the manner of two Horns, and shutting into a Fist his Thumb, with the other Fingers. Then in turning to *Epistemon*, he said, Lo here the true *Ollus* of *Martial*, who addicted and devoted himself wholly to the observing the Miseries, Crosses, and Calamities of others, whilst his own Wife, in the Interim, did keep an open Bawdy-house.

This Varlet is poorer than ever was *Irus*, and yet he is a proud, vaunting, arrogant, self-conceited, overweening, and more insupportable than Seventeen Devils; in one word, Πτωχαλάζων, which term of old was applied to the like beggarly strutting Coxcombs.

Come, let us leave this Madpash Bedlam, this hairbrain'd Fop, and give him leave to rave and dose his Belly-full, with his private and intimately acquainted Devils; who, if they were not the very worst of all the infernal Fiends, would never have daigned to serve such a knavish, barking Cur as this is. He hath not learnt the first Precept of Philosophy, which is, *Know thy self*: For whilst he braggeth and boasteth, that he can discern the least Mote in the Eye of another, he is not able to see the huge Block that puts out the sight of both his Eyes. This is such another *Polypragmon*, as is by *Plutarch* described: He is of the Nature of the *Lamian* Witches, who in forreign Places, in the Houses of Strangers, in Publick, and amongst the Common People, had a sharper and more piercing Inspection into their Affairs than any Lync; but at home, in their own proper Dwelling-Mansions, were blinder than Mold-Warps, and saw nothing at all: for their Custom was at their return from abroad, when they were by themselves in private, to take their Eyes out of their Head, from whence they were as easily removable as a Pair of Spectacles from their Nose, and to lay them up in a wooden Slipper, which for that purpose did hang behind the Door of their Lodging.

Panurge had no sooner done speaking, when *Her Trippa* took into his Hand a Tamarisk Branch. In this (quoth *Epistemon*) he doth very well, right and like an Artist, for *Nicander* calleth it the *Divinatory Tree*. Have you a mind (quoth *Her Trippa*) to have the truth of the matter yet more fully and amply disclosed unto you by *Pyromancy*, by *Aeromancy*, (whereof *Aristophanes* in his Clouds maketh great estimation) by *Hydromancy*, by *Leconomancy*, of old in prime request amongst the *Assyrians*, and throughly tried by *Hermolaus Barbarus*: Come hither, and I will shew thee, in this Platter-full of fair Fountain-water, thy future Wife lechering, and sercroupierising it with two swaggering Ruffians, one after another. Yea, but have a special care, (quoth *Panurge*) when thou comest to put thy Nose within my Arse, that thou forget not to pull off thy Spectacles. *Her Trippa* going on in his Discourse, said by *Catoptromancy*, likewise held in such account by the Emperor *Didius Julianus*, that by means thereof, he ever and anon foresaw all that which at any time did happen or befal unto him: Thou shalt not need to put on thy Spectacles; for in a Mirror thou wilt see her as clearly and manifestly Nebrundiated, and Billibodring-it, as if I should shew it in the Fountain of the Temple of *Minerva* near *Partras*. By *Coscinomancy*, most religiously observed of old, amidst the Ceremonies of the ancient *Romans*. Let us have a Sieve and Shiers, and thou shalt see Devils. By *Alphitomancy*, cried up by *Theocritus* in his *Pharmaceutria*. By *Aleuromancy*, mixing the Flower of Wheat with Oatmeal. By *Astragalomancy*, whereof I have the Plots and Models all at hand ready for the purpose. By *Tyromancy*, whereof we make some Proof in a great *Brehemont* Cheese, which I here keep by me. By *Giromancy*, if thou shouldst turn round Circles, thou mightest assure thy self from me, that they would fall always on the wrong side. By *Sternomancy*, which maketh nothing for thy Advantage, for thou hast an ill-proportion'd Stomach. By *Libanomancy*, for the which we shall need but a little Frankincense. By *Gastromancy*, which kind of ventral Fatiloquency was for a long time together used in *Ferrara* by Lady *Giacoma Rodogina*, the *Engastrimythian* Prophetess. By *Cephalomancy*, often practised amongst the *High-Germans*, in their boiling of an Asses Head upon burning Coals. By *Ceromancy*, where, by the means of Wax dissolved into Water, thou shalt see the Figure, Pourtrait, and lively Representation of thy future Wife, and of her Fredin Fredaliatory Belly thumping Blades. By *Capnomancy*; O the gallantest and most excellent of all Secrets! By *Axionomancy*, we want only a Hatchet and a Jeat-stone to be laid together upon a quick Fire of hot Embers. O how bravely *Homer* was versed in the Practice hereof towards *Penelope*'s Suitors! By *Onymancy*, for that we have Oyl and Wax. By *Tephromancy*, thou wilt see the Ashes thus aloft dispersed, exhibiting thy Wife in a fine Posture. By *Botanomancy*, for the nonce I have some few Leaves in reserve. By *Sicomancy*; O Divine Art in Fig-tree Leaves! By *Icthiomancy*, in ancient times so celebrated, and put in use by *Tiresias* and *Polydamas*, with the like certainty of event as was tried of old at the *Dina-ditch* within that Grove consecrated to *Apollo*, which is in the Territory of the *Lycians*. By *Choiramancy*: Let us have a great many Hogs, and thou shalt have the Bladder of one of them. By *Cheromomancy*, as the Bean is found in the Cake at the *Epiphany* Vigil. By *Anthropomancy*, practised by the *Roman* Emperor *Heliogabalus*; it is somewhat irksom, but thou wilt endure it well enough, seeing thou art destinated to be a Cuckold. By a *Sibylline* Stichomancy. By *Onomatomancy*: How do they call thee! Chaw, turd; (quoth *Panurge*). Or yet by *Alectryomancy*. If I should here with a Compass draw a round, and in looking upon thee, and considering thy Lot, divide the Circumference thereof into four and twenty equal parts, then form a several Letter of the Alphabet upon every one of them; and lastly, posit a Barley-Corn or two upon each of these so disposed Letters, I durst promise upon my Faith and Honesty, that if a young Virgin Cock be permitted to range alongst and athwart them, he should only eat the Grains which are set and placed upon these Letters, *A. C.u.c.k.o.l.d. T.h.o.u. s.h.a.l.t. b.e.* And that as fatidically as under the Emperor *Valence*, most perplexedly desirous to know the Name of him who should be his Successor to the Empire, the Cock Vaticinating and Alectryomantick, ate up the Pickles that were posited on the Letters *T.h.e.o.d.* Or for the more certainty, will you have a trial of your Fortune by the Art of Aruspiciny? by Augury? or by Extispicine? By Turdispicine, quoth *Panurge*. Or yet by the Mystery of *Negromancy*? I will, if you please, suddenly set up again, and revive some one lately deceased, as *Apollonius* of *Tyan* did to *Achilles*, and the *Pythoniss* in the Presence of *Saul*; which Body so raised up, and requickned, will tell us the Sum of all you shall require of him; no more nor less than at the Invocation of *Erictho*, a certain defunct Person, foretold to *Pompy* the whole Progress and Issue of the fatal Battle fought in the *Pharsalian* Fields? Or if you be afraid of the Dead, as commonly all Cuckolds are, I will make use of the Faculty of Sciomancy. Go, get thee gone, (quoth *Panurge*) thou Frantick Ass, to the Devil, and be buggered, filthy *Bordachio* that thou art, by some *Albanian*, for a Steeple-crown'd Hat. Why the Devil didst thou not counsel me as well to hold an Emerald, or the Stone of a *Hyena* under my Tongue? Or to furnish and provide my self with Tongues of Whoops, and Hearts of Green Frogs? Or to eat of the Liver or Milt of some Dragon? To the end that by those means I might, at the chanting and chirping of Swans and other Fowls, understand the Substance of my future Lot and Destiny, as did of old the Arabians in the Country of Mesopotamia? Fifteen Brace of Devils seize upon the Body and Soul of this horned Renegado, miscreant Cuckold, the Inchanter, Witch, and Sorcerer of Antichrist to all the Devils of Hell.

Let us return towards our King: I am sure he will not be well pleased with us, if he once come to get notice that we have been in the Kennel of this muffled Devil. I repent my being come hither. I would willingly dispence with a Hundred Nobles, and Fourteen Yeomans, on condition that he who not long since did blow in the bottom of my Breeches, should instantly with his squirting Spittle inluminate his Mustaches. O Lord God now! how the Villain hath besmoaked me with Vexation and Anger, with Charms and Witchcraft, and with a terrible Coyl and Stir of Infernal and *Tartarian* Devils! The Devil take him: Say *Amen*; and let us go drink. I shall not have any Appetite for my Victuals (how good Cheer soever I make) these two days to come, hardly these four.

CHAPTER XXVI

How Panurge consulteth with Friar Ihon, of the Funnels.

PANURGE was indeed very much troubled in mind, and disquieted at the words of *Her Trippa*, and therefore as he passed by the little Village of *Hugmes*, after he had made his Address to Fryar *Ihon*, in pecking at, rubbing and scratching his own left Ear, he said unto him, Keep me a little jovial and merry, my dear and sweet Bully, for I find my Brains altogether metagrabolized and confounded, and my Spirits in a most dunsical puzzle at the bitter talk of this Devilish, Hellish, Damned Fool: Hearken, my dainty Cod,

Mellow C.	Stuffed C.	Mounted C.
Lead-coloured C.	Speckled C.	Sleeked C.
	Finely metall'd C.	Diapred C.
Knurled C.	Arabian-like C.	Spotted C.
Suborned C.	Trussed up,	Master C.
Desired C.	Greyhound-like C.	Seeded C.

Lusty C.
Jupped C.
Milked C.
Calfeted C.
Raised C.
Odd C.
Steeled C.
Stale C.
Orange-tawny C.
Imbroidered C.
Glazed C.
Interlarded C.
Burger-like C.
Impoudred C.
Ebenized C.
Brasiliated C.
Organized C.
Passable C.
Trunkified C.
Furious C.
Packed C.
Hooded C.
Varnished C.
Renowned C.
Matted C.
Genetive C.
Gigantal C.
Oval C.
Claustral C.
Viril C.
Stayed C.
Massive C.
Manual C.
Absolute C.
Well-set C.
Gemel C.
Turkish C.
Burning C.
Thwacking C.
Urgent C.
Handsome C.
Prompt C.
Fortunate C.
Boxewood C.
Latten C.

Unbridled C.
Hooked C.
Researched C.
Encompassed C.
Strouting out C.
Jolly C.
Lively C.
Gerundive C.
Franked C.
Polished C.
Poudred Beef C.
Positive C.
Spared C.
Bold C.
Lascivious C.
Gluttonous C.
Resolute C.
Cabbage-like C.
Courteous C.
Fertil C.
Whizzing C.
Neat C.
Common C.
Brisk C.
Quick C.
Barelike C.
Partitional C.
Patronymick C.
Cockney C.
Auromercuriated C.
Robust C.
Appetizing C.
Succourable C.
Redoubtable C.
Affable C.
Memorable C.
Palpable C.
Barbable C.
Tragical C.
Transpontine C.
Digestive C.
Active C.
Vital C.
Magistral C.
Monachal C.

Subtil C.
Hammering C.
Clashing C.
Tingling C.
Usual C.
Exquisite C.
Trim C.
Succulent C.
Factious C.
Clammy C.
Fat C.
High-prised C.
Requisite C.
Laycod C.
Hand-filling C.
Insuperable C.
Agreeable C.
Formidable C.
Profitable C.
Notable C.
Musculous C.
Subsidiary C.
Satyrick C.
Repercussive C.
Convulsive C.
Restorative C.
Masculinating C.
Incarnative C.
Sigillative C.
Sallying C.
Plump C.
Thundering C.
Lechering C.
Fulminating C.
Sparkling C.
Ramming C.
Lusty C.
Houshold C.
Pretty C.
Astrolabian C.
Algebraical C.
Venust C.
Aromatizing C.
Trixy C.
Paillard C.

Gaillard C.
Broaching C.
Adle C.
Syndicated C.
Boulting C.
Snorting C.
Pilfring C.
Shaking C.
Bobbing C.
Chiveted C.
Fumbling C.
Topsiturvying C.
Raging C.
Piled up C.
Filled up C.
Manly C.
Idle C.
Membrous C.
Strong C.
Twin C.
Belabouring C.
Gentil C.
Stirring C.
Confident C.
Nimble C.
Roundheaded C.
Figging C.
Helpful C.
Spruce C.
Plucking C.
Ramage C.
Fine C.
Fierce C.
Brawny C.
Compt C.
Repaired C.
Soft C.
Wild C.
Renewed C.
Quaint C.
Starting C.
Fleshy C.

Auxiliary C.
New-vamped C.
Improved C.
Malling C.
Sounding C.
Batled C.
Burly C.
Seditious C.
Wardian C.
Protective C.
Twinkling C.
Able C.
Algoristical C.
Odoriferous C.
Pranked C.
Jocund C.
Routing C.
Purloyning C.
Frolick C.
Wagging C.
Ruffling C.
Jumbling C.
Rumbling C.
Thumping C.
Bumping C.
Cringeling C.
Berumpling C.
Jogging C.
Nobbing C.
Touzing C.
Tumbling C.
Fambling C.
Overturning C.
Shooting C.
Culeting C.
Jagged C.
Pinked C.
Arsiversing C.
Polished C.
Slasht C.
Hamed C.
Leisurely C.

Cut C.
Smooth C.
Depending C.
Independent C.
Lingring C.
Rapping C.
Reverend C.
Nodding C.
Disseminating C.
Affecting C.
Affected C.
Grapled C.
Stuffed C.
Well-fed C.
Flourished C.
Fallow C.
Sudden C.
Grasp-ful C.
Swillpow C.
Crushing C.
Creaking C.
Dilting C.
Ready C.
Vigorous C.
Scoulking C.
Superlative C.
Clashing C.
Wagging C.
Scriplike C.
Encremaster'd
 C.
Bouncing C.
Levelling C.
Fly-flap C.
Perinæ tegminal
 C.
Squat-Couching C.
Short-hung C.
The hypogastrian C.
Witness bearing C.
Testigerous C.
Instrumental C.

My Harcabuzing Cod, and Buttockstirring Ballock, Fryar *Ihon*, my Friend: I do carry a singular respect unto thee, and

honour thee with all my Heart, thy Counsel I hold for a choice
and delicate Morsel, therefore have I reserved it for the last Bit.
Give me thy Advice freely, I beseech thee; Should I marry or
no? Fryar *Ihon* very merrily, and with a sprightly chearfulness
made this Answer to him: Marry, in the Devil's Name, Why not:
What the Devil else shouldst thou do, but marry? Take thee a
Wife, and furbish her Harnish to some tune: Swinge her Skin-
coat, as if thou wert beating on Stock-fish, and let the repercus-
sion of thy Clapper from her resounding Metal, make a Noise,
as if a Double Peal of Chiming-Bells were hung at the Cremasters of thy Ballocks. As I say Marry, so do I understand, that
thou shouldst fall to work as speedily as may be: yea, my
meaning is, that thou oughtest to be so quick and forward therein, as on this same very day, before Sunset, to cause, proclaim
thy Banes of Matrimony, and make provision of Bedsteads. By
the Blood of a Hog's-pudding, till when wouldst thou delay the
acting of a Husband's part? Dost thou not know, and is it not
daily told unto thee, that the end of the World approacheth? We
are nearer it by three Poles, and half a Fathom, then we were
two days ago. The *Antichrist* is already born, at least it is so reported by many: the truth is, that hitherto the effects of his wrath
have not reached further than to the scratching of his Nurse and
Governesses: his Nails are not sharp enough as yet, nor have his
Claws attained to their full growth; he is little.

Crescat; Nos qui vivimus, multiplicemur. It is written so, and it
is holy stuff, I warrant you: The truth whereof is like to last as
long as a Sack of Corn may be had for a Penny, and a Punction
of pure Wine for Threepence. Would thou be content to be found
with thy Genitories full in the Day of Judgment? *Dum veneris
judicari.* Thou hast (quoth *Panurge*) a right, clear, and neat
Spirit, Fryar *Ihon*, my Metropolitan Cod; thou speakest in very
deed pertinently, and to purpose: That belike was the reason
which moved *Leander* of *Abydos* in *Asia*, whilst he was swimming
through the *Hellespontick* Sea, to make a Visit to his Sweetheart
Hero of *Sestus* in *Europe*, to pray unto *Neptune*, and all the other
Marine Gods, thus:

> *Now, whilst I go, have pity on me,*
> *And at my back returning drown me.*

He was loath, it seems, to die with his Cods overgorged: He was to be commended, therefore do I promise, that from henceforth no Malefactor shall by Justice be executed within my Jurisdiction of *Salmigondinois*, who shall not, for a day or two at least before, be permitted to culbut, and foraminate, Onocrotal-wise, that there remain not in all his vessels, to write a great Greek Γ; such a precious thing should not be foolishly cast away; he will perhaps therewith beget a Male, and so depart the more contentedly out of this Life, that he shall have left behind him one for one.

CHAPTER XXVII

How Fryar Ihon merrily, and sportingly counselleth Panurge.

BY Saint *Rigomer* (quoth Fryar *Ihon*) I do advise thee to nothing, (my dear Friend *Panurge*) which I would not do my self, were I in thy place: only have a special care, and take good heed thou soulder well together the Joynts of the double backed and two bellied Beast, and fortifie thy Nerves so strongly, that there be no discontinuance in the Knocks of the *Venerian* thwacking, else thou art lost, poor Soul: for if there pass long intervals betwixt the Priapising Feats, and that thou make an intermission of too large a time, that will befall thee, which betides the Nurses, if they desist from giving suck to Children, they lose their Milk; and if continually thou do not hold thy Aspersory Tool in exercise, and keep thy Mentul going, thy *Lactinician* Nectar will be gone, and it will serve thee only as a Pipe to piss out at, and thy Cods for a Wallet of lesser value than a Beggars Scrip. This is a certain truth I tell thee, Friend, and doubt not of it; for my self have seen the sad experiment thereof in many, who cannot now do what they would, because before they did not what they might have done. *Ex desuetudine amittuntur Privilegia.* Non-usage oftentimes destroys ones Right, say the learned Doctors of the Law: therefore, my *Billy*, entertain as well as possibly thou canst, that *Hypogastrian*, lower sort of Troglodytick People, that their chief pleasure may be placed in the case of sempiternal labouring. Give order that henceforth they live not like idle Gentlemen, idle upon their Rents and Revenues, but that they may work for their Livelyhood, by breaking ground within the *Paphian* Trenches. Nay truly (answered *Panurge*) Fryar *Ihon*, my left Ballock, I will believe thee, for thou dealest plain with me, and fallest down-right square upon the business, without going about the Bush with frivolous circumstances, and unnecessary reservations. Thou with the splendour of a piercing Wit, hast dissipated all the louring Clouds of anxious Apprehensions and Suspicions, which did intimidate and terrifie me: therefore the Heavens be pleased to grant to thee, at all She-conflicts, a stiff-standing Fortune. Well then, as thou hast said, so will I do, I will, in good Faith, Marry; in that point there shall be no failing, I promise thee, and shall have always by me pretty Girls clothed with the Name of my Wives Waiting-Maids, that lying under thy Wings, thou mayest be Night-Protector of their Sister-hood.

Let this serve for the first part of the Sermon. Hearken (quoth Fryar *Ihon*) to the Oracle of the Bells of *Varenes*; What say they? I hear and understand them (quoth *Panurge*) their Sound is by my Thirst, more uprightly fatidical, then that of *Jove's* Great Kettles in *Dodona*. Hearken; *Take thee a Wife, take thee a Wife, and marry, marry, marry: for if thou marry, thou shalt find good therein, herein, here in a Wife thou shalt find good*; *so marry, marry*. I will assure thee, that I shall be married, all the Elements invite and prompt me to it: let this Word be to thee a Brazen Wall, by diffidence not to be broken thorough. As for the Second part of this our Doctrine: Thou seemest in some measure to mistrust the readiness of my Paternity, in the practising of my Placket-Racket within the *Aphrodisian* Tennis-Court at all times fitting, as if the stiff God of Gardens were not favourable to me. I pray thee, favour me so much as to believe, that I still have him at a beck, attending always my Commandments, docile, obedient, vigorous, and active in all things, and every-where, and never stubborn or refractory to my will or pleasure.

I need no more, but to let go the Reins, and slacken the Leash, which is the Bellypoint, and when the Game is shewn unto him, say, Hey, *Jack*, to thy Booty, he will not fail even then to flesh himself upon his Prey, and tuzle it to some purpose. Hereby you may perceive, although my future Wife were as unsatiable and gluttonous in her Voluptuousness, and the Delights of Venery, as ever was the Empress *Messalina*, or yet the Marchioness in

England; and I desire thee to give credit to it, that I lack not for what is requisite to overloy the Stomach of her Lust, but have wherewith aboundingly to please her.

I am not ignorant that *Salomon* said, who indeed of that matter speaketh Clerk-like; and learnedly: as also how *Aristotle* after him declared for a truth, That for the greater part, the Lechery of a Woman is ravenous and unsatisfiable: nevertheless, let such as are my Friends, who read those passages, receive from me for a most real verity, that I for such a *gill*, have a fit *Jack*; and that, if Womens things cannot be satiated, I have an Instrument indefatigable; and Implement as copious in the giving, as can in craving be their *Vade Mecums*. Do not here produce ancient Examples of the *Paragons* of *Paillardise*, and offer to match with my Testiculatory Ability, the *Priapæan* Prowess of the fabulous Fornicators, *Hercules*, *Proculus*, *Cæsar*, and *Mahomet*, who in his *Alchoran* doth vaunt, that in his Cods he had the vigour of Threescore Bully Ruffians; but let no zealous Christian trust the Rogue, the filthy ribald Rascal is a Lyar. Shall thou need to urge Authorities, or bring forth the Instance of the *Indian* Prince, of whom *Theophrastus*, *Plinius*, and *Athenæus* testifie, that with the help of a certain Herb, he was able, and had given frequent Experiments thereof, to toss his sinewy Piece of Generation, in the Act of carnal Concupiscence, above Threescore and ten times in the space of Four and twenty hours. Of that I believe nothing, the number is supposititious, and too prodigally foisted in: Give no Faith unto it, I beseech thee, but prithee trust me in this, and thy credulity therein shall not be wronged; for it is true, and *Probatum est*, that my Pionier of Nature, the sacred *Ithyphallian* Champion, is of all stiff-intruding Blades the primest: Come hither my Ballockette, and hearken, Didst thou ever see the Monk of *Castres* Cowl? when in any House it was laid down, whether openly in view of all, or covertly out of the sight of any, such was the ineffable Vertue thereof for excitating and stirring up the people of both Sexes unto Lechery, that the whole Inhabitants and Indwellers, not only of that, but likeways of all the circumjacent places thereto, within three Leagues around it, did suddenly enter into Rut, both Beasts and Folks, Men and Women, even to the Dogs and Hogs, Rats and Cats.

I swear to thee, that many times heretofore I have perceived, and found in my *Codpiece* a certain kind of Energy, or efficacious Vertue, much more irregular, and of a greater Anomaly, then what I have related: I will not speak to thee either of House or Cottage, nor of Church or Market, but only tell thee, that once at the Representation of the *Passion*, which was acted at Saint *Mexents*, I had no sooner entred within the Pit of the Theater, but that forthwith, by the vertue and occult property of it, on a sudden all that were there, both Players and Spectators, did fall into such an exorbitant Temptation of Lust, that there was not Angel, Man, Devil, nor Deviless, upon the place, who would not then have Bricollitched it with all their Heart and Soul.

The Prompter forsook his Copy, he who played *Michael*'s part, came down to rights, the Devils issued out of Hell, and carried along with them most of the pretty little Girls that were there; yea, *Lucifer* got out of his Fetters; in a word: Seeing the huge Disorder, I disparked my self forth of that inclosed place, in imitation of *Cato* the *Censor*, who perceiving by reason of his presence, the *Floralian* Festivals out of order, withdrew himself.

CHAPTER XXVIII

How Friar Ihon comforteth Panurge in the doubtful matter of Cuckoldry.

I UNDERSTAND thee well enough, said Friar *Ihon*; but *time makes all things plain*. The most durable Marbre or Porphyr is subject to Old Age and Decay. Though for the present thou possibly be not weary of the Exercise, yet is it like, I will hear thee confess a few years hence, that thy Cods hang dangling downwards for want of a better Truss. I see thee waxing a little hoar-headed already; thy Beard by the Distinctions of grey, white, tawny and black, hath to my thinking the resemblance of a Map of the Terrestrial Globe, or Geographical Cart. Look attentively upon, and take Inspection of what I shall show unto thee. Behold there *Asia*, here are *Tygris* and *Euphrates*: Lo there *Africk*; here is the Mountain of the *Moon*, yonder thou mayest perceive the Fenny Marsh of *Nilus*. On this side lieth *Europe*: Dost thou not see the Abby of *Tileme?* This little Tuft, which is altogether white, is the *Hyperborean Hills*. By the thirst of my Throple, Friend, when Snow is on the Mountains, I say the Head and the Chin, there is not then any considerable Heat to be expected in the Valleys and Low-Countries of the Codpiece. By the Kibes of thy Heels (quoth *Panurge*) thou dost not understand the Topicks. When Snow is on the tops of the Hills, Lightning, Thunder, Tempest, Whirlwinds, Storms, Hurricanes, and all the Devils of Hell rage in the Valleys. Wouldst thou see the experience thereof, go to the Territory of the *Swissers*, and earnestly perpend with thy self there the Situation of the Lake of *Wendelberlick*, about four Leagues distant from *Berne*, on the *Syon*-side of the Land. Thou twittest me with my Grey Heirs, yet considerest not how I am of the Nature of Leeks, which with a white Head carry a green, fresh, streight, and vigorous Tail.

The truth is nevertheless, (why should I deny it) that I now and then discern in my self some indicative Signs of Old Age. Tell this, I prithee, to no body, but let it be kept very close and secret betwixt us two; for I find the Wine much sweeter now, more savoury to my taste, and unto my Palate of a better relish than formerly I was wont to do; and withal, besides mine accustomed manner, I have a more dreadful Apprehension than I ever heretofore have had of lighting on bad Wine. Note and observe that this doth argue and portend I know not what of the *West* and *Occident* of my time, and signifieth that the *South* and *Meridian* of mine Age is past. But what then? My Gentle Companion, that doth but betoken that I will hereafter drink so much the more. That is not, the Devil hale it, the thing that I fear; nor is there where my Shoo pinches. The thing that I doubt most, and have greatest reason to dread and suspect is, that through some long absence of our King *Pantagruel* (to whom I must needs bear Company, should he go to all the Devils of *Barathrum*) my future Wife shall make me a Cuckold. This is, in truth, the long and the short on't: For I am by all those whom I have spoke to menac'd and threatned with a Horned Fortune; and all of them affirm, it is the Lot to which from Heaven I am predestinated. Every one (answered Friar *Ihon*) that would be a Cuckold, is not one: If it be thy Fate to be hereafter of the number of that *Horned* Cattle, then may I conclude with an *Ergo*, thy

Wife will be beautiful, and *Ergo*, thou wilt be kindly used by her: Likewise with this *Ergo* thou shalt be blissed with the fruition of many Friends and Well-willers: And finally with this other *Ergo* thou shalt be saved, and have a place in *Paradise*. These are Monachal Topicks and Maxims of the Cloyster: Thou mayst take more liberty to sin: Thou shalt be more at ease than ever: There will be never the less left for thee, nothing diminished, but thy Goods shall increase notably: And if so be it was pre-ordinated for thee, wouldst thou be so impious as not to acquiesce in thy Destiny? Speak thou jaded Cod,

Faded C.	Felled C.	Untriped C.
Mouldy C.	Fleeted C.	Blasted C.
Musty C.	Cloyed C.	Cut off C.
Paultery C.	Squeezed C.	Beveraged C.
Senseless C.	Resty C.	Scarified C.
Foundred C.	Pounded C.	Dasht C.
Distempred C.	Loose C.	Slasht C.
Berayed C.	Coldish C.	Infeebled C.
Inveigled C.	Peckled C.	Whore-hunting C.
Dangling C.	Churned C.	Deteriorated C.
Stupid C.	Filiped C.	Chil C.
Seedless C.	Singlefied C.	Scrupulous C.
Soaked C.	Begrimed C.	Crazed C.
Lowting C.	Wrinkled C.	Tasteless C.
Discouraged C.	Fainted C.	Hacked C.
Surfeited C.	Extenuated C.	Flaggy C.
Peevish C.	Grim C.	Scrubby C.
Translated C.	Wasted C.	Drained C.
Forlorn C.	Inflamed C.	Haled C.
Unsavoury C.	Unhinged C.	Lolling C.
Worm-eaten C.	Scurfie C.	Drenched C.
Overtoiled C.	Stradling C.	Burst C.
Miserable C.	Putrefied C.	Stirred up C.
Steeped C.	Maimed C.	Mitred C.
Kneaded with cold	Overlechered C.	Pedling furnished
Water C.	Druggely C.	C.
Appealant C.	Mitified C.	Rusty C.
Swagging C.	Goat-ridden C.	Exhausted C.
Withered C.	Weakned C.	Perplexed C.
Broken reined C.	Asse-ridden C.	Unhelved C.
Defective C.	Puff-pasted C.	Fizled C.
Crestfallen C.	St. Anthonified C.	Leaprous C.

Bruised C.
Spadonick C.
Boughty C.
Mealy C.
Wrangling C.
Gangreened C.
Crustrisen C.
Ragged C.
Quelled C.
Bragodochio C.
Beggarly C.
Trepanned C.
Bedusked C.
Emasculated C.
Corked C.
Transparent C.
Vile C.
Antidated C.
Chopped C.
Pinked C.
Cup-glassified C.
Fruitless C.
Riven C.
Pursie C.
Fusty C.
Jadish C.
Fistulous C.
Languishing C.
Maleficiated C.
Hectick C.
Worn out C.
Ill-favoured C.
Duncified C.
Macerated C.
Paralytick C.
Degraded C.
Benummed C.
Bat-like C.
Fart-shotten C.
Sun-burnt C.
Pacified C.
Blunted C.
Rangling tasted C.
Rooted out C.
Costive C.

Hailed on C.
Cuffed C.
Buffeted C.
Whirreted C.
Robbed C.
Neglected C.
Lame C.
Confused C.
Unsavoury C.
Overthrown C.
Boulted C.
Trod under C.
Desolate C.
Declining C.
Stinching C.
Sorrowful C.
Murthered C.
Matachin-like C.
Besotted C.
Customerless C.
Minced C.
Exulcerated C.
Patched C.
Stupified C.
Annihilated C.
Spent C.
Foiled C.
Aguish C.
Disfigured C.
Disabled C.
Forcedless C.
Censured C.
Cut C.
Rifled C.
Undone C.
Corrected C.
Slit C.
Skittish C.
Spungy C.
Botched C.
Dejected C.
Jagged C.
Pining C.
Deformed C.
Mischieved C.

Cobled C.
Imbased C.
Ransacked C.
Despised C.
Mangy C.
Abased C.
Supine C.
Mended C.
Dismayed C.
Harsh C.
Beaten C.
Barred C.
Abandoned C.
Confounded C.
Lowtish C.
Born down C.
Sparred C.
Abashed C.
Unseasonable C.
Opprest C.
Grated C.
Falling away C.
Smalcut C.
Disordered C.
Lattised C.
Ruined C.
Exasperated C.
Rejected C.
Belammed C.
Fabricitant C.
Perused C.
Emasculated C.
Roughly handled C.
Examined C.
Crakt C.
Waiward C.
Hagled C.
Gleaning C.
Ill-favoured C.
Pulled C.
Drooping C.
Faint C.
Parched C.
Paultry C.

Cankred C.
Void C.
Vexed C.
Bestunk C.
Crooked C.
Brabling C.
Rotten C.
Anxious C.
Clouted C.
Tired C.
Proud C.
Fractured C.
Melancholy C.
Coxcombly C.
Base C.
Bleaked C.
Detested C.
Diaphanous C.
Unworthy C.
Checked C.
Mangled C.
Turned over C.
Harried C.
Flawed C.
Froward C.
Ugly C.
Drawn C.
Riven C.
Distasteful C.
Hanging C.
Broken C.
Limber C.
Effeminate C.
Kindled C.
Evacuated C.
Grieved C.
Carking C.
Disorderly C.
Empty C.
Disquieted C.
Besysted C.
Confounded C.
Hooked C.
Diverous C.
Wearied C.

Sad C.
Cross C.
Vain-glorious C.
Poor C.
Brown C.
Shrunkin C.
Abhorred C.
Troubled C.
Scornful C.
Dishonest C.
Reproved C.
Cocketed C.
Filthy C.
Shred C.
Chawned C.
Short-winded C.
Branchless C.
Chapped C.
Failing C.
Deficient C.
Lean C.
Consumed C.
Used C.
Puzled C.
Allayed C.
Spoiled C.
Clagged C.
Palsey-strucken C.
Amazed C.
Bedunsed C.
Extirpated C.
Banged C.
Stripped C.
Hoary C.
Winnowed C.
Decayed C.
Disastrous C.
Unhandsom C.
Stummed C.
Barren C.
Wretched C.
Feeble C.
Cast down C.
Stopped C.
Kept under C.

Stubborn C.
Ground C.
Retchless C.
Weather-beaten C.
Flayed C.
Bauld C.
Tossed C.
Flapping C.
Cleft C.
Meagre C.
Dumpified C.
Supprest C.
Hagged C.
Jawped C.
Havocked C.
Astonished C.
Dulled C.
Slow C.
Plucked up C.
Constipated C.
Blown C.
Blockify'd C.
Pommeled C.
All-to-be mawl'd C.
Fallen away C.
Unlucky C.
Steril C.
Beshitten C.
Appeased C.
Caitive C.
Woful C.
Unseemly C.
Heavy C.
Weak C.
Prostrated C.
Uncomely C.
Naughty C.
Laid flat C.
Suffocated C.
Held down C.
Barked C.
Hairless C.
Flamping C.
Hooded C.
Wormy C.

Besysted C.	Douf C.	Besmeared C.
Faulty C.	Clarty C.	Hollow C.
Bemealed C.	Lumpish C.	Pantless C.
Mortified C.	Abject C.	Guizened C.
Scurvy C.	Side C.	Demiss C.
Bescabbed C.	Choaked up C.	Refractory C.
Torn C.	Backward C.	Rensie C.
Subdued C.	Prolix C.	Frowning C.
Sneaking C.	Spotted C.	Limping C.
Bare C.	Crumpled C.	Raveled C.
Swart C.	Frumpled C.	Rammish C.
Smutched C.	State C.	Gaunt C.
Raised up C.	Corrupted C.	Beskimmered C.
Chopped C.	Beflowred C.	Scraggy C.
Flirted C.	Amated C.	Lank C.
Blained C.	Blackish C.	Swashring C.
Blotted C.	Underlaid C.	Moyling C.
Sunk in C.	Loathing C.	Swinking C.
Gastly C.	Ill-filled C.	Harried C.
Unpointed C.	Bobbed C.	Tugged C.
Beblistered C.	Mated C.	Towed C.
Wizened C.	Tawny C.	Misused C.
Begger-plated C.	Whealed C.	Adamitical C.

Balockatso to the *Devil*, my dear Friend *Panurge*, seeing it is so decreed by the Gods, wouldst thou invert the course of the Planets, and make them retrograde? Wouldst thou disorder all the Cœlestial Spheres? blame the Intelligences, blunt the Spindles, joynt the Wherves, slander the Spinning Quills, reproach the Bobbins, revile the Clew-bottoms, and finally ravel and untwist all the threads of both the warp and the waft of the weerd Sister *Parques*? What a Pox to thy Bones dost thou mean, stony Cod? Thou wouldst if thou couldst, a great deal worse than the Gyants of old intended to have done. Come hither, Billicullion; whether wouldst thou be jealous without cause, or be a Cuckold and know nothing of it? Neither the one nor the other (quoth *Panurge*) would I choose to be: But if I get an inkling of the matter, I will provide well enough, or there shall not be one stick of Wood within five hundred Leagues about me, whereof to make a Cudgel. In good Faith (Fryar *Ihon*) I speak now seriously unto thee, I think it will be my best not to marry: Hearken to what the Bells do tell me, now that we are nearer to them: *Do not Marry, Marry not, not, not, not, not*; *Marry, Marry not, not, not, not, not*: *If thou Marry, thou who miscarry, carry carry, thou'lt repent it, resent it, sent it: If thou Marry, thou a Cuckold, a Cou-cou-Cuckoe, Cou-cou-Cuckold thou shalt be.* By the worthy Wrath of God, I begin to be angry; this *Campanilian* Oracle fretteth me to the Guts, a *March-Hare* was never in such a Chaff as I am. O how I am vexed! you Monks and Fryars of the Cowl-pated and Hood-poll'd Fraternity, have you no Remedy nor Salve against this Malady of Graffing Horns in Heads? Hath Nature so abandoned Human-kind, and of her help left us so destitute, that married Men cannot know how to sail through the Seas of this mortal Life, and be safe from the Whirlpools, Quicksands, Rocks and Banks that lie alongst the Coast of Cornwall.

I will (said Fryar *Ihon*) shew thee a way, and teach thee an Expedient, by means whereof thy Wife shall never make thee a Cuckold without thy knowledge, and thine own consent. Do me the favour, I pray thee, (quoth *Panurge*) my pretty, soft, downy Cod; now tell it, *Billy*, tell it, I beseech thee. Take (quoth Fryar *Ihon*) *Hans Carvel*'s Ring upon thy Finger, who was the King of *Melinda*'s chief Jeweller; besides that, this *Hans Carvel* had the Reputation of being very skilful and expert in the Lapidary's Profession, he was a studious, learned, and ingenious Man, a Scientifick Person, full of Knowledge, a great Philosopher, of a sound Judgment, of a prime Wit, good Sence, clear spirited, an honest Creature, Courteous, Charitable, Giver of Alms, and of a Jovial Humour, a Boon Companion, and a Merry Blade, if ever there was any in the World: He was somewhat Gorbellied, had a little Shake in his Head, and in effect unwieldy of his Body; in his Old Age he took to Wife the Bailiff of *Concordat*'s Daughter, a young, fair, jolly, gallant, spruce, frisk, brisk, neat, feat, smirk, smug, compt, quaint, gay, fine, trixy, trim, decent, proper, graceful, handsom, beautiful, comly; and kind, a little too much to her Neighbours and Acquaintance.

Hereupon it fell out, after the expiring of a scantling of Weeks, that Master *Carvel* became as jealous as a Tygar, and entred into a very profound suspition that his new-marry'd Gixy did keep a Buttock-stirring with others: To prevent which inconveniency, he did tell her many tragical Stories of the total Ruine of several Kingdoms by Adultery; did read unto her the

Legend of chast Wives; then made some Lectures to her in the praise of the choice Virtue of Pudicity, and did present her with a Book in Commendation of Conjugal Fidelity: wherein the Wickedness of all Licentious Women was odiously detested; and withal, he gave her a Chain enrich'd with pure Oriental Saphires. Notwithstanding all this, he found her always more and more enclined to the reception of her Neighbour Cope-Mates, that day by day his Jealousie increased; in sequel whereof, one night as he was lying by her, whilst in his Sleep the rambling Fancies of the lecherous Deportments of his Wife, did take up the Celluls of his Brain, he dreamt that he encountred with the Devil, to whom he had discovered to the full the buzzing of his Head, and suspicion that his Wife did tread her Shooe awry; the Devil, he thought, in this perplexity, did, for his comfort, give him a Ring, and therewithal did kindly put it on his Middle-finger, saying *Hans Carvel*, I give thee this Ring, whilst thou carriest it upon that Finger, thy Wife shall never carnally be known by any other than thy self, without thy special knowledge and consent. Grammercy (quoth *Hans Carvel*) my Lord Devil; I renounce *Mahomet*, if ever it shall come off my Finger. The Devil vanished, as is his Custom; and then *Hans Carvel* full of Joy awaking, found that his Middle-finger was as far as it could reach within the *What-do-you-call-it* of his Wife. I did forget to tell thee, how his Wife, as soon she had felt the Finger there, said, in recoyling her Buttocks, Off, yes, nay, tut, pish, tush, aye, lord, that is not the Thing which should be put up in that Place. With this, *Hans Carvel* thought that some pilfering Fellow was about to take the Ring from him.

Is not this an infallible and sovereign Antidote? therefore, if thou wilt believe me, in imitation of this Example, never fail to have continually the Ring of thy Wife's Commodity upon thy Finger. When that was said, their Discourse and their Way ended.

CHAPTER XXIX

How Pantagruel Convocated together a Theologian, Physitian,
Lawyer, and Philosopher, for extricating Panurge out of the
perplexity wherein he was.

NO sooner were they come into the Royal Palace, but they, to
the full, made Report unto *Pantagruel* of the Success of their
Expedition; they shew him the Response of *Raminagrobis*.
When *Pantagruel* had read it over and over again, the oftner he
perused it, being the better pleased therewith; he said, in addressing his Speech to *Panurge*, I have not as yet seen any Answer
framed to your Demand, which affordeth me more Contentment: For in this his succinct Copy of Verses, he summarily, and
briefly, yet fully enough expresseth, how he would have us to
understand, that every one in the Project and Enterprize of Marriage, ought to be his own Carver, sole Arbitrator of his proper
Thoughts, and from himself alone take Counsel in the main and
peremptory closure of what his Determination should be, in
either his assent to, or dissent from it. Such always hath been
my Opinion to you; and when at first you spoke thereof to me,
I truly told you this very same thing: but tacitly you scorned my
Advice, and would not harbour it within your mind. I know for
certain, and therefore may I with the greater confidence utter
my conception of it, that *Philauty*, or Self-love, is that which
blinds your Judgment, and deceiveth you.

Let us do otherways, and that is this: Whatever we are, or
have, consisteth in Three Things; the Soul, the Body, and the
Goods: Now for the preservation of these Three, there are Three
sorts of Learned Men ordained, each respectively to have care
of that one which is recommended to his charge. *Theologues* are
appointed for the soul, *Physitians* for the Welfare of the Body,
and *Lawyers* for the Safety of our Goods: Hence it is, that it is
my Resolution to have on Sunday next with me at Dinner, a
Divine, a *Physitian*, and a *Lawyer*, that with those Three assembled thus together, we may in every Point and Particle confer at
large of your Perplexity. By St. *Picot* (answered *Panurge*) we
never shall do any good that way: I see it already, and you see

your self, how the World is vilely abused, as when with a Fox-tayl one claps another's Breech, to cajole him. We give our Souls to keep to the *Theologues*, who for the greater part are *Hereticks*: Our Bodies we commit to the *Physitians*, who never themselves take any *Physick*: And then we intrust our Goods to *Lawyers*, who never go to *Law* against one another. You speak like a Courtier, (quoth *Pantagruel*) but the first Point of your Assertion is to be denied: For we daily see how good *Theologues* make it their chief Business, their whole and sole Employment, by their Deeds, their Words, and Writings, to extirpate Errors and Heresies out of the Hearts of Men; and in their stead profoundly plant the true and lively Faith. The second Point you spoke of I com-mend: For whereas the Professors of the Art of *Medicine* give so good order to the *Prophylactick*, or *Conservative* part of their Faculty, in what concerneth their proper Healths, that they stand in no need of making use of the other Branch, which is the *Cur-ative*, or *Therapeutick*, by Medicaments. As for the Third, I grant it to be true: For learned *Advocates* and *Counsellors* at *Law* are so much taken up with the Affairs of others in their Consultations, Pleadings and such like Patrocinations of those who are their Clients, that they have no leisure to attend any Controversies of their own. Therefore, on the next ensuing *Sunday*, let the Divine be our goodly Father *Hippothadee*, the Physitian our honest Master *Rondibilis*, and the Legist our good Friend *Bridlegoose*: Nor will it be (to my thinking) amiss, that we enter into the *Pythagorick Field*, and chuse for an Assistant to the Three afore-named Doctors, our ancient faithful Acquaintance, the Philo-sopher *Trouillogan*; especially seeing a perfect Philosopher, such as is *Trouillogan*, is able positively to resolve all whatsoever Doubts you can propose. *Carpalin*, have you a care to have them here all Four on *Sunday* next at Dinner, without fail.

I believe (quoth *Epistemon*) that throughout the whole Country, in all the Corners thereof, you could not have pitched upon such other Four; which I speak not so much in regard of the most excellent Qualifications and Accomplishments where-with all of them are endowed, for the respective Discharge and Management of each his own Vocation and Calling, (wherein, without all doubt or controversy, they are the Paragons of the Land, and surpass all others) as for that *Rondibilis* is married now, who before was not: *Hippothadee* was not before, nor is yet: *Bridlegoose* was married once, but is not now: And *Trouillogan* is married now, who wedded was to another Wife before. Sir, if it may stand with your good liking, I will ease *Carpalin* of some parcel of his labour, and invite *Bridlegoose* my self, with whom I of a long time have had a very intimate familiarity, and unto whom I am to speak on the behalf of a pretty hopeful Youth, who now studieth at *Tholouse*, under the most learned, vertuous Doctor *Boissonnet*. Do what you deem most expedient, (quoth *Pantagruel*) and tell me, if my Recommendation can in any thing be steadable for the promoval of the good of that Youth, or otherwise serve for the bettering of the Dignity and Office of the worthy *Boissonnet*, whom I do so love and respect, for one of the ablest and most sufficient in his way, that any-where are extant. Sir, I will use therein my best Endeavours, and heartily bestir my self about it.

CHAPTER XXX

How the Theologue, Hippothadee, giveth Counsel to Panurge in the matter and business of his Nuptial Enterprize.

THE Dinner on the subsequent *Sunday* was no sooner made ready, than that the aforenamed invited Guests gave thereto their Appearance, all of them; *Bridlegoose* only excepted, who was the Deputy-Governor of the *Fonsbeton*. At the ushering in of the Second Service, *Panurge* making a low Reverence, spake thus: Gentlemen, the Question I am to propound unto you, shall be uttered in very few Words: *Should I marry or no?* If my Doubt herein be not resolved by you, I shall hold it altogether insolvable, as are the *Insolubilia de Aliaco*; for all of you are elected, chosen, and culled out from amongst others, every one in his own Condition and Quality, like so many picked Peas on a Carpet.

The Father *Hippothadee*, in obedience to the Bidding of *Pantagruel*, and with much Courtesie to the Company, answer'd exceedingly modestly after this manner: My Friend, you are pleased to ask Counsel of us; but first you must consult with your self. Do you find any trouble or disquiet in your Body, by the importunate stings and pricklings of the Flesh? That I do (quoth *Panurge*) in a hugely strong and almost irresistable measure: Be not offended, I beseech you, good Father, at the freedom of my Expression. No truly, Friend, not I (quoth *Hippothadee*) there is no reason why I should be displeased there-with: But in this Carnal Strife and Debate of yours, have you obtained from God the Gift and *special Grace* of Continency? In good Faith, not (quoth *Panurge.*) My Counsel to you in that case (my Friend) is, that you marry, (quoth *Hippothadee*) for you should rather choose to marry once, than to burn still in Fires of Concupiscence. Then *Panurge*, with a jovial Heart and a loud Voice, cried out, That is spoke gallantly, without circumbili-vaginating about and about, and never hit it in its centred Point. Grammercy, my good Father. In truth I am resolved now to marry, and without fail I shall do it quickly. I invite you to my Wedding: By the Body of a Hen, we shall make good Cheer, and be as merry as Crickets: You shall wear the Bridegroom's Colours: and if we eat a Goose, my Wife shall not rost for me. I will in-treat you to lead up the first Dance of the Brides Maids, if it may please you to do me so much Favour and Honour. There resteth yet a small Difficulty, a little Scruple, yea, even less than noth-ing, whereof I humbly crave your Resolution; Shall I be a Cuck-old, Father, yea, or no? By no means (answered *Hippothadee*) will you be Cuckolded, if it please God. O the Lord help us now (quoth *Panurge*) whither are we driven to, good Folks? To the *Conditionals*, which, according to the Rules and Precepts of the Dialectick Faculty, admit of all Contradictions and Impossi-bilities. *If my Transalpine Mule had Wings, my Transalpine Mule would fly.* If it please God I shall not be a Cuckold, but I shall be a Cuckold if it please him. Good God, if this were a Condition which I knew how to prevent, my Hopes should be as high as ever, nor would I despair: But you here send me to God's Privy Council, to the Closet of his little Pleasures. You, my *French* Countrymen, Which is the Way you take to go thither?

My honest Father, I believe it will be your best not to come to my Wedding: The clutter and dingle dangle noise of Mar-riage Guests will but disturb you, and break the serious Fancies of your Brain. You love Repose, with Solitude and Silence; I really believe you will not come: And then you Dance but indifferently, and would be out of Countenance at the first Entry. I will send you some good things to your Chamber together with the *Bride's Favour*, and there you may drink our Health, if it may stand with your good liking. My Friend, (quoth *Hippothadee*) take my Words in the Sence wherein I meaned them, and do not misinterpret me. When I tell you, *if it please God*, do I to you do any wrong therein? Is it an ill Expression? Is it a Blaspheming Clause or Reserve any way scandalous unto the World? Do not we thereby honour the Lord God Almighty, Creator, Protector, and Conserver of all things? Is not that a mean, whereby we do acknowledge him to be the sole Giver of all whatsoever is good? Do not we in that manifest our Faith, that we believe all things to depend upon his infinite and incomprehensible Bounty? and that without him nothing can be produced, nor after its Production be of any value, force, or power, without the concurring aid and favour of his assisting Grace? Is it not a canonical and authentick Exception, worthy to be premised to all our Undertakings? Is it not expedient, that what we propose unto our selves, be still referred to what shall be disposed of by the Sacred Will of God, unto which all things must acquiesce in the Heavens as well as on the Earth? Is not that verily a sanctifying of his Holy Name? My Friend, you shall not be a Cuckold, if it please God; nor shall we need to despair of the knowledge of his good Will and Pleasure herein, as if it were such an abstruse and mysteriously hidden Secret, that for the clear understanding thereof, it were necessary to consult with those of his Celestial Privy Council, or expresly make a Voyage unto the *Empyrean* Chamber, where Order is given for the effectuating of his most holy Pleasures.

The great God hath done us this good, and he hath declared and revealed them to us openly and plainly, and described them in the Holy Bible: There you will find that you shall never be a Cuckold, that is to say your Wife shall never be a Strumpet, if you make choice of one of a commendable Extraction, descended of honest Parents, and instructed in all Piety and Vertue: Such a one as hath not at any time hanted or frequented the Company or Conversation of those that are of corrupt and deprav'd Manners; one loving and fearing God, who taketh a singular delight in drawing near to him by Faith, and the cordial observing of his Sacred Commandments; And finally, one who standing in awe of the Divine Majesty, of the Most High, will be loth to offend Him, and lose the favourable Kindness of his Grace, through any defect of Faith, or transgression against the Ordinances of his Holy Law, wherein Adultery is most rigorously forbidden, and a close Adherence to her Husband alone most strictly and severely enjoyned; yea, in such sort, that she is to cherish, serve and love him above any thing, next to God, that meriteth to be beloved. In the interim, for the better schooling of her in these Instructions, and that the wholsom Doctrin of a Matrimonial Duty may take the deeper root in her Mind, you must needs carry your self so on your part, and your behaviour is to be such, that you are to go before her in a good Example, by entertaining her unfeignedly with a Conjugal Amity, by continually approving your self in all your Words and Actions a faithful and discreet Husband; and by living not only at home, and privately with your own Houshold and Family, but in the face also of all Men, and open view of the World, devotely, vertuously and chastly, as you would have her on her side to deport and demean her self towards you, as becomes a Godly, Loyal, and Respectful Wife, who maketh Conscience to keep inviolable the Tie of a Matrimonial Oath.

For as that *Looking-glass* is not the best, which is most deck'd with Gold and Precious-stones, but that which representeth to the Eye the liveliest Shapes of Objects set before it; even so that Wife should not be most esteemed who richest is, and of the noblest Race, but she who fearing God, conforms her self nearest unto the Humour of her Husband.

Consider how the *Moon* doth not borrow her Light from *Jupiter, Mars, Mercury,* or any other of the Planets, nor yet from any of those Splendid Stars which are set in the spangled Firmament; but from her Husband only, the bright *Sun,* which she receiveth from him more or less, according to the manner of his *Aspect,* and variously bestowed Eradiations. Just so should you be a Pattern to your Wife in Vertue, goodly Zeal and true Devotion; that by your Radiance in darting on her the *Aspect* of an Exemplary Goodness, she, in your imitation, may outshine the Luminaries of all other Women. To this effect, you daily must implore God's Grace to the protection of you both. You would have me then (quoth *Panurge*, twisting the Whiskers of his Beard on either side with the Thumb and Fore-Finger of his Left-Hand) to espouse and take to Wife the prudent and frugal Woman described by *Solomon*: Without all doubt she is dead, and truly, to my best remembrance, I never saw her; the Lord forgive me. Nevertheless, I thank you, Father; Eat this slice of Marchpane, it will help your Digestion; then shall you be presented with a Cup of Claret Hypocras, which is right healthful and stomached. Let us proceed.

CHAPTER XXXI

How the Physitian Rondibilis counselleth Panurge.

PANURGE continuing his Discourse, said, The first word which was spoken by him who guelded the Lubbardly quaffing Monks of *Saussiniac*, after that he had unstoned Friar *Corcil*, was this, *To the rest*. In like manner, I say, *to the rest*. Therefore I beseech you, my good Master *Rondibilis*, should *I marry or not?* By the raking pace of my Mule, quoth *Rondibilis*, I know not what Answer to make to this Problem of yours.

You say that you feel in you the *pricking Stings* of Sensuality, by which you are stirred up to Venery. I find in our Faculty of *Medicine*, and we have founded our Opinion therein upon the deliberate Resolution and final Decision of the ancient *Platonicks*, that *Carnal Concupiscence* is cooled and quelled five several ways.

First, By the means of *Wine*. I shall easily believe that, (quoth Friar *Ihon*) for when I am well whitled with the Juyce of the Grape, I care for nothing else so I may sleep. When I say (quoth *Rondibilis*) that *Wine* abateth Lust, my meaning is, *Wine* immoderately taken; for by Intemperancy proceeding from the excessive drinking of Strong Liquor, there is brought upon the Body of such a Swilldown Bouser a chillness in the Blood, a slackening in the Sinews, a Dissipation of the Generative Seed, a numbness and hebetation of the Senses, with a perversive wriness and Convulsion of the Muscles; all which are great Lets and Impediments to the Act of Generation. Hence it is that *Bacchus*, the God of Bibbers, Tiplers and Drunkards is most commonly painted Beardless, and clad in a Womans Habit, as a Person altogether Effeminate, or like a libbed Eunuch. *Wine* nevertheless taken moderately worketh quite contrary Effects, as is implied by the old Proverb, which saith, That *Venus* takes cold when not accompanied with *Ceres* and *Bacchus*. This Opinion is of great Antiquity, as appeareth by the Testimony of *Diodorus* the *Sicilian*, and confirmed by *Pausanias*, and universally held amongst the *Lampsacians*, that *Don Priapos* was the son of *Bacchus* and *Venus*.

Secondly, the Fervency of Lust is abated by certain *Drugs*, Plants, Herbs and Roots, which make the Taker cold, maleficiated, unfit for, and unable to perform the Act of Generation; as hath been often experimented in the Water-Lilly, *Heraclea*, *Agnus Castus*, Willow-twigs, Hemp-stalks, Woodbind, Honey suckle, Tamarisk, Chastree, Mandrake, Bennet, Kecbuglosse, the Skin of a *Hippopatam*, and many other such, which by convenient Doses, proportioned to the peccant Humour and Constitution of the Patient, being duly and seasonably received within the Body, what by their Elementary Vertues on the one side, and peculiar Properties on the other, do either benumb, mortifie and beclumpse with Cold the prolifick Semence; or scatter and disperse the Spirits, which ought to have gone along with, and conducted the Sperm to the places destinated and appointed for its reception. Or lastly, Shut up, stop and obstruct the ways, passages, and conduits through which the Seed should have been expelled, evacuated and ejected. We have nevertheless of those Ingredients, which being of a contrary Operation, heat the Blood, bend the Nerves, unite the Spirits, quicken the Senses, strengthen the Muscles, and thereby rouze up, provoke, excite and inable a Man to the vigorous Accomplishment of the Feat of Amorous Dalliance. I have no need of those, (quoth *Panurge*) God be thanked, and you my good Master. Howsoever I pray you take no exception or offence at these my Words; for what I have said was not out of any ill will I did bear to you, the Lord he knows.

Thirdly, The Ardour of Letchery is very much subdued and mated by frequent *Labour* and continual Toyling: For by painful Exercises and laborious working, so great a Dissolution is brought upon the whole Body, that the Blood which runneth alongst the Channels of the Veins thereof, for the Nourishment and Alimentation of each of its Members, hath neither time, leisure nor power to afford the Seminal Resudation, or super-fluity of the third Concoction, which Nature most carefully reserves for the conservation of the Individual, whose Preserva-tion she more heedfully regardeth than the propagating of the Species, and the multiplication of Humane Kind. Whence it is, that *Diana* is said to be chast, because she is never idle, but always busied about her Hunting; For the same reason was a Camp, or Leaguer of old called *Castrum*, as if they would have said *Castum*: Because the Soldiers, Wrestlers, Runners, Throwers of the Bar, and other such-like Athletick Champions, as are usually seen in a Military Circumvallation, do uncessantly travel and turmoil, and are in a perpetual stir and agitation. To this purpose *Hippocrates* also writeth in his Book, *De Aere, Aqua, et locis*: That in his time there were People in *Scythia* as impotent as Eunuchs, in the discharge of a Venerian Exploit; because that without any cessation, pause, or respit, they were never from off Horseback, or otherways assiduously employed in some troublesom and molesting Drudgery.

On the other part, in opposition and repugnancy hereto, the Philosophers say, *That Idleness is the Mother of Luxury*: When it was asked *Ovid*, Why *Egistus* became an Adulterer, he made no other Answer but this: *Because he was idle*. Who were able to rid the World of Loytring and Laziness, might easily frustrate and disappoint *Cupid* of all his Designs, Aims, Engines, and Devices, and so disable and appall him, that his Bow, Quiver, and Darts should from thenceforth be a meer needless Load and Burthen to him: for that it could not then lie in his power to strike, or wound any of either Sex, with all the Arms he had. He is not, I believe, so expert an Archer, as that he can hit the Cranes flying in the Air, or yet the young Stags, skipping through the Thic-kets, as the *Parthians* knew well how to do; that is to say, People moyling, swinking, and hurrying up and down, restless, and without repose. He must have those husht, still, quiet, lying at a stay, lither, and full of ease, whom he is able, though his Mother help him, to touch, much less to pierce with all his Arrows: In confirmation hereof, *Theophrastus* being asked on a time, What kind of Beast or Thing he judged a toyish, wanton Love to be?

He made Answer, *That it was a Passion of idle and sluggish Spirits*. From which pretty Description of tickling Love-tricks that of *Diogenes*'s hatching was not very discrepant, when he defined Leachery, *Occupation of Folks destitute of all other Occupation*.

For this cause the Syconian Engraver, *Canachus*, being desirous to give us to understand, that Sloath, Drouziness, Negligence, and Laziness were the prime Guardians and Governesses of Ribaldry, made the Statue of *Venus* (not standing, as other Stone-Cutters had used to do, but) sitting.

Fourthly, The tickling pricks of Incontinency are blunted by an eager Study; for from thence proceedeth an incredible resolution of the Spirits, that oftentimes there do not remain so many behind as may suffice to push and thrust forwards the Generative Resudation to the places thereto appropriated, and therewithal inflate the Cavernous Nerve; whose Office is to ejaculate the Moisture for the Propagation of Humane Progeny. Least you should think it is not so, be pleased but to contemplate a little the Form, Fashion, and Carriage of a Man exceeding earnestly set upon some Learned Meditation, and deeply plunged therein, and you shall see how all the Arteries of his Brain are stretched forth, and bent like the String of a Crossbow, the more promptly, dexterously, and copiously to suppeditate, furnish, and supply him with Store of Spirits, sufficient to replenish and fill up the Ventricles, Seats, Tunnels, Mansions, Receptacles, and Celluls of the common Sense; of the Imagination, Apprehension, and Fancy; of the Ratiocination, Arguing, and Resolution; as likewise of the Memory, Recordation, and Remembrance; and with great alacrity, nimbleness, and agility to run, pass, and course from the one to the other, through those Pipes, Windings, and Conduits, which to skilful Anatomists are perceivable, at the end of the *Wonderful Net*, where all the Arteries close in a terminating Point: which Arteries taking their rise and origine from the *left Capsul* of the Heart, bring through several Circuits, Ambages, and Anfractuosities the Vital, to subtilize and refine them to the Ætherial Purity of Animal Spirits. Nay, in such a studiously musing Person, you may espy so extravagant Raptures of one, as it were, out of himself, that all his Natural Faculties for that time will seem to be suspended from each their proper charge and office, and his exteriour

Senses to be at a stand. In a word, you cannot otherways choose then think, that he is by an extraordinary Extasie quite transported out of what he was, or should be; and that *Socrates* did not speak improperly, when he said, *That Philosophy was nothing else but a Meditation upon Death*. This possibly is the reason, why *Democritus* deprived himself of the Sense of Seeing, prizing at a much lower rate the loss of his Sight, than the diminution of his Contemplations; which he frequently had found disturbed by the vagrant, flying-out strayings of his unsetled and roving Eyes. Therefore is it, that *Pallas*, the Goddess of Wisdom, Tutress, and Guardianess of such as are diligently studious, and painfully industrious, is, and hath been still accounted a Virgin. The *Muses* upon the same Consideration are esteemed perpetual *Maids*: And the *Graces* for the like reason, have been held to continue in a sempiternal *Pudicity*.

I remember to have read, that *Cupid* on a time being asked of his Mother *Venus*, why he did not assault and set upon the *Muses*, his Answer was, *That he found them so fair, so sweet, so fine, so neat, so wise, so learned, so modest, so discreet, so courteous, so vertuous, and so continually busied and employed*: One in the Speculation of the Stars; another in the Supputation of Numbers; the Third in the Dimension of Geometrical Quantities; the Fourth in the Composition of Heroick Poems; the Fifth in the jovial Interludes of a Comick Strain; the Sixth in the stately Gravity of a Tragick Vein; the Seventh in the Melodious Disposition of Musical Airs; the Eighth in the compleatest manner of Writing Histories, and Books on all sorts of Subjects; and the Ninth in the Mysteries, Secrets, and Curiosities of all Sciences, Faculties, Disciplines, and Arts whatsoever, whether Liberal or Mechanick; that approaching near unto them, he unbended his Bow, shut his Quiver, and extinguished his Torch, through meer shame and fear, that by mischance he might do them some hurt or prejudice: Which done, he thereafter put off the Fillet wherewith his Eyes were bound, to look them in the Face, and to hear their Melody and Poetick Odes. There took he the greatest pleasure in the World; that many times he was transported with their Beauty and pretty Behaviour, and charmed asleep by the Harmony; so far was he from assaulting them, or interrupting their Studies. Under this Article may be comprised, what *Hippocrates* wrote in the aforecited Treatise concerning the *Scythians*, as also that in a Book of his entituled, *Of Breeding and Production*; where he hath affirmed, all such Men to be unfit for Generation, as have their *Parotid* Arteries cut; whose Situation is beside the Ears: For the reason given already, when I was speaking of the resolution of the Spirits, and of that Spiritual Blood, whereof the Arteries are the sole and proper Receptacles; and that likewise he doth maintain a large portion of the Parastatick Liquor, to issue and descend from the Brains and Backbone.

Fifthly, By the too frequent reiteration of the Act of Venery. There did I wait for you (quoth *Panurge*) and shall willingly apply it to my self, whilst any one that pleaseth may, for me, make use of any of the four preceding. That is the very same thing (quoth Fryar *Ihon*) which Father *Scyllino*, Prior of Saint *Victor*, at *Marseilles*, calleth by the Name of *Maceration, and taming of the Flesh*. I am of the same Opinion; and so was the Hermite of *Saint Radegonde*, a little above *Chinon*: For (quoth he) the Hermites of *Thebaida* can no more aptly or expediently macerate and bring down the Pride of their Bodies, daunt and mortifie their letcherous Sensuality, or depress and overcome the stubbornness and rebellion of the Flesh, than by *dufling* and *fanferluching* it Five and twenty, or Thirty times a day. I see *Panurge*, quoth *Rondibilis*, neatly featured, and proportioned in all the Members of his Body, of a good temperament in his Humors, well complexioned in his Spirits, of a competent Age, in an opportune Time, and of a reasonably forward Mind to be married: Truly, if he encounter with a Wife of the like Nature, Temperament, and Constitution, he may beget upon her Children worthy of some *Transpontine* Monarchy; and the sooner he marry, it will be the better for him, and the more conducible for his Profit, if he would see and have his Children in his own time well provided for. Sir, my worthy Master (quoth *Panurge*) I will do it, do not you doubt thereof; and that quickly enough, I warrant you. Nevertheless, whilst you were busied in the uttering of your Learned Discourse, this Flea which I have in mine Ear, hath tickled me more than ever. I retain you in the Number of my Festival Guests, and promise you, that we shall not want for Mirth, and good Chear enough; yea, over and above the ordinary Rate. And, if it may please you, desire your Wife to come along with you, together with her She-Friends and Neighbours: That is to be understood, and there shall be fair Play.

CHAPTER XXXII

How Rondibilis declareth Cuckoldry to be naturally one of the Appendances of Marriage.

THERE remaineth as yet, quoth *Panurge* going on in his Discourse, one small scruple to be cleared: you have seen heretofore, I doubt not, in the *Roman* Standards, *S.P.Q.R.* Si, Peu, Que, Rien: *Shall not I be a Cuckold?* By the Haven of Safety, cried out *Rondibilis*, what is this you ask of me? If you shall be a Cuckold: My Noble Friend, I am married, and you are like to be so very speedily: therefore be pleased from my Experiment in the matter, to write in your Brain, with a Steel-pen, this subsequent Ditton, *There is no married Man who doth not run the hazard of being made a Cuckold*. Cuckoldry naturally attendeth Marriage; the Shadow doth not more naturally follow the Body, then Cuckoldry ensueth after Marriage, to place fair Horns upon the Husband's Heads.

And when you shall happen to hear any Man pronounce these three Words: *He is married*: If you then say he is, hath been, shall be, or may be a Cuckold, you will not be accounted an unskilful Artist in framing of true Consequences. Tripes and Bowels of all the Devils, (cryes *Panurge*) what do you tell me? My dear Friend (answered *Rondibilis*) as *Hippocrates*, on a time, was in the very nick of setting forwards from *Lango* to *Polystilo*, to visit the Philosopher *Democritus*, he wrote a familiar Letter to his Friend *Dionoys*, wherein he desired him, That he would, during the interval of his absence, carry his Wife to the House of her Father and Mother, who were an honourable Couple, and of good Repute; because I would not have her at my Home (said he) to make abode in Solitude: yet notwithstanding this her Residence beside her Parents, do not fail (quoth he) with a most heedful care and circumspection to pry into her ways, and to espy what Places she shall go to with her Mother, and who those be that shall repair unto her: Not (quoth he) that I do mistrust her Vertue, or that I seem to have any diffidence of her Pudicity, and chast Behaviour; for of that I have frequently had good and real proofs: but I must freely tell you, *She is a Woman*; There lies the suspicion.

My worthy Friend, the Nature of Women is set forth before our Eyes, and represented to us by the *Moon*, in divers other things, as well as in this, that they squat, sculk, constrain their own Inclinations, and with all the Cunning they can, dissemble and play the Hypocrite in the sight and presence of their Husbands; who come no sooner to be out of the way, but that forthwith they take their advantage, pass the time merrily, desist from all labour, frolick it, gad abroad, lay aside their counterfeit Garb, and openly declare and manifest the interiour of their Dispositions; even as the *Moon*, when she is in *Conjunction* with the *Sun*, is neither seen in the Heavens, nor on the Earth, but in her *Opposition*, when remotest from him, shineth in her greatest fulness, and wholly appeareth in her brightest splendour whilst it is Night: *Thus Women are but Women*.

When I say *Womankind*, I speak of a Sex so frail, so variable, so changeable, so fickle, inconstant, and imperfect, that, in my Opinion, *Nature* (under favour nevertheless of the prime Honour and Reverence which is due unto her) did in a manner mistake the Road which she had traced formerly, and stray exceedingly from that Excellence of Providential Judgment, by the which she had created and formed all other things, when she built, framed, and made up the *Woman*. And having thought upon it a Hundred and five times, I know not what else to determine therein, save only that in the devising, hammering, forging and composing of the *Woman*, she hath had a much tenderer regard, and by a great deal more respectful heed to the delightful Consortship, and sociable Delectation of the *Man*, than to the Perfection and Accomplishment of the individual *Womanishness*, or *Muliebrity*. The divine Philosopher *Plato* was doubtful in what Rank of living Creatures to place and collocate them, whither amongst the *Rational Animals*, by elevating them to an upper Seat in the Specified Classis of *Humanity*; or with the *Irrational* by degrading them to a lower Bench on the opposite side, of a Brutal kind, and meer *Bestiality*: for Nature hath posited in a privy, secret, and intestine place of their Bodies, a sort of Member, (by some not impertinently termed an *Animal*)

426

which is not to be found in Men. Therein sometimes are ingendred certain Humours so saltish, brackish, clammy, sharp, nipping,
tearing, prickling, and most eagerly tickling, that by their stinging
Acrimony, rending Nitrosity, figging Itch, wrigling Mordicancy,
and smarting Salsitude, (for the said Member is altogether sinewy,
and of a most quick and lively feeling) their whole Body is
shaken and ebrangled, their Senses totally ravished and transported, the Operations of their Judgment and Understanding
utterly confounded, and all disordinate Passions and Perturbations of the Mind thoroughly and absolutely allowed, admitted,
and approved of; yea, in such sort, that if Nature had not been
so favourable unto them, as to have sprinkled their Forehead
with a little Tincture of Bashfulness and Modesty, you should
see them in a so frantick mood run mad after Lechery, and hye
apace up and down with hast and Lust, in quest of, and to fix
some Chamber-Standard in their *Paphian* Ground, that never
did the *Pretides, Mimallonides*, nor *Lyæan Thyads*, deport themselves in the time of their *Bacchanalian Festivals*, more shame-
lesly, or with a so affronted and brazen-faced Impudency;
because this terrible *Animal* is knit unto, and hath an union with
all the chief and most principal Parts of the Body, as to Anatomists is evident. Let it not here be thought strange that I should
call it an *Animal*, seeing therein I do no otherwise than follow
and adhere to the Doctrine of the *Academick* and *Peripatetick*
Philosophers. For if a proper Motion be a certain mark and
infallible token of the Life and Animation of the Mover, (as
Aristotle writeth) and that any such thing as *moveth of it self* ought
to be held *Animated*, and of a *Living Nature*; then assuredly *Plato*
with very good reason did give it the Denomination of an
Animal; for that he perceived and observed in it the proper and
self-stirring motions of Suffocation, Precipitation, Corrugation, and
of Indignation, so extremely violent, that often-times by them
is taken and removed from the Women all other sense and Moving
whatsoever, as if she were in a swounding *Lipothymy*,
benumming *Sincop, Epileptick*, Apoplectick Palsey, and true
resemblance of a pale-faced Death.

Furthermore, in the said *Member* there is a manifest discerning Faculty of Scents and Odours very perceptible to Women,
who feel it fly from what is rank and unsavoury, and follow

RABELAIS

fragrant and Aromatick Smells. It is not unknown to me how *Cl. Gallen* striveth with might and main to prove, that these are not proper and particular Notions proceeding intrinsically from the thing it self, but accidentally, and by chance. Nor hath it escaped my notice, how others of that Sect have laboured hardly, yea, to the utmost of their Abilities, to demonstrate that it is not a sensitive discerning or perception in it of the difference of Wafts and Smells, but meerly a various manner of Vertue and Efficacy, passing forth and flowing from the diversity of odoriferous Substances applied near unto it. Nevertheless, if you will studiously examine, and seriously ponder and weigh in *Critolaus*'s Balance the strength of their Reasons and Arguments, you shall find that they, not only in this, but in several other matters also of the like nature have spoken at random, and rather out of an ambitious Envy to check and reprehend their Betters, than for any design to make enquiry into the solid Truth.

I will not launch my little Skif any further into the wide Ocean of this Dispute, only will I tell you, that the Praise and Commendation is not mean and slender which is due to those honest and good Women, who living chastly and without blame, have had the power and virtue to curb, range and subdue that unbridled, heady and wild *Animal*, to an obedient, submissive and obsequious yielding unto Reason. Therefore here will I make an end of my Discourse thereon, when I shall have told you, that the said *Animal* being once satiated (if it be possible that it can be contented or satisfied) by that Aliment, which Nature hath provided for it out of the Epididymal Store-house of Man, all its former and irregular and disordered Motions are at an end, laid and asswaged; all its vehement and unruly Longings lulled, pacified and quieted, and all the furious and raging Lusts, Appetites and Desires thereof appeased, suppressed, calmed and extinguished. For this cause, let it seem nothing strange unto you, if we be in a perpetual danger of being *Cuckolds*; that is to say, such of us as have not wherewithal fully to satisfie the Appetite and Expectation of the voracious Animal. Ods fish! (quoth *Panurge*) have you no preventive Cure in all your Medicinal Art for hindring one's Head to be Horny-graffed at home, whilst his Feet are plodding abroad? Yes that I have, my gallant Friend, (answered *Rondibilis*) and that which is a

428

sovereign Remedy, whereof I frequently make use my self; and
that you may the better relish, it is set down and written in the
Book of a most famous Author, whose Renown is of a standing
of two thousand Years, Hearken and take good heed. You are
(quoth *Panurge*) by *Cocks-hobby*, a right honest Man, and I love
you with all my heart: Eàt a little of this Quince-Pye it is very
proper and convenient for the shutting up of the Orifice of the
Ventricle of the Stomach; because of a kind of astringent Styp-
ticity which is in that sort of Fruit, and is helpful to the first
Concoction. But what? I think I speak *Latin* before *Clerks*. Stay,
fill, I give you somewhat to drink out of this *Nestorian* Goblet.
Will you have another Draught of White *Hippocras*? Be not afraid
of the Squinzy: No: There is neither Squinant, Ginger, nor
Grains in it; only a little Choice Cinnamon, and some of the best
refined Sugar, with the delicious White-wine of the Growth of
that Vine, which was set in the Slips of the great Sorbaple,
above the Walnut-tree.

CHAPTER XXXIII

Rondibilis the Physitian's Cure of Cuckoldry.

At that time (quoth Rondibilis) when *Jupiter* took a View of the
State of his *Olympick* House and Family, and that he had made
the Calendar of all the Gods and Goddesses, appointing unto
the Festival of every one of them its proper day and season,
establishing certain fixed places and stations for the pronouncing of Oracles, and relief of travelling pilgrims, and ordaining
Victims, Immolations and Sacrifices suitable and correspondent
to the Dignity and Nature of the worshipped and adored Deity.
Did not he do (asked *Panurge*) therein, as *Tintouille* the Bishop
of *Auxerre* is said once to have done? This Noble Prelate loved
entirely the pure Liquor of the Grape, as every honest and judicious Man doth; therefore was it that he had an especial care
and regard to the Bud of the Vine-tree, as to the Great-Grand-
father of *Bacchus*. But so it is, that for sundry Years together he
saw a most pitiful Havock, Desolation and Destruction made
amongst the Sprouts, Shootings, Buds, Blossoms and Sciens of
the Vines, by hoary Frosts, Dank-fogs, hot Mists, unseasonable

Colds, chill Blasts, thick Hail, and other calamitous Chances of
foul Weather happening, as he thought, by the dismal inauspi-
ciousness of the Holy days of St. *George*, St. *Mary*, St. *Paul*, St.
Eutrope, Holy Rood, the *Ascension*, and other Festivals, in that
time when the Sun passeth under the Sign of *Taurus*; and thereupon harboured in his Mind this Opinion, That the aforenamed
Saints were *Saint* Hail-flingers, *Saint* Frost-senders, *Saint* Fog-
mongers, and *Saint* Spoilers of the Vine-buds; for which cause
he went about to have transmitted their Feasts from the Spring
to the Winter, to be celebrated between *Christmas* and *Epiphany*,
(so the Mother of the *three Kings* called it) allowing them with all
Honour and Reverence the liberty then to freeze, hail and rain
as much as they would; for that he knew that at such a time
Frost was rather profitable than hurtful to the Vine-buds, and in
their steads to have placed the Festivals of St. *Christopher*, St. *John*
the *Baptist*, St. *Magdalene*, St. *Ann*, St. *Domingo*, and St. *Lawrence*;
yea, and to have gone so far as to collocate and transpose
the middle of *August*, in and to the beginning of *May*; because,
during the whole space of their Solemnity, there was so little
danger of hoary Frosts and cold Mists, that no Artificers are then
held in greater Request, than the Afforder of Refrigerating
Inventions, Makers of Junkets, fit Disposers of cooling Shades,
Composers of green Arbours, and Refreshers of Wine.

Jupiter (said *Rondibilis*) forgot the poor Devil *Cuckoldry*, who
was then in the Court at *Paris*, very eagerly solliciting a pedling
Suit at Law for one of his Vassals and Tenants; within some few
days thereafter, (I have forgot how many) when he got full notice of the Trick, which in his absence was done unto him, he
instantly desisted from prosecuting Legal Processes, in the behalf of others, full of Sollicitude to pursue after his own business, lest he should be fore-closed: And thereupon he appeared
personally at the Tribunal of the great *Jupiter*, displayed before
him the importance of his preceding Merits, together with the
acceptable Services, which, in Obedience to his Commandments,
he had formerly performed; and therefore, in all humility,
begged of him, that he would be pleased not to leave him alone
amongst all the Sacred Potentates, destitute and void of Honour, Reverence, Sacrifices, and Festivals Ceremonies. To this
Petition, *Jupiter*'s Answer was excusatory, That all the Places

and Offices of his House were bestowed. Nevertheless, so importuned was he by the continual Supplications of Monsieur *Cuckoldry*, that he, in fine, placed him in the Rank, List, Roll, Rubrick and Catalogue; and appointed Honours, Sacrifices, and Festival Rites to be observed on Earth in great Devotion, and tendred to him with Solemnity.

The Feast, because there was no void, empty, nor vacant Place in all the Calendar, was to be celebrated jointly with, and on the same Day that had been consecrated to the Goddess *Jealousie*: His Power and Dominion should be over Married Folks, especially such as had handsom Wives: His Sacrifices were to be, Suspicion, Diffidence, Mistrust, a lowring, powting, Sullenness, Watchings, Wardings, Researchings, Plyings, Explorations, together with the Waylayings, Ambushes, narrow Observations, and malicious Doggings of the Husband's Scouts and Espials of the most privy Actions of their Wives. Herewithal every married Man was expresly and rigorously commanded to reverence, honour and worship him; to celebrate and solemnize his Festival with twice more respect than that of another Saint or Deity, and to immolate unto him, with all Sincerity and Alacrity of Heart, the above-mentioned Sacrifices and Oblations, under pain of severe Censures, Threatnings, and Comminations of these subsequent Fines, Mulcts, Amerciaments, Penalties and Punishments to be inflicted on the Delinquents; that Monsieur *Cuckoldry* should never be favourable nor propitious to them; that he should never help, aid, supply, succour, nor grant them any subventitious Furtherance, auxiliary Suffrage, or adminiculary Assistance; that he should never hold in any Reckoning, Account, or Estimation; that he should never daign to enter within their Houses, neither at the Doors, Windows, nor any other Place thereof; that he should never haunt nor frequent their Companies or Conversations; how frequently soever they should invocate him, and call upon his Name; and that not only he should leave and abandon them to rot alone with their Wives in a sempiternal Solitariness, without the benefit of the Diversion of any Copesmate or Corrival at all; but should withal shun and eschew them, fly from them, and eternally forsake and reject them as impious Hereticks and sacrilegious Persons, according to the accustom'd manner of other Gods, towards such as are too slack in offering up the Duties and Reverences which ought to be performed respectively to their Divinities: As is evidently apparent in *Bacchus* towards negligent Vine-dressers; in *Ceres* against idle Plow-men and Tillers of the Ground; in *Pomona* to unworthy Fruiterers and Coster-mongers; in *Neptune* towards dissolute Mariners and Seà-faring Men; in *Vulcan* towards loytering Smiths and Forgemen; and so throughout the rest.

Now, on the contrary, this infallible Promise was added, that unto all those who should make a *Holy Day* of the above-recited Festival, and cease from all manner of worldly Work and Negotiation, lay aside all their own most important occasions, and to be so watchless, heedless, and careless of what might concern the management of their proper Affairs, as to mind nothing else but a suspicious espying and prying into the secret Deportments of their Wives, and how to koop, shut up, hold at under, and deal cruelly and austeerly with them, by all the Harshness and Hardships that an implacable, and every way inexorable Jealousie can devise and suggest, conform to the sacred Ordinances of the afore-mentioned Sacrifices and Oblations, he should be continually favourable to them, should love them, sociably converse with them, should be Day and Night in their Houses, and never leave them destitute of his Presence. Now I have said, and you have heard my Cure.

Ha, ha, ha, (quoth *Carpalin* laughing) this is a Remedy yet more apt and proper than *Hans Carvel*'s Ring: The Devil take me if I do not believe it. The Humour, Inclination and Nature of Women is like the Thunder, whose force in its Bolt, or otherways, burneth, bruiseth, and breaketh only hard, massive and resisting Objects, without staying or stopping at soft, empty and yielding matters: For it pasheth into pieces the Steel Sword, without doing any hurt to the Velvet Scabbard which insheatheth it: It rusheth also, and consumeth the Bones, without wounding or endammaging the Flesh, wherewith they are vailed and covered: Just so it is, that Women for the greater part never bend the Contention, Subtilty, and contradictory Disposition of their Spirits, unless it be to do what is prohibited and forbidden.

Verily, (quoth *Hippothadee*) some of our Doctors averr for a truth, that the first Woman of the World, whom the *Hebrews* call *Eve*, had hardly been induced or allured into the Temptation of eating of the Fruit of the *Tree of Life*, if it had not been forbidden her so to do. And that you may give the more Credit to the Validity of this Opinion, consider how the cautelous and wily Tempter did commemorate unto her, for an antecedent to his *Enthymeme*, the *Prohibition* which was made to taste it, as being desirous to infer from thènce, *It is forbidden thee; therefore thou shouldst eat of it, else thou canst not be a Woman.*

CHAPTER XXXIV

How Women ordinarily have the greatest longing after things prohibited.

WHEN I was (quoth *Carpalin*) a Whoremaster at *Orleans*, the whole Art of Rhetorick in all its Tropes and Figures, was not able to afford unto me a Colour or Flourish of greater force and value; nor could I by any other form or manner of Elocution pitch upon a more perswasive Argument for bringing young beautiful married Ladies into the Snares of Adultery, through alluring and inticing them to tast with me of Amorous Delights, than with a lively Sprightfulness to tell them in down-right terms, and to remonstrate to them (with a great shew of Detestation of a Crime so horrid) how their Husbands were jealous. This was none of my Invention: It is written, and we have Laws, Examples, Reasons and daily Experiences confirmative of the same. If this Belief once enter into their Noddles, their Husbands will infallibly be *Cuckolds*; yea, by God, will they, (without swearing) although they should do like *Semiramis*, *Pasiphae*, *Egesta*, the Women of the *Isle Mandez* in *Egypt*, and other such like Queanish flurting Harlots, mentioned in the Writings of *Herodotus*, *Strabo*, and such like Puppies.

Truly (quoth *Panocrates*) I have heard it related, and it hath been told me for a Verity, that Pope *Jhon* 22. passing on a day through the Abby of *Toucherome*, was in all Humility required and besought by the Abbess, and other discreet Mothers of the said Convent, to grant them an Indulgence, by means whereof they might confess themselves to one another, alledging, That *Religious* Women were subject to some petty secret Slips and Imperfections, which would be a foul and burning shame for them to discover and to reveal to Men, how Sacerdotal soever their

Function were: but that they would freelier, more familiarly, and with greater chearfulness, open to each other their Offences, Faults, and Escapes, under the Seal of Confession. There is not any thing (answered the Pope) fitting for you to impetrate of me, which I would not most willingly condescend unto: but I find one inconvenience; you know, *Confession should be kept secret*: and Women are not able to do so. Exceeding well (quoth they) most Holy Father, and much more closely than the best of Men.

The said Pope on the very same day, gave them in keeping a pretty Box, wherein he purposely caused a little Linnet to be put, willing them very gently and courteously to lock it up in some sure and hidden place; and promising them, by the *Faith of a Pope*, that he should yield to their Request, if they would keep secret what was enclosed within that deposited Box: enjoyning them withal, not to presume one way nor other, directly or indirectly, to go about the opening thereof, under pain of the highest Ecclesiastical Censure, Eternal Excommunication. The Prohibition was no sooner made, but that they did all of them boyl with a most ardent desire to know, and see what kind of thing it was that was within it: they thought long already, that the Pope was not gone, to the end they might joyntly, with the more leisure and ease apply themselves to the Box-opening Curiosity.

The Holy Father, after he had given them his Benediction, retired and withdrew himself to the Pontifical Lodgings of his own Palace: but he was hardly gone three Steps from without the Gates of their *Cloyster*, when the good Ladies throngingly, and as in a hudled Crowd, pressing hard on the Backs of one another, ran thrusting and shoving who should be first at the setting open of the forbidden Box, and descrying of the *Quod latitat* within.

On the very next day thereafter, the Pope made them another Visit, of a full design, purpose, and intention (as they imagined) to dispatch the Grant of their sought and wished-for Indulgence: But before he would enter into any Chat or Communing with them, he commanded the Casket to be brought unto him: it was done so accordingly; but by your leave, the Bird was no more there. Then was it that the Pope did represent to their *Maternities*, how hard a matter and difficult it was for them to keep Secrets revealed to them in *Confession*, unmanifested to the Ears of others; seeing for the space of Four and twenty hours they were not able to lay up in secret a Box, which he had highly recommended to their Discretion, Charge and Custody.

Welcome, in good Faith, my dear Master, welcome: It did me good to hear you talk, the Lord be praised for all. I do not remember to have seen you before now, since the last time that you acted at *Monpelliers*, with our ancient Friends, *Anthony Saporra, Guy Bourguyer, Balthasar Noyer, Tolly, Ihon Quentin, Francis Robinet, Jhon Perdrier*, and *Francis Rabelais*, the Moral Comedy of him who had espoused and married a *Dumb Wife*. I was there, quoth *Epistemon*; the good honest Man, her Husband, was very earnestly urgent to have the Fillet of her Tongue untied, and would needs have her speak by any means: at his desire some pains were taken on her, and partly by the industry of the Physitian, other part by the expertness of the Surgeon, the *Encyliglotte*, which she had under her Tongue, being cut, she spoke and spoke again; yea, within few hours she spoke so loud, so much, so fiercely, and so long, that her poor Husband returned to the same Physitian for a Recipe to make her hold her Peace: There are (quoth the *Physitian*) many proper Remedies in our Art, to make dumb Women speak, but there are none, that ever I could learn therein, to make them silent. The only Cure which I have found out, is their Husband's *Deafness*. The Wretch became within few Weeks thereafter, by Vertue of some Drugs, Charms or Enchantments, which the *Physitian* had prescribed unto him, so *deaf*, that he could not have heard the Thundring of Nineteen hundred Canons at a *Salve*. His Wife perceiving, that indeed he was as *deaf* as a Door-nail, and that her Scolding was but in vain, sith that he heard her not, she grew stark mad.

Some time after, the Doctor asked for his Fee of the Husband; who answered, That truly he was *deaf*, and so was not able to understand what the tenure of his Demand might be. Whereupon the Leech bedusted him with a little, I know not what, sort of Powder; which rendred him a Fool immediately: so great was the stiltificating Vertue of that strange kind of pulverized Dose. Then did this Fool of a Husband, and his mad Wife joyn together, falling on the Doctor and the Surgeon, did so scratch, bethwack, and bang them, that they were left half dead upon the place, so furious were the Blows which they received: I never in my Life-time laughed so much, as at the acting of that Buffoonry.

Let us come to where we left off, (quoth *Panurge*) your Words being translated from the Clapper-dudgions to plain English, do signifie, that it is not very inexpedient that I marry, and that I should not care for being a *Cuckold*. You have there hit the Nail on the Head. I believe, Master Doctor, that on the day of my Marriage you will be so much taken up with your Patients, or otherways so seriously employed, that we shall not enjoy your Company: Sir, I will heartily excuse your absence.

> *Stercus et urina medici sunt prandia prima.*
> *Ex aliis paleas, ex istis collige grana.*

You are mistaken (quoth *Rondibilis*) in the Second Verse of our Distich; for it ought to run thus:

> *Nobis sunt signa, vobis sunt prandia digna.*

If my Wife at any time prove to be unwell, and ill at ease, I will look upon the Water which she shall have made in an Urinal-glass, (quoth *Rondibilis*) grope her Pulse, and see the disposition of her *Hypogaster*, together with her Umbilicary Parts, according to the Prescript Rule of *Hippocrates*, 2 *Aph.* 35. before I proceed any further in the Cure of her Distemper. No, no, (quoth *Panurge*) that will be but to little purpose; such a Feat is for the Practice of us that are Lawyers, who have the Rubrick, *De Ventre inspiciendo*: Do not therefore trouble your self about it, (Master Doctor) I will provide for her a Plaister of warm Guts. Do not neglect your more urgent occasions otherwhere, for coming to my Wedding, I will send you some supply of Victuals to your own House, without putting you to the trouble of coming abroad, and you shall always be my special Friend. With this approaching somewhat nearer to him, he clapp'd into his Hand, without the speaking of so much as one word, four *Rose Nobles*. *Rondibilis* did shut his Fist upon them right kindly; yet as if it had displeased him to make acceptance of such Golden Presents; he in a start, as if he had been wroth, said, He, he, he, he, he, there was no need of any thing, I thank you nevertheless; *From wicked Folks, I never get enough*; and *I from honest People refuse nothing*. I shall be always, Sir, at your Command. Provided that I pay you well, quoth *Panurge*. That (quoth *Rondibilis*) is understood.

CHAPTER XXXV

*How the Philosopher Trouillogan handleth the difficulty of
Marriage.*

As this Discourse was ended, *Pantagruel* said to the Philosopher
Trouillogan, Our loyal, honest, true and trusty Friend, the Lamp
from hand to hand is come to you; it falleth to your turn to give
an Answer, Should *Panurge*, pray you, marry, yea or no? He should
do both, quoth *Trouillogan*. What say you, asked *Panurge*? That
which you have heard, answered *Trouillogan*. What have I
heard? replied *Panurge*. That which I have said, replied *Trouillogan*. Ha, ha, ha, are we come to that pass? quoth *Panurge*. Let
it go nevertheless, I do not value it at a rush, seeing we can
make no better of the Game. But howsoever tell me, Should I
marry or no? Neither the one nor the other, answered *Trouillogan*. The Devil take me, quoth *Panurge*, if these odd Answers do
not make me dote, and may he snatch me presently away, if I
do understand you. Stay awhile until I fasten these Spectacles
of mine on this left Ear, that I may hear you better. With this
Pantagruel perceived at the Door of the great Hall, (which was
that day their Dining-Room) *Gargantua*'s little Dog, whose
Name was Kyne; for so was *Toby*'s Dog called, as is recorded.
Then did he say to these who were there present, Our King is
not far off, let us all rise. That word was scarcely sooner uttered,
than that *Gargantua* with his Royal Presence graced that banqueting and stately Hall. Each of their Guests arose to do their
King that Reverence and Duty which became them. After that
Gargantua had most affably saluted all the Gentlemen there
present, he said, Good Friends, I beg this favour of you, and
therein you will very much oblige me, that you leave not the
places where you sate, nor quit the Discourse you were upon.

Let a Chair be brought hither unto this end of the Table, and
reach me a Cup full of the strongest and best Wine you have,
that I may drink to all the Company. You are in Faith, all welcom, Gentlemen. Now let me know what Talk you were about.
To this *Pantagruel* answered, That at the beginning of the Second Service *Panurge* had proposed a Problematick Theme, to

wit, *Whether he should marry, or not marry?* That Father *Hippotha-dee*, and Doctor *Rondibilis* had already dispatched their Resolutions thereupon; and that just as his Majesty was coming in, the faithful *Trouillogan*, in the delivery of his Opinion, hath thus far proceeded, that when *Panurge* asked, whether he ought to *marry, yea or no*, at first he made this Answer, *Both together.* When this same Question was again propounded, his second Answer was, *Not the one nor the other. Panurge* exclaimeth, that those Answers are full of Repugnancies and Contradictions, protesting that he understands them not, nor what it is that can be meaned by them. If I be not mistaken, quoth *Gargantua*, I understand it very well: The Answer is not unlike to that which was once made by a Philosopher in ancient times, who being interrogated, if he had a Woman, whom they named him, to his Wife; *I have her*, quoth he, but *she hath not me*; possessing her, by her I am not possest. Such another Answer, quoth *Pantagruel*, was once made by a certain bouncing Wench of *Sparta*, who being asked, if at any time she had had to do with a Man? No (quoth she) *but sometimes Men have to do with me.* Well then (quoth *Rondibilis*) let it be a *Neuter* in Physick; as when we say a body is *Neuter*, when it is neither sick nor healthful; and a *Mean* in Philosophy; *that* by an Abnegation of both Extreams, and *this* by the Participation of the one and of the other: Even as when lukewarm Water is said to be both hot and cold; or rather, as when Time makes the Partition, and equally divides betwixt the two, a while in the one, another while, as long, in the other opposite extremity. The holy Apostle, (quoth *Hippothadee*) seemeth, as I conceive, to have more clearly explained this Point, when he said, *Those that are married, let them be as if they were not married*; and those that have Wives, let them be as if they had no Wives at all. I thus interpret (quoth *Pantagruel*) the having and not having of a Wife. To have a Wife, is to have the use of her in such a way as Nature hath ordained, which is for the Aid, Society and Solace of Man, and propagating of his Race: To have no Wife is not to be uxorious, play the Coward, and be lazy about her, and not for her sake to distain the Lustre of that Affection which Man owes to God; or yet for her to leave those Offices and Duties which he owes unto his Country, unto his Friends and Kindred; or for her to abandon and forsake his precious Studies, and other businesses of Account, to wait still on her Will, her Beck, and her Buttocks. If we be pleased in this Sense to take having and not having of a Wife, we shall indeed find no Repugnancy nor Contradiction in the Terms at all.

CHAPTER XXXVI

A Continuation of the Answer of the Ephectick and Pyrronian Philosopher Trouillogan.

You speak wisely, quoth *Panurge*, if the Moon were Green Cheese; such a Tale once piss'd my Goose: I do not think but that I am let down into that dark Pit, in the lowermost bottom whereof the truth was hid, according to the saying of *Heraclitus*. I see no whit at all, I hear nothing, understand as little, my Senses are altogether dull'd and blunted; truly I do very shrewdly suspect that I am enchanted. I will now alter the former style of my Discourse, and talk to him in another Strain. Our trusty Friend, stir not, nor imburse any; but let us vary the Chance, and speak without Disjunctives: I see already that these loose and ill-joined Members of an Enunciation do vex, trouble, and perplex you.

Now go on, in the Name of God, *Should I marry?*

Trouillogan. There is some likelyhood therein.

Panurge. But if I do not marry?

Trouil. I see in that no Inconvenience.

Pan. You do not?

Trouil. None, truly, if my Eyes deceive me not.

Pan. Yea, but I find more than Five Hundred.

Trouil. Reckon them.

Pan. This is an Impropriety of Speech, I confess; for I do no more thereby, but take a certain for an uncertain Number, and posit the determinate Term for what is indeterminate. When I say therefore Five Hundred, my meaning is, many.

Trouil. I hear you.

Pan. Is it possible for me to live without a Wife, in the Name of all the Subterranean Devils?

Trouil. Away with these filthy Beasts.

Pan. Let it be then in the Name of God; for my *Salmigondinish* People use to say, *To lie alone without a Wife, is certainly a brutish Life.* And such a Life also was it assevered to be by *Dido* in her Lamentations.

Trouil. At your Command.

Pan. By the Pody Cody, I have fished fair; where are we now? But will you tell me? Shall I marry?

Trouil. Perhaps.

Pan. Shall I thrive or speed well withal?

Trouil. According to the Encounter.

Pan. But if in my Adventure I encounter aright, as I hope I will, shall I be fortunate?

Trouil. Enough.

Pan. Let us turn the clean contrary way, and brush our former Words against the Wool; what if I encounter ill?

Trouil. Then blame not me.

Pan. But, of Courtesie, be pleased to give me some Advice: I heartily beseech you, what must I do?

Trouil. Even what thou wilt.

Pan. Wishy, washy; Trolly, Trolly.

Trouil. Do not invocate the Name of any thing, I pray you.

Pan. In the Name of God, let it be so: My Actions shall be regulated by the Rule and Square of your Counsel: What is it that you advise and counsel me to do?

Trouil. Nothing.

Pan. Shall I marry?

Trouil. I have no hand in it.

Pan. Then shall I not marry?

Trouil. I cannot help it.

Pan. If I never marry, I shall never be a Cuckold.

Trouil. I thought so.

Pan. But put the case that I be married.

Trouil. Where shall we put it?

Pan. Admit it be so then, and take my meaning in that sence.

Trouil. I am otherways employed.

Pan. By the Death of a Hog, and Mother of a Toad, O Lord, if I durst hazard upon a little Fling at the swearing Game, though privily and under Thumb, it would lighten the burthen of my Heart, and ease my Lights and Reins exceedingly; a little Patience nevertheless is requisite. Well then, if I marry, I shall be a Cuckold.

Trouil. One would say so.

Pan. Yet if my Wife prove a vertuous, wise, discreet and chaste woman, I shall never be Cuckolded.

Trouil. I think you speak congruously.

Pan. Hearken.

Trouil. As much as you will.

Pan. Will she be discreet and chaste? This is the only Point I would be resolved in.

Trouil. I question it.

Pan. You never saw her?

Trouil. Not that I know of.

Pan. Why do you then doubt of that which you know not?

Trouil. For a Cause.

Pan. And if you should know her.

Trouil. Yet more.

Pan. Page, my pretty little Darling, take here my Cap, I give it thee: Have a care you do not break the Spectacles that are in it; go down to the lower Court, Swear there half an hour for me, and I shall in compensation of that Favour swear hereafter for thee as much as thou wilt. But who shall Cuckold me?

Trouil. Some body.

Pan. By the Belly of the wooden Horse at *Troy*, Master *Somebody*, I shall bang, belam thee, and claw thee well for thy labour.

Trouil. You say so.

Pan. Nay, nay, that *Nick* in the dark Celler, who hath no white in his Eye, carry me quite away with him, if, in that case, whensoever I go abroad from the Palace of my Domestick Residence, I do not with as much Circumspection, as they use to ring Mares in our Country to keep them from being sallied by Stoned Horses, clap a *Bergamasco* Lock upon my Wife.

Trouil. Talk better.

Pan. It is *Bien chien chié chanté*, well cacked, and cackled; shitten, and sung in matter of Talk: Let us resolve on somewhat.

Trouil. I do not gainsay it.

Pan. Have a little patience, seeing I cannot on this side draw any Blood of you. I will try, if with the Launcet of my Judgment, I be able to bleed you in another Vein. Are you married, or are you not?

Trouil. Neither the one, nor the other, and both together.

Pan. O the good God help us; by the Death of a Buffle-ox, I sweat with the toyl and travel that I am put to, and find my Digestion broke off, disturbed, and interrupted for all my *Phrenes*, *Metaphrenes*, and *Diaphragmes*, Back, Belly, Midrif, Muscles, Veins, and Sinews are held in a suspence, and for a while discharged from their proper Offices, to stretch forth their several Powers and Abilities, for *Incornifistibulating*, and laying up into the Hamper of my Understanding, your various Sayings and Answers.

Trouil. I shall be no hinderer thereof.

Pan. Tush, for shame: Our faithful Friend, speak, Are you married?

Trouil. I think so.

Pan. You were also married before you had this Wife.

Trouil. It is possible.

Pan. Had you good Luck in your first Marriage?

Trouil. It is not impossible.

Pan. How thrive you with this Second Wife of yours?

Trouil. Even as it pleaseth my Fatal Destiny.

Pan. But what in good earnest? tell me: Do you prosper well with her?

Trouil. It is likely.

Pan. But on, in the Name of God: I vow, by the Burthen of Saint *Christopher*, that I had rather undertake the fetching of a Fart forth of the Belly of a dead Ass, than to draw out of you a positive and determinate Resolution: yet shall I be sure at this time to have a snatch at you, and get my Claws over you. Our trusty Friend, let us shame the Devil of Hell, and confess the verity: Were you ever a Cuckold? I say, you who are here, and not that other you who playeth below in the Tennis-Court?

Trouil. No, if it was not predestinated.

Pan. By the Flesh, Blood, and Body, I swear, reswear, forswear, abjure, and renounce, he evades and avoids, shifts, and escapes me, and quite slips and winds himself out of my Gripes and Clutches.

At these words *Gargantua* arose, and said, praised be the good God in all things, but especially for bringing the World into that height of Refinedness, beyond what it was when I first came to be acquainted therewith, that now the Learnedst and most prudent Philosophers are not ashamed to be seen entring in at the Porches and Frontispieces of the Schools of the *Pyrronian*, *Aporetick*, *Sceptick*, and *Ephectick* Sects: Blessed be the Holy Name of God, veritably, it is like henceforth to be found an Enterprize of much more easie undertaking, to catch Lyons by the Neck, Horses by the Main, Oxen by the Horns, Bulls by the Muzzle, Wolves by the Tail, Goats by the Beard, and flying Birds by the Feet, then to intrap such Philosophers in their words. Farewel, my worthy, dear, and honest Friends.

When he had done thus speaking, he withdrew himself from the Company; *Pantagruel*, and others with him would have followed and accompanied him, but he would not permit them so to do. No sooner was *Gargantua* departed out of the Banquetting-Hall, than that *Pantagruel* said to the invited Guests: *Plato*'s *Timee*, at the *Beginning* always of a solemn Festival Convention, was wont to count those that were called thereto; we on the contrary, shall at the Closure and *End* of this Treatment, reckon up our Number, One, Two, Three; Where is the Fourth? I miss my Friend *Bridlegoose*: Was not he sent for? *Epistemon* answered, That he had been at his House to bid and invite him; but could not meet with him: For that a Messenger from the Parliament of *Mirlingois*, in *Mirlingues*, was come for him, with a Writ of Summons, to cite and warn him personally to appear before the Reverend *Senators* of the High Court there, to vindicate and justifie himself at the Bar, of the Crime of *Prevarication* laid to his charge, and to be peremptorily instanced against him in a certain Decree, Judgment, or Sentence lately awarded, given and pronounced by him: and that therefore he had taken Horse, and departed in great hast from his own House; to the end, that without peril or danger of falling into a default, or contumacy, he might be the better able to keep the perfixed and appointed time.

I will (quoth *Pantagruel*) understand how that matter goeth; it is now above Forty Years, that he hath been constantly the Judge of *Fonsbeton*: during which space of time, he hath given four thousand Definitive Sentences: Of two thousand three hundred and nine whereof, although appeal was made by the Parties whom he had judicially condemned from his inferiour

Judicatory, to the Supream Court of the Parliament of *Mirling-ois*, in *Mirlingues* they were all of them nevertheless confirmed, ratified and approved of by an Order, Decree, and final Sentence of the said Sovereign Court, to the casting of the *Appellants*, and utter overthrow of the Suits wherein they had been foiled at Law, for ever and a day: that now in his old Age he should be personally summoned, who in all the foregoing time of his Life, hath demeaned himself so unblamably in the Discharge of the Office and Vocation he had been called unto; it cannot assuredly be, that such a change hath happened without some notorious Misfortune and Disaster: I am resolved to help and assist him in Equity and Justice to the uttermost extent of my power and ability. I know the Malice, Despight, and Wickedness of the World to be so much more now-a-days exaspered, increased, and aggravated by what it was not long since, that the best Cause that is, how just and equitable soever it be, standeth in great need to be succoured, aided and supported. Therefore presently, from this very instant forth, do I purpose, till I see the event and closure thereof, most heedfully to attend and wait upon it, for fear of some under-hand tricky Surprizal, Cavilling, Pettifoggery, or fallacious Quirks in Law, to his detriment, hurt, or disadvantage.

Then Dinner being done, and the Tables drawn and removed, when *Pantagruel* had very cordially and affectionately thanked his invited Guests, for the favour which he had enjoyed of their Company, he presented them with several rich and costly Gifts, such as Jewels, Rings set with precious Stones, Gold and Silver Vessels, with a great deal of other sort of Plate besides; and lastly, taking of them all his Leave, retired himself into an inner Chamber.

CHAPTER XXXVII

How Pantagruel perswaded Panurge to take Counsel of a Fool.

WHEN *Pantagruel* had withdrawn himself, he by a little sloping Window in one of the Galleries, perceived *Panurge* in a Lobbey not far from thence, walking alone, with the Gesture, Carriage, and Garb of a fond Dotard, raving, wagging, and shaking his

Hands, dandling, lolling and nodding with his Head, like a Cow bellowing for her Calf; and having then called him nearer, spoke unto him thus: You are at this present (as I think) not unlike to a Mouse intangled in a Snare, who the more that she goeth about to rid and unwind her self out of the Gin wherein she is caught, by endeavouring to clear and deliver her feet from the Pitch whereto they stick, the foulier she is bewrayed with it, and the more strongly pestered therein; even so is it with you: For the more that you labour, strive, and inforce your self to disincumber, and extricate your Thoughts out of the implicating Involutions and Fetterings of the grievous and lamentable Gins and Springs of Anguish and Perplexity; the greater difficulty there is in the relieving of you, and you remain faster bound than ever: nor do I know for the removal of this Inconveniency, any Remedy but one.

Take heed; I have often heard it said in a Vulgar Proverb, The *Wise may be instructed by a Fool*. Seeing the Answers and Responses of sage and judicious Men have in no manner of way satisfied you, take advice of some Fool; and possibly by so doing, you may come to get that Councel which will be agreeable to your own Heart's desire and contentment. You know how by the Advice and Councel and Prediction of *Fools*, many Kings, Princes, States, and Commonwealths have been preserved, several Battels gained, and divers doubts of a most perplexed Intricacy resolved: I am not so diffident of your Memory, as to hold it needful to refresh it with a Quotation of Examples, nor do I so far undervalue your Judgment, but that I think it will acquiesce in the Reason of this my subsequent Discourse.

As he who narrowly takes heed to what concerns the dextrous Management of his private Affairs, domestick Businesses and those Adoes which are confined within the streight-lac'd compass of one Family: who is attentive, vigilant, and active in the œconomick Rule of his own House; whose frugal Spirit never strays from home; who loseth no occasion, whereby he may purchase to himself more Riches, and build up new heaps of Treasure on his former Wealth; and who knows warily how to prevent the Inconveniences of Poverty, is called a worldly Wise Man, though perhaps in the second Judgment of the Intelligences which are above, he be esteemed a *Fool*. So on the contrary, is he most like (even in the thoughts of all Cœlestial Spirits) to be not only *sage*, but to *presage* Events to come by Divine Inspiration, who laying quite aside those Cares which are conducible to his Body or his Fortunes, and as it were departing from himself, rids all his Senses of Terrene Affections, and clears his Fancies of those plodding Studies, which harbour in the Minds of thriving Men: All which neglects of Sublunary Things are vulgarly imputed *Folly*.

After this manner, the Son of *Picus*, King of the *Latins*, that great Southsayer *Faunus*, was called *Fatuus*, by the witless Rabble of the common People. The like we daily see practised amongst the Commick Players, whose Drammatick Rolls, in distribution of the Personages, appoint the acting of the *Fool* to him who is the wisest of the Troop. In approbation also of this fashion, the *Mathematicians* allow the very same *Horoscope* to Princes, and to Sots. Whereof a right pregnant instance by them is given in the Nativities of *Æneas* and *Chorœbus*; the latter of which two is by *Euphorion* said to have been a *Fool*: and yet had with the former the same *Aspects*, and Heavenly *Genethlick* Influences.

I shall not, I suppose, swerve much from the purpose in hand, if I relate unto you, what *Ihon Andrew* said upon the Return of a *Papal Writ*, which was directed to the Mayor of *Rochel* and Burgesses; after him by *Panorm*, upon the same Pontifical Canon; *Barbatia*, on the *Pandects*; and recently by *Jason*, in his councels; concerning *Seyny Ihon* the noted Fool of *Paris*, and *Caillets* fore-great Grandfather. The Case is this:

At *Paris*, in the Roast-meat Cookery of the *Petit Chastelet*, before the Cook-shop of one of the Roast-meat Sellers of that Lane, a certain hungry Porter was eating his Bread, after he had by Parcels kept it a while above the Reek and Steam of a fat Goose on the Spit, turning at a great Fire, and found it so besmoaked with the Vapour, to be savoury; which the Cook observing, took no notice, till after having ravined his Penny Loaf, whereof no Morsel had been unsmoakified, he was about discamping and going away; but by your leave, as the Fellow thought to have departed thence shot-free, the Master-Cook laid hold upon him by the Gorget, demanded payment for the Smoak of his Roast-meat. The Porter answered, that he had sustained no loss at all; that by what he had done there was no Diminution made of the Flesh, that he had taken nothing of his, and that therefore he was not indebted to him in any thing: As for the Smoak in question, that, although he had not been there, it would howsoever have been evaporated: Besides that, before that time it had never been seen nor heard, that Roast-meat Smoak was sold upon the Streets of *Paris*. The Cook hereto replied, That he was not obliged nor any way bound to feed and nourish for nought a Porter whom he had never seen before with the Smoak of his Roast-meat; and thereupon swore, that if he would not forthwith content and satisfie him with present Payment for the Repast which he had thereby got, that he would take his crooked Staves from off his Back; which instead of having Loads thereafter laid upon them, should serve for Fuel to his Kitchen Fires. Whilst he was going about so to do, and to have pulled them to him by one of the bottom Rungs, which he had caught in his Hand, the sturdy Porter got out of his Gripes, drew forth the knotty Cudgel, and stood to his own Defence. The Altercation waxed hot in Words, which moved the gaping Hoydons of the sottish *Parisians* to run from all parts therabouts to see what the issue would be of that babling Strife and Contention. In the interim of this Dispute, to very good purpose, *Seiny Ihon* the Fool and Citizen of *Paris*, hapned to be there, whom the Cook perceiving, said to the Porter, Wilt thou refer and submit unto the noble *Seiny Ihon*, the Decision of the Difference and Controversie which is betwixt us? Yes, by the blood of a Goose, answered the Porter, I am content. *Seiny Ihon* the *Fool*, finding that the Cook and Porter had compromised the Determination of their Variance and Debate to the Discretion of his Award and Arbitriment; after that the Reasons on either side whereupon was grounded the mutual fierceness of their brawling Jar had been to the full displayed and laid open before him, commanded the Porter to draw out of the Fab of his Belt a piece of Money, if he had it. Whereupon the Porter immediately without delay, in Reverence to the Authority of such a Judicious Umpire, put the tenth part of a Silver *Phillip* into his Hand. This little *Phillip Seiny Ihon* took, then set it on his left Shoulder, to try by feeling if it was of a sufficient weight; after that, laying it on the palm of his Hand he made it ring and tingle, to understand by the Ear if it was of a good Alloy in the Metal whereof it was composed:

Thereafter he put it to the Ball or Apple of his Left Eye, to explore by the sight if it was well stamped and marked; all which being done, in a profound Silence of the whole doltish People, who were there Spectators of this Pageantry, to the great hope of the Cooks, and despair of the Porters Prevalency in the Suit that was in agitation, he finally caused the Porter to make it sound several times upon the Stal of the Cooks Shop. Then with a *Presidential Majesty* holding his Bable (Scepter-like) in his Hand, muffling his Head with a Hood of Martern Skins, each side whereof had the resemblance of an Ape's Face, sprucified up with Ears of pasted Paper, and having about his neck a bucked Ruff, raised, furrowed, and ridged, with Ponting Sticks of the shape and fashion of small Organ-Pipes; he first, with all the force of his Lungs, coughed two or three times, and then with an audible Voice pronounced this following Sentence, The Court declareth, *That the Porter, who ate his Bread at the Smoak of the Roast, hath civilly paid the Cook with the Sound of his Money*: And the said Court *Ordaineth*, That every one return to his own home, and attend his proper business, without Cost and Charges, and for a Cause. This Verdict, Award and Arbitriment of the *Parisian Fool*, did appear so equitable, yea, so admirable to the aforesaid *Doctors*, that they very much doubted, if the Matter had been brought before the *Sessions for Justice* of the said Place, or that the Judges of the *Rota* at *Rome* had been Umpires therein; or yet that the *Areopagites* themselves had been the Deciders thereof, if by any one part, or all of them together, it had been so judicially sententiated and awarded. Therefore advise, if you will be counselled by a *Fool*.

CHAPTER XXXVIII

How Triboulet is set forth and blazed by Pantagruel and Panurge.

BY my Soul, (quoth *Panurge*) that Overture pleaseth me exceedingly well; I will therefore lay hold thereon, and embrace it. At the very motioning thereof my very *Right Entral* seemeth to be widened and enlarged, which was but just now hard bound, contracted and costive: but as we have hitherto made choice of the

purest and most refined Cream of Wisdom and Sapience for our
Counsel, so would I now have to preside and bear the prime
Sway in our Consultation as were a *Fool* in the supreme degree.
Triboulet (quoth *Pantagruel*) is compleatly *foolish*, as I conceive.
Yes, truly, (answered *Panurge*) he is properly and totally a *Fool*, a

Pantagruel.	*Panurge.*
Fatal f.	Jovial f.
Natural f.	Mercurial f.
Celestial f.	Lunatick f.
Erratick f.	Ducal f.
Excentrick f.	Common f.
Ætherial and Junonian f.	Lordly f.
Arctick f.	Palatin f.
Heroick f.	Principal f.
Genial f.	Pretorian f.
Inconstant f.	Elected f.
Earthly f.	Courtly f.
Solacious and sporting f.	Primipilary f.
Jocund and wanton f.	Triumphant f.
Pimpled f.	Vulgar f.
Freckled f.	Domestick f.
Bell-tinging f.	Exemplary f.
Laughing and lecherous f.	Rare outlandish f.
Nimming and filching f.	Satrapal f.
Unpressed f.	Civil f.
First broached f.	Popular f.
Augustal f.	Familiar f.
Cesarine f.	Notable f.
Imperial f.	Favourized f.
Royal f.	Latinized f.
Patriarchal f.	Ordinary f.
Original f.	Transcendent f.
Loyal f.	Rising f.
Episcopal f.	Papal f.
Doctoral f.	Consistorian f.
Monachal f.	Conclavist f.
Fiscal f.	Bullist f.
Extravagant f.	Synodal f.
Writhed f.	Doating and raving f.
	Singular and surpassing f.

RABELAIS

Pantagruel.	*Panurge.*
Canonical f.	Special and excelling f.
Such another f.	Metaphysical f.
Graduated f.	Scatical f.
Commensal f.	Predicamental and cata-
Primolicentiated f.	gorick f.
Trainbairing f.	Predicable and enuncia-
Supererrogating f.	tory f.
Collateral f.	Decumane and superla-
Haunch and side f.	tive f.
Nestling, ninny, and	Dutiful and officious f.
youngling f.	Optical and perspective f.
Flitting, giddy, and un-	Algoristick f.
steddy f.	Algebraical f.
Brancher, novice, and	Cabalistical and masso-
cockney f.	retical f.
Hagard, cross, and fro-	Talmudical f.
ward f.	Algamalized f.
Gentle, mild, and tract-	Compendious f.
able f.	Abbreviated f.
Mail-coated f.	Hyperbolical f.
Pilfring and purloining f.	Anatomastical f.
Tail-grown f.	Allegorical f.
Gray-peckled f.	Tropological f.
Pleonasmical f.	Micher pincrust f.
Capital f.	Heteroclit f.
Hairbrained f.	Summist f.
Cordial F.	Abbridging f.
Intimate f.	Morrish f.
Hepatick f.	Leaden-sealed f.
Cushotten and swilling f.	Mandatory f.
Splenetick f.	Compassionate f.
Windy f.	Titulary f.
Legitimate f.	Crooching, showking,
Azymathal f.	ducking f.
Almicautarized f.	Grim, stern, harsh, and
Proportioned f.	wayward f.
Chinnified f.	Well-hung and timbred f.
Swollen and puffed	Ill-clawed, pounced and
up f.	pawed f.

Pantagruel.	*Panurge.*
Overcockrifedid and li-fied f.	Well-stoned f.
Corallery f.	Crabbed and unpleasing f.
Eastern f.	Winded and tainted f.
Sublime f.	Kitchen-haunting f.
Crimson f.	Lofty and stately f.
Ingrained f.	Spitrack f.
City f.	Architrave f.
Basely accoutred f.	Pedestal f.
Mast-headed f.	Tetragonal f.
Modal f.	Renowned f.
Second notial f.	Reumatick f.
Chearful and buxom f.	Flaunting and bragga-dochio f.
Solemn f.	Egregious f.
Annual f.	Humorous and capri-cious f.
Festival f.	
Recreative f.	
Boorish and counterfeit f.	Rude, gross, and absurd f.
Pleasant f.	
Privileged f.	Large-measured f.
Rustical f.	Bable f.
Proper and peculiar f.	Down-right f.
Ever ready f.	Broad-lifted f.
Diapasonal f.	Downsical-bearing f.
Resolute f.	Stale and overworn f.
Hieroglyphical f.	Sawcy and swaggering f.
Authentick f.	Full bulked f.
Worthy f.	Gallant and vainglorious f.
Precious f.	
Fanatick f.	Gorgeous and gawdy f.
Fantastical f.	Continual and intermit-ting f.
Lymphatick f.	
Panick f.	Rebasing and roundling f.
Limbicked and distilled f.	Prototypal and prece-denting f.
Comportable f.	
Wretched and heartless f.	Prating f.
Fooded f.	Catechetick f.
Thick and threefold f.	Cacodoxical f.
Damasked f.	Meridional f.

Pantagruel.	*Panurge.*
Fearny f.	Nocturnal f.
Unleavened f.	Occidental f.
Barytonant f.	Trifling f.
Pink and spot-poudered f.	Astrological and figure-flinging f.
Musket-proof f.	Genethliack and horo-scopal f.
Pendantick f.	
Strouting f.	Knavish f.
Wood f.	Idiot f.
Greedy f.	Blockish f.
Senseless f.	Beetle-headed f.
Godderlich f.	Grotesk f.
Obstinate f.	Impertinent f.
Contradictory f.	Quarrelsom f.
Pedagogical f.	Unmannerly f.
Daft f.	Captious and Sophistical f.
Drunken f.	
Peevish f.	Soritick f.
Prodigal f.	Catholoproton f.
Rash f.	Hoti and Dioti f.
Plodding f.	Aaplos and Catati f.

Pantagruel. If there was any reason why at *Rome* the *Quirinal* Holiday, of old, was called, The Feast of *Fools*; I know not why we may not for the like cause institute in *France* the *Tribouletick* Festivals, to be celebrated and solemnized over all the Land.

Panurge. If all *Fools* carried Cruppers.

Pantagruel. If he were the God *Fatuus*, of whom we have already made mention, the Husband of the Goddess *Fatua*, his Father would be *Good Day*, and his Grandmother *Good Even*.

Panurge. If all Fools *paced*, albeit he be somewhat wry-legg'd, he would overlay at least a Fathom at every Rake. Let us go toward him, without any further lingring or delay, we shall have, no doubt, some fine Resolution of him. I am ready to go, and long for the issue of our Progress impatiently. I must needs (quoth *Pantagruel*) according to my former Resolution of him, be present at *Bridlegoose*'s Tryal: Nevertheless, whilst I shall be upon my Journey towards *Mirelingues*, which is on the other side of the River of *Loire*, I will dispatch *Carpalin* to bring along with him from *Blois* the *Fool Triboulet*. Then was *Carpalin* instantly sent away, and *Pantagruel* at the same time, attended by his *Domesticks*, *Panurge*, *Epistemon*, *Ponocrates*, Fryar *Ihon*, *Gymnast*, *Rysotome*, and others, marched forward on the High Road to *Mirelingues*.

CHAPTER XXXIX

How Pantagruel was present at the tryal of Judge Bridlegoose, who decided Causes and Controversies in Law, by the Chance and Fortune of the Dice.

ON the Day following, precisely at the Hour appointed, *Pantagruel* came to *Mirelingues*: At his Arrival, the Presidents, Senators and Counsellors prayed him to do them the honour to enter in with them, to hear the Dicision of all the Causes, Arguments and Reasons, which *Bridlegoose* in his own Defence would produce, why he had pronounced a certain Sentence against the Subsidy-Assessor, *Toucheronde*; which did not seem very equitable to that *Centumviral Court. Pantagruel* very willingly condescended to their desire; and accordingly entring in, found *Bridlegoose* sitting within the middle of the Inclosure of the said Court of Justice; who immediately, upon the coming of *Pantagruel*, accompanied with the Senatorian Members of that worshipful Judicatory, arose, went to the Bar, had his Indictment read; and for all his Reasons, Defences, and Excuses, answered nothing else, but that he was become Old, and that his Sight of late was very much failed, and become dimmer than it was wont to be; instancing therewithal many Miseries and Calamities which Old Age bringeth along with it, and are concomitant to wrinkled Elders; which *not. per Archid., d. lxxxvj, c. tanta*: by reason of which Infirmity, he was not able so distinctly and clearly to discern the *Points* and *Blots* of the *Dice*, as formerly he had been accustomed to do: whence it might very well have happened, said he, as old dim-sighted *Isaac* took *Jacob* for *Esau*, that I after the same manner, at the Decision of Causes and Controversies in Law, should have been mistaken in taking a *Quatre* for a *Cinque*, or *Tre* for a *Deuce*: This, I beseech your Worship (quoth he) to take into your serious Consideration, and to have the more favourable opinion of my Uprightness (notwithstanding the *Prevarication* whereof I am accused, in the Matter of *Touche-*

rondy's Sentence) that at the time of that Decree's pronouncing, I only had made use of my small *Dice*; and your Worships (said he) knew very well, how by the most Authentick Rules of the Law, it is provided, That *the Imperfections of Nature* should never be *imputed* unto any for Crimes and Transgressions; as appeareth, *§ de re milit., l. qui cum uno; § de reg. jur., l. fere; § de edil. ed. per totum; § de term. mo., l. Divus Adrianus; resolu. per Lud. Ro. in. l.: si vero, § solu. matri.* And who would offer to do otherways, should not thereby accuse the Man, but Nature, and the All-seeing Providence of God, as is evident *in l. maximum vitium, C. de lib. praeter.*

What kind of *Dice* (quoth *Trinquamelle*, grand President of the said Court) do you mean, my Friend *Bridlegoose*? The *Dice* (quoth *Bridlegoose*) of Sentences at Law, Decrees, and peremptory Judgments, *Alea Judiciorum*, whereof is written, *Per doct. 26. q. ij. c. sors; l. nec emptio, § de contrah. empt.; l. quod debetur, § de pecul., et ibi Barthol.* And which your Worships do, as well as I, use, in this glorious Sovereign Court of yours: so do all other righteous Judges, in their Decision of Processes, and Final Determination of Legal Differences, observing that which hath been said thereof by *D. Henri. Ferraudet, et no. gl. in c. fin. de sortil. & l. sed cum ambo, § de judi., ubi doct.* Where mark, that Chance and Fortune, are good, honest, profitable and necessary for ending of, and putting a final closure to Dissensions and Debates in Suits at Law. The same hath more clearly been declared by *Bal. Bart. & Alex. C. communia de l. Si duo.* But how is it that you do these things? (asked *Trinquemelle.*) I very briefly (quoth *Bridlegoose*) shall answer you, according to the Doctrine and Instructions of *l. Ampliorem, § in refutatoriis, C. de appella.* Which is conform to what is said in *Gl. l. j. § quod met. cau. Gaudent brevitate moderni.* My Practice is therein the same with that of your other Worships, and as the Custom of the Judicatory requires, unto which our Law commandeth us to have regard, and by the Rule thereof still to direct and regulate our Actions and Procedures. *ut, no. extra. de consuet., c. ex literis, et ibi Innoc.:* for having well and exactly seen, surveyed, overlooked, reviewed, recognised, read, and read over again, turned and tossed over, seriously perused and examined the Bills of Complaint, Accusations, Impeachments, Indictments, Warnings, Citations,

Summonings, Comparitions, Appearances, Mandates, Commissions, Delegations, Instructions, Informations, Inquests, Preparatories, Productions, Evidences, Proofs, Allegations, Depositions, cross Speeches, Contradictions, Supplications, Requests, Petitions, Enquiries, Instruments of the Deposition of Witnesses, Rejoinders, Replies, Confirmations of former Assertions, Duplies, Triplies, Answers to Rejoinders, Writings, Deeds, Reproaches, disabling of Exceptions taken, Grievances, Salvation-Bills, Re-examination of Witnesses, Confronting of them together, Declarations, Denunciations, Libels, Certificates, Royal Missives, Letters of Appeal, Letters of Attorney, Instruments of Compulsion, Declinatories, Anticipatories, Evocations, Messages, Dismissions, Issues, Exceptions, dilatory Pleas, Demurs, Compositions, Injunctions, Reliefs, Reports, Returns, Confessions, Acknowledgments, Exploits, Executions, and other such-like Confects and Spiceries, both at the one and the other Side, as a good Judge ought to do, conform to what hath been noted thereupon. *Spec., de ordinario,* § *iij & tit. de offi. om. ju.,* § *fi., & de rescriptis praesenta.,* § *j.* I posit on the end of a Table in my Closet, all the Poaks and Bags of the *Defendant,* and then allow unto him the first hazard of the *Dice*; according to the usual manner of your other Worships. And it is mentioned, *l. Favorabiliores,* § *de reg. jur., et in c. cum sunt, eod. tit. lib. vj,* which saith, *Cum sunt partium jura obscura, reo potius favendum est quam actori.* That being done, I thereafter lay down upon the other end of the same Table, the Bags and Sachels of the Plaintiff, (as your other Worships are accustomed to do) *Visum Visu,* just over-against one another; for, *opposita, juxta se posita, magis elucescunt, ut not. in l. j,* § *videamus,* § *de his qui sunt sui vel alie. jur., et in l. munerum j. mixta,* § *de muner. et honor.* Then do I likeways, and semblably throw the *Dice* for him, and forthwith *livre* him his chance. But, (quoth *Trigamelle*) my Friend, how come you to know, understand and resolve the obscurity of these various and seeming contrary Passages in Law, which are laid claim to by the Suitors, and pleading Parties? Even just (quoth *Bridlegoose*) after the fashion of your other Worships; to wit, when there are many Bags on the one side, and on the other, I then use my little small *Dice* (after the customary manner of your other Worships) in obedience to the Law *Semper in stipulationibus,* § *de reg.*

jur. The Law verified, verifieth that, *eod. tit. Semper in obscuris quod nimium est sequimur*: Canonized in *c., in obscuris, eod. tit. lib. vj*. I have other large great *Dice*, fair, and goodly ones, which I employ in the fashion that your other Worships use to do, when the Matter is more plain, clear and liquid; that is to say, when there are fewer Bags. But when you have done all these fine things (quoth *Triquamel*) how do you, my Friend, award your Decrees, and pronounce Judgment? Even as your other Worships (answered *Bridlegoose*) for I give out Sentence in his favour, unto whom hath befallen the *best Chance* by *Dice*; Judiciary, Tribunian, Pretorial, what comes first: So our Laws command. *§. qui po. in pig., l. potior. leg. creditor., C. de consul., l. j, et de reg. jur., in vj: Qui prior est tempore potior est jure.*

CHAPTER XL

How Bridlegoose giveth Reasons, why he looked upon those Law-Actions which he decided by the Chance of the Dice.

YEA, but (quoth *Trinquamel*) my Friend, seeing it is by the Lot, Chance, and Throw of the Dice that you award your Judgments and Sentences, why do not you *livre* up these fair Throws and Chances the very same Day and Hour, without any further procrastination or delay, that the controverting Party-pleaders appear before you? To what use can those Writings serve you, those Papers, and other Procedures contained in the Bags and Poaks of the Law-Suitors? To the very same use (quoth *Bridlegoose*) that they serve your other Worships, They are behooful unto me, and serve my turn in three things very exquisite, requisite, and authentical. *First*, for *Formality* sake, the omission whereof, that it maketh all whatever is done, to be of no force nor value, is excellently well proved, by *Spec., tit. de instr. edi. et tit. de rescrip. praesent.* Besides, that it is not unknown to you, who have had many more Experiments thereof than I, how oftentimes in Judicial Proceedings, the *Formalities* utterly destroy the Materialities and Substances of the Causes and Matters agitated; for *forma mutata mutatur substantia, § ad exhib., l. Julianus; § ad leg. falcid., l. Si is qui quadringenta, et extra., de deci., c. ad audientiam, et de celebra. miss., c. in quadam.*

Secondly, They are useful and steadable to me, (even as unto your other Worships) in lieu of some other honest and healthful *Exercise.* The late Master *Othoman Vadat,* a prime Physitian, as you would say, *C. de comit. et archi., lib. xij,* hath frequently told me, That the lack and default of Bodily *Exercise,* is the chief, if not the sole and only cause of the little Health, and short Lives of all Officers of Justice, such as your Worships and I am. Which observation was singularly well, before him, noted and re-marked by *Bartholus in l. j. C. de senten. quæ pro eo quod:* therefore is it, that the Practice of such-like Exercitations is appointed to be laid hold on by your other Worships, and consequently not to be denied unto me, who am of the same Profession: *quia accessorium naturam sequitur principalis, de reg. jur. lib. VI et l. cum principalis, et l. nihil dolo., § eod. titu.; § de fidejusso., L. fidejussor, et extra. de offi. de leg.; c. j.* Let certain honest, and recreative Sports and Plays of Corporeal Exercises be allowed and ap-proved of; and so far, *§ de al. lus. et aleat., L. solent, et autent. ut omnes obediant, in princ., coll. vij, et § de praescript. verb., l. si gra-tuitam, et l. j. C. de spect., lib. xj.* Such also is the Opinion of *D. Thom. in secunda secundæ, quæst. clxviij.* Quoted in very good purpose, by *D. Al. de Rosa;* who, *Fuit magnus Practicus,* and a solemn Doctor, as *Barbatia* attesteth in *Principiis Consil.* Where-fore the Reason is evidently and clearly deduced, and set down before us, in *gl. in procemio §, § ne autem tertii: Interpone tuis inter-dum gaudia curis.* In every deed, one, in the Year a Thousand four hundred fourscore and sixth, having a Business concerning the Portion and Inheritance of a younger Brother, depending in the Court and Chamber of the four High Treasurers of *France,* whereinto assoon as ever I got leave to enter by a Pecuniary Permission of the Usher thereof, as your other Worships know very well, that *Pecuniæ obediunt omnia;* and there says *Baldus,* in *l. Singularia, § si certum pet., et Salic., in l. recepticia, C. de constit. pecun., et Card., in Cle. j, de baptis.;* I found them all recreating and diverting themselves at the Play called *Musse,* either be-fore or after Dinner; to me, truly, it is a thing altogether indif-ferent, whether of the two it was, provided that *Hic not.* that the Game of the *Musse* is honest, healthful, ancient, and lawful: *a Musco inventore, de quo C., de petit. haered., l. si post motam, & Mus-carii, id est:* Such as play and sport it at the *Musse,* are excusable in and by Law, *l. j, C., de excus. artif., lib. x.* And at the very same time was Master *Tielman Picquet*, one of the Players of that Game of *Musse*: There is nothing that I do better remember; for he laughed heartily, when his Fellow-Members of the aforesaid Judicial Chamber, spoiled their Caps in swinging of his Shoulders; he, nevertheless, did even then say unto them, that the banging and flapping of him to the wast, and havock of their Caps, should not at their return from the Palace to their own Houses, excuse them from their Wives: *per c. j, extra., de præsump., et ibi gl.* Now *resolutorie loquendo*, I should say, according to the stile and phrase of your other Worships, that there is no Exercise, Sport, Game, Play, nor Recreation in all this Palatine, Palacial, or Parliamentary World, more ariomatizing and fragrant, then to empty and void Bags and Purses: turn over Papers and Writings: quote Margins and Backs of Scrolls and Rolls; fill Panniers, and take inspection of Causes: *ex Bart. et Jo. de Pra., in l. falsa de condit. et demon. §.*

Thirdly, I consider as your own Worships use to do, that *Time* ripeneth and bringeth all things to maturity, that by *Time* every thing cometh to be made manifest and patent, and that *Time* is the Father of Truth and Vertue. *Gl. in l. j, C. de servit., Autent., de restit. et ea quæ pa., et Spec. tit. de requis. cons.* Therefore is it, that after the manner and fashion of your other Worships, I defer, protract, delay, prolong, intermit, surcease, pause, linger, suspend, prorogate, drive out, wyre-draw, and shift off the *Time* of giving a Definitive Sentence, to the end that the Suit or Process, being well vanned and winnowed, tost and canvassed to and fro: narrowly, precisely, and nearly garbelled, sifted, searched, and examined: and on all Hands exactly argued, disputed and debated, may, by success of *Time* come at last to its full ripeness and maturity: by means whereof, when the fatal hazard of the *Dice* ensueth thereupon, the Parties cast or condemned by the said *Aleatory Chance*, will with much greater patience, and more mildly and gently endure and bear up the disastrous Load of their Misfortune, than if they had been sentenced at their first arrival unto the Court: as, *no. glo. § de excu. tut., L. Tria onera: Portatur leviter, quod portat quisque libenter.* On the other part, to pass a Decree or Sentence, when the action is raw, crude, green, unripe, and unprepared as at the beginning, a danger would

ensue of a no less inconveniency, then that which the Physitians have been wont to say, befalleth to him in whom an *Im-
posthume* is pierced before it be ripe; or unto any other whose
Body is purged of a strong predominating Humour, before its
digestion: For as it is written, *in Autent., Haec constit. in inno.
const. prin.* So is the same repeated, *gl. in. c. Caeterum, extra., de
jura. calum.: quod Medicamenta morbis exhibent, hoc jura negotiis.*
Nature furthermore admonisheth and teacheth us, to gather
and reap, eat and feed on Fruits when they are ripe, and not
before. *Instit., de re. di., § is ad quem, et § de acti. empt., l. Julianus.*
To marry likewise our Daughters when they are ripe, and no
sooner. *§ de donat. int. vir. et uxo., l. Cum hic status, § Si quia sponsa,
et 27 q., j c., Sicut dicit gl.*

> *Jam matura thoro plenis adoleverat annis*
> *Virginitas.*

And in a word, she instructeth us to do nothing of any considerable Importance, but in a full maturity and ripeness. *xxiij
q. ij § ult. & xxxiij d. c. ult.*

CHAPTER XLI

How Bridlegoose relateth the History of the Reconcilers of Parties at variance in matters of Law.

I REMEMBER to the same purpose (quoth *Bridlegoose*, in continuing his Discourse) that in the time when at *Poictiers* I was a
student of Law under *Brocadium Juris*, there was at *Smerva* one
Peter Dandin, a very honest Man, careful Labourer of the Ground,
fine singer in a Church-Desk, of good Repute and Credit, and
older than the most aged of all your Worships, who was wont to
say, that he had seen the great and goodly good Man the *Council
of Lateran*, with his wide and broad brimmed red Hat; As also,
that he had beheld and looked upon the fair and beautiful *Pragmatical Sanction*, his Wife, with her huge Rosary or Patenotrian
Chapelet of Jeat-beads, hanging at a large Sky-coloured Ribbond. This honest Man compounded, attoned and agreed more
Differences, Controversies and Variances at Law than had been

459

determined, voided, and finished during his time in the whole Palace of *Poictiers*, in the Auditory of *Montmorillon*, and in the Town-house of the old *Partenay*. This amicable Disposition of his rendred him Venerable, and of great Estimation, Sway, Power and Authority throughout all the neighbouring places of *Chauvinie, Nouaille, Vivonne, Mezeaux, Estables*, and other bordering and circumjacent Towns, Villages, and Hamlets: All their Debates were pacified by him; he put an end to their brabling Suits at Law, and wrangling Differences. By his Advice and Counsels were Accords and Reconcilements no less firmly made, than if the Verdict of a Soveraign Judge had been interposed therein, although, in very deed, he was no Judge at all, but a right honest Man, as you may well conceive. *Arg. in l. sed si unius, § de jureju., et de verb. oblig., l. continuus.*

There was not a Hog killed within three Parishes of him, whereof he had not some part of the Haslet and Puddings. He was almost every day invited either to a Marriage, Banket, Christning Feast, an Uprising or Women-Churching Treatment, a Birth-day's Anniversary Solemnity, a merry Frollick Gossiping, or otherways to some delicious Entertainment in a Tavern, to make some Accord and Agreement between Persons at odds, and in debate with one another. Remark what I say; for he never yet setled and compounded a Difference betwixt any two at variance, but he streight made the Parties agreed and pacified, to drink together, as a sure and infallible Token and Symbol of a perfect and compleatly well cemented Reconciliation, sign of a sound and sincere Amity and proper Mark of a new Joy and Gladness to follow thereupon. *Ut no. per doct., § de peri. et comm. rei vend. l. j.* He had a Son whose Name was *Tenot Dandin*, a lusty young sturdy frisking Royster, so help me God, who likewise (in imitation of his Peace-making Father) would have undertaken and medled with the taking up of Variances, and deciding of Controversies betwixt disagreeing and contentious Parties, Pleaders as you know.

> *Sæpe solet similis filius esse patri,*
> *Et sequitur leviter filia matris iter.*

Ut ait gl., vj q., j c.: Si quis; g. de cons., d. v, c. j fi.; et est no. per doct., C. de impu. et aliis subst., l. ult. et l. legitimæ, § de stat. hom., gl.

in l. quod si nolit, § de edit. ed., l. quis, C. ad le. Jul. majest. Excipio
filios a moniali susceptos ex monacho, per gl. in c. Impudicas, xxvij q. I.
And such was his Confidence to have no worse Success than
his Father, he assumed unto himself the Title of *Law-strife-setler.*
He was likeways in these pacificatory Negotiations so active and
vigilant; for *vigilantibus jura subveniunt, ex l. pupillus, § quæ in*
fraud. cred., et ibid. l. non enim, et instit. in proœmio; that when he
had smelt, heard, and fully understood; *ut § si quad. pau. fec.,*
L. *Agaso, gl. in verbo olfecit i. nasum ad culum posuit*; that there was
any where in the Country a debatable matter at Law, he would
incontinently thrust in his Advice, and so forwardly intrude his
Opinion in the business, that he made no Bones of making offer,
and taking upon him to decide it, how difficult soever it might
happen to be, to the full contentment and Satisfaction of both
Parties: It is written, *Qui non laborat non manducat.* And the said
gl. § de dam. infect., l. quamvis: And *Currere* plus quæ le pas *vetulam*
compellit egestas. gl. § de lib. agnos., l. Si quis pro qua facit; l. si plures,
C. de cond. incer. But so huge great was his Misfortune in this his
Undertaking, that he never composed any difference, how little
soever you may imagine it might have been, but that instead of
reconciling the Parties at odds, he did incense, irritate, and exas-
perate them to a higher point of Dissention and Enmity than
ever they were at before. Your Worships know I doubt not that,

Sermo datur cunctis, animi sapintia paucis.

gl. § de alie. ju. mu. caus. fa., l. ij. This administred unto the
Tavern-keepers, Wine-drawers, and Vintners of *Smerva* an occasion to say, that under him they had not in the space of a
whole year so much *Reconciliation-Wine* (for so were they pleased
to call the good Wine of *Leguge*) as under his Father they had
done in one half hours time. It hapned a little while thereafter,
that he made a most heavy regret thereof to his Father, attribut-
ing the Causes of his bad Success in pacificatory Enterprizes to
the Perversity, Stubbornness, froward, cross and backward Inclinations of the People of his time, roundly boldly and irrever-
ently upbraiding, that if but a score of Years before the World
had been so wayward, obstinate, pervicacious, implacable,
and out of all Square, Frame and Order as it was then, his Father
had never attained to, and acquired the Honour and Title of

Strife-appeaser, so irrefragably, inviolably and irrevocably as he hath done; in doing whereof *Tenot* did heinously transgress against the Law which prohibiteth Children to reproach the Actions of their Parents. *Per gl. et Bar., l. iij, § Si quis, § de condi. ob caus., et autent., de Nup., § Sed quod sancitum, Coll. iiij*. To this the honest old Father answered thus: My Son *Dandin*, when *Don oportet* taketh place, this is the course which we must trace, *gl. C. de appell., l. eos etiam*: For the Road that you went upon was not the way to the Fullers Mill nor in any part thereof was the Form to be found wherein the Hare did sit. Thou hast not the skill and dexterity of setling and composing Differences. Why? Because thou takest them at the beginning in the very Infancy and Bud as it were, when they are green, raw, and indigestible; yet I know handsomly and featly how to compose and settle them all. Why? Because I take them at their Decadence, in their Weaning, and when they are pretty well digested. So saith *gl. dulcior est fructus post multa pericula ductus. L. non moriturus, C. de contrahend. et comit. stip.* Didst thou ever hear the vulgar proverb, *Happy is the Physitian whose coming is desired at the Declension of a Disease*? For the Sickness being come to a Crisis, is then upon the decreasing hand, and drawing towards an end, although the Physitian should not repair thither for the Cure thereof; whereby though Nature wholly do the work, he bears away the Palm and Praise thereof. My Pleaders after the same manner, before I did interpose my Judgment in the reconciling of them, were waxing faint in their Contestations, their Altercation Heat was much abated, and, in declining from their former Strife, they of themselves inclined to a firm Accommodation of their Differences; because there wanted Fuel to that Fire of burning, Rancour and despightful Wrangling, whereof the lower sort of Lawyers were the Kindlers: This is to say, their Purses were emptied of Coin, they had not a Win in their Fab, nor Penny in their Bag, wherewith to sollicit and present their Actions,

Deficiente pecu-, deficit omne, -nia.

There wanted then nothing but some Brother to supply the place of a Paranymph, Braul-broker, Proxenete or Mediator, who acting his part dextrously, should be the first broacher of the Motion of an Agreement, for saving both the one and the other Party from that hurtful and pernicious Shame, whereof he could not have avoided the Imputation, when it should have been said, that he was the first who yielded and spoke of a Reconcilement; and that therefore his Cause not being good, and being sensible where his Shoe did pinch him, was willing to break the Ice, and make the greater haste to prepare the way for a Condescendment to an amicable and friendly Treaty. Then was it that I came in pudding time, (*Dandin* my Son) nor is the fat of Bacon more relishing to boiled Pease, than was my Verdict then agreeable to them: This was my Luck, my Profit and good Fortune. I tell thee, my Jolly Son *Dandin*, that by this Rule and Method I could settle a firm Peace, or at least clap up a Cessation of Arms and Truce for many years to come betwixt the *Great King* and the *Venetian State*; the *Emperor* and the *Cantons* of *Swisserland*; the *English* and the *Scots*; and betwixt the Pope and the *Ferrarians*. Shall I go yet further: Yea, as I would have God to help me, betwixt the *Turk* and the *Sophy*, the *Tartars* and the *Muscoviters*. Remark well what I am to say unto thee, I would take them at that very instant nick of time, when both those of the one and the other side should be weary and tired of making War, when they had voided and emptied their own Cashes and Coffers of all Treasure and Coin, drained and exhausted the Purses and Bags of their Subjects, sold and morgaged their Domains and proper Inheritances, and totally wasted, spent and consumed the Munition, Furniture, Provision and Victuals that were necessary for the continuance of a Military Expedition. There I am sure, by God, or by his Mother, that would they, would they, in spight of all their Teeths, they should be forced to take a little Respit and Breathing-time, to moderate the Fury and cruel Rage of their ambitious Aims. This is the Doctrine in *gl. xxxvii. d. c. si quando.*

Odero, si potero, si non invitus amabo.

CHAPTER XLII

*How Suits at Law are bred at first, and how they come
afterwards to their perfect growth.*

FOR this Cause (quoth *Bridlegoose*) going on in his Discourse, I
temporise and apply my self to the Times, as your other Worships use to do, waiting patiently for the Maturity of the Process, full Growth and Perfection thereof in all its Members; to
wit, the Writings and the Bags. *Arg. in l. si major., C. commu. divi.
et de cons., d. j, c. Solennitates, et ibi gl.* A Suit in Law at its Production, Birth and first beginning, seemeth to me as unto your other
Worships, shapeless, without Form or Fashion, incompleat, ugly
and imperfect, even as a *Bare*, at his first coming into the World,
hath neither Hands, Skin, Hair nor Head, but is meerly an
inform, rude and ill-favoured piece and lump of Flesh; and
would remain still so, if his Dam out of the abundance of her
Affection to her hopeful Cub, did not with much licking put his
Members into that figure and shape which Nature had provided
for those of an *Arctick* and Ursinal kind. *Ut no. doct., § ad leg.
Aquil., l. ij, in fi.* Just so I see, as your other Worships do, Processes and Suits in Law at their first bringing forth, to be mem-
berless, without shape, deformed and disfigured; for that then
they consist only of one or two Writings, or Copies of Instruments, through which Defect they appear unto me as to your
other Worships, foul, loathsom, filthy and misshapen Beasts. But
when there are heaps of these Legiformal Papers packed, piled,
laid up together, impoaked, insacheled, and put up in Bags, then
is it that with a good reason we may term that Suit, to which, as
pieces, parcels, parts, portions and members thereof, they do
pertain and belong, well-formed and fashioned, big-limmed,
strong set, and in all and each of its Dimensions most compleatly
membred: Because *forma dat esse rei, l. Si is qui, § ad leg. Falci. in
c. cum dilecta, extra., de rescrip.; Barbatia, consil. 12., lib. 2.* And
before him, *Bald. in c. ulti. extra. de consue., et L. Julianus, § ad
exib., et L. Quæsitum, § de lega. iii.* The manner is such as is set
down *in gl. p. q. i. c. Paulus.*

Debile principium melior fortuna sequetur.

Like your other Worships, also the Sergeants, Catchpoles, Pursevants, Messengers, Summoners, Apparitors, Ushers, Doorkeepers, Pettifoggers, Attorneys, Proctors, Commissioners, Justices of the Peace, Judge Delegates, Arbitrators, Overseers, Sequestrators, Advocates, Inquisitors, Jurors, Searchers, Examiners, Notaries, Tabellions, Scribes, Scriveners, Clerks, Pregnatories, Secondaries and *Expedanean* Judges, *de quibus tit. est lib. iij Cod.* by sucking very much, and that exceeding forcibly, and licking at the Purses of the pleading Parties, they, to the Suits already begot and engendred, form, fashion, and frame Head, Feet, Claws, Talons, Beaks, Bills, Teeth, Hands, Veins, Sinews, Arteries, Muscles, Humours, and so forth, through all the Simulary and Dissimilary Parts of the whole; which Parts, Particles, Pendicles and Appurtenances, are the Law-poaks and Bags, *gl. de cons., d. iiij. c. accepisti. Qualis vestis erit, talia corda gerit. Hic notandum est* that in this respect the Pleaders, Litigants and Law-Suiters are happier than the Officers, Ministers, and Administrators of Justice: For *beatius est dare quam accipere, § comm., l. iij. et extra. de celebra. miss., c. cum Marthæ, et 24 q., j. c. Odi gl.*

Affectum dantis pensat censura tonantis.

Thus becometh the Action or Process, by their care and industry, to be of a compleat and goodly bulk, well shaped, framed, formed, and fashioned according to the *Canonical Gloss.*

Accipe, sume, cape, sunt verba placentia Papæ.

Which Speech hath been more clearly explained by *Alb. de Ros. in verbo Roma.*

Roma manus rodit, quas rodere non valet, odit.
Dantes custodit, non dantes spernit, & odit.

The Reason whereof is thought to be this:

Ad præsens ova cras pullis sunt meliora.

Ut est glo., in l. Quum hi, § de transac. Nor is this all, for the inconvenience of the contrary is set down in *gl. c. de allu., l. F.*:

465

Quum labor in damno est, crescit mortalis egestas.

In confirmation whereof we find, that the true Etymology and Exposition of the word *Process* is *Purchase, viz.* of good store of Money to the Lawyers, and of many Poaks, *id est, Prou-Sacks,* to the Pleaders, upon which Subject we have most Cœlestial Quips, Gybes, and Girds.

Litigando jura crescunt, litigando jus acquiritur.

Item gl. in c. illud, ext. de præsumpt., et C. de prob., l. instrumenta, l. Non epistolis, l. Non nudis,

Et si non prosunt singula, multa juvant.

Yea, but (asked *Trinquamelle*) how do you proceed, (my Friend) in Criminal Causes, the culpable and guilty Party being taken and seized upon, *Flagrante Crimine?* Even as your other Worships use to do (answered *Bridlegoose:) First,* I permit the Plaintiff to depart from the Court, enjoyning him not to presume to return thither, till he preallably, should have taken a good sound and profound Sleep, which is to serve for the prime Entry and Introduction to the legal carrying on of the Business. In the next place, a formal Report is to be made to me of his having slept. *Thirdly,* I issue forth a Warrant to convent him before me. *Fourthly,* He is to produce a sufficient and authentick Attestation, of his having thoroughly and entirely sleeped, conform to the *gl., 32 q. vij c. Si quis cum,*

Quandoque bonus dormitat Homerus.

Being thus far advanced in the Formality of the Process, I find that this Consopiating Act engendreth another Act, whence ariseth the articulating of a Member; that again produceth a Third Act, fashionative of another Member; which Third bringing forth a Fourth, Procreative of another Act: New Members in a no fewer Number are shapen and framed, one still breeding, and begetting another (as Link after Link, the Coat of Mail at length is made) till thus, Piece after Piece, by little and little, like Information upon Information, the Process be compleatly well formed, and perfect in all his Members. Finally, having proceeded this length, I have recourse to my *Dice,* nor is it to be thought, that this interruption, respit, or interpellation, is by me occasioned without very good reason inducing me thereunto, and a notable Experience of a most convincing and irrefragable force.

I remember, on a time, that in the Camp at *Stockholm*, there was a certain *Gascon* named *Gratinauld*, Native of the Town of *Saint Sever*, who having lost all his Money at Play, and consecutively being very angry thereat, as you know, *pecunia est alter sanguis, ut ait Anto. de Butrio in c. accedens., ij, extra., ut lit. non contest., et Bald. in l. si tuis., C. de op. li. per no., et l. advocati, C. de advo. div. jud.: Pecunia est vita hominis et optimus fidejussor in necessitatibus*: Did, at his coming forth of the Gaming-House, in the presence of the whole Company that was there, with a very loud Voice, speak in his own Language these following words: *Pao cap de bious, hillotz, que maulx de pippe bous tresbyre; ares que pergudes sont les mies bingt et quouatte baguettes, ta pla donnerien picz, truez et patactz. Sey degun de bous aulx qui boille truquar ambe iou à belz embiz.* Finding that none would make him any Answer, he passed from thence to that part of the Leaguer, where the huff, snuff, honder-sponder, swash-buckling *High-Germans* were, to whom he renewed these very Terms, provoking them to fight with him; but all the Return he had from them to his stout Challenge was only *Der Guascogner thut schich usz mitt eim jedem ze schlagen, aber er ist geneigter zu staelen; darumb, lieben fravven, hend serg zu unserm hausraut.* Finding also, that none of that Band of *Teutonick* Soldiers offered himself to the Combat, he passed to that quarter of the Leaguer where the *French* Free-booting Adventurers were encamped, and reiterating unto them, what he had before repeated to the *Dutch* Warriours, challenged them likewise to fight with him, and therewithal made some pretty little *Gasconado* frisking *Gambols*, to oblige them the more cheerfully and gallantly to cope with him in the Lists of a Duellizing Engagement; but no Answer at all was made unto him. Whereupon the *Gascon* despairing of meeting with any Antagonists, departed from thence, and laying himself down, not far from the Pavilions of the grand *Christian* Cavalier, *Crissie*, fell fast asleep. When he had throughly slept an hour or two, another adventurous and all-hazarding Blade of the Forlorn Hope of the lavishingly wasting Gamesters, having also lost all his Moneys, sallied forth with a Sword in his Hand, of a firm

Resolution to fight with the aforesaid *Gascon* seeing he had lost as well as he.

Ploratur lachrymis amissa pecunia veris,

saith the *Gl. de pœnitent. dist. 3, c. Sunt plures.* To this effect, having made enquiry and search for him throughout the whole Camp, and in sequel thereof found him asleep, he said unto him, Up, ho, good Fellow, in Name of all the Devils of Hell, rise up, rise up, get up; I have lost my Money as well as thou hast done, let us therefore go fight lustily together, grapple and scuffle it to some purpose: Thou may'st see that; and look, my Tuck is no longer than thy Rapier. The *Gascon*, altogether astonished at his unexpected Provocation, without altering his former Dialect, spoke thus: *Cap de sainct Arnault, quau seys tu, qui me rebeillez? Que man de tavverne te gyre. Ho, sainct Siobé, cap de Guascoigne, ta pla dormie iou, quand aquoest taquain me bingut estée.* The ventrous Royster inviteth him again to the Duel; but the *Gascon*, without condescending to his desire, said only this: *Hé, paovret, iou te esquinerie, ares que son pla reposat. Vayne un pauc qui te posar com iou; puesse truqueren.* Thus, in forgetting his Loss, he forgot the eagerness which he had to fight. In conclusion, after that the other had likeways slept a little they, instead of fighting, and possibly killing one another, went joyntly to a Sutler's Tent, where they drank together very amicably, each upon the pawn of his Sword. Thus, by a little Sleep was pacified the ardent Fury of two warlike Champions. There, Gossip, comes the Golden Word of Jhon Andr. *in c. ult. de sent. et re judic., libro sexto:*

Sedendo, & dormiendo fit anima prudens.

CHAPTER XLIII

How Pantagruel excuseth Bridlegoose, in the matter of Sentencing Actions at Law, by the Chance of the Dice.

WITH this *Bridlegoose* held his peace. Whereupon *Trinquamelle* bid them withdraw from the Court: Which accordingly was done; and then directed his Discourse to *Pantagruel* after this manner: It is fitting (most Illustrious Prince) not only by reason of the deep Obligations wherein this present *Parliament*, together with the whole Marquisate of *Merlingues*, stand bound to your Royal Highness, for the innumerable Benefits, which as effects of *meer Grace*, they have received from your incomparable Bounty; but for that excellent Wit also, prime Judgment, and admirable Learning wherewith Almighty God, the Giver of all Good Things, hath most richly qualified and endowed you, we tender and present unto you the Decision of this new, strange, and Paradoxical Case of *Bridlegoose*, who in your presence, to your both hearing and seeing, hath plainly confessed his final Judging and Determinating of Suit of Law, by the meer Chance and Fortune of the *Dice*: therefore do we beseech you, that you may be pleased to give Sentence therein, as unto you shall seem most just and equitable. To this *Pantagruel* answered: *Gentlemen*, It is not unknown to you, how my Condition is somewhat remote from the Profession of deciding Law-Controversies; yet seeing you are pleased to do me the Honour to put that Task upon me, instead of undergoing the Office of a *Judge*, I will become your humble *Supplicant*: I observe, *Gentlemen*, in this *Bridlegoose*, several things, which induce me to represent before you, that it is my opinion he should be pardoned. In the *First place* his *Old Age*; *Secondly*, his *Simplicity*: To both which Qualities our Statute and Common Laws, Civil and Municipal together, allow many Excuses for any slips or escapes, which through the invincible Imperfection of either, have been inconsiderately stumbled upon by a Person so qualified. *Thirdly, Gentlemen*, I must needs display before you another Case, which in Equity and Justice maketh much for the advantage of *Bridlegoose*; to wit, that this one, sole, and single fault of his, ought to be quite forgotten, abolished, and swallowed up, by that immense and vast Ocean of just Dooms and Sentences, which heretofore he hath given and pronounced: his Demeanours for these forty Years and upwards, that he hath been a Judge, having been so evenly balanced in the Scales of Uprightness, that Envy itself, till now, could not have been so impudent as to accuse and twit him with an Act worthy of a Check or Reprehension: As if a Drop of the Sea were thrown into the *Loire*, none could perceive, or say, that by this single Drop, the whole River should be salt and brackish.

Truly, it seemeth unto me, that in the whole Series of *Bridle-goose*'s Juridical Decrees, there hath been, I know not what, of extraordinary savouring of the unspeakable Benignity of God, that all those his preceding Sentences, Awards, and Judgments, have been confirmed and approved of by your selves, in this your own Venerable and *Sovereign Court*: for it is usual (as you know well) with him whose ways are inscrutable, to manifest his own ineffable Glory, in blunting the Perspicacy of the Eyes of the Wise, in weakening the Strength of potent Oppressors, in depressing the Pride of rich Extortioners, and in erecting, comforting, protecting, supporting, upholding, and shoaring up the poor, feeble, humble, silly, and foolish Ones of the Earth. But waving all these matters, I shall only beseech you, not by the Obligations which you pretend to owe to my Family, for which I thank you; but for that constant and unfeigned Love and Affection which you have always found in me, both on this and on the other side of *Loire*, for the Maintenance and Establishment of your Places, Offices, and Dignities, that for this one time, you would pardon and forgive him, upon these two Conditions: *First*, That he satisfie, or put a sufficient Surety for the Satisfaction of the Party wronged by the Injustice of the Sentence in question: For the fulfilment of this Article, I will provide sufficiently. And *Secondly*, That for his subsidiary Aid in the weighty Charge of Administring Justice, you would be pleased to appoint, and assign unto him some pretty, little, vertuous Counsellor, younger, learneder, and wiser than he, by the Square and Rule of whose Advice he may regulate, guide, temper, and moderate in times coming, all his Judiciary Procedures; or otherways, if you intend totally to depose him from his Office, and to deprive him altogether of the State and Dignity of a Judge, I shall cordially intreat you to make a Present and free Gift of him to me, who shall find in my Kingdoms Charges and Employments enough wherewith to imbusie him, for the bettering of his own Fortunes, and furtherance of my Service. In the mean time, I implore the Creator, Saviour and Sanctifier of all good things, in their Grace, Mercy and Kindness, to preserve you all now and evermore, World without end.

These words thus spoken, *Pantagruel* vayling his Cap, and making a Leg, with such a Majestick Garb as became a Person of his paramount Degree and Eminency, farewell'd *Trinquamelle* the President, and Master Speaker of that *Merlinguesian* Parliament, took his leave of the whole Court, and went out of the Chamber; at the Door whereof finding *Panurge, Epistemon*, Fryar *Ihon*, and others, he forthwith, attended by them, walked to the outer Gate, where all them immediately took Horse to return towards *Gargantua*. *Pantagruel* by the way related to them, from point to point, the manner of *Bridlegoose's* sententiating Differences at Law. Fryar *Ihon* said, that he had seen *Peter Dandin*, and was acquainted with him at that time when he sojourned in the Monastery of *Fontaine le Conte*, under the Noble Abbot *Ardillon*. *Gymnast* likewise affirmed, that he was in the Tent of the Grand *Christian* Cavallier *de Cressie*, when the *Gascon*, after his Sleep, made answer to the Adventurer. *Panurge* was somewhat incredulous in the Matter of Believing, that it was morally possible *Bridlegoose* should have been for such a long space of Time so continually fortunate in that *Aleatory* way of deciding Law-Debates. *Epistemon* said to *Pantagruel*, Such another Story, not much unlike to that, in all the Circumstances thereof, is vulgarly reported of the *Provost* of *Montlehery*. In good sooth, such a perpetuity of good Luck is to be wondred at. To have hit right twice or thrice in a Judgment so given by Haphazard, might have fallen out well enough, especially in Controversies that were ambiguous, intricate, abstruse, perplexed, and obscure.

CHAPTER XLIV

How Pantagruel relateth a strange History of the Perplexity of Humane Judgment.

SEING you talk (quoth *Pantagruel*) of dark, difficult, hard and knotty Debates, I will tell you of one controverted before *Cneius Dolabella*, Proconsul in *Asia*. The Case was this:

A Wife in *Smyrna* had of her first Husband a Child named *Abece*; he dying, she, after the expiring of a year and Day, married again, and to her Second Husband bore a Boy called *Edege*: A pretty long time thereafter it happened (as you know the Affection of Step-fathers and Step-dams is very rare, towards the

Children of the first Fathers and Mothers deceased) that this
Husband, with the help of his Son *Edege*, secretly, wittingly,
willingly and treacherously murthered *Abece*. The Woman came
no sooner to get Information of the Fact, that it might not go
unpunished, she caused kill them both, to revenge the Death
of her first Son. She was Apprehended, and carried before
Cneius Dolabella, in whose Presence she, without dissembling
any thing, confessed all that was laid to her Charge; yet alledged, that she had both Right and Reason on her side for the
killing of them. Thus was the State of the Question. He found
the Business so dubious and intricate, that he knew not what to
determin therein, nor which of the Parties to incline to. On the
one hand, it was an execrable Crime to cut off at once both her
Second Husband and her Son. On the other hand, the Cause of
the Murther seemed to be so natural, as to be grounded upon
the Law of Nations, and the rational Instinct of all the People
of the World; seeing they two together had feloniously and mur-
therously destroyed her first Son: Not that they had been in any
manner of way wronged, outraged or injured by him, but out of
an avaricious intent to possess his Inheritance. In this doubtful
Quandary and Uncertainty what to pitch upon, he sent to the
Areopagites then sitting at *Athens*, to learn and obtain their Advice
and Judgment. That Judicious Senate very sagely perpending
the Reasons of his Perplexity, sent him word to summon her
personally to compear before him, a precise Hundred Years
thereafter, to answer to some Interrogatories touching certain
Points, which were not contained in the Verbal Defence: Which
Resolution of theirs did import, that it was, in their opinion, a
so difficult and inextricable a Matter, that they knew not what
to say or judge therein. Who had decided that Plea by the Chance
and Fortune of the *Dice*, could not have erred nor awarded amiss,
on which side soever he had past his casting and condemnatory
Sentence: If against the Woman, she deserved Punishment for
usurping Sovereign Authority, by taking that Vengeance at her
own hand, the inflicting whereof was only competent to the
Supream Power, to administer Justice in Criminal Cases: If for her,
the just Resentment of a so atrocious Injury done unto her, in murthering her innocent Son, did fully excuse and vindicate her of any
Trespass or Offence about that Particular committed by her. But

this continuation of *Bridlegoose* for so many Years, still hitting the Nail on the Head, never missing the Mark, and always judging aright, by the meer throwing of the *Dice*, and the Chance thereof, is that which most astonisheth and amazeth me.

To answer (quoth *Epistemon*) categorically to that which you wonder at I must ingeniously confess and avow that I cannot; yet conjecturally to guess at the reason of it, I would refer the Cause of that marvellously long-continued happy Success in the Judiciary Results of his Definitive Sentences to the favourable *Aspect* of the Heavens, and Benignity of the *Intelligences*; who, out of their love to Goodness, after having contemplated the pure Simplicity and sincere Unfeignedness of Judge *Bridlegoose* in the acknowledgment of his Inabilities, did regulate that for him by Chance, which by the profoundest Act of his maturest Deliberation he was not able to reach unto. That likewise which possibly made him to diffide in his own Skill and Capacity, notwithstanding his being an expert and understanding Lawyer, for any thing that I know to the contrary, was the Knowledge and Experience which he had of the Antenomies, Contrarieties, Antilogies, Contradictions, Traversings and Thwartings of Law, Customs, Edicts, Statutes, Orders and Ordinances, in which dangerous Opposition, Equity and Justice being structured and founded on either of the opposite Terms, and a Gap being thereby opened for the ushering in of Injustice and Iniquity, through the various Interpretations of Self-ended Lawyers, being assuredly perswaded that the Infernal Calumniator who frequently transformeth himself into the likeness of a Messenger or Angel of Light, maketh use of these cross Glosses and Expositions in the Mouths and Pens of his Ministers and Servants, the perverse Advocates, bribing Judges, Law-monging Attorneys, prevaricating Counsellors, and other such-like Law-wrestling Members of a Court of Justice, to turn by those means Black to White, Green to Grey, and what is Streight to a Crooked ply; for the more expedient doing whereof, these *Diabolical* Ministers make both the Pleading Parties believe that their Cause is just and righteous; for it is well known, that there is no Cause, how bad soever, which doth not find an Advocate to patrocinate and defend it, else would there be no Process in the World, no Suits at Law, nor Pleadings at the Bar. He did in these Extremities, as I conceive, most humbly recommend the Direction of his Judicial Proceedings to the Upright Judge of Judges, God Almighty; did submit himself to the Conduct and Guideship of the Blessed Spirit, in the Hazard and Perplexity of the Definitive Sentence; and by this *Aleatory* Lot, did, as it were, implore and explore the Divine Decree of his *Good Will* and Pleasure, instead of that which we call the *Final Judgment of a Court*. To this effect, to the better attaining to his purpose, which was to judge righteously, he did in my opinion throw and turn the *Dice*, to the end, that by the Providence aforesaid, the best *Chance* might fall to him whose Action was uprightest, and backed with greatest Reason; in doing whereof, he did not stray from the Sense of *Talmudists*, who say, that there is so little harm in that manner of searching the Truth, that in the Anxiety and Perplexedness of Humane Wits, God oftentimes manifesteth the secret Pleasure of his Divine Will.

Furthermore, I will neither think nor say, nor can I believe, that the Unstreightness is so irregular, or the Corruption so evident, of those of the Parliament of *Mirlingois* in *Mirlingues*, before whom *Bridlegoose* was Arraigned for Prevarication, that they will maintain it to be a worse Practice to have the Decision of a Suit at law referred to the Chance and Hazard of a Throw of the *Dice*, hab nab, or luck as it will, than to have it remitted to, and past by the Determination of those whose *Hands* are full of *Blood*, and Hearts of wry Affections. Besides that, their principal Direction in all Law-matters, comes to their Hands from one *Tribonian*, a wicked, miscreant, barbarous, faithless, and perfidious Knave, so pernicious, injust, avaricious and perverse in his ways, that it was his ordinary custom to sell Laws, Edicts, Declarations, Constitutions and Ordinances, as at an Outroop or Putsale, to him who offered most for them. Thus did he shape Measures for the Pleaders, and cut their Morsels to them by and out of these little Parcels, Fragments, Bits, Scantlings and Shreds of the Law now in use, altogether concealing, suppressing, disanulling and abolishing the remainder, which did make for the total Law; fearing that if the whole Law were made manifest and laid open to the knowledge of such as are interested in it, and the learned Books of the ancient *Doctors* of the Law, upon the Exposition of the *Twelve Tables*, and *Prætorian* Edicts, his villanous Pranks, Naughtiness, and vile Impiety, should come to the publick Notice of the World. Therefore were it better in my conceit, that is to say, less inconvenient, that Parties at Variance in any Juridicial Case, should in the dark march upon Caltropes, than to submit the Determination of what is their Right to such unhallowed Sentences and horrible Decrees: As *Cato* in his time wished and advised, that every Judiciary Court should be paved with Caltropes.

CHAPTER XLV

How Panurge taketh advice of Triboulet.

ON the sixth Day thereafter *Pantagruel* was returned home, at the very same hour that *Triboulet* was by Water come from *Blois*. *Panurge*, at his Arrival, gave him a Hogs Bladder puffed up with Wind, and resounding, because of the hard Pease that were within it: Moreover, he did present him with a gilt Wooden Sword, a hollow Budget made of a Tortoise shell, an Osier Watled Wicker-Bottle-full of *Briton* Wine, and five and twenty Apples of the Orchard of *Blanduco*.

If he be such a Fool (quoth *Carpalin*) as to be won with Apples, there is no more Wit in his Pate, than in the Head of an Ordinary Cabbage. *Triboulet* girded the Sword and Scrip to his side, took the Bladder in his Hand, ate some few of the Apples, and drunk up all the Wine. *Panurge* very wistly and heedfully looking upon him, said, I never yet saw a Fool, (and I have seen ten thousand Franks worth of that kind of Cattle) who did not love to drink heartily, and by good long Draughts. When *Triboulet* had done with his *Drinking*, *Panurge* laid out before him, and exposed the Sum of the Business, wherein he was to require his Advice in eloquent and choice-sorted Terms, adorned with Flourishes of Rhetorick. But before he had altogether done, *Triboulet* with his Fist gave him a bouncing Whirret between the Shoulders, rendred back into his Hand again the empty Bottle, fillipped and flirted him on the Nose with the Hog's Bladder; and lastly, for a final resolution, shaking and wagging his Head strongly and disorderly, he answered nothing else but this, *By God, God; mad Fool; beware the Monk: Buzansay Hornepipe.*

These Words thus finished he slipt himself out of the Company, went aside, and ratling the Bladder, took a huge Delight in the melody of the rickling, crackling Noise of the Pease: After which time, it lay not in the power of them all to draw out of his Chaps the Articulate Sound of one Syllable; insomuch that when *Panurge* went about to interrogate him further, *Triboulet* drew his Wooden Sword, and would have stuck him therewith. I have fished fair now (quoth *Panurge*) and brought my Pigs to a fine Market. Have I not got a brave Determination of all my Doubts, and a Response in all things agreeable to the Oracle that gave it? He is a great *Fool* that is not to be denied; yet is he a greater *Fool* who brought him hither to me. That Bolt (quoth *Carpalin*) levels point-blank at me. But of the three, I am the greatest *Fool*, who did impart the Secret of my Thoughts to such an Idiot Ass, and Native Ninny.

Without putting our selves to any stir or trouble in the least (quoth *Pantagruel*) let us maturely and seriously consider and perpend the Gestures and Speech which he hath made and uttered: In them veritably (quoth he) have I remarked and observed some excellent and notable Mysteries, yea, of such important worth and weight, that I shall never henceforth be astonished, nor think strange, why the *Turks*, with a great deal of Worship and Reverence, Honour and Respect Natural Fools, equally with their Primest Doctors, Mufties, Divines and Prophets. Did not you take heed (quoth he) a little before he opened his Mouth to speak what a shogging, shaking and wagging his Head did keep? By the approved Doctrine of the ancient Philosophers, the customary Ceremonies of the most expert Magicians, and the received Opinions of the learnedest Lawyers, such a brangling Agitation and Moving should by us all be judged to proceed from, and be quickned and suscitated by the coming and Inspiration of the Prophetizing and Fatidical Spirit, which entring briskly: and on a sudden, into a shallow Receptacle of a debil Substance (for as you know, and as the Proverb shews it, *a little Head containeth not much Brains*) was the cause of that Commotion. This is conform to what is avouched by the most skilful Physicians, when they afirm, that Shakings and Tremblings fall upon the Members of a Humane Body, partly because of the Heaviness and violent Impetuosity of the

Burthen and Load that is carried, and other part, by reason of
the Weakness and Imbecillity that is in the vertue of the bearing
Organ: A manifest Example whereof appeareth in those, who
fasting, are not able to carry to their Head a great Goblet full of
Wine without a trembling and a shaking in the Hand that holds
it. This of old was accounted a Prefiguration and a mystical
pointing out of the *Pythian* Divineress, who used always before
the uttering of a Response from the *Oracle* to shake a Branch of
her Domestick Lawrel. *Lampridius* also testifieth that the Emperor *Heliogabalus*, to acquire unto himself the Reputation of a
Soothsayer, did, on several Holy Days of prime Solemnity, in the
Presence of the Fanatick Rabble, make the Head of his *Idol*, by
some slight within the Body thereof, publickly to shake. *Plautus*, in his *Asserie*, declareth likewise, that *Saurius*, whithersoever
he walked like one quite distracted of his Wits, keepeth such a
furious lolling and mad-like shaking of his Head, that he commonly affrighted those who casually met with him in his Way.
The said Author in another place shewing a Reason why *Char-
mides* shook and brangled his Head, averred that he was transported, and in an Extasie. *Catullus* after the same manner maketh
mention in his *Berecynthia* and *Atys*, of the place wherein the
Menades, *Bacchical* Women, She-Priests of the *Lyæan* God, and
demented Prophetesses, carrying Ivy Boughs in their Hands,
did shake their Heads. As in the like case amongst the *Gauls*,
the gelded Priests of *Cybele* were wont to do in the celebrating
of some Festivals, which according to the Sense of the ancient
Theologues, have from thence had their Denomination; for
κυβεσται signifieth to *turn round*, whirl about, shake the Head,
and play the part of one that is wry-necked.

Semblably *Titus Livius* writeth, that in the Solemnization time
of the *Bacchanalian* Fobedays at *Rome*, both Men and Women
seemed to Prophetize and Vaticinate, because of an affected
kind of wagging of the Head, shrugging of the Shoulders, and
Jectigation of the whole Body, which they used then most punctually. For the common Voice of the Philosophers, together
with the Opinion of the People, asserteth for an irrefragable
Truth, that Vaticination is seldom by the Heavens bestowed on
any, without the Concomitancy of a little Phrensie, and a Head
shaking, not only when the said presaging Vertue is infused, but

when the Person also therewith inspired declareth and manifesteth it unto others. The learned Lawyer *Julien*, being asked on a
time, if that Slave might be truly esteemed to be healthful and
in a good plight, who had not only convers'd with some furious,
maniack and enraged People, but in their Company had also
prophesied, yet without a Noddle-shaking Concussion,
answered, That seeing there was no Head-wagging at the time
of his Predictions, he might be held for sound and compotent
enough. Is it not daily seen how School-masters, Teachers,
Tutors and Instructors of Children, shake the Heads of their
Disciples, (as one would do a Pot in holding it by the Lugs) that
by this Erection, Vellication, stretching and pulling their Ears,
(which according to the Doctrine of the sage *Egyptians*, is a
Member consecrated to the *Memory*) they may stir them up to
recollect their scatter'd Thoughts, bring home those Fancies of
theirs, which perhaps have been extravagantly roaming abroad
upon strange and uncouth Objects, and totally range their Judgments, which possibly by disordinate Affections have been
made wild, to the Rule and Pattern of a wise, discreet, vertuous
and Philosophical Discipline: All which *Virgil* acknowledgeth to
be true, in the branglement of *Apollo Cynthius*.

CHAPTER XLVI

*How Pantagruel and Panurge diversly interpret the Words of
Triboulet.*

HE says you are a *Fool*; and what kind of *Fool*? A *mad* Fool, who
in your old Age would enslave your self to the Bondage of Matrimony, and shut your Pleasures up within a Wedlock, whose
Key some Ruffian carries in his Codpiece. He says furthermore,
beware of the *Monk*. Upon mine Honour, it gives me in my mind,
that you will be cuckolded by a *Monk*. Nay, I will engage mine
Honour, which is the most precious Pawn I could have in my
Possession, although I were sole and peaceable Dominator over
all *Europe*, *Asia*, and *Africk*, that if you marry, you will surely be
one of the horned Brotherhood of *Vulcan*. Hereby may you perceive how much I do attribute to the wise *Foolery* of our Morosoph *Triboulet*. The other Oracles and Responses did in the general

prognosticate you a Cuckold, without descending so near to the point of a particular Determination, as to pitch upon what Vocation, amongst the several sorts of Men, he should profess who is to be the Copesmate of your Wife, and Hornifyer of your proper self. Thus noble *Triboulet* tells it us plainly, from whose Words we may gather with all ease imaginary, that your Cuckoldry is to be infamous, and so much the more scandalous, that your Conjugal Bed will be incestuously contaminated with the Filthiness of a *Monkery* Lecher. Moreover he says, that you will be the *Hornepipe of Buzansay.* That is to say, well horned, hornified and cornuted: And as *Triboulet*'s Unkle asked from *Lewis* the Twelfth, for a younger Brother of his own who lived at *Blois*, the *Hornepipes* of *Buzansay*, for the Organ Pipes, through the mistake of one Word for another: Even so, whilst you think to marry a wise, humble, calm, discreet and honest Wife, you shall unhappily stumble upon one witless, proud, lowd, obstreperous, bawling, clamorous, and more unpleasant than any *Buzansay-hornepipe.* Consider withal, how he flirted you on the Nose with the *Bladder*, and gave you a sound thumping Blow with his Fist upon the ridge of the Back. This denotates and presageth, that you shall be banged, beaten and filliped by her; and that also she will steal of your Goods from you, as you stole the Hogs Bladder from the little boys of *Vaubreton.* Flat contrary (quoth *Panurge*) not that I would impudently exempt my self from being a Vassal in the Territory of *Folly*; I hold of that Jurisdiction, and am subject thereto, I confess it; and why should I not? for the whole World is *foolish.* In the old *Lorrain* Language (*fou* for *tou*) *All* and *Fool* were the same thing. Besides it is avouched by *Solomon*, that infinite is the number of *Fools*: From an Infinity nothing can be deducted or abated, nor yet by the Testimony of *Aristotle*, can any thing thereto be added or subjoyned. Therefore were I a *mad Fool*, if being a *Fool* I should not hold my self a Fool. After the same manner of speaking, we may aver the number of the mad and enraged Folks to be infinite. *Avicenne* maketh no Bones to assert, that the several kinds of *Madness* are infinite.

Though this much of *Triboulet*'s words tend little to my Advantage, how be it the Prejudice which I sustain thereby be common with me to all other Men, yet the rest of his Talk and

Gesture maketh altogether for me. He said to my Wife, *Be wary of the Monky*; that is as much, as if she should be chery, and take as much delight in a Monky as ever did the *Lesbia* of *Catullus* in her Sparrow; who will for his Recreation pass his time no less joyfully at the exercise of snatching Flies, than heretofore did the merciless Flycatcher *Domitian*. Withal he meant by another part of his Discourse, that she should be of a Jovial Country-like Humour, as gay and pleasing as a harmonious *Hornepipe* of *Saulian* or *Buzansay*. The veridical *Triboulet* did therein hint at what I liked well, as perfectly knowing the Inclinations and Propensions of my Mind, my natural Disposition, and the Biass of my interior Passions and Affections: For you may be assured, that my Humour is much better satisfied and contented with the pretty frolick rural discheveled Shepheardesses, whose Bums through their coarse Canvas Smocks smell of the Claver-grass of the Field, than with those great Ladies in Magnifick Courts, with their Flandan, Topknots and Sultana's, their Polvil, Postillo's and Cosmeticks. The homely sound likeways of a Rustical *Hornepipe*, is more agreeable to my Ears, than the curious Warblings and musical Quavering of Lutes, Teorbes, Viols, Rebecks and Violins. He gave me a lusty rapping thwack on my Back. What then? Let it pass in the Name and for the Love of God, as an Abatement of, and Deduction from so much of my future Pains in *Purgatory*. He did it not out of any evil intent: He thought belike to have hit some of the Pages: He is an honest *Fool*, and an innocent Changeling. It is a Sin to harbour in the Heart any bad Conceit of him. As for my self, I heartily pardon him. He flirted me on the Nose: In that there is no harm; for it importeth nothing else, but that betwixt my *Wife* and me there will occur some toyish wanton Tricks, which usually happen to all new married Folks.

CHAPTER XLVII

How Pantagruel and Panurge resolved to make a Visit to the Oracle of the Holy Bottle.

THERE is as yet another Point (quoth *Panurge*) which you have not at all considered on, although it be the chief and principal

Head of the matter. He put the *Bottle* in my Hand, and restored
it me again. How interpret you that Passage? What is the meaning
of that? He possibly (quoth *Pantagruel*) signifieth thereby, that
your *Wife* will be such a Drunkard, as shall daily take in her
Liquor kindly, and ply the Pots and *Bottles* apace. Quite otherways (quoth *Panurge*) for the *Bottle* was empty. I swear to you,
by the prickling brambly Thorn of St. *Fiacre* in Brie, that our
unique Morosoph whom I formerly termed the Lunatick *Triboulet*, referreth me, for attaining to the final Resolution of my
Scruple, to the Response-giving *Bottle:* Therefore do I renew
afresh the first Vow which I made, and here in your Presence
protest and make Oath by Styx and Acheron, to carry still Spectacles in my Cap, and never to wear a Codpiece in my Breeches,
until upon the Enterprize in hand of my Nuptial Undertaking,
I shall have obtained an Answer from the *Holy Bottle*. I am acquainted with a prudent, understanding, and discreet Gentleman, and besides a very good Friend of mine, who knoweth the
Land, Country, and Place where its *Temple* and *Oracle* is built
and posited: He will guide and conduct us thither sure and safely. Let us go thither, I beseech you: Deny me not, and say not,
Nay; reject not the Suit I make unto you, I intreat you. I will be
to you an *Achates*, a *Damis*, and heartily accompany you all along
in the whole Voyage, both in your going forth and coming back.
I have of a long time known you to be a great lover of Pere-
grination, desirous still to learn new things, and still to see what
you had never seen before.

Very willingly (quoth *Pantagruel*) I condescend to your Request. But before we enter in upon our Progress towards the
Accomplishment of so far a Journey, replenished and fraught
with eminent Perils, full of innumerable Hazards, and every way
stored with evident and manifest Dangers. What Dangers
(quoth *Panurge*, interrupting him)? Dangers fly back, run from,
and shun me whither soever I go seven Leagues around: As
in the Presence of the Soveraign a subordinate Magistracy is
eclipsed; or as Clouds and Darkness quite evanish at the bright
coming of a Radiant Sun; or as all Sores and Sicknesses did suddenly depart, at the approach of the Body of St. *Martin Aquande*:
Nevertheless (quoth *Pantagruel*) before we adventure to set forwards on the Road of our projected and intended Voyage, some

few Points are to be discussed, expedited and dispatched. *First*, Let us send back *Triboulet* to *Blois*, (which was instantly done, after that *Pantagruel* had given him a Frize Coat.) *Secondly*, Our Design must be backed with the Advice and Counsel of the King my Father. And *Lastly*, It is most needful and expedient for us, that we search for, and find out some *Sibylle* to serve us for a Guide, Truchman and Interpreter. To this *Panurge* made answer, That his Friend *Xenomanes* would abundantly suffice for the plenary Discharge and Performance of the *Sibyl*'s Office; and that furthermore, in passing through the *Lanternatory* Revelling Country, they should take along with them a learned and profitable *Lanterne*, which would be no less useful to them in their Voyage, than was that of the *Sibyl* to *Æneas* in his Descent to the *Elysian* Fields. *Carpalin* in the interim, as he was upon the conducting away of *Triboulet*, in his passing by, hearkened a little to the Discourse they were upon, then spoke out, saying, Ho, *Panurge*, Master Freeman, take my Lord *Debitis* at *Calais* alongst with you, for he is *Goud-fallot*, a good Fellow: He will not forget those who have been *Debitors*: These are *Lanternes*: Thus shall you not lack for both *Fallot* and *Lanterne*. I may safely with the little Skill I have (quoth *Pantagruel*) prognosticate, that by the way we shall engender no Melancholy; I clearly perceive it already: The only thing that vexeth me is, that I cannot speak the *Lanternatorie* Language. I shall (answered *Panurge*) speak for you all; I understand it every whit as well as I do mine own Maternal Tongue, I have been no less used to it than to the vulgar *French*.

> *Briszmarg d'algotbric nubstzne zos*
> *Isquebfz prusq; alborlz crinqs zacbac.*
> *Misbe disbarlkz morp nipp stancz bos.*
> *Strombtz Panrge walmap quost grufz bac.*

Now guess, Friend *Epistemon* what this is. They are (quoth *Epistemon*) Names of errand Devils, paissant Devils, and rampant Devils. These words of thine, dear friend of mine, are true (quoth *Panurge*) yet are they Terms used in the Language of the Court of the *Lanternish* People. By the way as we go upon our Journey I will make to thee a pretty little Dictionary, which notwithstanding shall not last you much longer than a Pair of new Shoes; thou shalt have learned it sooner than thou canst perceive the Dawning of the next subsequent Morning. What I have said in the foregoing *Tetrastick* is thus translated out of the *Lanternish* Tongue into our Vulgar Dialect.

> *All Miseries attended me, whilst I*
> *A Lover was, and had no good thereby:*
> *Of better Luck the married People tell,*
> Panurge *is one of those, and knows it well.*

There is little more then (quoth *Pantagruel*) to be done, but that we understand what the Will of the King my Father will be therein, and purchase his Consent.

CHAPTER XLVIII

How Gargantua sheweth, that the Children ought not to marry without the special Knowledge and Advice of their Fathers and Mothers.

No sooner had Pantagruel entred in at the Door of the Great Hall of the Castle, than that he encountred full but with the good honest *Gargantua* coming forth from the Council Board, unto whom he made a succinct and summary Narrative of what had pass'd and occurred worthy of his Observation in his Travels abroad since their last Interview: Then, acquainting him with the Design he had in hand, besought him that it might stand with his good Will and Pleasure to grant him leave to prosecute and go thorough-stitch with the Enterprize which he had undertaken. The good Man *Gargantua* having in one hand two great bundles of Petitions, indorsed and answered; and in the other some remembrancing Notes and Bills, to put him in mind of such other Requests of Supplicants, which albeit presented, had nevertheless been neither read nor heard, he gave both to *Ulrich Gallet*, his ancient and faithful Master of Requests; then drew aside *Pantagruel,* and with a Countenance more serene and jovial than customary, spoke to him thus: I praise God, and have great reason so to do, my most dear Son, that he hath been pleased to entertain in you a constant Inclination to vertuous Actions. I am well content that the Voyage which you have motioned to me be by you accomplished, but withal, I could wish you would have a mind and desire to marry, for that I see you are of competent years. *Panurge* in the mean while was in a readiness of preparing and providing for Remedies, Salves and Cures against all such Lets, Obstacles, and Impediments as he could in the height of his Fancy conceive might by *Gargantua* be cast in the way of their Itinerary Design. It is your Pleasure (most dear Father) that you speak? (answered *Pantagruel*). For my part I have not yet thought upon it. In all this Affair I wholly submit and rest in your good liking and Paternal Authority: For I shall rather pray unto God that he would throw me down stark dead at your Feet, in your Pleasure, then that against your pleasure I should be found married alive. I never yet heard that by any Law, whether Sacred or Profane, yea, amongst the rudest and most barbarous Nations in the World, it was allowed and approved of that Children may be suffered and tolerated to marry at their own good Will and Pleasure, without the Knowledge, Advice or Consent asked and had thereto of their Fathers, Mothers, and nearest Kindred. All Legislators every where upon the face of the whole Earth, have taken away and removed this Licentious Liberty from Children, and totally reserved it to the Discretion of the Parents.

My dearly beloved Son (quoth *Gargantua*) I believe you, and from my Heart thank God for having endowed you with the Grace of having both a perfect notice of, and entire liking to laudable and praise worthy things; and that through the Windows of your exterior Senses he hath vouchsafed to transmit unto the interiour faculties of your Mind, nothing but what is good and vertuous. For in my time there have been found on the Continent a certain Country, wherein are I know not what kind of *Pastophorian* Mole-catching Priests, who albeit averse from engaging their proper Persons into a Matrimonial Duty, like the Pontifical Flamens of *Cibele* in *Phrygia*, as if they were Capons and not Cocks; full of Lasciviousness, Salacity and Wantonness, who yet have nevertheless, in the matter of Conjugal Affairs, taken upon them to prescribe Laws and Ordinances to married Folks. I cannot goodly determine what I should most abhor, detest, loath and abominate, whether the Tyrannical Presumption of those dreaded Sacerdotal *Mole-catchers*, who not being willing to contain and coop up themselves within the Grates and Treillices of their own mysterious Temples, do deal in, meddle with, obtrude upon, and thrust their Sickles into Harvests of Secular Businesses quite contrary, and diametrically opposite to the Quality, State and Condition of their Callings, Professions, and Vocations; or the superstitious Stupidity and senceless Scrupulousness of married Folks, who have yielded Obedience, and submitted their Bodies, Fortunes and Estates to the Discretion and Authority of such odious, perverse, barbarous, and unreasonable Laws. Nor do they see that which is clearer than the Light and Splendour of the Morning Star, how all these Nuptial and Connubial Sanctions, Statutes and Ordinances have been decreed, made and instituted, for the sole Benefit, Profit and Advantage of the *Flaminal Mists*, and mysterious *Flamens*, and nothing at all for the good Utility of Emolument of the silly hood-winked married People; which administreth unto others a sufficient Cause for rendring these Church-men suspicious of Iniquity, and of an unjust and fraudulent manner of dealing, no more to be connived at nor countenanced, after that it be well weighed in the Scales of Reason, than if with a reciprocal Temerity the Laicks by way of Compensation would impose Laws to be followed and observed by those Mysts and Flamens; how they should behave themselves in the making and Performance of their Rites and Ceremonies, and after what manner they ought to proceed in the offering up, and immolating of their various Oblations, Victims and Sacrifices; seeing that besides the Edecimation and Tith-haling of their Gods, they cut off and take Parings, Shreddings, and Clippings of the Gain proceeding from the Labour of their Hands, and Sweat of their Brows, therewith to entertain themselves the better. Upon which Consideration in my Opinion, their Injunctions and Commands would not prove so pernicious and impertinent as those of the Ecclesiastick Power, unto which they had tendred their blind Obedience.

For as you have very well said, there is no place in the World where legally a Licence is granted to the Children to marry without the Advice and Consent of their Parents and Kindred. Nevertheless by those wicked Laws and *Mole-catching* Customs, whereat there is a little hinted in what I have already spoken to you, there is no scurvy, mezely, leprous or pocky Ruffian, Pander, Knave, Rogue, Skelm, Robber or Thief, pilloried, whipped and burn-marked in his own Country for his Crimes and Felonies, who may not violently snatch away and ravish what Maid soever he had a mind to pitch upon, how noble, how fair, how rich, honest and chast soever she be, and that out of the House of her own Father, in his own Presence, from the Bosom of her Mother, and in the sight and despight of her Friends and Kindred looking on a so woful Spectacle, provided that the Rascal Villain be so cunning as to associate unto himself some *Mystical Flamen*, who according to the Covenant made betwixt them two, shall be in hope some day to participate of the Prey.

Could the *Goths*, the *Scyths*, or *Messagets* do a worse or more cruel Act to any of the Inhabitants of a Hostile City, when after the loss of many of their most considerable Commanders, the expence of a great deal of Money, and a long Siege, they shall have stormed and taken it by a violent and impetuous Assault? May not these Fathers and Mothers (think you) be sorrowful and heavy-hearted, when they see an unknown Fellow, a Vagabond Stranger, a barbarous Lowt, a rude Curr, rotten, fleshless, putrified, scraggy, bily, botchy, poor, a forlorn Caitif and miserable Snake, by an open Rapt, snatch away before their own Eyes, their so fair, delicate, neat, well-behavioured, richly provided for, and healthful Daughters, on whose breeding and Education they had spared no Cost nor Charges, by bringing them up in an honest Discipline, to all the honourable and vertuous Employments becoming one of their Sex, descended of a noble Parentage, hoping by those commendable and industrious means in an opportune and convenient time to bestow them on the worthy Sons of their well-deserving Neighbours and ancient Friends, who had nourished, entertained, taught, instructed and schooled their Children with the same Care and Solicitude, to make them Matches fit to attain to the Felicity of a so happy Marriage; that from them might issue an Off-spring and Progeny no less Heirs to the laudable Endowments and exquisite Qualifications of their Parents whom they every way resemble, than to their Personal and Real Estates, Moveables and Inheritances? How doleful, trist and plangorous would such a Sight and Pageantry prove unto them? You shall not need to think that the

Collachrymation of the *Romans*, and their Confederates, at the Decease of *Germanicus Drusus*, was comparable to this Lamentation of theirs? Neither would I have you to believe, that the Discomfort and Anxiety of the *Lacedemonians*, when the *Greek Helen*, by the Perfidiousness of the Adulterous *Trojan Paris* was privily stollen away out of their Country, was greater or more pitiful than this ruthful and deplorable Collugency of theirs? You may very well imagine that *Ceres*, at the Ravishment of her Daughter *Proserpina*, was not more attristed, sad, nor mournful than they. Trust me, and your own Reason, that the loss of *Osiris* was not so regreatable to *Isis*; nor did *Venus* so deplore the Death of *Adonis*; nor yet did *Hercules* so bewail the straying of *Hylas*; nor was the Rapt of *Polyxena* more throbbingly resented and condoled by *Pyramus* and *Hecuba*, then this aforesaid Accident would be sympathetically bemoaned, grievous, ruthful and anxious to the wofully desolate and disconsolate Parents.

Notwithstanding all this, the greater part of so vilely abused Parents, are so timerous and afraid of Devils and Hobgoblins, and so deeply plunged in Superstition, that they dare not gainsay nor contradict, much less oppose and resist those unnatural and impious Actions, when the *Mole-catcher* hath been present at the perpetrating of the Fact, and a Party Contracter and Covenanter in that detestable Bargain. What do they do then? They wretchedly stay at their own miserable Homes, destitute of their well-beloved Daughters; the Fathers cursing the days and the hours wherein they were married; and the Mothers howling, and crying that it was not their fortune to have brought forth Abortive Issues, when they hapned to be delivered of such unfortunate Girls; and in this pitiful plight spend at best the remainder of their Time with Tears and Weeping for those their Children of and from whom they expected (and with good reason should have obtained and reaped) in these latter days of theirs, Joy and Comfort. Other Parents there have been, so impatient of that Affront and Indignity put upon them and their Families, that, transported with the Extremity of Passion, in a mad and frantick mood, through the Vehemency of a grievous Fury and raging Sorrow, have drowned, hanged, killed, and otherways put violent hands on themselves. Others again of that Parental Relation, have upon the reception of the like Injury,

been of a more magnanimous and heroick Spirit, who (in imitation, and at the Example of the Children of *Jacob*, revenging
upon the *Sichemits* the Rapt of their Sister *Dina*) having found the
Rascally Ruffian in the Association of his mystical *Mole-catcher*
closely and in hugger-mugger, conferring, parlying, and coming
with their Daughters, for the suborning, corrupting, depraving,
perverting and enticing these innocent, unexperienced Maids
unto filthy Lewdnesses, have, without any further Advisement
on the matter, cut them instantly into pieces, and thereupon
forthwith thrown out upon the Fields their so dismembred
Bodies, to serve for Food unto the Wolves and Ravens. Upon the
chivalrous, bold and couragious Atchievement of a so valiant,
stout and man-like Act, the other *Mole-catching Symmists* have
been so highly incensed, and have so chaffed, fretted and fumed
thereat, that Bills of Complaint and Accusations having been in
a most odious and detestible manner put in before the competent Judges, the *Arm of Secular Authority* hath with much Importunity and Impetuosity been by them implored and required,
they proudly contending, that the *Servants of God* would become
contemptible, if exemplary Punishment were not speedily taken
upon the Persons of the Perpetrators of such an enormous, horrid, sacrilegious, crying, heinous, and execrable Crime.

Yet neither by Natural Equity, by the Law of Nations, nor
by any Imperial Law whatsoever, hath there been found so much
as one Rubrick, Paragraph, Point or Tittle, by the which any
kind of Chastisement or Correction hath been adjudged due to
be inflicted upon any for their Delinquency in that kind. Reason
opposeth, and Nature is repugnant: For there is no vertuous
Man in the World, who, both naturally and with good reason,
will not be more hugely troubled in Mind, hearing of the News
of the Rapt, Disgrace, Ignominy and Dishonour of his Daughter,
than of her Death. Now any Man finding in hot Blood, one who
with a fore-thought Felony hath murthered his Daughter, may,
without tying himself to the Formalities and Circumstances of
a Legal Proceeding, kill him on a sudden, and out of hand, without incurring any hazard of being attainted and apprehended
by the Officers of Justice for so doing. What wonder is it then?
or how little strange should it appear to any rational Man, if a
Lechering Rogue, together with his *Mole-catching* Abetter, be

entrapped in the flagrant Act of suborning his Daughter, and stealing her out of his House, (though her self consent thereto) that the Father in such a case of Stain and Infamy by them brought upon his Family, should put them both to a shameful Death, and cast their Carcases upon Dunghils to be devoured and eaten up by Dogs and Swine, or otherwise fling them a little further off to the direption, tearing and rending asunder of their Joynts and Members by the wild Beasts of the Field?

Dearly beloved Son, have an especial Care, that after my Decease none of these Laws be received in any of your Kingdoms; for whilst I breath, by the Grace and Assistance of God I shall give good Order.

Seeing therefore you have totally referred unto my Discretion the Disposure of you in Marriage, I am fully of an Opinion, that I shall provide sufficiently well for you in that Point. Make ready and prepare your self for *Panurge*'s Voyage: Take along with you *Epistemon*, Friar *Ihon*, and such others as you will choose: Do with my Treasures what unto your self shall seem most expedient: None of your Actions, I promise you, can in any manner of way displease me. Take out of my Arcenal *Thalasse*, whatsoever Equipage, Furniture or Provision you please, together with such Pilots, Mariners and Truchmen, as you have a mind to; and with the first fair and favourable Wind set sail and make out to Sea in the Name of God our Saviour. In the mean while, during your Absence, I shall not be neglective of providing a *Wife* for you, nor of those Preparations, which are requisite to be made for the more sumptuous solemnizing of your Nuptials with a most splendid Feast, if ever there was any in the World, since the days of *Assuerus*.

CHAPTER XLIX

How Pantagruel did put himself in a readiness to go to Sea;
and of the Herb named Pantagruelion.

WITHIN very few days after that *Pantagruel* had taken his leave of the good *Gargantua*, who devoutly prayed for his Sons happy Voyage, he arrived at the Sea-Port, near to *Sammalo*, accompanied with *Panurge*, *Epistemon*, Friar *Ihon* of the *Funnels*, *Abbot* of

Theleme, and others of the Royal House, especially with *Xeno-manes* the great Traveller, and Thwarter of dangerous ways, who was come at the bidding and appointment of *Panurge*, of whose *Castlewick* of *Salmigondin* he did hold some petty Inheritance by the Tenure of a *Mesnefee*. *Pantagruel* being come thither, prepared and made ready for launching a Fleet of Ships, to the number of those which *Ajax* of *Salamine* had of old equipped, in Convoy of the *Græcian* Soldiery against the *Trojan* State. He likewise picked out for his use so many Mariners, Pilots, Sailors, Interpreters, Artificers, Officers and Soldiers, as he thought fitting; and therewithal made Provision of so much Victuals of all sorts, Artillery, Munition of divers kinds, Cloaths, Moneys, and such other Luggage, Stuff, Baggage, Chaffer and Furniture, as he deemed needful for carrying on the Design of a so tedious, long and perillous Voyage. Amongst other things, it was observed, how he caused some of his Vessels to be fraught and loaded with a great quantity of an Herb of his called *Pantagrue-lion*, not only of the green and raw sort of it, but of the confected also, and of that which was notably well befitted for present use after the fashion of Conserves. The Herb *Pantagruelion* hath a little Root somewhat hard and ruff, roundish, terminating in an obtuse and very blunt Point, and having some of its Veins, Strings or Filaments coloured with some spots of white, never fixeth it self into the ground above the profoundness almost of a Cubit, or Foot and a half; from the Root thereof proceedeth the only Stalk, orbicular, canelike, green without, whitish within, and hollow like the Stem of *Smyrnium, Olus Atrum*, Beans and Gentian, full of long threds, streight, easie to be broken, jogged, snipped, nicked and notched a little after the manner of Pillars and Columns, slightly furrowed, chamfered, guttred and channel'd, and full of Fibres, or Hairs like Strings, in which consisteth the chief Value and Dignity of the Herb, especially in that part thereof which is termed *Mesa*, as he would say the *Mean*; and in that other which hath got the Denomination of *Milasea*. Its height is commonly of five or six Foot; yet sometimes it is of such a tall Growth, as doth surpass the length of a Lance, but that is only when it meeteth with a sweet, easie, warm, wet and well-soaked Soil, (as is the ground of the Territory of *Olone*, and that of *Rosea*, near to *Preneste* in *Sabinia*) and that it want not for Rain enough about the Season of the *Fishers Holydays*, and the *Estival Solstice*. There are many Trees whose Height is by it very far exceeded, and you might call it *Dendromalache* by the Authority of *Theophrastus*. The Plant every year perisheth; the Tree, neither in the Trunk, Root, Bark or Boughs, being durable.

From the Stalk of this *Pantagruelian* Plant there issue forth several large and great Branches, whose Leaves have thrice as much length as breadth, always green, roughish and rugged like the Alcanet, or *Spanish* Buglose, hardish, slit round about like unto a Sickle, or as the Saxifragum, Betony, and finally ending as it were in the Points of a *Macedonian* Spear, or of such a Lancet as Surgeons commonly make use of in their Phlebotomizing Tiltings. The figure and shape of the Leaves thereof is not much different from that of those of the Ash-tree, or of *Egrimony*; the Herb it self so being like the *Eupatorian* Plant, that many skilful *Herbalists* have called it the *Domestick Eupator*, and the *Eupator* the wild *Pantagruelion*. These Leaves are in equal and parallel Distances spread around the Stalk, by the number in every Rank either of Five or Seven, Nature having so highly favoured and cherish'd this Plant, that she hath richly adorned it with these two *odd*, *divine* and *mysterious* Numbers. The Smell thereof is somewhat strong, and not very pleasing to nice, tender, and delicate Noses: The Seed inclosed therein mounteth up to the very top of its Stalk, and a little above it.

This is a numerous Herb; for there is no less abundance of it than of any other whatsoever. Some of these Plants are Spherical, some Romboid, and some of an oblong shape, and all of those either black, bright-coloured or tawny, rude to the touch, and mantled with a quickly-blasted-away Coat, yet such a one as is of a delicious Taste and Savour to all shrill and sweetly singing Birds, such as Linnets, Goldfinches, Larks, Canary-Birds, Yellowhammers, and others of that Airy chirping Quire; but it would quite extinguish the Natural Heat and Procreative Vertue of the Semence of any Man, who would eat much, and often of it. And although, that, of old, amongst the *Greeks* there was certain kinds of Fritters and Pancakes, Buns and Tarts made thereof, which commonly for a lickuorish Daintiness were presented the Table after Supper, to delight the Palat, and make the Wine relish the better. Yet is it of a difficult Concoction, and offensive to the Stomach; for it engendreth bad and un-wholsom Blood, and with its exorbitant Heat woundeth them with grievous, hurtful, smart and noysom Vapours. And as in divers Plants and Trees there are two Sexes, Male and Female, which is perceptible in Lawrels, Palms, Cypresses, Oaks, Holmes, the Daffadil, Mandrake, Fearn, the Agarick, Mushrum, Birth-wort, Turpentine, Penny-royal, Peony, Rose of the Mount, and many other such like. Even so, in this Herb there is a *Male* which beareth no Flower at all, yet it is very copious of, and abundant in Seed. There is likeways in it a *Female*, which hath great store and plenty of whitish Flowers, serviceable to little or no purpose; nor doth it carry in it Seed of any worth at all, at least comparable to that of the Male. It hath also a larger Leaf, and much softer than that of the Male; nor doth it altogether grow to so great a height. This *Pantagruelion* is to be sown at the first coming of the Swallows, and is to be plucked out of the Ground when the Grashoppers begin to be a little hoarse.

CHAPTER L

How the famous Pantagruelion ought to be prepared and wrought.

THE Herb *Pantagruelion* in *September*, under the Autumnal Equinox, is dressed and prepared several ways, according to the various Fancies of the People, and Diversity of the Climates wherein it groweth. The first Instruction which *Pantagruel* gave concerning it, was, to divest and dispoil the Stalk and Stem thereof of all its Flowers and Seeds, to macerate and mortifie it in Pond, Pool, or Lake-water, which is to be made run a little for five days together, if the Season be dry, and the Water hot; or for full nine or twelve days, if the weather be cloudish, and the Water cold: Then must it be parched before the Sun, till it be drained of its Moisture: After this it is in the Shadow, where the Sun shines not, to be peeled, and its Rind pulled off: Then are the Fibres and Strings thereof to be parted, (wherein, as we have already said, consisteth its prime Vertue, Price, and Efficacy) and severed from the woody part thereof, which is improfitable, and serveth hardly to any other use, than to make a clear and

glistering Blaze, to kindle the Fire, and for the Play, Pastime and
Disport of little Children, to blow up Hogs Bladders, and make
them rattle. Many times some use is made thereof by tipling,
sweet-lipped Bibbers, who out of it frame Quills and Pipes,
through which they with their Liquor- attractive Breath suck up
the new dainty Wine from the Bung of the Barrel. Some modern
Pantagruelists, to shun and avoid that manual Labour, which such
a separating and partitional Work would of necessity require,
employ certain *Catarractick* Instruments, composed and formed
after the same manner that the froward, pettish and angry *Juno*
did hold the Fingers of both her Hands interwovenly clenched
together, when she would have hindred the Childbirth Delivery of *Alcmena*, at the Nativity of *Hercules*; and athwart those
Cataracts they break and bruise to very Trash the woody parcels, thereby to preserve the better the Fibres, which are the
precious and excellent parts. In, and with this sole Operation
do these acquiesce and are contented, who, contrary to the
received Opinion of the whole Earth, and in a manner paradoxical to all Philosophers, gain their Livelihoods backwards, and
by recoiling. But those that love to hold it at a higher rate, and
prize it according to its Value, for their own greater Profit, do
the very same which is told us of the Recreation of the three
fatal Sister *Parques*, or of the nocturnal Exercise of the noble
Circe; or yet of the Excuse which *Penelope* made to her fond
wooing Youngsters and effeminate Courtiers, during the long
absence of her Husband *Ulysses*.

By these means is this Herb put into a way to display its
inestimable Vertues, whereof I will discover a part (for to relate
all is a thing impossible to do): I have already interpreted and
exposed before you the Denomination thereof. I find that Plants
have their Names given and bestowed upon them after several
ways: Some got the Name of him who first found them out,
knew them, sowed them, improved them by Culture, qualified
them to a tractability, and appropriated them to the uses and
subserviences they were fit for: As the *Mercuriale* from *Mercury*,
Panacee from *Panace* the Daughter of *Esculapius*, *Armois* from
Artemis, who is *Diana*; *Eupatorie* from the King *Eupator*; *Tele-
phion* from *Telephus*; *Euphorbium* from *Euphorbus*, King *Juba*'s
Physician; *Clymenos* from *Clymenus*; *Alchibiadium* from *Alcibiades*;

493

Gentiane from *Gentius* King of *Sclavonia*, and so forth, through a
great many other Herbs or Plants. Truly, in ancient Times, this
Prerogative of imposing the Inventors Name upon an Herb
found out by him, was held in a so great account and estimation,
that as a Controversie arose betwixt *Neptune* and *Pallas*, from
which of them two that Land should receive its Denomination,
which had been equally found out by them both together, though
thereafter it was called and had the Appellation of *Athens*, from
Athene, which is *Minerva*: Just so would *Lynceus* King of *Scythia*
have treacherously slain the young *Triptolemus*, whom *Ceres* had
sent to shew unto Mankind the Invention of Corn, which until
then had been utterly unknown, to the end, that after the murther of the Messenger (whose Death he made account to have
kept secret) he might, by imposing with the less suspicion of
false-dealing, his own Name upon the said found out Seed, acquire unto himself an immortal Honour and Glory, for having
been the Inventor of a Grain so profitable and necessary to, and
for the use of Humane Life. For the wickedness of which Treas-
onable Attempt he was by *Ceres* transformed into that wild
Beast, which by some is called a *Lynx*, and by others an *Oince*.
Such also was the Ambition of others upon the like occasion, as
appeareth by that very sharp Wars, and of a long continuance,
have been made of old betwixt some Residentary Kings in *Cap-
padocia*, upon this only Debate, of whose Name a certain *Herb*
should have the Appellation; by reason of which difference, so
troublesom and expensive to them all, it was by them called
Polemonion, and by us for the same Cause termed *Make-bate*.

Other Herbs and Plants there are, which retain the Names
of the Countries from whence they were transported: As the
Median Apples from *Media*, where they first grew; *Punick* Apples
from *Punicia*, (that is to say, *Carthage*;) *Ligusticum* (which we call
Louage) from *Liguria* the Coast of *Genoua*; *Rubarb* from a Flood
in *Barbary* (as *Ammianus* attesteth) called *Ru*; *Santonica* from a
Region of that Name; *Fenugreek* from *Greece*; *Gastanes* from a
Country so called; *Persicarie* from *Persia*; *Sabine* from a Territory
of that Appellation; *Stæchas* from the *Stæchad* Islands; *Spica Cel-
tica* from the Land of the *Celtick Gauls*; and so throughout a great
many other, which were tedious to enumerate. Some others
again have obtained their Denominations, by way of Antiphrasis,

or Contrariety; as, *Absinth*, because it is contrary to ψίντος; for it is bitter to the taste in drinking; *Holosteon*, as if it were all Bones, whilst on the contrary, there is no frailer, tenderer nor britler Herb in the whole Production of Nature than it.

There are some other sorts of Herbs, which have got their Names from their Vertues and Operations; as *Aristolochie*, because it helpeth Women in Child-birth; *Lichen*, for that it cureth the Disease of that Name; *Mallow*, because it mollifieth; *Callithricum*, because it maketh the Hair of a bright Colour; *Alyssum*, *Ephemerum*, *Bechium*, *Nasturtium*, *Aneban*, and so forth through many more.

Other some there are which have obtained their Names from the admirable Qualities which are found to be in them; as *Heliotropium* (which is the Marigold) because it followeth the Sun; so that at the Sun rising it displayeth and spreads it self out, at his ascending it mounteth, at his declining it waineth; and when he is set it is close shut: *Adianton*, because although it grow near unto watry Places, and albeit you should let it lie in Water a long time, it will nevertheless retain no Moisture nor Humidity: *Hierachia*, *Eringium*, and so throughout a great many more. There are also a great many Herbs, and Plants, which have retained the very same Names of the Men and Women who have been metamorphosed and transformed in them; as from *Daphne*, the Lawrel is called also *Daphne; Myrrhe*, from *Myrrha* the Daughter of *Cinarus*; *Pythis*, from *Pythis; Cinara*, (which is the Artichock) from one of that name; *Narcissus*, with *Saffran*, *Similax*, and divers others.

Many Herbs likewise have got their Names of those things which they seem to have some Resemblance; as *Hippuris*, because it hath the likeness of a Horse's Tail; *Alopecuris*, because it representeth in similitude the Tail of a Fox; *Psyllion*, from a Flea which it resembleth; *Delphinium*, for that it is like a *Dolphin* Fish; *Buglosse* is so called, because it is an Herb like an Oxes Tongue; *Iris*, so called, because in its Flowers it hath some resemblance of the Rain-bow; *Myosata*, because it is like the Ear of a Mouse; *Coronopus*, for that it is of the likeness of a Crows Foot: A great many other such there are, which here to recite were needless. Furthermore, as there are Herbs and Plants which have had their Names from those of Men, so by a reciprocal

Denomination have the Surnames of many Families taken their Origin from them; as the *Fabii, à fabis*, Beans; the *Pisons, à pisis*, Peas; the *Lentuli*, from *Lentils*; the *Cicerons, à Ciceribus, vel Ciceris*, a sort of Pulse call'd *Cichepeason*, and so forth. In some Plants and Herbs, the resemblance or likeness hath been taken from a higher Mark or Object, as when we say, *Venus* Navil, *Venus* Hair, *Venus* Tub, *Jupiter*'s Beard, *Jupiter*'s Eye, *Mars*'s Blood, the *Hermodactyl* or *Mercury*'s Fingers, which are all of them Names of Herbs, as there are a great many more of the like Appellation. Others again have received their Denomination from their Forms; such as the *Trefoil*, because it is three-leaved; *Pentaphylon*, for having five Leaves; *Serpolet*, because it creepeth along the ground; *Helixine, Petast, Myrobalon*, which the *Arabians* call *Been*, as if you would say an *Ackorne*, for it hath a kind of resemblance thereto, and withall is very oily.

CHAPTER LI

Why it is called Pantagruelion, and of the admirable Vertues thereof.

By such like means of attaining to a Denomination (the fabulous ways being only from thence excepted; for the Lord forbid that we should make use of any Fables in this a so venerable History) is this *Herb* called *Pantagruelion*; for *Pantagruel* was the Inventor thereof: I do not say, of the Plant it self, but of a certain use which it serves for, exceeding odious and hateful to Thieves and Robbers, unto whom it is more contrarious and hurtful than the *Strangle-weed, Choakfitch*, is to the Flax, the Cats-tail to the Brakes, the Sheavgrass to the Mowers of Hay, the Fitches to the Chickny-Pease, the Darnel to Barley, the Hatchet Fitch to the Lentil Pulse, the *Antramium* to the Beans, Tares to Wheat, Ivy to Walls, the Water Lilly to lecherous Monks, the Birchin Rod to the Scholars of the College of *Navarre* in *Paris*, Colewort to the Vine-tree, Garlick to the Loadstone, Onyons to the Sight, Fearn-seed to Women with Child, Willow-grain to vicious Nuns, the Yew-tree Shade to those that sleep under it, Wolfsbane to Wolves and Libbards, the Smell of Fig-tree to mad Bulls, Hemlock to Goslings, Purslane to the Teeth, or Oil to Trees: For we

have seen many of those Rogues, by vertue and right application of this Herb, finish their Lives, *short* and *long*, after the manner of *Phillis* Queen of *Thracia*, of *Bonosus* Emperor of *Rome*, of
Amata King *Latinus*'s Wife, of *Iphis, Autolicus, Lycambe, Arachne,
Phædra, Leda, Achius* King of *Lydia*, and many thousands more;
who were chiefly angry and vexed at this Disaster therein, that
without being otherways sick, evil disposed in their Bodies, by
a Touch only of the *Pantagruelian*, they came on a sudden to
have the passage obstructed, and their Pipes (through which
were wont to bolt so many jolly Sayings, and to enter so many
luscious Morsels) stopped, more cleaverly, than ever could have
done the Squinancy.

Others have been heard most wofully to lament, at the very
instant when *Atropos* was about to cut the thred of their Life,
that *Pantagruel held them by the Gorge*. But (well-a-day) it was not
Pantagruel; he never was an Executioner: It was the *Pantagruelion*, manufactured and fashioned into an Halter, and serving in
the Place and Office of a Cravat. In that verily they *solæcised*,
and spoke improperly, unless you would excuse them by a
Trope, which alloweth us to posit the *Inventor* in the place of the
invented; as when *Ceres is* taken for *Bread*, and *Bacchus* put instead of *Wine*. I swear to you here, by the good and frolick Words
which are to issue out of that Wine-bottle which is a cooling
below in the Copper Vessel full of Fountain Water, that the
noble *Pantagruel* never snatch'd any Man by the Throat, unless
it was such a one as was altogether careless and neglective of
those obviating Remedies, which were preventive of the Thirst
to come.

It is also termed *Pantagruelion* by a Similitude: For *Pantagruel*, at the very first minute of his Birth, was no less tall than
this Herb is long, whereof I speak unto you, his measure having
been then taken the more easie, that he was born in the Season
of the great Drowth, when they were busiest in the gathering of
the said *Herb*, to wit, at that time when *Icarus*'s Dog, with his
fiery bawling and barking at the Sun, maketh the whole World
Troglodytick, and enforceth People every-where to hide themselves in Dens and subterranean Caves. It is likeways called
Pantagruelion, because of the notable and singular Qualities,
Vertues and Properties thereof: For as *Pantagruel* hath been the

Idea, Pattern, Prototype and Exemplary of all *Jovial* Perfection and Accomplishment, (in the truth whereof, I believe there is none of you, Gentlemen Drinkers, that putteth any question) so in this *Pantagruelion* have I found so much Efficacy and Energy, so much Compleatness and Excellency, so much Exquisiteness and Rarity, and so many admirable Effects and Operations of a transcendent Nature, that if the Worth and Virtue thereof had been known, when those *Trees*, by the Relation of the *Prophet*, made Election of a Wooden *King* to rule and govern over them, it without all doubt would have carried away from all the rest the Plurality of Votes and Suffrages.

Shall I yet say more? If *Oxilus* the Son of *Orius* had begotten this Plant upon his Sister *Hamadryas*, he had taken more delight in the Value and Perfection of it alone, than in all his eight Children, so highly renowned by our ablest *Mythologians*, that they have sedulously recommended their Names to the never-failing Tuition of an eternal Remembrance. The eldest Child was a Daughter, whose Name was *Vine*; the next born was a Boy, and his Name was *Fig-tree*; the third was called *Walnut-tree*; the fourth *Oak*; the fifth *Sorbaple-tree*; the sixth *Ash*; the seventh *Poplar*; and the last had the Name of *Elm*, who was the greatest *Surgeon* in his time. I shall forbear to tell you, how the Juyce or Sap thereof, being poured and distilled within the Ears, killeth every kind of Vermin, that by any manner of Putrefaction cometh to be bred and engendred there; and destroyeth also any whatsoever other Animal that shall have entred in thereat. If likewise you put a little of the said Juyce within a Pale or Bucket full of Water, you shall see the Water instantly turn and grow thick therewith, as if it were Milk-Curds, whereof the Virtue is so great, that the Water thus curded, is a present Remedy for Horses subject to the Cholick, and such as strike at their own Flanks: The Root thereof well boiled, mollifieth the Joynts, softneth the hardness of shrunk in Sinews, is every way comfortable to the Nerves, and good against all Cramps and Convulsions, as likewise all cold and knotty Gouts. If you would speedily heal a Burning, whether occasioned by Water or Fire, apply thereto a little raw *Pantagruelion*, that is to say, take it so as it cometh out of the Ground, without bestowing any other Preparation or Composition upon it: but have a special care to change it for some fresher in lieu thereof, as soon as you shall find it waxing dry upon the Sore.

Without this *Herb*, Kitchins would be detested, the Tables of Dining-Rooms abhorred, although there were great Plenty and Variety of most Dainty and sumptuous Dishes of Meat set down upon them; and the choicest Beds also, how richly soever adorned with Gold, Silver, Amber, Ivory, Porphyr, and the mixture of most precious Metals, would without it yield no Delight or Pleasure to the Reposers in them: Without it Millers could neither carry Wheat, nor any other kind of Corn to the Mill; nor would they be able to bring back from thence Flour, or any other sort of Meal whatsoever. Without it, how could the Papers and Writs of Lawyers Clients be brought to the Bar? Seldom is the Mortar, Lime, or Plaister, brought to the Work-house without it. Without it, how should the Water be drawn out of a Draw-Well? In what case would Tabellions, Notaries, Copists, Makers of Counterpanes, Writers, Clerks, Secretaries, Scriveners, and such-like Persons, be without it? Were it not for it, what would become of the Toll-rates and Rent-rolls? Would not the Noble Art of Printing perish without it? Whereof could the Chassis or Paper-Windows be made? How should the Bells be rung? The Altars of *Isis* are adorned therewith; the *Pastophorian* Priests are therewith clad and accoutred; and whole Human Nature covered and wrapped therein, at its first position and production in, and into this World: All the Lanifick Trees of *Seres*, the Bumbast and Cotton Bushes in the Territories near the *Persian* Sea and Gulf of *Bengala*; the *Arabian* Swans, together with the Plants of *Maltha*, do not all of them cloath, attire, and apparel so many Persons as this one *Herb* alone. Soldiers are now-a-days much better sheltered under it, than they were in former times, when they lay in Tents covered with Skins. It overshadows the Theatres and Amphitheaters from the Heat of a scorching Sun: It begirdeth and encompasseth Forests, Chases, Parks, Copses, and Groves, for the pleasure of Hunters: It descendeth into the Salt and Fresh of both Sea and River-Waters, for the profit of Fishers: By it are Boots of all sizes, Buskins, Gamashes, Brodkins, Gambados, Shooes, Pumps, Slippers, and every cobled Ware wrought and made steddable for the Use of Man: By it the Butt and Rover-bows are strong, the Cross-bows bended, and the Slings made fixed: And,

as it were an *Herb* every whit as *holy* as the *Verveine*, and reverenced
by Ghosts, Spirits, Hobgoblins, Fiends and Phantoms, the Bodies
of deceased Men are never buried without it.

I will proceed yet further, by the means of this fine *Herb*, the
invisible Substances are visibly stopped, arrested, taken, detained,
and, Prisoner-like, committed to their receptive Goals. Heavy and
ponderous Weights are by it heaved, lifted up, turned, veered,
drawn, carried, and every way moved quickly, nimbly, and easily, to the great Profit and Emolument of Humane Kind. When
I perpend with my self these and such-like marvellous Effects
of this wonderful *Herb*, it seemeth strange unto me, how the
Invention of so useful a Practice did escape, through so many
by-past Ages, the Knowledge of the ancient *Philosophers*, considering the inestimable Utility which from thence proceeded;
and the immense Labour, which without it, they did undergo in
their pristine Elucubrations. By virtue thereof, through the
retention of some Aerial Gusts, are the huge Rambarges, mighty
Gallioons, the large Floyts, the *Chiliander*, the *Myriander* Ships
launched from their Stations, and set a going at the Pleasure and
Arbitriment of their Rulers, Conners and Steersmen. By the help
thereof those remote Nations, whom Nature seemed so unwilling to have discovered to us, and so desirous to have kept them
still *in abscondito*, and hidden from us, that the Ways through
which their Countries were to be reached unto, were not only
totally unknown, but judged also to be altogether impermeable
and inaccessible, are now arrived to us, and we to them.

Those Voyages outreached Flights of Birds, and far surpass'd the Scope of Feather'd Fowls, how swift soever they had
been on the Wing, and notwithstanding that advantage which
they have of us in swimming through the Air. *Taproban* hath
seen the Heaths of *Lapland*, and both the *Java's* the *Riphæan*
Mountains, wide distant *Phebol* shall see *Theleme*, and the *Islanders* drink of the Flood *Euphrates*; By it the chill-mouthed
Boreas hath surveyed the parched Mansions of the torrid *Auster*,
and *Eurus* visited the Regions which *Zephirus* hath under his
Command; yea, in such sort have Interviews been made, by the
assistance of this *Sacred Herb*, that maugre Longitudes and Latitudes
and all the Variation of the Zones, the *Periæcian* People, and the
Antoecian, Amphiscian, Heteroscian, and *Periscian*, have oft tendred

and received mutual Visits to and from other, upon all the Climates. These strange Exploits bred such Astonishment to the Celestial *Intelligencies*, to all the *Marine* and *Terrestrial* Gods, that they were on a sudden all afraid: From which Amazement, when they saw how, by means of this bless'd *Pantagruelion*, the *Arctick* People look'd upon the *Antarctick*, scoured the *Antlantick* Ocean, passed the *Tropicks*, pushed through the *Torrid Zone*, measured all the *Zodiack*, sported under the *Equinoctial*, having both *Poles* level with their *Horizon*; they judged it high time to call a Council, for their own Safety and Preservation.

The *Olympick* Gods being all and each of them affrighted at the sight of such Atchievements, said, *Pantagruel* hath shapen Work enough for us, and put us more to a Plunge, and nearer our Wits End, by this sole *Herb* of his, than did of old the *Aloids*, by overturning Mountains. He very speedily is to be married, and shall have many Children by his Wife: It lies not in our Power to oppose this Destiny; for it hath passed through the Hands and Spindles of the *Fatal Sisters*, Necessity's inexorable Daughters. Who knows but by his Sons may be found out an *Herb* of such another Vertue, and prodigious Energy, as that by the Aid thereof, in using it aright according to their Fathers Skill, they may contrive a way for Human Kind to pierce into the high Aerian Clouds, get up unto the Spring-head of the Hail, take an Inspection of the Snowy Sources, and shut and open as they please the Sluces from whence proceed the Flood-gates of the Rain; then prosecuting their Ætherial Voyage, they may step in unto the Lightning Work-house and Shop, where all the Thunderbolts are forged, where seizing on the Magazin of Heaven, and Storehouse of our Warlike Fire Munition, they may discharge a bouncing Peal or two of thundring Ordinance, for Joy of their Arrival to these new supernal Places; and charging those Tonitrual Guns afresh, turn the whole force of that Artillery against our selves, wherein we most confided; Then is it like they will set forward to invade the Territories of the *Moon*, whence passing through both *Mercury* and *Venus*, the *Sun* will serve them for a *Torch*, to shew the way from *Mars* to *Jupiter* and *Saturn*: We shall not then be able to resist the Impetuosity of their Intrusion, nor put a stoppage to their entring in at all whatever Regions, Domicils or Mansions of the Spangled

Firmament they shall have any mind to see, to stay in, to travel through for their Recreation: All the Celestial Signs together, with the Constellations of the Fixed Stars, will joyntly be at their Devotion then: Some will take up their Lodging at the *Ram*, some at the *Bull*, and others at the *Twins*; some at the *Crab*, some at the *Lion* Inn, and others at the Sign of the *Virgin*: some at the *Balance*, others at the *Scorpion*, and others will be quartered at the *Archer*; some will be harboured at the *Goat*, some at the *Waterpourer*'s Sign, some at the *Fishes*; some will lie at the *Crown*, some at the *Harp*, some at the Golden *Eagle*, and the *Dolphin*; some at the *Flying Horse*, some at the *Ship*, some at the great, some at the little *Bear*; and so throughout the glistning Hostories of the whole twinkling Asteristick Welkin: There will be Sojourners come from the Earth, who longing after the Tast of the sweet Cream, of their own scumming off, from the best Milk of all the Dairy of the *Galaxy*, will set themselves at Table down with us, drink of our *Nectar* and *Ambrosia*, and take to their own Beds at Night for Wives and Concubines our fairest *Goddesses*, the only means whereby they can be *Deify'd*. A Junto hereupon being convocated, the better to consult upon the manner of obviating a so dreadful Danger, *Jove*, sitting in his Presidential Throne, asked the Votes of all the other Gods, which, after a profound Deliberation amongst themselves on all Contingencies, they freely gave at last, and then resolved unanimously to withstand the Shock of all whatsoever sublunary Assaults.

CHAPTER LII

How a certain kind of Pantagruelion is of that nature, that the Fire is not able to consume it.

I HAVE already related to you great and admirable things; but if you might be induced to adventure upon the hazard of believing some other Divinity of this Sacred *Pantagruelion*, I very willingly would tell it you. Believe it if you will, or otherways believe it not, I care not which of them you do, they are both alike to me, it shall be sufficient for my Purpose to have told you the Truth, and the Truth I will tell you: But to enter in thereat, because it is of a knaggy, difficult and rugged access, this is the

Question which I ask of you, If I had put within this Bottle two Pints, the one of Wine, and the other of Water, throughly and exactly mingled together, how would you unmix them? After what manner would you go about to sever them, and separate the one Liquor from the other in such sort, that you render me the Water apart, free from the Wine, and the Wine also pure without the intermixture of one drop of Water; and both of them in the same measure, quantity and taste that I had embottled them? Or to state the Question otherways, if your Carmen and Mariners, intrusted for the Provision of your Houses, with the bringing of a certain considerable number of Tuns, Punchions, Pipes, Barrels and Hogsheads of *Graves* Wine, or of the Wine of *Orleans, Beaune* and *Mirevaux*, should drink out the half, and afterwards with Water fill up the other empty halves of the Vessels as full as before; as the *Limosins* use to do in their Carriages by Wains and Carts of the Wines of *Argenton* and *Sangaultier*. After that, how would you part the Water from the Wine, and purifie them both in such a case? I understand you well enough; your meaning is, that I must do it with an *Ivy* Funnel: That it is written, it is true, and the Verity thereof explored by a thousand Experiments; you have learned to do this Feat before I see it: But those that have never known it, nor at any time have seen the like, would hardly believe that it were possible. Let us nevertheless proceed.

But put the case we were now living in the Age of *Silla, Marius, Cæsar*, and other such *Roman* Emperors; or that we were in the time of our ancient *Druids*, whose Custom was to burn and calcine the dead Bodies of their Parents and Lords, and that you had a mind to drink the Ashes or Cinders of your Wives or Fathers in the infused Liquor of some good White-wine, as *Artemisia* drunk the Dust and Ashes of her Husband *Mausolus*; or otherways, that you did determine to have them reserved in some fine Urn, or Reliquary Pot, how would you save the Ashes apart, and separate them from those other Cinders and Ashes into which the Fuel of the Funeral and bustuary Fire hath been converted? Answer if you can; by my Figgins, I believe it will trouble you so to do.

Well, I will dispatch, and tell you, that if you take of this Celestial *Pantagruelion* so much as is needful to cover the Body of the Defunct, and after that you shall have inwrapped and bound therein as hard and closely as you can the Corps of the said deceased Persons, and sewed up the Folding-sheet with thread of the same stuff, throw it into the Fire, how great or ardent soever it be it matters not a Straw, the Fire through this *Pantagruelion* will burn the Body, and reduce to Ashes the Bones thereof, and the *Pantagruelion* shall be not only not consumed, nor burnt, but also shall neither lose one Atom of the Ashes inclos'd within it, nor receive one Atom of the huge bustuary heap of Ashes resulting from the blazing Conflagration of things combustible laid round about it, but shall at last, when taken out of the Fire, be fairer, whiter, and much cleaner than when you did put it in at first: Therefore is it called *Asbeston*, which is as much as to say *incombustible*. Great plenty is to be found thereof in *Carpasia*, as likewise in the Climate *Diasienes*, at very easie rates. O how rare and admirable a thing it is, that the Fire which devoureth, consumeth and destroyeth all such things else, should cleanse, purge and whiten this sole *Pantagruelion Carpasian Asbeston*! If you mistrust the Verity of this Relation, and demand for further Confirmation of my Assertion a visible Sign, as the *Jews*, and such incredulous Infidels use to do; take a fresh Egg, and orbicularly (or rather ovally) infold it within this Divine *Pantagruelion*; when it is so wrapped up, put it in the hot Embers of a Fire, how great or ardent soever it be, and having left it there as long as you will, you shall at last, at your taking it out of the Fire, find the Egg roasted hard, and as it were burnt, without any Alteration, Change, Mutation, or so much as a Calefaction of the Sacred *Pantagruelion*: For less than a Million of Pounds *Sterling*, modified, taken down and amoderated to the twelfth part of one Four Pence Half-penny Farthing, you are able to put it to a trial, and make Proof thereof.

Do not think to overmatch me here, by *paragoning* with it, in the way of a more eminent Comparison, the *Salamander*. That is a Fib; for albeit a little ordinary Fire, such as is used in Dining-Rooms and Chambers, gladden, chear up, exhilerate, and quicken it, yet may I warrantably enough assure, that in the flaming fire of a Furnace, it will, like any other animated Creature, be quickly suffocated, choaked, consumed and destroyed. We have seen the Experiment thereof, and *Galen* many ages ago hath clearly demonstrated and confirmed it, *Lib.* 3. *De temperamentis*. And *Dioscorides* maintaineth the same Doctrine, *Lib.* 2. Do not here instance in competition with this Sacred *Herb* the *Feather Allum*, or the wooden Tower of *Pyree*, which *Lucius Sylla* was never able to get burnt; for that *Archelaus*, Governour of the Town for *Mithridates* King of *Pontus*, had plaistered it all over on the out-side with the said *Allum*. Nor would I have you to compare therewith the *Herb*, which *Alexander Cornelius* called *Eonem*, and said that it had some resemblance with that *Oak* which bears the *Misselto*; and that it could neither be consumed, nor receive any manner of prejudice by Fire, nor by Water, no more than the *Misselto*, of which was built (said he) the so renowned Ship *Argos*. Search where you please for those that will believe it, I in that Point desire to be excused. Neither would I wish you to parallel therewith (although I cannot deny but that it is of a very marvellous Nature) that sort of Tree which groweth alongst the Mountains of *Brianson* and *Ambrun*, which produceth out of his *Root* the good *Agarick*; from its *Body* it yieldeth unto us a so excellent *Rosin*, that *Galen* hath been bold to equal it to the *Turpentine*: Upon the delicate Leaves thereof it retaineth for our use that sweet Heavenly Honey, which is called the *Manna*: And although it be of a gummy, oily, fat and greasie Substance, it is notwithstanding unconsumable by any Fire. It is in *Greek* and Latin called *Larix*. The *Alpinesi* name it *Melze*. The *Antenodites* and *Venetians* term it *Larege*; which gave occasion to that Castle in *Piedmont* to receive the Denomination of *Larignum*, by putting *Julius Cæsar* to a stand at his return from amongst the *Gauls*.

Julius Cæsar commanded all the Yeomans, Boors, Hinds, and other Inhabitants in, near unto, and about the *Alps* and *Piedmont*, to bring all manner of Victuals and Provisions for an Army to those places, which on the Military Road he had appointed to receive them for the use of his marching Soldiery; to which Ordinance all of them were obedient, save only those as were within the Garrison of *Larignum*; who, trusting in the natural Strength of the Place, would not pay their Contribution. The Emperor purposing to chastise them for their refusal, caused his whole Army to march streight towards that Castle, before the Gate whereof was erected a *Tower*, built of huge big Sparrs and Rafters of the *Larch* Tree, fast bound together with Pins and

Pegs of the same Wood, and interchangeably laid on one another, after the fashion of a Pile or Stack of Timber, set up in the Fabrick thereof to such an apt and convenient heighth, that from the Parapet above the Portcullis they thought with Stones and Leavers to beat off and drive away such as should approach thereto.

When *Cæsar* had understood that the chief Defence of those within the Castle did consist in Stones and Clubs, and that it was not an easie matter to sling, hurl, dart, throw, or cast them so far as to hinder the Approaches, he forthwith commanded his men to throw great store of Bavins, Faggots and Fascines round about the Castle; and when they had made the Heap of a competent height to put them all in a fair Fire, which was thereupon incontinently done; the Fire put amidst the Faggots was so great and so high, that it covered the whole Castle, that they might well imagine the Tower would thereby be altogether burnt to Dust, and demolished. Nevertheless, contrary to all their Hopes and Expectations, when the Flames ceased, and that the Faggots were quite burnt and consumed, the Tower appeared as whole, sound and entire as ever. *Cæsar*, after a serious Consideration had thereof, commanded a Compass to be taken, without the distance of a Stones cast from the Castle round about it there, with Ditches and Entrenchments to form a Blockade; which when the *Lorignians* understood, they rendred themselves upon Terms: And then, by a Relation from them it was that *Cæsar* learned the admirable Nature and Vertue of this *Wood*; which, of it self, produceth neither Fire, Flame nor Coal; and would therefore in regard of that rare Quality of *Incombustibility*, have been admitted into this Rank and Degree of a true *Pantagruelional* Plant; and that so much the rather, for that *Pantagruel* directed that all the Gates, Doors, Angiports, Windows, Gutters, frettized and embowed Cielings, Cans, and other whatsoever wooden Furniture in the Abby of *Theleme* should be all materiated of this kind of Timber. He likewise caused to cover therewith the Sterns, Stems, Cook-rooms or Laps, Hatches, Decks, Coursies, Bends and Walls of his Carricks, Ships, Gallions, Galleys, Brigantines, Foysts, Frigates, Crears, Barks, Floyts, Pinks, Pinnaces, Huys, Catches, Capers, and other Vessels of his *Thalassian* Arcenal; were it not that the Wood or Timber of the *Larch-tree*, being put within a large and ample Furnace full of huge vehemently flaming Fire, proceeding from the Fuel of other sorts and kinds of Wood, cometh at last to be corrupted, consumed, dissipated and destroyed, as are Stones in a Lime-kill: But this *Pantagruelion Asbeston* is rather by the Fire renewed and cleansed, than by the Flames thereof consumed or changed. Therefore,

> Arabians, Indians, Sabæans,
> *Sing not in Hymns and* Io Pæans;
> *Your Incense, Myrrh, or Ebony:*
> *Come, here, a nobler* Plant *to see;*
> *And carry home, at any rate,*
> *Some Seed, that you may propagate.*
> *If in your Soil it takes, to Heaven*
> *A thousand thousand Thanks be given;*
> *And say with* France, *it goodly goes*
> *Where the* Pantagruelion *grows.*

THE FOURTH BOOK

OF THE HEROICK DEEDS AND SAYINGS
OF THE GOOD PANTAGRUEL

THE AUTHORS EPISTLE
DEDICATORY

TO THE MOST ILLUSTRIOUS PRINCE
AND MOST REVEREND
ODET, CARDINAL DE CHASTILLON

YOU know, *Most Illustrious Prince*, how often I have been and am daily prest by great Numbers of Eminent Persons, to proceed in the Pantagruelian Fables; they tell me that many languishing, sick and disconsolate Persons perusing them, have deceiv'd their Grief, pass'd their Time merrily, and been inspir'd with new Joy and Comfort. I commonly answer, That I aim'd not at Glory and Applause, when I diverted my self with writing; but only design'd to give by my Pen, to the absent who labour under Affliction, that little help which at all times I willingly strive to give to the Present that stand in need of my Art, and Service. Sometimes I at large relate to them, how *Hippocrates* in several places, and particularly in *Lib.* 6. *Epidem*, describing the Institution of the Physician his Disciple, and also *Soranus* of *Ephesus, Orbasius, Galen, Hali Abbas*, and other Authors, have descended to particulars in the prescription of his Motions, Deportment, Looks, Countenance, Gracefulness, Civility, Cleanliness of Face, Cloaths, Beard, Hair, Hands, Mouth, even his very Nails; as if he were to play the Part of a Lover, in some Comedy, or enter the Lists to Fight some Enemy. And indeed the practice of Physic is properly enough compar'd by *Hippocrates* to a Fight, and also to a Farce acted between three Persons, the Patient, the Physician, and the Disease. Which Passage has sometimes put me in mind of *Julia*'s saying to *Augustus* her Father. One day she came before him in a very gorgeous loose lascivious Dress; which very much displeas'd him, though he did not much discover his discontent. The next day, she put on another, and in a modest Garb, such as the chast *Roman* Ladies wore, came into his presence. The kind Father could not then forbear expressing the pleasure which he took to see her, so much alter'd, and said to her, *Oh! how much more this Garb becomes, and is commendable in the Daughter of* Augustus! But she, having her excuse ready, answered, *This day*, Sir, *I drest my self to please my Father's Eye; yesterday to gratifie that of my Husband*. Thus, disguis'd in looks and garb, nay even, as formerly was the Fashion, with a rich and pleasant Gown with four sleeves which was called *Philonium*, according to *Petrus Alexandrinus in* 6. *Epidem*. a Physician might answer to such as might find the *Metamorphosis* indecent: *Thus have I accoutred my self, not that I am Proud of appearing in such a Dress; but for the sake of my Patient, whom alone I wholly design to please, and no ways offend or dissatisfie*. There is also a Passage in our Father *Hippocrates*, in the Book I have nam'd, which causes some to sweat, dispute and labour; not indeed to know whether the Physician's frowning, discontented, and morose Look render the Patient sad, and his joyful, serene and pleasing Countenance rejoyce him, for Experience teaches us that this is most certain; But whether such Sensations of grief, or pleasure, are produc'd by the Apprehension of the Patient observing his motions and qualities in his Physician, and drawing from thence conjectures of the end, and catastrophe of his disease, as, by his pleasing Look, joyful and desirable Events, and by his sorrowful and unpleasing Air, sad and dismal Consequences; or whether those Sensations be produced by a transfusion of the serene or gloomy, aerial or terrestrial, joyful or melancholic Spirits of the Physician, into the Person of the Patient, as it is the Opinion of *Plato, Averroes* and others.

Above all things the best Authors have given particular directions to Physicians about the Words, Discourse, and Converse, which they ought to have with their Patients, every one aiming at one point, that is, to rejoyce them without offending *God*, and in no ways whatsoever to vex or displease them. Which causes *Herophilus* much to blame that Physician who being ask'd by a Patient of his, *Shall I die?* impudently made him this Answer:

Patroclus *dy'd, whom all allow,*
By much, a better Man than you.

Another who had a mind to know the state of his distemper, asking him after our merry *Patelin*'s way: *Well, Doctor, do's not my Water tell you I shall die?* He foolishly answered, No; if *Latona* the Mother of those lovely Twins, *Phœbus* and *Diana*, begot thee. *Galen, lib.* 4. *Comment.* 6. *Epidem.* blames much also *Quintus* his Tutor, who, a certain noble Man of *Rome*, his Patient saying to him, *You have been at breakfast, my Master, your Breath smells of Wine*; answered arrogantly, *yours smells of Fever, which is the better smell of the two? Wine or a putrid Fever?* But the Calumny of certain *Cannibals, Misanthropes*, perpetual Eaves-droppers, has been so foul and excessive, that it had conquered my patience; and I had resolv'd not to write one jot more. For the least of their Detractions were, that my Books are all stuffed with various Heresies, of which nevertheless they could not show one single Instance; much indeed of Comical and facetious fooleries, neither offending God nor the King: (And truly I own they are the Subject, and only Theme of these Books). But of heresy, not a Word, unless they interpreted wrong and against all use of Reason, and common Language, what, I had rather suffer a thousand deaths, if it were possible, than have thought; as who should make Bread to be *stone*, a fish to be a *Serpent*, & an Egg to be a *Scorpion*. This, my Lord, emboldned me once to tell you, as I was complaining of it in your presence, that if I did not esteem my self a better Christian, than they show themselves towards me, and if my life, writings, words, nay thoughts betray'd to me one single spark of heresy, or I should in a detestable manner fall into the Snares of the Spirit of Detraction, Διάβολος, that by their means raises such Crimes against me; I would then like the *Phœnix* gather dry Wood, kindle a fire, and burn my self in the midst of it. You were then pleas'd to say to me, That King *Francis* of Eternal memory, had been made sensible of those false accusations: And that having caused my Books, (mine, I say, because several false, and infamous have been wickedly layd to me,) to be carefully, and distinctly read to him by the most learned, and faithful Anagnost in this

Kingdom, he had not found any Passage suspitious; and that he abhorr'd a certain envious, ignorant, hypocritical Informer, who grounded a mortal heresy on an N put instead of an M by the carelessness of the Printers.

As much was done by his Son, our most gracious, virtuous, and blessed Sovereign, *Henry*, whom Heaven long preserve; so that he granted you his Royal privilege, and particular protection, for me against my slandering adversaries.

You kindly condescended since, to confirm me these happy News at *Paris*, and also lately when you visited my Lord Cardinal *du Bellay*, who for the benefit of his health, after a lingring distemper, was retired to St. *Maur*, that Place (or rather Paradise) of salubrity, serenity, conveniency, and all desireable Country-Pleasures.

Thus, *my Lord*, under so glorious a Patronage, I am emboldened once more to draw my pen, undaunted now and secure; with hopes that you will still prove to me against the power of Detraction, a second *Gallic Hercules* in Learning, Prudence and Eloquence, and *Alexicacos* in virtue, power and authority; you, of whom I may truly say what the wise Monarch *Solomon* saith of *Moses* that great Prophet, and Captain of *Israel*; *Ecclesiast.* 45. *A Man fearing and loving God, who found favour in the sight of all flesh, whose memorial is blessed. God made him like to the glorious saints, and magnified him so, that his enemies stood in fear of him; and for him made Wonders: made him glorious in the sight of Kings, gave him a Commandment for his People, and by him shew'd his light; he sanctified him in his faithfulness, and meekness, and chose him out of all Men. By him he made us to hear his Voice, and caused by him the Law of life and knowledge to be given.*

Accordingly, if I shall be so happy as to hear any one commend those merry Composures, they shall be adjur'd by me to be oblig'd, and pay their Thanks to you alone, as also to offer their prayers to *Heaven* for the continuance and encrease of your Greatness; and to attribute no more to me, than my humble and ready obedience to your Commands: For by your most honourable Incouragement, you at once have inspir'd me with Spirit, and with Invention; and without you my heart had fail'd me, and the fountain-head of my Animal Spirits had been dry. May the Lord keep you in his blessed Mercy.

My Lord,
  Your most humble and
    most devoted Servant,

FRANCIS RABELAIS,
Physician.

Paris this 28th of
  January, MDLII.

THE AUTHORS PROLOGUE

GOOD *People, God save and keep you: Where are you? I can't see you; stay – I'll saddle my Nose with Spectacles – Oh, Oh! 'twill be fair anon, I see you. Well, you have had a good Vintage, they say; this is no bad News to Frank you may swear; you have got an infallible Cure against Thirst, rarely perform'd of you, my Friends! You, your Wives, Children, Friends, and Families are in as good Case as heart can wish; 'tis well, 'tis as I'd have it: God be praised for it, and if such be his will, may you long be so. For my part I am thereabouts, thanks to his blessed Goodness; and by the means of a little* Pantagruelism, *(which you know is a certain Jollity of Mind pickled in the scorn of Fortune) you see me now Hale, and Cheery, as sound as a Bell, and ready to drink, if you will. Would you know why I'm thus, Good People? I'll e'en give you a positive answer—such is the Lord's Will, which I obey and revere; it being said in his Word, in great Derision to the* Physician, *neglectful of his own Health,* Physician, *heal thy self.*

Galen *had some knowledge of the Bible, and had convers'd with the Christians of his time, as appears* Lib. 11. de Usu Partium; Lib. 2. de differentiis Pulsuum, cap. 3. *and* ibid. Lib. 3. cap. 2. *and* Lib. de rerum affectibus *(if it be* Galen's*) Yet 'twas not for any such Veneration of Holy Writ that he took Care of his own Health. No, 'twas for fear of being twitted with the Saying so well known among* Physicians.

ʼΙατρὸς ἄλλων, αὐτὸς ἕλκεσι βρύων.

He boasts of healing (Poor and Rich),
Yet is himself all over Itch.

This made him boldly say, that he did not desire to be esteem'd a Physician, *if from his twenty eighth Year to his old Age he had not liv'd in perfect health, except some ephemerous* Fevers, of which he soon rid*

---

* Fevers, that last but a Day, and are Cured with Rest.

himself; Yet he was not naturally of the soundest Temper, his Stomach being evidently bad. Indeed, as he saith, Lib. 5. de Sanitate tuendâ, that Physician *will hardly be thought very carefull of the health of others, who neglects his own.* Asclepiades *boasted yet more than this; for he said that he had articled with Fortune not to be reputed a* Physician, *if he could be said to have been sick, since he began to practise Physic, to his latter Age, which he reach'd, lusty in all his Members, and Victorious over Fortune, till at last the Old Gentleman unluckily tumbled down from the Top of a certain ill-propt and rotten Stair-Case; and so there was an end of him.*

If by some Disaster Health is fled from your Worships to the right or to the left, above or below, before or behind, within or without, far or near, on this side or t'other side, wheresoever it be, may you presently, with the help of the Lord meet with it; having found it, may you immediately claim it, seize it and secure it. The Law allows it; the King would have it so: nay, you have my advice for't; neither more nor less than the Law-Makers of Old did fully impower a Master to claim and seize his run-away Servant whereever he might be found. Ods-bodikins, is it not written and warranted by the Ancient Customs of this so Noble, so rich, so flourishing Realm of France, That the Dead seizes the Quick?* *See what has been declar'd very lately in that Point by that Learned, Wise, Courteous and Just Civilian* Andrè Tiraquell, *one of the Judges in the most Honourable Court of* Parliament *at Paris. Health is our Life, as* Antiphron *the* Sicyonian *wisely has it, without Health Life is no Life, 'tis not living Life.* Ἄβίος βίος, βίος αβίωτος. *Without Health Life is only a Languishment and an Image of Death. Therefore, you that want your Health, that is to say,* that are Dead, Seize the Quick; *secure Life to your selves, that is to say,* Health.

I have this hope in the Lord, that he will hear our Supplications, considering with what Faith and Zeal we Pray, and that he will grant this our Wish, because 'tis moderate and mean. Mediocrity was held by the ancient Sages to be Golden, *that is to say, precious, prais'd by all Men, and pleasing in all Places. Read the Sacred Bible, you'll find, the Prayers of those who ask'd moderately were never unanswered. For Example, little dapper* Zacheus, *whose Body and Reliques the Monks*

---

* That is, the Death of a Person gives a Right to his Heir to seize what he has left.

of St. Garlick, *near* Orleans, *boast of having, and nickname him*
St. Sylvanus: *he only wished to see our Blessed Saviour near* Jerusalem.
*'Twas but a small Request, and no more than any Body then might
pretend to. But alas! he was but low built, and one of so diminutive a
Size among the Crowd couldn't so much as get a Glimpse of him: well
then he struts, stands on Tip-Toes, bustles and bestirring his stumps,
shoves and makes way, and with much adoe clambers up a Sycamor.
Upon this, the Lord who knew his sincere Affection, presented himself
to his sight, and was not only seen by him, but heard also: Nay, what's
more, he came to his House, and blest his Family.*

One of the Sons of the Prophets in Israel, *felling Wood near the
River* Jordan, *his Hatchet forsook the Helve and fell to the Bottom of
the River; so he pray'd to have it again ('twas but a small Request,
mark ye me,) and having a strong Faith, he did not throw the Hatchet
after the Helve, as some Spirits of Contradiction say by way of scandalous Blunder, but the Helve after the Hatchet, as you all properly
have it. Presently two great Miracles were seen, up springs the Hatchet
from the Bottom of the Water, and fixes it self to its old acquaintance
the Helve. Now had he wish'd to coach it to Heaven in a Fiery Chariot
like* Elias, *to multiply in Seed like* Abraham, *be as rich as* Job, *strong
as* Sampson, *and beautiful as* Absalom, *would he have obtain'd it,
d'ye think? I' troth, my Friends, I question it very much.*

*Now I talk of moderate wishes in point of Hatchet (But hark 'e me,
be sure you don't forget when we ought to drink) I'll tell you what's
written among the Apologues of wise* Æsop *the* Frenchman, *I mean
the* Phrygian *and* Trojan, *as* Max. Planudes *makes him; from which
People, according to the most faithful Chroniclers the noble* French *are
descended:* Ælian *writes that he was of* Thrace, *and* Agathias *after*
Herodotus, *that he was of* Samos; *'tis all one to* Frank.

In his time liv'd a poor honest Country Fellow of Gravot, Tom
Wellhung *by Name, a Wood-cleaver by Trade, who in that low
Drudgery made shift so, to pick up a sorry Livelyhood. It happen'd that
he lost his Hatchet. Now tell me who had ever more Cause to be vex'd
than poor* Tom? *alas, his whole Estate and Life depended on his
Hatchet; by his Hatchet he earn'd many a fair Penny of the best Wood-
mongers or Log-merchants, among whom he went a Jobbing; for want
of his Hatchet he was like to starve, and had Death but met him six
Days after without a Hatchet, the grim Fiend would have mow'd him
down in the Twinkling of a Bedstaff. In this sad Case he began to be in*

a heavy Taking, and call'd upon Jupiter *with most eloquent Prayers (for you know, Necessity was the Mother of Eloquence) with the Whites of his Eyes turn'd up towards Heaven, down on his Marrowbones, his arms rear'd high, his fingers stretched wide, and his head bare, the poor wretch without Ceasing was roaring out by way of Litany at every Repetition of his Supplications, my Hatchet, Lord* Jupiter, *my Hatchet, my Hatchet; only my Hatchet, O* Jupiter, *or money to buy another, and nothing else; Alas, my poor hatchet!*

Jupiter *happen'd then to be holding a grand Council about certain urgent affairs, and old Gammer* Cybele *was just giving her opinion, or if you had rather have it so, it was Young* Phœbus *the Beau: but in short,* Tom's *Out-cry and Lamentations were so loud that they were heard with no small amazement at the Council Board, by the whole Consistory of the Gods. What a Devil have we below, quoth* Jupiter, *that howls so horridly? By the Mud of* Styx, *haven't we had all along and haven't we here still enough to do to set to rights a World of damn'd puzzling Businesses of Consequence? We made an end of the Fray between* Presthan *King of* Persia, *and* Soliman *the Turkish Emperor; we have stopp'd up the Passages between the* Tartars *and the* Moscovites; *answer'd the Xeriff's Petition, done the same to that of* Golgots Rays; *the State of* Parma's *dispatch'd, so is that of* Maydemburg, *that of* Mirandola, *and that of* Africa, *that Town on the* Mediterranean *which we call* Aphrodisium; Tripoli *by carelesness has got a new Master, her hour was come.*

Here are the Gascons *Cursing and damning, demanding the Restitution of their Bells.*

In yonder Corner are the Saxons, Easterlings, Ostrogoths, *and* Germans, *Nations formerly invincible, but now* Aberkeids, *Bridled, Curb'd and brought under by a Paultry Diminutive crippled Fellow: they ask us Revenge, Relief, Restitution of their former good Sence and Ancient Liberty.*

But what shall we do with this same Ramus *and this* Galland *with a Pox to 'em, who surrounded with a swarm of their Scullions, Blackguard, Ragamuffins, Sizers, Vouchers and Stipulators, set together by the Ears, the whole University of* Paris? *I am in a sad quandary about it, and for the Heart's Blood of me can't tell yet with whom of the two to side.*

Both seem to me notable Fellows, and as true Cods as ever piss'd; the one has Rose-Nobles, I say fine and weighty ones; the other would gladly have some too. The one knows something: the other's no Dunce. The one loves the better sort of men, the other's belov'd by 'em. The one is an old cunning Fox, the other with Tongue and Pen, Tooth and Nail falls foul on the ancient Orators and Philosophers, and barks at them like a Cur.

What think'st thou of it, say, thou bawdy Priapus? *I have found thy Council just before now,* Et habet tua mentula mentem.

King Jupiter, *answer'd* Priapus, *standing up and taking off his Cowle, his Snout uncas'd and rear'd up, fiery and stifly propt, Since you compare the one to a yelping snarling Cur, and the other to sly* Reynard the Fox, *my Advice is with submission, that without fretting or puzling your Brains any further about 'em, without any more ado you e'en serve 'em both as in the Days of Yore you did the Dog and the Fox. How?* ask'd Jupiter, *when? who were they? where was it? You have a rare Memory for ought I see, return'd* Priapus! *This right Worshipful Father* Bacchus, *whom we have here Nodding with his Crimson Phyz, to be reveng'd on the* Thebans, *had got a Fairy Fox, who whatever mischief he did, was never to be caught or wrong'd by any Beast that wore a Head.*

The Noble Vulcan *here present had fram'd a Dog of Monesian Brass, and with long Puffing and Blowing put the Spirit of Life into him: he gave it you, you gave it your Miss* Europa, *Miss* Europa *gave it* Minos, Minos *gave it* Procris, Procris *gave it* Cephalus. *He was also of the Fairy kind, so that like the Lawyers of our age, he was too hard for all other sorts of Creatures, nothing could escape the Dog: Now who should happen to meet but these two? What do you think they did? Dog by his Destiny was to take Fox, and Fox by his Fate was not to be taken.*

The Case was brought before your Council; you protested that you would not act against the Fates; and the Fates were contradictory. In short, the End and Result of the Matter was, that to reconcile two contradictions was an impossibility in Nature. The very Pang put you into a sweat, some Drops of which happ'ning to light on the Earth produced what the Mortals call Collyflowers. *All our Noble Consistory for want of a Categorical Solution were seiz'd with such a horrid Thirst, that above seventy eight Hogsheads of Nectar were swill'd down at that sitting. At last you took my advice, and transmogriphy'd 'em into Stones, and immediately got rid of your Perplexity, and a Truce with Thirst was proclaim'd thro' this vast* Olympus. *This was the Year of flabby Cods near* Teumessus *between* Thebes *and* Chalcis.

After this manner, 'tis my Opinion that you should petrifie this Dog and this Fox. The Metamorphosis will not be incongruous; for they both bear the name of Peter. And because, according to the Lymosin *Proverb, To make an Oven's Mouth there must be three Stones, you may associate them with Master* Peter du Coignet, *whom you formerly petrified for the same Cause. Then those three dead Pieces shall be put in an equilateral Trigone, somewhere in the great Temple at* Paris, *in the middle of the Porch, if you will, there to perform the Office of Extinguishers, and with their Noses put out the lighted Candles, Torches, Tapers and Flambeaux; since, while they liv'd, they still lighted ballock-like the Fire of Faction, Division, Ballock Sects, and wrangling among those idle bearded Boys, and Students. And this will be an everlasting Monument to show that those puny self-conceited Pedants, Ballock framers, were rather contemn'd than condemn'd by you.* Dixi, *I have said my Say.*

You deal too kindly by them, said Jupiter, *for ought I see, Monsieur* Priapus. *You don't use to be so kind to every Body, let me tell you: For as they seek to eternize their names, it would be much better for them to be thus chang'd into hard stones, than to return to Earth and putrefaction. But now to other Matters: Yonder behind us towards the* Tuscan *Sea, and the Neighbourhood of* Mount Appennin, *do you see what Tragedies are stirr'd up by certain topping Ecclesiastical Bullies? This hot Fit will last its time, like the* Limosins *Ovens, and then will be cool'd, but not so fast.*

We shall have sport enough with it, but I foresee one inconveniency; for me thinks we have but little store of Thunder-Ammunition, since the time that you, my Fellow Gods, for your Pastime, lavish'd them away to bombard New Antioch, *by my particular permission; as since, after your Example, the stout Champions, who had undertaken to hold the Fortress of* Dindenarois *against all Comers, fairly wasted their Powder with shooting at Sparrows; and then, not having wherewith to defend themselves in time of need,* valiantly *surrendred to the Enemy, who were already packing up their Awls, full of madness and despair, and thought on nothing but a shameful Retreat. Take care this be remedied, Son* Vulcan; *Rouse up your drowsie* Cyclopes, Asteropes, Brontes, Arges, Polyphemus, Steropes, Pyracmon, *and so forth; set them at work, and make them drink as they ought.*

Never spare Liquor to such as are at hot work. Now let us dispatch this bawling fellow below; you Mercury, *go see who it is? And know what he wants.* Mercury *lookt out at heaven's trap door, through which as I am told, they hear what's said here below; by the way, one might well enough mistake it for the scuttle of a Ship; tho* Icaromenippus *said it was like the mouth of a Well: The light-heel'd Deity saw that it was honest* Tom, *who ask'd for his lost Hatchet; and accordingly he made his report to the Synod. By* Jove, *said* Jupiter, *we are finely hop'd up, as if we had nothing else to do here but to restore lost hatchets. Well, he must then have it for all this, for so 'tis written in the Book of Fate, (Do you hear?) as well as if it was worth the whole Dutchy of* Milan. *The truth is, the Fellow's Hatchet is as much to him as a Kingdom to a King. Come, come, let no more words be scattered about it, let him have his Hatchet again.*

Now, let us make an end of the difference betwixt the Levites *and* Mole-catcher *of* Landerousse. *Whereabouts were we?* Priapus *was standing in the chimney corner, and having heard what* Mercury *had reported, said in a most courteous and Jovial manner; King* Jupiter, *while by your order and particular Favour, I was Garden-keeper general on Earth; I observed that this word Hatchet is equivocal to many things: for it signifies a certain instrument, by the means of which Men fell and cleave Timber. It also signifies (at least I am sure it did formerly) a Female soundly and frequently Thumpthumpriggletickletwiddletoby'd: thus I perceiv'd that every Cock of the game us'd to call his Doxie his Hatchet, for with that same Tool (this he said lugging out and exhibiting his nine inch Knocker) they so strongly and resolutely shove and drive in their helves, that the Females remain free from a fear Epidemical amongst their Sex,* viz. *that from the bottom of the Male's Belly the said Instrument should dangle at his heel for want of such Feminine props. And I remember, (for I have a* Member, *and a* Memory *too, ay, and a fine Memory large enough to fill a butter* Firkin): *I remember, I say, that one Day of Tubilustre [Horn Fair] at the Festivals of Good-man* Vulcan *in May, I heard* Josquin Des prez, Olkegan, Hobreths, Agricola, Brumel, Camelin, Vigoris, dela Fage, Bruyer, Prioris, Seguin, dela Rue, Midy, Moulu, Mouton, Gascoigne, Loiset, Compere, Penet, Fevin, Rousee, Richard Fort, Rousseau, Consilion, Constantio Festi, Jacquet, *and* Bercan *melodiously singing the following Catch on a pleasant green.*

> Long *John* to bed went to his Bride,
> And laid a Mallet by his side:

What means this Mallet, *John*, saith she?
Why! 'tis to wedge thee home, quoth he.
Alas! cried she, the Man's a Fool:
What need you use a wooden Tool?
When lusty *John* do's to me come,
He never shoves but with his Bum.

Nine Olympiads *and an* Intercalary *Year after* (*I have a rare member, I would say memory, but I often make Blunders in the symbolisation and colligance of those two Words*) *I heard* Adrian Viellard, Gombert, Janequin Arcader, Claudin, Certon, Machicourt, Auxerre, Villiers, Sandrin, Sohier, Hesdin, Morales, Passereau, Maille, Maillart, Jacotin, Hurteur, Verdelot, Carpentras, l'Heriner, Cadeac, Doublet, Vermunt, Bouteiller, Lupi, Pagnier, Millet, Du Mollin, Alaire, Maraut, Morpin, Gendre, *and other merry lovers of Musick, in a private Garden, under some fine shady Trees round about a Bulwark of Flaggons, Gammons, Pasty's, with several* Coated Quails, *and* lac'd Mutton, *waggishly singing.*

Since Tools without their Hafts are useless Lumber,
And Hatchets without Helves are of that Number;
That one may go in t'other, and may match it,
I'll be the Helve, and thou shalt be the Hatchet.

Now would I know what kind of Hatchet this Bawling Tom *wants? This threw all the venerable Gods and Goddesses into a fit of Laughter like any Microcosm of Flyes; and even set limping* Vulcan *a hopping and jumping* smoothly *three or four times for the sake of his Dear. Come, come, said* Jupiter *to* Mercury, *run down immediately, and cast at the poor Fellow's Feet three Hatchets; his own, another of Gold, and a third of Massy Silver, all of one size: Then having left it to his will to take his choice, if he take his own, and be satisfyed with it, give him t'other two. If he take another chop his head off with his own; and henceforth serve me all those losers of hatchets after that manner. Having said this,* Jupiter, *with an awkward turn of his head, like a Jackanapes swallowing of Pills, made so dreadful a phyz, that all the Vast* Olympus *quak'd again. Heaven's Foot-Messenger, thanks to his low crown'd narrow-brim'd Hat, and plume of Feathers, Heel-pieces, and running Stick with Pidgeon Wings, flings himself out at Heavens Wicket thro the idle Desarts of the Air, and in a trice nimbly alights upon the Earth, and throws at Friend* Tom's *Feet the three Hatchets; saying to him; thou hast bawl'd long enough to be a dry, thy Prayers and request are granted by* Jupiter; *see which of these three is thy Hatchet, and take it away with thee.* Wellhung *lifts up the Golden Hatchet, peeps upon it, and finds it very heavy; then staring on* Mercury, *cries Cods zouks this is none of mine; I won't ha 't. The same he did with the Silver one, and said, 'Tis not this neither, you may e'en take them again. At last, he takes up his own Hatchet, examines the end of the Helve, and finds his mark there; then ravish'd with Joy, like a Fox that meets some straggling Poultry, and sneering from the tip of the nose, he cried By the mass, This is my Hatchet, Master God; if you will leave it me, I will sacrifice to you a very good and huge Pot of Milk, brim full cover'd with fine Strawberryes next Ides of May.*

Honest Fellow, said Mercury, *I leave it thee, take it, and because thou hast wish'd and chosen moderately, in point of Hatchet, by* Jupiter's *command, I give thee these two others; thou hast now where-with to make thy self rich: Be honest. Honest* Tom *gave* Mercury *a whole Cartload of Thanks, and rever'd the most great* Jupiter. *His old Hatchet he fastens close to his Leathern girdle; and girds it above his Breech like* Martin *of* Cambray: *The two others, being more heavy, he lays on his Shoulder. Thus he plods on trudging over the Fields, keeping a good countenance amongst his Neighbours and fellow Parishioners, with one merry saying or other after* Patelin's *way. The next Day having put on a clean white Jacket, he takes on his back the two precious Hatchets, and comes to* Chinon *the famous City, noble City, ancient City, yea the first City, in the World, according to the Judgment and assertion of the most learned Massoreths. At* Chinon *he turned his silver Hatchet into fine* Testons, *Crown-pieces and other white Cash; his golden Hatchet into fine Angels, curious Ducats, substantial* Ridders, *Spankers, and Rose Nobles. Then with them purchases a good Number of Farms, Barns, Houses, Out-Houses, Thatch-Houses, Stables, Meadows, Orchards, Fields, Vineyards, Woods, arable Lands, Pastures, Ponds, Mills, Gardens, Nurseries, Oxen, Cows, Sheep, Goats, Swine, Hogs, Asses, Horses, Hens, Cocks, Capons, Chickens, Geese, Ganders, Ducks, Drakes, and a World of all other necessaries, and in a short time became the richest Man in the Country, nay, even richer than that limping Scrapegood* Maulevrier. *His Brother Bumpkins and the Yeomen and other Country-Puts thereabouts, perceiving his good Fortune, were not a little amaz'd, insomuch, that their former pity of poor* Tom *was soon chang'd into an Envy of his so great and unexpected Rise; and as they could not for their Souls devise how this came about,*

524

they made it their Business to pry up and down, and lay their Heads together, to enquire, seek and inform themselves by what means, in what place, on what day, what hour, how, why and wherefore he had come by this great Treasure.

At last, hearing it was by Losing his Hatchet, ha, ha! said they, was there no more to do, but to lose a Hatchet, to make us rich? Mum for that; 'tis as easie as pissing a Bed, and will cost but little; are then at this time the Revolutions of the Heavens, the Constellations of the Firmament, and Aspects of the Planets such, that whosoever shall lose a Hatchet, shall immediately grow rich? ha, ha, ha, by Jove, *you shall e'en be lost, an 't please you, my dear Hatchet. With this they all fairly lost their Hatchets out of hand. The Devil of one that had a Hatchet left; he was not his Mother's Son, that did not lose his Hatchet. No more was Wood fell'd or cleav'd in that Country thro' want of Hatchets. Nay, the Æsopian Apologue even saith, that certain pretty Country Gents, of the lower Class, who had sold* Wellhung *their little Mill and little Field, to have wherewithal to make a Figure at the next Muster, having been told that this Treasure was come to him by that only means, sold the only Badge of their Gentility, their Swords, to purchase Hatchets to go lose them, as the silly Clodpates did, in hopes to gain store of Chink by that Loss.*

You would have truly sworn they had been a parcel of your petty spiritual Usurers, Rome-bound, selling their All, and borrowing of others to buy store of Mandates *a Pennyworth of a New made Pope.*

Now they cry'd out and bray'd and pray'd and bawl'd and lamented and invok'd Jupiter; *my* Hatchet! *my* Hatchet! Jupiter, *my* Hatchet! *On this side, my* Hatchet, *on that side, my* Hatchet, *ho, ho, ho, ho,* Jupiter, *my* Hatchet. *The Air round about rung again with the Crys and Howlings of these rascally Losers of Hatchets.*

Mercury *was nimble in bringing them Hatchets; to each offering that which he had lost, another of Gold, and a third of Silver.*

Every He still was for that of Gold, giving Thanks in abundance to the great Giver Jupiter; *but in the very nick of time, that they bow'd and stoop'd to take it from the ground, whip, in a trice,* Mercury *lopp'd off their Heads, as* Jupiter *had commanded; and of Heads, thus cut off, the number was just equal to that of the lost Hatchets.*

You see how it is now; you see how it goes with those who in the simplicity of their hearts wish and desire with Moderation. Make warning by this, all you greedy, fresh-water Shirks, who scorn to wish for any thing under Ten Thousand Pounds: and do not for the future run on impudently, as I have sometimes heard you wishing, Would to God, I have now one hundred seventy eight Millions of Gold; Oh! how I should tickle it off! The Dewse on you, what more might a King, an Emperor, or a Pope wish for? For that reason, indeed, you see that after you have made such hopeful wishes, all the good that comes to you of it is the Itch or the Scab, and not a Cross in your Breeches to scare the Devil that tempts you to make these Wishes; no more than those two Mumpers, wishers after the Custom of Paris; one of whom only wish'd to have in good old Gold as much as hath been spent, bought and sold in Paris since it's first Foundations were laid, to this hour; all of it valued at the price, sale, and rate of the dearest Year in all that space of Time. Do you think the Fellow was bashful? had he eaten sowre Plums unpeel'd? were his Teeth on edge, I pray you? The other wish'd Our Lady's Church brim full of steel Needles, from the Flowr to the top of the roof, and to have as many Ducats as might be cram'd into as many bags as might be sow'd with each and every one of those Needles, till they were all either broke at the point or eye. This is to wish with a vengeance! What think you of it? What did they get by 't, in your Opinion? Why, at night both my Gentlemen had kyb'd Heels, a tetter in the Chin, a Churchyard Cough in the Lungs, a Catarrh in the Throat, a swinging Boyl at the Rump, and the Devil of one musty Crust of a brown George the poor Dogs had to scour their Grinders with. Wish therefore for Mediocrity, and it shall be given unto you, and over and above yet; that is to say, provided you bestir your selves manfully, and do your best in the mean time.

Ay, but say you, God might as soon have given me seventy eight thousand as the thirteenth part of one half; for he is Omnipotent, and a million of Gold is no more to him than one Farthing. Oh, ho, pray tell me who taught you to talk at this rate of the Power and Predestination of God, poor silly People? Peace, Tush, St, St, St, fall down before his sacred Face, and own the Nothingness of your Nothing.

Upon this, O ye that labour under the affliction of the Gout, I ground my hopes, firmly believing, that if so it pleases the Divine Goodness, you shall obtain Health; since you wish and ask for nothing else, at least for the present. Well, stay yet a little longer with half an Ounce of Patience.

The Genouese do not use, like you, to be satisfied with wishing Health alone, when after they have all the live long Morning been in a brown study, talk'd, ponder'd, ruminated, and resolv'd in their Counting-houses, of whom and how they may squeeze the Ready, *and who by their Craft must be hook'd in, wheadled, bubl'd, sharp'd, over-reach'd and chous'd, they go to the Exchange, and greet one another with a* sanita and guadagno, Messer; *health and gain to you, Sir. Health alone will not go down with the greedy Curmudgeons, they over and above must wish for gain, with a Pox to 'em; ay and for the fine Crowns, or* scudi di guadagno; *whence, Heaven be praised, it happens many a time, that the silly Wishers and Woulders are baulk'd and get neither. Now, my Lads, as you hope for good health, cough once aloud with Lungs of Leather; Take me off three swindging Bumpers; Prick up your Ears; and you shall hear me tell Wonders of the noble and good* Pantagruel.

THE FOURTH BOOK

CHAPTER I

*How Pantagruel went to sea, to visit the oracle of Bacbuc,
alias the Holy Bottle.*

In the Month of *June*, on *Vesta*'s Holydays, the very numerical
day on which *Brutus*, conquering *Spain*, taught its strutting Dons
to truckle under him, and that niggardly Miser *Crassus* was
routed and knock'd on the head by the *Parthians*, *Pantagruel*
took his leave of the good *Gargantua*, his Royal Father. The
old Gentleman, according to the laudable Custom of the Primitive Christians, devoutly pray'd for the happy Voyage of his
Son and his whole Company, and then they took Shipping at
the Port of *Thalassa*. *Pantagruel* had with him *Panurge*, Fryar
Jhon des Entomeures, alias of the *Funnels, Epistemon, Gymnast,
Eusthenes, Rhizotome, Carpalin, cum multis aliis,* his ancient Servants
and Domestics. Also *Xenomanes*, the great Traveller, who had
cross'd so many dangerous Roads, Dikes, Ponds, Seas, and so
forth, and was come sometime before, having been sent for by
Panurge.

For certain good Causes and Considerations him thereunto
moving, he had left with *Gargantua*, and marked out, in his Great
and Universal Hydrographical *Chart*, the Course which they
were to steer to Visit the Oracle of the *Holy Bottle, Bacbuc*. The
number of Ships was such as I described in the Third Book,
convoyed by a like number of *Triremes*, Men of War, *Gallions*
and *Feluccaes* well Rigg'd, Caulkt, and Stor'd with a good quantity of *Pantagruelion*.

All the Officers, Droggermen, Pilots, Captains, Mates, Boat-
swains, Mid shipmen, Quarter masters and Sailers, met in the
Thalamege, Pantagruel's principal Flag-Ship, which had in her Stern
a huge large Bottle, half Silver well polish'd, the other Half Gold,
Inamel'd with Carnation, whereby it was easy to guess that

white and red were the colours of the Noble Travellers, and that they went for the Word of the *Bottle*.

On the Stern of the Second was a Lanthorn like those of the Antients, industriously made with *Diaphanous* Stone, implying that they were to pass by *Lanternland*. The Third Ship had for her Device a fine deep *China* Ewre. The Fourth, a double-handed Jar much like an ancient Urn. The Fifth, a famous Kan made of Sperm of Emerald. The Sixth, a Monk's Mumping Bottle made of the four Mettals together. The Seventh, an Ebony Funnel all imboss'd and wrought with Gold after the *Tauchic* manner. The Eighth, an Ivy Goblet very precious, inlaid with Gold. The Ninth, a Cup of fine *Obriz* Gold. The Tenth, a Tumbler of Aromatic Agaloch (you call it *Lignum Aloes*) edg'd with *Cyprian* Gold, after the *Azemine* make. The Eleventh, a Golden Vine-Tub of *Mozaic* Work. The Twelfth, a Runlet of unpolish'd Gold, covered with a small Vine of large *Indian* Pearl of *Topiarian* Work. Insomuch that there was no Man, however in the Dumps, musty, sower look'd, or Melanchollic he were, not even excepting that blubbering Whiner *Heraclitus*, had he been there, but, seeing this Noble Convoy of Ships and their Devises, must have been seized with present gladness of Heart, and smiling at the Conceit, have said that the Travellers were all honest Topers, true Pitcher-men, and have judged by a most sure Prognostication, that their Voyage both outward and homeward bound, would be performed in Mirth and perfect Health.

In the *Thalamege* where was the general meeting, *Pantagruel* made a short but sweet Exhortation, wholy back'd with Authorities from Scripture upon Navigation; which being ended, with an audible Voice Prayers were said in the presence and hearing of all the Burghers of *Thalassa*, who had flock'd to the Mole to see them take Shipping. After the Prayers, was melodiously sung a *Psalm* of the Holy King *David*, which begins, *When Israel went out of Ægypt;* and that being ended, Tables were plac'd upon Deck, and a Feast speedily serv'd up. The *Thalassians* who had also born a Chorus in the *Psalm*, caus'd store of belly Timber to be brought out of their Houses. All drank to them, they drank to all; which was the cause that none of the whole Company gave up what they had eaten, nor were Sea-sick with a pain at the Head and Stomach, which inconveniency they could not so easily have prevented by drinking, for some time before, Salt-Water either alone or mixt with Wine, using Quinces, Citron-peel, Juice of Pomgranats, sowrish Sweat-Meats, fasting a long time, covering their Stomachs with Paper, or following such other idle Remedies, as foolish Physicians prescribe to those that go to Sea.

Having often renewed their Tiplings, each Mother's Son retired on board his own Ship, and set Sail all so fast with a merry Gale at South East, to which point of the Compass the Chief Pilot, *James Brayer* by Name, had shap'd his Course, and fixt all things accordingly. For seeing that the Oracle of the *Holy Bottle* lay near *Catay*, in the upper *India*, his advice and that of *Xenomanes* also, was, not to steer the Course which the *Portuguese* use, while sayling through the *Torrid Zone*, and Cape *Bona Speranza* at the South Point of *Africk* beyond the *Equinoctial Line*, and losing sight of the Northern Pole their Guide, they make a prodigious long Voyage; but rather to keep as near the Parallel of the said *India* as possible, and to tack to the Westard of the said Pole, so that winding under the North, they might find themselves in the Latitude of the Port of *Olone*, without coming nearer it, for fear of being shut up in the Frozen Sea; whereas following this Canonical Turn by the said Parallel, they must have that on the right to the Eastward, which at their departure was on their left.

This prov'd a much shorter Cut; for without Shipwreck, Danger, or loss of Men, with uninterrupted good Weather, except one day near the Island of the *Macreons*, they perform'd in less than four Months the Voyage of Upper *India*, which the *Portuguese*, with a thousand Inconveniencies and innumerable Dangers, can hardly compleat in three Years. And it is my Opinion, with Submission to better Judgments, that this Course was perhaps steer'd by those *Indians* who Sail'd to *Germany*, and were honourably received by the King of the *Swedes*, while *Quintus Metellus Celer* was Proconsul of the *Gauls*, as *Corn. Nepos*, *Pomponius Mela*, and *Pliny* after them tell us.

CHAPTER II

How Pantagruel bought many rarities in the island of
Medamothy.

THAT day and the two following, they neither discovered Land
nor any thing new; for they had formerly Sailed that way; but on
the fourth they made an Island call'd *Medamothy*, of a fine and
delightful Prospect, by reason of the vast number of Light-
Houses and high Marble Towers in its Circuit, which is not less
than that of *Canada*. *Pantagruel*, enquiring who Govern'd there,
heard that it was King *Philophanes*, absent at that time upon
account of the Marriage of his Brother *Philotheamon* with the
Infanta of the *Kingdom* of *Engys*.

Hearing this, he went ashoar in the Harbour, and while every
Ship's Crew Water'd, pass'd his time in viewing divers Animals,
Fishes, Birds, and other exotic and foreign Merchandises which
were along the Walks of the Mole, and in the Markets of the
Port. For it was the third day of the great and famous Fair of
the Place, to which the chief Merchants of *Africa* and *Asia*
resorted. Out of these Fryar *Jhon* bought him two rare Pictures,
in one of which, the Face of a Man that brings in an Appeal, was
drawn to the Life, and in the other, a Servant that wants a Master,
with every needful Particular, Action, Countenance, Looks,
Gate, Feature and Deportment; being an Original, by Master
Charles Charmois, principal Painter to King *Megistus*; and he paid
for them in the Court Fashion, with *Congé* and *Grimace*. *Panurge*
bought a large Picture copied and done from the Needle-Work
formerly wrought by *Philomela*, shewing to her Sister *Progne*
how her Brother-in-law *Tereus* had by force hansell'd her Copy-
hold, and then cut out her Tongue, that she might not (as Women
will) tell tales. I vow and swear by the handle of my Paper Lanthorn, that it was a gallant, a mirific, nay a most admirable Piece.
Nor do you think, I pray you, that in it was the Picture of a Man
playing the Beast with two Backs with a Female, this had been
too silly and gross; no, no; 'twas another-guise thing, and much
plainer. You may, if you please, see it at *Theleme*, on the left
hand, as you go into the high Gallery. *Epistemon* bought another

wherein were painted to the Life, the *Ideas* of *Plato* and the *Atoms* of *Epicurus*. *Rhizotome* purchased another, wherein *Echo* was drawn to the Life. *Pantagruel* caused to be bought by *Gymnast*, the Life and Deeds of *Achilles* in Seventy eight pieces of Tapestry four Fathom long, and three Fathom broad, all of *Phrygian* Silk imboss'd with Gold and Silver; the Work beginning at the Nuptials of *Peleus* and *Thetis*, continuing to the Birth of *Achilles*; his Youth describ'd by *Statius Papinius*; his warlike Atchievements celebrated by *Homer*; his Death and Exequies written by *Ovid* and *Quintus Calaber*; and ending at the appearance of his Ghost, and *Polyxene*'s Sacrifice Rehearsed by *Euripides*.

He also caus'd to be bought three fine young Unicorns; one of them a Male of a Chesnut colour, and two grey dappled Females; also a Tarand whom he bought of a *Scythian* of the *Geloni*'s Country.

A Tarand is an Animal as big as a Bullock, having a Head like a Stag, or a little bigger, two stately Horns with large Branches, cloven Feet, Hair long like that of a furr'd Muscovite, I mean a Bear, and a Skin almost as hard as Steel Armor. The *Scythian* said that there are but few Tarands to be found in *Scythia*, because it varieth its colour according to the diversity of the places where it grazes and abides, and represents the colour of the Grass, Plants, Trees, Shrubs, Flowers, Meadows, Rocks, and generally of all things near which it comes. It hath this common with the Sea Pulp, or Polypus, with the Thoes, with the Wolves of *India*, and with the Chamælion, which is a kind of a Lizard so wonderful, that *Democritus* hath written a whole Book of its Figure, and Anatomy, as also of its Virtue and Propriety in Magic. This I can affirm, that I have seen it change its colour not only at the approach of things that have a colour, but by its own voluntary impulse, according to its fear or other affections: as for example, upon a green Carpet, I have seen it certainly become green; but having remain'd there some time, it turn'd yellow, blue, tann'd, and purple in course, in the same manner as you see a Turky Cock's Comb change colour according to its Passions. But what we found most surprizing in this Tarand, is, that not only its Face and Skin, but also its Hair could take whatever colour was about it. Near *Panurge* with his Kersy Coat, its Hair used to turn grey; near *Pantagruel* with his Scarlat Mantle, its Hair and Skin grew red; near the *Pilot* drest after the fashion of the *Isiacs* of *Anubis* in *Ægypt*, its Hair seem'd all white; which two colours the Chamælion can't borrow.

When the Creature was free from any fear or affection, the colour of its Hair was just such as you see that of the Asses of *Meung*.

CHAPTER III

How Pantagruel received a Letter from his Father Gargantua, and of the strange way to have speedy news from far distant places.

WHILE *Pantagruel* was taken up with the Purchase of those foreign Animals, the noise of ten Guns and Culverins, together with a loud and joyful Cheer of all the Fleet was heard from the Mole. *Pantagruel* look'd towards the Haven, and perceived that this was occasioned by the Arrival of one of his Father *Gargantua*'s *Celoces*, or Advice-Boat named the *Chelidonia*, because on the Stern of it, was carv'd in *Corinthian* Brass a Sea Lark, which is a Fish as large as a Dare-fish of *Loire*, all Flesh and no Bone, with cartilaginous Wings (like a Bat's) very long and broad, by the means of which, I have seen them fly about three Fathom above Water about a Bow-shot. At *Marseillis* 'tis call'd *Lendole*. And indeed that Ship was as light as a Lark, so that it rather seem'd to fly on the Sea than to sail. *Malicorn*, *Gargantua*'s Esq; Carver, was come in her, being sent expresly by his Master to have an Account of his Son's Health and Circumstances, and to bring him Credentials. When *Malicorn* had Saluted *Pantagruel*, before the Prince opened the Letters, the first thing he said to him, was, Have you here the *Gozal*, the Heavenly Messenger? Yes, Sir, said he, here it is swadled up in this Basket. It was a grey Pigeon taken out of *Gargantua*'s Dove-house, whose young ones were just hatch'd when the Advice-Boat was going off.

If any ill Fortune had befallen *Pantagruel*, he would have fasten'd some black Ribbon to its Feet; but because all things had succeeded happily hitherto, having caus'd it to be undrest, he ty'd to its Feet a white Ribbon, and without any further delay, let it loose. The Pigeon presently flew away cutting the Air with an incredible speed, as you know that there is no flight like a Pigeon's, especially when it hath Eggs or Young Ones, through the extream Care which Nature hath fixt in it to relieve, and be with its Young; insomuch that in less than two hours it compass'd in the Air, the long Tract which the Advice Boat with all her diligence, with Oars and Sails, and a fair Wind, had gone through in no less than three Days and three Nights, and was seen (as it went into the Dove-House) in its Nest. Whereupon *Gargantua* hearing that it had the white Ribbon on, was joyful and secure of his Son's welfare. This was the Custom of the noble *Gargantua* and *Pantagruel*, when they would have speedy News of something of great Concern, as the event of some Battel either by Sea or Land; the surrendring or holding out of some strong Place; the determination of some difference of Moment; the safe or unhappy Delivery of some Queen or great Lady; the Death or Recovery of their sick Friends or Allies, and so forth. They used to take the *Gozal*, and had it carried from one to another by the Post, to the Places whence they desir'd to have News. The *Gozal* bearing either a black or white Ribbon, according to the Occurrences and Accidents, us'd to remove their doubts at its return, making in the space of one hour, more way through the Air, than thirty Post-Boys could have done in one natural day. May not this be said to redeem and gain time with a vengeance, think you? For the like Service therefore, you may believe as a most true thing, that, in the Dove-Houses of their Farms, there were to be found all the Year long, store of Pigeons hatching Eggs or rearing their young. Which may be easily done in *Aviaries* and *Voleries*, by the help of *Saltpeter* and the sacred Herb *Vervain*.

The *Gozal* being let fly, *Pantagruel* perus'd his Father *Gargantua*'s Letter, the Contents of which were as followeth.

My Dearest Son,—*The Affection that naturally a Father bears a beloved Son, is so much increased in me, by reflecting on the particular Gifts which by the Divine Goodness have been heaped on thee, that since thy departure, it hath often banished all other Thoughts out of my Mind; leaving my Heart wholly possess'd with Fear, lest some misfortune has attended thy Voyage: for thou knowest that fear was ever the*

attendant of true and sincere Love. Now because (as Hesiod *saith*) A
good beginning of any thing is the half of it; *or,* well begun's half
done, *according to the old saying; to free my Mind from this anxiety, I
have expressly dispatch'd* Malicorn, *that he may give me a true account
of thy Health at the beginning of thy Voyage. For if it be good, and such
as I wish it, I shall easily foresee the rest.*

*I have met with some diverting Books, which the Bearer will deliver
thee, thou mayst read them when thou wantest to unbend and ease thy
Mind from thy better Studies; He will also give thee at large the News
at Court. The Peace of the Lord be with thee. Remember me to* Panurge,
Fryar Jhon, Epistemon, Xenomanes, Gymnast, *and thy other
principal Domestics.* Dated at our Paternal Seat this 13th day of
June. Thy Father and Friend,

Gargantua.

CHAPTER IV

*How Pantagruel writ to his Father Gargantua, and sent him
several Curiosities.*

PANTAGRUEL having persued the Letter, had a long Conference with the Esquire *Malicorn,* insomuch, that *Panurge* at
last interrupting them, ask'd him, Pray, Sir, when do you design
to drink? When shall we drink? When shall the Worshipful Esquire drink? What a Devil have you not talk'd long enough to
drink? 'Tis a good motion, answer'd *Pantagruel,* go, get us something ready at the next Inn; I think 'tis the *Centaur.* In the mean
time he writ to *Gargantua* as followeth, to be sent by the aforesaid Esquire.

Most Gracious Father,—*As our Senses and Animal Faculties are
more discompos'd at the News of Events unexpected, tho' desir'd (even
to an immediate dissolution of the Soul from the Body) than if those
accidents had been foreseen; so the coming of* Malicorn *hath much sur-
prized and disordered me. For I had no hopes to see any of your Servants, or to hear from you, before I had finished our Voyage, and
contented my self with the dear Remembrance of your August Majesty,
deeply impress'd in the hindmost Ventricle of my Brain, often representing you to my Mind.*

But since you have made me happy beyond expectation, by the perusal of your Gracious Letter, and the Faith I have in your Esquire, hath reviv'd my Spirits by the News of your welfare; I am as it were compell'd to do what formerly I did freely, that is, first to praise the Blessed Redeemer, who by his Divine Goodness preserves you in this long enjoyment of perfect Health; then to return you eternal Thanks for the fervent Affection which you have for me your most humble Son and unprofitable Servant.

Formerly a Roman, *named* Furnius, *said to* Augustus *who had received his Father into Favour, and Pardoned him after he had sided with* Anthony, *that by that Action the Emperor had reduc'd him to this extremity,* That for want of Power to be Grateful, both while he liv'd and after it, he should be oblig'd to be tax'd with Ingratitude. *So I may say, That the excess of your Fatherly Affection, drives me into such a streight, that I shall be forced to live and die ungrateful; unless that Crime be redress'd by the Sentence of the* Stoicks, *who say,* That there are three parts in a Benefit, the one of the Giver, the other of the Receiver, the third of the Remunerator; and that the Receiver rewards the Giver when he freely receives the Benefit, and always remembers it; as on the contrary, That Man is most ungrateful who despises and forgets a Benefit. *Therefore being overwhelmed with infinite Favours, all proceeding from your extream goodness, and on the other side wholly uncapable of making the smallest Return, I hope at least to free my self from the imputation of Ingratitude, since they can never be blotted out of my mind; and my Tongue shall never cease to own, that to thank you as I ought transcends my Capacity.*

As for us, I have this assurance in the Lord's Mercy and Help, that the end of our Voyage will be answerable to its beginning, and so it will be entirely performed in Health and Mirth. I will not fail to set down in a Journal a full Account of our Navigation, that at our return you may have an exact Relation of the whole.

I have found here a Scythian *Tarand, an Animal strange and wonderful for the variations of colour on its Skin and Hair, according to the distinction of neighbouring Things; It is as tractable and easily kept as a Lamb; be pleased to accept of it.*

I also send you three young Unicorns, which are the tamest of Creatures.

I have confer'd with the Esquire, and taught him how they must be fed; these cannot graze on the Ground, by reason of the long Horn on their Fore-head, but are forced to brouze on Fruit-Trees, or on proper Racks, or to be fed by Hand with Herbs, Sheaves, Apples, Pears, Barly, Rye, and other Fruits, and Roots being plac'd before them.

I am amazed that Ancient Writers should report them to be so Wild, Furious, and Dangerous, and never seen alive: Far from it, you will find that they are the mildest things in the World, provided thay are not maliciously offended. Likewise, I send you the Life and Deeds of Achilles in curious Tapestry; assuring you that whatever Rarities of Animals, Plants, Birds, or precious Stones, and others, I shall be able to find and purchase in our Travels, shall be brought to you, God willing, whom I beseech by his blessed Grace, to preserve you. From Medamothy, this 16th of June. Panurge, Fryar Jhon, Epistemon, Xenomanes, Gymnast, Eusthenes, Rhizotome, and Carpalim, having most humbly kissed your Hand, return your Salute a thousand times. Your most Dutiful Son and Servant,

Pantagruel.

While *Pantagruel* was writing this Letter, *Malicorn* was made welcom by all with a thousand goodly Good-Morows and How-d'y's; they clung about him so, that I cannot tell you how much they made of him, how many Humble Services, how many *from my Love and to my Love* were sent with him. *Pantagruel* having writ his Letters, sat down at Table with him, and afterwards presented him with a large Chain of Gold weighing eight hundred Crowns; between whose Septenary Links, some large Diamonds, Rubies, Emeralds, *Turky* Stones, and Unions were alternatively set in. To each of his Bark's Crew, he order'd to be given five hundred Crowns. To *Gargantua* his Father, he sent the Tarand covered with a Cloth of Gold, brocaded with Sattin, and the Tapistry containing the Life and Deeds of *Achilles*, with the three Unicorns in Friz'd Cloth of Gold Trappings. And so they left *Medamothy. Malicorn* to return to *Gargantua; Pantagruel* to proceed in his Voyage, during which, *Epistemon* read to him the Books which the Esquire had brought: And because he found them jovial and pleasant, I shall give you an account of them, if you earnestly desire it.

CHAPTER V

How Pantagruel met a Ship with Passengers returning from Lantern-Land.

ON the fifth day we began already to wind by little and little about the *Pole*, going still farther from the *Equinoctial Line*, we discovered a Merchant Man to the Windward of us. The Joy for this was not smal on both sides, in hopes to hear News from Sea, and those in the Merchant-Man from Land. So we bore upon 'em, and coming up with them, we Hal'd them, and finding them to be *Frenchmen* of *Xaintonge*, back'd our Sails and lay by to talk to them. *Pantagruel* heard that they came from *Lantern-Land*, which added to his joy, and that of the whole Fleet. We enquir'd about the State of that Country, and the way of living of the *Lanterns*; and were told, that about the latter end of the following *July*, was the time prefix'd for the meeting of the General Chapter of the *Lanterns*; and that if we arrived there at that time, as we might easily, we should see a Handsom, Honourable, and jolly Company of *Lanterns*; and that great Preparations were making, as if they intended to *Lanternise* there to the purpose. We were told also, That if we touch'd at the great Kingdom of *Gebarin*, we should be Honourably received and Treated by the Sovereign of that Country, King *Ohabé*, who as well as all his Subjects, speaks *Touraine French*.

While we were listening to these News, *Panurge* fell out with one *Dingdong* a Drover or Sheep-Merchant of *Taillebourg*. The occasion of the Fray was thus.

This same *Dingdong* seeing *Panurge* without a Codpiece, with his Spectacles fastened to his Cap, said to one of his Comrades, Prithee, look, is not there here a fine Medal of a Cuckold? *Panurge* by reason of his Spectacles, as you may well think, heard more plainly by half with his Ears than usually; which caused him (hearing this) to say to the sawcy Dealer in Mutton, in kind of Pet,

How the Devil should I be one of the hornified Fraternity, since I am not yet a Brother of the Marriage Noose, as thou art, as I guess by thy ill-favour'd Phyz?

Yea verily, quoth the Grazier, I am Married, and would not be otherwise for all the pairs of Spectacles in *Europe*; nay, not for all the Magnifying Gim-Cracks in *Africa*; for I have got me the Cleverest, Prettiest, Handsomest, Properest, Neatest, Tightest, Honestest, and Soberest piece of Woman's Flesh for my Wife, that is in all the whole Country of *Xaintonge*, I'll say that for her, and a Fart for all the rest. I bring her home a fine and eleven inch long branch of Red Coral, *for her Christmass-Box*, what hast thou to do with it? What's that to thee? Who art thou? Whence comest thou, O dark Lanthorn of Antichrist? Answer if thou art of God? I ask thee, *by the way of Question*, said *Panurge* to him very seriously, if with the Consent and Countenance of all the Elements, I had Gingumbob'd, Codpiec'd, and Thumpthumpriggledtickledtwidl'd thy so Clever, so Pretty, so Handsom, so Proper, so Neat, so Tight, so Honest, and so Sober Female Importance, insomuch, that the Stiff Deity that has no fore-cast, *Priapus*, (who dwells here at Liberty, all Subjection of fastened Codpieces or Bolts, Bars, and Locks, Abdicated) remain'd sticking in her natural *Christmass-box* in such a lamentable manner, that it were never to come out, but Eternally should stick there, unless thou didst pull it out with thy Teeth; what wouldst thou do? Wouldst thou everlastingly leave it there, or wouldst thou pluck it out with thy Grinders? Answer me, O thou Ram of *Mahomet*, since thou art one of the Devil's Gang. I would, reply'd the Sheep Monger, take thee such a woundy cut on this Spectacle-bearing Lug of thine, with my trusty Bilbo, as would smite thee dead as a Herring. Thus having taken Pepper in the Nose, he was lugging out Sword; but alas, Curs'd Cows have short Horns, it stuck in the Scabbard; as you know that at Sea, cold Iron will easily take rust, by reason of the excessive and Nitrous Moistness. *Panurge* so smitten with Terror, that his Heart sunk down to his Midriff, scower'd off to *Pantagruel* for help: But Fryar *Jhon* laid hand on his slashing Scymiter that was new ground, and would certainly have dispatch'd *Dingdong* to rights, had not the Skipper and some of his Passengers beseech'd *Pantagruel* not to suffer such an out-rage to be committed on Board his Ship. So the matter was made up, and *Panurge* and his Antagonist shak'd Fists, and drank in course to one another, in token of a perfect Reconciliation.

CHAPTER VI

*How the Fray being over, Panurge Cheapened one of
Dingdong's Sheep.*

THIS Quarrel being hush'd, *Panurge* tipp'd the wink upon *Epistemon* and Friar *Jhon*, and taking them aside; Stand at some distance out of the way, said he, and take your share of the
following Scene of Mirth; you shall have rare Sport anon, if my
Cake ben't Dough, and my Plot do but take. Then addressing
himself to the Drover, he took off to him a Bumper of good
Lantern Wine. The other pledg'd him briskly and courteously.
This done, *Panurge* earnestly entreated him to sell him one of
his Sheep: But the other answered him, Is it come to that,
Friend and Neighbour, would you put tricks upon Travellers?
Alas, how finely you love to play upon poor Folk! Nay, you
seem a rare Chapman, that's the truth on't. Oh what a mighty
Sheep-Merchant you are! In good faith you look liker one of the
Diving Trade than a buyer of Sheep. Adzookers, what a Bless-
ing it would be to have ones Purse well lin'd with Chink near
your Worship at a Tripe-House when it begins to thaw!
Humph, Humph, did not we know you well, you might serve
one a slippery trick! Pray do but see, good People, what a
mighty Conjurer the fellow would be reckon'd. Patience, said
Panurge; but waving that, be so kind as to sell me one of your
Sheep, come, how much? What do you mean, Master of mine,
answered the other? They are long Wool Sheep, from these did
Jason take his *Golden Fleece*. The Gold of the House of *Burgundy*
was drawn from them. Zwoons, Man, they are Oriental Sheep,
Topping Sheep, Fatted Sheep, Sheep of Quality. Be it so, said
Panurge, but sell me one of them, I beseech you, and that for a
cause, paying you ready Money upon the Nail, in good and lawful Occidental Currant Cash; wilt say how much? Friend,
Neighbour, answered the Seller of Mutton, hark 'e me a little,
on the other Ear.

 Panurge. On which side you please; I hear you.
 Dingdong. You are a going to *Lantern-Land*, they say.
 Panurge. Yea verily.

Ding. To see Fashions?

Panurge. Even so.

Ding. And be Merry?

Panurge. And be Merry.

Ding. Your Name is as I take it, *Robin Mutton?*

Panurge. As you please for that, sweet Sir.

Ding. Nay, without offence.

Panurge. So I would have it.

Ding. You are, as I take it, the King's Jester, aren't you?

Panurge. Ay, ay, any thing.

Ding. Give me your Hand,—humph, humph, you go to see Fashions, you are the King's Jester, your Name is *Robin Mutton*! Do you see this same Ram? His Name too is *Robin.* Here *Robin, Robin, Robin:* Baea, Baea, Baea, Hath he not a rare Voice?

Panurge. Ay marry has he, a very fine and harmonious Voice.

Ding. Well, this bargain shall be made between you and me, Friend, and Neighbour, we will get a pair of Scales, then you *Robin Mutton* shall be put into one of them, and *Tup Robin* into the other. Now I'll hold you a Peck of *Busch Oysters*, that in Weight, Value, and Price, he shall outdo you, and you shall be found light in the very numerical manner, as when you shall be Hang'd and Suspended.

Patience, said *Panurge*, but you would do much for me, and your whole Posterity, if you would Chaffer with me for him, or some other of his Inferiors. I beg it of you; good your Worship, be so kind. Hark 'e, Friend of mine, answered the other, with the Fleece of these your fine *Roan* Cloth is to be made, your *Lemster* superfine Wooll is mine Arse to 't; meer Flock in comparison: of their Skin the best *Cordivant* will be made, which shall be sold for *Turky* and *Montelimart*, or for *Spanish* Leather at least. Of the Guts shall be made Fiddle and Harp Strings, that will sell as dear as if they came from *Munican* or *Aquileia*. What do you think on 't, hah? If you please, sell me one of them, said *Panurge*, and I am yours for ever. Look, here's ready Cash. What's the Price? This he said, exhibiting his Purse stuffed with new *Henricuses*.

CHAPTER VII

Which if you read, you'll find how Panurge bargain'd with Dingdong.

NEIGHBOUR, my Friend, answer'd *Dingdong*, they are Meat for None but Kings and Princes; their Flesh is so delicate, so Savory, and so dainty, that One would swear, it melted in the Mouth. I bring them out of a Country where the very Hogs, God be with us, live on nothing but mirabolans. The Sows in their Styes when they lie in, (saving the honour of this good Company) are fed only with Orange Flowers. But, said *Panurge*, drive a Bargain with me for one of them, and I will pay you for't like a King, upon the honest Word of a true Trojan: come come, what do you ask? Not so fast, *Robin*, answer'd the Trader, these Sheep are lineally descended from the very family of the Ram that wafted *Phrixus* and *Helle* over the Sea, since call'd the *Hellespont*. A Pox on 't, said *Panurge*, you are *Clericus vel addiscens!* *Ita* is a Cabbage, and *Verè* a Leek, answered the Merchant. But *rr, rrr, rrrr, rrrrr*, hoh *Robin, rr, rrrrrrr*, you don't understand that Gibberish, do you? Now I think on 't, over all the fields, where they piss, Corn grows as fast as if the Lord had piss'd there; they need neither be till'd, nor dung'd. Besides, Man, your Chymists extract the best Saltpeter in the World out of their Urin: nay, with their very Dung (with reverence be it spoken) the Doctors in our Country make Pills that cure seventy eight kinds of Diseases; the least of which is the Evil of St. *Eutropius* of *Xaintes*, from which good Lord deliver us! Now what do you think on 't, Neighbour, my Friend? The truth is, they cost me money, that they do! Cost what they will, cry'd *Panurge*, trade with me for one of them, paying you well. Our friend, quoth the quack-like Sheep-man, do but mind the wonders of Nature that are found in those Animals, even in a member which one would think were of no use. Take me but these horns, and bray them a little with an Iron-pestle, or with an Andiron, which you please, 'tis all one to me; then bury them where-ever you will, provided it be where the Sun may shine, and water them frequently; in a few months I'll engage you will have the best

Asparagus in the World, not even excepting those of *Ravenna*. Now come and tell me whether the Horns of you other Knights of the Bulls Feather, have such a virtue and wonderful propriety?

Patience, said *Panurge*. I don't know whether you be a Scholar or no, pursued *Dingdong*: I have seen a World of Scholars, I say great Scholars, that were cuckolds, I'l assure you. But hark you me, if you were a Scholar, you should know that in the most inferiour members of those Animals (which are the feet) there is a bone (which is the heel) the *Astragalus*, if you will have it so, wherewith, and with that of no other Creature breathing, except the *Indian* Ass, and the Dorcades of *Libya*, they us'd in old times to play at the Royal game of Dice, whereat *Augustus* the Emperour won above fifty thousand Crowns one Evening. Now such Cuckolds as you will be hang'd ere you get half so much at it. Patience, said *Panurge*, but let us dispatch. And when, my Friend and Neighbour, continu'd the canting Sheep-seller, shall I have duely prais'd the inward Members, the Shoulders, the Legs, the Knuckles, the Neck, the Breast, the Liver, the Spleen, the Tripes, the Kidneys, the Bladder, wherewith they make Footballs, the Ribs, which serve in *Pigmy-land* to make little Crossbows to pelt the Cranes with Cherry-stones; the Head which with a little Brimstone serves to make a miraculous decoction to loosen and ease the belly of costive Dogs. A Turd on 't, said the Skipper to his preaching Passenger, what a fidle fadle have we here? There is too long a Lecture by half, sell him one if thou wilt; if thou won't, don't let the Man lose more time. I hate a gibble gabble and a rimble ramble Talk, I am for a Man of Brevity. I will for your sake, reply'd the Holder-forth: but then he shall give me three Livers French Money for each, and pick and chuse. 'Tis a woundy Price, cry'd *Panurge*, in our Country I could have five, nay six for the Money; see that you do not overreach me, Master. You are not the first Man whom I have known, to have fallen, even sometime to the indangering, if not breaking of his own Neck, for endeavouring to rise all at once. A Murrain seize thee for a blockheaded Booby, cry'd the angry seller of Sheep; by the worthy vow of our Lady of *Charroux*: the worst in this Flock is four times better than those which the *Coraxians* in *Tuditania*, a Country of *Spain*, us'd to sell for a Gold

Talent each; and how much do'st thou think, thou Hybernian Fool, that a Talent of Gold was worth? Sweet Sir, you fall into a Passion I see, return'd *Panurge*: Well, hold, here is your Money. *Panurge* having paid his Money, chose him out of all the Flock a fine topping Ram, and as he was hawling it along crying out and bleating, all the rest hearing and bleating in Consort star'd, to see whither their brother-Ram should be carried. In the mean while the Drover was saying to his Shepherds, Ah! How well the Knave could chuse him out a Ram, the whoreson has Skill in Cattle; on my honest Word I reserv'd that very piece of Flesh for the Lord of *Cancale*, well knowing his disposition; for the good Man naturally is overjoy'd when he holds a good siz'd handsom shoulder of Mutton, instead of a left-handed racket in one hand, with a good sharp Carver in the other; got wot how he belabours himself then.

CHAPTER VIII

How Panurge caus'd Dingdong and his Sheep to be drowned in the Sea.

ON a Sudden, you would wonder how the thing was so soon done; for my Part I can't tell you, for I had not leisure to mind it; our friend *Panurge* without any further tittle tattle, throws you his Ram over board into the middle of the Sea bleating and making a sad noise. Upon this all the other Sheep in the Ship crying and bleating in the same tone, made all the hast they could to leap nimbly into the Sea one after another, and great was the throng who should leap in first after their Leader. It was impossible to hinder them; for you know that it is in the Nature of Sheep always to follow the first, wheresoever it goes; which makes *Aristotle lib. 9. de Hist. Animal.* mark them for the most silly and foolish Animals in the World. *Dingdong* at his wit's End, and stark staring Mad like a Man who saw his Sheep destroy and drown themselves before his Face, strove to hinder and keep them back with might and main, but all in vain; they all, one after t' other, frisk'd and jump'd into the Sea, and were lost: at last he laid hold on a huge sturdy one by the fleece upon the deck of the Ship, hoping to keep it back, and so to save that and the rest; but the Ram was so strong that it proved too hard for him, and carried its Master into the Herring-Pond, in spight of his Teeth; where 'tis supposed he drank somewhat more than his Fill: So that he was drowned, in the same manner, as one-eyed *Polyphemus*'s Sheep carried out of the Den *Ulysses* and his Companions: The like happen'd to the Shepherds and all their gang, some laying hold on their beloved Tup, this by the horns, t' other by the Legs, a third by the Rump, and others by the fleece; till in fine they were all of them forc'd to Sea, and drowned like so many Rats. *Panurge* on the gunnel of the Ship with an Oar in his hand, not to help them, you may swear, but to keep them from swimming to the Ship, and saving themselves from drowning, preach'd and canted to them all the while like any little Fryar *Maillard*, or another Fryar *John Burgess*, laying before them Rhetorical common places concerning the miseries of this Life, and the blessings and felicity of the next; assuring them that the Dead were much happier than the Living in this vale of misery, and promising to erect a stately Cenotaphe and Honorary Tomb to every one of them on the highest Summit of Mount *Cenis* at his return from *Lantern* land; wishing them nevertheless, in case they were not yet dispos'd to shake hands with this Life, and did not like their salt Liquor, they might have the good luck to meet with some kind Whale which might set them ashore safe and sound, on some bless'd Land of *Gotham* after a famous Example.

The Ship being clear'd of *Dingdong* and his Tups: Is there ever another sheepish Soul left lurking on board, cried *Panurge*? Where are those of *Toby Lamb*, and *Robin Ram*, that sleep whilst the rest are a feeding? Faith I can't tell my self. This was an old coaster's Trick: What think'st thou of it, Fryar *Jhon*, hah? Rarely perform'd, answer'd Fryar *Jhon*, only methinks that as formerly in War on the Day of Battle, a double Pay was commonly promis'd the Soldiers for that Day; for if they overcame, there was enough to pay them; and if they lost, it would have been shameful for them to demand it, as the cowardly *Foresters* did after the Battle of *Cerizoles*: Likewise, my Friend, you ought not to have paid your Man, and the Mony had been sav'd. A Fart for the Money, said *Panurge*, have I not had above fifty thousand pounds worth of sport? Come now, let's begon, the Wind is fair,

hark you me, my Friend *Jhon*, Never did Man do me a good
Turn but I return'd or at least acknowledg'd it: No, I scorn to
be ungrateful, I never was, nor ever will be: Never did Man do
me an ill one without rueing the Day that he did it, either in this
World or the next. I am not yet so much a fool neither. Thou
damn'st thy self like any old Devill, quoth Fryar *Jhon*. It is written *Mihi vindictum*, &c. matter of breviary, Mark ye me; that's
holy stuff.

CHAPTER IX

*How Pantagruel Arrived at the Island of Ennasin, and of the
strange ways of being akin in that Country.*

WE had still the Wind at South South West, and had been a
whole day without making Land. On the third day at the Flyes
up-rising, which, you know, is some two or three hours after the
Sun's, we got sight of a Triangular Island, very much like *Sicily*
for its Form and Situation. It was called the Island of *Alliances*.

The People there are much like your Carrot-pated *Poitevins*,
save only that all of them, Men, Women, and Children, have
their Noses shap'd like an Ace of Clubs. For that reason the
ancient Name of the Country was *Ennasin*. There were all akin,
as the Mayor of the place told us, at least they boasted so.

You People of the other World, esteem it a wonderful thing,
that, out of the Family of the *Fabii* at *Rome*, on a certain day,
which was the 13th of *February*, at a certain Gate, which was the
Porta Carmentalis, since nam'd *Scelerata*, formerly situated at the
foot of the *Capitol*, between the *Tarpeian Rock* and the *Tyber*,
March'd out against the *Veientes* of *Etruria*, three hundred and
six Men bearing Arms, all related to each other, with five thousand other Soldiers every one of them their Vassals, who were
all slain near the River *Cremera*, that comes out of the Lake of
Beccano. Now from this same Country of *Ennasin* in case of need,
above three hundred thousand all Relations, and of one Family,
might March out.

Their degrees of Consanguinity and Alliance are very strange,
for being thus akin and allied to one another, we found that
none was either Father or Mother, Brother or Sister, Uncle or

Aunt, Nephew or Neece, Son-in-Law or Daughter-in-Law, God-Father or God-Mother to the other, unless truly, a tall flat-nos'd old fellow, who, as I perceiv'd, call'd a little shitten ars'd Girl of three or four years old, Father, and the Child call'd him Daughter.

Their distinction of degrees of Kindred was thus, a Man us'd to call a Woman my *Lean Bit*; the Woman call'd him my *Porpus*. Those, said Fryar *Jhon*, must needs stink damnably of Fish, when they have rub'd their Bacon one with t' other. One smiling on a young bucksom Baggage, said, good morrow dear *Curry-Comb*: she to return him his Civility, said, The like to you my *Steed*. Hah! Hah! Hah! said *Panurge*, that's pretty well i' faith, for indeed it stands her in good stead to Curry-comb this Steed. Another greeted his Buttock with a farewel, my *Case*: she reply'd, Adieu *Tryal*. By St. *Winifred*'s Placket, cry'd *Gymnast*, this Case has been often try'd. Another ask'd a she Friend of his, How is't, *Hatchet*? she answer'd him, at your service, dear *Helve*. Odds Belly, saith *Carpalin*, this Helve and this Hatchet are well match'd. As we went on, I saw one who, calling his she Relation, styl'd her my *Crum*, and she call'd him my *Crust*.

Quoth one to a brisk, plump, juicy Female, I am glad to see you, dear *Tap*: so am I to find you so merry, sweet *Spiggot*, reply'd she. One call'd a wench his *Shovel*, she call'd him her *Peal*. One nam'd his, my *Slipper*, and she him, my *Foot*. Another my *Boot*, she my *Shasoon*.

In the same degree of Kindred, one call'd his, my *Butter*, she call'd him, my *Eggs*; and they were akin just like a Dish of Butter'd Eggs. I heard one call his, my *Tripe*, and she him, my *Faggot*. Now I could not for the Heart's Blood of me pick out or discover what Parentage, Alliance, Affinity, or Consanguinity was between them, with reference to our Custom, only they told us, that she was Faggot's Tripe: [*Tripe de Faggot* means the smallest sticks in a Faggot.] Another Complementing his Convenient, said, yours, my *Shell*; she reply'd, I was yours before, sweet *Oyster*: I reckon, said *Carpalin*, she hath gutted his Oyster. Another long-shank'd ugly Rogue, mounted upon a pair of high-heel'd Wooden Slippers, meeting a strapping, fusty squobb'd Dowdy, says to her, how'st my *Top*? she was short upon him, and arrogantly reply'd, never the better for you, my *Whip*. By

St. *Anthony*'s Hog, said *Xenomanes*, I believe so, for how can this
Whip be sufficient to lash this Top?

A College-Professor well provided with Cod, and poudered
and prink'd up, having a while discoursed with a great Lady,
taking his leave, with these words, Thank you *Sweet Meat*; she
cry'd, there needs no thanks, *Sower Sauce*. Saith *Pantagruel*, this
is not altogether incongruous, for sweet Meat must have sower
Sawce. A Wooden Loggerhead said to a young Wench, 'Tis long
since I saw you *Bag*, all the better, cry'd she, *Pipe*. Set 'em
together, said *Panurge*, then blow in their Arses, 'twill be a Bagpipe. We saw after that a diminutive hump-back'd Gallant, pretty
near us, taking leave of a she relation of his, thus, Fare thee
well, Friend *Hole*; she repartee'd, save thee, Friend *Peg*. Quoth
Fryar *Jhon*, what could they say more, were he all Peg and she
all Hole: But now would I give something to know if every
Crany of the Hole can be stopp'd up with that same Peg.

A Baudy Batchelor talking with an old Trout, was saying,
Remember it, *Rusty Gun*. I won't fail, said she, *Scowrer*. Do you
reckon these two to be akin, said *Pantagruel* to the Mayor? I
rather take them to be Foes; in our Country a Woman would
take this as a mortal affront. Good People of t' other World,
reply'd the Mayor, you have few such and so near Relations as
this Gun and Scowerer are to one another; for they both came
out of one Shop. What, was the Shop their Mother, quoth *Panurge*? What Mother, said the Mayor, does the Man mean? That
must be some of your Worlds Affinity; we have here neither
Father nor Mother: Your little paultry fellows that live on t' other
side the Water, poor Rogues, Booted with Wisps of Hay, may
indeed have such, but we scorn it. The good *Pantagruel* stood
gazing and listning, but at these words he had like to have lost
all Patience; ὡς καὶ νῦν ὁ ἑρμηνευτής Π. M.

Having very exactly viewed the Situation of the Island, and
the way of living of the *Ennased* Nation, we went to take a Cup
of the Creature at a Tavern where there happen'd to be a Wedding after the manner of the Country; bating that shocking Custom, there was special good Chear.

While we were there, a pleasant Match was struck up betwixt a Female call'd *Pear* (a tight thing as we thought, but by
some who knew better things, said to be quaggy and flabby) and

a young soft Male, call'd *Cheese*, somewhat sandy. In our Country indeed we say, *Il ne fut onc tel marriage, qu'est de la Poire et du Fromage*, There's no Match like that made between the Pear and the Cheese; and in many other Places good store of such Bargains have been driven. Besides, when the women are at their last Prayers, 'tis to this day a noted saying, *That after Cheese comes nothing*.

In another Room I saw them marrying an old greasy Boot to a young pliable Buskin. *Pantagruel* was told, that young Buskin took old Boot *to have and to hold*, because she was of special Leather, in good case and wax'd, sear'd, liquor'd, and greas'd to the purpose, even tho' it had been for the Fisherman that went to Bed with his Boots on. In another Room below I saw a young Brogue taking a young Slipper *for better for worse*: Which, they told us, was neither for the sake of her Piety, Parts, or Person, but for the fourth comprehensive P, Portion; the Spankers, Spur-royals, Rose-Nobles, and other Coriander Seed with which she was quilted all over.

CHAPTER X

How Pantagruel went ashoar at the Island of Chely, where he saw King St. Panigon.

WE sail'd right before the Wind which we had at West, leaving those odd *Alliancers* with their Ace of Clubs Snouts, and having taken height by the Sun, stood in for *Chely*, a large, Fruitful, Wealthy, and well Peopled Island. King St. *Panigon* first of the Name Reign'd there, and attended by the Princes his Sons, and the Nobles of his Court, came as far as the Port to receive *Pantagruel*, and conducted him to his Palace, near the Gate of which, the Queen attended by the Princesses her Daughters and the Court Ladies, received us. *Panigon* directed her and all her Retinue to salute *Pantagruel* and his Men with a Kiss; for such was the Civil Custom of the Country; and they were all fairly buss'd accordingly, except Fryar *Jhon*, who stept aside and sneak'd off among the King's Officers. *Panigon* us'd all the entreaties imaginable, to persuade *Pantagruel* to tarry there that day and the next, but he would needs be gone, and excus'd himself upon the opportunity of Wind and Weather, which being oftener desir'd than enjoy'd, ought not to be neglected when it comes. *Panigon* having heard these reasons, let us go, but first made us take off some five and twenty or thirty Bumpers each.

Pantagruel returning to the Port, miss'd Fryar *Jhon*, and ask'd why he was not with the rest of the Company? *Panurge* could not tell how to excuse him, and would have gone back to the Palace to call him, when Fryar *Jhon* overtook them, and merrily cry'd, Long live the noble *Panigon*; as I love my Belly, he minds good Eating, and keeps a noble House, and a dainty Kitchen; I have been there, Boys, every thing goes about by dozens, I was in good hopes to have stufed my Puddings there like a Monk! What! always in a Kitchin, Friend? (said *Pantagruel*) By the Belly of St. *Cramcapon*, quoth the Fryar, I understand the Customs and Ceremonies which are us'd there, much better than all the formal Stuff, antick Postures, and nonsensical Fidle-fadle that must be us'd with those Women, *magni, magna, Shittencumshita*, Cringes, Grimaces, Scrapes, Bowes, and Congées; double Honours this way, tripple Salutes that way, the Embrace, the Grasp, the Squeeze, the Hug, the Leer, the Smack, *baso las manos de vostra merce, de vostra Maesta*. You are most *tarabin, tarabas, Stront*, that's downright *Dutch*, why all this ado? I don't say but a Man might be for a bit by the by and away, to be doing as well as his Neighbours; but this little nasty Cringing and Curtising made me as mad as any *March Devil*. You talk of kissing Ladies; by the Worthy and Sacred Frock I wear, I seldom venture upon 't, lest I be serv'd as was the Lord of *Guyercharois*. What was it, said *Pantagruel*, I know him; he is one of the best Friends I have?

He was invited to a Sumptuous Feast, said Fryar *Jhon*, by a Relation and Neighbour of his, together with all the Gentlemen and Ladies in the Neighbourhood. Now some of the latter, expecting his coming, drest the Pages in Womens Cloths, and *finified* them like any Babies, then order'd them to meet my Lord at his coming, near the Draw-bridge; so the *Complementing Monsieur* came, and there kiss'd the Petticoated Lads with great formality. At last the Ladies who minded Passages in the Gallery, burst out with Laughing, and made signs to the Pages to take off their dress; which the good Lord having observed, the Devil a bit he durst make up to the true Ladies to kiss them, but said,

That since they had disguis'd the Pages, by his Great Grandfather's Helmet, these were certainly the very Foot-men and
Grooms still more cunningly disguis'd. Ods Fish, *Da jurandi*,
why do not we rather remove our humanities into some good
warm Kitchin of God, that noble Laboratory? and there admire
the turning of the Spits, the harmonious rattling of the Jacks and
Fenders, criticise on the Position of the Lard, the temperature
of the Potages, the preparation for the *Dessert*, and the order of
the Wine Service? *Beati Immaculati in via*, matter of Breviary,
my Masters.

CHAPTER XI

Why Monks love to be in Kitchens.

THIS, said *Epistemon*, is spoke like a true *Monk* I mean like a
right *Monking Monk*, not a *bemonk'd* monastical *Monkling*. Truly
you put me in mind of some passages that happen'd at *Florence*
some twenty Years ago in a Company of studious Travellers,
fond of visiting the Learned, and seeing the Antiquities of *Italy*,
among whom I was. As we view'd the situation and beauty of
Florence, the structure of the Dome, the Magnificence of the
Churches, and Palaces, We strove to outdo one another in giving them their due; when a certain *Monk* of *Amiens*, *Bernard Lardon* by name, quite angry, scandaliz'd, and out of all Patience,
told us: I don't know what the Devill you can find in this same
Town, that's so much to be cry'd up; For my Part, I have look'd
and por'd and star'd as well as the best of you, I think my Eye
sight's as clear as another body's, and what can one see after all?
There are fine Houses indeed, and that's all. But the Cage does
not feed the Birds: God and *Monsieur* St. *Bernard* our good Patron be with us, in all this same Town I have not seen one poor
Lane of roasting Cooks, and yet I have not a little look'd about,
and sought for so necessary a part of a Commonwealth; Ay, and
I dare assure you that I have pry'd up and down with the exact-
ness of an Informer; as ready to number both to the right and
left how many and on what side we might find most roasting
Cooks, as a Spy would be to reckon the Bastions of a Town:
Now at *Amiens*, in four, nay five times less ground than we have

trod in our contemplations, I could have shown you above fourteen Streets of roasting Cooks, most ancient, Savoury, and Aromatic. I can't imagin what kind of pleasure you can have taken
in gazing on the *Lyons* and *Africans* (so methinks you call their
Tigers) near the *Belfrey*, or in ogling the *Porcupines* and *Estridges*
in the Lord *Philip Strozzi*'s Palace. Faith and Troth, I had rather
see a good fat Goose at the Spit. This Porphyry, those Marbles
are fine; I say nothing to the contrary, but our Cheesecakes at
Amiens are far better in my mind; These antient Statues are well
made; I am willing to believe it; but by St. *Ferreol* of *Abbeville*,
we have young Wenches in our Country which please me better
a thousand times.

What is the reason, ask'd Fryar *Jhon*, that *Monks* are always
to be found in Kitchins; and Kings, Emperours and Popes are
never there? Is there not, said *Rhizotome*, some latent Vertue
and specific propriety hid in the Kettles, and Pans, which, as
the Loadstone attracts Iron, draws the *Monks* there, and cannot
attract Emperors, Popes, or Kings? or is it a natural induction
and inclination fix'd in the frocks and cowls which of it self
leads and forceth those good Religious Men into Kitchins,
whether they will or no? He would speak of forms following matter, as *Averroës* names them, answer'd *Epistemon*: Right, said
Fryar *Jhon*.

I'll not offer to solve this problem, said *Pantagruel*; for it is
somewhat ticklish, and you can hardly handle it without coming
off scurvily; but I'll tell you what I have heard.

Antigonus King of *Macedon* one day coming into one of the
Tents, where his Cooks use to dress his Meat, and finding there
Poet Antagoras frying a Conger, and holding the pan himself, merrily ask'd him, Pray, Mr. *Poet*, was *Homer* frying Congers when
he writ the Deeds of *Agamemnon*? *Antagoras* readily answer'd;
But do you think, Sir, that when *Agamemnon* did them, he made
it his business to know if any in his Camp were frying Congers?
The King thought it an Indecency that a *Poet* shou'd be thus a
frying in a Kitchin; and the *Poet* let the King know that it was a
more indecent thing for a King to be found in such a place: I'll
clap another story upon the Neck of this, quoth *Panurge*, and
will tell you what *Briton Villandray* answer'd one day to the Duke
of *Guise*.

They were saying that at a certain Battle of King *Francis* against *Charles* the Fifth, *Briton* arm'd *Capape* to the Teeth, and mounted like St. *George*; yet sneak'd off, and play'd least in sight during the Ingagement. Blood and Oons, answer'd *Briton*, I was there and can prove it easily; nay, even where you, my Lord, dar'd not have been. The Duke began to resent this as too rash and sawcy; But *Briton* easily appeas'd him, and set them all a laughing. I gad, my Lord, quoth he, I kept out of harm's way; I was all the while with your Page *Jack*, sculking in a certain place where you had not dar'd hide your head as I did. Thus discoursing they got to their Ships, and left the *Island* of *Chely*.

CHAPTER XII

How Pantagruel pass'd by the Land of Pettifogging, and of the strange way of living among the Catchpoles.

STEERING our Course forwards the next Day we pass'd by *Pettifogging*, a Country all blurr'd and blotted, so that I could hardly tell what to make on 't. There we saw some Pettifoggers and Catchpoles, Rogues that will hang their Father for a Groat. They neither invited us to eat or drink, but with a multiplyed train of scrapes and cringes, said they were all at our service, for the *Legem pone*.

One of our *Droggermen* related to *Pantagruel* their strange way of living, diametrically oppos'd to that of our modern *Romans*: for at *Rome* a world of Folks get an honest livelyhood by Poysoning, Drubbing, Lambasting, Stabbing and Murthering; but the *Catchpoles* earn theirs by being Thrash'd, so that if they were long without a tight Lambasting, the poor Dogs with their Wives and Children would be starv'd. This is just, quoth *Panurge*, like those who, as *Galen* tells us, cannot erect the Cavernous nerve towards the Equinoctial Circle, unless they are soundly flogg'd. By St. *Patrick*'s Slipper, who ever should jirk me so, would soon in stead of setting me right, throw me off the Saddle, in the Devil's Name.

The way is this, said the Interpreter, when a *Monk*, Levite, close fisted Usurer or Lawyer owes a grudge to some neighboring Gentleman, he sends to him one of those *Catchpoles* or

Apparitors, who nabs, or at least cites him, serves a Writ or Warrant upon him; thumps, abuses and affronts him impudently by natural instinct, and according to his pious instructions; in so much that if the Gentleman hath but any guts in his Brains, and is not more stupid than a *Girin* Frog, he will find himself oblig'd either to apply a Faggot-stick or his sword to the Rascal's Jobbornol, give him the gentle lash, or make him cut a caper out at the Window by way of Correction. This done, *Catchpole* is rich for four Months at least, as if *Bastinadoes* were his real harvest; for the *Monk*, Levite, Usurer or Lawyer will reward him roundly, and my Gentleman must pay him such swindging damages, that his acres may bleed for 't, and he be in danger of miserably rotting within a stone Doublet, as if he had struck the King.

Quoth *Panurge*, I know an excellent remedy against this; us'd by the Lord of *Basché*; what is it? said *Pantagruel*. The Lord of *Basché*, said *Panurge*, was a brave honest noble-spirited Gentleman, who at his return from the long war in which the Duke of *Ferrara*, with the help of the *French*, bravely defended himself against the fury of Pope *Julius* II. was every Day cited, warn'd and prosecuted at the Suit and for the Sport and Fancy of the fat Prior of St. *Louant*.

One Morning as he was at breakfast with some of his Domestics (for he lov'd to be sometimes among them) he sent for one *Loir* his Baker and his Spouse, and for one *Oudart* the Vicar of his Parish, who was also his Butler, as the Custom was then in *France*; then said to them before his Gentleman and other Servants: You all see how I am daily plagu'd with these rascally *Catchpoles*, truly if you do not lend me your helping hand, I am finally resolv'd to leave the Country, and go fight for the *Sultan*, or the Devill, rather than be thus eternally tees'd. Therefore to be rid of their damn'd Visits, hereafter, when any of them come here, be ready you Baker and your Wife, to make your personal appearance in my great Hall in your wedding Cloaths, as if you were going to be affianc'd; here take these Ducats, which I give you to keep you in a fitting Garb. As for you, Sir *Oudart*, be sure you make your personal appearance there in your fine Surplice and Stole, not forgetting your Holy Water, as if you were to wed them. Be you there also, *Trudon*, said he to his Drummer, with your Pipe and Taber. The form of Matrimony must be read, and

555

the Bride kiss'd, then all of you, as the Witnesses use to do in this Country, shall give one another the remembrance of the Wedding, (which you know is to be a blow with your Fist, bidding the Partie struck remember the Nuptials by that token) this will but make you have the better Stomach to your Supper: but when you come to the Catchpole's turn, thrash him thrice and threefold, as you would a Sheaf of green Corn, don't spare him, maul him, drub him, lambast him, swinge him off, I pray you. Here, take these Steel Gantlets, covered with Kid, Head, Back, Belly, and Sides, give him blows innumerable; he that gives him most, shall be my best Friend. Fear not to be call'd to an account about it, I'll stand by you; for the blows must seem to be given in jest, as it is Customary among us at all Weddings.

Ay, but how shall we know the Catchpole, said the Man of God, all sorts of People daily resort to this Castle? I have taken care of that, reply'd the Lord. When some fellow either on foot or on a scurvy Jade, with a large broad Silver Ring on his Thumb comes to the door, he is certainly a Catchpole: the Porter having civilly let him in, shall ring the Bell, then be all ready, and come into the Hall, to act the Tragi-Comedy, whose Plot I have now laid for you.

That numerical day, as Chance would have it, came an old fat ruddy Catchpole; having knock'd at the Gate, and then piss'd, as most Men will do, the Porter soon found him out, by his large greasie Spatterdashes, his Jaded hollow flank'd Mare, his Bag full of Writs and Informations dangling at his Girdle, but above all, by the large Silver hoop on his left Thumb.

The Porter was civil to him, admitted him in kindly, and rung the Bell briskly. As soon as the Baker and his Wife heard it, they clapp'd on their best Clothes, and made their personal appearance in the Hall, keeping their Gravities like a new made Judge. The *Domine* put on his Surplice and Stole, and as he came out of his Office, met the Catchpole, had him in there, and made him suck his Face a good while, while the Gantlets were drawing on all hands, and then told him, you are come just in Pudding time, my Lord is in his right Cue; we shall feast like Kings anon, here's to be swingding doings, we have a Wedding in the House, here, drink and cheer up, pull away.

THE FOURTH BOOK

While these two were at it hand to fist, *Basché*, seeing all his People in the Hall in their proper Equipage, sends for the Vicar. *Oudart* comes with the Holy Water Pot, follow'd by the Catchpole, who as he came into the Hall, did not forget to make good store of aukward Cringes, and then serv'd *Basché* with a Writ. *Basché* gave him *Grimace* for *Grimace*, slipp'd an Angel into his Mutton Fist, and pray'd him to assist at the Contract and Ceremony. Which he did. When it was ended, Thumps and Fisticuffs began to fly about among the Assistants; but when it came to the Catchpole's turn, they all lay'd on him so unmercifully with their Gantlets, that they at last settled him, all stunn'd, and batter'd, bruis'd and mortify'd, with one of his Eyes black and blue, eight Ribs bruis'd, his Brisket sunk in, his *Omoplates* in four quarters, his under Jaw-bone in three pieces, and all this in jest and no harm done. God wot how the *Levite* belabour'd him, hiding within the long Sleeve of his Canonical Shirt, his huge Steel Gantlet lin'd with Ermin, for he was a strong built *Ball*, and an old Dog at Fisticuffs. The Catchpole, all of a bloody Tyger-like hue, with much ado, crawl'd home to *l'Isle Bouchart*, well pleas'd and edify'd however with *Basché*'s kind reception, and with the help of the good Surgeons of the place, liv'd as long as you'd have him. From that time to this not a word of the business; the memory of it was lost with the sound of the Bells that rung for Joy at his Funeral.

CHAPTER XIII

How, like Master Francis Villon, the Lord of Basché commended his Servants.

THE Catchpole being pack'd off on blind Sorrel (so he call'd his one Ey'd Mare) *Basché* sent for his Lady, her Women and all his Servants into the Arbour of his Garden; had Wine brought, attended by good store of Pasties, Hams, Fruit, and other Table-Ammunition for a Nuncion, drank with them joyfully, and then told them this Story.

Master *Francis Villon*, in his old Age, retir'd to St. *Maixent* in *Poitou*, under the Patronage of a good honest Abbot of the place. There to make sport for the Mob, he undertook to get the *Passion* acted after the way and in the Dialect of the Country. The parts being distributed, the Play having been rehears'd, and the Stage prepar'd, he told the Mayor and Aldermen, that the Mystery might be ready after *Niort* Fair, and that there only wanted Properties and necessaries, but chiefly Clothes fit for the parts; so the Mayor and his Brethren took care to get them.

Villon, to dress an old Clownish Father Grey Beard, who was to represent God the *Father*, begg'd of Fryar *Stephen Tickletoby*, Sacristan to the *Franciscan* Fryars of the place, to lend him a Cope and a Stole. *Tickletoby* refus'd him, alledging that by their Provincial Statutes, it was rigorously forbidden to give or lend any thing to Players. *Villon* reply'd, That the Statute reached no farther than Farces, Drolls, Anticks, loose and dissolute Games, and that he ask'd no more than what he had been allow'd at *Brussels* and other Places. *Tickletoby*, notwithstanding, peremptorily bid him provide himself elsewhere if he would, and not to hope for any thing out of his Monastical Wardrobe. *Villon* gave an account of this to the Players, as of a most abominable action; adding, that God would shortly revenge himself, and make an example of *Tickletoby*.

The *Saturday* following he had notice given him, that *Tickletoby* upon the Filly of the Convent (so they call a young Mare that was never leap'd yet) was gone a Mumping to St. *Ligarius*, and would be back about two in the afternoon. Knowing this, he made a Cavalcade of his Devils of the *Passion* through the Town. They were all rigg'd with Wolves, Calves, and Rams Skins, lac'd and trimm'd with Sheeps Heads, Bulls Feathers, and large Kitchin Tenter-Hooks, girt with broad Leathern Girdles, whereat hang'd dangling huge Cow Bells and Horse Bells, which made a horrid din. Some held in their Claws black Sticks full of Squibs and Crackers, others had long lighted pieces of wood, upon which at the corner of every street they flung whole handfuls of Rosin dust, that made a terrible fire and smoak: having thus led them about, to the great diversion of the Mob, and the dreadful fear of little Children, he finally carried them to an entertainment at a Summer-House without the Gate that leads to St. *Ligarius*.

As they came near the place, he spy'd *Tickletoby* afar off, coming home from Mumping, and told them in Maceronic Verse,

THE FOURTH BOOK

Hic est Mumpator natus de gente Cucowli,
*Qui solet antiquo scrappas portare bisacco.**

A Plague on his Fryarship (said the Devils then) the lowsy
Beggar would not lend a poor Cope to the Fatherly Father, let
us fright him. Well said, cry'd *Villon*; but let us hide our selves
till he comes by, and then charge home briskly with your Squibs
and burning Sticks. *Tickletoby* being come to the place, they all
rush'd on a sudden into the Road to meet him, and in a frightful
manner threw fire from all sides upon him and his Filly Foal,
ringing and tingling their Bells, and howling like so many real
Devils, hho, hho, hho, hho, brrou, rrou, rrourrs, rrrourrs, hoo,
hou, hou, hho, hho, hhoi, Fryar *Stephen*, don't we play the Devils
rarely? The Filly was soon scar'd out of her seven Senses, and
began to start, to funk it, to squirt it, to trot it, to fart it, to bound
it, to gallop it, to kick it, to spurn it, to calcitrate it, to winse it,
to frisk it, to leap it, to curvet it, with double Jirks, and bum-
motions; in so much that she threw down *Tickletoby*, tho' he held
fast by the Tree of the Pack-Saddle with might and main: now
his Traps and Stirrups were of Cord, and on the right side, his
Sandal was so entangled and twisted, that he could not for the
Hearts blood of him get out his foot. Thus he was dragg'd about
by the Filly through the Road, scratching his bare Breech all the
way, she still multiplying her kicks against him and straying for
fear, over Hedge and Ditch; in so much that she trepann'd his
thick Skull so, that his Cockle Brains were dash'd out near the
Osanna or *High Cross*. Then his Arms fell to pieces, one this way
and t' other that way, and even so were his Legs serv'd at the
same time: Then she made a bloody havock with his Puddings,
and being got to the Convent, brought back only his right Foot
and twisted Sandal, leaving them to guess what was become of
the rest.

Villon seeing that things had succeeded as he intended, said
to his Devils, you will Act rarely, Gentlemen Devils, you will
Act rarely; I dare engage you'll top your Parts. I defie the Devils
of *Saumur, Douay, Montmorillon, Langez, St. Espain, Angers*; nay,
by Gad, even those of *Poictiers*, for all their bragging and vapouring, to match you.

* A Monk's double Pouch.

Likewise, Friends, said *Basché*, I foresee, that hereafter you will act rarely this Tragical Farce, since the very first time you have so skilfully hamper'd, bethwack'd, belamm'd, and bebump'd the Catchpole. From this day I double your Wages. As for you, my Dear (said he to his Lady) make your Gratifications as you please; you are my Treasurer, you know. For my part, first and foremost, I drink to you all. Come on, box it about, 'tis good and cool. In the second place, you, Mr. Steward, take this Silver Bason, I give it you freely. Then, you, my Gentleman of the Horse, take these two Silver gilt Cups, and let not the Pages be Horse-whip'd these three Months. My Dear, let them have my best white Plumes of Feathers with the Gold Buckles to them. Sir *Oudart*, this Silver Flaggon falls to your share: this other I give to the Cooks. To the *Valets de Chambre*, I give this Silver Basket; to the Grooms this Silver gilt Boat; to the Porter these two Plates: to the Hostlers these ten Porringers. *Trudon*, take you these Silver Spoons and this Sugar-Box. You Footmen, take this large Salt. Serve me well, and I'll remember you. For on the word of a Gentleman, I had rather bear in War one hundred blows on my Helmet in the Service of my Country, than be once cited by these Knavish Catchpoles, meerly to humour this same gorbelly'd Prior.

CHAPTER XIV

A *further Account of Catchpoles who were drub'd at Basché's House.*

FOUR days after, another young long-shank'd rawbon'd Catchpole coming to serve *Basché* with a Writ at the fat Prior's request, was no sooner at the Gate, but the Porter smelt him out, and rung the Bell; at whose second pull, all the Family understood the Mystery. *Loire* was kneading his Dough, his Wife was sifting Meal; *Oudart* was toping in his Office; the Gentlemen were playing at Tennis; the Lord *Basché* at In and Out with my Lady; the Waitingmen and Gentlewomen at Push-Pin; the Officers at Lanterlue, and the Pages at Hot-cockles, giving one another smart bangs. There were all immediately inform'd that a Catchpole was Hous'd.

Upon this, *Oudart* put on his Sacerdotal, and *Loire* and his Wife their Nuptial Badges. *Trudon* Pip'd it, and then Taber'd it like mad, all made haste to get ready, not forgetting the Gantlets. *Basché* went into the outward Yard; there the Catchpole meeting him, fell on his Marrowbones; beg'd of him not to take it ill, if he serv'd him with a Writ at the Suit of the fat Prior; and in a pathetic Speech, let him know that he was a publick person, a Servant to the Monking Tribe, Apparitor to the *Abbatial* Mytre, ready to do as much for him, nay, for the least of his Servants, whensoever he would imploy and use him.

Nay, truly, said the Lord, you shall not serve your Writ till you have tasted some of my good *Quinquenays* Wine and been a Witness to a Wedding which we are to have this very minute. Let him drink and refresh himself, added he, turning towards the *Levitical* Butler, and then bring him into the Hall. After which, Catchpole well stuffed and moisten'd, came with *Oudart* to the place where all the Actors in the Farce stood ready to begin. The sight of their Game set them a laughing, and the Messenger of Mischief grinn'd also for Company's sake. Then the Mysterious words were mutter'd to and by the Couple, their Hands join'd, the Bride buss'd, and all besprinkled with Holy Water. While they were bringing Wine and Kickshaws, Thumps began to trot about by dozens. The Catchpole gave the *Levite* several blows. *Oudart* who had his Gantlet hid under his Canonical Shirt, draws it on like a Mittin, and then with his clench'd Fist, souce he fell on the Catchpole, and maul'd him like a Devil; the junior Gantlets dropt on him likewise like so many battering Rams. Remember the Wedding by this, by that, by these blows, said they. In short they stroak'd him so to the purpose that he piss'd Blood out at Mouth, Nose, Ears, and Eyes, and was bruis'd, sore, batter'd, bebump'd, and crippled at the Back, Neck, Breast, Arms, and soforth. Never did the Batchelors at *Avignon* in Carnival time play more melodiously at *Raphe*, than was then play'd on the Catchpole's Microcosm: at last down he fell.

They threw a great deal of Wine on his Snout, ty'd round the Sleeve of his Doublet a fine yellow and green Favour, and got him upon his snotty Beast, and God knows how he got to *l'Isle Bouchart*, where I cannot truly tell you whether he was dress'd

and look'd after or no, both by his Spouse and the able Doctors
of the Country, for the thing never came to my Ears.

The next day they had a third part to the same Tune, because it did not appear by the lean Catchpole's Bag, that he had
serv'd his Writ. So the fat Prior sent a new Catchpole at the head
of a brace of Bums for his *Guard du Corps* to Summon my Lord.
The Porter ringing the Bell, the whole Family was overjoy'd,
knowing that it was another Rogue. *Basché* was at Dinner with
his Lady and the Gentlemen, so he sent for the Catchpole, made
him sit by him, and the Bums by the Women, and made them
eat till their Bellies crack'd with their Breeches unbutton'd.
The Fruit being serv'd, the Catchpole arose from Table, and
before the Bums cited *Basché*, *Basché* kindly ask'd him for a Copy
of the Warant, which the other had got ready: he then takes
Witness and a Copy of the Summons. To the Catchpole and his
Bums he order'd four Ducats for Civility Money. In the mean
time all were withdrawn for the Farce. So *Trudon* gave the
Alarm with his Tabor. *Basché* desir'd the Catchpole to stay and
see one of his Servants married, and witness the Contract of
Marriage, paying him his Fee. The Catchpole slap dash was
ready, took out his Ink-horn, got Paper immediately, and his
Bums by him.

Then *Loire* came into the Hall at one door, and his Wife with
the Gentlewomen at another in Nuptial Accoutrements. *Oudart*,
in *Pontificalibus* takes them both by the hands, asketh them
their will; giveth them the Matrimonial Blessing, and was very
Liberal of Holy Water. The Contract Written, Sign'd, and Register'd, on one side was brought Wine and Comfits; on the other,
White and Orange-tauny-colour'd Favours were distributed; on
another, Gantlets privately handed about.

CHAPTER XV

*How the Ancient Custom at Nuptials is renewed by the
Catchpole.*

THE Catchpole having made shift to get down a swindging
Streaker of Briton Wine, said to *Basché*, Pray, Sir, what do
you mean? You do not give one another the Memento of the

Wedding. By St. *Joseph*'s Wooden Shoe all good Customs are forgot. We find the Form, but the Hare's scamper'd; and the Nest, but the Birds are flown. There are no true Friends now-a-days. You see how in several Churches the Ancient Laudable Custom of Tippling on account of the blessed St. *O. O.* at *Christmass* is come to nothing. The World is in its Dotage, and Dooms-day is certainly coming all so fast. Now come on; The Wedding, the Wedding, the Wedding, remember it by this. This he said, striking *Basché* and his Lady, then her Women and the *Levite*. Then the Tabor beat a point of War, and the Gantlets began to do their Duty, insomuch that the Catchpole had his Crown crack'd in no less than nine places. One of the Bums had his right Arm put out of joint, and the other his upper Jaw-bone or Mandibule dislocated; so that it hid half his Chin, with a denudation of the *Uvula* and sad loss of the Molar, Masticatory and Canine Teeth. Then the Tabor beat a Retreat; the Gantlets were carefully hid in a trice, and sweet Meats afresh distributed to renew the Mirth of the Company. So they all drank to one another, and especially to the Catchpole and his Bums. But *Oudart* Curs'd and Damn'd the Wedding to the pit of Hell, complaining that one of the Bums had utterly disincornifistibulated his nether Shoulder blade. Nevertheless he scorn'd to be thought a Flincher, and made shift to tope to him on the square.

The Jawless Bum shrug'd up his Shoulders, join'd his Hands, and by signs beg'd his Pardon; for speak he could not. The sham Bridegroom made his moan, That the crippled Bum had struck him such a horrid thump with his Shoulder-of-Mutton-Fist on the nether Elbow, that he was grown quite esperruquanchuzelubelouzerireliced down to his very Heel, to the no small loss of Mistress Bride.

But what harm had poor I done (cry'd *Trudon* hiding his left Eye with his Kerchief, and shewing his Tabor crack'd on one side) they were not satisfied with thus poaching, black-and-bluing, and morrambouzevezengouzequoquemorgasacbaquevezinemaffreliding my poor Eyes, but they have also broke my harmless Drum. Drums indeed are commonly beaten at Weddings; (and 'tis fit they should) but Drummers are well entertained, and never beaten. Now let *Belzebub* e'en take the Drum to make his Devilship a Night-Cap. Brother, said the lame Catchpole,

never fret thy self, I will make thee a present of a fine, large, old
Patent, which I have here in my Bag, to patch up thy Drum, and
for Madam St. *Ann*'s sake I pray thee forgive us. By'r Lady of
River, the blessed Dame, I meant no more harm than the Child
unborn. One of the Querries who hopping and halting like a
mumping Cripple, mimick'd the good limping Lord *de la Roche
Posay*, directed his Discourse to the Bum with the pouting Jaw,
and told him, What, Mr. *Manbound*, was it not enough thus to
have morcrocastebezasteverestegrigeligoscopapopondrillated
us all in our upper Members with your botch'd Mittens, but you
must also apply such morderegripippiatabirofreluchambure-
lurecaquelurintimpaniments on our Shin-Bones with the hard
tops and extremities of your cobbl'd Shoes? Do you call this
Childrens play? By the *Mass* 'tis no Jest. The Bum wringing his
Hands, seem'd to beg his Pardon, muttering with his Tongue,
mon, mon, mon, vrelon, von, von, like a Dumb Man. The Bride
crying laught, and laughing cry'd, because the Catchpole was
not satisfied with drubbing her without choice or distinction of
Members, but had also rudely rous'd and tous'd her, pull'd off
her Topping, and not having the Fear of her Husband before
his Eyes, treacherously trepignemanpenillorifrizonoufrestur-
fumbledtumbled and squeez'd her lower parts. The Devil go
with it, said *Basché*, there was much need indeed that this same
Master King (this was the Catchpole's Name) should thus break
my Wife's Back: however I forgive him now; these are little
Nuptial Caresses. But this I plainly perceive, that he cited me
like an Angel, and drubb'd me like a Devil. He hath something
in him of Fryar *Thumpwell*. Come, for all this I must drink to
him, and to you likewise his trusty Esquires. But said his Lady,
Why hath he been so very liberal of his manual kindness to me,
without the least provocation? I assure you, I by no means like
it; but this I dare say for him, that he hath the hardest Knuckles
that ever I felt on my Shoulders. The Steward held his left Arm
in a Scarf, as if it had been rent and torn in twain: I think it was
the Devil, said he, that mov'd me to assist at these Nuptials;
shame on ill luck, I must needs be meddling, with a Pox,
and now see what I have got by the Bargain, both my Arms are
wretchedly engoulevezinemassdandbruis'd. Do you call this a
Wedding? By St. *Briget*'s Tooth, I had rather be at that of a Tom

T—d-Man; this is o' my word e'en just such another Feast as was that of the *Lapithes*, describ'd by the Philosopher of *Samosate*. One of the Bums had lost his Tongue. The two other, tho' they had more need to complain, made their excuse as well as they could, protesting that they had no ill design in this Dumbfounding; begging that for goodness sake they would forgive them; and so tho' they could hardly budge a foot, or wag along, away they crawl'd. About a Mile from *Basché*'s Seat, the Catchpole found himself somewhat out of sorts. The Bums got to *l'Isle Bouchart*, publickly saying, That since they were born, they had never seen an honester Gentleman than the Lord of *Basché*, or civiller People than his, and that they had never been at the like Wedding (which I verily believe) but that it was their own faults, if they had been tickled off, and toss'd about from Post to Pillar, since themselves had began the beating. So they liv'd I can't exactly tell you how many days after this. But from that time to this it was held for a certain truth, That *Basché*'s Money was more pestilential, mortal and pernicious to the Catchpoles and Bums, than were formerly the *Aurum Tholosanum*, and the *Sejan* Horse to those that possessed them. Ever since this, he lived quietly, and *Basché*'s *Wedding grew into a common Proverb*.

CHAPTER XVI

How Fryar Jhon made tryal of the Nature of the Catchpoles.

THIS Story would seem pleasant enough, said *Pantagruel*, were we not to have always the fear of God before our Eyes. It had been better, said *Epistemon*, if those Gantlets had fallen upon the fat Prior: Since he took a pleasure in spending his Mony, partly to vex *Basché*, partly to see those Catchpoles bang'd, good lusty thumps would have done well on his shav'd Crown, considering the horrid Concussions now-a days among those puny Judges. What harm had done those poor Devils the Catchpoles. This puts me in mind, said *Pantagruel*, of an ancient *Roman* named *L. Neratius*; he was of Noble Blood, and for some time was rich; but had this Tyrannical Inclination, that whenever he went out of doors, he caus'd his Servants to fill their Pockets with Gold and Silver, and meeting in the street your spruce Gallants and better sort of Beaux, without the least provocation, for his fancy he us'd to strike them hard on the Face with his Fist, and immediately after that, to appease them and hinder them from complaining to the Magistrates, he would give them as much Money as satisfied them according to the Law of the twelve Tables. Thus he us'd to spend his Revenue, beating People for the price of his Money. By St. *Bennet*'s Sacred Boot, quoth Fryar *Jhon*, I will know the truth of it presently.

This said, he went on shoar, put his hand in his Fob, and took out twenty Ducats, then said with a loud voice in the hearing of a shoal of the Nation of Catchpoles, Who will earn twenty Ducats, for being beaten like the Devil? Io, Io, Io, said they all; you will cripple us for ever, Sir, that's most certain, but the Money is tempting. With this they were all thronging who should be first, to be thus pretiously beaten. Fryar *Jhon* singl'd him out of the whole knot of these Rogues in grain, a red Snout Catchpole, who upon his right Thumb wore a thick broad Silver Hoop, wherein was set a good large Toadstone. He had no sooner pick'd him out from the rest, but I perceiv'd that they all mutter'd and grumbl'd, and I heard a young thin-jaw'd Catchpole, a notable Scholar, a pretty Fellow at his Pen, and, according to publick report, much cry'd up for his honesty at *Doctors Commons*, making his complaint, and muttering; because this same crimson Phyz carry'd away all the Practice, and that if there were but a score and a half of Bastinadoes to be got, he would certainly run away with eight and twenty of them. But all this was look'd upon to be nothing but meer Envy.

Fryar *Jhon* so unmercifully thrash'd, thump'd and belabour'd Red-Snout, Back and Belly, Sides, Legs and Arms, Head, Feet, and so forth, with the home and frequently repeated application of one of the best Members of a Faggot, that I took him to be a dead Man; then he gave him the twenty Ducats, which made the Dog get on his Legs, pleas'd like a little King, or two. The rest were saying to Fryar *Jhon*, Sir, Sir, Brother Devil, if it please you to do us the favour to beat some of us for less Money, we are all at your Devilship's command, Bags, Papers, Pens and all. Red-Snout cry'd out against them, saying with a loud voice, Body of me, you little Prigs, will you offer to take the Bread out of my

Mouth? will you take my Bargain over my Head? Would you draw and inveigle from me my Clients and Customers? Take notice, I summon you before the Official this day se'night; I will Law and Claw you like any old Devil, that I will. — Then turning himself towards Fryar *Jhon*, with a smiling and joyful Look, he said to him, Reverend Father in the Devil, if you have found me a good Hide, and have a mind to divert your self once more, by beating your humble Servant, I will bate you half in half this time, rather than lose your Custom, do not spare me, I beseech you; I am all, and more than all yours, good Mr. Devil, Head, Lungs, Tripes, Guts and Garbage, and that at a Penniworth I'll assure you. Fryar *Jhon* ne'er heeded his proffers, but e'en left them. The other Catchpoles were making Addresses to *Panurge*, *Epistemon*, *Gymnast*, and others, entreating them charitably to bestow upon their Carcasses a small beating, for otherwise they were in danger of keeping a long Fast: but none of them had a Stomach to it. Sometime after, seeking fresh Water for the Ship's Company, we met a couple of old Female Catchpoles of the place, miserably howling and weeping in Consort. *Pantagruel* had kept on Board, and already had caus'd a Retreat to be sounded. Thinking they might be related to the Catchpole that was bastinado'd, We ask'd them the occasion of their grief. They reply'd, That they had too much cause to weep; for that very hour, from an exalted Triple Tree, two of the honestest Gentlemen in Catchpole-land had been made to cut a Caper on nothing. Cut a Caper on nothing? said *Gymnast*, my Pages use to cut Capers on the Ground; to cut a Caper on nothing should be hanging and choaking, or I am out. Ay, ay, said Fryar *Jhon*, you speak of it like St. *Jhon de la Palisse*.

We ask'd them why they treated those worthy Persons with such a choaking Hempen Sallat? They told us they had only borrow'd, *alias* stoln the Tools of the *Mass*, and hid them under the handle of the Parish. This is a very Allegorical way of speaking, said *Epistemon*.

CHAPTER XVII

*How Pantagruel came to the Islands of Tohu and Bohu, and of
the strange death of Widenostrils, the Swallower of Windmils.*

THAT day *Pantagruel* came to the two *Islands* of *Tohu* and *Bohu*,
where the Devill a bit we could find any thing to fry with: For,
one *Widenostrils*, a huge Giant had swallowed every individual
Pan, Skillet, Kettle, frying-Pan, dripping-Pan, and Brass and Iron
Pot in the Land, for want of Windmils, which were his daily
food. Whence it happen'd that somewhat before Day, about the
hour of his digestion, the greedy Churle was taken very Ill, with
a kind of a Surfeit or Crudity of stomach, occasion'd (as the
Physicians said) by the weakness of the concocting faculty of
his stomach, naturally dispos'd to digest whole Windmils at a
gust; yet unable to consume perfectly the Pans and Skillets;
though it had indeed pretty well digested the Kettles and Pots,
as they said they knew by the *Hypostases* and *Encoresmes* of four
Tubs of second-hand Drink, which he had evacuated at two
different times that morning. They made use of diverse
remedies according to art, to give him ease: But all would not
do, the Distemper prevailed over the remedies, in so much that
the famous *Widenostrils* dy'd that morning, of so strange a death,
that I think you ought no longer to wonder at that of the Poet
Æschylus's. It had been foretold him by the Sooth-sayers, that he
would dye on a certain Day, by the ruin of something that should
fall on him; that fatal day being come in its Turn, he remov'd
himself out of Town, far from all Houses, Trees, or any other
things that can fall, and indanger by their ruin; and stay'd in a
large field, trusting himself to the open Sky, there very secure
as he thought, unless indeed the Sky should happen to fall,
which he held to be impossible. Yet they say that the Larks are
much afraid of it, for if it should fall, they must all be taken.

The *Celtz* that once liv'd near the *Rhine*, (they are our noble
valiant *French*) in ancient Times were also afraid of the Sky's
falling; for being ask'd by *Alexander* the great, what they fear'd
most in this World, hoping well they would say that they
fear'd none but him, considering his great Atchievements,

they made answer, That they fear'd nothing but the Sky's falling; however, not refusing to enter into a confederacy with so
brave a King: If you believe *Strabo, Lib. 7.* and *Arrian, Lib. I.*

Plutarch also in his Book of the Face that appears on the body
of the Moon, speaks of one *Phænaces* who very much fear'd the
Moon should fall on Earth, and piti'd those that live under that
Planet, as the *Æthiopians* and *Taprobanians*, if so heavy a Mass
ever happened to fall on them; and would have fear'd the like
of Heaven and Earth, had they not been duely propp'd up and
born by the Atlantic Pillars, as the ancients believ'd, according
to *Aristotle*'s testimony, *Lib. 5. Metaphis.* Notwithstanding all
this, poor *Æschylus* was kill'd by the fall of the shell of a *Tortoise*,
which falling from betwixt the Claws of an Eagle high in the
Air, just on his head, dash'd out his brains.

Neither ought you to wonder at the death of another Poet, I
mean old Jolly *Anacreon*, who was choak'd with a grape-stone:
nor at that of *Fabius* the Roman *Prætor* who was smothered with
a single Goat's-hair as he was supping up a porringer of Milk.
Nor at the death of that bashfull Fool who by holding in his
Wind, and for want of letting out a Bumgunshot dy'd suddenly
in the presence of Emperor *Claudius*. Nor at that of the *Italian*,
buried on the *Via Flaminia* at *Rome* who in his Epitaph, com-
plains that the bite of a she-Puss on his little Finger was the
cause of his death. Nor of that of *Q. Lecanius Bassus*, who dyed
suddenly of so small a prick with a needle on his left thumb,
that it could hardly be descern'd. Nor of *Quenelault*, a *Norman*
Physician who dy'd suddenly at *Montpellier*, meerely for having
sideways took a worm out of his hand with a Pen-knife. Nor of
Philomenes, whose Servant having got him some new Figs, for
the first course of his dinner, whilst he went to fetch wine, a
straggling welhung Ass got into the House, and seeing the figs
on the Table, without further invitation soberly fell to: *Philomenes*
coming into the Room and nicely observing with what gravity
the Ass eat its Dinner, said to his Man who was come back;
Since thou hast set Figs here for this reverend Guest of ours to
eat, methinks it's but reason thou also give him some of this
Wine to drink. He had no sooner said this, but he was so excessively pleased, and fell into so exorbitant a fit of Laughter, that
the use of his spleen took that of his breath utterly away, and he

immediately dy'd. Nor of *Spurius Saufeius*, who dy'd supping up
a soft Egg as he came out of a bath. Nor of him who, as *Boccace*
tells us, dy'd suddenly by picking his grinders with a Sage-stalk.
Nor of *Philipot Placut*, who being brisk and hale, fell dead as he
was paying an old debt; which causes perhaps many not to pay
theirs, for fear of the like accident. Nor of the Painter *Zeuxis* who
kill'd himself with laughing at the sight of the Antick *Jobbernol*
of an old hagg drawn by him. Nor in short of a thousand more
of which Authors write, as *Verrius*, *Pliny*, *Valerius*, *J. Baptista
Fulgosius*, and *Bacabery* the elder. In short, Gaffer *Widenostrils*
choak'd himself with eating a huge lump of fresh Butter at the
mouth of a hot Oven, by the advice of *Physicians*.

They likewise told us there, that the King of *Cullan* in *Bohu*
had routed the *Grandees* of King *Mecloth*, and made sad work
with the Fortresses of *Belima*.

After this, we sail'd by the Islands of *Nargues* and *Zargues*;
also by the Islands of *Teleniabin* and *Geneliabin*, very fine and
fruitful in Ingredients for Clysters: and then by the Islands of
Enig and *Evig*, on whose account formerly the Landgrave of
Hesse was swindg'd off with a vengeance.

CHAPTER XVIII

How Pantagruel met with a great Storm at Sea.

THE next day we espied nine Sail that came spooning before
the Wind; they were full of *Dominicans*, *Jesuits*, *Capuchins*, *Hermits*, *Austins*, *Bernardins*, *Celestins*, *Theatins*, *Egnatins*, *Amadeans*,
Cordeliers, *Carmelites*, *Minims*, and the Devil and all of other holy
Monks and Fryars, who were going to the Council of *Chesil*, to
sift and garble some Articles of Faith against the new Hereticks;
Panurge was overjoy'd to see them, being most certain of good
luck, for that day, and a long train of others. So having courteously saluted the goodly Fathers, and recommended the salvation of his precious Soul to their Devout Prayers and private
Ejaculations, he caus'd seventy eight dozen of *Westphalia* Hams,
Unites of Pots of Caviar, Tens of *Bolonia* Sawsages, Hundreds
of Botargoes, and Thousands of fine Angels, for the Souls of the
dead, to be thrown on board their Ships. *Pantagruel* seem'd

metagraboliz'd, dozing, out of sorts, and as melancholick as a Cat;
Fryar *Jhon* who soon perceiv'd it, was enquiring of him whence
should come this unusual sadness? When the Master, whose
Watch it was, observing the fluttering of the Ancient above the
Poop, and seeing that it began to overcast, judg'd that we should
have Wind, therefore he bid the Boatswain call hands upon
Deck, Officers, Sailers, Fore-Mast Men, Swabbers, and Cabbin-
boys, and even the Passengers; made 'em first settle their Top-
sails, take in their Spreet-sail; then he cry'd, in with your
Top-sails, lower the Fore-sail, Tallow under the Parrels, brade
up close all them Sails, strike your Top-Masts to the Cap, make
all sure with your Sheeps-feet, Lash your Guns fast. All this was
nimbly done. Immediately it blow'd a Storm, the Sea began to
roar, and swell Mountain high: the Rut of the Sea was great, the
Waves breaking upon our Ships Quarter, the North West Wind
bluster'd and overblow'd; boisterous gusts; dreadful clashings
and deadly scuds of Wind whistled through our Yards, and made
our Shrouds rattle again. The Thunder grumbled so horridly,
that you would have thought Heaven had been tumbling about
our Ears; at the same time it Lighten'd, Rain'd, Hail'd; the sky
lost its transparent hue, grew dusky, thick and gloomy, so that
we had no other Light than that of the Flashes of Lightning and
rending of the Clouds: the Hurricans, Flaws and sudden Whirlwinds began to make a Flame about us by the Lightnings, Fiery
Vapours, and other Aerial Ejaculations. Oh! how our Looks
were full of amazement and trouble, while the sawcy Winds did
rudely lift up above us the Mountainous Waves of the Main.
Believe me, it seem'd to us a lively Image of the Chaos, where
Fire, Air, Sea, Land, and all the Elements, were in a refractory
Confusion. Poor *Panurge*, having, with the full Contents of the
inside of his Doublet, plentifully fed the Fish, greedy enough
of such odious Fare, sat on the Deck all in a heap, with his Nose
and Arse together, most sadly cast down, moping and half dead;
invok'd and call'd to his Assistance all the blessed he and she
Saints he could muster up, swore and vow'd to confess in time
and place convenient, and then bawl'd out frightfully, Steward,
Maistre d'Hotel, see hoe, my Friend, my Father, my Uncle,
pr'ythee let's have a piece of Powder'd Beef or Pork; we shall
drink but too much anon, for ought I see, eat little and drink the

more shall hereafter be my Motto, I fear. Would to our dear
Lord, and to our blessed, worthy, and sacred Lady, I were now,
I say, this very minute of an hour, well on shoar on *Terra firma*,
hale and easie. O twice and thrice happy those that plant Cabbages! O Destinies, why did you not *Spin* me for a Cabbage
Planter? O how few are they to whom *Jupiter* hath been so
favourable as to Predestinate them to plant Cabbage! They
have always one Foot on the ground and the other not far from
it. Dispute who will of Felicity, and *summum bonum*, for my part,
whosoever *plants* Cabbage, is now by my Decree proclaim'd
most happy; for as good a reason as the Philosopher *Pyrrho* being
in the same danger, and seeing a Hog near the shoar eating
some scatter'd Oats, declar'd it happy in two respects, first, because it had plenty of Oats, and besides that it was on shoar.
Hah, for a Divine and Princely Habitation, commend me to the
Cows Floor.

Murther! This Wave will sweep us away, blessed Saviour! O,
my Friends! a little Vinegar. I sweat again with meer agony.
Alas, the Misen Sail's split, the Gallery's wash'd away, the Masts
are sprung, the Main Top Mast Head dives into the Sea; the
Keel is up to the Sun; our Shrouds are almost all broke, and
blown away. Alas! Alas! Where is our main Course? *Ael is ver-
looren by Godt*, our Top-Mast is run adrift. Alas! Who shall have
this Wreck? Friend, lend me here behind you one of these
Wales. Your Lanthorn is fallen, my Lads. Alas! don't let go the
main tack nor the Bowlin. I hear the Block crack, is it broke? For
the Lord's sake, let us save the Hull, and let all the Rigging be
damn'd. Be be be bous, bous, bous. Look to the Needle of your
Compass, I beeseech you, good Sir *Astrophel*, and tell us, if you
can, whence comes this Storm, my Heart's sunk down below
my Midriff. By my troth I am in a sad fright; bou, bou, bou, bous,
bous, I am lost for ever. I conskite my self for meer madness and
fear. Bou, bou, bou, bou, Otto to to to to ti. Bou, bou bou, ou,
ou ou, bou, bou, bous. I sink, I'm drowned, I'm gone, good
People, I'm drowned.

CHAPTER XIX

What Countenances Panurge and Fryar Jhon kept during the Storm.

PANTAGRUEL having first implor'd the help of the Great and Almighty Deliverer, and pray'd publickly with fervent Devotion, by the Pilot's advice held titely the Mast of the Ship. Fryar *Jhon* had strip'd himself to his Waistcoat, to help the Seamen. *Epistemon, Ponocrates*, and the rest did as much. *Panurge* alone sate on his Breech upon Deck, weeping, and howling. Fryar *Jhon* espy'd him, going on the Quarter-Deck, and said to him: Odzoons, *Panurge* the Calf, *Panurge* the Whiner, *Panurge* the Brayer, would it not become thee much better to lend us here a helping hand, than to lie lowing like a Cow, as thou dost, sitting on thy Stones like a bald breech'd Baboon? Be, be, be, bous, bous, bous, return'd *Panurge*, Fryar *Jhon*, my Friend, my good Father, I am drowning, my dear Friend! I drown; I am a dead Man, my dear Father in God, I am a dead Man, my Friend: your cutting Hanger cannot save me from this: Alas! Alas! We are above *Ela*. Above the pitch, out of Tune, and off the Hinges. Be, be, be, bou, bous. Alas! we are now above *G sol re ut*. I sink, I sink, hah, my Father, my Uncle, my All. The Water is got into my Shooes by the Collar; bous, bous, bous, paisch, hu, hu, hu, he, he, he, ha, ha, I drown. Alas! Alas! Hu, hu, hu, hu, hu, hu, hu, be be bous, bous, bobous, bobous, ho, ho, ho, ho, ho. Alas! Alas! Now am I like your Tumblers, my Feet stand higher than my Head: Would to Heaven I were now with those good, holy Fathers bound for the Council, whom we met this morning, so Godly, so Fat, so Merry, so Plump and Comely. Holos, holos, holas, alas, alas. This Devilish Wave (*mea culpa, Deus*) I mean this wave of God will sink our Vessel. Alas, Fryar *Jhon*, my Father, my Friend, Confession, here I am down on my Knees, *Confiteor*; your holy Blessing. Come hither and be damn'd thou pitiful Devil and help us (said Fryar *Jhon*) who fell a swearing and cursing like a Tinker; in the Name of thirty Legions of black Devils, come, will you come? Don't let us swear at this time, said *Panurge*, Holy Father, my Friend, don't swear, I beseech you; to morrow as much as you please. Holos, holos, alas, our Ship leaks. I drown, alas, alas, I will give eighteen hundred thousand Crowns to any one that will set me on shoar all beray'd, and bedawb'd as I am now, if ever there was a Man in my Country in the like pickle. *Confiteor*, alas! a word or two of Testament or Codicil at least. A thousand Devils seize the Cuck-oldy Cow-hearted Mungril, cry'd Fryar *Jhon*; Ods Belly, art thou talking here of making thy Will, now we are in danger, and it behoveth us to bestir our stumps lustily, or never. Wilt thou come, ho Devil? Midship-man my Friend, O the rare Lieuten-ant, here *Gymnast*, here on the Poop. We are by the *Mass*, all beshit now, our Light is out. This is hastening to the Devil as fast as it can. – Alas, bou, bou, bou, bou, bou, alas, alas, alas, alas, said *Panurge*, was it here we were born to perish? Oh! hoh! Good People, I drown, I die. *Consummatum est*. I am sped.—*Magna, gna, gna*, said Fryar *Jhon*. Fye upon him, how ugly the shitten Howler looks.—Boy, Younker, see hoyh.—Mind the Pumps, or the Devil choak thee.—Hast thou hurt thy self? Zoons, here fasten it to one of these Blocks. On this side in the Devil's Name, hay—so my Boy.—Ah Fryar *Jhon*, said *Panurge*, good Ghostly Father, dear Friend, don't let us swear, you sin. Oh ho, Oh ho, be be be bous, bous, bhous, I sink, I die, my Friends. I die in Charity with all the World. Farewell, *In manus*. Bohous, bhous, bhousowwauwaus. St. *Michael* of *Aure*! St. *Nicholas*! now, now or never. I here make you a solemn Vow and to our Saviour, that if you stand by me but this time, I mean if you set me ashoar out of this danger, I will build you a fine large little Chappel or two between *Cande* and *Monsoreau*, where neither Cow nor Calf shall feed. Oh ho, oh ho. Above eighteen Palefuls or two of it are got down my Gullet, bous, bhous, bhous, bhous, how damn'd bitter and Salt it is.—By the virtue (said Fryar *Jhon*) of the Blood, the Flesh, the Belly, the Head, if I hear thee again howling, thou Cuckoldly Cur, I'll maul thee worse than any Sea Wolf. Ods fish, why don't we take him by the Lugs, and throw him over board to the bottom of the Sea? Here, Sailor, ho honest Fellow. Thus, thus, my Friend, hold fast above.—In truth here is a sad Lightning and Thundering; I think that all the Devils are got loose, 'tis Holy-day with 'em, or else Madam *Proserpine* is in Child's Labour, all the Devils dance a Morrice.

574

CHAPTER XX

How the Pilots were forsaking their Ships in the greatest stress of Weather.

OH, said *Panurge*, you sin, Fryar *Jhon*, my former Crony, former, I say, for at this time I am no more, you are no more. It goes against my Heart to tell it you; for I believe this swearing doth your spleen a great deal of good; as it is a great ease to a Wood-Cleaver to cry hem, at every blow; and as one who plays at Nine Pins, is wonderfully help'd, if, when he hath not thrown his Bowl right, and is like to make a bad cast, some *ingenious* stander-by leans and screws his Body half way about, on that side which the Bowl should have took to hit the Pins. Nevertheless you offend, my sweet Friend. But what do you think of eating some kind of Cabirotadoes? Wouldn't this secure us from this Storm? I have read that the Ministers of the Gods *Cabiri* so much celebrated by *Orpheus, Apollonius, Pherecides, Strabo, Pausanias,* and *Herodotus,* were always secure in time of Storm. He doats, he raves, the poor Devil, said Fryar *Jhon.* A thousand, a million, nay, a hundred millions of Devils seize the hornifi'd Doddipole. Lend's a Hand here, hoh, Tiger, wouldst thou? Here on the Starboard side; Ods me, thou Buffalo's-Head stuffed with Relicks, what Ape's *Pater Noster* art thou muttering and chattering here between thy Teeth? That Devil of a Sea calf is the Cause of all this Storm, and is the only Man who doth not lend a helping hand. By G— if I come near thee, I'll fetch thee out by the Head and Ears with a vengeance, and chastise thee like any Tempestative Devil. Here Mate, my Lad, hold fast till I have made a double knot. O' brave Boy! Would to Heaven thou wert Abbot of *Talemouze,* and that he that is, were Guardian of *Croullay.* Hold Brother *Ponocrates,* you will hurt your self Man. *Epistemon,* pr'ythee stand off out of the Hatch-way. Methinks I saw the Thunder fall there but just now. Con the Ship, so ho—Mind your Steerage. Well said, thus, thus, steady, keep her thus, get the Long Boat clear.—Steady. Ods fish, the Beakhead is stav'd to pieces. Grumble, Devils, fart, belch, shite a T—d o' the Wave. If this be Weather, the Devil's a Ram. Nay,

by G— a little more would have wash'd me clear away into the
Current. I think all the Legions of Devils hold here their Provincial Chapter, or are Polling, Canvasing and Wrangling for the
Election of a New Rector.—Starboard; well said.—Take heed;
have a care of your Noddle, Lad, in the Devil's Name. So ho,
Starboard, Starboard. Be, be, be, bous, bous, bous, cry'd *Panurge*, bous, bous, be, be, be, bous, bous, I am lost. I see neither
Heaven nor Earth; of the four Elements we have here only Fire
and Water left. Bou, bou, bou, bous, bous, bous. Would it were
the pleasure of the worthy Divine Bounty, that I were at this
present hour in the Close at *Sevillé*, or at *Innocent*'s the Pastry-
Cook, over against the painted Wine-Vault at *Chinon*, though I
were to strip to my Doublet, and bake the *petty Pasties* my self.

Honest Man, could not you throw me ashoar, you can do a
World of good things, they say. I give you all *Salmigondinois*, and
my large Shore full of Whilks, Cockles and Periwinkles, if by
your industry, I ever set Foot on firm ground. Alas, alas, I drown.
Hark'ee, my Friends, since we cannot get safe into Port, let us
come to an Anchor into some Road, no matter whither. Drop all
your Anchors, let us be out of danger I beseech you. Here honest Tar get you into the Chains and heave the Lead, an't please
you. Let us how now many Fathom water we are in. Sound,
Friend, in the Lord *Harry*'s Name. Let us know, whether a Man
might here drink easily without stooping. I am apt to believe
One might. Helm a lee, hoh, cry'd the Pilot. Helm a lee, a Hand
or two at the Helm, About Ships with her, Helm a lee, Helm a
lee.—Stand off from the Leech of the Sail.—Hoh, Belay, here
make fast below, hoh, Helm a lee, lash sure the Helm a lee, and
let her drive. Is it come to that, said *Pantagruel*, our good Saviour
then help us. Let her lie under the Sea, cry'd *James Brahier*, our
chief Mate, let her drive. To Prayers, to Prayers, let all think on
their Souls, and fall to Prayers; nor hope to scape but by a Miracle. Let us, said *Panurge*, make some good pious kind of Vow,
alas, alas, alas, bou, bou, be be be bous, bous, bous, Oho, Oho,
Oho, Oho, let us make a Pilgrim; come, come, let every Man
club his Penny towards it, come on. Here, here, on this side, said
Fryar *Jhon* in the Devil's Name. Let her drive, for the Lord's
sake unhang the Rudder, hoh, let her drive, let her drive, and
let us drink, I say of the best and most cheering, d'ye hear,

Steward, produce, exhibit, for d'ye see this, and all the rest will as well go to the Devil out of hand. A Pox on that Windbroaker *Æolus* with his Flusterblusters, Sirrah, Page, bring me here my Drawer (for so he call'd his Breviary) stay a little here, hawl Friend, thus—Odzoons, here's a deal of Hail and Thunder to no purpose. Hold fast above, I pray you. When have we *All-Saints* Day? I believe 'tis the unholy holy day of all the Devil's Crew. Alas, said *Panurge*, Fryar *Jhon* damns himself here as black as Buttermilk for the noance. Oh what a good Friend I lose in him. Alas, alas, there is anothergats Bout than last year's. We are falling out of *Scylla* into *Charybdis*. Oho! I drown. *Confiteor*, one poor Word or two by way of Testament, Fryar *Jhon* my Ghostly Father, good Mr. Abstractor, my Crony, my *Achates*, *Xenomanes*, my All. Alas I drown, two Words of Testament here upon this Ladder.

CHAPTER XXI

A Continuation of the Storm, with a short Discourse on the Subject of making Testaments at Sea.

To make ones last Will, said *Epistemon*, at this time that we ought to bestir our selves and help our Seamen, on the penalty of being drown'd, seems to me as idle and ridiculous a Maggot as that of some of *Cæsar*'s Men, who at their coming into the *Gauls*, were mightily busi'd in making Wills and Codicils, be-moan'd their Fortune, and the absence of their Spouses and Friends at *Rome*, when it was absolutely necessary for them to run to their Arms, and use their utmost Strength against *Ariovistus* their Enemy.

This also is to be as silly, as that jolt-headed Loblolly of a Carter, who, having laid his Waggon fast in a Slough, down on his Marrow-bones, was calling on the strong-Back'd Deity *Hercules*, might and main, to help him at a dead lift, but all the while forgot to goad on his Oxen, and lay his Shoulder to the Wheels, as it behoved him, as if a *Lord have mercy upon us* alone, would have got his Cart out of the Mire.

What will it signify to make your Will now? For either we shall come off, or drown for't. If we scape, it will not signifie a straw to us; for Testaments are of no value or Authority, but by the death of the Testators. If we are drown'd, will it not be drown'd too? Pr'ythee who will transmit it to the Executors? Some kind Wave will throw it ashoar, like *Ulysses*, reply'd *Panurge*, and some King's Daughter, going to fetch a Walk in the fresco on the Evening, will find it, and take care to have it prov'd and fulfill'd; nay, and have some stately *Cenotaph* erected to my Memory, as *Dido* had to that of her good Man *Sichæus*; *Æneas* to *Deiphobus* upon the *Trojan* shoar near *Rhœte*; *Andromache* to *Hector* in the City of *Buthrot*; *Aristotle* to *Hermias* and *Eubulus*; the *Athenians* to the Poet *Euripides*; the *Romans* to *Drusus* in *Germany*, and to *Alexander Severus* their Emperor in the *Gauls*; *Argentier* to *Callaischre*; *Xenocrates* to *Lisidices*; *Timares* to his Son *Teleutagoras*; *Eupolis* and *Aristodice* to their Son *Theotimus*; *Onestes* to *Timocles*; *Callimachus* to *Sopolis* the Son of *Dioclides*; *Catullus* to his Brother; *Statius* to his Father; *Germain* of *Brie* to *Hervé* the *Breton* Tarpawlin. Art thou mad, said Fryar *Jhon*, to run on at this rate? Help here, in the name of five hundred thousand millions of Cartloads of Devils, help; may a Shanker gnaw thy Moustachio's, and three rows of Pock-royals and Colly-flowers cover thy Bum and Turd-barrel instead of Breeches and Codpiece. Codsooks, our Ship is almost overset. Ods death, how shall we clear her? 'Tis well if she don't founder. What a Devilish Sea there runs? She'll neither try, nor hull, the Sea will overtake her, so we shall never scape, the Devil scape me. Then *Pantagruel* was heard to make a sad Exclamation, saying with a loud voice, Lord save us, we perish: Yet not as we would have it, but thy holy Will be done. The Lord and the blessed Virgin be with us said *Panurge*: Holos, alas, I drown, be be be bous, be bous bous: *In manus*. Good Heaven, send me some Dolphin to carry me safe on shoar, like a pretty little *Arion*: I shall make shift to sound the Harp if it be not unstrung. Let nineteen Legions of black Devils seize me, said Fryar *Jhon*, (the Lord be with us, whisper'd *Panurge* between his chattering Teeth) If I come down to thee, I'll shew thee to some purpose, that the Badge of thy Humanity dangles at a Calves Breech, thou ragged horn'd Cuckoldy Booby; mgna, mgnan, mgnan: Come hither and help us thou great weeping Calf, or may thirty millions of Devils leap on thee; wilt thou come, Sea-Calf? Fye, how ugly the howling Whelp looks! What, always the same Ditty? Come on now my bonny Drawer. This he said, opening his Breviary, come forward, thou and I must be somewhat serious for a while, let me peruse thee stiffly. *Beatus vir qui non abiit*. Pshaw, I know all this by heart; let's see the Legend of Monsieur St. *Nicholas*.

Horrida *Tempestas montem* turbavit *acutum*.

Tempest was a mighty Flogger of Lads at *Mountague College*. If *Pedants* be damn'd for whipping poor little innocent wretches their Scholars, he is, upon my Honour by this time fix'd within *Ixion*'s Wheel lashing the cropt ear bobtail'd Cur that gives it motion. If they are sav'd for having whipp'd innocent Lads, he ought to be above the—

CHAPTER XXII

An End of the Storm.

SHOAR, Shoar, cry'd *Pantagruel*, Land to, my Friends, I see Land, pluck up a good spirit, Boys, 'tis within a kenning, so we are not far from a Port—I see the Sky clearing up to the North-wards —Look to the South-east! Courage my Hearts, said the Pilot, now she'll bear the hullock of a Sail, the Sea is much smoother, some hands aloft, to the main Top—Put the Helm a weather— Steady, Steady—Hall your aftermisen bowlins—Hawl, Hawl, Hawl—Thus, Thus, and no nearer. Mind your Steerage, bring your main Tack aboard—Clear your Sheats; Clear your bow- lins; Port, Port, Helm a lee—Now, to the Sheat on the star- board-side, thou Son of a Whore. Thou art mightily pleas'd, honest Fellow, quoth Fryar *Jhon*, with hearing him make mention of thy Mother. Loff, Loff, cry'd the Quarter-master that con'd the Ship, keep her full, Loff the Helm. Loff, it is, answer'd the Steer- man; keep her thus.—Get the Bonnets fix'd.—Steady, Steady.

That's well said, said Fryar *Jhon*, now this is something like a Tanzy. Come, Come, Come, Children be nimble—Good.— Loff, Loff.—Thus.—helm a weather. That's well said and thought on. Methinks the Storm is almost over. It was high time, faith; however, the Lord be thanked.—Our Devils begin to scamper.—Out with all your Sails.—Hoist your Sails.—

Hoist.—That's spoke like a Man, Hoist, Hoist.—Here agod's name honest *Ponocrates*, thou'rt a lusty fornicator, the whore-Son will get none but Boys; *Eusthenes*, thou art a notable Fellow. —Run up to the fore-top-Saile.—Thus, Thus.—Well said, i-faith, Thus, Thus. I dare not fear any thing all this while, for it is a Holy-day. Vea, Vea, Vea! Husah! This shout of the Sea-men is not amiss, and pleases me, for it is Holy-day: Keep her full, Thus.—Good. Chear up my merry Mates all, cry'd out *Epistemon*, I see already *Castor* on the Right. Be, be, bous, bous, bous, said *Panurge*, I am much afraid it is the Bitch *Helen*. 'Tis truly *Mixarchagenas*, return'd *Epistemon*, if thou likest better that denomination which the *Argives* gives him. Ho, Ho! I see Land too; let her bear in with the Harbour, I see a good many People on the Beach: I see a light on an *Obeliscolychny*. Shorten your Sails, said the Pilot, fetch the sounding-Line, we must double that point of Land, and mind the Sands.—We are clear of them, said the Sailers. Soon after, away she goes, quoth the Pilot, and so doth the rest of our Fleet: Help came in good season.

By St. *John*, said *Panurge*, This is spoke somewhat like: O the sweet Word! There's the Soul of Musick in't: Mgna, mgna, mgna, said Fryar *Jhon*: If ever thou tast a drop on 't, let the Devil's-Dam tast me, thou Ballocky Devil. Here honest Soul, here's a full Sneacker of the very best. Bring the Flagons, Dost hear, *Gymnast*, and that same large Pasty Jambic, Gammonic, as you will have it.—Take heed you pilot her in Right.

Cheer up, cry'd out *Pantagruel*, cheer up, my Boys: Let's be our selves again, do you see yonder close by our Ship, two Barks, three Sloops, five Ships, eight Pinks, four Yawls, and six Frigats, making towards us, sent by the good People of the neighbour-ing Island to our Relief. But who is this *Ucalegon* below, that cry's and makes such a sad moan? Were it not that I hold the Mast firmly with both my hands, and keep it streighter than two hundred tacklings—I'd.—It is (said Fryar *Jhon*) that poor Devil *Panurge*, who is troubled with a Calf's ague; he quakes for fear when his belly's full. If, said *Pantagruel*, he hath been afraid during this dreadfull Hurricane, and dangerous Storm, provided (waving that) he hath done his part like a Man, I do not value him a Jot the less for it. For as to fear in all Encounters, is the mark of a heavy, and cowardly Heart, as *Agamemnon* did, who for that reason, is ignominously tax'd by *Achilles* with having Dogs Eyes, and a Stags Heart; so, not to fear when the case is evidently dreadful, is a sign of want or smallness of Apprehension.

Now if any thing ought to be feard, in this Life, next to offending God, I will not say it is death; I will not meddle with the Disputes of *Socrates* and the Academies, that death of it self is neither bad nor to be fear'd: But I will affirm that this kind of death by Shipwrack is to be fear'd or nothing is. For as *Homer* saith, it is a grievous, dreadfull, and an unnatural thing to perish at Sea. And indeed *Æneas*, in the Storm that took his Fleet near *Sicily*, was griev'd that he had not dy'd by the Hand of the brave *Diomedes*, and said that those were three nay four times happy who perish'd with *Troy*. No Man here hath lost his Life; the Lord our Saviour be eternally prais'd for it: But in truth here is a Ship sadly out of order. Well, we must take care to have the damage repair'd. Take heed we do not run a ground and billage her.

CHAPTER XXIII

How Panurge play'd the Good Fellow when the Storm was over.

WHAT Cheer ho? fore and aft? quoth *Panurge*, Oh ho! All is well, the Storm is over. I beseech ye, be so kind as to let me be the first that is set on shoar; for I would by all means a little untruss a point.—Shall I help you still, here, let me see, I'll coyle this Rope; I have plenty of courage, and of fear as little as may be. Give it me yonder, honest Tar—No, no, I have not a bit of fear. Indeed that same Decumane Wave that took us fore and aft somewhat alter'd my Pulse.—Down with your Sails, well said, how now, Fryar *Jhon*, you do nothing? Is it time for us to drink now? Who can tell but St. *Martin*'s running Footman *Belzebuth* may still be hatching us some further mischief? Shall I come and help you again! Pork and Pease choak me, if I do not heartily repent, tho' too late, not having followed the Doctrine of the good Philosopher who tells us, *That to walk by the Sea, and to navigate by the Shoar, are very safe and pleasant things*; just as 'tis to go on foot when we hold our Horse by the Bridle.—Hah, hah,

hah, by G— all goes well.—Shall I help you here, too? Let me see, I'll do this as it should be, or the Devil's in 't.

Epistemon (who had the inside of one of his Hands all fleea'd and bloody, having held a Tackling with might and main) hearing what *Pantagruel* had said, told him, You may believe, my Lord, I had my share of fear, as well as *Panurge*, yet I spar'd no Pains in lending my helping Hand. I consider'd, that since by fatal and unavoidable necessity, we must all die, it is the blessed Will of God that we die this or that hour, and this or that kind of death; nevertheless we ought to implore, invoke, pray, beseech, and supplicate him; but yet we must not stop there; it behoveth us also to use our endeavours on our side, and, as the Holy Writ saith, *to cooperate with him*.

You know what *C. Flaminius* the Consul said, when by *Hannibal*'s Policy he was penn'd up near the Lake of *Peruse* alias *Thrasymene*, *Friends* (said he to his Soldiers) *you must not hope to get out of this place barely by Vows or Prayers to the Gods; no, 'tis by Fortitude and Strength we must escape, and cut ourselves a way with the edge of our Swords, through the midst of our Enemies.*

Sallust likewise makes *M. Portius Cato* say this, *The help of the Gods is not obtain'd by idle Vows, and Womanish Complaints; 'tis by Vigilance, Labour, and repeated Endeavours that all things succeed according to our Wishes and Designs.*

If a Man in time of need and danger is negligent, heartless, and lazy, in vain he implores the Gods; they are then justly angry and incens'd against him. The Devil take me, said Fryar *Jhon* (I'll go his halves, quoth *Panurge*) if the Close of *Sevillé* had not been all gather'd, vintag'd, glean'd and destroy'd, if I had only sung *Contra hostium insidias* (matter of Breviary) like all the rest of the Monking Devils, and had not bestir'd my self to save the Vineyard as I did, dispatching the Truant *Piccaroons* of *Lerné* with the Staff of the Cross.

Let her sink or swim a Gods Name, said *Panurge*, all's one to Fryar *Jhon*, he doth nothing; his Name is Fryar *Jhon Doelittle*; for all he sees me here a sweating and puffing to help with all my might this *honest Tar* first of the Name.—Hark you me, dear Soul, a word with you—but pray be not angry; How thick do you judge the Planks of our Ship to be? Some two good inches and upwards, return'd the Pilot, don't fear. Odskilderkins, said

Panurge, it seems then we are within two Fingers breadth of Damnation. Is this one of the nine Comforts of Matrimony? Ah, dear Soul, you do well to measure the danger by the Yard of Fear. For my part I have none on 't, my name is *William Dreadnought*. As for Heart, I have more than enough on 't; I mean none of your Sheeps Heart; but of Wolf's Heart, the Courage of a Bravoe; by the Pavilion of *Mars*, I fear nothing but Danger.

CHAPTER XXIV

How Panurge was said to have been afraid, without reason,
during the Storm.

GOOD morrow, Gentlemen, said *Panurge*, Good morrow to you all, You are in very good Health, thanks to Heaven, and your selves? You are all heartily wellcome, and in good time. Let us go on shoar—Here, *Coxen*, get the Ladder over the Gunnel, Man the sides, Man the pinnace, and get her by the Ships side.— Shall I yet lend you a hand here? I am stark mad for want of business, and would work like any two yoaks of Oxen.—Truly this is a fine Place, and these look like a very good People.— Children, do you want me still in any thing, do not spare the sweat of my Body, for godsake. *Adam* (that is *Man*) was made to labour and work, as the Birds were made to fly; our Lord's Will is that we get our bread with the sweat of our brows, not idling and doing nothing like this tatterdemallion of a *Monk* here, this Fryar *Jack*, who is fain to drink to hearten himself up, and dyes for fear.—Rare weather.—I now find the answer of *Anacharsis*, the noble *Philosopher*, very proper; being ask'd what Ship he reckon'd the safest; he reply'd, that which is in the Harbour: he made a yet better repartie, said *Pantagruel*, when some body inquiring which is greater, the number of the living, or that of the dead? He ask'd them, amongst which of the two they reckon'd those that are at Sea? ingeniously implying, that they are continually in danger of death, dying live, and living dye. *Portius Cato* also said that there were but three things of which he would repent; That is, if ever he had trusted his Wife with his secret, if he had idled away a day, and if he had ever gone by Sea, to a place which he could visit by Land. By this dignified

Frock of mine, said Fryar *Jhon* to *Panurge*, Friend, thou hast been afraid during the Storm, without cause or reason; for thou wert not born to be drowned, but rather to be hang'd, and exalted in the Air, or to be roasted in the midst of a jolly bonfire. My Lord, would you have a good Cloak for the Rain? Leave me off your Wolf and Badger-skin Mantle: Let *Panurge* but be flead, and cover your self with his hide. But do not come near the Fire, nor near your Blacksmith's Forges a God's name, for in a moment you would see it in ashes. Yet be as long as you please in the Rain, Snow, Hail, nay, by the Devil's maker, throw your self or dive down to the very bottom of the Water, I'll ingage you'll not be wet at all. Have some winter Boots made of it, they'le never take in a drop of Water; make Bladders of it to lay under Boys, to teach them to swim, instead of Corks, and they will learn without the least danger. His Skin then, said *Pantagruel*, should be like the herb called, true maidens Hair, which never takes wet nor moistness, but still keeps dry, though you lay it at the bottom of the Water as long as you please, and for that reason is call'd *Adiantos*.

Friend *Panurge*, said Fryar *Jhon*, I pray thee never be afraid of Water, thy life for mine, thou art threatn'd with a contrary Element. Ay, ay, reply'd *Panurge*, but the Devil's Cooks dote sometimes, and are apt to make horrid blunders as well as others, often putting to boyle in water what was design'd to be roasted on the fire, like the head Cooks of our Kitchin, who often lard Partridges, Queests and Stockdoves with intent to roast them, one wou'd think, but it happens sometimes, that they e'en turn the Partridges into the Pot to be boyl'd with Cabbages, the Queests with leek Porradge, and the Stockdoves with Turnips.

But hark you me, good Friends, I protest before this noble Company, that as for the Chappel which I vow'd to Monsieur St. *Nicholas*, between *Cande*, and *Monsoreau*, I *honestly* mean that it shall be a Chappel, alias a Lymbeck of Rose-water, which shall be where neither Cow nor Calf shall be fed, for between you and I I intend to throw it to the bottom of the Water. Here is a rare Rogue for yee, said *Eusthenes*; here's a pure Rogue, a Rogue in grain, a Rogue enough, a Rogue and a half. He is re-solv'd to make good the *Italian* Proverb, *Passato el pericolo è gabato el Santo*.

The Devil was sick, the Devil a Monk wou'd be;
The Devil was well, and the Devil a Monk he'd be.

CHAPTER XXV

How after the Storm, Pantagruel went on shoar in the Islands
of the Macreons.

IMMEDIATELY after, we went a shoar at the Port of an Island, which they call'd the Island of the *Macreons*; the good People of the place receiv'd us very honourably. An old *Macrobius* (so they call'd their eldest Elderman) desir'd *Pantagruel* to come to the Town-house to refresh himself, and eat something, but he would not budge a foot, from the Mole, till all his Men were landed. After he had seen them, he gave order they should all change Cloaths, and that some of all the Stores in the Fleet, should be brought on shoar that every ship's Crew might live well, which was accordingly done; and God wot how they all top'd, and carrouz'd; the People of the Place brought them Provisions in abundance. The *Pantagruelists* return'd them more: As the truth is, their's were somewhat damag'd by the late Storm. When they had well stuffed the insides of their Doublets, *Pantagruel* desired every one to lend their help to repair the damage, which they readily did. It was easy enough to refit there; for all the Inhabitants of the Island were Carpenters, and all such Handicrafts as are seen in the *Arsenale* at *Venice*. None but the largest Island was inhabited, having three Ports, and ten Parishes; the rest being over-run with Wood and desert, much like the Forest of *Arden*. We entreated the old *Macrobius* to shew us what was worth seeing in the Island, which he did; and in the desert and dark Forest, we discover'd several old ruined Temples, Obeliscs, Pyramids, Monuments, and ancient Tombs, with diverse Inscriptions, and Epitaphs, some of them in hieroglyphic Characters, others in the *Gothic* Dialect, some in the *Arabic, Agarenian, Sclavonian*, and other Tongues: of which *Epistemon* took an exact Account. In the interim *Panurge* said to Fryar *Jhon*, is this the island of the *Macreons*? *Macreon* signifies in Greek an old Man, or one much stricken in years. What's that to me, said Fryar *Jhon*, how can I help it? I was not in the Country when they Christen'd it. Now I think on 't, quoth *Panurge*, I believe the Name of *Makerel* [that's a *Bawd* in French] was deriv'd from it; for, procuring is the Province of the old, as Buttock-riggling is that of the young. Therefore I don't know but this may be the Bawdy or Mackrel Island, the Original and Prototype of the Island of that name at *Paris*. Let's go and drudge for Cock-Oysters. Old *Macrobius* ask'd in the *Ionick* Tongue, how, and by what industry and labour *Pantagruel* got to their Port that day, there having been such blustering weather, and such a dreadful Storm at Sea. *Pantagruel* told him, that the Almighty preserver of mankind had regarded the Simplicity, and sincere Affection of his Servants, who did not travel for Gain or sordid Profit, the sole design of their Voyage being a studious desire to know, see, and visit the Oracle of *Bacbuc*, and take the word of the Bottle upon some difficulties offer'd by one of the Company; nevertheless this had not been without great Affliction, and evident danger of Shipwrack. After that, he ask'd him what he judg'd to be the cause of that terrible Tempest, and if the adjacent Seas were thus frequently subject to Storms, as in the Ocean are the *Ratz* of *Sammaieu*, *Maumusson*, and in the *Mediterranean* Sea the Gulph of *Sataly*, *Montargentan*, *Piombino*, *Capo Melio* in the *Morea*, the *Streights* of *Gibraltar*, *Faro di Messina*, and others.

CHAPTER XXVI

*How the good Macrobius gave us an Account of the Mansion,
and decease of the Heroes.*

THE good *Macrobius* then answer'd; Friendly Strangers, this Island is one of the *Sporades*, not of your *Sporades* that lie in the *Carpathian* Sea, but one of the *Sporades* of the Ocean; in former times rich, frequented, wealthy, populous, full of Traffic, and in the Dominions of the Ruler of *Britain*; but now by Course of time, and in these latter Ages of the world, poor and desolate as you see. In this dark Forest, above Seventy eight thousand *Persian* Leagues in Compass, is the dwelling-place of the *Dæmons* and Heroes, that are grown old, and we believe that some one of them dy'd Yesterday; since the Comet, which we saw for three days before together, shines no more: and now 'tis likely, that at his Death there arose this horrible Storm; for while they are alive all Happiness attends both this and the adjacent Islands, and a setled Calm and Serenity. At the Death of every one of them we commonly hear in the Forest loud and mournful groans, and the whole Land is infested with Pestilence, Earthquakes, Inundations and other Calamities; the Air with Fogs and obscurity, and the Sea with Storms and Hurricanes. What you tell us seems to me likely enough, said *Pantagruel*; For as a Torch or Candle, as long as it hath Life enough and is lighted, shines round about, disperses its Light, delights those that are near it, yields them its Service and Clearness, and never causes any pain or displeasure; but as soon as 'tis extinguished, its Smoak and Evaporation infects the Air, offends the By-standers, and is noisome to all; so, as long as those noble and renowned Souls inhabit their Bodies, Peace, Profit, Pleasure, and Honour never leave the places where they abide; but as soon as they leave them, both the Continent and the adjacent Islands are annoyed with great Commotions; in the Air, Fogs, Darkness, Thunder, Hail, Tremblings, Pulsations, Arietations of the Earth, Storms and Hurricanes at Sea, together with sad Complaints amongst the People, Broaching of Religions, Changes in Governments, and Ruins of Commonwealths.

We had a sad Instance of this lately, said *Eustemon*, at the Death of that valiant and learned Knight *William du Bellay*, during whose Life *France* enjoy'd so much Happiness, that all the rest of the World look'd upon it with Envy, sought Friendship with it, and stood in awe of its Power; but soon after his Decease it hath for a considerable time been the Scorn of the rest of the World.

Thus, said *Pantagruel, Anchises* being dead at *Drepany* in *Sicily, Æneas* was dreadfully tosst and endanger'd by a Storm; and perhaps for the same reason *Herod*, that Tyrant and cruel King of *Judea*, finding himself near the Pangs of a horrid kind of Death, (for he dy'd of a *Phthiriasis*, devour'd by Vermin and Lice; as before him dy'd *L. Scylla, Pherecides* the *Syrian* Preceptor, *Pythagoras*, the Greek Poet *Alcmæon* and others) and foreseeing that the *Jews* would make Bonfires at his Death, caus'd all the Nobles and Magistrates to be summoned to his *Seraglio* out of all the Cities, Towns, and Castles of *Judæa*, fraudulently pretending that he had some things of moment to impart to them. They made their personal Appearance; whereupon he caus'd them all to be shut up in the *Hippodrome* of the *Seraglio*; then said to his Sister *Salome*, and *Alexander* her Husband; I am certain that the *Jews* will rejoice at my Death, but if you will observe and perform what I will tell you, my Funeral shall be honourable, and there will be a general Mourning; As soon as you shall see me dead, let my Guards, to whom I have already given strict Commission to that purpose, kill all the Noblemen and Magistrates that are secur'd in the *Hippodrome*. By these means all *Jewry* shall in spite of themselves be oblig'd to mourn and lament, and Foreigners will imagine it to be for my death, as if some Heroic Soul had left her Body. A desperate Tyrant wish'd as much, when he said, *When I dye, let Earth and Fire be mix'd together*, which was as good as to say, let the whole world perish: Which Saying the Tyrant *Nero* alter'd, saying *While I live*, as *Suetonius* affirms it. This detestable saying of which *Cicero, lib. 3. de Finib.* and *Seneca, lib. 2. de Clementia*, make mention, is ascrib'd to the Emperour *Tiberius*, by *Dion Nicæus*, and *Suidas*.

CHAPTER XXVII

Pantagruel's Discourse of the Decease of Heroic Souls; and of the dreadful Prodigies that happen'd before the Death of the late Lord de Langey.

I would not, continu'd *Pantagruel*, have miss'd the Storm that hath thus disorder'd us, were I also to have miss'd the Relation of these things told us by this good *Macrobius*. Neither am I unwilling to believe what he said of a Comet that appears in the Sky some days before such a Decease. For some of those Souls are so Noble, so Pretious, and so Heroic, that Heaven gives us notice of their departing, some days before it happens. And as a Prudent Physician seeing by some Symptoms that his Patient draws towards his end, some days before, gives notice of it to his Wife, Children, Kindred, and Friends, that, in that little time he hath yet to live, they may admonish him to settle all things in his Family, to tutor and instruct his Children as much as he can, recommend his Relict to his Friends, in her Widowhood, declare what he knows to be necessary about a Provision for the Orphans, that he may not be surpriz'd by Death without making his Will, and may take care of his Soul and Family; In the same manner the Heavens, as it were, joyful for the approaching reception of those blessed Souls, seem to make Bonfires by those Comets and blazing Meteors, which they at the same time kindly design should Prognosticate to us here, that in few days one of those venerable Souls is to leave her Body, and this terrestrial Globe. Not altogether unlike this, was what was formerly done at *Athens* by the Judges of the *Areopagus*. For when they gave their Verdict to cast or clear the Culprits that were try'd before them, they us'd certain notes according to the substance of the Sentences; by Θ, signifying Condemnation to Death; by T. Absolution; by A. Ampliation or a Demur, when the case was not sufficiently examin'd. Thus having publickly set up those Letters, they eas'd the Relations and Friends of the Prisoners, and such others as desir'd to know their Doom, of their Doubts. Likewise by these Comets, as in etherial Characters, the Heavens silently say to us, Make haste, Mortals, if you would know or learn of these blessed Souls any thing concerning the publick good or your private Interest; for their Catastrophe is near, which being past, you will vainly wish for them afterwards.

The good-natur'd Heavens still do more; and, that Mankind may be declared unworthy of the injoyment of those Renown'd Souls, they fright and astonish us with Prodigies, Monsters, and other foreboding Signs, that thwart the Order of Nature.

Of this we had an instance several Days before the decease of the Heroik Soul of the Learned and Valiant *Chevalier de Langey*, of whom you have already spoken. I remember it, said *Epistemon*, and my Heart still trembles within me when I think on the many dreadful Prodigies that we saw five or six days before he dy'd. For the Lords of *D'assier, Chemant*, one-ey'd *Mailly*, St. *Ayl, Villeneufue-la-Guyart*, Master *Gabriel*, Physician of *Savillan, Rabelais, Cohuau, Massuau, Majorici, Bullou, Cercu*, alias *Bourgmaistre, Francis Proust, Ferron, Charles Girard, Francis Bourré*, and many other Friends and Servants to the Deceased, all dismay'd, gaz'd on each other, without uttering one word; yet not without foreseeing that *France* wou'd in a short time be depriv'd of a Knight so accomplish'd and necessary for its Glory and

Protection, and that Heaven claim'd him again as its due. By the tufted Tip of my Cowle, cry'd Fryar *Jhon*, I am e'en resolv'd to become a Scholar before I die: I have a pretty good Headpiece of my own, you must own: Now pray give me leave to ask you a civil Question; Can these same Heroes and Demi-gods, you talk of, die? May I never be damn'd, if I was not so much a Lobcock as to believe they had been Immortal like so many fine Angels; Heav'n forgive me! but this most Reverend Father *Macroby* tells us, *They die at last.* We all must, return'd *Pantagruel.*

The *Stoicks* held them all to be Mortal, except one, who alone is Immortal, Impassible, Invisible. *Pindar* plainly saith, That there is no more Thread, that is to say, no more Life spun from the Distaff and Flax of the hard-hearted Fates for the Goddesses *Hamadryades*, than there is for those Trees that are preserv'd by them, which are good sturdy downright Oaks, whence they derived their Original, according to the Opinion of *Callimachus*, and *Pausanias* in *Phoci*; with whom concurs *Martianus Capella.* As for the Demigods, *Fauns, Satyrs, Sylvans, Hobgoblins, Ægpanes, Nymphs, Heroes*, and *Dæmons*, several Men have, from the total Sum, which is the result of the divers Ages Calculated by *Hesiod*, reckon'd their Life to be 9720 Years, that sum, consisting of four special numbers orderly arising from one, the same added together and multiplied by four every way, amounts to forty; these forties being reduced into Triangles by five times, make up the total of the foresaid Number. See *Plutarch*, in his Book about the Cessation of Oracles.

This, said Fryar *Jhon*, is not matter of Breviary; I may believe as little or as much of it as you and I please. I believe, said *Pantagruel*, that all Intellectual Souls are exempted from *Atropos*'s Scissers. They are all Immortal, whether they be of Angels, of Dæmons, or Human: Yet I'll tell you a story concerning this, that's very strange, but is written and affirmed by several learned Historians.

CHAPTER XXVIII

How Pantagruel related a very sad story of the Death of the Heroes.

EPITHERSES the Father of *Æmilian* the *Rhetorician*, sailing from *Greece* to *Italy*, in a Ship freighted with divers Goods, and Passengers, at night, the wind fail'd 'em near the *Echinades*, some Islands that lie between the *Morea* and *Tunïs*, and the Vessel was driven near *Paxos*. When they were got thither, some of the passengers being asleep, others awake, the rest eating and drinking, a Voice was heard that call'd aloud *Thamous*; which Cry surpris'd them all. This same *Thamous* was their Pilot, an *Egyptian* by Birth, but known by Name only to some few Travellers. The Voice was heard a second time calling *Thamous*, in a frightful Tone, and none making answer but trembling and remaining silent, the Voice was heard a third time, more dreadful than before.

This caus'd *Thamous* to answer; Here am I, What do'st thou call me for? What wilt thou have me do? Then the Voice louder than before, bad him publish when he should come to *Paloda*, That the Great God *Pan* was dead.

Epitherses related, that all the Mariners, and Passengers, having heard this, were extreamly amaz'd and frighted; and that consulting among themselves, whether they had best conceal or divulge what the Voice had enjoyn'd *Thamous* said, his advice was, That if they happen'd to have a fair wind, they should proceed without mentioning a word on 't; but if they chanc'd to be becalm'd, he wou'd publish what he had heard: Now when they were near *Paloda* they had no Wind, neither were they in any Current. *Thamous* then getting up on the top of the Ship's forecastle, and casting his Eyes on the Shoar, said that he had been commanded to proclaim, that the great God *Pan* was dead. The words were hardly out of his Mouth, when deep Groans, great Lamentations, and Shrieks, not of one Person, but of many together, were heard from the Land.

The News of this, (many being present then) was soon spread at *Rome*; insomuch that *Tiberius*, who was then Emperor, sent for this *Thamous*, and having heard him, gave credit to his words; and inquiring of the Learned in his Court and at *Rome*, who was that *Pan*? He found by their relation, that he was the Son of *Mercury* and *Penelope*; as *Herodotus*, and *Cicero* in his Third Book of the Nature of the Gods, had written before.

For my part, I understand it of that Great Saviour of the Faithfull, who was shamefully put to Death at *Jerusalem*, by the envy and wickedness of the Doctors, Priests, and Monks of the *Mosaic* Law. And methinks, my Interpretation is not improper; for he may lawfully be said in the Greek Tongue, to be *Pan*, since he is our *All*. For all that we are, all that we live, all that we have, all that we hope, is him, by him, from him, and in him; he is the good *Pan*, the great Shepherd, who, as the loving Sheperd *Corydon* affirms, hath not only a tender Love and Affection for his Sheep, but also for their Shepherds. At his death, complaints, sighs, fears and lamentations were spread through the whole *Fabric* of the universe, whether Heaven, Land, Sea, or Hell.

The time also concurs with this Interpretation of mine; for this most good, most mighty *Pan*, our only Saviour, dyed near *Jerusalem*, during the Reign of *Tiberius Cæsar*. *Pantagruel* having ended this discourse, remain'd silent, and full of Contemplation; a little while after, we saw the tears flow out of his eyes as big as Ostridg's Eggs. God take me presently if I tell you one single syllable of a Lye in the matter.

CHAPTER XXIX

How Pantagruel sail'd by the Sneaking Island where Shrove-tide reign'd.

THE Jovial Fleet being refitted and repair'd, new Stores taken in, the *Macreons* over and above satisfy'd, and pleas'd with the Money spent there by *Pantagruel*, our Men in better humour yet than they us'd to be if possible, we merrily put to sea the next day near Sun-set, with a delicious fresh Gale.

Xenomanes show'd us afar off the Sneaking Island, where reign'd *Shrovetide*, of whom *Pantagruel* had heard much talk formerly; for that Reason, he would gladly have seen him in

Person, had not *Xenomanes* advis'd him to the contrary: First because this wou'd have been much out of our way; and then, for the lean Cheer which he told us, was to be found at that Prince's Court, and indeed all over the Island.

You can see nothing there for your Money (said he) but a huge Greedy-Guts, a tall woundy swallower of hot Wardens and Muscles, a Longshank'd Mole-catcher, an over-grown Bottler of hay, a Mossy-chin'd, Demy-giant with a double shaven Crown, of Lantern Breed, a very great Loytering Noddy-peak'd youngster, banner-bearer to the Fish-eating Tribe, Dictator of Mustard-land, Flogger of little Children, Calciner of Ashes, Father and Foster-father to Physicians, swarming with Pardons, Indulgencies, and Stations; a very honest Man; a good Catholic and as brimfull of Devotion as ever he can hold.

He weeps the Three fourth parts of the day, and never assists at any Weddings; but, give the Devil his due, he's the most industrious Larding-stick, and Scure-maker in forty Kingdoms. About Six Years ago, as I pass'd by Sneaking Land, I brought home a large Scure from thence, and made a Present of it to the Butchers of *Quande*, who set a great value upon them, and that for a Cause: sometime or other, if ever we live to come back to our own Country, I will shew you two of them fasten'd on the great Church-Porch. His usual Food is pickled Coats of Mail, salt Helmets and Head-pieces, and salt Sallads; which sometimes makes him piss Pins and Needles. As for his Cloathing, 'tis Comical enough o' Conscience, both for make and colour; for he wears Gray and Cold, nothing before, and nought behind, with the Sleeves of the same.

You will do me a Kindness, said *Pantagruel*, if as you have described his Cloths, Food, Actions, and Pastimes, you will also give me an Account of his Shape, and Disposition in all his Parts. Prithee do, dear Cod, said Fryar *Jhon*, for I have found him in my Breviary, and then follow the Moveable Holy-days. With all my heart, answer'd *Xenomanes*, We may chance to hear more of him as we touch at the Wild Island, the Dominion of the Squob *Chitterlings* his Enemies; against whom he is eternally at odds; and were it not for the help of the noble *Carnaval* their Protector, and good Neighbour, this Meagre-look'd Lozelly *Shrovetide* would long before this have made sad work among them, and rooted them out of their Habitation. Are these same *Chitterlings*, said Fryar *Jhon*, Male or Female, Angels or Mortals, Women or Maids? They are, reply'd *Xenomanes*, Female in Sex, Mortal in kind, some of them Maids, others not. The Devil have me, said Fryar *Jhon*, if I been't for them. What a shameful disorder in Nature is it not, to make War against Women? Let's go back, and hack the Villain to pieces.—What! meddle with *Shrovetide*, cry'd *Panurge*, in the Name of *Belzebub*, I am not yet so weary of my Life: No, I'm not yet so mad as that comes to. *Quid juris?* Suppose we should find our selves pent up between the *Chitterlings* and *Shrovetide*? between the Anvil and the Hammers? Shankers, and Buboes; stand off; Godzooks let's make the best of our way. I bid you Good-night, sweet Mr. *Shrovetide*; I recommend to you the *Chitterlings*, and pray don't forget the Puddings.

CHAPTER XXX

How Shrove-tide is anatomiz'd and describ'd by Xenomanes.

As for the inward Parts of *Shrovetide*, said *Xenomanes*, his *Brain*, is (at least it was in my time) in Bigness, Colour, Substance and Strength, much like the left Cod of a He-hand-worm.

The *Ventricles* of his said Brain, like an Augre.

The Worm-like *Excrescence*, like a Christmas-Box.

The *Membranes*, like a Monk's Cowle.

The *Funnel*, like a Mason's Chissel.

The *Fornix*, like a Casket.

The *Glandula pinealis*, like a Bag-pipe.

The *Rete Admirable*, like a Gutter.

The *Dug-like Processes*, like a Patch.

The *Tympanums*, like a Whirly-Gig.

The *Rocky bones*, like a Goose-wing.

The *Nape* of the *Neck*, like a Paper Lanthorn.

The *Nerves*, like a Pipkin.

The *Uvula*, like a Sack-butt.

The *Palate*, like a Mittain.

The *Spittle*, like a Shuttle.

The *Almonds*, like a Telescope.

The *Bridge* of his *Nose*, like a Wheel-barrow.

The *Head* of the *Larynx*, like a Vintage Basket.

The *Stomach*, like a Belt.

The *Pylorus*, like a Pitchfork.

The *Windpipe*, like an Oyster-Knife.

The *Throat*, like a Pincushion stuff'd with Oakham.

The *Lungs*, like a Prebend's Fur-gown.

The *Heart*, like a Cope.

The *Mediastin*, like an earthen Cup.

The *Pleura*, like a Crows-bill.

The *Arteries*, like a Watch-coat.

The *Midriff*, like a Mounteer-Cap.

The *Liver*, like a double-Tongu'd Mattock.

The *Veins*, like a Sash-Window.

The *Spleen*, like a Catcal.

The *Guts*, like a Trammel.

The *Gall*, like a Coopers Ads.

The *Entrails*, like a Gantlet.

The *Mesentery*, like a Abbot's Myter.

The *Hungry Gut*, like a Button.

The *Blind Gut*, like a Breast-plate.

The *Colon*, like a Bridle.

The *Arse-Gut*, like a Monk's Leathern Bottle.

The *Kidneys*, like a Trowel.

The *Loyns*, like a Padlock.

The *Ureters*, like a Pot-hook.

The *Emulgent Veins*, like two Gilly-flowers.

The *Spermatick Vessels*, like a Cully-mully-puff.

The *Parastata's*, like an Ink-pot.

The *Bladder*, like a Stone-bow.

Its *Neck*, like a Mill-Clapper.

The *Mirach*, or lower Parts of the *Belly*, like a High crown'd Hat.

The *Siphach*, or its *Inner Rind*, like a Wooden Cuff.

The *Muscles* like a pair of Bellows.

The *Tendons*, like a Hawking Glove.

The *Ligaments*, like a Tinker's Budget.

The *Bones*, like three-corner'd Cheese-Cakes.

The *Marrow*, like a Wallet.

The *Cartilages*, like a Field Tortoise, *alias* a Mole.

The *Glandules* in the *Mouth*, like a Pruning-Knife.

The *Animal Spirits*, like swindging Fisty-cuffs.

The *Blood* fermenting, like a multiplication of flurts on the Nose.

The *Urin*, like a Fig-pecker.

The *Sperm*, like a hundred of Tenpenny-Nails.

And his Nurse told me, That being Married to *Mid-Lent*, he only begot a good number of Local Adverbs, and certain double *Fasts*.

His *Memory* he had like a Scarf.

His *Common Sence*, like a buzzing of Bees.

His *Imagination*, like the Chime of a Set of Bells.

His *Thoughts*, like a flight of Starlings.

His *Conscience*, like the unnestling of a parcel of young Herns.

His *Deliberations*, like a Set of Organs.

His *Repentance*, like the Carriage of a double Canon.

His *Undertakings*, like the Ballast of a Galion.

His *Understanding*, like a torn Breviary.

His *Notions*, like Snails crawling out of Strawberries.

His *Will*, like three Filberts in a Porrenger.

His *Desire*, like six Trusses of Hay.

His *Judgment*, like a Shoing-horn.

His *Discretion*, like the truckle of a Pully.

His *Reason*, like a Cricket.

CHAPTER XXXI

Shrovetide's outward parts Anatomiz'd.

SHROVETIDE, continued *Xenomanes*, is somewhat better proportioned in his outward Parts, excepting the seven Ribs which he had over and above the common shape of Men.

His Toes *were like a Virginal on an Organ.*

His Nails, *like a Gimlet.*

His Feet, *like a Guitar.*

His Heels, *like a Club.*

The Soles *of his* Feet, *like a Crucible.*

His Legs, *like a Hawk's Lure.*

His Knees, *like a Joynt-Stool.*

His Thighs, *like a Steel Cap.*

His Hips, *like a Wimble.*

His Belly *as big as a Tun, button'd after the old Fashion, with a Girdle riding over the middle of his Bosom.*

His Navel, *like a Cymbal.*

His Groyn, *like a Minc'd Pye.*

His Member, *like a Slipper.*

His Purse, *like an Oyl-Cruet.*

His Genitals, *like a Joyners Plainer.*

Their Erecting Muscles, *like a Racket.*

The Perineum, *like a Flageolet.*

His Arse hole, *like a Crystal-Looking-Glass.*

His Bum, *like a Harrow.*

His Loyns, *like a Butter-pot.*

The Peritonæum, *or* Caul *wherein his* Bowels *were wrapp'd, like a Billiard-Table.*

His Back, *like an overgrown rack-bent Cross-Bow.*

The Vertebræ, *or* Joynts *of his* Back-bone, *like a Bagpipe.*

His Ribs, *like a Spinning-Wheel.*

His Brisket, *like a Canopy.*

His Shoulder-Blades, *like a Mortar.*

His Breast, *like a Game at Nine-Pins.*

His Paps, *like a Horn-Pipe.*

His Arm-pits, *like a Chequer.*

His Shoulders, *like a Hand-barrow.*

His Arms, *like a Riding-Hood.*

His Fingers, *like a Brotherhood's Andirons.*

The Fibulæ, *or lesser* Bones *of his* Legs, *like a pair of Stilts.*

His Shin-bones, *like Sickles.*

His Elbows, *like a Mouse-Trap.*

His Hands, *like a Curry-Comb.*

His Neck, *like a Talboy.*

His Throat, *like a Felt to distil* Hippocras.

The Knob *in his* Throat, *like a Barrel, where hang'd two brazen Wens, very fine and harmonious, in the shape of an Hour-glass.*

His Beard, *like a Lanthorn.*

His Chin, *like a Mushrom.*

His Ears, *like a pair of Gloves.*

His Nose, *like a Buskin.*

His Nostrils, *like a Forehead-Cloth.*
His Eye-brows, *like a Dripping-pan.*
On his left Brow, *was a mark of the shape and bigness of an Urinal.*
His Eye-lids, *like a Fiddle.*
His Eyes, *like a Comb-box.*
His Optick Nerves, *like a Tinder box.*
His Forehead, *like a false Cup.*
His Temples, *like the Cock of a Cistern.*
His Cheeks, *like a pair of Wooden Shoes.*
His Jaws, *like a Cawdle Cup.*
His Teeth, *like a Hunter's Staff. Of such Colts Teeth as his, you will find one at* Colonges les Royaux *in* Poictou, *and two at* la Brosse *in* Xaintonge, *on the Celler-door.*
His Tongue, *like a Jews-Harp.*
His Mouth, *like a Horse-Cloth.*
His Face *imbroider'd like a Mule's Pack-Saddle.*
His Head *contriv'd like a Still.*
His Skull, *like a Pouch.*
The Suturæ, *or Seams of his* Skull, *like the* Annulus Piscatoris, *or the* Fisher's Signet.
His Skin, *like a Gabardine.*
His Epidermis, *or outward* Skin, *like a Boulting-Cloth.*
His Hair, *like a Scrubbing-Brush.*
His Fur, *such as abovesaid.*

CHAPTER XXXII

A Continuation of Shrovetide's Countenance.

'TIS a wonderful thing, continued *Xenomanes,* to hear and see the State of *Shrovetide.*
If he chanc'd to Spit, it was whole Baskets full of Gold-finches.
If he blow'd his Nose, it was pickl'd Grigs.
When he Wept, it was Ducks with Onion Sauce.
When he Trembl'd, it was large Venison Pasties.
When he did Sweat, it was Old Ling with Butter Sauce.
When he Belch'd, it was Bushels of Oysters.
When he Sneez'd, it was whole Tubs full of Mustard.
When he Cough'd, it was Boxes of Marmalade.

When he Sob'd, it was Water-Cresses.

When he Yawn'd, it was Pots full of Pickl'd Pease.

When he Sigh'd, it was dry'd Neats Tongues.

When he Whistled, it was a whole Scuttle full of green Apes.

When he Snoar'd, it was a whole Pan-full of fry'd Beans.

When he Frown'd, it was Sows'd Hogs-Feet.

When he spoke, it was course brown Russet Cloth; so little it was like Crimson Silk with which Parisatis *desir'd that the words of such as spoke to her Son* Cyrus, *King of* Persia, *should be interwoven.*

When he Blow'd, it was Indulgence-Money boxes.

When he Wink'd, it was Butter'd Buns.

When he Grumbled, it was March Cats.

When he Nodded, 'twas Iron-bound Waggons.

When he made Mouths, it was broken Staves.

When he Mutter'd, it was Lawyers Revels.

When he Hopp'd about, it was Letters of Licence and Protections.

When he stepp'd back, it was Sea Cockle shells.

When he Slabber'd, it was common Ovens.

When he was Hoarse, it was an entry of Morrice-Dancers.

When he broke Wind, it was Duns-Cows-Leather Spatter-dashes.

When he Funk'd, it was Wash'd Leather Boots.

When he scratch'd himself, it was new Proclamations.

When he sung, it was Pease in Cods.

When he Evacuated, it was Mushroms and Morilles.

When he Puffed, it was Cabbages with Oyl, alias Caules Ambolif.

When he Talk'd, it was the last years Snow.

When he Dreamt, it was of a Cock and a Bull.

When he gave nothing, so much for the Bearer.

If he Thought to himself, it was Whimsies and Maggots.

If he Doz'd, it was Leases of Lands.

What is yet more strange, he us'd to work doing Nothing, and did nothing, tho' he work'd; Carous'd Sleeping, and slept carousing, with his Eyes open like the Hares in our Country, for fear of being taken Napping by the *Chitterlings* his inveterate Enemies; Biting he Laugh'd, and laughing bit; Eat nothing Fasting, and fasted eating nothing; mumbled upon Suspicion, drank by Imagination; Swam on the tops of high Steeples, dry'd his Clothes in Ponds and Rivers; Fish'd in the Air, and there

us'd to catch *Decumane* Lobsters; Hunted at the bottom of the
Herring-Pond, and caught their *Ibices, Stamboucs, Shamois*, and
other wild Goats; us'd to put out the Eyes of all the Crows
which he took sneakingly; fear'd nothing but his own shadow,
and the cries of fat Kids; us'd to gad abroad some days like a
Truant School-boy; play'd with the Ropes of Bells on Festival
days of Saints; made a Mallet of his fist, and writ on hairy Parchment Prognostications and Almanacks with his huge Pincase.

Is that the Gentleman, said Fryar *Jhon*, he is my Man: this is
the very Fellow I lookt for; I'll send him a Challenge immediately. This is, said *Pantagruel*, a strange and monstrous sort of a
Man, if I may call him a Man. You put me in mind of the Form
and Looks of *Amodunt* and *Dissonance*. How were they made,
said Fryar *Jhon*? may I be peel'd like a raw Onion if ever I heard
a word of them. I'll tell you what I read of them in some ancient
Apologues, reply'd *Pantagruel*.

Physis (that is to say Nature) at her first Burthen, begat
Beauty, and Harmony, without Carnal Copulation, being of her
self very Fruitful and Prolifick: *Antiphysis*, who ever was the
Counter part of Nature, immediately out of a malicious Spight
against her for Beautiful and Honourable Productions, in opposition, begat *Amodunt* and *Dissonance*, by Copulation with *Tellu-
mon*. Their heads were round like a Football, and not gently
flatted on both sides like the common shape of Men. Their ears
stood prick'd up like those of Asses; their Eyes, as hard as those
of Crabs, and without Brows, star'd out of their Heads, fix'd on
Bones like those of our Heels; their Feet were round like Tennis-
Balls; their Arms and Hands turn'd backwards towards their
Shoulders, and they walk'd on their Heads, continually turning
round like a Ball, topsie-turvy Heels over Head.

Yet (as you know that Apes esteem their Young the handsomest in the World) *Antiphysis* extolld her Offspring and strove
to prove, that their shape was handsomer and neater, than that
of the Children of *Physis*; saying that thus to have *Spherical* Heads,
and Feet, and walk in a circular Manner, wheeling round, had
something in it of the perfection of the divine Power, which
makes all beings eternally turn in that fashion; and that to have
our Feet uppermost, and the Head below them, was to imitate
the Creator of the universe, the Hair being like the roots, and

the Legs like the branches of Man; for Trees are better planted in the Earth by the roots, than they could be by their branches. By this demonstration, she imply'd that her Children were much more to be prais'd, for being like a standing Tree, than those of *Physis* that made the figure of a Tree upside down: As for the Arms and Hands, she pretended to prove that they were more justly turn'd towards the shoulders, because that part of the Body ought not to be without a defence, while the fore part is duly fenc'd with Teeth, which a Man cannot only use to chew, but also to defend himself against those things that offend him. Thus by the testimony, and astipulation of the brute Beasts, she drew all the witless herd, and mob of Fools into her opinion, and was admir'd by all brainless and nonsensical People.

Since that, she begot the hypocritical Tribes of evesdropping dissemblers, superstitious Popemongers and Priestridden Biggots, the Frantic Pistolets, the Scrapers of Benefices, Apparitors with the Devil in them, and other Grinders and Squeezers of Livings, your mad Herb-stinking Hermits, gulliguted dunces of the Cowl, Church-vermin, false zealots, devourers of the Substance of Men, and many more other deform'd and ill-favour'd Monsters, made in spight of Nature.

CHAPTER XXXIII

How Pantagruel discover'd a Monstrous Physetere, or Whirlpool, near the Wild Island.

ABOUT Sun set coming near the Wild Island, *Pantagruel* spy'd afar off a huge monstrous *Physetere*, a sort of a Whale (which some call a Whirl pool,) that came right upon us neighing, snorting, rais'd above the Waves higher than our main Tops, and spouting Water all the way into the Air, before it self, like a large River falling from a Mountain: *Pantagruel* showed it to the Pilot, and to *Xenomanes*.

By the Pilot's advice the Trumpets of the Thalamege were sounded, to warn all the Fleet to stand close and look to themselves: This Alarm being given, all the Ships, Gallions, Frigats, Brigantines, (according to their Naval discipline) placed themselves in the Order and Figure of a Y. [Upsilon,] the Letter of

Pythagoras, as Cranes do in their flight, and like an Angle, in whose Cone and Basis the Thalamege plac'd her self ready to fight smartly: Fryar *Jhon* with the Granadeers, got on the Forecastle.

Poor *Panurge* began to Cry and Howl worse than ever *Babillebabou*, said he, shrugging up his shoulders, quivering all over with fear, There will be the Devil upon Dun. This is a worse Business than That t' other Day; let us fly, let us fly; Old Nick take me if it is not *Leviathan*, describ'd by the noble Prophet *Moses*, in the Life of Patient *Job*. It will swallow us all, Ships and Men, Shag, Rag, and Bobtail, like a dose of Pills. Alas, it will make no more of us, and we shall hold no more room in its hellish Jaws, than a Sugar-plum in an Asse's Throat. Look, look, 'tis upon us, let's wheel off, whip it away and get ashoar. I believe 'tis the very individual Sea Monster, that was formerly design'd to devour *Andromeda*; we are all undone. Oh! for some valiant *Perseus* here now to kill the Dog.

I'll do its business presently, said *Pantagruel*; fear nothing. Odds-belly, said *Panurge*, remove the cause of my Fear then; when, the Devil, would you have a Man be afraid, but when there is so much Cause? If your Destiny be such as Fryar *Jhon* was saying a while ago (reply'd *Pantagruel*) you ought to be afraid of *Pyrois*, *Eöus*, *Æthon*, and *Phlegon*, the Suns Coach-horses that breath Fire at the Nostrils, and not of Physeters that spout nothing but Water at the Snout and Mouth. Their Water will not endanger your Life; and that Element will rather save and preserve, than hurt or endanger you.

Ay, ay, trust to that, and hang me, quoth *Panurge*, yours is a very pretty Fancy; Od's Fish, did I not give you a sufficient account of the Elements Transmutation, and the Blunders that are made of Roast for Boyld, and Boyld for Roast? Alas, here 'tis: I'le go hide my self below. We are dead Men every Mother's Son of us; I see upon our main Top that merciless Hagg *Atropos* with her Scizzers new ground, ready to cut our Threads all at one Snip. Oh! how dreadful and abominable thou art; Thou hast drown'd a good many, besides us, who never made their Brags of it. Did it but spout good brisk, dainty, delicious White-wine, instead of this damn'd bitter Salt-water, one might better bear with it, and there would be some cause to be Patient; like that

English Lord, who being doom'd to dye, and had leave to choose what kind of Death he would, chose to be drown'd in a Butt of Malmsie. Here it is.—Oh, oh, Devil, Sathanas, Leviathan, I can't abide to look upon thee, thou art so abominable Ugly.—Go to the Bar, go take the Pettifoggers.

CHAPTER XXXIV

How the monstrous Physetere was slain by Pantagruel.

THE *Physetere* coming between the Ships and the Gallions, threw water by whole Tuns upon them, as if it had been the *Catadupes* of the *Nile* in *Ethiopia*. On the other side, Arrows, Darts, Gleaves, Javelins, Spears, Harping Irons, and Partizans flew upon it like Hail. Fryar *Jhon* did not spare himself in it. *Panurge* was half dead for fear. The Artillery roar'd and thunder'd like mad, and seem'd to gawl it in good earnest, but did but little good; for the great Iron and Brass-Cannon-shot entring its Skin, seem'd to melt like Tiles in the Sun.

Pantagruel then considering the weight and Exigency of the matter, stretched out his Arms, and shew'd what he could do. You tell us, and it is recorded that *Commodus* the *Roman* Emperour could shoot with a Bow so dextrously that at a good distance he would let fly an Arrow through a Child's Fingers, and never touch them. You also tell us of an *Indian* Archer, who liv'd when *Alexander* the *Great* conquer'd *India*, and was so skilful in drawing the Bow, that at a considerable distance he would shoot his Arrows through a Ring, tho' they were three Cubits long, and their Iron so large and weighty that with them he us'd to pierce steel Cutlasses, thick Shields, steel Breast plates, and generally what he did hit, how firm, resisting, hard and strong soever it were. You also tell us wonders of the Industry of the ancient *Francks*, who were preferred to all others in point of Archery, and when they hunted either Black or Dun Beasts, us'd to rub the head of their Arrows with Hellebore, because the flesh of the Venison struck with such an Arrow was more tender, dainty, wholesome, and delicious (paring off nevertheless the part that was touch'd round about.) You also talk of the *Parthians* who us'd to shoot backwards more dextrously than other Nations forwards; and also celebrate the Skill of the *Scythians* in that Art, who sent once to *Darius* King of *Persia* an Embassador that made him a present of a Bird, a Frog, a Mouse and five Arrows, without speaking one word; and being ask'd what those Presents meant, and if he had Commission to say any thing, answer'd that he had not; Which puzzl'd and gravell'd *Darius* very much; till *Gobrias*, one of the seven Captains that had kill'd the *Magi* explain'd it, saying to *Darius*, By these Gifts and *Offerings* the *Scythians* silently tell you, that except the *Persians* like Birds fly up to Heaven, like Mice hide themselves near the Centre of the Earth, or like Frogs dive to the very bottom of Ponds and Lakes, they shall be destroyed by the Power and Arrows of the *Scythians*.

The Noble *Pantagruel* was without Comparison, more admirable yet in the Art of Shooting and Darting; for with his dreadful Piles and Darts, nearly resembling the huge Beams that support the Bridges of *Nantes, Saumur, Bergerac*, and at *Paris* the Millers and the Changers Bridges, in length, size, weight, and Iron-work, he at a Mile's distance would open an Oyster and never touch the edges; he would snuff a Candle without putting it out; would shoot a Magpy in the Eye, take off a Boot's under-soal, or a Riding-hood's lining, without sollyng them a bit; turn over every leaf of Fryar *Jhon*'s Breviary one after another, and not tear one.

With such Darts, of which there was good store in his Ship, at the first blow he ran the *Physetere* in at the Forehead so furiously, that he pierced both its Jaws and Tongue, so that from that time to this it no more open'd its Guttural Trap-door, nor drew and spouted water. At the second blow he put out its right Eye, and at the third its left; and we had All the pleasure to see the *Physetere* bearing those three Horns in its Forehead, somewhat leaning forwards in an equilateral Triangle.

Mean while it turn'd about to and fro staggering and straying like one stunn'd, blinded, and taking his leave of the World. *Pantagruel* not satisfied with this, let fly another Dart, which took the Monster under the Tail likewise sloping; then with three other on the Chyne in a perpendicular Line divided its Flank from the Tail to the Snout at an equal distance; then he larded it with fifty on one side, and after that to make even work, he darted as many on its other side; so that the Body of the *Physetere* seem'd like the hulk of a Gallion with three Masts, join'd by a competent Dimension of its Beams, as if they had been the Ribs and Chainwales of the Keel, which was a pleasant sight. The *Physetere* then giving up the Ghost, turn'd it self upon its Back, as all dead Fishes do, and being thus overturn'd with the Beams and Darts upside down in the Sea, it seem'd a *Scolopendria*, or *Centipede*, as that Serpent is describ'd by the ancient Sage *Nicander*.

CHAPTER XXXV

How Pantagruel went on shoar at the Wild Island, the ancient abode of the Chitterlings.

THE Boat's Crew of the Ship *Lantern* tow'd the *Physetere* ashoar on the Neighbouring shoar (which happen'd to be the Wild Island) to make an Anatomical Dissection of its Body, and save the fat of its Kidneys, which, they said, was very useful and necessary for the Cure of a certain Distemper which they call'd want of Money. As for *Pantagruel* he took no manner of notice of the Monster, for he had seen many such, nay bigger in the *Gallick Ocean*. Yet he condescended to land in the Wild Island, to dry and refresh some of his Men (whom the *Physetere* had wetted and bedawb'd) at a small Desert Sea-port towards the South, seated near a fine pleasant Grove, out of which flow'd a delicious Brook of fresh, clear, and purling Water; here they pitch'd their Tents, and set up their Kitchins, nor did they spare Fewel.

Every one having shifted, as they thought fit, Fryar *Jhon* rang the Bell, and the Cloth was immediately laid, and Supper brought in. *Pantagruel* eating chearfully with his Men, much about the second Course, perceiv'd certain little sly Chitterlings clammering up a high Tree near the Pantry as still as so many Mice. Which made him ask *Xenomanes*, what kind of Creatures these were, taking them for Squirrels, Weesels, Martins, or Hermins. They are Chitterlings, reply'd *Xenomanes*: This is the Wild Island, of which I spake to you this morning: There hath been an irreconcilable War this long time between them and *Shrovetide* their malicious and ancient Enemy: I believe that the noise of the Guns which we fir'd at the *Physetere* hath alarm'd 'em, and made them fear their Enemy was come with his Forces to surprise them, or lay the Island waste, as he hath often attempted to do, tho' he still came off but blewly, by reason of the care and vigilance of the Chitterlings, who (as *Dido* said to *Æneas*'s Companions that would have landed at *Carthage* without her Leave or Knowledge) were forc'd to watch and stand upon their Guard, considering the malice of their Enemy and the Neighbourhood of his Territories.

Pray, dear Friend, said *Pantagruel*, if you find that by some honest means we may bring this War to an end, and reconcile them together, give me notice of it: I will use my Endeavours in it, with all my Heart, and spare nothing on my side to moderate and accommodate the points in dispute between both Parties.

That's impossible at this time, answer'd *Xenomanes*. About four years ago, passing Incognito by this Country, I endeavour'd to make a Peace, or at least a long Truce among them, and I had certainly brought them to be good Friends and Neighbours, if both one and the other Parties would have yielded to one single Article. *Shrovetide* would not include in the Treaty of Peace the Wild Puddings, nor the Highland Sawsages, their ancient Gossips and Confederates. The Chitterlings demanded that the Fort of *Caques* might be under their Government, as is the Castle of *Sulloaoir,* and that a parcel of I don't know what stinking Villains, Murtherers, Robbers, that held it then, should be expell'd. But they could not agree in this, and the terms that were offer'd seem'd too hard to either Party. So the Treaty broke off, and nothing was done. Nevertheless, they became less severe, and gentler Enemies than they were before: But since the denunciation of the National Council of *Chesil*, whereby they were roughly handled, hamper'd, and cited, whereby also *Shrovetide* was declared filthy, beshitten, and beray'd, in case he made any League, or Agreement with them, they are grown wonderful inveterate, Incens'd, and Obstinate against one another, and there is no way to remedy it. You might sooner reconcile Cats and Rats, or Hounds and Hares together.

CHAPTER XXXVI

How the Wild Chitterlings laid an Ambuscado for Pantagruel.

WHILE *Xenomanes* was saying this, Fryar *Jhon* spy'd twenty five or thirty young slender-shap'd Chitterlings posting as fast as they could towards their Town, Citadel, Castle, and Fort of *Chimney*, and said to *Pantagruel*, I smell a Rat, there will be here the Devil upon two sticks, or I am much out. These worshipful Chitterlings may chance to mistake you for *Shrovetide*, tho' you are not a bit like him. Let us once in our lives leave our Junketing for a while, and put our selves in a posture to give 'em a Belly full of fighting, if they would be at that sport. There can be no false Latin in this, said *Xenomanes*, Chitterlings are still Chitterlings, always double-hearted, and treacherous.

Pantagruel then arose from Table, to visit and scoure the Thicket, and return'd presently, having discover'd on the left an Ambuscade of squob Chitterlings; and on the right, about half a League from thence, a large Body of huge Giant-like arm'd Chitterlings rang'd in Battalia along a little Hill, and marching furiously towards us at the sound of Bagpipes, Sheep's-Paunches and Bladders, the merry Fifes and Drums, Trumpets and Clarions, hoping to catch us as *Moss* caught his Mare. By the conjecture of seventy eight Standards which we told, we guess'd their Number to be two and forty thousand, at a modest computation.

Their Order, proud Gate, and resolute Looks, made us judge that they were none of your raw paultry Links, but old Warlike Chitterlings and Sawsages. From the foremost Ranks to the Colours they were all arm'd *Cap a pié* with small Arms, as we reckon'd them at a distance, yet very sharp, and case-harden'd. Their right and left Wings were lin'd with a great number of Forrest-Puddings, heavy Patti-pans, and Horse Sawsages, all of them tall and proper Islanders, Banditti, and Wild.

Pantagruel was very much daunted, and not without cause, tho' *Epistemon* told him that it might be the use and custom of the *Chitterlingonians* to welcom and receive thus in Arms their foreign Friends; as the Noble Kings of *France* are received and saluted at their first coming into the chief Cities of the Kingdom, after their advancement to the Crown. Perhaps, said he, it may be the usual Guard of the Queen of the place; who having notice given her, by the Junior Chitterlings of the Forlorn-hope, whom you saw on the Tree, of the arrival of your fine and pompous Fleet, hath judg'd that it was without doubt some rich and potent Prince, and is come to visit you in Person.

Pantagruel little trusting to this, call'd a Council to have their advice at large in this doubtful case. He briefly shew'd them how this way of reception with Arms, had often, under colour of Compliment and Friendship been fatal to the Parties so receiv'd. Thus, said he, the Emperor *Antonius Caracalla* at one time destroy'd the Citizens of *Alexandria*; and at another time cut off the Attendants of *Artabanus* King of *Persia*, under color of Marrying his Daughter: Which, by the way, did not pass unpunish'd, for a while after, this cost him his life.

Thus *Jacob*'s Children destroy'd the *Sichemites*, to revenge the Rape of their Sister *Dina*. By such another hypocritical trick, *Galienus* the *Roman* Emperor put to death the Military Men in *Constantinople*. Thus, under colour of Friendship, *Antonius* inticed *Artavasdes* King of *Armenia*, then having caused him to be bound in heavy Chains, and shackled, at last put him to death.

We find a thousand such instances in History; and K. Charles the 6th is justly commended for his Prudence to this day, in that, coming back Victorious over the *Ghenters* and other *Flemmings* to his good City of *Paris*, and when he came to *Bourget*, (a League from thence) hearing that the Citizens with their Mallets (whence they got the Name of *Maillotins*) were march'd out of Town in Battalia twenty thousand strong, he would not go into the Town till they had laid down their Arms, and retired to their respective homes, tho' they protested to him, that they had taken Arms with no other design, than to receive him with the greater demonstration of Honour and Respect.

CHAPTER XXXVII

*How Pantagruel sent for Colonel Mawl-Chitterling, and
Colonel Cut-Pudding; with a discourse well worth your
hearing, about the Names of places and persons.*

THE Resolution of the Council was, That, let things be how
they would, it behov'd the *Pantagruelists* to stand upon their
Guard. Therefore *Carpalim* and *Gymnast* were order'd by *Pantagruel*, to go for the Soldiers that were on board the Cup-Gally,
under the Command of Colonel *Mawl-Chitterling*, and those
on board the Vine-Tub-Frigat, under the Command of Colonel
Cut-Pudding the younger. I'll ease *Gymnast* of that trouble, said
Panurge who wanted to be upon the Run: You may have occasion for him here. By this worthy Frock of mine, quoth Fryar
Jhon, thou hast a mind to slip thy neck out of the Collar, and
absent thy self from the Fight, thou white-liver'd Son of a Dunghill; upon my virginity, thou'llt never come back. Well, there
can be no great loss in thee; for thou would'st do nothing here
but Howl, Bray, Weep, and dishearten the good Sholdiers. I'll
certainly come back, said *Panurge*, Fryar *Jhon*, my Ghostly Father,
and speedily too: do but take care that these Plaguy *Chitterlings*
don't board our Ships; all the while you'l be a Fighting, I'l pray
heartily for your Victory after the example of the valiant Captain and guide of the People of *Israel, Moses*; having said this he
wheel'd off.

Then said *Epistemon* to *Pantagruel*, the Denomination of
these two Colonels of yours, *Mawl-Chitterling* and *Cut-Pudding*
promiseth us Assurance, Success and Victory, if those *Chitterlings* should chance to set upon us. You take it rightly, said *Pantagruel*, and it pleaseth me to see you foresee and prognosticate
our Victory by the Names of our Colonels.

This Way of foretelling by Names, is not new, it was in Old
times celebrated, and religiously observed by the *Pythagoreans*.
Several great Princes and Emperors have formerly made good
use of it. *Octavianus Augustus* Emperor of the *Romans* meeting
on a day a Country Fellow nam'd *Eutychius*, (that is, fortunate)
driving an Ass nam'd *Nicon* (that is in Greek *Victorian*) mov'd by

the Signification of the Ass's, and Ass-driver's Names, remain'd
assur'd of all Prosperity and Victory.

The Emperour *Vespasian*, being once all alone at Prayers in
the Temple of *Serapis*, at the sight and unexpected coming of a
certain Servant of his nam'd *Basilides*, (that is Royal) whom he
had left Sick a great way behind, took hopes and assurance of
obtaining the Empire of the *Romans*. *Regilian* was chosen Emperour by the Soldiers for no other reason, but the Signification
of his Name. See the *Cratyle* of the divine *Plato* (By my Thirst I
will read it, said *Rhizotome*; I hear you so often quote it) see how
the *Pythagoreans*, by reason of the names and numbers conclude
that *Patroclus* was to fall by the hand of *Hector*, *Hector* by *Achilles*,
Achilles by *Paris*, *Paris* by *Philoctetes*. I am quite lost in my understanding, when I reflect upon the admirable Invention of *Pythagoras*, who by the number, either even or odd, of the Syllables of
every Noun would tell you of what side a Man was Lame, Hulch-
back'd, Blind, Gouty, troubled with the Palsie, Pleurisie, or any
other Distemper, incident to humane kind, allotting even numbers to the Right, and odd ones to the Left side of the Body.

Indeed, said *Epistemon*. I saw this way of Syllabising, try'd at
Xaintes at a general Procession in the Presence of that Good,
Virtuous, Learned and just President *Brian Vallée*, Lord of *Dou-
hait*. When there went by a Man or Woman that was either Lame,
Blind of one Eye, or Hump-back'd, he had an Account brought
him of his or her Name, and if the Syllables of the Name were
of an odd number, immediately without seeing the Persons he
declar'd them to be deform'd, Blind, Lame, or crooked of the
Right side; and of the Left, if they were even in number: and
such indeed we ever found them.

By this Syllabical invention, said *Pantagruel*, the Learned have
affirm'd, that *Achilles* kneeling was wounded by the Arrow of
Paris in the Right heel, for his name is of odd Syllables: (here
we ought to observe that the Ancients us'd to kneel the Right
foot.) And that *Venus* was also wounded before *Troy* in the
Left hand; for her Name in Greek is Ϝροίτη, of four Syllables;
Vulcan Lam'd of his Left foot, for the same reason; *Phillip* King
of *Macedon* and *Hannibal*, blind of the Right eye: not to speak of
Sciatica's, broken Bellies, and *Hemicrania's*, which may be distinguish'd by this *Pythagorean* Reason.

THE FOURTH BOOK

But returning to Names, Do but consider how *Alexander* the Great, Son to King *Philip*, of whom we spoke just now, compass'd his Undertaking, meerly by the Interpretation of a Name. He had besieged the strong City of *Tyre*, and for several Weeks battered it with all his Power; but all in vain; his Engines and Attempts were still baffled by the *Tyrians*. Which made him finally resolve to raise the Siege to his great Grief, foreseeing the great Stain, which such a shameful Retreat would be to his Reputation. In this Anxiety and Agitation of mind he fell asleep, and dreamt that a Satyr was come into his Tent capering, skipping, and tripping it up and down with his Goatish hoofs, and that he strove to lay hold on him. But the Satyr still slip'd from him, till at last having pen'd him up into a Corner, he took him: With this he awak'd; and telling his Dream to the Philosophers, and Sages of his Court, they let him know, that it was a Promise of Victory from the Gods, and that he should soon be Master of *Tyre*; the word *Satyros* divided into two being *Sa Tyros*, and signifying *Tyre* is thine; and in truth, at the next Onset he took the Town by Storm, and by a compleat Victory, reduc'd that stubborn People to Subjection.

On the other hand, see how by the Signification of one word, *Pompey* fell into despair. Being overcome by *Cæsar* at the Battel of *Pharsalia*, he had no other way left to escape but by flight; which attempting by Sea, he arriv'd near the Island of *Cyprus*, and perceiv'd on the shoar near the City of *Paphos*, a beautiful and stately Palace; Now asking the Pilot what was the name of it, he told him, that it was call'd κακοβασιλέα, that is, *Evil-King*; which struck such a dread and terror in him, that he fell into Despair, as being assured of loosing shortly his Life; insomuch that his Complaints, Sighs, and Groans were heard by the Mariners and other Passengers. And indeed a while after a certain strange Peasant call'd *Achillas* cut off his Head.

To all these Examples might be added what happen'd to *L. Paulus Æmilius*, when the Senate elected him Emperour, that is, Chief of the Army which they sent against *Perses* King of *Macedon*; that Evening returning home to prepare for his Expedition, and kissing a little Daughter of his call'd *Trasia*, she seem'd somewhat sad to him. What is the matter, said he, my Chicken, why is my *Trasia* thus sad and Melancholly? Daddy, (reply'd the Child) *Persa* is dead; this was the Name of a little

Bitch which she lov'd mightily. Hearing this, *Paulus* took assurance of a Victory over *Perses*.

If time would permit us to discourse of the Sacred Hebrew writ, we might find a hundred noted Passages evidently shewing how religiously they observ'd Proper names, and their Significations. He had hardly ended this Discourse, when the two Colonels arrived with their Soldiers, all well arm'd and resolute. *Pantagruel* made them a short Speech, intreating them to behave themselves bravely, in case they were attackt; for he cou'd not yet believe that the *Chitterlings* were so treacherous, but he bad them by no means to give the first offence; giving them *Carnaval* for the Watch-word.

CHAPTER XXXVIII

How Chitterlings are not to be slighted by Men.

You shake your empty Noddles now, jolly Topers, and don't believe what I tell you here any more than if it were some Tale of a Tub: Well, well, I can't help it. Believe it if you will; if you won't, let it alone. For my part, I very well know what I saw. It was in the wild Island, in our Voyage to the Holy Bottle, I tell you the Time and Place, what would you have more? I would have you call to mind the strength of the ancient Giants that undertook to lay the high Mountain *Pelion* on the top of *Ossa*, and set among those the shady *Olympus*, to dash out the Gods Brains, unnestle them and scour their Heavenly Lodgings. Their's was no small strength, you may well think, and yet they were nothing but *Chitterlings* from the Waste downwards, or at least, Serpents, not to tell a Lye for the matter.

The Serpent that tempted *Eve* too was of the *Chitterling* kind, and yet it is recorded of him, that he was more subtle than any Beast of the Field. Even so are *Chitterlings*: Nay, to this very hour they hold in some Universities that this same Tempter was the *Chitterling* call'd *Ithyphallus*, or *Standing*, into which was transform'd bawdy *Priapus* Arch-seducer of Females in Paradise, that is, a Garden in Greek.

Pray now tell me, Who can tell but that the *Switzers* now so bold and warlike were formerly *Chitterlings*? For my part, I would not take my Oath to the contrary. The *Himantopodes*, a Nation very famous in *Ethiopia*, according to *Pliny*'s Description, are *Chitterlings*, and nothing else. If all this will not satisfie your Worships, or remove your Incredulity, I would have you forthwith (I mean drinking first, that nothing be done rashly) visit *Lusignan*, *Parthenay*, *Vouant*, *Mervant*, and *Pouzauges* in *Poictou*. There you will find a Cloud of Witnesses, not of your Affidavit-Men of the right stamp, but Credible, time out of mind, that will take their Corporal Oath, on *Rigome*'s Knuckle-bone, that *Mellusine* their first Founder, or Foundress, which you please, was Woman from the Head to the Prick-purse, and thence downwards was a Serpentine *Chitterling*, or if you'll have it otherwise, a *Chitterlingdiz*'d Serpent. She nevertheless had a genteel and noble Gate, imitated to this very Day by your Hop-Merchants of *Britanny* in their *Paspié* and Country Dances.

What do you think was the cause of *Erichthonius*'s being the first Inventor of Coaches, Litters, and Chariots? Nothing but because *Vulcan* had begot him with *Chitterlingdiz*'d Legs, which to hide, he chose to ride in a Litter rather than on Horse-back; for *Chitterlings* were not yet in esteem at that time.

The *Scythian* Nymph *Ora* was likewise half Woman and half *Chitterling*; and yet seem'd so beautiful to *Jupiter*, that nothing could serve him but he must give her a touch of his Godship's kindness; and accordingly had a brave Boy by her call'd *Colaxes*, and therefore, I would have you leave off shaking your empty Noddles at this, as if it were a Story, and firmly believe that nothing is truer than the Gospel.

CHAPTER XXXIX

How Fryar Jhon joyn'd with the Cooks to fight the Chitterlings.

FRYAR *Jhon*, seeing these furious *Chitterlings* thus boldly march up, said to *Pantagruel*; here will be a rare Battel of Hobby-horses, a pretty kind of Puppet-show Fight for ought I see; Oh! What mighty Honour and wonderful Glory will attend our Victory? I would have you only be a bare Spectator of this Fight, and for any thing else leave me and my men to deal with them. What men? said *Pantagruel*. Matter of Breviary, reply'd Fryar *Jhon*:

How came *Potiphar* who was Head Cook of *Pharoah*'s Kitchins, he that bought *Joseph*, and whom they said *Joseph* might have made a Cuckold, if he had not been a *Joseph*; how came he I say, to be made General of all the Horse in the Kingdom of *Egypt*? Why was *Nabuzardan*, King *Nebuchadonozor*'s Head-Cook chosen, to the Exclusion of all other Captains, to besiege and destroy *Jerusalem*? I hear you, reply'd *Pantagruel*; By St. *Christopher*'s Whiskers, said Fryar *Jhon*, I dare lay a Wager that it was because they had formerly engaged *Chitterlings*, or Men as little valu'd; whom to rout, conquer, and destroy, Cooks are without comparison, more fit than *Cuirassiers* and *Gens d'Armes* arm'd at all Points, or all the Horse and Foot in the world.

You put me in mind said *Pantagruel*, of what is written amongst the Facetious and merry Sayings of *Cicero*. During the *more than Civil Wars* between *Cæsar* and *Pompey*, tho' he was much Courted by the first, he naturally lean'd more to the side of the latter; now one day, hearing that the *Pompejans* in a certain *Rencontre* had lost a great many Men, he took a Fancy to visit their Camp. There he perceiv'd little Strength, less Courage, but much disorder. From that time, foreseeing that things would go ill with them, as it since happen'd, he began to Banter now one and then another, and be very Free of his cutting Jests: so some of *Pompey*'s Captains playing the good Fellows to shew their assurance, told him, Do you see how many Eagles we have yet? (They were then the Devise of the *Romans* in War) They might be of use to you, reply'd *Cicero*, if you had to do with Magpies.

Thus seeing we are to fight *Chitterlings*, pursued *Pantagruel*, you infer thence that it is a Culinary War, and have a mind to joyn with the Cooks. Well, do as you please. I'll stay here in the mean time, and wait for the event of the Battel.

Fryar *Jhon* went that very moment among the Sutlers into the Cooks Tents, and told them in a pleasing manner, I must see you Crown'd with Honour and Triumph this day, my Lads; To your Arms are reserv'd such Atchievments, as never yet were perform'd within the Memory of Man. Od's Belly, do they make nothing of the valiant Cooks? Let us go fight yonder fornicating *Chitterlings*, I'll be your Captain: But first let's drink, Boys—come on—Let us be of good Cheer. Noble Captain, return'd the Kitchin Tribe, this was spoken like your self, brave-ly offer'd: Huzza! we are all at your Excellency's Command, and will live and dye by you. Live, live, said Fryar *Jhon*, a God's Name; but dye by no means. That's the *Chitterlings* lot, they shall have their Belly full on 't: Come on then, let us put our selves in Order; *Nabuzardan's the word*.

CHAPTER XL

How Fryar Jhon fitted up the Sow: and of the Valiant Cooks that went into it.

THEN by Fryar *Jhon*'s Order the Engineers and their Work-men fitted up the great Sow that was in the Ship *Leathern-Bottle*. It was a wonderful Machine, so contriv'd, that by the means of large Engines that were round about it in Rows, it throw'd forked Iron Bars, and four squar'd Steel Boults; and in its Hold two hundred Men at least could easily fight, and be shelter'd. It was made after the Model of the Sow of *Riole*, by the means of which *Bergerac* was re-taken from the *English* in the Reign of *Charles* the sixth.

Here are the Names of the Noble and Valiant Cooks who went into the Sow, as the *Greeks* did into the *Trojan* Horse.

Sowre Sawce.	*Crisp Pig.*	*Sop in Pan.*
Sweet Meat.	*Greasy Slouch.*	*Pick-foul.*
Greedy Gut.	*Fatgut.*	*Mustard-pot.*
Licorish Chops.	*Bray-mortar.*	*Calfs Pluck.*
Sows'd Pork.	*Lick-sawce.*	*Hogs Haslet.*
Slap Sawce.	*Hog's Foot.*	*Chopt-phiz.*
Cock-Broth.	*Hodgepodge.*	*Gallymaufrey.*
Slipslop.	*Carbonadoe.*	

All these Noble Cooks in their Coat of Arms did bear in a Field Gules, a Larding-pin Vert, charg'd with a Chevron Ar-gent.

Lard, Hogs Lard.	*Pinch Lard.*	*Snatch Lard.*
Nible Lard.	*Top Lard.*	*Gnaw Lard.*
Filch Lard.	*Pick Lard.*	*Scrape Lard.*
Fat Lard.	*Save Lard.*	*Chew Lard.*

Gaillard (by *Syncope*) born near *Rambouillet*: The said Culinary Doctor's name was *Gaillard-lard*; in the same manner as you use to *Idolatrous* for *Idololatrous*.

Stiff Lard.	Cut Lard.	Waste Lard.
Watch Lard.	Mince Lard.	Ogle-Lard.
Sweet Lard.	Dainty Lard.	Weigh Lard.
Eat Lard.	Fresh Lard.	Gulch Lard.
Snap Lard.	Rusty Lard.	Eye Lard.
Catch Lard.		

Names unknown among the *Marranes* and *Jews*.

Balloky.	Thirsty.	Porridge Pot.
Pick Sallat.	Kitchin Stuff.	Lick Dish.
Broyl Rasher.	Verjuice.	Salt Gullet.
Conny Skin.	Save Dripping.	Snail Dresser.
Dainty Chops.	Water-Creese.	Soupe-Monger.
Pye Wright.	Scrape Turnip.	Browis Belly.
Pudding-pan.	Trivet.	Chine Picker.
Toss-pot.	Monsieur Ragoust.	Suck Gravy.
Mustard Sawce.	Crack Pipkin.	Macaroon.
Claret Sawce.	Scrape Pot.	Scure Maker.
Swill Broth.		

Smell-Smock, he was afterwards taken from the Kitchin and remov'd to Chamber Practice, for the Service of the Noble Cardinal *Hunt Venison*.

Rot Rost.	Hogs Gullet.	Fox Tail.
Dishclout.	Sir Loyne.	Fly Flap.
Save Sewet.	Spit Mutton.	Old Grizle.
Fire Fumbler.	Friter Fryer.	Ruff Belly.
Pillicock.	Flesh Smith.	Saffron Sawce.
Long Tool.	Cram Gut.	Strutting Tom.
Prick Pride.	Tuzzymussy.	Slash'd Snout.
Prick-Madam.	Jacket Liner.	Smutty Face.
Pricket.	Guzzle Drink.	

Mondam that first invented *Madam*'s Sawce, and for that discovery, was thus called in the *Scotch-French* Dialect.

Loblolly.	Sloven.	Trencher-man.
Slabber Chops.	Swallow-pitcher.	Goodman Goosecap.
Scrum Pot.	Wafer-Monger.	Munch Turnip.
Gully Guts.	Snap Gobbet.	Pudding-bag.

Rinse Pot.	*Scurvy Phiz.*	*Pig-sticker.*
Drink-spiller.		

Robert, he invented *Robert*'s Sawce, so good and necessary for Roasted Coneys, Ducks, Fresh Pork, Poach'd Eggs, Salt Fish, and a thousand other such Dishes.

Cold Eel.	*Frying-pan.*	*Big Snout.*
Thornback.	*Man-of Dough.*	*Lick-finger.*
Gurnard.	*Sawce-Doctor.*	*Titt Bit.*
Grumbling Gut.	*Waste Butter.*	*Sauce-box.*
Alms-scrip.	*Shitbreech.*	*All Fours.*
Taste all.	*Thick Brawn.*	*Whimwham.*
Scrap Merchant.	*Tom T—d.*	*Basterost.*
Belly-timberman.	*Mouldy Crust.*	*Gaping Hoyden.*
Hashee.	*Hasty.*	*Calf Pluck.*
Frig-palat.	*Red Herring.*	*Leather Breeches.*
Powdering-tub.	*Cheese Cake.*	

All these Noble Cooks went into the Sow, Merry, Cheery, Hale, Brisk, old Dogs at Mischief, and ready to fight stoutly; Fryar *Jhon*, ever and anon waving his huge Scimiter, brought up the Reer, and double-lock'd the Doors on the inside.

CHAPTER XLI

How Pantagruel broke the Chitterlings at the Knees.

THE Chitterlings advanc'd so near, that *Pantagruel* perceiv'd that they stretched their Arms, and already began to charge their Lances, which caus'd him to send *Gymnast* to know what they meant, and why they thus, without the least provocation, came to fall upon their old trusty Friends, who had neither said nor done the least ill thing to them. *Gymnast* being advanc'd near their Front, bow'd very low, and said to them as loud as ever he could; We are Friends, we are Friends; all, all of us your Friends, yours, and at your command, we are for *Carnaval* your old Confederate. Some have since told me, that he mistook and said *Cavernal* instead of *Carnaval*.

Whatever it was, the word was no sooner out of his Mouth, but a huge wild Squob-Sawsage, starting out of the Front of their main Body, would have grip'd him by the Collar. By the

Helmet of *Mars*, said *Gymnast*, I'll swallow thee, but thou shalt only come in in chips and slices; for, big as thou art, thou could'st never come in whole. This spoke, he lugs out his trusty Sword, *Kiss-mine-Arse*, (so he call'd it) with both his Fists, and cut the Sawsage in twain. Bless me how fat the foul Thief was! It puts me in mind of the huge Bull of *Berne* that was slain at *Marignan* when the drunken *Switzers* were so mawl'd there. Believe me, it had little less than four inches Lard on its Punch.

The Sawsage's job being done, a Crowd of others flew upon *Gymnast*, and had most scurvily drag'd him down, when *Pantagruel* with his Men came up to his relief. Then began the Martial Fray, higledy pickledy. *Mawl Chitterling* did mawl Chitterlings, *Cut Pudding* did cut Puddings; *Pantagruel* did break the Chitterlings at the Knees; Fryar *Jhon* play'd at least in sight within his Sow, viewing and observing all things; when the *Patty-pans* that lay in Ambuscado, most furiously sallied out upon *Pantagruel*.

Fryar *Jhon*, who lay snug all this while, by that time perceiving the Rout and Hurly-burly, set open the doors of his Sow, and sallied out with his merry *Greeks*, some of them arm'd with Iron Spits, others with Andirons, Racks, Fire-Shouvels, Frying-pans, Kettles, Grid Irons, Oven Forks, Tongs, Dripping-pans, Brooms, Iron-pots, Mortars, Pestles, all in Battle array like so many House breakers, hollowing and roaring out all together most frightfully, *Nabuzardan, nabuzardan, nabuzardan*. Thus shouting and hooting they fought like Dragons, and charg'd through the *Patty-pans*, and *Sawsages*. The *Chitterlings* perceiving this fresh reinforcement, and that the others would be too hard for 'em, betook themselves to their Heels, scampering off with full speed, as if the Devil had been come for them. Fryar *Jhon* with an Iron Crow knock'd them down as fast as Hops; his Men too were not sparing on their side. Oh! What a woeful sight it was! The field was all over strow'd with heaps of dead or wounded *Chitterlings*; and History relates, that had not Heav'n had a hand in it, the *Chitterling* Tribe had been totally routed out of the World, by the Culinary Champions. But there happened a wonderful thing, you may believe as little or as much of it as you please.

From the North flew towards us a huge, fat, thick, grizly Swine, with long and large Wings like those of a Windmil, its

Plumes red Crimson, like those of a *Phenicoptere* (which in *Languedoc* they call *Flaman*) its Eyes were red and flaming like a Carbuncle, its Ears green like a *Prasin* Emerald, its Teeth like a Topaze, its Tail long and black like Jet, its Feet white, diaphanous, and transparent like a Diamond, somewhat broad and of the splay-kind, like those of Geese, and as Queen *Dick*'s us'd to be at *Tholose* in the days of Yore. About its Neck it wore a Gold Collar round which were some *Ionian* Characters, whereof I could pick out but two words 'ΥΣ ΑΘΗΝΑΝ: *Hog teaching Minerva*.

The Sky was clear before, but at that Monster's appearance, it chang'd so mightily for the worse, that we were all amaz'd at it. As soon as the *Chitterlings* perceiv'd the flying Hog, down they all threw their Weapons and fell on their Knees, lifting up their Hands joyn'd together, without speaking one word, in a posture of Adoration. Fryar *Jhon* and his Party kept on mincing, felling, braining, mangling, and spitting the *Chitterlings* like mad; But *Pantagruel* sounded a Retreat, and all Hostility ceas'd. The Monster, having several times hover'd backwards and forwards between the two Armies, with a Tail-shot voided above twenty seven Buts of Mustard on the ground; then flew away through the Air, crying all the while, *Carnaval, Carnaval, Carnaval*.

CHAPTER XLII

How Pantagruel held a treaty with Niphleseth Queen of the Chitterlings.

THE Monster being out of sight, and the two Armies remaining silent, *Pantagruel* demanded a parly with the Lady *Niphleseth*, Queen of the Chitterlings who was in her Chariot by the Standards, and it was easily granted. The Queen alighted, courteously receiv'd *Pantagruel*, and was glad to see him. *Pantagruel* complain'd to her of this breach of Peace: But she civilly made her excuse, telling him that a false information had caus'd all this mischief, her Spies having brought her word, that *Shrovetide* their mortal foe was landed, and spent his time in examining the Urin of *Physeteres*.

She therefore intreated him to pardon them their offence, telling him, that Sir-reverence was sooner found in Chitterlings

than Gall; and offering, for her self, and all her successors, to
hold of him and his the whole Island and Country, to obey him
in all his Commands, be friends to his friends, and foes to his
foes; and also to send every Year, as an acknowledgment of their
homage, a tribute of seventy eight thousand Royal Chitterlings,
to serve him at his first Course at Table, six months in the Year:
which was punctually perform'd. For, the next Day, she sent
the aforesaid quantity of Royal Chitterlings to the good *Gargantua*, under the Conduct of young *Niphleseth* Infanta of the Island.

The good *Gargantua* made a Present of them to the great
King of *Paris*: But by change of Air, and for want of Mustard (the
natural Balsam and restorer of Chitterlings) most of them dyed.
By the great King's particular Grant they were buried in heaps,
in a part of *Paris*, to this day call'd *La Rue pavée d'Andouilles, The
Street pav'd with Chitterlings*. At the Request of the Ladies at his
Court, young *Niphleseth* was preserv'd, honourably us'd, and
since that married to heart's content; and was the Mother of
many Children, for which heav'n be prais'd.

Pantagruel civilly thank'd the Queen, forgave all Offences,
refus'd the offer she had made of her Country, and gave her a
pretty little Knife: after that, he ask'd several nice Questions
concerning the Apparition of that flying Hog? she answer'd,
That it was the Idea of *Carnaval*, their Tutelary *God*, in time of
War, first Founder and Original of all the Chitterling-race, for
which reason he resembled a Hog, for Chitterlings drew their
Extraction from Hogs.

Pantagruel asking to what purpose, and curative Indication,
he had voided so much Mustard on the Earth? The Queen reply'd,
That Mustard was their *Sang-real*, and celestial Balsam, of
which laying but a little in the wounds of the fallen Chitterlings,
in a very short time the wounded were heal'd, and the dead
restor'd to life. *Pantagruel* held no further Discourse with the
Queen, but retir'd a ship board: The like did all the Bon Companions with their Implements of Destruction and their huge
Sow.

CHAPTER XLIII

How Pantagruel went into the Island of Ruach.

TWO Days after, we arriv'd at the Island of *Ruach*; and I swear to you, by the Celestial Hen and Chickens, that I found the way of living of the People so strange and wonderfull, that I can't for the heart's Blood of me half tell it you. They live on nothing but Wind, eat nothing but Wind, and drink nothing but Wind. They have no other Houses but weather-cocks. They sow no other Seeds but the three sorts of Windflowers, Rue, and herbs that may make One break wind to the purpose, these scowre them off carefully. The common sort of People, to feed themselves, make use of feather, paper or linnen Fans, according to their Abilities; As for the Rich they live by the means of Wind-mills.

When they wou'd have some noble Treat, the Tables are spread under one or two Wind-mills: There they feast as merry as beggars; and during the Meal, their whole talk is commonly of the goodness, excellency, salubrity and rarity of Winds; as you jolly Topers, in your Cups, Philosophize and Argue upon Wines. The one praises the South-east; the other the South-west. This the West and by South, and this the East and by North, another the West, and another the East, and so of the rest. As for Lovers, and amorous Sparks, no Gale for them like a smock Gale. For the sick, they use Bellows, as we use Clysters among us.

Oh! (said to me a little diminutive swoln Bubble) that I had now but a bladderfull of that same good *Languedoc* Wind, which they call *Cierce*: The famous Physician *Scurron*, passing one day by this Country, was telling us that it was so strong that it will make nothing of overturning a loaded Waggon: Oh! what good wou'd it not do my oedipodic Legg. The biggest are not the best, but, said *Panurge*, rather would I had here a large Butt of the same good *Languedoc* Wine that grows at *Mireveux, Cante-perdrix*, and *Frontignan*.

I saw a good likely sort of a Man there, much resembling *Ventrose*, tearing and fuming in a grievous Fret with a tall burly Groom and a pimping little Page of his, laying them on, like the

Devil, with a buskin: Not knowing the cause of his anger, at first I thought that all this was by the Doctor's advice, as being a thing very healthy to the Master to be in a Passion, and to his Man to be bang'd for 't. But at last I heard him taxing his Man with stealing from him, like a Rogue as he was, the better half of a large leathern Bag of an excellent southerly Wind, which he had carefully lay'd up, like a hidden Reserve, against the cold weather.

They neither Exonerate, Piss, nor Spit in that Island, but to make amends, they belch, fizle, funk, and give Tailshots in abundance. They are troubled with all manner of distempers: And indeed, all distempers are engendred and proceed from Ventosities, as *Hippocrates* demonstrates, *lib. de Flatibus*. But the most epidemical among them, is the wind-Colick. The remedies which they use are large Blisters, whereby they void store of Windiness. They all dye of Dropsies, and Tympanies, the Men farting, and the Women fizling, so that their Soul takes her leave at the back-door.

Some time after, walking in the Island, we met Three hare-brain'd airy Fellows, who seem'd mightily pufft up, and went to take their pastime, and view the *Pluvers* who live on the same diet as themselves, and abound in the Island. I observ'd that, as you, true Topers, when you travell, carry flasks, leathern bottles, and small runlets along with you, so each of them had at his girdle a pretty little pair of bellows. If they happen'd to want wind, by the help of those pretty bellows they immediately drew some fresh and cool, by Attraction, and Reciprocal Expulsion: For, as you well know, Wind, essentially defin'd, is nothing but fluctuating and agitated Air.

A while after we were commanded in the King's name, not to receive for three hours any Man or Woman of the Country on board our ships. Some having stole from him a rousing fart of the very individual Wind which old Goodman *Æolus* the Snoarer gave *Ulysses*, to conduct his Ship, when ever it should happen to be becalm'd: Which fart the King kept religiously like another *Sangreal*, and perform'd a world of wonderfull Cures with it, in many dangerous diseases, letting loose and distributing to the Patient only as much of it as might frame a Virginal Fart; that is, if you must know, what our *Sanctimonials*, alias *Nuns*, in their Dialect call ringing backwards.

CHAPTER XLIV

How a small Rain lays a high Wind.

PANTAGRUEL commended their Government and way of living, and said to their *Hypenemian* Mayor, If you approve *Epicurus*'s Opinion, placing the *summum bonum* in Pleasure (I mean pleasure that's easie and free from toil) I esteem you happy; for your Food being Wind, costs you little or nothing; since you need but blow. True, Sir, return'd the Mayor; but alas, nothing is perfect here below: For too often, when we are at Table feeding on some good blessed Wind of God, as on Celestial Manna, merry as so many Fryars, down drops on a sudden some small Rain, which lays our Wind, and so robs us of it; thus many a Meal is lost for want of Meat.

Just so, quoth *Panurge, Jenin Toss-pot* of *Quinquenois* evacuating some Wine of his own burning on his Wife's Posteriors, laid the ill fum'd Wind that blow'd out of their Centre as out of some Magisterial Æolipyle. Here's a kind of a Whim on that Subject which I made formerly:

> *One Evening, when* Toss-pot *had been at his Buts,*
> *And* Joane *his fat Spouse cramm'd with Turnips her Guts,*
> *Together they pigg'd; nor did Drink so besot him,*
> *But he did what was done when his Daddy begot him.*

> *Now when, to recruit, he'd fain have been snoaring,*
> Joane's *Back-door was filthily puffing and roaring:*
> *So for spight he bepiss'd her, and quickly did find,*
> *That a very small Rain lays a very high Wind.*

We are also plagu'd yearly with a very great Calamity, cry'd the Mayor; for a Giant call'd *Widenostrils*, who lives in the Island of *Tohu*, comes hither every Spring, to purge by the advice of his Physicians, and swallows us, like so many Pills, a great number of Windmils and of Bellows also, at which his Mouth waters exceedingly.

Now this is a sad Mortification to us here, who are fain to fast over three or four whole Lents every year for this, besides certain petty Lents, Ember-Weeks, and other Orison and Starving-tides.

And have you no Remedy for this? ask'd *Pantagruel*. By the
Advice of our *Mezarims*, reply'd the Mayor, about the time that
he uses to give us a Visit, we Garrison our Windmills with good
store of Cocks and Hens. So the first time that the greedy Thief
swallow'd them, they had like to have done his business at
once, for they crow'd and cackl'd in his Maw, and flutter'd up
and down athwart and along in his Stomach, which threw the
Glutton into a Lipothymy, Cardiac Passion, and dreadful and
dangerous Convulsions, as if some Serpent creeping in at his
Mouth, had been frisking in his Stomach.

Here is a comparative *as* altogether incongruous and impertinent, cry'd Fryar *Jhon*, interrupting them, for I have formerly
heard, that if a Serpent chance to get into a Man's Stomach, it
will not do him the least hurt, but will immediately get out, if
you do but hang the Patient by the Heels, and lay a Pan full of
warm Milk near his Mouth. You were told this, said *Pantagruel*,
and so were those who gave you this account; but none ever saw
or read of such a Cure. On the contrary, *Hippocrates*, in his fifth
Book of *Epidem*. writes, *That such a case happening in his time, the
Patient presently died of a Spasm and Convulsion*.

Besides the Cocks and Hens, said the Mayor, continuing his
Story, all the Foxes in the Country whip'd into *Widenostril*'s
Mouth, posting after the Poultry, which made such a stir with
Reynard at their Heels, that he grievously fell into Fits each minute
of an hour.

At last by the advice of a *Baden* Enchanter, at the time of the
Paroxysm, he us'd to flea a Fox by way of Antidote: Since that,
he took better advice, and easies himself with taking a Clyster
made with a Decoction of Wheat and Barly-Corns, and of Livers
of Goslins; to the first of which the Poultry run, and the Foxes
to the latter. Besides, he swallows some of your Badgers or Fox-
Dogs by the way of Pills and Bolus's. This is our misfortune.

Cease to fear, good People, cry'd *Pantagruel*, This huge *Widenostrils*, this same Swallower of Windmills, is no more, I'll assure
you; he dy'd, being stifled and choak'd with eating a lump of
fresh Butter, at the Mouth of a hot Oven by the advice of his
Physicians.

CHAPTER XLV

How Pantagruel went ashoar in the Island of Popefig-Land.

THE next Morning, we arriv'd at the Island of *Popefigs*, formerly a rich and free People call'd the *Gaillardets*, but now alas,
miserably poor, and under the Yoke of the *Papimen*. The Occasion of it was this.

On a certain yearly high Holy-day, the Burger-Master, Syndics and topping Rabbies of the *Gaillardets* chanc'd to go into
the Neighbouring Island of *Papimany* to see the Festival, and
pass away the time. Now one of them having espy'd the Pope's
Picture, (with the sight of which, according to a laudable Custom, the People were bless'd on High-offering Holy-days)
made mouths at it and cry'd, A Fig for 't, as a sign of manifest
Contempt and Derision. To be reveng'd of this Affront, the
Papimen some days after, without giving the others the least warning, took Arms, and surpriz'd, destroy'd, and ruin'd the whole
Island of the *Gaillardets*, putting the Men to the Sword, and sparing none but the Women and Children, and those too only on
Condition to do what the Inhabitants of *Milan* were condemn'd
to, by the Emperor *Frederick Barbarossa*.

These had rebell'd against him in his absence, and ignomi-
niously turn'd the Empress out of the City, mounting her a
Horse-back on a Mule call'd *Thacor*, with her Breech foremost towards the Old jaded Mule's head, and her Face turn'd towards
the Crupper. Now *Frederick* being return'd, master'd them, and
caus'd so careful a Search to be made, that he found out, and got
the famous Mule *Thacor*. Then the Hangman, by his Order, clap'd
a Fig into the Mule's Jimcrack, in the Presence of the inslav'd
Citts that were brought into the middle of the great Market-
Place, and proclaim'd, in the Emperor's Name, with Trumpets,
That whosoever of them would save his own Life, should publickly pull the Fig out with his Teeth, and after that put it in
again in the very individual Cranny whence he had draw'd it,
without using his hands; and that whoever refused to do this,
should presently swing for 't, and die in his Shoes. Some sturdy
Fools, standing upon their *Punctilio*, chose *Honourably* to be

hang'd, rather than submit to so shameful, and abominable a Disgrace; and others, less nice in Point of Ceremony, took heart of Grace, and ev'n resolv'd to have at the Fig, and a Fig for 't, rather than make a worse Figure with a hempen Collar, and die in the Air, at so short Warning: accordingly, when they had neatly pick'd out the Fig with their Teeth from old *Thacor*'s Snatch-blatch, they plainly show'd it the Heads-man, saying, *Ecco lo Fico!* (behold the Fig.)

By the same Ignominy the rest of these poor distress'd *Gaillardets* sav'd their Bacon, becoming Tributaries and Slaves, and the Name of *Pope-Figs* was given them, because they had said, A *Fig for the Pope's Image.* Since this, the poor Wretches never prosper'd, but every Year the Devil was at their Doors, and they were plagu'd with Hail, Storms, Famine and all manner of Woes, as an everlasting Punishment for the Sin of their Ancestors and Relations. Perceiving the Misery and Calamity of that Generation, we did not care to go further up into the Country, contenting our selves with going into a little Chappel near the Haven to take some Holy water. It was dilapidated and ruin'd, wanting also a Cover (like St. *Peter* at *Rome*). When we were in, as we dip'd our Fingers in the sanctifi'd Cistern, we spy'd in the middle of that Holy Pickle a Fellow muffled up with Stoles all under water, like a diving Duck, except the tip of his Snout to draw his Breath. About him, stood three Priests, true shavelings, clean shorn and poll'd, who were muttering strange words to the Devils out of a Conjuring Book.

Pantagruel was not a little amaz'd at this, and, inquiring what kind of sport these were at, was told, that, for Three years last past, the Plague had so dreadfully rag'd in the Island, that the better half of it had been utterly depopulated, and the Lands lay Fallow without Owners. Now the mortality being over, this same Fellow, who was crept into the Holy Tub, having a large piece of Ground; chanc'd to be Sowing it with White winter Wheat; at the very minute of an hour that a kind of a Silly sucking Devil, who could not yet Write or Read, or Hail and Thunder, unless it were on Parsly or Colworts, had got leave of his Master *Lucifer* to go into this Island of *Pope-figs*, where the Devils were very familiar with the Men and Women, and often went to take their Pastime.

This same Devil being got thither, directed his Discourse to the Husband-man, and ask'd him what he was doing. The poor Man told him, that he was Sowing this ground with Corn to help him to subsist the next Year. Ay, but the Ground is none of thine, Mr. *Plough-jobber*, cry'd the Devil, but mine: for, since the time that you mock'd the *Pôpe*, all this Land has been proscrib'd, adjudg'd, and abandon'd to us. However, to sow Corn is not my Province; therefore I will give thee leave to sow the Field; that is to say, provided we share the Profit. I will, reply'd the Farmer. I mean, said the Devil, that, of what the Land shall bear, two Lots shall be made, one of what shall grow above Ground, the other of what shall be cover'd with Earth; the right of chusing belongs to me, for I am a Devil of noble and ancient Race; thou art a base Clown. I therefore chuse what shall lye under Ground, take thou what shall be above. When dost thou reckon to reap, hah? About the middle of *July*, quoth the Farmer. Well, said the Devil, I'll not fail thee then: In the mean time, slave as thou oughtest. Work, Clown, work: I am going to tempt to the pleasing Sin of whoring, the Nuns of *Dryfart*, the Sham-saints of the Cowle, and the Gluttonish Crew; I am more than sure of these. There needs but meet, and the Job's done; true Fire and Tinder, touch and take; down falls Nun, and up gets Fryar.

CHAPTER XLVI

How a Junior Devil was fool'd by a Husband-man of Popefig-Land.

IN the middle of *July*, the Devil came to the place aforesaid, with all his Crew at his Heels, a whole Quire of the younger Fry of Hell, and having met the Farmer, said to him; Well, Clod-pate, how hast thou done, since I went? Thou and I must now share the Concern. Ay, Master Devil, quoth the Clown, 'tis but reason we should. Then he and his Men began to cut and reap the Corn: and on the other side the Devil's Imps fell to work, grubbing up, and pulling out the stubble by the Root.

The Country-man had his Corn thrash'd, Winnow'd it, put it into Sacks, and went with it to Market. The same did the Devil's Servants, and sate them down there by the Man, to sell their Straw. The Country-man sold off his Corn at a good rate, and with the Money fill'd an old kind of a Demy-Buskin, which was fasten'd to his Girdle; but the Devil a Sous the Devils took; far from taking Hansel, they were flouted, and jeer'd by the Country Louts.

Market being over, quoth the Devil to the Farmer, Well Clown thou hast chous'd me once, 'tis thy Fault; chouse me twice, 'twill be mine. Nay, good Sir Devil, reply'd the Farmer, how can I be said to have chous'd you, since 'twas your worship that chose first. The truth is that by this trick you thought to cheat me, hoping that nothing would spring out of the Earth for my share, and that you should find whole under Ground the Corn which I had sow'd, and with it tempt the Poor and Needy, the close Hypocrite, or the Covetous Gripe, thus making them fall into your snares. But troth, you must e'en go to School yet, you are no Conjurer, for ought I see: for, the Corn that was sow'd is dead and rotten, its Corruption having caus'd the generation of that which you saw me sell: so you chose the worst, and therefore are curs'd in the Gospel. Well, talk no more on 't, quoth the Devil: what can'st thou sow our Field with for next Year? If a Man would make the best on 't, answer'd the Ploughman, 'twere fit he sow it with Radish. Now cry'd the Devil, thou talkst like an honest Fellow, Bumpkin, well, sow me good store of Radish, I'll see and keep them safe from storms, and will not hail a bit on them; but harke'e me, this time I bespeak for my share what shall be above ground, what's under shall be thine: Drudge on, Looby, drudge on. I am going to tempt hereticks, their Souls are dainty victuals when broil'd in Rashers and well powder'd. My Lord *Lucifer* has the griping in the guts, they'l make a dainty warm dish for his Honour's Maw.

When the season of Radishes was come, our Devil fail'd not to meet in the Field with a train of rascally underlings, all waiting Devils, and finding there the Farmer and his Men, he began to cut and gather the Leaves of the Radishes. After him the Farmer with his Spade digg'd up the Radishes, and clapt them up into pouches. This done, the Devil, the Farmer, and their gangs, hy'd them to Market, and there the Farmer presently made good Mony of his Radishes; but the poor Devil took nothing, nay, what was worse he was made a common

laughing-stock by the gaping hoydons. I see thou hast play'd
me a scurvy trick, thou villainous Fellow, (cry'd the angry
Devil), at last I am fully resolv'd e'en to make an end of the
Business between thee and my self about the Ground, and
these shall be the Terms; We'll chapperclaw each other, and
whoever of us two shall first cry *hold*, shall quit his share of the
Field, which shall wholly belong to the Conqueror. I fix the
Time for this Tryal of Skill on this day se'night: Assure thy self
that I'll claw thee off like a Devil. I was going to tempt your
Fornicators, Bayliffs, Perplexers of Causes, Scriveners, forgers
of Deeds, two-handed Counsellors, prevaricating Sollicitors,
and other such vermine; but they were so civill as to send me
word by an Interpreter, that they are all mine already: Besides,
our Master *Lucifer* is so cloy'd with their Souls, that he often
sends them back to the smutty Scullions and slovenly Devils,
of his Kitchin, and they scarce go down with him, unless now
and then, when they are high-season'd.

Some say there is no Breakfast like a Student's, no dinner
like a Lawyer's, no afternoon's nunchion like a Vintner's, no
supper like a Tradesman's, no second supper like a serving
Wench's, and none of these Meals together like a frockifi'd
Hobgoblin's. All this is true enough; accordingly at my Lord
Lucifer's first Course Hobgoblings, *alias* Imps in Cowles, are a
standing Dish. He willingly us'd to breakfast on Students; but,
alas, I do not know by what Ill Luck, they have of late years
join'd the holy Bible to their Studies; so the Devil a one we can
get down among us, and I verily believe that unless the Hypocrites of the Tribe of *Levi* help us in it; taking from the inlightned
Book-mongers their St. *Paul*, either by Threats, Revilings,
Force, Violence, Fire and Faggot, we shall not be able to hook-
in any more of them, to nibble at below. He dines commonly on
Counsellors, Mischief-mongers, Multipliers of Law-Suits, such
as wrest and pervert Right and Law, and Grind and Fleece the
Poor: He never fears to want any of these. But who can endure
to be wedded to a Dish?

He said t' other Day at a full Chapter, that he had a great
mind to eat the Soul of one of the Fraternity of the Cowle that
had forgot to speak for himself, in his Sermon, and he promis'd
double Pay, and a large Pension, to any one that should bring

him such a Titbit piping-hot. We all went a hunting after such
a Rarity, but came home without the Prey; for they all admonish
the good Women to remember their Convent. As for afternoon
Nunchions, he has left them off, since he was so wofully grip'd
with the Colic, his Fosterers, Sutlers, Char-Coalmen, and boyling Cooks having been sadly mawl'd and pepper'd off in the
Northern Countries.

His high Devil-ship sups very well on Tradesmen, Usurers,
Apothecaries, Cheats, Coyners, and Adulterers of Wares. Now
and then when he is on the merry pin, his second supper is of
serving Wenches who, after they have by stealth soak'd their
Faces with their Masters good Liquor, fill up the Vessel with it
at second-hand, or with other stinking Water.

Well, drudge on, Boor, drudge on; I am going to tempt the
Students of *Trebisonde*, to leave Father and Mother, forgo for
ever the establish'd and common Rule of living; disclaim and
free themselves from obeying their lawfull Sovereign's Edicts,
live in absolute Liberty, proudly despise every one, laugh at all
Mankind, and taking the fine jovial little *Cap* of *Poetic License*,
become so many pretty Hobgoblins.

CHAPTER XLVII

How the Devil was deceived by an Old Woman of Popefig-Land.

THE Country *Lob* trudg'd home very much concern'd and
thoughtfull, you may swear; in so much that his good Woman,
seeing him thus look moping, ween'd that something had been
stolen from him at market; but when she had heard the cause of
his affliction, and seen his Budget well lin'd with Coyn, she bad
him be of good Cheer, assuring him that he'd be never the worse
for the scratching Bout in question, wishing him only to leave her
to manage that business, and not trouble his head about it: for
she had already contriv'd how to bring him off cleverly. Let
the worst come to the worst, said the Husbandman, it will be
but a scratch, for I'll yield at the first stroke, and quit the Field.
Quit a Fart, reply'd the Wife, he shall have none of the
Field, rely upon me and be quiet, let me alone to deal with him.
You say he's a pimping little Devil, that's enough; I'll soon

make him give up the Field, I'll warrant you: Indeed had he been a great Devil, it had been somewhat.

The Day that we landed in the Island happen'd to be that which the Devil had fix'd for the Combat. Now the Country-man, having like a good *Catholic* very fairly *confessed himself* and *received*, betimes in the morning, by the Advice of his Vicar had hid himself, all but the snout, in the holy Water-stock in the Posture in which we found him: And just as they were telling us this story, News came that the old Woman had fool'd the Devil, and gain'd the Field: You may not be sorry perhaps to hear how this happen'd.

The Devil, you must know, came to the poor Man's Door and rapping there, cry'd so hoe, ho the House, hoe Clod-pate, where art thou? Come out with a vengeance, come out with a wannion, come out and be damn'd; now for clawing; then brisk-ly and resolutely entring the House, and not finding the Country Man there, he spy'd his Wife lying on the Ground pitiously weeping and howling: What's the matter? ask'd the Devil, where is he? What does he? Oh! that I knew where he is, reply'd Threescore and five, the wicked Rogue, the Butcherly Dog, the Murtherer: he has spoyl'd me, I am undone, I dye of what he has done me. How, cry'd the Devil, what is it? I'll tickle him off for you by and by. Alas, cry'd the old Dissembler, he told me, the Butcher, the Tyrant, the Tearer of Devils, that he had made a match to scratch with you this Day, and to try his Clawes, he did but just touch me with his little Finger, here betwixt the Legs, and has spoyl'd me for ever. Oh! I am a dead Woman, I shall never be my self again: do but see! nay, and besides he talk'd of going to the Smiths to have his Pounces sharpen'd and pointed. Alas, you are undone, Mr. Devil; good Sir, scamper quickly, I am sure he won't stay; save your self, I beseech you; while she said this, she uncover'd her self up to the Chin, after the manner in which the *Persian* Women met their Children, who fled from the Fight, and plainly shew'd her What de'e call them. The frighted Devil, seeing the enormous Solution of the Continuity in all its dimensions, blest himself, cry'd out, *Mahon, Demiourgon, Megæra, Alecto, Persephone*: s'Life, catch me here when he comes! I am gon, s'Death what a gash! I resign him the Field.

Having heard the Catastrophe of the Story, we retired a ship-board, not being willing to stay there any longer. *Pantagruel* gave to the Poors-Box of the Fabrick of the Church, eighteen thousand gold Royals in commiseration of the Poverty of the People, and the Calamity of the Place.

CHAPTER XLVIII

How Pantagruel went ashoar at the Island of Papimany.

HAVING left the desolate Island of the *Popefigs*, we sailed for the space of a day very fairly and merrily, and made the blessed Island of *Papimany*. As soon as we had dropt Anchor in the Road, before we had well-moor'd our Ship with ground Tackle, four Persons in different Garbs row'd towards us in a Skiff. One of them was dress'd like a Monk in his Frock, draggle-tail'd and Booted: the other like a Falkoner with a Lure and a long-wing'd Hawk on his Fist: the third like a Sollicitor, with a large Bag, full of Informations, Subpœna's, Breviates, Bills, Writs, Cases, and other Implements of Pettifogging. The fourth look'd like one of your Vine Barbers about *Orleans*, with a *jantee* pair of Canvass Trowzers, a Dosser and a Pruning Knife at his Girdle.

As soon as the Boat had clap'd them on Board, they all with one Voice ask'd, Have you seen him, good Passengers, have you seen him? Who, ask'd *Pantagruel*? You know who, answer'd they. Who is it, ask'd Fryar *Jhon*, s'blood and oonds, I'll thrash him thick and threefold? This he said, thinking that they enquir'd after some Robber, Murtherer, or Church-breaker. Oh wonderful, cry'd the four, do not you foreign People know the *One*? Sirs, reply'd *Epistemon*, we do not understand those Terms; but if you will be pleas'd to let us know who you mean, we'll tell you the truth of the matter without any more ado. We mean, said they, *he that is*; did you ever see him? *He that is*, return'd *Pantagruel*, according to our Theological Doctrine, is God, who said to *Moses*, *I am that I am*: We never saw him, nor can he be beheld by Mortal Eyes. We meant nothing less than that supream God who rules in Heaven, reply'd they, we spoke of the God on Earth, did you ever see him? Upon my Honour, cry'd *Carpalim*, they mean the *Pope*. Ay, ay, answer'd *Panurge*, yea verily, Gentlemen, I have seen three of them, whose sight has not much better'd me. How! cry'd they, our Sacred *Decretals* inform us, that there never is more than one living. I mean successively, one after the other, return'd *Panurge*, otherwise I never saw more than one at a time.

O thrice and four times happy People, cry'd they, you are welcom and more than double-welcom! They then kneel'd down before us, and would have kiss'd our Feet, but we would not suffer it, telling them, that, should the Pope come thither in his own Person, 'tis all they could do to him. No, certainly, answer'd they, for we have already resolv'd upon the matter. We would kiss his bare Arse, without boggling at it, and eke his two Pounders; for he has a pair of them, the Holy Father, that he has; we find it so by our fine *Decretals*, otherwise he could not be Pope. So that according to our subtile *Decretalin* Philosophy, this is a necessary Consequence; he is Pope, therefore he has Genitories; and, should Genitories no more be found in the World, the World could no more have a Pope.

While they were talking thus, *Pantagruel* enquir'd of one of their Coxwain's Crew, who those Persons were? he answer'd, that they were the four Estates of the Island, and added that we should be made as welcom as Princes, since we had seen the Pope. *Panurge* having been acquainted with this by *Pantagruel*, said to him in his Ear, I swear and Vow, Sir, 'tis even so, he that has patience may compass any thing. Seeing the Pope had done us no good, now in the Devil's name, 'twill do us a great deal. We then went ashoar, and the whole Country, Men, Women and Children came to meet us as in a solemn Procession. Our four Estates cry'd out to them with a loud voice; they have seen him, they have seen him, they have seen him. That Proclamation being made, all the Mob kneeled down before us, lifting up their Hands towards Heaven, and crying; O happy Men! O most happy. And this Acclamation lasted above a quarter of an hour.

Then came the *Busby* of the Place, with all his Pedagogues, Ushers, and School-boys, whom he Magisterially flogg'd, as they us'd to whip Children in our Country, formerly when some Criminal was hang'd, that they might remember it. This displeas'd *Pantagruel*, who said to them; Gentlemen, if you do not leave off whipping these poor Children, I'm gone. The People

were amaz'd hearing his Stentorean Voice; and I saw a little
Hump with long Fingers, say to the *Hypodidascal*; What! In the
name of Wonder, do all those that see the Pope, grow as tall as
yon huge Fellow that threatens us? Ah! How I shall think time
long, till I have seen him too, that I may grow and look as big.
In short, the Acclamations were so great, that *Homenas* (so they
call their Bishop) hasten'd thither on an unbridled Mule, with
green Trappings, attended by his *Aposts* (as they said) and his
Supposts or Officers, bearing Crosses, Banners, Standards, Can-
opies, Torches, Holy-water Pots, &c. He too wanted to kiss
our Feet (as the good *Christian Valfinier* did to Pope *Clement*)
saying, that one of their *Hypophetes*, that's one of the Scavengers,
Scowrers and Commentators of their Holy Decretals, had written, that, in the same manner as the Messiah, so long and so
much expected by the *Jews*, at last appear'd among them; so on
some happy day of God the Pope would come into that Island;
and that, while they waited for that blessed time, if any who had
seen him at *Rome*, or elsewhere, chanc'd to come among them,
they should be sure to make much of them, feast them plentifully, and Treat them with a great deal of Reverence. However,
we civilly desir'd to be excus'd.

CHAPTER XLIX

*How Homenas Bishop of Papimany shew'd us the Uranopet
Decretals.*

HOMENAS then said to us: 'Tis enjoyn'd us by our Holy Decretals to visit Churches first, and Taverns after. Therefore, not
to decline that fine Institution, let us go to Church; we shall
afterwards go to Feast our selves. Man of God, quoth Fryar *Jhon*,
do you go before, we'll follow you; you spoke in the matter
properly and like a good Christian; 'tis long since we saw any
such. For my part, this rejoyces my mind very much, and I verily
believe that I shall have the better Stomach after it: well, 'tis a
happy thing to meet with good Men! Being come near the Gate
of the Church, we spy'd a huge thick Book, gilt and cover'd all
over with precious Stones, as Rubies, Emeralds, and Pearls,
more, or at least as valuable as those which *Augustus* consecrated

to *Jupiter Capitolinus*. This Book hang'd in the Air, being
fasten'd with two thick Chains of Gold to the *Zoophore* of the
Porch. We look'd on it, and admir'd it. As for *Pantagruel*,
he handled it, and dandled it, and turn'd it as he pleas'd, for he
could reach it without straining; and he protested, that whenever
he touch'd it, he was seiz'd with a pleasant tickling at his Fingers
end, new Life and Activity in his Arms, and a violent temptation in his Mind to beat one or two Sergeants or such Officers,
provided they were not of the Shaveling-kind. *Homenas* then
said to us, The Law was formerly given to the *Jews* by *Moses*,
written by God himself; at *Delphos* before the Portal of *Apollo*'s
Temple, this Sentence, ΓΝΩΘΙ ΣΕΑΥΤΟΝ, was found written with
a Divine Hand, and sometime after it was also seen, and as
Divinely written and transmitted from Heaven. *Cybele*'s Shrine
was brought out of Heaven into a Field, call'd *Penisunt* in *Phrygia*;
so was that of *Diana* to *Tauris*, if you will believe *Euripides*; the
Oriflambe, or Holy Standard was transmitted out of Heaven to
the Noble and most Christian Kings of *France* to fight against
the Unbelievers. In the Reign of *Numa Pompilius*, second King
of the *Romans*, the famous Copper Buckler call'd *Ancile*
was seen to descend from Heaven. At *Acropolis* near *Athens*,
Minerva's Statue formerly fell from the Empyreal Heaven. In
like manner, the sacred Decretals, which you see, were written
with the hand of an Angel of the Cherubin-kind; you Outlandish
People will hardly believe this, I fear. Little enough of Conscience, said *Panurge*.—And then, continued *Homenas*, they
were miraculously transmitted to us here from the very Heaven
of Heavens in the same manner as the River *Nile* is call'd
Diipetes, by *Homer* the Father of all Philosophy (the holy Decretals always excepted.) Now because you have seen the Pope,
their Evangelist and everlasting Protector, we will give you
leave to see and kiss them on the Inside, if you think it meet.
But then you must fast three Days before, and Canonically confess, nicely and strictly mustering up, and inventorising your
Sins great and small, so thick that one single Circumstance of
them may not scape you, as our holy Decretals, which you see,
direct. This will take up some time. Man of God, answered *Panurge*, we have seen and descry'd Decrees and eke Decretals
enough o' Conscience, some on Paper other on Parchment fine

and gay like any painted Paper Lantern, some on Vellom, some in Manuscript, and others in Print; so you need not take half this Pains to shew us these. We'll take the Good-will for the Deed, and thank you as much as if we had. Ay, Marry, said *Homenas*; but you never saw these that are Angelically written. Those in your Country, are only Transcripts from ours, as we find it written by one of our old Decretaline Scoliasts. For me; Do not spare me, I do not value the Labour, so I may serve you; do but tell me whether you will be confest, and fast only three short little days of God? As for shriving, answer'd *Panurge*, there can be no great harm in 't, but this same Fasting, Master of mine, will hardly down with us at this time; for we have so very much over-fasted our selves at Sea, that the Spiders have spun their Cobwebs over our Grinders. Do but look on this, good Fryar *Jhon des Entomeures*, (*Homenas* then courteously Demy-clip'd him about the Neck) some Moss is growing in his Throat, for want of bestirring and exercising his Chaps. He speaks the Truth, vouch'd Fryar *Jhon*; I have so much fasted, that I'm almost grown hump-shoulder'd. Come then, let's go into the Church, said *Homenas*; and pray forgive us, if for the Present we do not sing you a fine high Mass: The hour of Mid-day is past, and after it our sacred Decretals forbid us to sing Mass, I mean your high and lawful Mass. But I'll say a low and dry one for you. I had rather have one moisten'd with some good *Anjou* Wine, cry'd *Panurge*; fall to, fall to your low Mass, and dispatch. Od's Bodikins, quoth Fryar *Jhon*, it frets me to the Guts that I must have an empty Stomach at this time of day. For had I eaten a good Breakfast, and fed like a Monk, if he should chance to sing us the *Requiem æternam dona eis, domine*, I had then brought thither Bread and Wine for the *Traits* passes, (those that are gone before.) Well, Patience; Pull away, and save a Tide; short and sweet, I pray you, and this for a Cause.

CHAPTER L

How Homenas shew'd us the Arch-Type, or Representation of a Pope.

MASS being mumbled over, *Homenas* took a huge bundle of Keys out of a Trunk near the Head Altar, and put Thirty two of them into so many Keyholes, put back so many Springs, then with Fourteen more master'd so many Padlocks, and at last open'd an Iron-Window strongly barr'd above the said Altar. This being done, in token of great Mystery, he cover'd himself with wet Sackcloth, and drawing a Curtain of Crimson Sattin, shew'd us an Image daub'd over coursly enough, to my thinking; then he touch'd it with a pretty long stick, and made us all kiss the part of the Stick that had touch'd the Image. After this, he said to us, What think you of this Image? It is the Likeness of a Pope, answer'd *Pantagruel*; I know it by the Tripple Crown, his Furr'd *Aumusse*, his Rochet, and his Slipper. You are in the right, said *Homenas*; it is the Idea of that same good God on Earth, whose coming we devoutly await, and whom we hope one day to see in this Country. O happy, wish'd for, and much expected day; and happy, most happy, you whose propitious Stars have so far favour'd you as to let you see the living and real Face of this good God on Earth, by the single sight of whose Picture we obtain full Remission of all the Sins which we remember, that we have committed, as also a Third part, and Eighteen *Quarantaines* of the Sins which we have forgot: And indeed we only see it on high annual Holy days.

This caus'd *Pantagruel* to say that it was a Work like those which *Dædalus* us'd to make; since tho' it were deform'd and ill drawn, nevertheless some divine Energy in Point of Pardons lay hid and conceal'd in it. Thus, said Fryar *Jhon*, at *Sevillé*, the rascally Beggers being one Evening on a Solemn Holy-day at Supper in the Spittle, one bragg'd of having got Six *Blancs*, or Two pence Halfpeny; another, Eight *Liards*, or Two pence, a Third Seven *Carolus*'s, or Six pence; but an old Mumper made his Vaunts of having got three Testons, or five Shillings: Ah, but (cry'd his Comrades) thou hast a Leg of god. As if continu'd

637

Fryar *Jhon*, some divine Vertue could lye hid in a stenching ulcerated rotten Shanck. Pray, said *Pantagruel*, when you are for telling us some such nauseous Tale, be so kind as not to forget to provide a *Bason*, Fryar *Jhon*; I'll assure you, I had much ado to forbear bringing up my Breakfast: Fy, I wonder a Man of your Coat is not asham'd to use thus the Sacred name of God, in speaking of things so filthy and abominable; Fy, I say: If among your monking Tribes such an abuse of Words is allow'd, I beseech you leave it there, and do not let it come out of the Cloysters. Physicians, said *Epistemon*, thus attribute a kind of Divinity to some Diseases; *Nero* also extoll'd Mushrooms, and in a *Greek* Proverb term'd them divine Food, because with them he had Poyson'd *Claudius* his Predecessor. But methinks, Gentlemen, this same Picture is not over-like our late Popes. For I have seen them, not with their *Pallium, Aumusse* or *Rochet* on, but with Helmets on their Heads, more like the Top of a *Persian* Turbant; and while the Christian Commonwealth was in Peace, they alone were most furiously and cruelly making War. This must have been then, return'd *Homenas*, against the Rebellious, Heretical Protestants; Reprobates, who are disobedient to the Holiness of this good God on Earth. 'Tis not only lawful for him to do so, but it is enjoyn'd him by the Sacred Decretals, and if any dare transgress one single *Iota* against their Commands, whether they be Emperors, Kings, Dukes, Princes, or Commonwealths, he is immediately to pursue them with Fire and Sword, strip them of all their Goods, take their Kingdoms from them, proscribe them, Anathematize them, and destroy not only their Bodies, those of their Children, Relations and others, but Damn also their Souls to the very bottom of the most hot and burning *Caldron* in Hell. Here, in the Devil's Name, said *Panurge*, the People are no Hereticks, such as was our *Raminagrobis*, and as they are in *Germany* and *England*. You are *Christians* of the best Edition, all pick'd and cull'd, for ought I see. Ay, marry are we, return'd *Homenas*, and for that reason we shall all be sav'd. Now let us go and bless our selves with Holy-water, and then to Dinner.

CHAPTER LI

Table-Talk in Praise of the Decretals.

Now Topers, pray observe that while *Homenas* was saying his dry Mass, three Collectors, or Licens'd Beggers of the Church, each of them with a large Basin went round among the People, saying with a loud Voice; *Pray remember the blessed Men who have seen his Face.* As we came out of the Temple they brought their Basins brim full of *Papimany* Chink to *Homenas*, who told us, that it was plentifully to Feast with; and that, of this Contribution and voluntary Tax, one part should be laid out in good Drinking, another in good Eating, and the remainder in both; according to an admirable Exposition hidden in a Corner of their Holy Decretals; which was perform'd to a T, and that at a noted Tavern not much unlike that of *Will*'s at *Amiens*. Believe me we tickled it off there with copious Cramming, and numerous Swilling.

I made two notable Observations at that Dinner; the one that there was not one Dish serv'd up, whether of Cabrittas, Capons, Hogs (of which latter there's great Plenty in *Papimany*) Pigeons, Coneys, Leverets, Turkeys or others, without abundance of Magistral *Stuff*; the other, that every Course and the Fruit also were serv'd up by unmarried Females of the Place, tight Lasses, I'll assure you, Waggish, Fair, Good-condition'd and Comely, Spruce, and fit for Business. They were clad all in fine long white *Albes* with two Girts, their Hair interwoven with narrow Tape, and purple Ribbond, stuck with Roses, Gilly-flowers, Marjoram, Daffidowndillies, Thyme and other sweet Flowers.

At every Cadence, they invited us to drink and bang it about, dropping us neat and gentile Court'sies: Nor was the sight of them unwelcome to all the Company; and as for Fryar *Jhon*, he leer'd on them sideways, like a Cur that steals a Capon. When the first course was taken off, the Females melodiously sung us an Epode in Praise of the *Sacrosanct* Decretals; and then the second Course being serv'd up *Homenas* joyful and cheery, said to one of the she Buttlers, Light here, *Claricia*. Immediately one of the Girls brought him a Tall-boy brim-full of *Extravagant*

Wine. He took fast hold of it and fetching a deep sigh said to *Pantagruel*; My Lord, and you my good Friends, Here's t' ye, with all my Heart: You are all very welcome. When he had tipp'd that off, and given the Tall-boy to the pretty Creature, he lifted up his Voice and said; O most holy *Decretals*, how good is good Wine found through your means. This is the best Jest we have had yet, observ'd *Panurge*; But 'twould still be better, if they could turn bad Wine into Good.

O *Seraphic Sextum*! (continu'd *Homenas*,) how necessary are you not to the Salvation of poor Mortals. O *Cherubic Clementinæ*! how perfectly the perfect institution of a true Christian is contain'd and describ'd in you! O *Angelical Extravagants*! How many poor Souls that wander up and down in mortal Bodies, throw this vale of Misery, would perish, were it not for you! When, ha! When shall this special gift of grace be bestow'd on Man kind, as to lay aside all other Studies and Concerns, to use you, to peruse you, to understand you, to know you by heart, to practise you, to incorporate you, to turn you into blood, and incenter you into the deepest Ventricles of their Brains, the inmost Marrow of their Bones, and most intricate Labyrinth of their Arteries? Then, ha then, and no sooner than then, nor otherwise than thus shall the World be happy! While the Old Man was thus running on, *Epistemon* arose and softly said to *Panurge*; For want of a close stool, I must e'en leave you for a moment or two; this *Stuff* has unbung'd the Orifice of my Mustard-Barrel, but I'll not tarry long.

Then, ah then, continu'd *Homenas*, no Hail, Frost, Ice, Snow, Overflowing, or *Vis-major*: Then plenty of all earthly goods here below. Then uninterrupted and eternal Peace throw the universe, an End of all Wars, plunderings, drudgeries, robbing, assassinates, unless it be to destroy these cursed Rebels the Heretics. Oh then, Rejoycing, Cheerfulness, Jollity, Solace, Sports and delicious Pleasures, over the Face of the Earth. Oh! What great Learning, inestimable Erudition, and Godlike Precepts, are knit, link'd, rivetted and mortais'd in the Divine Chapters of these eternal Decretals?

Oh! How wonderfully, if you read but one demy Canon, short Paragraph, or single Observation of these *Sacrosanct* Decretals, how wonderfully, I say, do you not perceive to kindle in your Hearts, a furnace of divine Love, Charity towards your

Neighbour (provided he be no Heretic,) bold Contempt of all casual and sublunary Things, firm Content in all your affections, and extatic Elevation of Soul even to the third Heaven!

CHAPTER LII

A Continuation of the Miracles caus'd by the Decretals.

WISELY, Brother *Timothy*, quoth *Panurge*, did am, did am; he says blew; But for my part I believe as little of it as I can. For, one Day by chance I happen'd to read a Chapter of them at *Poictiers* at the most Decretalipotent *Scotch* Doctor's, and Old Nick turn me into Bumfodder, if this did not make me so Hidebound and costive, that for four or five Days I hardly scumber'd one poor butt of Sir-reverence; and that too was full as dry and hard, I protest, as *Catullus* tells us were those of his Neighbour *Furius*.

> *Nec toto decies cacas in anno,*
> *Atque id durius est fabâ, et lapillis:*
> *Quod tu si manibus teras, fricesque*
> *Non unquam digitum inquinare posses.*

Oh, ho, cry'd *Homenas*, by 'r Lady, it may be you were then in the state of Mortal sin, my Friend. Well turn'd, cry'd *Panurge*, this was of a new strain é gad.

One day, said Fryar *John*, at *Sevillé* I had apply'd to my posteriors by the way of hind-Towel a leaf of an old *Clementinæ*, which our Rent-gatherer *John Guimard* had thrown out into the green of our Cloyster: now the Devil broyl me like a Black-pudding if I wasn't so abominably plagu'd with chaps, chawns and piles at the Fundament, that the Orifice of my poor Nockandroe was in a most wofull Pickle for I don't know how long. By 'r Lady, cry'd *Homenas*, 'twas a plain Punishment of God, for the sin that you had committed in beraying that sacred Book, which you ought rather to have kiss'd and ador'd, I say with an adoration of *Latria*, or of *Hyperdulia* at least: The *Panormitan* never told a Lye in the matter.

Saith *Ponocrates*, at *Montpelier*, *John Choüart* having bought of the *Monks* of St. *Olary* a delicate set of Decretals written on fine large Parchment of *Lamballe*, to beat Gold between the leaves, not so much as a piece that was beaten in them came to good, but all were dilacerated and spoil'd. Mark this, cry'd *Homenas*, 'twas a Divine punishment and vengeance.

At *Mans*, said *Eudemon*, *Francis Cornu*, Apothecary, had turn'd an old Set of *Extravagantes* into waste Paper; may I never stir, if whatever was lapt up in them was not immediately corrupted, rotten and spoyl'd; incense, Pepper, Cloves, Cinnamon, Saffron, Wax, Cassia, Rhubarb, Tamarinds, all, Drugs and Spices, were lost without exception. Mark, mark, quoth *Homenas*, an effect of Divine Justice! This comes of putting the Sacred Scriptures to such prophane uses.

At *Paris*, said *Carpalim*, *Snip Groignet* the Taylor had turn'd an old *Clementinæ* into Patterns and Measures, and all the Clothes that were cut on them were utterly spoil'd and lost; Gowns, Hoods, Cloaks, Cassocks, Jerkins, Jackets, Wastcoats, Capes, Doublets, Petticoats, *Corps de Robes*, Vardingals, and soforth. *Snip* thinking to cut a Hood would cut you out a Codpiece; instead of a Cassock he'd make you a high Crown'd Hat; for a Wastcoat he'd shape you out a Rochet; on the Pattern of a Doublet he'd make you a thing like a Frying-pan; then his Journey-men, having stitch'd it up, did jagg it and pink it at the bottom, and so it look'd like a pan to fry Chesnuts; instead of a Cape he made a Buskin; for a Vardingale he shap'd a Montero-Cap; and thinking to make a Cloak he'd cut out a pair of your big out-stroutting *Switzers* Breeches with panes like the outside of a Tabor. In so much that *Snip* was condemn'd to make good the Stuffs to all his Customers; and to this day poor Cabbidge's hair grows through his Hood, and his Arse through his Pocket-holes. Mark, an effect of Heavenly wrath and vengeance, cry'd *Homenas*.

At *Cahusac*, said *Gymnast*, a match being made by the Lords of *Estissac* and Vicount *Lausun* to shoot at a Mark, *Perotou* had taken to pieces a set of Decretals, and set one of the Leaves for the White to shoot at; now I sell, nay I give and bequeath for ever and aye the Mould of my Doublet to fifteen hundred Hampers full of black Devils, if ever any Archer in the Country (tho they are singular Marksmen in *Gujenne*) could hit the White. Not the least bit of the Holy Scrible was contaminated or touch'd; nay, and *Sansornin* the Elder who held Stakes, swore to us, *Figues dioures*, hard Figs (his greatest Oath) that he had openly, visibly and manifestly seen the Bolt of *Carquelin* moving right to the round Circle in the middle of the White, and that just on the point when it was going to hit and enter, it had gone aside above seven foot and four inches wide of it towards the Bakehouse.

Miracle! (cry'd *Homenas*) Miracle, Miracle! *Clerica*, come Wench, light, light here, Here's to you all Gentlemen; I vow you seem to me very sound Christians. While he said this, the Maidens began to snicker at his elbow, grinning, giggling and twittering among themselves. Fryar *Jhon* began to paw, neigh and whinny at the Snout's end, as one ready to leap, or at least to play the Ass, and to get up and ride tantivy to the Devil like a Beggar on Horseback.

Methinks, said *Pantagruel*, a Man might have been more out of Danger near the White of which *Gymnast* spoke, than was formerly *Diogenes* near another. How's that? ask'd *Homenas*, what was it? Was he one of our Decretalists? Rarely fallen in again e'gad, said *Epistemon* returning from Stool, I see he will hook his Decretals in, tho' by the Head and Shoulders.

Diogenes, said *Pantagruel*, one Day for Pastime, went to see some Archers that shot at Butts, one of whom was so unskilful, that, when it was his turn to shoot, all the bystanders went aside, lest he should mistake them for the Mark. *Diogenes* had seen him shoot extremly wide off it, so when the other was taking aim a second time, and the People remov'd at a great distance to the right and left of the White, he placed himself close by the Mark, holding that place to be the safest, and that so bad an Archer would certainly hit any other.

One of the Lord *d'Estissac*'s Pages at last found out the Charm, pursued *Gymnast*, and by his Advice *Perotou* put in another White made up of some Papers of *Pouillac*'s Law Suit, and then every one shot cleverly.

At *Landerousse*, said *Rhizotome*, at *John Delif*'s Wedding were very great doings, as 'twas then the Custom of the Country. After Supper, several Farces, Interludes, and Comical Scenes were acted: they had also several Morrice-dances with Bells and Tabors; and divers sorts of Masques, and Mummers were let in. My School-fellows and I, to grace the Festival to the best of our

Power (for fine white and purple Liveries had been given to all of us in the Morning) contriv'd a merry Mask with store of Cockle-shells, shells of Snails, Periwinkles, and such other. Then for want of Cuckoe-pint or Priest-pintle, Louse-bur, Clote, and Paper, we made our selves false Faces with the Leaves of an old *Sextum*, that had been thrown by and lay there for any one that would take it up, cutting out holes for the Eyes, Nose and Mouth. Now did you ever hear the like since you were born? When we had play'd our little Boyish Antick Tricks, and came to take off our sham-faces, we appear'd more hideous and ugly than the little Devils that acted the *Passion* at *Douay*: For our Faces were utterly spoyl'd at the places which had been touch'd by those leaves; one had there the Small Pox, another God's Token, or the Plague spot, a third the Crinckums, a fourth the Measles, a fifth Botches Pushes and Carbuncles; in short, he came off the least hurt who only lost his Teeth by the bargain. Miracle, bawl'd out *Homenas*, Miracle!

Hold, hold, cry'd *Rhizotome*, 'tisn't yet time to clap; my Sister *Kate*, and my Sister *Ren* had put the Crepines of their Hoods, their Ruffles, Snuffekins, and Neck-Ruffs new wash'd starch'd and iron'd, into that very Book of Decretals; for, you must know, it was cover'd with thick Boards and had strong Clasps; now, by the virtue of God—Hold, interrupted *Homenas*, what God do you mean? There is but one, answer'd *Rhizotome*. In Heaven, I grant, reply'd *Homenas*, but we have another here on Earth, d'ye see. Ay marry, have we, said *Rhizotome*, but on my Soul I protest I had quite forgot it—well then, by the virtue of God the Pope, their Pinners, Neck-ruffs, Bibs, Coifs, and other Linnen turn'd as black as a Char-coal-man's Sack. Miracle, cry'd *Homenas*! Here, *Clerica*, light me here, and pr'ythee, Girl, observe these rare Stories. How comes it to pass then, ask'd Fryar *Jhon*, that People say,

> Ever since *Decrees* had *Tails*
> And *Gens-d'Arms* lugg'd heavy Mails,
> Since each Monk would have a Horse,
> All went here from bad to worse.

> *Depuis que* Decrets *eurent* Ales,
> *Et* Gens-d'Armes *porterent Males*,

Moines allerent à Cheval,
En ce monde abonda à tout mal.

I understand you, answered *Homenas*; this is one of the quirks and little satyres of the new fangl'd Hereticks.

CHAPTER LIII

How, by the Virtue of the Decretals, Gold is subtilly drawn out
of France to Rome.

I WOULD, said *Epistemon*, it had cost me a pint of the best Tripe that ever can enter into Gut, so we had but compar'd with the Original, the dreadful Chapters, *Exercrabilis. De multa. Si plures. De Annatis per totum. Nisi essent. Cum ad Monasterium. Quod dilectio. Mandatum*; and certain others that draw every year out of *France* to *Rome*, four hundred thousand Ducats and more.

Do you make nothing of this, ask'd *Homenas*? Tho' methinks, after all, 'tis but little if we consider that *France* the *most Christian*, is the only Nurse, the See of *Rome* has. However find me in the whole World a Book, whether of Philosophy, Physic, Law, Mathematicks, or other humane Learning, nay, even, by *my* God, of the Holy Scripture it self, that will draw as much Money thence? None, none, pshaw, tush, blurt, pish, none can: You may look till your Eyes drop out of your Head; nay, till Dooms-day in the afternoon, before you can find another of that Energy; I'll pass my word for that.

Yet these Devillish Heretics refuse to learn and know it. Burn 'em, tear 'em, nip 'em with hot Pincers, drown 'em, hang 'em, spit 'em at the Bunghole, pelt 'em, paut 'em, bruise 'em, beat 'em, cripple 'em, dismember 'em, cut 'em, gut 'em, bowell 'em, paunch 'em, thrash 'em, slash 'em, gash 'em, chop 'em, slice 'em, slit 'em, carve 'em, saw 'em, bethwack 'em, pare 'em, hack 'em, hew 'em, mince 'em, flea 'em, boyl 'em, broyl 'em, roast 'em, toast 'em, bake 'em, fry 'em, crucifie 'em, crush 'em, squeeze 'em, grind 'em, batter 'em, burst 'em, quarter 'em, unlimb 'em, bebump 'em, bethump 'em, belamme 'em, belabour 'em, pepper 'em, spitchcock 'em, and carbonade 'em on Gridirons, these wicked Heretics; Decretalifuges, Decretalicides, worse than Homicides, worse than Parricides, Decretalictones of the Devil of Hell.

As for you other good People, I most earnestly pray and beseech you to believe no other thing, think on, say, undertake, or do no other thing than what's contain'd in our Sacred Decretals, and their Corallaries, this fine *Sextum*, these fine *Clementinæ*, these fine *Extravagantes*. O Deific Books! So shall you enjoy Glory, Honour, Exaltation, Wealth, Dignities, and Preferments in this World; be rever'd, and dreaded by all, preferr'd, Elected, and Chosen above all Men.

For, there is not under the Cope of Heaven, a condition of Men out of which you'll find Persons fitter to do and handle all things, than those who by Divine Prescience, Eternal Predestination, have applied themselves to the Study of the Holy Decretals.

Would you chuse a worthy Emperor, a good Captain, a fit General in time of War, one that can well forsee all inconveniences, avoid all dangers, briskly and bravely bring his Men on to a Breach or Attack, still be on sure grounds, always overcome without loss of his Men, and know how to make a good use of his Victory? Take me a Decretist.—No, no, I mean a Decretalist. Ho, the foul Blunder, whisper'd *Epistemon*.

Would you in time of Peace, find a Man capable of wisely governing the State of a Commonwealth, of a Kingdom, of an Empire, of a Monarchy, sufficient to maintain the Clergy, Nobility, Senate and Commons in Wealth, Friendship, Unity, Obedience, Virtue and Honesty? Take a Decretalist.

Would you find a Man who, by his exemplary Life, Eloquence, and pious Admonitions, may in a short time without effusion of humane blood Conquer the Holy Land, and bring over to the Holy Church the misbelieving *Turks, Jews, Tartars, Muscovites, Mammelus*, and *Sarrabovites*? Take me a Decretalist.

What makes in many Countries, the People Rebellious and deprav'd, Pages sawcy and mischievous, Students sottish and duncical? Nothing but that their Governors, Esquires, and Tutors were not Decretalists.

But what, on your Conscience, was it d' ye think that establish'd, confirm'd and authoris'd these fine Religious Orders with whom you see the Christian World every where adorn'd, grac'd and illustrated as the Firmament is with its glorious Stars? The Holy Decretals.

What was it that founded, underpropt, and fix'd, and now maintains, nourishes and feeds the devout Monks and Fryars in Convents, Monasteries and Abbeys, so that did they not daily and mightily pray without ceasing, the World would be in evident danger of returning to its Primitive Chaos? The Sacred Decretals.

What makes, and daily encreases the famous and celebrated Patrimony of St. *Peter* in plenty of all Temporal, Corporeal and Spiritual Blessings? The Holy Decretals.

What made the Holy Apostolick See and Pope of *Rome* in all times, and at this present so dreadful in the Universe, that all Kings, Emperors, Potentates, and Lords willing nilling must depend on him, hold of him, be Crown'd, confirm'd, and Authoris'd by him, come thither to strike sail, buckle, and fall down before his Holy Slipper, whose Picture you have seen? The mighty Decretals of God.

I will discover you a great secret; The Universities of your World have commonly a Book either open or shut in their Arms and Devises; what Book do you think it is? Truly, I do not know, answer'd *Pantagruel*, I never read it. It is the Decretals, said *Homenas*, without which the Priviledges of all Universities would soon be lost. You must own I have taught you this, ha, ha, ha, ha, ha.

Here *Homenas* began to belch, to fart, to funk, to laugh, to slaver, and to sweat; and then he gave his huge greasie four-corner'd Cap to one of the Lasses, who clapt it on her pretty head with a deal of joy after she had lovingly buss'd it, as a sure token that she should be first married. *Vivat*, cry'd *Epistemon*, *fifat, bibat, pipat*.

O Apocalyptic Secret, continued *Homenas*! light, light, *Clerica*, light here with double Lanterns. Now for the Fruit, Virgins.

I was saying then, that giving your selves thus wholly to the study of the Holy Decretals, you'll gain Wealth and Honour in this World; I add, that in the next you'll infallibly be saved in the blessed Kingdom of Heaven, whose Keys are given to *Our* good God and Decretaliarch. O *My* good God, whom I adore and never saw, by thy special Grace open unto us, at the Point of

Death at least, this most Sacred Treasure of our Holy Mother Church, whose Protector, Preserver, Buttler, Chief Larder, Administrator, and Disposer thou art; and take care, I beseech thee, O Lord, that the precious works of Supererogation, the goodly Pardons do not fail us in time of need; so that the Devils may not find an opportunity to gripe our precious Souls, and the dreadful Jaws of Hell may not swallow us. If we must pass thro' Purgatory, *Thy* Will be done. It is in thy Power to draw us out of it when thou pleasest. Here *Homenas* began to shed huge hot briny Tears, to beat his Brest, and kiss his Thumbs in the shape of a Cross.

CHAPTER LIV

How Homenas gave Pantagruel some Bon-Christian Pears.

EPISTEMON, Fryar *Jhon*, and *Panurge* seeing this doleful Catastrophe began under the cover of their Napkins to cry, Meeow, Meeow, Meeow, feigning to wipe their Eyes all the while as if they had wept. The Wenches were doubly diligent and brought Brimmers of *Clementine* Wine to every one, besides store of Sweetmeats, and thus the Feasting was reviv'd.

Before we arose from Table, *Homenas* gave us a great quantity of fair large Pears; saying, Here, my good Friends, these are singular good Pears; you'll find none such anywhere else, I dare warrant. Every Soil bears not every thing you know: *India* alone boasts black *Ebony*, the best Incense is produced in *Sabæa*, the Sphragitid Earth at *Lemnos*; So this Island is the only Place where such fine Pears grow. You may, if you please, make Seminaries with their Pippins, in your Country.

I like their Taste extremely, said *Pantagruel*; if they were slic'd and put into a Pan on the Fire with Wine and Sugar, I fancy they would be very wholsome Meat for the Sick as well as for the Healthy; Pray, what do you call 'em? No otherwise than you've heard, reply'd *Homenas*; we are a plain down-right sort of People, as God would have it, and call Figs, Figs; Plumbs, Plumbs; and Pears, Pears. Truly, said *Pantagruel*, if I live to go home, (which I hope will be speedily, God willing) I'll set and graff some in my Garden in *Touraine* by the Banks of the

Loire, and will them call *Bon-Christian* or *Good-Christian* Pears; for I never saw better Christians than are these good *Papimans*. I'd like him two to one better yet, said Fryar *Jhon*, would he but give us two or three Cart-loads of yon buxome Lasses. Why, what wou'd you do with them, cry'd *Homenas*? Quoth Fryar *Jhon*, No harm, only bleed the kind-hearted Souls straight between the two great Toes with certain clever Lancets of the right stamp: By which Operation, *Good-Christian* Children would be inoculated upon them, and the Breed be multiplied in our Country, in which there are not many over good, the more's the Pity.

Nay, verily reply'd *Homenas*, We cannot do this, for you would make them tread their Shoes awry, crack their Pipkins, and spoil their Shapes: You love Mutton I see, you'll run at Sheep, I know you by that same Nose and Hair of yours, tho' I never saw your Face before. Alas, alas, how kind you are! And wou'd you indeed Damn your precious Soul? Our Decretals forbid this: Ah, I wish you had them at your Fingers-end. Patience, said Fryar *Jhon*: But, *Si tu non vis dare, præsta quæsumus*; matter of Breviary; as for that I defie all the world, and I fear no Man that wears a Head and a Hood, tho' he were a *Chrystallin*, I mean, a *Decretalin* Doctor.

Dinner being over, we took our leave of the Right Reverend *Homenas*, and of all the good People, humbly giving thanks; and to make them amends for their kind Entertainment, Promised them that at our coming to *Rome* we would make our Applications so effectualy to the Pope, that he would speedily be sure to come to Visit them in Person. After this, we went o' Board.

Pantagruel, by an Act of Generosity, and as an Acknowledgment for the Sight of the Pope's Picture, gave *Homenas* Nine pieces of double friz'd Cloth of Gold to be set before the Grates of the Window. He also caus'd the Church-Box for its Repairs and Fabrick, to be quite fill'd with double-Crowns of Gold, and order'd Nine hundred and Fourteen Angels to be deliver'd to each of the Lasses, who had waited at Table, to buy them Husbands when they could get them.

CHAPTER LV

How Pantagruel, being at Sea, heard various unfrozen words.

WHEN we were at Sea Junketting, Tipling, Discoursing, and telling Stories, *Pantagruel* rose and stood up to look out; then ask'd us, Do you hear nothing, Gentlemen? Methinks I hear some People talking in the Air; yet I can see no Body; Hark! According to his Command we listen'd, and with full Ears suck'd in the Air, as some of you suck Oysters, to find if we could hear some sound scatter'd through the Sky; and to lose none of it, like the Emperor *Antoninus*, some of us laid their hands hollow next to their Ears: But all this wou'd not do, nor cou'd we hear any Voice. Yet *Pantagruel* continued to assure us he heard various Voices in the Air, some of Men, and some of Women.

At last we began to Fancy that we also heard something, or at least that our Ears tingled, and the more we listen'd, the plainer we discern'd the Voices, so as to distinguish Articulate Sounds. This mightily frighted us, and not without cause, since we could see nothing, yet heard such various Sounds and Voices of Men, Women, Children, Horses, etc. insomuch that *Panurge* cry'd out, Cods Belly, there's no fooling with the Devil; we are all beshit; let's fly. There is some Ambuscado here abouts. Fryar *Jhon* art thou here, my Love? I pr'y thee stay by me old Boy: hast thou got thy swindging Tool? See that it do not stick in the Scabbard; thou never scour'st it half as it should be. We are undone. Hark! They are Guns, Gad judge me; Let's fly, I do not say with hands and feet, as *Brutus* said at the Battel of *Pharsalia*, I say with Sails and Oars; Let's whip it away, I never find my self to have a bit of Courage at Sea; In Cellars and elsewhere I have more than enough. Let's fly, and save our Bacon. I do not say this for any fear that I have; for I dread nothing but Danger; that I don't: I always say it that shou'dn't. The Free-Archer of *Baignolet* said as much. Let's hazard nothing therefore, I say, lest we come off blewly. Tack about, Helm a Lee! thou Son of a Batchelor. Would I were now well in *Quinquenois*, tho' I were never to Marry. Hast away; let's make all the Sail we can, they'll be too hard for us, we are not able to cope with them,

THE FOURTH BOOK

they are ten to our one, I'll warrant you; nay, and they are on their Dunghil, while we do not know the Country. They'll be the Death of us. We'll lose no Honour by flying; *Demosthenes* saith, That the Man that runs away may fight another time. At least, let us retreat to the Lee-ward. Helm a Lee; Bring the main Tack aboard, Hawl the Bowlins, Hoist the Top-Gallants, we are all dead Men: get off in the Devil's name, get off.

Pantagruel hearing the sad Outcry which *Panurge* made, said, who Talks of flying? Let's first see who they are, perhaps they may be Friends; I can discover no Body yet, tho' I can see a hundred Miles round me: But let's consider a little; I have read, that a Philosopher nam'd *Perron* was of Opinion, that there were several Worlds that touch'd each other in an Equilateral Triangle; in whose Centre, he said, was the dwelling of Truth; and that the words, Ideas, Copies and Images of all things past, and to come resided there: round which was the Age, and that with Success of Time part of them us'd to fall on mankind like Rhumes and Mildews, just as the Dew fell on *Gideon*'s Fleece, till the Age was fulfilled.

I also remember, continu'd he, that *Aristotle* affirms *Homer*'s Words to be flying, moving, and consequently animated. Besides, *Antiphanes* said, that *Plato*'s Philosophy was like words which being spoken in some Country during a hard Winter are immediately congeal'd, frozen up and not heard; for what *Plato* taught young Lads, could hardly be understood by them, when they were grown Old: Now, continu'd he, we should Philosophise and Search whether this be not the place where those words are thaw'd.

You'd wonder very much, should this be the Head and Lyre of *Orpheus*. When the *Thracian* Women had torn him to Pieces, they threw his Head and Lyre into the River *Hebrus*; down which they floated to the *Euxine* Sea, as far as the Island of *Lesbos*, the Head continually uttering a doleful Song, as it were, lamenting the Death of *Orpheus*, and the Lyre with the Wind's impulse, moving its strings, and Harmoniously *Accompanying* the Voice. Let's see if we cannot discover them hereabouts.

CHAPTER LVI

*How among the Frozen Words, Pantagruel found some odd
ones.*

THE Skipper made answer; Be not afraid, my Lord, we are on
the Confines of the Frozen Sea, on which about the beginning
of last Winter happen'd a great and bloody Fight between the
Arimaspians and the *Nephelibates*. Then the words and cries of
Men and Women, the hacking, slashing, and hewing of Battle-
axes, the shocking, knocking, and joulting of Armours, and Har-
nesses, the neighing of Horses, and all other Martial din and
noise, froze in the Air; And now the rigour of the Winter being
over by the succeeding serenity and warmth of the Weather,
they melt and are heard.

By jingo, quoth *Panurge*, the Man talks somewhat like, I believe him; but cou'dn't we see some of 'em? Methinks I have
read that on the edge of the Mountain on which *Moses* receiv'd
the *Judaic* Law, the People saw the Voices sensibly.—Here,
here, said *Pantagruel*, here are some that are not yet thaw'd. He
then throw'd us on the Deck whole handfulls of frozen Words,
which seem'd to us like your rough Sugar-Plumbs, of many colours, like those us'd in Heraldry, some Words *Gules* [This means
also Jests and merry sayings] some *Vert*, some *Azur*, some *Black*,
some *Or*, [This means also fair words;] and when we had somewhat warm'd them between our Hands, they melted like Snow,
and we really heard them, but cou'd not understand them, for
it was a Barbarous Gibberish; one of them only that was pretty
big, having been warm'd between Fryar *Jhon*'s Hands, gave a
sound much like that of Chesnuts when they are thrown into
the Fire without being first cut, which made us all start. This
was the report of a Field-piece in its time, cry'd Fryar *Jhon*.

Panurge pray'd *Pantagruel* to give him some more; but *Pantagruel* told him, that to give words, was the Part of a Lover. Sell
me some then, I pray you, cry'd *Panurge*. That's the part of a
Lawyer, return'd *Pantagruel*; I would sooner sell you Silence,
tho' at a dearer Rate, as *Demosthenes* formerly sold it by the means
of his *Argentangina* or Silver Squinsey.

However, he threw three or four Handfulls of them on the Deck, among which I perceiv'd some very sharp words, and some bloody words, which the Pilot said, us'd sometimes to go back and recoil to the place whence they came, but 'twas with a slit weesand; we also saw some terrible words, and some others not very pleasant to the Eye.

When they had been all melted together, we heard a strange noise, hin, hin, hin, hin, his, tick, tock, taack, brededin, brededack, frr, frr, frr, bou, bou, bou, bou, bou, bou, bou, bou, track, track, trr, trr, trr, trrr, trrrrrr, on, on, on, on, on, on, ououououon, gog, magog, and I do not know what other barbarous words, which the Pilot said, were the noise made by the Charging Squadrons, the shock and neighing of Horses.

Then we heard some large ones go off like Drums and Fifes, and others like Clarions and Trumpets. Believe me, we had very good sport with them. I wou'd fain have sav'd some merry odd words, and have preserv'd them in Oyl, as Ice and Snow are kept, and between clean Straw. But *Pantagruel* would not let me, saying, that 'tis a folly to hoard up what we are never like to want, or have always at hand, odd, quaint, merry and fat words of *Gules* never being scarce among all good and jovial *Pantagruelists*.

Panurge somewhat vex'd Fryar *Jhon*, and put him in the pouts; for he took him at his word, while he dreamt of nothing less. This caus'd the Fryar to threaten him with such a piece of Revenge as was put upon *G. Jousseaume*, who having taken the merry *Patelin* at his Word, when he had overbid himself in some Cloth, was afterwards fairly taken by the Horns like a Bullock, by his jovial Chapman, whom he took at his Word like a Man. *Panurge* well knowing that threaten'd folks live long, bobb'd, and made mouths at him, in token of Derision, then cry'd, would I had here the *Word* of the *Holy Bottle*, without being thus oblig'd to go farther in Pilgrimage to her.

CHAPTER LVII

*How Pantagruel went ashoar at the Dwelling of Gaster, the
first Master of Arts in the World.*

THAT Day *Pantagruel* went ashore in an Island, which for Situation and Governor may be said not to have its fellow. When you just come into it, you find it rugged, craggy, barren, unpleasant to the Eye, painful to the Feet, and almost as inaccessible as the Mountain of *Dauphiné*, which is somewhat like a Toadstool, and was never climb'd, as any can remember, by any but *Doyac*, who had the charge of King *Charles* the Eighth's Train of Artillery.

This same *Doyac* with strange Tools and Engines, gain'd that Mountain's top, and there he found an old Ram. It puzzl'd many a wise Head to guess how it got thither. Some said, that some Eagle, or great Horn-Coot, having carry'd it thither while 'twas yet a Lambkin, it had got away and sav'd it self among the Bushes.

As for us, having with much toil and sweat overcome the difficult ways at the entrance, we found the top of the Mountain so fertile, healthful, and pleasant, that I thought I was then in the true Garden of *Eden* or Earthly Paradice, about whose Situation our good Theologues are in such a quandary, and keep such a pother.

As for *Pantagruel*, he said, That here was the Seat of *Arete* (that's as much as to say, Virtue) describ'd by *Hesiod*; this however, with submission to better Judgments. The Ruler of the place was one Master *Gaster*, the first Master of Arts in this World; for if you believe that Fire is the great Master of Arts, as *Tully* writes, you very much wrong him and your self; alas, *Tully* never believ'd this. On the other side, if you fancy *Mercury* to be the first Inventer of Arts, as our ancient *Druids* believ'd of old, you are mightily beside the Mark. The Satirist's Sentence, that affirms Master *Gaster* to be Master of all Arts, is true. With him peacefully resided old Goody *Penia* alias *Poverty*, the Mother of the Ninety Nine Muses, on whom *Porus* the Lord of *Plenty* formerly begot *Love*, that Noble Child, the Mediator of Heaven and Earth, as *Plato* affirms in his *Symposio*.

We were all oblig'd to pay our homage and swear Allegiance to that mighty Sovereign; for he is Imperious, Severe, Blunt, Hard, Uneasie, Inflexible; you cannot make him believe, represent to him, or persuade him any thing.

He do's not hear; and as the *Egyptians* said, That *Harpocrates* the God of Silence nam'd *Sigalion* in *Greek* was *Astomé*, that is, without a Mouth; so *Gaster* was created without Ears, even like the Image of *Jupiter* in *Candia*.

He only speaks by Signs, but those Signs are more readily obey'd by every one, than the Statutes of Senates, or Commands of Monarchs; neither will he admit the least Lett, or delay in his Summons. You say, that when a Lyon roars all the Beasts at a considerable distance round about, as far as his Roar can be heard, are seiz'd with a shivering. This is written, 'Tis true, I have seen it. I assure you, that at Master *Gaster*'s Command, the very Heavens tremble, and all the Earth shakes, his Command is call'd, *Do this or dye*: Needs must whom the Devil drives, there's no gain-saying of it.

The Pilot was telling us how on a certain Time, after the manner of the Members that mutin'd against the Belly, as *Æsop* describes it, the whole Kingdom of the *Somates* went off into a direct Faction against *Gaster*, resolving to throw off his Yoke, but they soon found their mistake and most humbly submitted, for otherwise they had all been Famish'd.

What Companies soever he is in, none dispute with him for Precedence or Superiority, he still goes first, tho' Kings, Emperors, or even the Pope were there. So he held the first Place at the Council of *Basle*, tho some will tell you that the Council was tumultuous by the Contentions and Ambition of many for Priority.

Every one is busied, and labours to serve him; and indeed, to make amends for this, he do's this good to Mankind, as to invent for them All Arts, Machines, Trades, Engines, and Crafts: he even instructs Brutes in Arts which are against their Nature, making Poets of Ravens, Jack-Daws, chattering Jays, Parrots and Starlings, and Poetresses of Magpies, teaching them to utter human Languages, Speak and Sing; and All for the Gut. He reclaims and tames Eagles, Gerfaulcons, Faulcons gentle, Sakers, Lanniers, Gosse-hawks, Sparhawks, Merlins, Hagards, Passengers, Wild rapacious Birds; so that setting them free in the Air, whenever he thinks fit, as high and as long as he pleases, he keeps them suspended, straying, flying, hovering, and courting him above the Clouds: then on a sudden he makes them stoop and come down amain from Heaven next to the Ground; and all for the Gut.

Elephants, Lions, Rhinocerotes, Bears, Horses, Mares, and Dogs, he teaches to Dance, Prance, Vault, Fight, Swim, hide themselves, fetch and carry what he pleases; and all for the Gut.

Salt and fresh-water Fish, Whales, and the Monsters of the Main, he brings up from the bottom of the Deep; Wolves he forces out of the Woods, Bears out of the Rocks, Foxes out of their Holes, and Serpents out of the Ground; and all for the Gut.

In short, he is so unruly, that in his Rage he devours all Men and Beasts; as was seen among the *Vascons*, when *Q. Metellus* besieg'd them in the *Sertorian* Wars; among the *Saguntines* besieg'd by *Hannibal*; among the *Jews* besieg'd by the *Romans*, and Six hundred more; and all for the Gut. When his Regent *Penia* takes a Progress, where ever she moves, all Senates are shut up, all Statutes repeal'd, all Orders and Proclamations vain: she knows, obeys, and has no Law. All shun her, in every Place chusing rather to expose themselves to Shipwracks at Sea, and venture through Fire, Rocks, Caves and Precipices, than be seiz'd by that most dreadful Tormentor.

CHAPTER LVIII

How at the Court of the Master of Ingenuity, Pantagruel detested the Engastrimythes, and the Gastrolaters.

AT the Court of that great Master of Ingenuity, *Pantagruel* observ'd two sorts of troublesom and too officious Apparitors, whom he very much detested. The first, were call'd *Engastrimythes*; the others, *Gastrolaters*.

The first pretended to be descended of the Ancient Race of *Euricles*; and for this brought the Authority of *Aristophanes*, in his Comedy call'd, *The Wasps*; whence of old they were call'd *Euriclians*, as *Plato* writes, and *Plutarch* in his Book of the *Cessation of Oracles*. In the Holy Decrees *26 Qu. 3.* they are stil'd *Ventriloqui*; and the same Name is given them in *Ionian* by *Hippocrates*, in his Fifth Book of *Epid.* as Men who speak from the Belly. *Sophocles* calls them *Sternomantes*. These were Southsayers, Enchanters, Cheats, who gull'd the Mob, and seem'd not to speak and give Answers from the Mouth; but from the Belly.

Such a one, about the Year of our Lord 1513, was *Jacoba Rodogina*, an Italian Woman of mean Extract; from whose Belly, we, as well as an infinite Number of others at *Ferrara*, and elsewhere, have often heard the Voice of the Evil Spirit speak, low, feeble and small indeed; but yet very distinct, articulate and intelligible, when she was sent for, out of Curiosity, by the Lords and Princes of the *Cisalpine* Gaul. To remove all Manner of Doubt, and be assur'd that this was not a Trick, they us'd to have her Stripp'd stark naked, and caus'd her Mouth and Nose to be stopp'd. This Evil Spirit would be call'd *Curl'd-Pate*, or *Cincinnatulo*, seeming pleas'd when any call'd him by that Name; at which, he was always ready to Answer. If any Spoke to him of things past or present, he gave pertinent Answers, sometimes to the Amazement of the Hearers; but, if of things to come, then the Devil was gravell'd, and us'd to Lye as fast as a Dog can Trot. Nay, sometimes he seem'd to own his Ignorance, instead of an Answer, letting out a rouzing Fart, or muttering some Words with barbarous and uncouth Inflexions, and not to be understood.

As for the *Gastrolaters*, they stuck close to one another in Knots and Gangs. Some of them Merry, Wanton, and Soft as so many Milksops; others lowring, grim, dogged, demure and crabbed, all idle, mortal foes to business, spending half their Time in sleeping, and the rest in doing nothing, a Rent-charge and dead unnecessary Weight on the Earth, as *Hesiod* saith; afraid (as we judg'd) of offending or lessening their Paunch. Others were mask'd, disguis'd, and so oddly dress'd, that 'twould have done you good to have seen them.

There's a Saying, and several Ancient Sages write, That the Skill of Nature appears wonderful in the Pleasure which she seems to have taken in the Configuration of Sea-shells, so great is their Variety in figures, colours, streaks, and inimitable shapes. I protest the Variety we perceiv'd in the Dresses of the *Gastrolatrous Coquillons* was not less. They all own'd *Gaster* for their Supreme God, ador'd him as a God, offer'd him Sacrifices as to their Omnipotent Deity, own'd no other God, serv'd, lov'd, and honour'd him above all things.

You would have thought that the Holy Apostle spoke of those, when he said, *Phil*. Chap. 3. *Many walk of whom I have told you often, and now tell you even weeping, that they are Enemies of the Cross of Christ: whose End is Destruction, whose God is their Belly.* Pantagruel compar'd them to the Cyclops *Polyphemus*, whom *Euripides* brings in speaking thus, I only Sacrifice to my self (not to the Gods) and to this Belly of Mine, the greatest of all the Gods.

CHAPTER LIX

Of the ridiculous Statue Manduce; and how and what the Gastrolaters Sacrifice to their Ventripotent God.

WHILE we fed our Eyes with the sight of the Phyzzes and Actions of these lozelly Gulligutted *Gastrolaters*, we on a sudden heard the Sound of a Musical Instrument call'd a Bell, at which all of them plac'd themselves in Rank and File as for some mighty Battel, every one according to his Office, Degree and Seniority.

In this Order, they mov'd towards Master *Gaster*, after a plump, young, lusty gorbellied Fellow, who on a long Staff fairly gilt, carried a wooden Statue grossly carv'd and as scurvily daub'd o'er with Paint, such a one as *Plautus*, *Juvenal* and *Pomp. Festus* describe it. At *Lions* during the Carnaval 'tis call'd *Maschecrouste*, or *Gnaw crust*; they call'd this *Manduce*.

It was a monstrous, ridiculous, hideous Figure, fit to fright little Children: Its Eyes were bigger than its Belly, and its Head larger than all the rest of its Body, well Mouth-cloven however, having a goodly Pair of wide, broad Jaws, lin'd with two Rows of Teeth, upper Teer and under Teer, which, by the Magic of a small Twine hid in the hollow part of the Golden Staff, were made to clash, clatter and rattle dreadfully one against another, as they do at *Metz* with St. *Clement*'s Dragon.

Coming near the *Gastrolaters*, I saw they were follow'd by a great number of fat Waiters and Tenders laden with Baskets, Dossers, Hampers, Dishes, Wallets, Pots and Kettles: Then under the Conduct of *Manduce*, and singing I don't know what

Dithyrambics, Crepalocomes and *Epenons*, opening their Baskets and Pots, they offer'd their God,

White Hippocras
  with dry Toasts.
White-Bread.
Brown-Bread.
Carbonadoes,
  six sorts.
Brawn.
Sweet-breads.
Fricasses nine sorts.

Monastical Browess.
  Gravy-soupe.
Hotch-pots.
Soft-bread.
Houshold Bread.
Capirotadoes.
Cold Loins of Veal with
  Spice.
Zinziberine.

Beatille-Pyes.
Brewess.
Marrow-Bones,
  Toast and Cabbidge.
Hashes.

Eternal Drink intermix'd. Brisk delicate White-wine led the Van, Claret and Champaign follow'd, cool, nay, as cold as the very Ice, I say, fill'd and offer'd in large Silver Cups: Then they offer'd,

Chitterlings garnish'd
  with Mustard.
Saucidges.
Neats Tongues.
Hung Beef.
Chines and Pease.

Hogs-haslets.
Scotch Collops.
Puddings.
Cervelats.
Bolonia Sawcidges.

Hams.
Brawn-Heads.
Powder'd Venison;
  with Turnips.
Pickled Olives.

All this associated with Sempiternal Liquor. Then they hous'd within his Muzzle,

Legs of Mutton with
  Shallots.
Ollas.
Lumber-Pyes, with hot
  Sauce.
Ribs of Pork, with
  Onion Sauce.
Roast Capons basted
  with their own
  Dripping.
Caponets.
Caviar and Toast.
Fawns, Deer.
Hares, Leverets.
Partridges, & young
  Partridges.
Pluvers.

Dwarfe herons.
Teals.
Duckers.
Bittors.
Shovelers.
Curlues.
Wood-hens.
Coots with Leeks.
Fat Kids.
Shoulders of Mutton
  with Capers.
Sir-Loins of Beef.
Breasts of Veal.
Phesants and Phesant
  poots.
Peacocks.
Storks.

Woodcocks.
Snipes.
Hortolans.
Turkey-Cocks,
  Hen-Turkeys and
  Turkey-poots.
Stock-doves, and
  Wood-culvers.
Pigs with Wine sauce.
Blackbirds, Owsels,
  and Rayles.
Moor-hens.
Bustards and Bustard
  poots.
Fig-peckers.
Young Guiny hens.
Flemmings.

Cignets.
A Renforcement of
    Vinegar intermixt.
Venison Pasties.
Lark Pyes.
Dormise Pyes.
Cabretto Pasties.
Roe-buck Pasties.
Pigeon Pyes.
Kid Pasties.
Capon Pyes.
Bacon Pyes.
Souc'd Hogs feet.
Fry'd Pasty crust.
Forc'd Capons.
Parmesan Cheese.
Red and Pale
    Hippocras.
Gold-peaches.
Artichokes.
Dry and wet
    Sweet-meats, 78
    sorts.

Boyl'd Hens and fat
    Capons maronated.
Pullets with Eggs.
Chickens.
Rabbets and sucking
    Rabbets.
Quails and young
    Quails.
Pigeons Squobbs and
    Squeakers.
Herons and young
    Herons.
Feldivers.
Olaves.
Thrushes.
Young Sea-Ravens.
Geese, Goslins.
Queests.
Widgeons.
Mavises.
Grouses.
Turtles.
Doe-Connys.

Hedge hogs.
Snytes.
Then large Puffs.
Thistle-Finches.
Whore's-Farts.
Fritters.
Cakes, sixteen sorts.
Crisp Wafers.
Quince Tarts.
Curds and Cream.
Whipp'd Cream.
Preserv'd
    Myrabolans.
Gellies.
Welch Barrapyclids.
Macaroons.
Tarts, twenty sorts.
Lemon Cream,
    Rasberry Cream,
    & c.
Comfits, 100 Colours.
Cream Wafers.
Cream Cheese.

Vinegar brought up the Reer to wash the Mouth, and for fear of the Squinsy: Also Toasts to scower the Grinders.

CHAPTER LX

What the Gastrolaters Sacrific'd to their God on interlarded Fish-Days.

PANTAGRUEL did not like this Pack of Rascally Scoundrels with their manifold Kitchen Sacrifices, and would have been gone, had not *Epistemon* prevail'd with him to stay and see the End of the Farce; he then ask'd the Skipper, what the idle Lobcocks us'd to sacrifice to their gorbellied God on interlarded Fish-days? For his first Course, said the Skipper, they give him

Caviar.
Botargoes.
Fresh Butter.
Pease soupe.

Spinage.
Fresh Herrings
    full-roed.
Salats, a hundred

Varieties, of Creeses,
    sodden Hop-tops,
    Bishops-Cods,

Sellery, Sives, Rampions, Jew's-Ears, (a sort of Mushrooms that sprout out of old Elders), Sparagus, Woodbind, and a World of others. Red-herrings. Pilchards. Anchovies. Fry of Tunny. Colly flowers. Beans. Salt Salmon. Pickled Griggs. Oysters in the Shell.

Then he must drink or the Devil would gripe him at the Throat; This therefore they take care to prevent, and nothing's wanting. Which being done, they give him *Lampreys* with *Hippocras* sawce.

Gurnards. Salmon-Trouts. Barbels great and small. Roaches. Cockrells. Menews. Thornbacks. Sleeves. Sturgeons. Sheath fish. Mackerels. Maids. Plaice. Fry'd Oysters. Cockles. Prawnes. Smelts. Rock-fish. Gracious Lords. Sword fish. Skate-fish. Lamprills. Jegs. Pickerells. Golden Carps. Burbates. Salmons. Salmon-perls. Dolphins. Barn Trouts.

Miller's-Thumbs. Preeks. Bret-fish. Flounders. Sea nettles. Mullets. Gudgeons. Dabs and Sandings. Haddocks. Carpes. Pykes. Botitoes. Rochets. Sea-Bears. Sharplings. Tunnyes. Silver Eels. Chevins. Cray-fish. Pallours. Shrimps. Congers. Porposes. Bases. Shads. Murenes, a sort of Lampreys. Graylings. Smys. Turbots.

Trouts not above a foot long. Salmons. Meagers. Sea-Breams. Halibuts. Soles. Dog's-tongue or Kind-fool. Muskles. Lobsters. Great Prawnes. Dace. Bleaks. Tenches. Ombers. Fresh Cods. Dried Melwells. Darefish. Fausens, and Griggs. Eel-pouts. Tortoises. Serpents, i.e. Wood-Eeles. Dorces. Moor-game. Pearches. Loaches. Crab-fish. Snails and Whelks. Froggs.

If, when he had cramm'd all this down his Guttural Trap-door, he did not immediately make the Fish swim again in his Paunch, Death would pack him off in a trice; Special care is taken to Antidote his Godship with Vine-tree-Syrup. Then is sacrific'd to him, *Haberdines, Poor-Jack*, minglemangled mish-mash'd, &c.

Eggs fry'd, beaten,	*the Embers, toss'd in*	*Sea-Batts.*
butter'd, poach'd,	*the Chimney, & c.*	*Cod's-Ounds.*
hardened, boyl'd,	*Stock-fish.*	*Sea-Pikes.*
broyl'd, stew'd, slic'd,	*Green-fish.*	
roasted in		

Which to concoct and digest the more easily, Vinegar is multiply'd. For the latter part of their Sacrifices they offer,

Rice Milk and hasty Pudding.	*Stew'd Prunes, and bak'd Bullies.*	*Raisins.*
Butter'd Wheat and Flummery.	*Pistachoes or Fistick-Nuts.*	*Dates.*
Watergruel, and Milk-Porradge.	*Figgs.*	*Chestnuts and Wallnuts.*
Frumenty and Bonyclaber.	*Almond-Butter.*	*Filberds.*
	Skirret-Root.	*Parsenips.*
	White-Pot.	*Artichoakes.*

Perpetuity of Soaking with the whole.

'Twas none of their Fault, I'll assure you, if this same God of theirs was not publickly, preciously and plentifully serv'd in his Sacrifices, better yet than *Heliogabalus*'s Idol; nay, more than *Bell* and the *Dragon* in *Babylon* under King *Balshazzar*. Yet *Gaster* had the Manners to own that he was no God, but a poor, vile, wretched Creature. And as King *Antigonus*, first of the Name, when one *Hermodotus*, (as Poets will flatter, especially Princes) in some of his Fustian dubb'd him a God, and made the Sun adopt him for his Son, said to him, My *Lasanophore* (or in plain English, my Groom of the Close stool) can give thee the Lye; so Master *Gaster* very civilly us'd to send back his bigotted Worshipers to his Close-stool, to see, smell, taste, philosophise and examin what kind of Divinity they could pick out of his Sir-reverence.

CHAPTER LXI

How Gaster invented Means to get and preserve Corn.

THESE Gastrolatrous Hobgoblins being withdrawn, *Pantagruel* carefully minded the famous Master of Arts, *Gaster*. You know that by the Institution of Nature, Bread has been assign'd him for Provision and Food, and that as an addition to this Blessing, he should never want the means to get Bread.

Accordingly, from the beginning he invented the Smith's Art and Husbandry to manure the ground that it might yield him Corn; he invented Arms, and the Art of War to defend Corn; Physick and Astronomy, with other parts of Mathematicks, which might be useful to keep Corn a great number of Years in safety from the injuries of the Air, Beasts, Robbers and Purloiners; he invented Water, Wind and Hand-Mills, and a thousand other Engines to grind Corn, and turn it into Meal, Leaven to make the Dough ferment, and the use of Salt to give it a savour, for he knew that nothing bred more Diseases than heavy, unleaven'd, unsavoury Bread.

He found a way to get Fire to Bake it; Hour-glasses, Dials and Clocks to mark the time of its Baking; and as some Countries wanted Corn, he contriv'd means to convey some out of one Country into another.

He had the Wit to pimp for Asses and Mares, Animals of different *Species*, that they might Copulate for the Generation of a third, which we call Mules, more strong and fit for hard Service than the other two. He invented Carts and Waggons to draw him along with greater ease; and as Seas and Rivers hindred his Progress, he devis'd Boats, Gallies and Ships (to the astonishment of the Elements) to waft him over to barbarous, unknown, and far distant Nations, thence to bring, or thither to carry Corn.

Besides, seeing that, when he had tilled the ground, some years the Corn perish'd in it for want of Rain in due season, in others rotted, or was drown'd by its excess, sometimes spoil'd by Hail, eat by Worms in the Ear, or beaten down by Storms, and so his Stock was destroy'd on the ground; we were told that ever since the days of *Yore*, he has found out a way to Conjure the Rain down from Heaven only with cutting certain Grass, common enough in the Field, yet known to very few, some of which was then shown us: I took it to be the same as the Plant, one of whose Boughs being dipp'd by *Jove*'s Priest into the *Agrian* Fountain, on the *Lycian* Mountain in *Arcadia* in time of Drought, rais'd Vapours which gather'd into Clouds, and then dissolv'd into Rain, that kindly moisten'd the whole Country.

Our Master of Arts was also said to have found a way to keep the Rain up in the Air, and make it fall into the Sea; also to annihilate the Hail, suppress the Winds, and remove Storms as the *Methanensians* of *Trœzene* us'd to do. And as in the Fields, Thieves and Plunderers sometimes stole and took by force the Corn and Bread which others had toyl'd to get, he invented the Art of building Towns, Forts, and Castles, to hoard and secure that staff of Life; on the other hand, finding none in the Fields, and hearing that it was hoarded up and secur'd in Towns, Forts, and Castles, and watch'd with more care than ever were the Golden Pippins of the *Hesperides*, he turn'd Ingenier, and found ways to beat, storm, and demolish Forts and Castles with Machines, and Warlike Thunderbolts, battering Rams, Balists, and Catapults, whose shapes were shown us, not over-well understood by our Ingeniers, Architects, and other Disciples of *Vitruvius*, as Master *Philebert de l'Orme*, King *Megistus*'s principal Architect, has own'd to us.

And seeing that sometimes all these Tools of Destruction were baffled by the cunning subtilty, or the subtle cunning (which you please) of Fortifiers, he lately invented Cannons, Field-pieces, Culverins, Bombards, Basilisko's, Murthering Instruments that dart Iron, Leaden, and Brazen Balls, some of them outweighing huge Anvils; this by the means of a most dreadful Powder, whose Hellish Compound and Effect has even amazed Nature, and made her own her self out-done by Art; the *Oxydracan* Thunders, Hails and Storms, by which the people of that Name immediately destroy'd their Enemies in the Field, being but meer Pot-guns to these. For, one of our great Guns, when us'd, is more dreadful, more terrible, more diabolical, and maims, tears, breaks, slays, mows down, sweeps away more Men, and causes a greater Consternation and Destruction than a hundred Thunderbolts.

CHAPTER LXII

How Gaster invented an Art to avoid being hurt or touch'd by Cannon Balls.

GASTER having secur'd himself with his Corn within strong Holds, has sometimes been attack'd by Enemies, his Fortresses, by that thrice threefold curst Instrument, levell'd and destroy'd, his dearly beloved Corn and Bread snatch'd out of his Mouth, and sack'd by a Titannick Force, therefore he then sought means to preserve his Walls, Bastions, Rampiers, and Sconces from Cannon-shot, and to hinder the Bullets from hitting him, stopping them in their flight, or at least from doing him, or the Besiegers and Walls any damage; he show'd us a tryal of this, which has been since us'd by *Fronton*, and is now common among the Pastimes and harmless Recreations of the *Thelemites*. I'll tell you how he went to work, and pray for the future be a little more ready to believe what *Plutarch* affirms to have try'd; Suppose a Herd of Goats were all scampering as if the Devil drove 'em, do but put a bit of *Eringo* into the Mouth of the hindmost *Nanny*, and they will all stop stock-still, in the time you can tell three.

Thus *Gaster*, having caus'd a Brass Faulkon to be charg'd, with a sufficient quantity of Gunpowder, well purg'd from its Sulphur, and curiously made up with fine Camphir, he then had a suitable Ball put into the Piece, with twenty four little pellets like Hail-shot, some round, some pearl fashion, then taking his aim, and levelling it at a Page of his, as if he would have hit him on the Breast, about sixty strides off the Piece, half way between it and the Page in a right Line, he hang'd on a Gibbet by a Rope a very large Siderite or iron-like Stone, otherwise call'd *Herculean*, formerly found on *Ida* in *Phrygia* by one *Magnes* as *Nicander* writes, and commonly call'd Load-stone; Then he gave Fire to the Prime on the Piece's Touch-hole, which in an instant consuming the Powder, the Ball and Hail-shot, were with incredible violence and swiftness hurried out of the Gun at its Muzzle, that the Air might penetrate to its Chamber, where otherwise would have been a *Vacuum*; which Nature abhors so much that this Universal Machine, Heaven, Air, Land, and Sea, would sooner return to the Primitive *Chaos* than admit the least void any where. Now the Ball and small shot which threaten'd the Page with no less than quick Destruction, lost their impetuosity, and remain'd suspended and hovering round the Stone, nor did any one of them, notwithstanding the fury with which they rush'd, reach the Page.

Master *Gaster* could do more than all this yet, if you'll believe me, for he invented a way how to cause Bullets to fly backwards, and recoyl on those that sent 'em, with as great a force, and in the very numerical parallel for which the Guns were planted. And indeed, why should he have thought this difficult, seeing the Herb *Ethiopis* opens all Locks whatsoever, and an *Echineis* or *Remora*, a silly weakly Fish, in spight of all the Winds that blow from the 32 Points of the Compass, will in the midst of a Hurricane make you the biggest First Rate remain stock still as if she were becalm'd, or the Blustering Tribe had blown their last; nay, and with the Flesh of that Fish preserv'd with Salt, you may fish Gold out of the deepest Well that was ever sounded with a Plummet, for it will certainly draw up the precious Metal, since *Democritus* affirm'd it.

Theophrastus believ'd and experienc'd that there was an Herb at whose single touch an Iron Wedge tho never so far driven into a huge log of the hardest Wood that is, would presently come out, and 'tis this same Herb your *Hickways*, alias *Woodpeckers* use, when with some mighty Ax any one stops up the hole of their Nests, which they industriously dig and make in the Trunk of some sturdy Tree. Since Stags and Hinds when deeply wounded with Darts, Arrows, and Bolts, if they do but meet the Herb call'd *Dittany*, which is common in *Candia*, and eat a little of it, presently the shafts come out, and all's well again; even as kind *Venus* cur'd her Beloved By-blow *Æneas*, when he was wounded on the right Thigh with an Arrow by *Juturna Turnus*'s Sister. Since the very Wind of Laurels, Fig-trees, or Sea-calves, makes the Thunder sheer off, insomuch that it never strikes them. Since at the sight of a Ram, mad Elephants recover their former Sences; since mad Bulls coming near wild

Fig-trees call'd *Caprifici* grow tame, and will not budge a foot, as if they had the Cramp. Since the Venomous rage of Vipers is asswag'd, if you but touch them with a Beechen Bough. Since also *Euphorion* writes, that in the Isle of *Samos*, before *Juno*'s Temple was Built there, he had seen some Beasts call'd *Neades*, whose voice made the neighbouring places gape and sink into a Chasm and Abyss. In short, since Elders grow of a more pleasing Sound, and fitter to make Flutes in such places where the crowing of Cocks is not heard, as the Ancient Sages have writ, and *Theophrastus* relates; as if the crowing of a Cock dull'd, flatten'd and perverted the Wood of the Elder, as it is said to astonish and stupify with fear that strong and resolute Animal, a Lion.

I know that some have understood this of wild Elder, that grows so far from Towns or Villages that the crowing of Cocks cannot reach near it; and doubtless that sort ought to be preferr'd to the stenching common Elder that grows about decay'd and ruin'd places; but others have understood this in a higher sence, not litteral, but allegorical, according to the method of the *Pythagoreans*. As when it was said that *Mercury*'s Statue could not be made of every sort of Wood, to which Sentence they give this sence; That *God is not to be worshipp'd in a vulgar form, but in a chosen and religious manner.*

In the same manner by this Elder, which grows far from places where Cocks are heard, the Ancients meant, that the wise and studious ought not to give their minds to trivial or vulgar Musick, but to that which is Celestial, Divine, Angelical, more abstracted and brought from remoter parts, that is from a Region where the crowing of Cocks is not heard; for, to denote a solitary and unfrequented place, we say, Cocks are never heard to crow there.

CHAPTER LXIII

How Pantagruel fell asleep near the Island of Chaneph, and of the Problems propos'd to be solv'd when he wak'd.

THE next day merrily pursuing our Voyage we came in sight of the Island of *Chaneph*, where *Pantagruel*'s Ship could not arrive, the Wind chopping about, and then failing us, so that we were becalm'd, and could hardly get o' head, tacking about from Starboard to Larboard, and Larboard to Starboard, tho' to our Sails we had added Drablers.

With this accident we were all out of sorts, moping, drooping, metagrabolized, as dull as *Dun* in the Mire, in *C sol fa ut* flat out of Tune, off the hinges, and I don't know howish, without caring to speak one single syllable to each other.

Pantagruel was taking a Nap, slumbering and nodding on the Quarter-deck, by the Cuddy, with an *Heliodorus* in his hand, for still 'twas his custom to sleep better by Book than by Heart.

Epistemon was Conjuring with his Astrolabe to know what Latitude we were in.

Fryar *Jhon* was got into the Cook-room examining by the Ascendant of the Spits, and the Horoscope of Ragousts and Fricassees what time o' day it might then be.

Panurge (sweet Baby!) held a stalk of *Pantagruelion*, alias *Hemp*, next his Tongue, and with it made pretty Bubbles and Bladders.

Gymnast was making Tooth-pickers with Lentisk.

Ponocrates, dozing, doz'd, and dreaming dream'd, tickled himself to make himself laugh, and with one Finger scratch'd his Noddle where it did not itch.

Carpalim with a Nut-shell, and a Trencher of *Verne*, [that's a Card in *Gascony*] was making a pretty little merry Wind-mill, cutting the Card long-ways into four slips, and fastning them with a Pin to the Convex of the Nut, and its Concave to the tarr'd side of the Gunnel of the Ship.

Eusthenes bestriding one of the Guns, was playing on it with his Fingers, as if it had been a Trump-marine.

Rhizotome with the soft Coat of a Field-Tortoise, alias eclip'd a Mole, was making himself a Velvet Purse.

Xenomanes was patching up an old weather-beaten Lantern with a Hawk's Jesses.

Our Pilot (good Man!) was pulling Maggots out of the Seamen's Noses.

At last Fryar *Jhon* returning from the Fore-castle, perceiv'd that *Pantagruel* was awake. Then breaking this obstinate silence, he briskly and cheerfully asked him, how a Man should kill Time, and raise good Weather, during a Calm at Sea?

Panurge, whose Belly thought his Throat cut, back'd the Motion presently, and ask'd for a Pill to purge Melancholy?

Epistemon also came on, and ask'd how a Man might be ready to bepiss himself with Laughing, when he has no heart to be merry?

Gymnast arising, demanded a Remedy for a dimness of Eyes.

Ponocrates, after he had a while rub'd his Noddle, and shak'd his Ears, ask'd, How one might avoid Dog-sleep? Hold, cry'd *Pantagruel*, the Peripateticks have wisely made a Rule, that all Problems, Questions and Doubts which are offer'd to be solv'd, ought to be certain, clear, and intelligible; What do you mean by Dog-sleep? I mean, answer'd *Ponocrates*, to sleep fasting in the Sun at Noon-day, as the Dogs do.

Rhizotome, who lay stooping on the Pump, rais'd his drowsy Head, and lazily yawning, by natural sympathy, set almost every one in the Ship a yawning too; then ask'd for a Remedy against Oscitations and Gapings?

Xenomanes, half puzzled, and tir'd out with new vamping his antiquated Lantern, ask'd, How the Hold of the Stomach might be so well ballasted and freighted from the Keel to the Main-hatch with Stores well stowed, that our human Vessels might not heeld, or be walt, but well trimm'd, and stiff?

Carpalim twirling his diminutive Wind-mill, ask'd how many Motions are to be felt in Nature before a *Gentleman* may be said to be hungry?

Eusthenes hearing them talk, came from between Decks, and from the Capstern call'd out to know why a Man that's fasting, bit by a Serpent also fasting, is in greater danger of death than when Man and Serpent have eat their Breakfasts? Why a Man's fasting-spittle is poysonous to Serpents and venomous Creatures?

One single solution may serve for all your Problems, Gentlemen, answer'd *Pantagruel*, and one single Medicine for all such symptoms and accidents. My answer shall be short, not to tire you with a long needless train of pedantick Cant: The Belly has no Ears, nor is it to be fill'd with fair words; you shall be answer'd to content by signs and gestures. As formerly at *Rome*, *Tarquin* the Proud, its last King, sent an answer by signs to his Son *Sextus*, who was among the *Gabii*, (saying this, he pull'd the String of a little Bell, and Fryar *Jhon* hurried away to the

Cook-room.) The Son having sent his Father a Messenger to know how he might bring the *Gabii* under a close subjection; the King mistrusting the Messenger, made him no Answer, and only took him into his Privy-garden, and in his presence with his Sword lopt off the Heads of the tall Poppies that were there. The Express return'd without any other dispatch, yet having related to the Prince what he had seen his Father do, he easily understood that by those signs he advis'd him to cut off the Heads of the chief Men in the Town, the better to keep under the rest of the people.

CHAPTER LXIV

How Pantagruel gave no answer to the Problems.

PANTAGRUEL then ask'd, what sorts of People dwell'd in that Damn'd Island? They are, answer'd *Xenomanes*, all Hypocrites, holy Mountebanks, Tumblers of Beads, Mumblers of *Ave Maries*, spiritual Comedians, sham Saints, Hermits, all of them poor Rogues, who like the Hermit of *Lormont*, between *Blaye* and *Bordeaux*, live wholly on Alms given them by Passengers. Catch me there if you can, cry'd *Panurge*, may the Devil's Head-cook conjure my Bum-gut into a pair of Bellows, if ever you find me among them. Hermits, sham Saints, living Forms of Mortification, holy Mountebanks, avaunt, in the Name of your Father Sathan get out of my sight; when the Devil's a Hog you shall eat Bacon. I shall not forget yet a while our fat *Concilipetes* of *Chesil*; O that *Beelzebub* and *Astaroth* had counsell'd them to hang themselves out of the way, and they had done't, we had not then suffer'd so much by devilish Storms as we did for having seen 'em. Harkee me, dear Rogue, *Xenomanes*, my Friend, I pr'y thee, are these Hermits, Hypocrites, and Eves-droppers, Maids or Married? Is there any thing of the Femine Gender among them? Could a Body Hypocritically take there a small hypocritical Touch? Will they lye backwards, and let out their fore-rooms? There's fine Question to be ask'd, cry'd *Pantagruel*! Yes, yes, answer'd *Xenomanes*, you may find there many goodly Hypocritesses, jolly spiritual Actresses, kind Hermitesses, Women that have a plaguy deal of Religion; then there's the Copies of 'em, little Hypocritillons, Sham-sanctitos, and Hermitillons; Foh, away with them, cry'd Fryar *Jhon*, a young Saint an old Devil, (mark this, an old Saying, and as true a one, as a young Whore an old Saint.) Were there not such, continu'd *Xenomanes*, the Isle of *Caneph* for want of a multiplication of Progeny, had long ere this been desert and desolate.

Pantagruel sent them by *Gymnast* in the Pinnace seventy eight thousand fine pretty little Gold Half-Crowns, of those that are mark'd with a Lantern. After this he ask'd, What's o' Clock? Past nine, answer'd *Epistemon*. 'Tis then the best time to go to Dinner, said *Pantagruel*, for the sacred Line so celebrated by *Aristophanes* in his Play call'd *Concionatores*, is at hand, never failing when the shadow is decempedal.

Formerly among the *Persians* Dinner-time was at a set hour only for Kings; as for all others, their Appetite and their Belly was their Clock; when that chim'd, they thought it time to go to Dinner. So we find in *Plautus* a certain Parasite making a heavy do, and sadly railing at the Inventors of Hour-glasses and Dials, as being unnecessary things, there being no Clock more regular than the Belly.

Diogenes being ask'd at what times a Man ought to eat, answer'd, The Rich when he is hungry, the Poor when he has any thing to eat. Physicians more properly say, that the Canonical Hours are,

> *To rise at five, to dine at nine,*
> *To sup at five, to sleep at nine.*

The famous King *Petosiris*'s Magick was different—Here the Officers for the Gut came in, and got ready the Tables and Cupboards, laid the Cloth, whose sight and pleasant smell were very comfortable; and brought Plates, Napkins, Salts, Tankards, Flaggons, Tall-boys, Ewers, Tumblers, Cups, Goblets, Basons, and Cisterns.

Fryar *Jhon* at the head of the Stewards, Sewers, Yeomen of the Pantry, and of the Mouth, Tasters, Carvers, Cup-bearers, and Cupboard-keepers, brought four stately Pasties, so huge that they put me in mind of the four Bastions at *Turin*; 'ods Fish, how manfully did they storm them! What havock did they make with the long train of Dishes that came after them, how bravely

did they stand to their Pan puddings, and pay'd off their Dust!
How merrily did they soak their Noses!

The Fruit was not yet brought in, when a fresh gale at West
and by North began to fill the Main-course, Misen-sail, Fore-
sail, Tops, and Top-gallants; for which Blessing they all sung
divers Hymns of Thanks and Praise.

When the Fruit was on the Table, *Pantagruel* ask'd, Now tell
me, Gentlemen, are your Doubts fully resolv'd or no? I gape
and yawn no more, answer'd *Rhizotome*; I sleep no longer like a
Dog, said *Ponocrates*; I have clear'd my Eye-sight, said *Gymnast*;
I have broke my Fast, said *Eusthenes*; so that for this whole Day
shall be secure from the danger of my Spittle

Aspes.	Cychriodes.	Shrew-mice.
Amphisbenes.	Cafezates.	Miliares.
Anerudutes.	Cauhares.	Megalaunes.
Abedissimons.	Snakes.	Spitting Asps.
Alhartraz.	Cuhersks, Two-tongu'd	Porphyri.
Ammobates.	Adders.	Pareades.
Apimaos.	Amphibious Serpents.	Phalangs.
Alhatrabans.	Cenchrynes.	Pemphredons.
Aractes.	Cockatrices.	Pine-tree-worms.
Asterions.	Dipsades.	Rutelæ.
Alcharates.	Domeses.	Worms.
Arges.	Dryinades.	Rhagia.
Spiders.	Dragons.	Rhaganes.
Starry Lizards.	Elopes.	Salamanders.
Attelabes.	Enhydrides.	Sloe-worms.
Ascalabotes.	Fanuises.	Stellions.
Hæmorrhoids.	Galeotes.	Scorpenes.
Basilisks.	Harmenes.	Scorpions.
Fitches.	Handons.	Horn-worms.
Sucking Water-snakes.	Icles.	Scalavotins.
Black Wag leg-flies.	Jarraries.	Solofuidars.
Spanish flies.	Ilicines.	Deaf-Asps.
Catoblepes.	Pharao's Mice.	Horse-Leeches.
Horn'd Snakes.	Kesudures.	Salt-haters.
Caterpillars.	Sea-hares.	Rot Serpents.
Crocodiles.	Chalcidic Newts.	Stink-fish.
Toads.	Footed Serpents.	Stuphes.
Night-mares.	Manticores.	Sabtins.
Mad Dogs.	Mulures.	Blood-sucking-flies.
Colotes.	Mouse-serpents.	Hornfretters.

Scolopendres.   *Blind-worms.*   *Teristals.*
Tarantolas.   *Tetragnathias.*   *Vipers, &c.*

CHAPTER LXV

How Pantagruel past the Time with his Servants.

IN what Hierarchy of such venemous Creatures do you place *Panurge*'s future Spouse, ask'd Fryar *Jhon*? Art thou speaking ill of Women, cry'd *Panurge*, thou mangy Scoundrel, thou sorry, noddy-peak'd, shaveling Monk? By the *Cenomanic Paunch* and *Gixie*, said *Epistemon*, *Euripides* has written, and makes *Andromache* say it, that by Industry, and the help of the Gods, Men had found Remedies against all poisonous Creatures; but none was yet found against a bad Wife.

This flaunting *Euripides*, cry'd *Panurge*, was gabbling against Women every foot, and therefore was devour'd by Dogs, as a Judgment from Above; as *Aristophanes* observes—Let's go on, let him speak that's next. I can leak now like any Stone-horse, said then *Epistemon*. I am, said *Xenomanes*, full as an Egg and round as a Hoop; my Ship's Hold can hold no more, and will now make shift to bear a steddy Sail. Said *Carpalim*, A Truce with Thirst, a Truce with Hunger; They're strong, but Wine and Meat are stronger. I'm no more in the Dumps, cry'd *Panurge*, my Heart's a Pound lighter. I'm in the right Cue now, as brisk as a Body-Louse, and as merry as a Beggar. For my part, I know what I do when I drink; and 'tis a true thing (though 'tis in your *Euripides*) that is said by that jolly Toper *Silenus*, of blessed Memory, that

> *The Man's emphatically Mad,*
> *Who drinks the Best, yet can be sad.*

We must not fail to return our humble and hearty Thanks to the Being, who, with this good Bread, this cool delicious Wine, these good Meats and rare Dainties, removes from our Bodies and Minds these Pains and Perturbations, and, at the same time, fills us with Pleasure and with Food.

But methinks, Sir, you did not give an Answer to Fryar *Jhon*'s Question; which, as I take it, was, how to raise good Weather?

Since you ask no more than this easie Question, answer'd *Pantagruel*, I'll strive to give you satisfaction, and some other time we'll talk of the rest of the Problems, if you will.

Well then, Fryar *Jhon* ask'd how good Weather might be rais'd: have we not rais'd it? Look up, and see our full Top-sails; Hark! how the Wind whistles through the Shrouds, what a stiff Gale it blows; observe the Rattling of the Tacklings, and see the Sheats, that fasten the Main-sail behind; the force of the Wind puts them upon the stretch. While we pass'd our time merrily, the dull Weather also pass'd away, and while we rais'd the Glasses to our Mouths, we also rais'd the Wind by a secret sympathy in Nature.

Thus *Atlas* and *Hercules* clubb'd to raise and underprop the falling Sky, if you'll believe the wise Mythologists; but they rais'd it some half an inch too high; *Atlas* to entertain his Guest *Hercules* more pleasantly, and *Hercules* to make himself amends for the thirst which sometime before had tormented him in the Deserts of *Africa*.—Your good Father, said Fryar *Jhon*, interrupting him, takes care to free many People from such an inconveniency; for I have been told by many venerable Doctors, that his chief Butler *Turelupin* saves above eighteen hundred Pipes of Wine yearly, to make Servants and all comers and goers drink before they are a dry.—As the Camels and Dromedaries of a Caravan, continued *Pantagruel*, use to drink for the thirst that's past, for the present, and for that to come, so did *Hercules*; and being thus excessively rais'd, this gave a new motion to the Sky, which is that of Titubation and Trepidation, about which our crack-brain'd Astrologers make such a pother.—This, said *Panurge*, makes the saying good,

> *While jolly Companions carrouse it together,*
> *A fig for the Storm; it gives way to good Weather.*

Nay, continued *Pantagruel*, some will tell you, that we have not only shortned the time of the Calm, but also much disburthen'd the Ship, not like *Æsop*'s Basket, by easing it of the Provision, but by breaking our Fasts, and that a man is more Terrestrial and heavy when fasting, than when he has eaten and drank, even as they pretend that he weighs more dead than living. However 'tis you'll grant they are in the right, who take their Mornings draught, and Breakfast before a long Journey, then say that the Horses will perform the better, and that a Spur in the Head, is worth two in the Flank; or in the same Horse Dialect;

> That a Cup in the Pate
> Is a Mile in the Gate.

Don't you know that formerly the *Amycleans* worshiped the Noble Father *Bacchus* above all other Gods, and gave him the Name of *Psila*, which in the *Dorick* Dialect signifies *Wings*; for, as the Birds raise themselves by a towering flight with their Wings above the Clouds; so with the help of soaring *Bacchus*, the powerful Juice of the Grape, our Spirits are exalted to a pitch above themselves, our Bodies are more sprightly, and their Earthly Parts become soft and plyant.

CHAPTER LXVI

How by Pantagruel's Order the Muses were saluted near the Isle of Ganabim.

THIS fair wind and as fine talk brought us in sight of a high Land, which *Pantagruel* discovering afar off, shew'd it *Xenomanes*, and ask'd him, do you see yonder to the Leeward a high Rock with two tops, much like Mount *Parnassus* in *Phocis*? I do plainly, answer'd *Xenomanes*, 'tis the Isle of *Ganabim*; have you a mind to go ashoar there? No, return'd *Pantagruel*. You do well indeed, said *Xenomanes*, for there is nothing worth seeing in the place. The People are all Thieves; yet there is the finest Fountain in the World, and a very large Forest towards the right top of the Mountain. Your Fleet may take in Wood and Water there.

He that spoke last spoke well, quoth *Panurge*, let us not by any means be so mad as to go among a parcel of Thieves and Sharpers. You may take my word for 't, this Place is just such another, as, to my knowledge, formerly were the Islands of *Sark* and *Herm* between the smaller and the greater *Britain*; such as were the *Poneropolis* of *Philip* in *Thrace*; Islands of Thieves, Banditti, Picaroons, Robbers, Ruffians, and Murtherers, worse than *Raw-head* and *Bloody-bones*, and full as honest as the Senior

Fellows of the College of *Iniquity*, the very out-casts of the County-Gaol's Common-side. As you love your self, do not go among 'em; if you go, you'll come off but bluely, if you come off at all. If you will not believe me, at least believe what the good and wise *Xenomanes* tells you: for may I never stir if they are no worse than the very *Canibals*, they would certainly eat us alive. Do not go among 'em, I pray you, 'twere safer to take a Journey to Hell. Hark, by Cob's Body, I hear 'em ringing the Alarm-Bell most dreadfully, as the *Gascons* about *Bourdeaux* us'd formerly to do against the Commissaries and Officers for the Tax on Salt, or my ears tingle. Let's shear off.

Believe me, Sir, said Fryar *Jhon*, let's rather land, we'll rid the World of that Vermin, and inn there for nothing. Old Nick go with thee for me, quoth *Panurge*. This rash hair-brain'd Devil of a Fryar fears nothing, but ventures and runs on like a mad Devil as he is, and cares not a Rush what becomes of others; as if every one was a Monk like his Fryarship; a Pox on grinning Honour, say I. Go to, return'd the Fryar, thou mangy Noddy-peak! thou forlorn druggle-headed Sneaksby! And may a Million of black Devils Anatomise thy Cockle Brain. The Hen-hearted Rascal is so cowardly, that he berays himself for fear, every day. If thou art so afraid, Dunghill, don't go, stay here and be hang'd, or go and hide thy Logger-head under Madam *Proserpine*'s Petticoat.

Panurge hearing this, his Breech began to make Buttons, so he slunk in in an instant, and went to hide his Head down in the Bread-room among the musty Biscuits, and the Orts, and Scraps of broken Bread.

Pantagruel in the mean time said to the rest, I feel a pressing retraction in my Soul, which, like a Voice, admonishes me not to land there. Whenever I have felt such a motion within me, I have found my self happy in avoiding what it directed me to shun, or in undertaking what it prompted me to do, and I never had occasion to repent following its Dictates.

As much, said *Epistemon*, is related of the Dæmon of *Socrates*, so celebrated among the *Academics*. Well then, Sir, said Fryar *Jhon*, while the Ship's Crew water, have you a mind to have good sport? *Panurge* is got down somewhere in the Hold, where he is crept into some corner and lurks like a Mouse in a Cranny;

let 'em give the word for the Gunner to fire yon Gun over the Round-house on the Poop; this will serve to salute the *Muses* of this *Antiparnassus*; besides, the Powder does but decay in it. You are i' th' right, said *Pantagruel*; here, give the word for the Gunner.

The Gunner immediately came, and was order'd by *Pantagruel* to fire that Gun, and then charge it with fresh Powder, which was soon done; the Gunners of the other Ships, Frigats, Gallions, and Gallies of the Fleet hearing us fire, gave every one a Gun to the Island; which made such a horrid noise, that you'd have sworn Heav'n had been tumbling about our Ears.

CHAPTER LXVII

How Panurge bewray'd himself for fear; and of the huge Cat Rodilardus, which he took for a puny Devil.

PANURGE like a wild addle-pated giddy Goat, sallies out of the Bread Room in his Shirt, with nothing else about him but one of his Stockins, half on half off, about his Heel, like a rough-footed Pigeon, his Hair and Beard all bepowdered with Crums of Bread, in which he had been over Head and Ears, and a huge and mighty Pusse partly wrapt up in his other Stockin. In this Equipage, his Chops moving like a Monkey's who's a Louse-hunting, his Eyes staring like a dead Pig's, his Teeth chattering, and his Bum quivering, the poor Dog fled to Fryar *Jhon*, who was then sitting by the Chain-Wales of the Starboard-side of the Ship, and pray'd him heartily to take pity on him, and keep him in the safeguard of his trusty Bilbo, swearing by his share of Papimany that he had seen all Hell broke loose.

Woe's me, my *Jackee* (cry'd he) my dear *Johny*, my old Crony, my Brother, my Ghostly Father, all the Devils keep Holy-day, all the Devils keep their Feast to day, Man; Pork and Pease choak me, if ever thou sawest such preparations in thy life for an Infernal Feast. Dost thou see the Smoke of Hell's Kitchins? (This he said shewing him the Smoke of the Gun-powder above the Ships). Thou never sawest so many damn'd Souls since thou wast born; and so fair, so bewitching they seem, that one would swear they are *Stygian Ambrosia*. I thought at first, (God forgive me) they had been *English* Souls, and I don't know but that this Morning, the Isle of Horses near *Scotland* was sack'd with all the *English* who had surpris'd it, by the Lords of *Termes* and *Essay*.

Fryar *Jhon*, at the approach of *Panurge*, was entertain'd with a kind of smell that was not like that of Gun-powder, nor altogether so sweet as Musk; which made him turn *Panurge* about, and then he saw that his Shirt was dismally bepah'd, and beray'd with fresh Sir-reverence. The retentive Faculty of the Nerve which restrains the Muscle call'd *Sphincter* ('tis the Arse-hole an't please you) was relaxated by the violence of the fear which he had been in during his fantastic Visions. Add to this the thundering noise of the shooting, which seems more dreadful between Decks than above. Nor ought you to wonder at such a mishap, for one of the Symptoms and Accidents of Fear is, that it often opens the wicket of the Cupboard wherein second-hand-meat is kept for a time. Let's illustrate this noble Theme with some Examples.

Messer Pantolfe de la Cassina of *Siena*, riding Post from *Rome*, came to *Chamberry*, and alighting at honest *Vinet*'s, took one of the Pitch-forks in the Stable; then turning to the Inn-keeper, said to him *Da Roma in qua io non son andato del Corpo. Di gratia piglia in mano questa forcha, e fa mi paura.* I have not had a Stool since I left Rome; I pray thee take this Pitch-fork and fright me. *Vinet* took it, and made several offers, as if he would in good earnest have hit the Signor, but all in vain; so the *Sienese* said to him, *Si tu non fai altramente, tu non fai nulla: Pero sforzati di adoperarli piu guagliardamente*; If thou dost not go another way to work, thou hadst as good do nothing; therefore try to bestir thy self more briskly. With this, *Vinet* lent him such a swinging stoater with the Pitch-fork sowce between the Neck and the Collar of his Jerkin, that down fell *Signore* on the ground Arsy-versy with his spindle-shanks wide straggling over his Pole. Then mine Host sputtering, with a full-mouth'd laugh, said to his Guest, By *Belzebub's* Bum-gut, much good may do you, *Signore Italiano*, take notice this is *Datum Camberiaci*, given at *Chamberry*. 'Twas well the *Sienese* had untruss'd his Points and let down his Drawers; for this Physick work'd with him as soon as he took it, and as copious was the evacuation, as that of nine Buffeloes, and fourteen missificating Arch-lubbers. Which

Operation being over, the mannerly *Sienese* courteously gave mine Host a whole bushel of thanks, saying to him, *Io ti ringratio, bel messere; cosi faciendo tu m'ai esparagnata la speza d'un Servitiale*: I thank thee, good Landlord; by this thou hast e'en sav'd me the expence of a Clyster.

I'll give you another Example of *Edward* the Fifth, King of *England*. Master *Francis Villon* being banish'd *France*, fled to him, and got so far into his Favour as to be privy to all his Houshold Affairs. One day the King being on his Close-stool, show'd *Villon* the Arms of *France*, and said to him, Dost thou see what respect I have for thy French Kings? I have none of their Arms any where but in this Back-side near my Close-stool. Od's Life, said the *Buffoon*, how Wise, Prudent, and careful of your Health, your Highness is! How carefully your learned Doctor *Thomas Linacre* looks after you! He saw that, now you grow old, you are inclin'd to be somewhat Costive, and every day were fain to have an Apothecary, I mean, a Suppository or Clyster thrust into Royal *Nockandroe*, so he has, much to the purpose, induc'd you to place here the Arms of *France*; for the very sight of them puts you into such a dreadful Fright, that you immediately let fly, as much as would come from eighteen squattering *Bonasi* of *Peonia*: and if they were painted in other Parts of your house, by *Jingo*, you would presently conskite your self where-ever you saw them: Nay, had you but here a Picture of the great *Oriflamb* of *France*, Od's-bodikins, your Tripes and Bowels would be in no small Danger of dropping out at the Orifice of your Posteriors.—But henh, henh, *atque iterum* henh.

> *A silly Cockney am I not,*
> *As ever did from* Paris *come?*
> *And with a Rope and Sliding-knot*
> *My neck shall know what weighs my Bum.*

A Cockney of short reach, I say, shallow of Judgment, and judging shallowly to wonder, that you should cause your Points to be untrussed in your Chamber before you came into this Closet; by 'r Lady, at first I thought your Close-stool had stood behind the Hangings, or your Bed, otherwise it seem'd very odd to me you should untruss so far from the place of Evacuation. But now I find I was a Gull, a Wittal, a Woodcock, a meer Ninny, a

Jolt-head, a Noddy, a Changeling, a Calf-lolly, a Doddipole. You do wisely, by the Mass, you do wisely; for had not you been ready to clap your hind Face on the Mustard-Pot as soon as you came within sight of these Arms, mark ye me, Cop's Body, the bottom of your Breeches had supply'd the Office of a Close-stool.

Fryar *Jhon* stopping the handle of his Face with his Left-hand, did, with the Fore-finger of the Right, point out *Panurge*'s Shirt to *Pantagruel*; who, seeing him in this Pickle, scar'd, appall'd, shivering, raving, staring, beray'd, and torn with the Claws of the famous Cat *Rodilardus*, could not chuse but Laugh, and said to him, Pr'ythee what wouldst thou do with this Cat? With this Cat, quoth *Panurge*, the Devil scratch me, if I did not think it had been a young Soft-chin'd Devil, which, with this same Stocking instead of Mittain, I had snatch'd up in the great Hutch of Hell, as Thievishly as any Sizar of *Montague* College could ha' done. The Devil take *Tybert*, I feel it has all bespink'd my poor Hide, and drawn on it to the Life I don't know how many Lobster's Whiskers: with this he threw his Boar-Cat down.

Go, go, said *Pantagruel*, be bath'd and clean'd, calm your Fears, put on a clean Shirt, and then your Cloaths. What! do you think I am afraid? cry'd *Panurge*: Not I, I protest; by the Testicles of *Hercules*, I am more hearty and stout, tho' I say it that should not, than if I had swallow'd as many Flyes as are put into plumb Cakes, and other Paste at *Paris*, from *Midsummer* to *Christmas*— But what's this? hah! oh, oh, how the Devil came I by this? Do you call this what the *Cat* left in the Malt, Filth, Dirt, Dung, Dejection, fœcal Matter, Excrement, Stercoration, Sir-reverence, Ordure, Second-hand-meat, Fewmets, Stronts, Scybal or Syparathe? 'Tis *Hybernian* Saffron, I protest, Hah, hah, hah, 'tis *Irish* Saffron by *Shaint Pawtrick*. And so much for this time. Selah, Let's drink.

THE FIFTH BOOK

OF THE HEROICK DEEDS AND SAYINGS OF THE GOOD PANTAGRUEL

THE AUTHORS PROLOGUE

INDEFATIGABLE *Topers, and you Thrice precious Martyrs of the Smock, give me leave to put a serious Question to your Worships, while you are idly stroaking your Codpieces, and I my self not much better employ'd: Pray, Why is it that People say, that men are not such Sots now-a-days as they were in the days of Yore? Sot is an old word, that signifies a Dunce, Dullard, Jolthead, Gull, Wittal, or Noddy, one without Guts in his Brains, whose Cockloft is unfurnish'd, and in short, a Fool. Now would I know, Whether you would have us understand by this same Saying, as indeed you logically may, That formerly men were Fools, and this Generation is grown Wise? How many and what dispositions made them Fools? How many and what dispositions were wanting to make 'em Wise? Why were they Fools? How should they be Wise? Pray, how came you to know that men were formerly Fools? How did you find that they are now Wise? Who the Devil made 'em Fools? Who a God's Name made 'em Wise? Who d'ye think are most, those that lov'd Mankind Foolish, or those that love it Wise? How long has it been Wise? How long otherwise? Whence proceeded the foregoing Folly? Whence the following Wisdom? Why did the old Folly end now, and no later? Why did the Modern Wisdom begin now, and no sooner? What were we the worse for the former Folly? What the better for the succeeding Wisdom? How should the Ancient Folly be come to nothing? How should this same new Wisdom be started up and establish'd?*

Now answer me, an't please you; I dare not adjure you in stronger Terms, Reverend Sirs, lest I make your pious fatherly Worships in the least uneasie. Come, pluck up a good heart, speak the Truth, and shame the Devil. Be cheery, my Lads, and if you are for me, take me off three or five Bumpers to the best, while I make an halt of the first part of the Sermon; then answer my Question. If you are not, avaunt! avoid Satan! For I swear by my great Grandmother's Placket (and that's a horrid Oath!) that if you don't help me to solve that puzzling Problem, I will, nay, I already do repent, having propos'd it: For still I must

683

*remain netled and gravell'd, and the Devil a bit I know how to get off.
Well, what say you? I' faith, I begin to smell you out. You are not yet
dispos'd to give me an Answer; nor I neither, by these Whiskers. Yet to
give some Light into the business, I'll e'en tell you what had been
anciently foretold in the matter, by a Venerable Doc, who being mov'd
by the Spirit in a Prophetic Vein, wrote a Book eclip'd* The Prelatical
Bagpipe. *What d'ye think the Old Fornicator saith? Hearken, you old
Noddies, hearken now or never.*

> The Jubilee's Year, when all, like Fools, were shorn,
> Is about thirty (*Trente*) supernumerary.
> O want of Veneration! Fools they seem'd,
> But, persevering, with long Briefs, at last
> No more they shall be gaping greedy Fools:
> For they shall shell the Shrub's delicious Fruit,
> Whose Flow'r they in the Spring so much had fear'd.

> *L'an Jubilé que tout le monde raire*
> *Fadas se feist, est supernumeraire*
> *Audessus* Trente, *O peu de reverence*!
> *Fat il sembloit, mais, en perseverance*
> *De long Brevets, fat plus ne gloux sera;*
> *Car le doux fruict de l'herbe esgoussera*
> *Dont tant craignoit la fleur en prime vere.*

*Now you have it, what do you make on 't? The Seer is Ancient, the
Style Laconic, the Sentences dark, like those of* Scotus, *though they treat
of matters dark enough in themselves. The best Commentators on that
good Father take the Jubilee after the Thirtieth, to be the years that are
included in this present Age till 1550,* [there being but one Jubilee
every fifty Years.] *Men shall no longer be thought Fools next Green
Pease Season.*

The Fools whose Number, as Solomon *certifies, is infinite, shall go
to pot like a parcel of mad Bedlamites as they are; and all manner of
Folly shall have an end, that being also numberless, according to*
Avicenna, Maniæ infinitæ sunt species. *Having been driven back
and hidden towards the Centre, during the rigour of the Winter, 'tis
now to be seen on the Surface, and buds out like the Trees. This is as
plain as a Nose in a man's Face; you know it by experience, you see it.
And it was formerly found out by that great good Man* Hippocrates,
Aphorism. Veræ etenim maniæ, etc. *The World therefore, wisifying*

it self, shall no longer dread the Flower and Blossoms of Beans every coming Spring; that is, as you may believe, Bumper in Hand, and Tears in Eyes in the woful time of Lent, which us'd to keep them company.

Whole Cartloads of Books that seem'd florid, flourishing and flowry, gay and gawdy as so many Butterflies; but in the main were tiresome, dull, soporiferous, irksome, mischievous, crabbed, knotty, puzzling, and dark as those of Whining Heraclytus, *as unintelligible as the Numbers of* Pythagoras, *that King of the Bean according to* Horace: *Those Books, I say, have seen their best days, and shall soon come to nothing, being deliver'd to the executing Worms, and merciless Petty-Chandlers; such was their Destiny, and to this they were Predestinated.*

In their stead Beans in Cod are started up; that is, these Merry and Fructifying Pantagruelian *Books, so much sought now-a-days, in expectation of the following Jubilee's period; to the Study of which Writings all People have given their Minds; and accordingly have gain'd the Name of Wise.*

Now, I think, I have fairly solv'd and resolv'd your Problem; then reform and be the better for it. Hem once or twice like Hearts of Oak, stand to your Pan-puddings, and take me off your Bumpers, Nine go downs, and Huzza! since we are like to have a good Vintage, and Misers hang themselves: Oh! they'll cost me an Estate in Hempen Collars if fair Weather hold. For I hereby promise to furnish them with twice as much as will do their business, on free cost, as often as they will take the pains to dance at a Rope's end, providently to save Charges, to the no small disappointment of the Finisher of the Law.

Now my Friends, that you may put in for a share of this new Wisdom, and shake off the antiquated Folly, this very moment, scratch me out of your scrouls, and quite discard the symbol of the old Philosopher with the Golden Thigh, by which he has forbidden you to eat Beans: For you may take it for a truth granted among all Professors in the Science of good eating, that he enjoyn'd you not to taste of them, only with the same kind intent that a certain fresh-water Physitian had, when he did forbid to Amer, *late Lord of* Camelotiere, *Kinsman to the Lawyer of that Name, the Wing of the Partridge, the Rump of the Chicken, and the Neck of the Pigeon, saying,* Ala mala, Rumpum dubium, Collum bonum pelle remotâ. *For the Dunsical Dog-leech was so selfish, as to reserve them for his own dainty Chops, and allowed his poor*

Patients little more than the bare Bones to pick, lest they should over-load their squeemish Stomachs.

To the Heathen Philosopher succeeded a pack of Capusions, Monks, who forbid us the use of Beans, that is, Pantagruelian Books. They seem to follow the Example of Philoxenus and Gnatho, Sicilians of fulsome Memory, the Ancient Master-Builders of their Monastick Cramgut Voluptuousness; who when some dainty Bit was serv'd up at a Feast, filthily us'd to spit on it, that none but their nasty selves might have the stomach to eat of it, though their lickerish Chops watered never so much after it.

So those hideous, snotty, pthisicky, eves-dropping, musty, moving Forms of Mortification, both in publick and private, curse those dainty Books, and like Toads spit their Venom upon them.

Now though we have in our Mother-Tongue several excellent Works in Verse and Prose, and, Heav'n be prais'd, but little left of the Trash and Trumpery stuff of those dunsical Mumblers of Avemaries, and the barbarous foregoing Gothick Age; I have made bold to chuse to chirrup and warble my plain Ditty, or as they say, to whistle like a Goose among the Swans, rather than be thought deaf among so many pretty Poets and Eloquent Orators. And thus I am prouder of Acting the Clown, or any other under-part among the many Ingenious Actors in that Noble Play; than of herding among those Mutes, who, like so many shadows and Cyphers, only serve to fill up the House, and make up a number, gaping and yawning at the Flies, and pricking up their Lugs, like so many Arcadian Asses at the striking up of the Musick, thus silently giving to understand, that their Fopships are tickled in the right Place.

Having taken this Resolution, I thought it would not be amiss to move my Diogenical Tub, that you might not accuse me of living without Example. I see a swarm of our Modern Poets and Orators, your Collinets, Marots, Drouets, Saingelais, Salels, Masuels, and many more; who having commenc'd Masters in Apollo's Academy on Mount Parnassus, and drunk Brimmers at the Caballin Fountain, among the Nine merry Muses, have rais'd our Vulgar Tongue and made it a noble and everlasting Structure. Their Works are all Parian Marble, Alebaster, Porphiry, and Royal Ciment, they treat of nothing but Heroick Deeds, Mighty things, grave and difficult matters, and this in a Crimson Alamode Rhetorical Style. Their Writings are all Divine Nectar, rich, racy, sparkling, delicate and luscious Wine. Nor does our

Sex wholly engross this Honour; Ladies have had their share of the Glory: One of them of the Royal Blood of France, *whom it were a Prophanation but to name here, surprizes the Age at once by her transcendent and Inventive Genius in her Writings, and the admirable Graces of her Style. Imitate those great Examples, if you can, for my part I cannot. Every one, you know, cannot go to* Corinth. *When* Solomon *built the Temple, all could not give Gold by handfuls.*

Since then 'tis not in my Power to improve our Architecture as much as they, I am e'en resolv'd to do like Renault *of* Montauban; *I'll wait on the Masons, set on the Pot for the Masons, cook for the Stone-cutters; and since it was not my good luck to be cut out for one of them, I will live and die the Admirer of their Divine Writings.*

As for you, little envious Prigs, snarling, bastard, puny Criticks, you'll soon have rail'd your last: Go hang your selves, and chuse you out some well-spread Oak, under whose shade you may swing in state, to the admiration of the gaping Mob; you shall never want Rope enough. While I here solemnly protest before my Helicon, in the Presence of my Nine Mistresses the Muses, that if I live yet the Age of a Dog, ek'd out with that of three Crows, sound Wind and Limbs, like the old Hebrew *Captain* Moses, Xenophilus *the* Musicianer, *and* Demonax *the* Philosopher, *by Arguments no ways impertinent, and Reasons not to be disputed, I will prove, in the teeth of a parcel of Brokers and Retailers of Ancient Rhapsodies, and such mouldy Trash, That our Vulgar Tongue is not so mean, silly, poor, and contemptible, as they pretend. Nor ought I to be afraid of I know not what Botchers of old thredbare stuff a hundred and a hundred times clouted up and piec'd together; wretched Bunglers, that can do nothing but new vamp old rusty Saws; beggarly Scavengers, that rake even the muddiest Canals of Antiquity for scraps and bits of* Latin, *as insignificant as they are often uncertain. Beseeching our Grandees of* Witland, *that, as when formerly* Apollo *had distributed all the Treasures of his Poetical Exchequer to his Favourites, little hulchback'd* Æsop *got for himself the Office of Apologuemonger: In the same manner, since I do not aspire higher, they would not deny me that of Puny* Riparographer, *or Riffraff-scribler of the Sect of* Pyrrhicus.

I dare swear they will grant me this; for they are all so kind, so good-natur'd, and so generous, that they'll ne'er boggle at so small a Request. Therefore both dry and hungry Souls, Pot and Trenchermen, fully enjoying those Books, perusing, quoting them in their merry

Conventicles, and observing the great Mysteries of which they treat, shall gain a singular Profit and Fame; as in the like case was done by Alexander *the Great, with the Books of Prime Philosophy compos'd by* Aristotle.

O rare! Belly on Belly! what Swillers, what Twisters will there be!

Then be sure, all you that take care not to die of the Pip, be sure, I say, you take my Advice, and stock your selves with good store of such Books, as soon as you meet with them at the Booksellers, and do not only shell those Beans in Cods, but e'en swallow them down like an Opiat Cordial, and let them be in you, *I say, let them be* within you: *Then shall you find, my Beloved, what good they do to all clever Shellers of Beans.*

Here is a good handsome Basketful of them, which I here lay before your Worships; they were gather'd in the very individual Garden whence the former came. So I beseech you, Reverend Sirs, with as much Respect as e'er was paid by Dedicating Author, to accept of the Gift, in hopes of somewhat better against next Visit the Swallows give us.

THE FIFTH BOOK

CHAPTER I

How Pantagruel arriv'd at the Ringing Island, and of the noise that we heard.

PURSUING our Voyage, we sail'd three days without discovering any thing; on the fourth we made Land. Our Pilot told us, That it was the *Ringing Island*, and indeed we heard a kind of a confus'd and often-repeated Noise, that seem'd to us at a great distance not unlike the sound of great, middle-siz'd and little Bells rung all at once as 'tis customary at *Paris, Tours, Gergeau, Nantes*, and elsewhere on high Holidays; and the nearer we came to the Land, the louder we heard that Jangling.

Some of us doubted that this was the *Dodonan* Kettles, or the *Portico* call'd *Heptaphone* in *Olympia*, or the Eternal humming of the *Colossus* rais'd on *Memnon's* Tomb in *Thebes* of *Egypt*, or the horrid Din that us'd formerly to be heard about a Tomb at *Lipara*, one of the *Eolian* Islands. But this did not square with Chorography.

I don't know, said *Pantagruel*, but that some swarms of Bees here abouts may be taking a Ramble in the Air, and so the Neighbourhood make this dingle-dangle with Pans, Kettles, and Basons, the Coribanting Cimbals of *Cybele*, Grand-mother of the gods, to call them back. Let's hearken! when we were nearer, among the everlasting Ringing, we heard the indefatigable Singing (as we thought) of some Men. For this Reason, before we offer'd to land on the *Ringing Island, Pantagruel* was of opinion that we should go in the Pinnace to a small Rock, near which we discover'd an Hermitage, and a little Garden. There we found a diminutive old Hermit, whose name was *Braguibus*, born at *Glenay*. He gave us a full Account of all the Jangling, and regal'd us after a strange sort of a fashion; four live-long-days did he make us fast, assuring us, That we should not be admitted into the *Ringing Island* otherwise, because 'twas then one of the four *Fasting*, or *Ember-Weeks*. As I love my Belly, quoth *Panurge*, I by no means understand this Riddle; Methinks this should rather be one of the four Windy-weeks; for while we fast, we are only puff'd up with wind. Pray now, good Father Hermit, have not you here some other pastime besides Fasting; methinks 'tis somewhat of the leanest, we might well enough be without so many *Palace-holidays*, and those fasting *Times* of yours. In my *Donatus*, quoth Fryar *Jhon*, I could find yet but three *Times* or *Tenses*, the Preterit, the Present, and the Future, doubtless here the fourth ought to be a work of Supererogation. That *Time* or *Tense*, said *Epistemon*, is *Aorist*, deriv'd from the Preterimperfect Tense of the *Greeks*, admitted in War, and odd Cases: *Patience per force, is a Remedy for a Mad-Dog*. Saith the Hermit, 'tis as I told you, fatal to go against this, whoever does it, is a rank Heretick, and wants nothing but Fire and Faggot, that's certain. To deal plainly with you, my dear *Pater*, cri'd *Panurge*, being at Sea, I much more fear being wet, than being warm, and being drown'd than being burnt.

Well, however, let us fast a God's Name; yet I have fasted so long, that it has quite undermin'd my Flesh, and I fear that at last the Bastions of this Bodily Fort of mine will fall to ruin. Besides, I am much more afraid of vexing you in this same Trade of Fasting, for the Devil a bit I understand any thing in it, and it becomes me very scurvily, as several People have told me, and I am apt to believe them. For my part, I have no great Stomach to Fasting; for alas, 'tis as easie as pissing a Bed, and a Trade of which any body may set up, there needs no Tools. I am much more enclin'd not to fast for the future; for to do so, there's some Stock required, and some Tools are set a work. No matter, since you are so stedfast, and have us fast, let's fast as fast as we can, and then breakfast in the name of Famine; now we are come to these *esurial* idle Days. I vow, I had quite put them out of my head long ago. If we must fast, said *Pantagruel*, I see no other Remedy but to get rid of it as soon as we can, as we wou'd out of a bad way. I'll in that space of time somewhat look over my Papers, and examine whether the Marine Study be as good as ours at Land. For *Plato*, to describe a silly, raw, ignorant Fellow, compares him to those that are bred on

Ship-board, as we would do to one bred up in a Barrel; who never saw anything but through the Bunghole.

To tell you the short and long of the matter, our Fasting was most hideous and terrible; for, the first day we fasted at Fisti-cuffs, the second at Cudgels, the third at Sharps, and the fourth at Blood and Wounds; such was the Order of the Fairies.

CHAPTER II

How the Ringing Island had been inhabited by the Siticines,
who were become Birds.

HAVING fasted as aforesaid, the Hermit gave us a Letter for one whom he call'd *Albiam Camar*, Master *Ædituus* of the *Ringing Island*; but *Panurge* greeting him, call'd him, Master *Antitus*. He was a little quear old Fellow, bald pated, with a Snout whereat you might easily have lighted a Card-match, and a Phiz as red as a Cardinal's Cap. He made us all very welcome, upon the Hermit's Recommendation, hearing that we had fasted, as I have told you.

When we had well stuff'd our Puddings, he gave us an Account of what was Remarkable in the Island; affirming, That it had been at first inhabited by the *Siticines*; but that according to the course of Nature, as all things, you know, are subject to change, they were become Birds.

There I had a full Account of all that *Atteius Capito*, *Paulus*, *Marcellus*, *A. Gellius*, *Athenæus*, *Suidas*, *Ammonius* and others had writ of the *Siticines* and *Sicinnists*; and then we thought we might as easily believe the Transmutations of *Nectimene*, *Progne*, *Itys*, *Alcyone*, *Antigone*, *Tereus*, and other Birds. Nor did we think it more reasonable to doubt of the Transmogrification of the *Macrobian* Children into Swans, or that of the Men of *Pallene* in *Thrace* into Birds, as soon as they have bath'd themselves in the *Tritonic* Lake. After this, the Devil a word we could get out of him but of Birds and Cages.

The Cages were spacious, costly, magnificent, and of admir-able Architecture. The Birds were large, fine, and neat accord-ingly; looking as like the men in my Country, as one Pea do's like another; for they eat and drank like men, muted like men,

endued or digested like men, farted like men, but stunk like
Devils, slept, bill'd and trod their Females like men, but somewhat oftener; in short, had you seen and examin'd 'em from
Top to Toe, you would have laid your head to a Turnip, that
they had been meer Men. However, they were nothing less, as
Master *Ædituus* told us; assuring us at the same time, that they
were neither Secular nor Layic; and truth is, the diversity of
their Feathers and Plumes, did not a little puzzle us.

Some of them were all over as white as Swans, others as black
as Crows, many as grey as Owls, others black and white like
Magpies, some all red like Red-birds, and others purple and white
like some Pigeons. He call'd the Males, Clerghawks, Monkhawks,
Priesthawks, Abbothawks, Bishhawks, Cardinhawks, and one
Popehawk, who is a Species by himself. He call'd the Females,
Clergkites, Nunkites, Priestkites, Abbesskites, Bishkites, Car-
dinkites, and Popekites.

However, said he, as Hornets and Drones, will get among
the Bees, and there do nothing but buzz, eat and spoil everything; so, for these last Three hundred Years, a vast Swarm of
Bigottello's flockt I don't know how among these goodly Birds
every fifth full Moon, and have bemuted, bewray'd, and conskited the whole Island. They are so hard-favoured and monstrous,
that none can abide 'em. For their wry Necks make a figure like
a crooked Billet; their Paws are hairy like those of rough-footed
Pigeons; their Claws and Pounces, belly and breech like those
of the *Stymphalid Harpies*. Nor is it possible to root them out; for
if you get rid of one, strait four and twenty new ones fly thither.

There had been need of another Monster-hunter, such as
was *Hercules*, for Fryar *Jhon* had like to have run distracted about
it, so much he was nettled and puzzled in the matter. As for the
good *Pantagruel*, he was e'en serv'd as was Messer *Priapus*, contemplating the Sacrifices of *Ceres*, for want of Skin.

CHAPTER III

How there is but one Popehawk in the Ringing Island.

WE then ask'd Master *Ædituus* why there was but one *Popehawk*, among such numbers of venerable Birds, multiply'd in all

their Species? He answer'd, That such was the first Institution and fatal Destiny of the Stars. That the *Clerghawks* begot the *Priesthawks* and *Monkhawks*, without carnal Copulation, as some Bees are born of a young Bull. The *Priesthawks* beget the *Bishhawks*, the *Bishhawks* the stately *Cardinhawks*, and the stately *Cardinhawks*, if they live long enough, at last come to be *Popehawk*.

Of this last kind, there never is more than one at a time, as in a Bee hive there is but one King, and in the World is but one Sun.

When the *Popehawk* dies, another arises in his stead out of the whole Brood of *Cardinhawks*, that is, as you must understand it all along, without carnal Copulation. So that there is in that Species an individual Unity, with a perpetuity of Succession, neither more nor less than in the *Arabian* Phœnix.

'Tis true, that about Two thousand seven hundred and sixty Moons ago, two *Popehawks* were seen upon the Face of the Earth; but then you never saw in your lives such a woful Rout and Hurly-burly as was all over this Island. For all these same Birds did so peck, clapper-claw and maul one another all that time, that there was the Devil and all to do, and the Island was in a fair way of being left without Inhabitants. Some stood up for this *Popehawk*, some for t' other. Some, struck with a dumness, were as mute as so many Fishes; the Devil a Note was to be got out of them; Part of the merry Bells here were as silent as if they had lost their Tongues, I mean their Clappers.

During these troublesome Times, they call'd to their Assistance the Emperours, Kings, Dukes, Earls, Barons, and Commonwealths of the World that live on t' other side the Water; nor was this Schism and Sedition at an end, till one of them died, and the Plurality was reduc'd to Unity.

We then ask'd what mov'd those Birds to be thus continually chanting and singing? he answer'd, that it was the Bells that hang'd on the Tops of their Cages. Then he said to us, Will you have me make these *Monkhawks* whom you see bardocucullated with a Bag, such as you use to still Brandy, sing like any Wood-Larks? Pray do, said we. He then gave half a dozen pulls to a little Rope, which caus'd a diminutive Bell to give us many Tingtings, and presently a parcel of *Monkhawks* ran to him as if the Devil had drove 'em, and fell a singing like mad.

Pray Master, cry'd *Panurge*, if I also rang this Bell, could I make those other Birds yonder with Red-herring-colour'd Feathers, sing? Ay, marry wou'd you, return'd *Ædituus*. With this *Panurge* hang'd himself (by the hands, I mean) at the Bell-Rope's end, and no sooner made it speak, but those smoak'd Birds hy'd them thither, and began to lift up their Voices, and make a sort of an untowardly hoarse noise, which I grudge to call singing. *Ædituus* indeed told us, that they fed on nothing but Fish, like the Herns and Cormorants of the World, and that they were a fifth kind of *Cucullati* newly stamp'd.

He added, That he had been told by *Robert Valbringue*, who lately pass'd that way in his Return from *Africa*, that a sixth kind was to fly hither out of hand, which he call'd *Capushawks*, more grum, vinegar-fac'd, brainsick, froward, and loathsome, than any kind whatsoever in the whole Island. *Africa*, said *Pantagruel*, still uses to produce some new and monstrous Thing.

CHAPTER IV

How the Birds of the Ringing Island were all Passengers.

SINCE you have told us, said *Pantagruel*, how the Popehawk is begot by the Cardinhawks, the Cardinhawks by the Bishhawks, and the Bishhawks by the Priesthawks, and the Priesthawks by the Clerghawks, I would gladly know whence you have these same Clerghawks. They are all of them Passengers, return'd *Ædituus*, and come hither from t' other world; part out of a vast Countrey call'd *Want-o'-Bread*; the rest out of another toward the *West*, which they style, *Too-many-of-'em*. From these two Countries flock hither every year, whole Legions of these Clerghawks, leaving their Fathers, Mothers, Friends and Relations.

This happens when there are too many Children, whether Male or Female, in some good Family of the latter Countrey; insomuch that the House would come to nothing, if the Paternal Estate were shar'd among them all; (*as Reason requires, Nature directs, and God commands*). For this cause, Parents use to rid themselves of that Inconveniency, by packing off the Younger Fry, and forcing them to seek their Fortune in this *Isle Bossart*, (Crooked Island.) I suppose he means *l'Isle Bouchart*, near *Chinon*, cry'd *Panurge*. No, reply'd t' other, I mean *Bossart* (Crooked); for there is not one in ten among them, but is either crooked, crippled, blinking, limping, ill-favour'd, deform'd, or an unprofitable load to the earth.

'Twas quite otherwise among the Heathens, said *Pantagruel*, when they us'd to receive a Maiden among the number of Vestals; for *Leo Antistius* affirms that it was absolutely forbidden to admit a Virgin into that Order, if she had any Vice in her Soul, or Defect in her Body, tho' it were but the smallest Spot on any part of it. I can hardly believe, continued *Ædituus*, that their *Dams* on t' other side the Water go Nine Months with them; for they cannot endure them Nine Years, nay, scarce Seven, sometimes in the House: But by putting only a Shirt over the other Cloaths of the Young Urchins, and lopping off I don't well know how many Hairs from their Crowns, mumbling certain apostrophis'd and expiatory words, they visibly, openly, and plainly, by a Pythagorical *Metempsychosis*, without the least hurt, transmogrify them into such Birds as you now see; much after the fashion of the *Egyptian* Heathens, who us'd to constitute their *Isiacs*, by shaving them, and making them put on certain *Linostoles*, or Surplices. However, I don't know, my good Friends, but that these She-things, whether Clergkites, Monkites, and Abesskites, (that should not) instead of singing some plaisant Verses and *Charisters*, such as us'd to be sung to *Oromasis* by *Zoroaster*'s Institution, may be bellowing out such *Cataretes* and *Scythropys*, (curs'd, lamentable, and wretched Imprecations) as were usually offer'd to the *Arimanian* Dæmon; being thus in Devotion for their *kind* Friends and Relations, that transform'd them into Birds, whether when they were Maids, or Thornbacks, in their Prime, or at their last Prayers.

But the greatest number of our Birds come out of *Want-o'-bread*, which tho' a barren Countrey, where the days are of a most tedious lingring length, overstocks this whole Island with the lower Class of Birds. For hither flie the *Assaphis* that inhabit that Land, either when they are in danger of passing their time scurvily for want of Belly-timber, being unable, or, what's more likely, unwilling to take heart of grace, and follow some honest lawful calling, or too proud-hearted and lazy to go to service in some sober Family. The same is done by your frantick

Inamoradoes, who when cross'd in their wild Desires, grow stark-staring mad, and chuse this Life suggested to them by their despair, too cowardly to make them swing like their Brother *Iphis* of doleful Memory. There is another sort, that is, your Gaol birds, who having done some Rogue's Trick, or other heinous Villany, and being sought up and down to be truss'd up, and made to ride the Two or Three-legg'd Mare that groans for them, warily scour off, and come here to save their Bacon: Because all these sorts of Birds are here provided for, and grow in an instant as fat as Hogs, tho' they came as lean as Rakes: For having the Benefit of the *Clergy*, they are as safe as Thieves in a Mill, within this Sanctuary.

But, ask'd *Pantagruel*, Do these Birds never return to the world where they were hatch'd? Some do, answer'd *Ædituus*; formerly very few, very seldom, very late, and very unwillingly. However, since some certain Ecclypses, by the virtue of the Celestial Constellations, a great Crowd of them fled back to the World. Nor do we fret or vex our selves a jot about it; for those that stay, wisely sing, *The fewer, the better Cheer*; and all those that fly away first, cast off their Feathers here among these Nettles and Bryars.

Accordingly we found some thrown by there; and as we look'd up and down, we chanc'd to light on what some people will hardly thank us for having discover'd; and thereby hangs a Tale.

CHAPTER V

Of the dumb Knighthawks of the Ringing Island.

THESE Words were scarce out of his mouth, when some Five and twenty or Thirty Birds flew towards us: They were of a Hue and Feather like which we had not yet seen any thing in the whole Island. Their Plumes were as changeable as the Skin of the Chamelion, and the Flower of *Tripolion*, or *Tenerion*. They had all under the Left Wing a Mark like two Diameters dividing a Circle into equal parts, or (if you had rather have it so) like a Perpendicular Line falling on a Right Line. The Marks which each of them bore, were much of the same shape, but of different Colours; for some were White, others Green, some Red, others Purple, and some Blue. Who are those, ask'd *Panurge*, and how do you call them? They are Mongrels, quoth *Ædituus*.

We call them Knighthawks, and they have a great number of rich *Commanderies*, (fat Livings) in your World. Good your Worship, said I, make them give us a Song, an 't please you, that we may know how they sing. They scorn your words, cry'd *Ædituus*, they are none of your Singing Birds; but to make amends, they feed as much as the best two of them all. Pray, where are their Hens, where are their Females? said I. They have none, answer'd *Ædituus*. How comes it to pass then, ask'd *Panurge*, that they are thus bescabb'd, bescurf'd, all embroider'd o'er the Phiz with Carbuncles, Pushes, and Pockroyals; Some of which undermine the handles of their Faces. This same Fashionable and Illustrious Disease, quoth *Ædituus*, is common among that kind of Birds, because they are pretty apt to be toss'd on the Salt Deep.

He then acquainted us with the occasion of their coming. This, next to us, said he, looks so wistfully upon you, to see whether he may not find among your Company a stately gaudy kind of huge dreadful Birds of Prey, which yet are so untoward, that they ne'er could be brought to the *Lure*, nor to Perch on the Glove. They tell us that there are such in your World, and that some of them have goodly Garters below the knee, with an Inscription about them, which condemns him (*qui mal y pense*) who shall think ill of it, to be bewray'd and conskited. Others are said to wear the Devil in a String before their Paunches; and others a Ram's skin. All that's true enough, good Master *Ædituus*, quoth *Panurge*, but we have not the honour to be acquainted with their Knightships.

Come on, cry'd *Ædituus* in a merry mood, we have had Chat enough o' Conscience! let's e'en go Drink,—And Eat, quoth *Panurge*. Eat, reply'd *Ædituus*, and Drink bravely old Boy; Twist like Plough-jobbers, and Swill like Tinkers, Pull away and save Tide; for nothing is so dear or precious as Time, therefore we'll be sure to put it to a good use.

He wou'd fain have carried us first to bathe in the *Bagnio's* of the Cardinhawks, which are goodly delicious places, and have us lick'd over with precious Ointments by the Alyptes *alias* Rubbers, as soon as we should come out of the Bath. But

Pantagruel told him, that he could Drink but too much without that: He then led us into a spacious delicate Refectuary, or Fratrie-room, and told us, *Braguibus* the Hermit made you Fast Four days together; now, contrarywise, I'll make you Eat and Drink of the Best, four Days through-stitch before you budge from this place. But hark-ye-me, cry'd *Panurge*, mayn't we take a Nap in the mean time? Ay, ay, answer'd *Ædituus*, that's as you shall think good, for he that Sleeps, Drinks. Good Lord! how we liv'd! what good Bub! what dainty Cheer! Oh what an honest Cod was this same *Ædituus*!

CHAPTER VI

How the Birds are cramm'd in the Ringing Island.

PANTAGRUEL look'd I don't know howish, and seem'd not very well pleas'd with the Four days Junketting which *Ædituus* enjoyn'd us. *Ædituus*, who soon found it out, said to him, you know, Sir, that seven days before Winter, and seven days after, there is no Storm at Sea: For then the Elements are still, out of respect for the Halcyons, or Kingfishers, Birds sacred to *Thetis*, which then lay their Eggs and hatch their Young near the Shoar. Now here the Sea makes it self amends for this long Calm; and whenever some Foreigners come hither, it grows Boisterous and Stormy for four days together. We can give no other reason for it, but that it is a piece of its Civility, that those who come among us may stay whether they will or no, and be copiously Feasted all the while with the incomes of the Ringing. There-fore pray don't think your time lost, for willing, nilling, you'll be forc'd to stay; unless you are resolv'd to encounter *Juno*, *Neptune*, *Doris*, *Æolus* and his Fluster-blusters; and in short, all the pack of ill-natur'd left-handed Godlings and *Vejoves*. Do but resolve to be cheary, and fall to briskly.

After we had pretty well staid our stomachs, with some tight snatches, Fryar *Jhon* said to *Ædituus*, For ought I see, you have none but a parcel of Birds and Cages in this Island of yours, and the Devil-a-bit of one of them all that sets his hand to the Plough, or Tills the Land, whose Fat he devours: Their whole Business is to be frolick, to chirp it, to whistle it, to warble it, to sing it, and roar it merrily night and day; Pray then, if I may be so bold, Whence comes this Plenty and Overflowing of all dainty Bits and good Things which we see among you? From all the other World, return'd *Ædituus*, if you except some part of the *Northern* Regions, who of late Years have stirr'd up the *Jakes*; Mum! they may chance e're long to rue the day they did so; their Cows shall have Porrage, and their Dogs Oats; there will be work made among them, that there will: Come, a Fig for 't, let's drink,—But, pray what Country Men are you? *Tourain* is our Countrey, answer'd *Panurge*; Cod so, cry'd *Ædituus*, you were not then hatch'd of an ill Bird, I'll say that for you, since the blessed *Tourain* is your Mother. For from thence there comes hither every year such a vast store of good Things, that we were told by some folks of the Place that happen'd to touch at this Island, that your Duke of *Tourain*'s Income will not afford him to eat his Belly-full of Beans and Bacon [a good Dish spoil'd between *Moses* and *Pythagoras*] because his Predecessors have been more than liberal to these most holy Birds of ours, that we might here munch it, twist it, cram it, gorge it, craw it, riot it, junket it, and tickle it off, stuffing our Puddings with dainty Pheasants, Partridges, Pullets with Eggs, fat Capons of *Loudunois*, and all sorts of Venison and wild Foul. Come Box it about, Tope on my Friends. Pray do but see yon jolly Birds that are Perch'd together, how Fat, how Plump, and in good Case, they look with the Income that *Tourain* yields us! And in faith they Sing rarely for their good Founders, that's the truth on 't. You never saw any *Arcadian* Birds mumble more fairly than they do over a Dish, when they see these two gilt Battoons, or when I Ring for them these great Bells that you see above their Cages. Drink on, Sirs, whip it away, *verily* Friends, 'tis very fine Drinking to day, and so 'tis every day o' the week; then Drink on, Toss it about; here's to you with all my Soul, you are most heartily Welcome: Never spare it, I pray you, fear not we should ever want good Bub, and Belly-Timber; for, look here, though the Sky were of Brass, and the Earth of Iron, we should not want wherewithal to stuff the Gut, though they were to continue so Seven or Eight Years longer than the Famine in *Egypt*. Let us then with Brotherly Love and Charity refresh our selves here with the Creature.

Woons, Man, cry'd *Panurge*, what a rare time you have on 't in this World! Pshaw, return'd *Ædituus*, this is nothing to what we shall have in t' other: The *Elizian* Fields will be the least that can fall to our Lot. Come, in the mean time let's Drink here, come here's to thee old Fuddlecap.

Your first *Siticines*, said I, were superlatively wise, in devising thus a means for you to compass whatever all men naturally covet so much, and so few, or (to speak more properly) none can enjoy together; I mean, a Paradice in this Life, and another in the next; sure you were born wrapt in your Mother's smickits. O happy Creatures! O more than Men! would I had the luck to fare like you.

CHAPTER VII

How Pantagruel came to the Island of the Apedefers, or Ignoramus's, with long Claws, and Crooked Paws, and of terrible Adventures and Monsters there.

As soon as we had cast Anchor and had mor'd the Ship, the Pinnace was put over the Ship's side, and Mann'd by the Coxswain's Crew. When the good *Pantagruel* had prayed publickly, and given thanks to the Lord that had deliver'd him from so great a Danger, he stept into it with his whole Company, to go on shore, which was no ways difficult to do; for as the Sea was Calm, and the Winds laid, they soon got to the Cliffs. When they were set on shore, *Epistemon*, who was admiring the Scituation of the Place, and the strange shape of the Rocks, discover'd some of the Natives. The first he met, had on a short Purple Gown, a Doublet cut in Pains like a *Spanish* Leather Jerkin; half-sleeves of Satin, and the upper part of them Leather, a Coif like a Black Pot tipp'd with Tin; he was a good likely sort of a Body, and his name, as we heard afterwards, was *Double-fee*. *Epistemon* ask'd him, how they call'd those strange Craggy Rocks and Deep Vallies? He told him it was a Colony, brought out of *Attorney-land*, and call'd *Process*; and that if we forded the River somewhat further beyond the Rocks, we should come into the Island of the *Apedefers*. By the Memory of the *Decretals*, ask'd Fryar *Jhon*, tell us, I pray you, what you honest men here live on? Could not a man take a chirping Bottle with you, to taste your Wine? I can see nothing among you but Parchment, Ink-horns and Pens. We live on nothing else, return'd *Double-fee*; and all who live in this place must come through my hands. How, quoth *Panurge*, are you a Shaver then, do you fleece 'em? ay, ay, their Purse, answer'd *Double-fee*, nothing else. By the Foot of *Pharao*, cry'd *Panurge*, the De'll a Sous you'll get of me. How-ever, sweet Sir, be so kind as to shew an honest man the way to those *Apedefers*, or Ignorant People, for I come from the Land of the Learned, where I did not learn over much.

Still talking on, they got to the Island of the *Apedefers*, for they were soon got over the Ford. *Pantagruel* was not a little taken up with admiring the Structure and Habitation of the People of the Place. For they live in a swindging Wine-press, fifty steps up to it; you must know there are some of all sorts, little, great, private, middlesiz'd, and so forth. You go through a large *Peristile, alias* a long Entry set about with Pillars, in which you see in a kind of Landskip the Ruins of almost the whole World; besides so many great Robbers Gibbets, so many Gal-lows and Racks, that 'tis enough to fright you out of your seven Senses. *Double-fee* perceiving that *Pantagruel* was taken up with Contemplating those things, Let us go further, Sir, said he to him, all this is nothing yet. Nothing, quoth he, cri'd Fryar *Jhon*, By the soul of my over-heated Codpiece, Friend *Panurge* and I here shake and quiver for meer hunger. I had rather be drink-ing, than staring on those Ruins. Pray come along, Sir, said *Double-fee*. He then led us into a little Wine-press that lay back-wards in a blind Corner, and was call'd *Pithies* in the Language of the Country. You need not ask whether Master *Jhon* and *Panurge* made much of their sweet selves there; 'tis enough that I tell you, there was no want of *Bolonia* Sawcidges, Turky-poots, Capons, Bustards, Malmesy, and all other sorts of good Belly-Timber, very well drest.

A pimping Son of ten Fathers, who, for want of a better, did the Office of a Butler, seeing that Fryar *Jhon* had cast a Sheep's eye at a choice Bottle that stood near a Cupboard by it self, at some distance from the rest of the *Bottellic* Magazine, like a Jack in an Office, said to *Pantagruel*, Sir, I perceive that one of your Men here is making love to this Bottle, he ogles it, and would fain caress it; but I beg that none offer to meddle with it; for 'tis

reserv'd for their Worships. How, cri'd *Panurge*, there are some
Grandees here then I see: 'Tis Vintage-time with you, I perceive.

Then *Double-fee* led us up a private Stair-case, and shew'd us
into a Room, whence, without being seen, out at a Loop-hole,
we could see their Worships in the great Wine-press, where none
could be admitted without their leave. Their Worships, as he
call'd them, were about a score of fusty Crackropes and Gallow-
clappers, or rather more, all posted before a Bar, and staring at
each other like so many dead Pigs: Their Paws were as long as
a Crane's Foot, and their Claws four and twenty Inches long at
least; for you must know, they are injoin'd never to pair off the
least Chip of them, so that they grow as crooked as a Welch
Hook, or a Hedging Bill.

We saw a swindging Bunch of Grapes that are gather'd and
squeez'd in that Country, brought in to them. As soon as it was
laid down, they clapp'd it into the Press, and there was not a bit
of it out of which each of them did not squeeze some Oil of
Gold. Insomuch, that the poor Grape was tri'd with a Witness,
and brought off so drain'd and pick'd, and so dry, that there was
not the least moisture, juice or substance left in it, for they had
prest out its very quintessence.

Double-fee told us they had not often such huge Bunches, but,
let the worst come to the worst, they were sure never to be without others in their Press. But hark you me, Master of mine, ask'd
Panurge, Have they not some of different growth? ay marry have
they, quoth *Double-fee*; do you see here this little Bunch, to which
they are going to give t' other wrinch; 'Tis of Tyth-growth you
must know; they crush'd, wrung, squeez'd and strain'd out the
very heart's blood of it but t' other day, but it did not bleed
freely, the Oil came hard, and smelt of the Priest's Chest; so that
they found there was not much good to be got out of 't. Why
then, said *Pantagruel*, do they put it again into the Press? only,
answer'd *Double-fee*, for fear there should still lurk some Juice
among the Husks, and Hullings, in the Mother of the Grape.
The Devil be damn'd, cry'd Fryar *Jhon*, do you call these same
Folks illiterate Lobcocks, and Dunsical Doddipoles? May I be
broil'd like a Red-herring, if I don't think they are wise enough
to skin a Flint, and draw Oil out of a Brick-wall. So they are, said

Double-fee, for they sometimes put Castles, Parks, and Forests into the Press, and out of them all extract *Aurum potabile*. You mean, *Portabile*, I suppose, cri'd *Epistemon, such as may be born*. I mean as I said, repli'd *Double-fee, Potabile, such as may be drunk*; for it makes them drink many a good Bottle more than otherwise they should.

But I cannot better satisfy you as to the growths of the Vine-tree Syrup that is here squeez'd out of Grapes, than in desiring you to look your self yonder in that Back-yard, where you'll see above a thousand different growths that lie a waiting to be squeez'd every moment. Here are some of the publick, and some of the private growth; some of the Builders, Fortifications, Loans, Gifts and Gratuities, Escheats, Forfeitures, Fines and Recoveries, Penal Statutes, Crown-Lands and Demesne, Privy-Purse, Post-Office, Offerings, Lordships of Mannors, and a world of other growths for which we want Names. Pray, quoth *Epistemon*, tell me of what growth is that great one with all those little *Grapelings* about it. Oh, oh! return'd *Double-fee*, that plump one is of the Treasury, the very best growth in the whole Countrey; whenever any one of that growth is squeez'd, there is not one of their Worships but gets Juice enough out of it to soak his Nose six Months together. When their Worships were up, *Pantagruel* desir'd *Double-fee* to take us into that great Wine-press, which he readily did. As soon as we were in, *Epistemon*, who understood all sorts of Tongues, began to shew us many Devises on the Press which was large and fine, and made of the Wood of the Cross (at least *Double-fee* told us so.) On each part of it were Names of every thing in the Language of the Countrey. The Spindle of the Press was call'd *Receipt*; the Trough, *Cost and Damages*; the Hole for the Vice-pin, *State*; the Side-boards, *Money paid into the Office*; the great Beam, *Respit of homage*; the Branches, *Radiatur*; the Side-beams, *Recuperetur*; the Fats, *Ignoramus*;* the two-handled Baskets, *the Rolls*; the Treading place, *Acquittance*; the Dossers, *Validation*; the Panniers, *Authentic Decrees*; the Pailes, *Potentials*; the Funnel, *Quietus est*.

By the Queen of the Chitterlings, quoth *Panurge*, all the Hieroglyphics of *Egypt* are mine A— to this *Jargon*. Why! here's a

---

* *plus Valeur*. I don't know what it means.

parcel of Words full as analogous as Chalk and Cheese, or a Cat and a Cart-wheel! But why, pr'y thee, Dear *Double-fee*, do they call these Worshipful Dons of yours, Ignorant Fellows? Only, said *Double-fee*, because they neither are or ought to be Clerks, and all must be ignorant as to what they transact here; nor is there to be any other Reason given, but, *The Court hath said it; The Court will have it so; The Court has decreed it*. Cop's Body, quoth *Panurge*, they might full as well have call'd 'em *Necessity*; for *Necessity has no Law*.

From thence, as he was leading us to see a thousand little puny Presses, we spy'd another paltry Bar, about which sate four or five ignorant waspish Churls, of so testy, fuming a Temper, and so ready to take Pepper in the Nose for Yea and Nay, that a Dog would not have liv'd with 'em. They were hard at it with the lees and dregs of the Grapes, which they grip'd over and over again, might and main, with their clench'd Fists. They were call'd *Contractors*, in the Language of the Countrey: These are the ugliest, mishapen, grim-look'd Scrubbs, said Fryar *Jhon*, that ever were beheld with or without Spectacles. Then we pass'd by an infinite number of little pimping Wine-presses, all full of Vintage-mongers, who were picking, examining, and raking the Grapes with some Instruments call'd *Bills of Charge*.

Finally, We came into a Hall down Stairs, where we saw an overgrown curst mangy Curr with a pair of Heads, a Wolf's Belly, and Claws like the Devil of Hell. The Son of a Bitch was fed with *Cost*; for he liv'd on a *Mulctiplicity* of *Fine Amonds*, and Amercia-ments, by Order of their Worships, to each of whom the Monster was worth more than the best Farm in the Land. In their Tongue of Ignorance, they call'd him *Twofold*. His Dam lay by him, and her hair and shape was like her Whelp's; only she had four Heads two Male, and two Female, and her Name was *Fourfold*. She was certainly the most curs'd and dangerous Creature of the place, except her Grandam, that had been kept lockt up in a Dungeon, time out of mind, and her Name was *Refusing of Fees*.

Fryar *Jhon*, who had always twenty yards of Gut ready empty, to swallow a Gallimaufry of Lawyers, began to be somewhat out of humour, and desir'd *Pantagruel* to remember he had not din'd, and bring *Double-fee* along with him. So, away we went; and as we march'd out at the Back-gate, whom should we meet but an old piece of Mortality in Chains; he was half Ignorant, and half Learned, like an Hermaphrodite of Satan. The Fellow was all caparison'd with Spectacles, as a Tortoise is with Shells, and liv'd on nothing but a sort of Food, which, in their Gibberish, was call'd *Appeals*. *Pantagruel* ask'd *Double-fee*, of what Breed was that Prothonotary, and what Name they gave him? *Double-fee* told us, that, time out of mind, he had been kept there in Chains, to the great Grief of their Worships, who starv'd him; and his Name was *Review*. By the Pope's sanctify'd Two-pounders, cry'd Fryar *Jhon*, I don't much wonder at the meager Cheer which this old Chuff finds among their Worships, do but look a little on the weather-beaten Scratch *Toby*, Friend *Panurge*; by the sacred Tip of my Cowle, I'll lay Five Pounds to a Hazel-Nutt, the foul Thief has the very Looks of *Gripe-me-now*. These same Fellows here, ignorant as they be, are as sharp and knowing as other Folk. But were it my Case, I'd send him packing with a Squib in his Breech, like a Rogue enough as he is. By my oriental Barnicles, quoth *Panurge*, honest Fryar, thou'rt in the Right; for if we but examin that treacherous *Review*'s ill-favour'd Phiz, we find that the filthy Snudge is yet more mischievous and ignorant than these *Ignorant* Wretches here; since they (honest Dunces!) grapple and glean with as little harm and pother as they can, without any long Fiddle-come-farts or Tantalizing in the Case; nor do they dally and demur in your Suit, but, in two or three words, whip-stitch, in a trice, they finish the Vintage of the Close, bating you all those damn'd tedious Interlocutories, Examinations and Appointments, which frets to the hearts-blood your *Furr'd Law-cats*.

CHAPTER VIII

How Panurge related to Master Ædituus, the Fable of the Horse and the Ass.

WHEN we had cramm'd and cramm'd again, *Ædituus* took us into a Chamber that was well furnish'd, hung with Tapestry, and finely gilt. Thither he caus'd to be brought store of Mirabolans, Cashou, Green Ginger preserv'd, with plenty of Hypocras, and delicious Wine. With these Antidotes, that were like a sweeter *Lethe*, he invited us to forget the hardships of our Voyage; and at the same time he sent plenty of Provisions on board our Ships that rid in the Harbour. After this, we e'en jogg'd to Bed for that Night, but the Devil-a-bit poor Pilgarlic could sleep one wink, the everlasting jingle-jangle of the Bells kept me awake whether I would or no.

About midnight *Ædituus* came to wake us, that we might drink. He himself shew'd us the way, saying, You Men of t' other World say That Ignorance is the Mother of all Evil; and so far you are right; yet for all that, you don't take the least care to get rid of it, but still plod on, and live in it, with it, and by it; for which cause a plaguy-deal of mischief lights on you every day, and you are right enough serv'd; you are perpetually ailing somewhat, making a moan, and never right. 'Tis what I was ruminating upon just now. And, indeed, Ignorance keeps you here fasten'd in Bed, just as that Bully-rock *Mars* was detain'd by *Vulcan*'s Art; for all the while you don't mind that you ought to spare some of your Rest, and be as lavish as you can of the Goods of this famous Island. Come, come, you shou'd have eaten three Breakfasts already, and take this from me for a certain Truth, That if you wou'd consume the Mouth-Ammunition of this Island, you must rise betimes; Eat them, they multiply; Spare them, they diminish.

For Example: Mow a Field in due Season, and the Grass will grow thicker and better; don't mow it, and in a short time 'twill be floor'd with Moss. Let's drink, and drink again my Friends; come, let's all carouse it. The leanest of our Birds are now singing to us all; we'll drink to them if you please. Let's take off one, two, three, nine Bumpers, *Non Zelus, sed Charitas*.

When Day peeping in the East, made the Sky turn from Black to Red, like a boiling Lobster, he wak'd us again to take a Dish of Monastical Browess. From that time we made but one Meal that only lasted the whole Day; so that I cannot well tell how I may call it, whether Dinner, Supper, Nunchion, or After-Supper; only to get a Stomach, we took a turn or two in the Island, to see and hear the blessed singing Birds.

At Night *Panurge* said to *Ædituus*, Give me leave, sweet Sir, to tell you a merry Story of something that happen'd some three and twenty Moons ago in the Countrey of *Chastelleraudland*.

706

On the First of *April*, a certain Gentleman's Groom, *Roger* by Name, was walking his Master's Horses in some fallow ground. There 'twas his good Fortune to find a pretty Shepherdess, feeding her bleating Sheep, and harmless Lambkins, on the Brow of a neighbouring Mountain, in the shade of an adjacent Grove: Near her, some frisking Kids tripp'd it o'er a green Carpet of Nature's own spreading, and to compleat the Pastoral Landskip, There stood an Ass. *Roger*, who was a Wag, had a Dish of Chat with her, and after some If's, And's, and But's, Hem's, and Heigh's on her side, got her in the mind to get up behind him, to go and see his Stable, and there take a Bit by the bye in a Civil way. While they were holding a parley, the Horse directing his discourse to the Ass, (for all Brute Beasts spoke that year in divers places) whisper'd these words in his Ear: Poor Ass, how I pity thee! Thou slavest like any Hack, I read it on thy Crupper; thou do'st well however, since God has created thee to serve Mankind; thou art a very honest Ass: But not to be better Rub'd down, Curricomb'd, Trap'd, and Fed than thou art, seems to me indeed to be too hard a Lot. Alas! thou art all Rough-coated, in ill Plight; Jaded, Foundred, Crestfallen, and Drooping like a Mooting Duck, and Feedest here on nothing but coarse Grass, or Bryars and Thistles: Therefore do but Pace it along with me, and thou shalt see how we noble Steeds, made by Nature for War, are Treated; come, thou'lt lose nothing by coming, I'll get thee a taste of my Fare. I' troth Sir, I can but love you and thank you, return'd the Ass; I'll wait on you, good Mr. Steed. Methinks, Gaffer Ass, you might as well have said, Sir *Grandpaw* Steed. Oh! Cry mercy, good Sir *Grandpaw*, return'd the Ass; we Country Clowns are somewhat gross, and apt to knock Words out of joint. However, an 't please you, I'll come after your Worship at some distance, lest for taking this Run my Side should chance to be Firk'd and Curried with a Vengeance, as 'tis but too often, the more's my sorrow.

The Shepherdess being got behind *Roger*, the Ass follow'd, fully resolv'd to Bate like a Prince with *Roger*'s Steed. But when they got to the Stable, the Groom who spy'd the Grave Animal, order'd one of his Underlings to welcome him with the Pitchfork, and Curricomb him with a Cudgel. The Ass who heard this, recommended himself *Mentally* to the God *Neptune*, and

was packing off, thinking, and syllogizing within himself thus;
Had not I been an Ass, I had not come here among great Lords,
when I must needs be sensible that I was only made for the Use
of the small Vulgar; *Æsop* had given me a fair warning of this, in
one of his Fables. Well, I must e'en scamper, or take what follows. With this he fell a Trotting, and Winsing, and Yerking,
and Calcitrating, *alias* Kicking, and Farting, and Funking, and
Curvetting and Bounding, and Springing, and Galloping full drive,
as if the Devil had been come for him *in propriâ personâ*.

The Shepherdess who saw her Ass scour off, told *Roger* that
'twas her Cattle, and desir'd he might be kindly us'd, or else she
would not stir her foot over the Threshold. Friend *Roger* no sooner
knew this, but he order'd him to be fetch'd in, and that my Master's Horses should rather chop Straw for a Week together, than
my Mistress's Beast should want his Belly full of Corn.

The most difficult point was to get him back; for in vain the
youngsters complimented and cox'd him to come; I dare not,
said the Ass, I am bashful; and the more they strove by fair
means to bring him with them the more the stubborn Thing was
untoward, and flew out at heels; Insomuch that they might have
been there to this hour, had not his Mistress advis'd them to toss
Oats in a Sive, or in a Blanket, and call him, which was done,
and made him wheel-about, and say; Oats with a witness, Oats
shall go to pot, *adveniat*; Oats will do, there's Evidence in the
Case; but none of the Rubbing down, none of the Firking. Thus
Melodiously Singing, for as you know that *Arcadian* Bird's Note
is very Harmonious, he came to the young Gentlemen of the
Horse, *alias* Blackgarb, who brought him into the Stable.

When he was there, they plac'd him next to the great Horse,
his Friend, Rub'd him down, Curricom'd him, laid clean Straw
under him up to his Chin, and there he lay at Rack and Manger;
the first stuff'd with sweet Hay, the latter with Oats; which when
the Horse-*Valets-de-Chambre* sifted, he clap'd down his Lugs to
tell them by Signs that he would Eat it but too well without
sifting, and that he did not deserve so great an honour.

When they had well Fed, quoth the Horse to the Ass, Well,
poor Ass, how is it with thee now? How dost thou like this Fare?
Thou wert so nice at first, a body had much ado to get thee
hither. By the Fig, Answered the Ass, which one of our Ancestors

Eating, *Philemon* dyed Laughing, this is all sheer Ambrosia, good Sir *Grandpaw*. But what would you have an Ass say? Methinks all this is yet but half Cheer: don't your Worships here use now and then to take a leap? What Leaping dost thou mean? ask'd the Horse, the Devil leap thee, dost thou take me for an Ass? I' troth, Sir *Grandpaw*, quoth the Ass, I am somewhat a Blockhead you know, and can't for the heart's blood of me learn so fast the Court-way of speaking of you Gentlemen-horses; I mean don't you *Stallionize* it sometimes here among your metal'd Fillies? Tush, whisper'd the Horse, speak lower; for, by Bucephalus, if the Grooms but hear thee, they'll maul and belam me and thee thrice and three-fold; so that thou'lt have but little stomach to a leaping bout. Cod so, man, we dare not so much as grow stiff at the tip of the lowermost snout, tho' 'twere but to leak or so, for fear of being Jirk'd and Paid out of our Letchery. As for any thing else we are as happy as our Master, and perhaps more. By this Packsaddle, my old Acquaintance, quoth the Ass, I have done with you, a fart for thy Litter and Hay, and a fart for thy Oats: Give me the Thistles of our Fields, since there we leap when we list: Eat less, and leap the more, I say; 'tis Meat, Drink and Cloath to us. Ah! Friend *Grandpaw*, it would do thy heart good to see us at a Fair when we hold our Provincial Chapter! Oh! how we Leap it while our Mistresses are selling their Goslins and other Poultry! With this they parted: *Dixi*: I have done.

Panurge then held his Peace: *Pantagruel* would have had him to have gone on to the end of the Chapter: but *Ædituus* said, A word to the wise is enough; I can pick out the meaning of that Fable, and know who is that Ass and who the Horse; but you are a bashful youth I perceive: Well, know that there's nothing for you here, scatter no words. Yet, return'd *Panurge*, I saw but e'en now a pretty kind of cooing Abbeykite as white as a Dove, and her I had rather ride than lead. May I never stir, if she is not a dainty bit, and very worth a Sin or two. Heav'n forgive me! I meant no more harm in it than you; may the harm I meant in it befal me presently.

CHAPTER IX

How with much ado we got a sight of the Popehawk.

OUR Junketing and Banquetting held on at the same Rate the third day, as the two former. *Pantagruel* then earnestly desir'd to see the *Popehawk*; but *Ædituus* told him, it was not such an easy matter to get a sight of him. How, ask'd *Pantagruel*, has he *Plato*'s Helmet on his Crown, *Gyges*'s Ring on his Pounces, or a *Cameleon* on his Breast, to make him invisible when he pleases? No, Sir, return'd *Ædituus*, but he is naturally of pretty difficult access; however I'll see and take care that you may see him if possible. With this he left us piddling; then within a quarter of an hour came back, and told us the *Popehawk* is now to be seen; so he led us, without the least noise, directly to the Cage where-in he sate drooping, with his Feathers staring about him, attended by a Brace of little *Cardinhawks*, and six lusty fusty *Bishhawks*.

Panurge star'd at him like a dead Pig, examining exactly his Figure, Size, and Motions. Then with a loud voice he said, A Curse light on the hatcher of the ill Bird, o' my word this is a filthy *Whoophooper*. Tush, speak softly, said *Ædituus*, By G— he has a pair of Ears, as formerly *Michael de Metiscone* remark'd. What then, return'd *Panurge*, so hath a Whoopcat. So, said *Ædituus*, if he but hear you speak such another blasphemous word, you had as good be damn'd: Do you see that Basin yonder in his Cage? Out of it shall sally Thunderbolts and Lightnings, Storms, Bulls, and the Devil and all, that will sink you down to Peg-Trantums an hundred Fathom under ground. 'Twere better to drink and be merry, quoth Fryar *Jhon*.

Panurge was still feeding his Eyes with the sight of the *Pope-hawk*, and his Attendants, when somewhere under his Cage he perceiv'd a *Madgehowlet*; with this he cry'd out, By the Devil's-maker's Master, there's Roguery in the Case; they put Tricks upon Travellers here more than any where else, and would make us believe that a T—d's a Sugar-loaf. What damn'd cousening, gulling, and Coney-catching have we here! Do you see this *Madgehowlet*? by *Minerva* we are all beshit. Odsoons, said

Ædituus, speak softly, I tell you, 'tis no *Madgehowlet*, no she-thing, on my honest word, but a male and a noble Bird.

May we not hear the *Popehawk* sing, ask'd *Pantagruel*? I dare not promise that, return'd *Ædituus*, for he only sings and eats at his own time; so don't I, quoth *Panurge*, Poor Pilgarlic is fain to make every body's time his own; if they have time, I find time; Come then, let us go drink if you will. Now this is something like a Tansy, said *Ædituus*; you begin to talk somewhat like, still speak in that fashion, and I'll secure you from being thought an Heretic. Come on, I am of your mind.

As we went back to have t' other fuddling Bout, we spy'd an old green-headed *Bishhawk*, who sate moping with his Mate and three jolly *Bitter* Attendants, all snoring under an Arbor. Near the old Chuff stood a buxom *Abbeskite*, that sung like any Linet; and we were so mightily tickl'd with her singing, that I vow and swear we could have wish'd all our Members but one turn'd into Ears, to have had more of the melody. Quoth *Panurge*, This pretty Cherubin of Cherubins is here breaking her Head with chanting to this huge, fat, ugly-face, who lies grunting all the while like a Hog as he is. I'll make him change his Note presently in the Devil's Name. With this he rang a Bell that hung over the *Bishhawk*'s Head; but, tho' he rang and rang again, the Devil-a-bit *Bishhawk* would hear; the lowder the sound, the lowder his snoring. There was no making him sing. By G— quoth *Panurge*, You old Buzzard, if you won't sing by fair means, you shall by foul. Having said this, he took up one of *St. Stephen*'s Loaves, *alias* a Stone, and was going to hit him with it about the middle. But *Ædituus* cry'd to him, Hold, hold, honest Friend, strike, wound, poyson, kill and murther all the Kings and Princes in the World, by Treachery, or how thou wilt, and as soon as thou wouldst, unnestle the Angels from their Cockloft, *Popehawk* will pardon thee all this. But never be so mad as to meddle with these sacred Birds, as much as thou lov'st the profit, welfare and life not only of thy self, and thy Friends and Relations alive or dead, but also of those that may be born hereafter to the thousandth Generation; for so long thou wouldst entail misery upon them. Do but look upon that Basin. Cat-so! let us rather drink then, quoth *Panurge*. He that spoke last, spoke well, Mr. *Antitus*, quoth Fryar *Jhon*; while we are looking on these devilish Birds,

711

we do nothing but blaspheme; and while we are taking a Cup, we do nothing but praise God. Come on then, let's go drink: How well that word sounds!

The third day (after we had drank, as you must understand) *Ædituus* dismiss'd us. We made him a Present of a pretty little *Perguois* Knife, which he took more kindly than *Artaxerxes* did the Cup of cold Water that was given him by a Clown. He most courteously thank'd us, and sent all sorts of Provisions aboard our Ships, wish'd us a prosperous Voyage and Success in our undertakings, and made us promise and swear by *Jupiter* of Stone to come back by his Territories. Finally, he said to us, Friends, pray note that there are many more Stones in the world than men; take care you don't forget it.

CHAPTER X

How we arriv'd at the Island of Tools.

HAVING well ballasted the holds of our Human Vessels we weigh'd Anchor, hois'd up Sail, stow'd the Boats, set the Land, and stood for the Offing with a fair loom Gale, and for more hast unparrell'd the Misen yard, and lanch'd it and the Sail over her Lee-quarter, and fitted Gives to keep it steady, and boom'd it out; so in three days we made the Island of *Tools*, that is altogether uninhabited. We saw there a great number of Trees which bore Mattocks, Pickaxes, Crows, weeding Hooks, Sythes, Sickles, Spades, Trowels, Hatchets, hedging Bills, Saws, Addes, Bills, Axes, Sheers, Pincers, Bolts, Piercers, Augres and Wimblers.

Others bore Dags, Daggers, Poniards, Bayonets, Square-bladed Tucks, Stilettoes, Poinadoes, Skenes, Penknives, Puncheons, Bodkins, Swords, Rapiers, Backswords, Cutlasses, Semiters, Hangers, Falchions, Glaives, *Raillons*, Whittles and Whinyards.

Whoever would have any of these needed but to shake the Tree, and immediately they dropp'd down as thick as Hops, like so many ripe Plumbs; nay, what's more, they fell on a kind of Grass call'd Scabbard, and sheath'd themselves in it cleverly. But when they came down there was need of taking care lest they happen'd to touch the Head, Feet, or other Parts of the

Body. For they fell with the point downwards, and in they stuck, or slit the *continuum* of some Member, or lopp'd it off like a Twig; either of which generally was enough to have kill'd a man though he were a hundred year old, and worth as many thousand Spankers, Spur-royals and Rose-Nobles.

Under some other Trees, whose Names I can't justly tell you, I saw some certain sorts of Weeds that grew and sprouted like Pikes, Lances, Javelins, Javelots, Darts, Dartlets, Halbarts, Boar-spears, Eelspears, Partisans, Tridentes, Prongs, Trout-staves, Spears, Half-pikes and Hunting-Staffs. As they sprouted up and chanc'd to touch the Tree, strait they met with their Heads, Points and Blades, each suitable to its Kind, made ready for them by the Trees over them; as soon as every individual Wood was grown up, fit for its Steel; even like the Childrens Coats that are made for them as soon as they can wear them, and you wean them of their Swadling Clothes; nor do you mutter, I pray you, at what *Plato, Anaxagoras* and *Democritus* have said; Od's fish! they were none of your Lower-Form Gimcracks; were they?

Those Trees seem'd to us Terrestrial Animals, in no wise so different from Brute Beasts as not to have Skin, Fat, Flesh, Veins, Arteries, Ligaments, Nerves, Cartilages, Kernels, Bones, Marrow, Humours, *Matrices*, Brains and Articulations; for they certainly have some, since *Theophrastus* will have it so; but in this point they differ'd from other Animals, that their Heads, that is, the part of their Trunks next to the Root are downwards; their Hair, that is, their Roots, in the Earth; and their Feet, that is their Branches, upside down; as if a man should stand on his Head with outstretch'd Legs. And as you, batter'd Sinners, on whom *Venus* has bestow'd something to remember her, feel the approach of Rains, Winds, Cold, and every Change of Weather, at your *Ischiatic* Legs, and your *Omoplates*, by means of the perpetual Almanac which she has fix'd there; So these Trees have notice given them by certain sensations which they have at their Roots, Stocks, Gums, Paps or Marrow, of the growth of the Staffs under them; and accordingly they prepare suitable Points and Blades for them beforehand. Yet as all things, except God, are sometimes subject to Error, Nature its self is not free from it, when it produceth Monstrous things: likewise I observ'd something amiss in these Trees. For a Half-pike that grew up high enough to reach the Branches of one of these Instrument-iferous Trees, happen'd no sooner to touch them, but instead of being join'd to an Iron-head, it impal'd a stubb'd Broom at the Fondament. Well, no matter, 'twill serve to sweep the Chimney. Thus a *Pertusan* met with a Pair of Garden-shears; Come, all's good for something, 'twill serve to nip off little Twigs, and destroy Catterpillars. The Staff of a Halbert got the Blade of a Sythe, which made it look like an Hermaphrodite; happy be lucky, 'tis all a case, 'twill serve for some Mower. Oh 'tis a great Blessing to put our trust in the Lord! As we went back to our Ships, I spy'd behind I don't know what Bush, I don't know what Folks, doing I don't know what business, in I don't know what posture, scowring I don't know what Tools, in I don't know what manner, and I don't know what place.

CHAPTER XI

How Pantagruel arriv'd at the Island of Sharping.

WE left the Island of Tools to pursue our Voyage, and the next Day stood in for the Island of Sharping, the true Image of *Fontainbleau*; for the Land is so very lean there, that the Bones, that is the Rocks, shoot through its Skin. Besides, 'tis sandy, barren, and unpleasant. Our Pilot shew'd us there two little square Rocks, which had eight equal Points in the shape of a Cube; they were so white, that I might have mistaken them for Alabaster or Snow, had he not assur'd us they were made of Bone.

He told us that twenty chance Devils, very much fear'd in our Countrey, dwelt there in six different Stories, and that the biggest Twins or Braces of them were call'd Sixes, and the smallest Amb'sace; the rest Cinques, Quaters, Treys and Dewses. When they were conjur'd up, otherwise coupled, they were call'd either Sice cincq, Sice quater, Sice trey, Sice dewse, and Sice ace; or Cincq quater, Cincq trey, and so forth. I made there a shrewd Observation; would you know what 'tis, Gamesters? 'Tis that there are very few of you in the world but what call upon and invoke the Devils. For the Dice are no sooner thrown on the board, and the greedy gazing Sparks have hardly said, *two sixes, Frank*, but *six Devils damn it*, cry as many of them; if amb's ace, then, *A Brace of Devils broil me*, will they say. *Quater Deuse, Tom; the Dewse take it*, cries another, and so on to the end of the Chapter. Nay, they don't forget sometimes to call the Black Cloven-footed Gentlemen by their Christen-names and Sir-names; and what's stranger yet, they use them as their greatest Cronies, and make them so often the Executors of their Wills, not only giving themselves, but every body and every thing to the Devil, that there's no doubt but he takes care to seize, soon or late, what's so zealously bequeath'd him, Indeed 'tis true, *Lucifer* do's not always immediately appear by his lawful Attornies; but alas! 'tis not for want of good will; he is really to be excus'd for his delay, for what the Devil would you have a Devil do? he and his black Guards are then at some other places, according to the priority of the persons that call on them: There-fore pray let none be so venturesom as to think, that the Devils are deaf and blind.

He then told us, that more Wrecks had happen'd about those Square-rocks, and a greater loss of Body and Goods, than about all the *Syrtes, Sylla's* and *Charibdes, Sirens, Strophades* and *Gulphs* in the Universe. I had not much ado to believe it, remembring, that formerly amongst the wise *Egyptians, Neptune* was describ'd in Hieroglyphics by the first Cube, *Apollo* by an Ace, *Diana* by a Duce, *Minerva* by seven, and so forth.

He also told us that there was a Phial of *Sang real*, a most divine thing, and known but to a few. *Panurge* did so sweeten up the Syndics of the place, that they blest us with the sight of 't; but it was with three times more pother and ado, with more Formalities and antick Tricks, than they shew the Pandects of *Justinian* at *Florence*, or the Holy *Veronica* at *Rome*. I never saw, such a sight of Flambeaux, Torches and *Hagio's*, sanctifi'd Tapers, Rush-Lights, and Farthing Candles, in my whole life. After all, that which was shewn us, was only the ill-fac'd coun-tenance of a roasted Conny.

All that we saw there worth speaking of, was a good face set upon an ill game, and the shells of the two Eggs formerly laid up and hatch'd by *Læda*, out of which came *Castor* and *Pollux*, fair *Helen*'s Brothers. These same Syndics sold us a piece of 'em for a Song, I mean, for a morsel of bread. Before we went, we bought a parcel of Hats and Caps of the Manufacture of the place, which, I fear, will turn to no very good account: Nor are those who shall take 'em off our hands, more likely to commend their wearing.

CHAPTER XII

How we past through the Wicket, inhabited by Gripe-men-all,
Arch-Duke of the Furr'd Law-cats.

FROM thence *Condemnation* was pass'd by us: 'Tis another damn'd barren Island, whereat none for the world car'd to touch. Then we went through the *Wicket*, but *Pantagruel* had no mind to bear us company, and 'twas well he did not, for we were nabb'd there, and clapp'd into *Lob's-Pound* by Order of *Gripe-men-all*, Arch-Duke of the *Furr'd Law-cats*, because one of our Company wou'd ha' put upon a Serjeant some Hats of the *sharping* Island.

The *Furr'd Law-cats* are most terrible and dreadful Monsters, they devour little Children, and trample over Marble-Stones. 'Pray tell me, Noble Topers, do they not deserve to have their Snouts slit? The Hair of their Hides do's n't lie outward, but inwards; and every Mother's Son of 'em for his Devise wears a gaping Pouch, but not all in the same manner; for some wear it ty'd to their Neck Scarf-wise, others upon the Breech, some on the Paunch, others on the Side, and all for a Cause, with Reason and Mystery: They have Claws so very strong, long, and sharp, that nothing can get from 'em, that is once fast between their Clutches: Sometimes they cover their Heads with Mortar-like Caps, at other times with *mortify'd* Caparisons.

As we enter'd their Den, said a common Mumper to whom we had given half a *Teston, Worshipful Culprits, God send you a good Deliverance*. Examine well said he, the Countenance of these stout Props and Pillars of this Catch coin Law and *Iniquity*; and pray observe, that if you still live but Six Olympiads, and the Age of two Dogs more, you'll see these *Furr'd Law-cats* Lords of all *Europe*, and in peaceful Possession of all the Estates and Dominions belonging to it; unless by Divine Providence what's got over the Devil's Back is spent under his Belly; or the Goods which they unjustly get, perish with their Prodigal Heirs: Take this from an Honest *Poor* Beggar.

Among 'em reigns the *Sixth Essence*; by the means of which they gripe all, devour all, conskite all, burn all, draw all, hang all, quarter all, behead all, murther all, imprison all, waste all, and ruin all, without the least notice of Right or Wrong: For among *them* Vice is call'd Virtue; Wickedness Piety; Treason Loyalty; Robbery Justice; *Plunder* is their Motto, and when acted by them is approv'd by all Men, except the Heretics: and all this they do, because they dare; their Authority is Sovereign and Irrefragable.

For a sign of the Truth of what I tell you, you'll find that there the Mangers are above the Racks. Remember hereafter, that a Fool told you this; and if ever Plague, Famine, War, Fire, Earthquakes, Inundations, or other Judgments befal the World, do not attribute them to the Aspects and Conjunctions of the Malevolent Planets, to the Abuses of the Court of *Romania*, or the Tyranny of Secular Kings and Princes, to the Impostures of the false Zealots of the Cowl, Heretical Bigots, False Prophets and Broachers of Sects, to the Villany of griping Usurers, Clippers and Coiners, or to the Ignorance, Impudence, and Imprudence of Physicians, Surgeons, and Apothecaries, nor to the Lewdness of Adulteresses and Destroyers of By-blows; but charge 'em all wholly and solely to the inexpressible, incredible and inestimable Wickedness and Ruin, which is continually hatch'd, brew'd, and practis'd in the Den of those *Furr'd Law-cats*. Yet 'tis no more known in the world, than the *Cabala* of the *Jews*, the more's the Pity; and therefore 'tis not detested, chastis'd, and punish'd, as 'tis fit it shou'd be. But shou'd all their Villany be once display'd in its true Colours, and expos'd to the people, there never was, is, nor will be any Spokesman so sweet-mouth'd, whose fine colloguing Tongue cou'd save 'em; nor any Laws so rigorous and Draconic, that cou'd punish 'em as they deserve; nor yet any Magistrate so powerful, as to hinder their being burnt alive in their Conyboroughs without Mercy: Even their own *Furr'd Kittlings*, Friends and Relations would abominate 'em.

For this reason, as *Hannibal* was solemnly sworn by his Father *Amilcar* to pursue the *Romans* with the utmost hatred, as long as ever he liv'd; so, my late Father has enjoin'd me to remain here *without*, till God Almighty's Thunder reduce them

717

there *within* to Ashes, like other presumptuous *Titans*, Prophane Wretches, and Opposers of God; since Mankind is so inur'd to their Oppressions, that they either do not remember, foresee, or have a sense of the Woes and Miseries which they have caused; or if they have, either will, dare, or cannot root 'em out.

How! said *Panurge*, say you so! Catch me there and hang me! Damme, Let's march off! This Noble Beggar has scar'd me worse than the Thunder would do them. Upon this we were filing off; but alas! we found our selves trapp'd: The Door was double lock'd and barricado'd. Some Messengers of ill news told us, 'twas full as easy to get in there, as to get into Hell, and as hard for some to get out. Ay, there indeed lay the Difficulty: For there is no getting loose without a Pass and Discharge in due Course from the Bench. This for no other reason than because Folks go easier out of a Church than out of a Spunging-house, and they could not have our Company when they would. The worst on 't was when we got thro' the Wicket, for we were carry'd to get out our Pass or Discharge, before a more dreadful Monster than ever was read of in the Legends of Knight-Erranty: They call'd him *Gripe-men-all*: I can't tell what to compare it to, better than to a *Chymæra*, a *Sphynx*, a *Cerberus*; or to the Image of *Osiris*, as the *Egyptians* represented him, with Three Heads, one of a Roaring Lion, t' other of a Fawning Curr, and the last of a Howling Prowling Wolf, twisted about with a Dragon, biting his Tail, surrounded with Fiery Rays. His Hands were full of Gore, his Talons like those of the Harpies, his Snout like a Hawk's Bill, his Fangs or Tusks like those of an overgrown brindled Wild-Boare, his Eyes were flaming like the Jaws of Hell, all cover'd with Mortars interlac'd with Pestles, and nothing of his Arms was to be seen but his Clutches. His Hutch, and That of the *Warren cats* his Collaterals, was a long, spick-and-span new Rack, a top of which, (as the Mumper told us) some large, stately Mangers were fix'd in the Reverse. Over the Chief Seat was the Picture of an Old-woman holding the case or Scabbord of a Sickle in her Right-hand, a Pair of Scales in her Left, with Spectacles on her Nose: The Cups of the Balance were a Pair of Velvet-Pouches; the one full of *Bullion*, which overpois'd t' other, empty and long, hoisted higher than the middle of the Beam: I'm of opinion that it was the true Effigies of Justice *Gripe-men-all*; far different from the Institution of the ancient *Thebans*, who set up the Statues of their *Dicastes* without Hands, in Marble, Silver, or Gold, according to their Merit, even after their Death.

When we made our Personal Appearance before him, a sort of I don't-know-what men, all cloath'd with I don't-know-what Bags and Pouches, with long Scrowls in their Clutches, made us sit down upon a Cricket: [*Such as Criminals sit on when they are Try'd in* France.] Quoth *Panurge* to 'em, Good my Lords, I'm very well as I am; I'd as lieve stand, an 't please you. Besides, this same Stool is somewhat of the lowest for a Man that has new Breeches and a short Doublet. Sit you down, said *Gripe-men-all* again, and look that you don't make the Court bid you twice. Now, continu'd he, The Earth shall immediately open its Jaws, and swallow you up to quick Damnation, if you don't answer as you should.

CHAPTER XIII

How Gripe-men-all propounded a Riddle to us.

WHEN we were sate, *Gripe-men-all*, in the middle of his furr'd cats, call'd to us in a hoarse, dreadful Voice; Well, come on, give, give me presently—an answer. Well, come on, mutter'd *Panurge* between his Teeth; give, give me presently—a comforting Dram. Hearken to the Court, continu'd *Gripe-men-all*.

AN ENIGMA

A Young tight Thing, as Fair as may be,
Without a Dad Conceiv'd a Baby;
And brought him forth, without the Pother
In Labour made by teeming Mother.
Yet the curs'd Brat fear'd not to Gripe her,
But gnaw'd for haste her sides, like Viper.
Then the black Upstart boldly sallies,
And walks and flies o're Hills and Vallies.
Many fantastick Sons of Wisdom,
Amaz'd, foresaw their own in his Doom,
And thought, like an old *Græcian* Noddy,
A Human Spirit mov'd his Body.

ENIGME

Une bien jeune et toute blondelette
Conceut un fils Ethiopien sans pere;
Puis l'enfanta sans douleur la tendrette
Quoy qu'il sortit comme fait la vipere,
L'ayant rongé, en moult grand vitupere
Tout l'un des Flancs, pour son impatience,
Depuis, passa monts & vaux sans fiance,
Par l'Air volant, en terre cheminante;
Tant qu'estonna l'amy de sapience,
Qui l'estimoit estre humain animant.

Give, give me out of hand—an Answer to this Riddle, quoth *Gripe-men-all*. Give, give me—leave to tell you, good good, my Lord, answer'd *Panurge*, That if I had but a *Sphynx* at home, as *Verres* one of your Precursors had, I might then solve your *Enigma* presently; but verily, good my Lord, I was not there; and as I hope to be sav'd, am as innocent in the matter as the Child unborn. Foh, give me—a better Answer, cry'd *Gripe-men-all*, or by Gold, this shall not serve your turn; I'll not be paid in such Coin: if you have nothing better to offer, I'll let your Rascalship know, that it had been better for you to have fallen into *Lucifer*'s own Clutches, than into ours. Do'st thou see 'em here, Sirrah? hah? and do'st thou prate here of thy being Innocent, as if thou could'st be deliver'd from our Racks and Tortures for being so! Give me—Patience! Thou Widgeon, our Laws are like Cob-webs; your silly little Flies are stopt, caught, and destroy'd there; but your stronger Birds break them, and force and carry them which way they please. Likewise don't think we are so mad as to set up our Nets to snap up your great Robbers and Tyrants: No, they are somewhat too hard for us, there's no medling with them; for they would make no more of us, than we make of the little ones: But you paultry, silly, Innocent Wretches, must make us amends; and by Gold, we will *Innocentise* your Fopship with a Wannion, you never were so innocentis'd in your days.

Fryar *Jhon* hearing him run on at that mad rate, had no longer the power to remain silent, but cry'd to him, High-dey! Prithee, Mr. Devil in a Coif, would'st thou have a man tell thee more than he knows? has-n't the Fellow told you he does not know a

THE FIFTH BOOK

word of the business? his Name's *Twyford*. A Plague rot you,
won't Truth serve your turns? Why, how-now, Mr. *Prate-a-pace*,
(cry'd *Gripe-men-all*, taking him short) Marry come up, who
made you so sawcy as to open your Lips before you were spoken
to? Give me—Patience! By Gold! this is the first time since I
reign, that any one has had the impudence to speak before he
was bidden. How came this Mad Fellow to break loose? (Villain, thou liest, said Fryar *Jhon*, without stirring his lips.) Sirrah,
sirrah, continued *Gripe-men-all*, I doubt thou'lt have business
enough on thy hands, when it comes to thy turn to answer.
(Damme, thou liest, said Fryar *Jhon*, silently.) Do'st thou think,
continu'd my Lord, thou'rt in the Wilderness of your foolish
University, wrangling and bawling among the idle, wandring Searchers and Hunters after Truth? By Gold, we have here other
Fish to fry, we go another-gat's way to work, that we do: By
Gold, People here must give Categorical Answers to what they
don't know. By Gold, they must confess they have done those
things which they have not and ought not to have done. By
Gold, they must protest that they know what they never knew
in their lives: And after all, *Patience per Force* must be their only
remedy, as well as a Mad Dog's. Here silly Geese are pluck'd,
yet cackle not. Sirrah, Give me—an Account, Whether you had
a Letter of Attorney, or whether you were fee'd, or no, that you
offer'd to bawl in another man's Cause? I see you had no Authority to speak, and I may chance to have you wed to something
you won't like. Oh, you Devils, cry'd Fryar *Jhon*, Proto-Devils,
Panto-Devils, you would wed a Monk, would you? Ho ha, ho ha,
a Heretick, a Heretick, I'll give thee out for a rank Heretick.

CHAPTER XIV

How Panurge solv'd Gripe-men-all's Riddle.

GRIPE-MEN-ALL, as if he had not heard what Fryar *Jhon* said,
directed his Discourse to *Panurge*, saying to him, Well, what
have you to say for your self, Mr. *Rogue-enough*, hah! Give, give
me out of hand—an Answer. Say! quoth *Panurge*, why, what
would you have me say? I say, that we are damnably beshit,
since you give no heed at all to the Equity of the Plea, and the

721

Devil sings among you; let this Answer serve for all, I beseech you, and let us go about our business; I am no longer able to hold out, as gad shall judge me.

Go to, go to, cry'd *Gripe-men-all*; When did you ever hear that for these three hundred Years last past any body ever got out of this Weel, without leaving something of his behind him. No, no, get out of the Trap if you can, without losing Leather, Life, or at least some Hair, and you'll have done more than ever was done yet. For why, this would bring the Wisdom of the Court into question, as if we had took you up for nothing, and dealt wrongfully by you. Well, by hook or by crook we must have something out of you. Look ye, 'tis a folly to make a Rout for a fart and a doe; one word's as good as twenty; I have no more to say to thee, but that as thou likest thy former entertainment, thou'lt tell me more of the next; for 'twill go ten times worse with thee, unless, by Gold, you give me—a Solution to the Riddle I propounded. Give,—give it, without any more ado, I say.

By Gold, quoth *Panurge*, 'tis a black Mite, or Weevil, which is born of a white Bean, and sallies out at the hole which he makes, gnawing it: The Mite being turn'd into a kind of a Fly, sometimes walks and sometime flies over Hills and Dales. Now *Pythagoras* the Philosopher, and his Sect, besides many others, wondering at its Birth in such a place, (which makes some argue for equivocal Generation) thought that by a *Metempsycosis* the Body of that Insect was the Lodging of an Human Soul. Now were you *Men* here, after your welcom'd Death, according to his Opinion, your Souls wou'd most certainly enter into the Body of Mites or Weevils; for in your present state of life you are good for nothing in the world, but to gnaw, bite, eat, and devour all things; so in the next you'll e'en gnaw and devour your Mothers very sides, as the Vipers do. Now, by Gold, I think I have fairly solv'd and resolv'd your Riddle.

May my Bawble be turn'd into a Nut-cracker, quoth Fryar *Jhon*, if I could not almost find in my heart to wish that what comes out at my Bunghole were Beans, that these evil Weevils might feed as they deserve.

Panurge then, without any more ado, threw a large Leathern Purse stuff'd with Gold Crowns [*Escus au Soleil*] among them:

The Furr'd Law-Cats no sooner heard the jingling of the Chink, but they all began to bestir their Claws, like a parcel of Fiddlers running a Division; and then fell to 't, squimble, squamble, catch that catch can. They all said aloud, These are the Fees, these are the Gloves; now this is somewhat like a Tanzy: Oh, 'twas a pretty Trial, a sweet Trial, a dainty Trial. O' my word they did not starve the Cause; these are none of your sniveling *Forma Pauperis's*: No, they are Noble Clients, Gentlemen every Inch of them. By Gold, 'tis Gold, quoth *Panurge*, good old Gold, I'll assure you.

Saith *Gripe-men-all*, The Court upon a full Hearing, (of the Gold, quoth *Panurge*) and *weighty* Reasons *given*, finds the Prisoners *Not guilty*; and accordingly orders 'em to be discharg'd out of Custody, paying their Fees. Now, Gentlemen, proceed, go forwards, said he to us; we have not so much of the Devil in us, as we have of his Hue; tho' we are Stout, we are Merciful.

As we came out at the *Wicket*, we were conducted to the Port by a Detachment of certain Highland-Griffins, *scribere cum dashoes*, who advised us, before we came to our Ships, not to offer to leave the place, till we had made the usual Presents, first to the Lady *Gripe-men-all*, then to all the Furr'd Law-Pusses; otherwise *we must return to the place from whence we came*. Well, well, saith Fryar *Jhon*, we'll fumble in our Fobs, examine every one of us his Concern, and e'en give the Women their due; we'll ne'er boggle or stick out on that account; as we tickled the Men in the Palm, we'll tickle the Women in the right place. Pray, Gentlemen, added they, don't forget to leave somewhat behind you for us poor Devils to drink your Healths. O Lawd! never fear, answer'd Fryar *Jhon*, I don't remember that I ever went any where yet where the poor Devils are not mention'd and encourag'd.

CHAPTER XV

How the Furr'd Law Cats live on Corruption.

FRYAR *Jhon* had hardly said those words ere he perceiv'd Seventy Eight Gallies and Frigats just arriving at the Port. So he hied him thither to learn some News; and as he ask'd what

Goods they had o' board, he soon found that their whole Cargo was Venison, Hares, Capons, Turkeys, Pigs, Swine, Bacon, Kids, Calves, Hens, Ducks, Teals, Geese, and other Poultry and Wild-fowl.

He also spy'd among these some Pieces of Velvet, Satin and Damask. This made him ask the New-comers whither and to whom they were going to carry those dainty Goods? They answer'd that they were for *Gripe-men-all*, and the Furr'd Law-Cats.

Pray, asked he, what's the true name of all these things, in your Countrey Language? *Corruption*, they repli'd. If they live on Corruption, said the Friar, they'll perish with their Generation; May the Devil be damn'd, I have it now: Their Fathers devour'd the good Gentlemen, who, according to their state of life, us'd to go much a Hunting and Hawking to be the better inur'd to Toil in time of War; for Hunting is an Image of a Martial Life; and *Xenophon* was much in the right on 't, when he affirm'd that Hunting had yielded a great Number of excellent Warriors, as well as the *Trojan* Horse. For my part I am no Scholar, I have it but by hearsay, yet I believe it. Now the Souls of those brave Fellows, according to *Gripe-men-all*'s Riddle, after their decease, enter into Wild-boars, Stags, Roe-bucks, Herns, and such other Creatures, which they lov'd, and in quest of which they went while they were men; and these Furr'd Law-Cats having first destroy'd and devour'd their Castles, Lands, Demesnes, Possessions, Rents and Revenues, are still seeking to have their Blood and Soul in another Life. What an honest Fellow was that same Mumper who had forewarn'd us of all these things, and bid us take notice of the *Mangers* above the *Racks*!

But, said *Panurge* to the New-comer, how do you come by all this Venison? methinks the Great King has issued out a Proclamation, strictly inhibiting the destroying of Stags, Does, Wild-boars, Roe-bucks, or other Royal Game, on pain of Death. All this is true enough answer'd one of the rest: But the great King is so good and gracious, you must know, and these Furr'd Law-Cats so curst and cruel, so mad and thirsting after Christian Blood, that we have less cause to fear in trespassing against that Mighty Sovereign's Commands, than reason to hope to live, if we do not continually stop the mouths of these Furr'd Law-Cats with such Bribes and Corruption. Besides, added he, tomorrow *Gripe-men-all* marries a Furr'd Law-Puss of his to a high and mighty Double-furr'd Law-Tibert.

Formerly we us'd to call them *Chop-hay*; but alas, they are not such *neat* Creatures now as to eat any, or Chew the Cud. We call them Chop-Hares, Chop-Partridges, Chop-Woodcoks, Chop-Pheasants, Chop-pullets, Chop-Venison, Chop-Connies, Chop-Pigs; for they scorn to feed on coarser Meat. A T—d for their Chops, cry'd Frier *Jhon*, next year we'll have 'em called Chop-Dung, Chop-Stront, Chop-Filth.

Would you take my Advice, added he to the Company? What is it, answer'd we? Let's do two things, return'd he; First, Let's secure all this Venison and Wild-fowl, (I mean paying well for them:) for my part I am but too much tir'd already with our Salt-meat, it heats my Flanks so horribly; In the next place let's go back to the Wicket, and destroy all these devilish Furr'd Law-Cats. For my part, quoth *Panurge*, I know better things, catch me there, and hang me; No, I am somewhat more inclin'd to be fearful than bold, I love to sleep in a whole skin.

CHAPTER XVI

How Fryar Jhon talks of rooting out the Furr'd Law-cats.

VERTUE of the Frock, quoth Friar *Jhon*, what kind of a Voyage are we making? A shitten one o' my word; the Devil of any thing *we do* but fizzling, farting, funking, squattering, dozing, raving, and *doing nothing*. Ods Belly, 'tisn't in my Nature to lie idle, I mortally hate it; unless I am doing some Heroic Deed every foot, I can't sleep one wink o' nights. Dam it, did you then take me along with you for your Chaplain, to sing Mass and shrive you? By *Maunday-Thursday*, the first of ye all that comes to me on such an Account shall be fitted; for, the only Penance I'll enjoin shall be, that he immediately throw himself headlong over-board into the Sea like a wicked Cow-hearted Son of ten Fathers; this in deduction of the Pains of Purgatory.

What made *Hercules* such a famous Fellow, d'ye think? nothing, but that while he travell'd he still made it his business to rid the World of Tyrannies, Errors, Dangers, and Drudgeries, he still put to death all Robbers, all Monsters, all venemous Serpents and hurtful Creatures. Why then do we not follow his Example, doing as he did in the Countries through which we pass? He destroy'd the *Stymphalides*, the *Lernæan Hydra*, *Cacus*, *Antheus*, the *Centaurs*, and what not; I am no *Clericus*, those that are such, tell me so.

In imitation of that noble By-blow, let's destroy and root out these wicked Furr'd Law-Cats, that are a kind of Ravenous Devils; thus we shall remove all manner of Tyranny out of the Land. *Mawmet*'s Tutor swallow me Body and Soul, Tripes and Guts, if I would stay to ask your help or advice in the matter, were I but as strong as he was. Come, he that would be thought a Gentleman, let him storm a Town: Well then, shall we go? I dare swear we'll do their business for them with a wet Finger; they'll bear it, never fear; since they could swallow down more foul Language that came from us, than ten Sows and their Babies could swill Hogwash. Dam 'em, they don't value all the ill words or dishonour in the world at a Rush, so they but get the Coin into their Purses, though they were to have it in a shitten Clout. Come, we may chance to kill 'em all, as *Hercules* would have done, had they liv'd in his time. We only want to be set to work by another *Eurystheus*, and nothing else for the present; unless it be what I heartily wish them, That *Jupiter* may give 'em a short visit only some two or three hours long, and walk among their Lordships in the same Equipage that attended him when he came last to his Miss *Semele*, jolly *Bacchus*'s Mother.

'Tis a very great Mercy, quoth *Panurge*, that you have got out of their Clutches; for my part, I have no stomach to go there again; I'm hardly come to my self yet, so scar'd and appall'd I was; my hair still stands up an end when I think on 't; and most damnably troubled I was there, for three very weighty Reasons. First, Because I was troubled. Secondly, Because I was troubled. Thirdly and lastly, Because I was troubled. Heark'n to me a little on thy *right* side, Friar *Jhon*, my *left* Cod, since thou'lt not hear at the other: Whenever the Maggot bites thee, to take a Journey down to Hell, and visit the Tribunal of *Minos*, *Eacus*, and *Rhadamantus*, do but tell me, and I'll be sure to bear thee company, and never leave thee, as long as my name's *Panurge*, but will wade over *Acheron*, *Styx*, and *Cocytus*, drink whole Bumpers of *Lethe*'s Water, (tho I mortally hate that Element) and even pay thy Passage to that bawling cross-grain'd Ferryman *Charon*. But as for that damn'd *Wicket*, if thou art so weary of thy life as to go thither again, thou may'st e'en look for some body else to bear thee company; for I'll not move one step that way, e'en rest satisfy'd with this positive Answer. By my good-will, I'll not stir a foot to go thither as long as I live, any more than *Calpe* will come over to *Abyla*. [Calpe *is a Mountain in* Spain, *that faces another, call'd* Abyla *in* Mauritiania, *both said to have been sever'd by* Hercules.] Was *Ulysses* so mad as to go back into the *Cyclops*'s Cave to fetch his Sword? No marry was he not. Now I have left nothing behind me at the Wicket through forgetfulness, why then should I think of going thither?

Well, quoth Fryar *Jhon*, as good sit still as rise up and fall; what can't be cur'd, must be endur'd. But, pr'ythee, let's hear one another speak. Come, wert thou not a wise Doctor, to fling away a whole Purse of Gold on those mangy Scoundrels? Hah? A Squinzy choak thee, we were too rich, were we? Had it not been enough to have thrown the Hell-hounds a few cropt Pieces of white Cash?

How could I help it, returned *Panurge*? Did you not see how *Gripe-men-all* held his gaping Velvet-Pouch, and every Moment roar'd and bellow'd, *By Gold, give, give me out of hand; By Gold, give, give, give me presently.* Now, thought I to my self, we shall never come off scotfree; I'll e'en stop their Mouths with Gold, that the Wicket may be open'd, and we may get out; the sooner the better. And I judg'd that lowsy Silver would not do the business; for, d'ye see, Velvet-Pouches don't use to gape for little paultry clipt Silver, and small Cash: No, they are made for Gold, my Friend *Jhon*, that they are my dainty Cod. Ah! when thou hast been larded, basted, and roasted, as I was, thou'lt hardly talk at this rate, I doubt. But now what's to be done—we are enjoin'd by them to go for Wards.

The Scabby Slabberdegullions still waited for us at the Port, expecting to be greas'd in the Fist as well as their Masters. Now when they perceiv'd that we were ready to put to Sea, they came to Fryar *Jhon*, and begg'd that we might not forget to gratify the Apparitors before we went off, according to the Assessment for the Fees at our Discharge. Hell and Damnation, cry'd Fryar *Jhon*, Are you here still, ye Blood-hounds, ye citing, scribling Imps of Satan? Rot you, Am I not vext enough already, but you must have the impudence to come and plague me, ye scurvy Fly-catchers you? By Cob's-Body I'll gratify your Ruffianships as you deserve, I'll *Apparitorize* you presently, with a Wannion, that I will. With this he lugg'd out his slashing Cutlas, and, in a mighty heat, came out of the Ship, to cut the cousening Varlets into Stakes, but they scamper'd away, and got out of sight in a Trice.

However, there was somewhat more to do; for some of our Sailors, having got leave of *Pantagruel* to go o' shoar, while we were had before *Gripe-men-all*, had been at a Tavern near the Haven to make much of themselves, and roar it, as Seamen will do when they come into some Port. Now I don't know whether they had paid their Reck'ning to the full or no; but, however it was, an old fat Hostess meeting Friar *Jhon* on the Key, was making a woful Complaint, before a Sergeant, Son-in-law to one of the Furr'd Law-Cats, and a Brace of Bums his Assistants.

The Friar, who did not much care to be tir'd with their impertinent Prating, said to them, Harkee me, ye lubbardly Gnat-snappers, Do you presume to say, that our Seamen are not honest Men? I'll maintain they are, ye Dotterels, and will prove it to your brazen Faces, by *Justice*; I mean this trusty piece of cold Iron by my side; with this, he lugg'd it out, and flourish'd with it. The forlorn Lobcocks soon shew'd him their Backs, betaking themselves to their heels: But the old fusty Landlady kept her ground, swearing, like any Butter-whore, that the Tarpawlins were very honest Cods; but that they had only forgot to pay for the Bed on which they had lay'n after Dinner, and she ask'd Five-pence *French* Money for the said Bed. May I never sup, said the Friar, if it be not Dog-cheap; they are sorry Guests, and unkind Customers, that they are; they don't know when they have a Penniworth, and will not always meet with such Bargains; Come, I my self will pay you the Money, but I would willingly see it first.

The Hostess immediately took him home with her, and shew'd him the Bed, and having prais'd it for all its good *qualifications*, said that she thought, as Times went, she was not out

THE FIFTH BOOK

of the way, in asking Five-pence for 't. Friar *Jhon* then gave her
the Five-pence, and she no sooner turn'd her back, but he presently began to rip up the Ticking of the Feather-bed and Bolster,
and throw'd all the Feathers out at the window. In the mean
time the old Hag came down, and roar'd out for help, crying out
Murther, to set all the Neighbourhood in an Uproar. Yet she
also fell to gathering the Feathers that flew up and down in the
Air, being scatter'd by the wind. Friar *Jhon* let her bawl on, and,
without any further ado, march'd off with the Blanket, Quilt,
and both the Sheets, which he brought aboard undiscover'd; for
the Air was dark'ned with the Feathers, as it uses sometimes to
be with Snow. He gave them away to the Sailors, then said to
Pantagruel, that Beds were much cheaper at that place than in
Chinnonois, tho' we have there the famous Geese of *Pantile*; for
the old Bedlam had ask'd him but Five-pence for a Bed, which
in *Chinnonois* had been worth above Twelve *Francs*.*

CHAPTER XVII

*How we went For-wards, and how Panurge had like to have
been kill'd.*

WE put to Sea that very moment, steering our Course For-*wards*
and gave *Pantagruel* a full account of our Adventures, which so
deeply struck him with compassion, that he wrote some Elegies
on that Subject, to divert himself during the Voyage. When we
were safe in the Port, we took some Refreshment, and took in
fresh water and wood. The People of the place, who had the
countenance of jolly Fellows, and boon Companions, were all
of them For-*ward* Folks, bloated and pufft up with Fat; and we
saw some who slash'd and pink'd their Skin, to open a passage
to the Fat, that it might swell out at the slits and gashes which
they made: neither more nor less than the shitbreech Fellows
in our Countrey bepink and cut open their Breeches, that the
Tafety on the inside may stand out and be puff'd up. They said
that what they did was not out of Pride or Ostentation, but

* *There were several sorts of* Francs *then, some worth about Eighteen pence, others
four or five shillings.*

because otherwise their Skins would not hold them without much pain. Having thus slash'd their Skin, they us'd to grow much bigger, like the young Trees, on whose Barks the Gardeners make Incisions, that they may grow the better.

Near the Haven there was a Tavern which *forwards* seem'd very fine and stately; we repair'd thither, and found it fill'd with People of the Forward Nation, of all Ages, Sexes, and Conditions; so that we thought some notable Feast or other was getting ready: But we were told that all that Throng were Invited to the Bursting of mine Host, which caus'd all his Friends and Relations to hasten thither.

We did not understand that Jargon, and therefore thought that in that Countrey, by that Bursting they meant some Merrymeeting or other, as we do in ours, by Betrothing, Wedding, Groaning, Christening, Churching [*of Women*,] Shearing [*of Sheep*,] Reaping [*of Corn*,] or Harvest home, and many other Junketing Bouts that end in *ing*. But we soon heard that there was no such matter in hand.

The Master of the House, you must know, had been a Goodfellow in his time, lov'd heartily to wind up his Bottom, to bang the Pitcher, and lick his Dish; he us'd to be a very fair swallower of gravy Soupe, a notable accountant in matter of Hours; and his whole life was one continual Dinner, like mine Host at *Rouillac*. But now having Farted out much Fat for Ten years together, and water'd the Marigolds with much Wine of his own Burning, according to the Custom of the Countrey, he was drawing towards his Bursting hour; for neither the inner thin kell wherewith the Intrals are cover'd, nor his skin that had been jagg'd and mangl'd so many years, were able to hold and enclose his Guts any longer, or hinder them from forcing their way out; like a Wine-Vessel whose Sides fly out. Pray, quoth *Panurge*, is there no remedy, no help, for the poor Man, good People? Why don't you swaddle him round with good tight Girts, or secure his natural Tub with a strong Sorbopple-tree-hoop? Nay, Why don't you Iron-bind him, if needs be? This would keep the Man from Flying out and Bursting. The word was not yet out of his mouth, when we heard something give a loud Report, as if a huge sturdy Oak had been split in two; then some of the Neighbours told us, that the Bursting was over, and that the Clap, or Crack, which we heard, was the last Fart: And so there was an End of mine Host.

This made me to call to mind a Saying of the venerable Abbot of *Castillers*, the very same who never car'd to hump his Maids but when he was *in Pontificalibus*. That Pious Person, being much dunn'd, teiz'd, and importun'd by his Relations to resign his Abbey in his old Age, said and profess'd, That he would not Strip till he were ready to go to bed; and that the *last Fart* which his Reverend Paternity was to *utter*, shou'd be the *Fart of an Abbot*.

CHAPTER XVIII

How our Ships were Stranded, and we were reliev'd by some People that were Subject to Queen Whims [qui tenoient de la Quinte].

WE weighed and set Sail with a merry Westerly Gale, when about Seven Leagues off [Twenty two Miles] some gusts or scuds of Wind suddenly arose, and the Wind veering and shifting from Point to Point, was, as they say, like an old Woman's Breech, at no certainty; so we first got our Starboard Tacks Aboard, and Haled off our Lee Sheets. Then the Gusts encreas'd, and by fits blow'd all at once from several Quarters; yet we neither setled nor braded up close our Sails, but only let fly the Sheets, not to go against the Master of the Ship's Direction; and thus having let go amain, lest we should spend our Topsails, or the Ship's Quick-side should lye in the Water and she be overset, we lay by and run adrift, that is, in a Landlopers phrase, we temporis'd it. For he assur'd us, that as these gusts and whirlwinds would not do us much good, so they could not do us much harm, considering their easiness and pleasant strife, as also the clearness of the Sky, and calmness of the Current. So that we were to observe the Philosopher's Rule, *Bear, and Forbear*; that is, Trim, or go according to the Time.

However, these Whirlwinds and Gusts lasted so long, that we persuaded the Master to let us go and lye at Trie with our main Course; that is, to hale the Tack Aboard, the Sheet close aft, the Boling set up, and the Helm tied close Aboard; so after a Stormy Gale of wind we broke through the whirlwind. But 'twas like falling into *Scylla* to avoid *Carybdis*, [*out of the Frying-pan into the Fire.*] For we had not Sail'd a League, ere our Ships were Stranded upon some Sands, such as are the Flats of St. *Maixant*.

All our Company seem'd mightily disturb'd, except Fryar *Jhon*, who was not a jot daunted, and with sweet Sugar-plumb-words comforted now one, and then another, giving them hopes of speedy assistance from above, and telling them that he had seen *Castor* at the Main-yard-arm. Oh! that I were but now ashoar, cry'd *Panurge*, that's all I wish, for my self (at present) and that you who like the Sea so well, had each man of you Two hundred thousand Crowns; I would fairly let you set up Shop on these Sands, and wou'd get a fat Calf dress'd, and a hundred of Fag-gots, [*i.e. Bottles of Wine*] cool'd for you against you come ashoar. I freely consent never to mount a Wife, so you but set me ashoar, and mount me on a Horse that I may go home; no matter for a Servant, I'll be contented to serve my self; I am never bet-ter treated, than when I'm without a Man. Faith old *Plautus* was in the right on 't, when he said, The more Servants the more Crosses; for such they are, even supposing they could want what they all have but too much of, a Tongue, that most buisy, dan-gerous and pernicious Member of Servants; accordingly 'twas for their sakes alone, that the Racks, and Tortures for Confes-sion were invented, tho' some Foreign Civilians in our time have *uncivily* drawn alogical and unreasonable Consequences from it.

That very moment we spy'd a Sail that made toward us: when it was close by us, we soon knew what was the Lading of the Ship, and who was aboard of her. She was full Freighted with Drums: I was acquainted with many of the Passengers that came in her, who were most of 'em of good Families; among the rest, *Harry Cottiral*, an old Tost, who had got a swinging Ass's Touchtripe fasten'd to his waste, as the Good women's Beads are to their Girdle. In his left hand he held an overgrown greasy foul Cap, such as your Scald-pated *Fellows* wear, and in the right a huge Cabbage-stump.

As soon as he saw me he was over-joy'd, and bawl'd out to me, What Cheer ho? How dost like me now? Behold the true *Algamana*, (this he said shewing me the Asses Ticklegizard.) This Doctor's Cap is my true *Elixir*; and this (continu'd he, shaking the Cabbage-stump in his Fist) is *Lunaria Major*, you old Noddy, I have 'em, old Boy, I have 'em; we'll make 'em when thou'rt come back. But pray, Father, said I, whence come you? Whither are you bound? What's your Lading? Have you smelt the salt deep? To these Four Questions he answer'd, From Queen *Whims*; for *Touraine*; *Alchymy*; to the very Bottom.

Whom have you got o'board, said I? Said he, Astrologers, Fortunetellers, Alchymists, Rhimers, Poets, Painters, Projectors, Mathematicians, Watchmakers, Sing-songs, *Musitioners*, and the Devil and all of others that are Subject to Queen *Whims.**
They have very fair *legible Patents* to shew for 't, as any body may see. *Panurge* had no sooner heard this, but he was upon the High-Rope, and began to rail at them like mad. What o' Devil d'ye mean, cry'd he, to sit idly here like a pack of loitering Sneaks-bies, and see us stranded, while you may help us, and tow us off into the Current! A plague o' your *Whims*, you can make all things whatsoever they say, so much as good Weather, and little Children, yet won't make haste to fasten some Hawsers and Cables, and get us off. I was just coming to set you a'float, quoth *Harry Quottiral*; by *Trismegistus* I'll clear you in a Trice. With this he caus'd 7532810 huge Drums to be unheaded on one side, and set that open side so that it fac'd the end of our Streamers and Pendants; and having fastened them to good Tacklings, and our Ship's Head to the Stern of theirs, with Cables fasten'd to the Bits abaft the Manger in the Ship's Loof, they tow'd us off ground at one pull; so easily and pleasantly, that you'd have wonder'd at it, had you been there. For the Dub-o-dub rattling of the Drums, with the soft noise of the Gravel, which murmuring disputed us our way, and the merry Cheers and Huzzaes of the Sailors, made an Harmony almost as good as that of the Heavenly Bodies when they roul and are whirl'd round their Spheres; which rattling of the Celestial wheels, *Plato* said he heard some nights in his sleep.

We scorn'd to be behind-hand with 'em in Civility, and grate-fully gave 'em store of our Sawsidges and Chitterlings, with which we fill'd their Drums; and we were just a hoisting Two

---

* La Quinte, *This means a fantastick Humour, Maggots, or a foolish Giddiness of Brains; and also, a fifth, or the Proportion of Five in Musick, & c.*

and sixty Hogsheads of Wine out of the Hold, when two huge
Whirlpools with great Fury made towards their Ship, spouting
more water than is in the River *Vienne* [*Vigenna*] from *Chinon* to
Saumur: To make short, All their Drums, all their Sails, their
Concerns, and themselves were sows'd, and their very Hoze
were water'd by the Collar.

Panurge was so overjoy'd seeing this, and laugh'd so heartily,
that he was forc'd to hold his sides, and it set him into a Fit of
the Cholic for two hours and more. I had a mind, quoth he, to
make the Dogs drink, and those honest Whirlpools e'gad have
sav'd me that Labour and that Cost. There's Sawce for them;
ἄριστον μὲν ὕδωρ, Water's good, saith a Poet, let 'em *Pindarise*
upon 't; they never car'd for fresh water, but to wash their
Hands or their Glasses. This *good* Salt water will stand 'em in
good stead for want of *Sal Armoniac* and Nitre in *Geber*'s Kitchin.

We could not hold any further Discourse with 'em; for the
former Whirlwind hinder'd our Ship from feeling the Helm.
The Pilot advis'd us henceforwards to let her run adrift and follow the stream, not busying our selves with any thing, but making much of our Carcasses. For, our only way to arrive safe at the
Queendom of Whims, was to trust to the Whirlwind, and be led
by the Current.

CHAPTER XIX

How we arriv'd at the Queendom of Whims, or Enthelechy.

WE did as he directed for about twelve hours, and on the Third
day the Sky seem'd to us somewhat clearer, and we happily arriv'd
at the Port of *Mateotechny*, not far distant from *Queen-Whims*, *alias*
the *Quintessence*.

We met full-but on the Key a great number of Guards and
other Military Men that garison'd the *Arsenal*; and we were
somewhat frighted at first, because they made us all lay down
our Arms, and in a haughty manner ask'd us whence we came?

Cousin, quoth *Panurge* to him that ask'd the Question, we are
of *Touraine*, and come from *France*, being ambitious of paying
our Respects to the Lady *Quintessence*, and visit this famous
Realm of *Enthelechy*.

What do you say? cry'd they: Do you call it *Enthelechy* or *Endelechy*? Truly, truly, sweet Cousins, quoth *Panurge*, we are a silly sort of grout-headed Lobcocks, an 't please you; be so kind as to forgive us, if we chance to knock words out of joint; as for any thing else, we are dowright honest fellows, and true hearts.

We have not ask'd you this question without a cause, said they; for a great number of others who have pass'd this way from your Country of *Touraine*, seem'd as meer joltheaded Doddipoles, as ever were scor'd o're the Coxcomb, yet spoke as correct as other Folks. But there has been here from other Countries a pack of I know not over-weening self-conceited Prigs, as moody as so many Mules, and as stout as any Scotch Lairds, and nothing would serve these, forsooth, but they must wilfully wrangle and stand out against us at their coming: and much they got by it, after all: Troth we e'en fitted them, and claw'd 'em off with a vengeance, for all they look'd so big and so grum. Pray tell me, Do's your time lie so heavy upon you in your world, that you don't know how to bestow it better than in thus impudently talking, disputing and writing of our Sovereign Lady? There was much need that your *Tully*, the Consul, should go and leave the Care of his Commonwealth, to busie himself idly about her; and after him, your *Diogenes Laertius* the Biographer, and your *Theodorus Gaza* the Philosopher, and your *Argiropilus* the Emperor, and your *Bessario* the Cardinal, and your *Politian* the Pedant, and your *Budeus* the Judge, and your *Lascaris* the Embassador, and the Devil and all of those you call Lovers of Wisdom; whose number, it seems, was not thought great enough already, but lately your *Scaliger, Brigot, Chambrier, Francis Fleury*, and I can't tell how many such other junior sneaking Flyblows must take upon 'em to encrease it.

A Squincy gripe the Cods-headed Changelings at the Swallow, and eke at the cover-weesel; we shall make 'em;—But the Dewse take 'em; (they flatter the Devil here, and *smoothify* his name, quoth *Panurge*, between his Teeth:) You don't come here, continu'd the Captain, to uphold 'em in their Folly, you have no Commission from them to this Effect; well then, we'll talk no more on 't.

Aristotle, that first of Men and peerless Pattern of all Philosophy, was our Sovereign Lady's Godfather; and wisely and properly gave her the Name of *Entelechy*. Her true Name then

is *Entelechy*, and may he be in Tail beshit, and entail a Shit-a-bed
Faculty, and nothing else on his Family, who dares call her by
any other Name; for whoever he is, he do's her wrong, and is a
very impudent Person. You are heartily welcome, Gentlemen;
with this they coll'd and clipt us about the neck, which was no
small Comfort to us, I'll assure you.

Panurge then whisper'd me; Fellow-Traveller, quoth he, hast
thou not been somewhat afraid this Bout? a little, said I. To tell
you the truth of 't, quoth he, never were the *Ephraimites* in a
greater fear and quandary when the *Gileadites* kill'd and drowned
them for saying *Sibboleth*, instead of *Shibboleth*: And among
Friends, let me tell you, that perhaps there is not a man in the
whole Country of *Beauce*, but might easily have stopt my Bunghole with a Cart-load of Hay.

The Captain afterwards took us to the Queen's Palace, leading us silently with great Formality. *Pantagruel* would have said
something to him; but the other, not being able to come up to
his heighth, wish'd for a Ladder, or a very long Pair of Stilts;
then said, *Patience*, if it were our Sovereign Lady's Will, we'd be
as tall as you; well, we shall, when she pleases.

In the first Galleries we saw great numbers of sick persons,
differently plac'd according to their Maladies. The *Leprous*
were apart; those that were poison'd, on one side; those that had
got the Plague on another: Those that had the Pox, in the first
Rank; and the rest accordingly.

CHAPTER XX

How the Quintessence cur'd the sick with a Song.

THE Captain show'd us the Queen, attended with her Ladies
and Gentlemen, in the second Gallery. She look'd young, tho'
she was at least Eighteen hundred Years old; and was handsom,
slender, and as fine as a Queen, that is, as hands cou'd make her.
He then said to us, 'Tis not yet a fit time to speak to the Queen,
be you but mindful of her doings in the mean while.

You have Kings in your World, that fantastically pretend to cure
some certain Diseases; as for Example, *Scrophube* or Wens, swell'd
Throats, nick-nam'd the King's Evil, and Quartan Agues, only

with a touch: Now our Queen cures all manner of Diseases, without so much as touching the sick, but barely with a Song, according to the nature of the Distemper; he then shew'd us a Set of Organs, and said, that when it was touch'd by her, those miraculous Cures were perform'd. The Organ was indeed the strangest that ever Eyes beheld; for the Pipes were of *Cassia Fistula* in the Cod; the Top and Cornish of *Guayacum*; the Bellows of *Rhubarb*; the Pedals of *Turbith*; and the Clavier or Keys of *Scammony*.

While we were examining this wonderful new make of an Organ, the Leprous were brought in by her Abstractors, Spodizators, Masticators, Pregustics, Tabachins, Chachanins, Neemanins, Rabrebans, Nereins, Rozuins, Nedibins, Nearins, Segamions, Perazons, Chesepins, Sarins, Sotrins, Aboth, Enilins, Archasdarpenins, Mebins, Giborins, and other Officers, for whom I want names; so she plaid 'em I don't know what sort of a Tune or Song, and they were all immediately cur'd.

Then those who were poyson'd were had in, and she had no sooner given them a Song, but they began to find a use for their Legs, and up they got. Then came on the Deaf, the Blind and the Dumb, and they too were restor'd to their lost Senses with the same Remedy; which did so strangely amaze us (and not without reason, I think) that down we fell on our faces, remaining prostrate like men ravish'd in Extasy, and were not able to utter one word, thro' the excess of our Admiration, till she came, and having touch'd *Pantagruel* with a fine fragrant Nosegay of white Roses which she held in her hand, thus made us recover our Senses and get up. Then she made us the following Speech in *Byssin* Words, such as *Parisatis* desir'd should be spoken to her Son *Cyrus*, or at least of Crimson Alamode.

The Probity that scintillizes in the Superficies of your Persons, informs my ratiocinating Faculty, in a most stupendous manner, of the radiant Virtues, latent within the precious Caskets and Ventricles of your Minds. For, contemplating the mellifluous Suavity of your thrice discreet Reverences, 'tis impossible not to be perswaded with Facility that neither your Affections nor your Intellects are vitiated with any defect, or Privation of liberal and exalted Sciences; far from it, all must judge that in you are lodg'd a *Cornucopia*, and *Encyclopedia*, an unmeasurable Profundity of Knowledge in the most peregrine and sublime Disciplines; so frequently the Admiration, and so rarely the Concomitants of the imperite vulgar. This gently compels me, who in preceding Times indefatigably kept my private Affections absolutely subjugated, to condescend to make my Application to you in the trivial Phrase of the Plebeian World; and assure you, that you are well, most well, most heartily well, more than most heartily welcome.

I have no hand at making of Speeches, quoth *Panurge* to me privately; prithee, man, make answer to her for us if thou canst; this would not work with me, however, neither did *Pantagruel* return a word; so that Queen-*Whims*, or Queen *Quintessence* (which you please) perceiving that we stood as mute as Fishes, said: Your Taciturnity speaks you not only Disciples of *Pythagoras*, from whom the venerable Antiquity of my Progenitors in successive propagation was eman'd and derives its Original: but also discovers, that, through the Revolution of many Retrograde Moons, you have in *Egypt* press'd the Extremities of your Fingers, with the hard Tenants of your Mouths, and scalptiz'd your heads with frequent Applications of your Unguicules. In the School of *Pythagoras*, Taciturnity was the Symbol of abstracted and superlative Knowledge; and the silence of the *Egyptians* was agnited as an expressive manner of Divine Adoration: This caus'd the Pontifs of *Hieropolis* to Sacrifice to the great Deity in silence, impercussively, without any vociferous or obstreperous Sound. My design is not to enter into a Privation of Gratitude towards you; but by a vivacious formality, tho' matter were to abstract it self from me, excentricate to you my Cogitations.

Having spoken this, she only said to her Officers, *Tabachins a Panacea*; and strait they desir'd us not to take it amiss, if the Queen did not invite us to dine with her; for she never eat any thing at Dinner but some Categories, Jecabots, Eminins, Dimions, Abstractions, Harborins, Chelimins, second Intentions, Caradoths, Antitheses, Metempsycoses, transcendent Prolepsies and such other light Food.

Then they took us into a little Closet, lin'd through with Alarums, where we were treated God knows how. 'Tis said, that *Jupiter* writes whatever is transacted in the World, on the *Diphthera* or Skin of the *Amalthæan* Goat that suckled him in

Crete, which Pelt serv'd him instead of a Shield against the *Titans*, whence he was Nicknam'd *Egiochus*. Now, as I hate to drink water, Brother Topers, I protest, it would be impossible to make Eighteen Goat-skins hold the Description of all the good Meat they brought before us; tho' it were written in Characters as small as those in which were penn'd *Homer's Iliads*, which *Tully* tells us he saw enclos'd in a Nut-shell.

For my part, had I one hundred Mouths, as many Tongues, a Voice of Iron, a Heart of Oak, and Lungs of Leather, together with the mellifluous *Abundance* of *Plato*; yet I never could give you a full account of a Third part of a second of the whole.

Pantagruel was telling me, that he believ'd the Queen had given the Symbolic Word us'd among her Subjects to denote Sovereign good Chear, when she said to her *Tabachins*, *A Panacea*; just as *Lucullus* us'd to say, In *Apollo*, when he design'd to give his Friends a singular Treat, tho' sometimes they took him at unawares, as among the rest, *Cicero* and *Hortensius* sometimes us'd to do.

CHAPTER XXI

How the Queen pass'd her Time after Dinner.

WHEN we had din'd, a Chachanin led us into the Queen's Hall, and there we saw how, after Dinner, with the Ladies and Princes of her Court, she used to sift, searse, boult, range, and pass away time, with a fine large white and blew Silk Sieve. We also perceiv'd how they reviv'd Ancient Sports, diverting themselves together at

1. *Cordax*.	8. *Calabrismes*.
2. *Emmelia*.	9. *Molossia*.
3. *Sicinnis*.	10. *Cernophorum*.
4. *Iambics*.	11. *Monodia*.
5. *Persica*.	12. *Terminalia*.
6. *Phrygia*.	13. *Floralia*.
7. *Thracia*.	14. *Pyrrhice*.

And a thousand other Dances.*

* A sort of Country-dance. 2. A still Tragick-dance. 3. Dancing and Singing us'd at Funerals. 4. Cutting Sarcasms and Lampoons. 5. The *Persian*-dance. 6. Tunes, whose Measure inspir'd Men with a kind of

Afterwards she gave orders that they should show us the Apartments and Curiosities in her Palace; accordingly we saw there such new strange and wonderful things, that I am still ravish'd in Admiration every time I think of 't. However, nothing surpriz'd us more than what was done by the Gentlemen of her Houshold, Abstractors, Perazons, Nedibins, Spodizators, and others, who freely and without the least dissembling, told us, That the Queen their Mistress did all impossible things, and cur'd Men of incurable Diseases; and they, her Officers, us'd to do the rest.

I saw there a young Parazon cure many of the new Consumption, I mean the Pox, tho' they were never so pepper'd; had it been the rankest *Roan*-Ague [*Anglicè*, the *Covent-garden Gout*] 'twas all one to him, touching only their *Dentiform Vertebra* thrice with a piece of a Wooden-shooe, he made them as wholesome as so many Sucking-pigs.

Another did thoroughly cure Folks of Dropsies, Tympanies, Ascites, and Hyposarcidies, striking them on the Belly nine times with a Tenedian Satchel, without any Solution of the Continuum.

Another cur'd all manner of Fevers and Agues, on the spot, only with hanging a Fox-tail on the left-side of the Patient's Girdle.

One remov'd the Tooth-ach only with washing the Root of the aking Tooth with Elder-Vinegar, and letting it dry half an hour in the Sun.

Another, the Gout, whether hot or cold, natural or accidental, barely making the Gouty-person shut his Mouth, and open his Eyes.

I saw another ease nine good Gentlemen of St. *Francis*'s* Distemper, in a very short space of time, having clapt a Rope

---

Divine Fury. 7. The *Thracian*-movement. 8. Smutty Verses. 9. A Measure to which the *Molossi* of *Epirus* danc'd a certain Morice. 10. A Dance with Bowls or Pots in their Hands. 11. A Song where one sings alone. 12. Sports at the Holidays of the God of Bounds. 13. Dancing naked at *Flora*'s Holidays. 14. The *Trojan*-dance in Armour.

* *A Consumption in the Pocket, or want of Money; those of St.* Francis's *Order must carry none about 'em.*

about their Necks, at the end of which hang'd a Box with ten thousand Gold Crowns in 't.

One with a wonderful Engine, throw'd the Houses out at the Windows, by which means they were purg'd of all Pestilential Air.

Another cur'd of all the three kinds of Hectics, the Tabid, Atrophes, and Emaciated, without bathing, Tabian Milk, Dropax, *alias* Depilatory, or other such Medicaments: Only turning the Consumptive for three Months into Monks; and he assur'd me, that if they did not grow fat and plump in a Monastick way of living, they never would be fatten'd in this World, either by Nature, or by Art.

I saw another surrounded with a Croud of two sorts of Women; some were young, quaint, clever, neat, pretty, juicy, tight, brisk, buxom, proper, kind-hearted, and as right as my Leg, to any Man's thinking. The rest were old, weather-beaten, over-ridden, toothless, blear-ey'd, tough, wrinkled, shrivell'd, tawny, mouldy, ptysicky, decrepit hags, beldams, and walking Carcasses. We were told that his Office was to cast anew those She-pieces of Antiquity, and make them such as the pretty Creatures whom we saw, who had been made young again that day, recovering at once the Beauty, Shape, Size, and Disposition, which they enjoy'd at Sixteen, except their Heels that were now much shorter than in their former Youth.

This made them yet more apt to fall backwards when ever any Man happen'd to touch 'em, than they had been before. As for their Counterparts, the old Mother-scratch-tobies, they most devoutly waited for the blessed hour, when the Batch that was in the Oven was to be drawn, that they might have their turns, and in a mighty haste they were pulling and hawling the Man like mad, telling him, that 'tis the most grievous and intollerable thing in Nature, for the Tail to be o'fire, and the Head to scare away those who should quench it.

The Officer had his hands full, never wanting *Patients*; neither did his place bring him in little, you may swear. *Pantagruel* ask'd him, whether he could also make old Men young again? He said, he could not. But the way to make them new men, was to get 'em to cohabit with a new-cast Female; for thus they caught that fifth kind of Crinckams, which some call Pellade; in Greek, 'Οφίασις; that makes them cast off their old Hair and Skin, just as the Serpents do; and thus their Youth is renew'd like the *Arabian* Phœnix's. This is the true Fountain of Youth, for there the Old and Decrepit become Young, Active and Lusty.

Just so, as *Euripides* tell us, *Iolaus* was transmogrifi'd; and thus *Phaon*, for whom kind-hearted *Sappho* run wild, grew young again for *Venus*'s use; so *Tithon* by *Aurora*'s means; so *Æson* by *Medea*, and *Jason* also, who, if you'll believe *Pherecides*, and *Simonides*, was new-vamped and died by that Witch; and so were the Nurses of Jolly *Bacchus*, and their Husbands, as *Eschinus* relates.

CHAPTER XXII

How Queen Whim's Officers were employ'd; and how the said Lady retain'd us among her Abstractors.

I THEN saw a great number of the Queen's Officers, who made Black-a-moors white, as fast as Hops, just rubbing their Bellies with the Bottom of a Pannier.

Others with three Couples of Foxes in one Yoke, plow'd a Sandy-shoar, and did not lose their Seed.

Others wash'd burnt Tiles, and made them lose their Colour.

Others extracted Water out of Pumice-Stones, braying them a good while in a Mortar, and chang'd their substance.

Others sheer'd Asses, and thus got Long-fleece-wooll.

Others gather'd Barberries and Figs off of Thistles.

Others stroak'd He-goats by the Dugs, and sav'd their Milk in a Sieve; and much they got by it.

Others taught Cows to dance, and did not lose their fidling.

Others pitch'd Nets to catch the Wind, and took Cock-lobsters in them.

I saw a young *Spodizator*, who very artificially got Farts out of a dead Ass, and sold 'em for five pence an Ell.

Another did putrifie Beetles. O the dainty Food!

Poor *Panurge* fairly casted up his Accompts, and gave up his half-penny, [*i.e. vomited*] seeing an *Archasdarpenin*, who laid a huge plenty of Chamberlee to putrifie in Horse-dung, mish-mash'd with abundance of *Christian* Sir Reverence; pugh, fie upon him, nasty Dog. However, he told us, that with this sacred

Distillation, he *water'd* Kings and Princes, and made their *sweet* Lives a Fathom or two the longer.

Others built Churches to jump over the Steeples.

Others set Carts before the Horses, and began to flay Eels at the Tail; neither did those Eels cry before they were hurt, like those of *Melun*.

Others out of nothing made great things, and made great things to return to nothing.

Others cut Fire into Stakes with a Knife, and drew Water with a Fish-net.

Others made Chalk of Cheese, and Honey of a Dog's T—d.

We saw a knot of others, about a Baker's dozen in Number, tippling under an Arbour. They top'd out of jolly bottom-less Cups, four sorts of cool, sparkling, pure delicious Vine-tree Syrup, which went down like Mother's Milk; and Healths and Bumpers flew about like Lightning. We were told, that these true Philosophers were fairly multiplying the Stars by drinking till the Seven were Fourteen, as brawny *Hercules* did with *Atlas*.

Others made a Virtue of Necessity, and the best of a bad Market, which seem'd to me a very good piece of Work.

Others made Alchymy [*i.e. Sir-reverence*] with their Teeth, and clapping their Hind-retort to the Recipient, made scurvy Faces, and then squeez'd.

Others in a large *Grass-plat*, exactly measur'd how far the Fleas could go at a Hop, a Step, and Jump; and told us, that this was exceeding useful for the Ruling of Kingdoms, the Conduct of Armies, and the Administration of Commonwealths. And that *Socrates*, who first had got Philosophy out of Heaven, and from idle and trifling, made it profitable and of moment, us'd to spend half his Philosophizing time in measuring, the leaps of Fleas, as *Aristophanes*, the *Quintessential*, affirms.

I saw two *Giborins* by themselves, keeping Watch on the top of a Tower; and we were told, they guarded the Moon from the Wolves.

In a blind Corner, I met four more very hot at it, and ready to go to Logger-heads. I ask'd what was the cause of the stir and ado, the mighty coil and pother they made? And I heard that for four live-long-days, those over-wise Roisters had been at it

743

ding-dong, disputing on three high, more than Metaphysical Propositions, promising themselves Mountains of Gold by solving them: The first was concerning a He-asse's Shadow: The second, of the Smoke of a Lanthorn: And the third, of Goat's Hair, whether it were Wool or no? We heard that they did not think it a bit strange, that two Contradictions in Mode, Form, Figure, and Time, should be true. Tho' I'll warrant the *Sophists* of *Paris* had rather be unchrist'ned than own so much.

While we were admiring all those men's wonderful doings, the Evening Star already twinkling; the Queen (God bless her) appear'd attended with her Court, and again amaz'd and dazled us. She perceiv'd it, and said to us;

What occasions the Aberrations of humane Cogitations through the perplexing Labyrinths and Abysses of Admiration, is not the Source of the Effects, which sagacious Mortals visibly experience to be the consequential Result of Natural Causes; 'Tis the Novelty of the Experiment, which makes Impressions on their conceptive, cogitative Faculties, that do not previse the facility of the Operation adequately, with a subact and sedate Intellection, associated with diligent and congruous Study. Consequently let all manner of Perturbation abdicate the Ventricles of your Brains, if any one has invaded them while you were contemplating what is transacted by my Domestick Ministers. Be Spectators and Auditors of every particular Phænomenon, and every individual Proposition, within the extent of my Mansion, satiate your selves with all that can fall here under the Consideration of your Visual or Auscultating Powers, and thus emancipate your selves from the Servitude of Crassous Ignorance. And that you may be induc'd to apprehend how sincerely I desire this, in consideration of the studious Cupidity, that so demonstratively emicates at your external Organs, from this present Particle of time I retain you as my Abstractors. *Geber*, my Principal *Tabachin*, shall Register and Initiate you at your Departing.

We humbly thank'd her Queenship, without saying a word, accepting of the Noble Office she conferr'd on us.

CHAPTER XXIII

How the Queen was serv'd at Dinner, and of her way of eating.

QUEEN *Whims* after this, said to her Gentlemen, The Orifice of the Ventricule, that Ordinary Embassador for the Alimentation of all Members, whether Superior or Inferior, Importunes us to restore by the Apposition of Indoneous Sustenance, what was dissipated by the internal Calidity's Action on the Radical Humidity. Therefore Spodizators, Chesinins, Necmanins, and Perazons, be not culpable of Dilatory Protractions in the Apposition of every re-roborating Species, but rather let 'em pullulate and super-abound on the Tables. As for you, Nobilissim *Præstustators*, and my Gentilissim *Masticators*, your frequently experimented Industry internected with perdiligent Sedulity, and sedulous Perdiligence, continually adjuvates you to perficiate all things in so expeditious a manner that there is no necessity of exciting in you a Cupidity to consummate them. Therefore I can only suggest to you still to operate, as you are assuefacted indefatigably to operate.

Having made this *fine* Speech, she retir'd for a while with part of her Women, and we were told, that 'twas to bathe, as the Ancients did, more commonly than we use now-a-days to wash our Hands before we eat. The Tables were soon plac'd, the Cloath spread, and then the Queen sate down; she eat nothing but Cœlestial Ambrosia, and drank nothing but Divine Nectar: As for the Lords and Ladies that were there, they as well as we, far'd on as rare, costly, and dainty Dishes, as ever *Apicius* wot or dream'd of in his Life.

When we were as round as Hoops, and as full as Eggs, with stuffing the Gut, an *Olla* Podrida* was set before us, to force Hunger to come to terms with us, in case it had not granted us a Truce; and such a huge vast thing it was, that the Plate which *Pythius Althius* gave King *Darius*, would hardly have cover'd it. The *Olla* consisted of several sorts of Pottages, Salads, Fricasees, *Saugrenees*, Cabirotadoes, Rost and Boil'd-meat, Carbonadoes,

---

* *Some call it an* Olio. Rabelais *Pot-Pourry.*

RABELAIS

swindging pieces of Powder'd-beef, good old Hams, dainty *So-mates*, Cakes, Tarts, a world of Curds after the Morisk-way, fresh Cheese, Gellies and Fruits of all sorts. All this seem'd to me good and dainty; however the sight of it made me sigh; for alas; I could not taste a bit on't; so *full* I had *fill'd* my Puddings before, and a Belliful's a Belliful you know. Yet I must tell you what I saw, that seem'd to me odd enough o' Conscience; 'twas some Pasties in Paste; and what should those Pasties in Paste be, d'ye think, but Pasties in Pots? At the bottom I perceiv'd store of Dice, Cards, *Tarots*,* Luettes,* Chessmen, and Che-quers, besides full Bowles of Gold Crowns, for those who had a mind to have a Game or two, and try their Chance. Under this, I saw a Jolly Company of Mules in stately Trappings, with Vel-vet foot-cloaths, and a Troop of Ambling Nags, some for Men, and some for Women; besides, I don't know how many Litters all lin'd with Velvet, and some Coaches of *Ferrara*-make; all this for those who had a mind to take the Air.

This did not seem strange to me; but if any thing did, 'twas certainly the Queen's way of eating, and truly 'twas very new, and very odd; for she chew'd nothing, the good Lady; not but that she had good sound Teeth, and her meat requir'd to be *masticated*; but such was her Highness's Custom. When her *Præ-gustators* had tasted the meat, her *Masticators* took it and chew'd it most nobly; for their dainty Chops and Gullets were lin'd through with Crimsin Satin with little Welts, and Gold Purls, and their Teeth were of delicate White Ivory; thus, when they had chew'd the Meat ready for her Highness's Maw, they pour'd it down her Throat through a Funnel of fine Gold, and so on to her Craw. For that reason, they told us, she never visited a Close-stool but by Proxy.

* *Great Cards on which many different things are figured.*
* *Pieces of Ivory to play withal.*

746

CHAPTER XXIV

How there was a Ball in the manner of a Tournament, at which Queen Whim was present.

AFTER Supper, there was a Ball in the Form of a Tilt or Turnament, not only worth seeing, but also never to be forgotten. First, the Floor of the Hall was cover'd with a large piece of Velveted white and yellow chequer'd Tapistry, each Chequer exactly Square, and three full spans in breadth.

Then thirty two young Persons came into the Hall; sixteen of them array'd in Cloath of Gold; and of these, eight were young Nymphs, such as the Ancients describ'd *Diana*'s Attendants; the other eight were a King, a Queen, two Wardens of the Castle, two Knights, and two Archers. Those of the other Band were clad in Cloath of Silver.

They posted themselves on the Tap'stry in the following manner: The Kings on the last Line on the fourth Square, so that the Golden King was on a White Square, the Silver'd King on a Yellow Square, and each Queen by her King; the Golden Queen on a Yellow Square, and the Silver'd Queen on a White one, and on each side stood the Archers to guard their Kings and Queens; by the Archers the Knights, and the Wardens by them. In the next Row before 'em stood the eight Nymphs; and between the two Bands of Nymphs, four rows of Squares stood empty.

Each Band had its Musicians, eight on each side dress'd in its Livery; the one with Orange-colour'd Damask, the other with White, and all plaid on different Instruments most melodiously and harmoniously, still varying in Time and Measure as the Figure of the Dance requir'd. This seem'd to me an admirable thing, considering the numerous diversity of Steps, Back-steps, Bounds, Rebounds, Jerts, Paces, Leaps, Skips, Turns, *Coupés*, Hops, Leadings, Risings, Meetings, Flights, Embuscadoes, Moves, and Removes.

I was also at a loss, when I strove to comprehend how the Dancers could so suddenly know what every different Note meant; for they no sooner heard this or that sound but they plac'd themselves in the place which was denoted by the

Musick, tho' their Motions were all different. For the Nymphs that stood in the first File, as if they design'd to begin the Fight, march'd strait forwards to their Enemies from Square to Square, unless it were the first step, at which they were free to move over two steps at once. They alone never fall back, [which is not very natural to other Nymphs,] and if any one of them is so lucky as to advance to the opposite King's Row, she is immediately crown'd Queen of her King, and after that, moves with the same State, and in the same manner as the Queen; but till that happens, they never strike their enemies but forwards, and obliquely in a diagonal Line. However, they make it not their chief business to take their Foes; for if they did, they would leave their Queen expos'd to the adverse Parties, who then might take her.

The Kings move and take their Enemies on all sides square-ways, and only step from a white Square into a yellow one, and *vice versa*, except at their first step the Rank should want other Officers than the Wardens; for then they can set 'em in their place, and retire by him.

The Queens take a greater Liberty than any of the rest, for they move backwards and forwards all manner of ways in a straight line, as far as they please, provided the place be not fill'd with one of her own Party, and diagonally also keeping to the Colour on which she stands.

The Archers move backwards or forwards, far and near, never changing the Colour on which they stand.

The Knights move, and take in a lineal manner, stepping over one Square, tho' a Friend or a Foe stand upon it, posting themselves on the second Square to the right or left, from one Colour to another, which is very unwelcome to the adverse Party, and ought to be carefully observ'd, for they take at unawares.

The Wardens move, and take to the right or left, before or behind them, like the Kings, and can advance as far as they find places empty; which liberty the Kings take not.

The Laws which both sides observe, is at the end of the Fight, to besiege and enclose the King of either Party, so that he may not be able to move; and being reduc'd to that extremity, the Battle is over, and he loses the Day.

Now to avoid this, there is none of either Sex of each Party, but is willing to sacrifice his or her Life, and they begin to take one another on all sides in time, as soon as the Musick strikes up. When any one takes a Prisoner, he makes his Honours, and striking him gently in the hand, puts him out of the Field of Combate, and encamps where he stood.

If any of the Kings chance to stand where he might be taken, it is not lawful for any of his Adversaries that had discover'd him, to lay hold on him; far from it they are strictly enjoyn'd humbly to pay him their Respects, and give him notice, saying, God preserve you, Sir, that his Officers may relieve and cover him; or he may remove, if unhappily he cou'd not be reliev'd. However, he is not to be taken, but greeted with a *Good morrow*, the others bending the Knee; and thus the Turnament uses to end.

CHAPTER XXV

How the Thirty-two Persons at the Ball fought.

THE two Companies having taken their Stations, the Musick struck up, and with a Martial-sound, which had something of horrid in it, like a Point of War, rouz'd and allarm'd both Parties, who now began to shiver, and then soon were warm'd with War-like rage; and having got in a readiness to fight desperately, impatient of delay, stood waiting for the Charge.

Then the Musick of the Silver'd Band ceas'd playing, and the Instruments of the Golden-side alone were heard, which denoted that the Golden-party attack'd. Accordingly a new Movement was play'd for the Onset, and we saw the Nymph, who stood before the Queen, turn to the left towards her King, as it were to ask leave to fight; and thus saluting her Company at the same time, she mov'd two Squares forwards, and saluted the adverse Party.

Now the Musick of the Golden Brigade ceas'd playing, and their Antagonists began again. I ought to have told you, That the Nymph, who began by saluting her Company, had by that Formality also given them to understand that they were to fall on. She was saluted by them in the same manner with a full turn to the left, except the Queen, who went aside towards her King to the right; and the same manner of Salutation was observed on both sides during the whole Ball.

The Silver'd Nymph that stood before her Queen likewise mov'd, as soon as the Musick of her Party sounded a Charge; her Salutations, and those of her side, were to the right, and her Queen's to the left. She mov'd into the second Square forwards, and saluted her Antagonists, facing the first Golden Nymph, so that there was not any distance between them, and you would have thought they two had been going to fight, but they only strike side-ways.

Their Comrades, whether Silver'd or Golden, follow'd 'em in an intercalary Figure, and seem'd to Skirmish awhile, till the Golden Nymph, who had first enter'd the List, striking a Silver'd Nymph in the hand on the right, put her out of the Field, and set her self in her place. But soon the Musick playing a new Measure, she was struck by a Silver'd Archer, who after that, was oblig'd himself to retire. A Silver'd Knight then sally'd out, and the Golden Queen posted her self before her King.

Then the Silver'd King, dreading the Golden Queen's Fury, remov'd to the right, to the Place where his Warden stood, which seem'd to him strong and well guarded.

The two Knights on the left, whether Golden or Silver'd, march'd up, and on either side took up many Nymphs, who could not retreat, principally the Golden Knight, who made this his whole business: But the Silver'd Knight had greater Designs, dissembling all along, and even sometimes not taking a Nymph when he could have done it, still moving on till he was come up to the main Body of his Enemies, in such a manner, that he saluted their King with a *God save you, Sir.*

The whole Golden Brigade quak'd for fear and anger, those words giving notice of their King's danger; not but that they could soon relieve him, but because their King being thus saluted, they were to lose their Warden on the right Wing, without any hopes of a Recovery. Then the golden King retir'd to the Left, and the silver'd Knight took the golden Warden, which was a mighty Loss to that Party. However, they resolv'd to be reveng'd, and surrounded the Knight that he might not escape; he try'd to get off, behaving himself with a great deal of Gallantry, and his Friends did what they could to save him, but at last he fell into the golden Queen's hands and was carried off.

Her Forces not yet satisfied, having lost one of their best men, with more Fury than Conduct mov'd about, and did much mischief among their Enemies: The silver'd Party warily dissembled, watching their opportunity to be even with them, and presented one of their Nymphs to the golden Queen, having laid an Ambuscado, so that the Nymph being taken, a golden Archer had like to have seiz'd the silver'd Queen. Then the golden Knight undertakes to take the silver'd King and Queen, and says, good morrow. The silver'd Archer salutes them, and was taken by a golden Nymph, and she her self by a silver'd one.

The Fight was obstinate and sharp: The Wardens left their Posts, and advanc'd to relieve their Friends. The Battle was doubtful, and Victory hover'd over both Armies. Now the Silver Host charge and break through their Enemy's Ranks, as far as the Golden King's Tent, and now they are beaten back; The golden Queen distinguishes her self from the rest by her mighty Atchievements, still more than by her Garb and Dignity; for at once she takes an Archer, and going side-ways, seizes a silver'd Warden. Which Thing the silver'd Queen perceiving, she came forwards, and rushing on with equal Bravery, takes the last Golden Warden, and some Nymphs. The two Queens fought a long while hand to hand; now striving to take each other by Surprize, then to save themselves, and sometimes to guard their Kings. Finally, the golden Queen took the silver'd Queen; but presently after, she her self was taken by the silver'd Archer.

Then the silver'd King had only three Nymphs, an Archer, and a Warden left; and the golden, only three Nymphs and the right Knight, which made them fight more slowly and warily than before. The two Kings seem'd to mourn for the Loss of their loving Queens, and only studied and endeavour'd to get new ones out of all their Nymphs, to be rais'd to that Dignity, and thus be married to them. This made them excite those brave Nymphs to strive to reach the farthest Rank, where stood the King of the contrary Party, promising them certainly to have them Crown'd if they could do this. The golden Nymphs were beforehand with the others, and one of their number was created a Queen, who was drest in Royal Robes, and had a Crown set on her head. You need not doubt, the silver'd Nymphs made also what haste they could to be Queens; one of them was within a step of the Coronation Place; but there the golden Knight lay ready to intercept her, so that she could go no farther.

The new golden Queen resolv'd to shew her self valiant and worthy of her Advancement to the Crown, atchiev'd great Feats of Arms. But in the mean time, the silver'd Warden takes the golden Knight who guarded the Camp; and thus there was a new silver'd Queen, who, like the other, strove to excel in Heroic Deeds at the beginning of her Reign. Thus the Fight grew hotter than before. A thousand Stratagems, Charges, Rallyings, Retreats and Attacks were try'd on both sides; till at last the silver'd Queen, having by stealth advanc'd as far as the golden King's Tent, cry'd, God save you, Sir. Now none but his new Queen could relieve him; so she bravely came and expos'd herself to the utmost Extremity to deliver him out of it. Then the silver'd Warden with his Queen, reduc'd the golden King to such a stress, that to save himself, he was forc'd to lose his Queen; but the golden King took him at last. However, the rest of the golden Party were soon taken; and that King being left alone, the silver'd Party made him a low Bow; crying, *Good morrow, Sir*; which denoted that the silver'd King had got the Day.

This being heard, the Musick of both Parties loudly proclaim'd the Victory. And thus the first Battel ended, to the unspeakable Joy of all the Spectators.

After this the two Brigades took their former Stations, and began to tilt a second time, much as they had done before; only the Music play'd somewhat faster than at the first Battel, and the motions were altogether different. I saw the golden Queen sally out one of the first, with an Archer and a Knight, as it were angry at the former Defeat, and she had lik'd to have fallen upon the silver'd King in his Tent among his Officers; but having been baulk'd in her Attempt, she skirmish'd briskly, and overthrew so many silver'd Nymphs and Officers, that it was a most amazing sight. You wou'd have sworn she had been another *Penthesilea*; for she behav'd her self with as much Bravery as that *Amazonian* Queen did at *Troy*.

But this havock did not last long; for the silver'd Party, exasperated by their Loss, resolv'd to perish, or stop her Progress; and having posted an Archer in Ambuscado on a distant Angle, together with a Knight Errant, her Highness fell into their hands, and was carried out of the Field. The rest were soon routed, after the taking of their Queen; who without doubt, from that time resolv'd to be more wary, and keep near her King, without venturing so far amidst her Enemies, unless with more Forces to defend her. Thus the silver'd Brigade once more got the Victory.

This did not dishearten or deject the golden Party; far from it, they soon appear'd again in the Field to face their Enemies; and being posted as before, both the Armies seem'd more resolute and chearful than ever. Now the martial Consort began, and the Music was above a *Hemiole* the quicker, according to the Warlike *Phrygian Mode*, such as was invented by *Marsias*.

Then our *Combatants* began to wheel about and charge with such a swiftness, that in an instant they made four moves, besides the usual Salutations. So that they were continually in Action, flying, hovering, jumping, vaulting, tumbling, curvetting, with petauristical Turns and Motions, and often intermingled.

Seeing them turn about on one Foot after they had made their Honours, we compar'd them to your Tops or Giggs, such as Boys use to whip about; making them turn round so swiftly, that they sleep, as they call it, and motion cannot be perceiv'd, but resembles rest its contrary: So that if you make a Point or Mark on some part of one of those Gigs, 'twill be perceiv'd not as a Point, but as a continual Line, in a most divine manner, as *Cusanus* has *wisely* observ'd.

While they were thus warmly engag'd, we heard continually the Claps and *Episemasies* which those of the two Bands reiterated at the taking of their Enemies; and this, join'd to the variety of their Motions and Music, would have forc'd Smiles out of the most severe *Cato*, the never-laughing *Crassus*, the *Athenian* Man-hater *Timon*; nay, even the whining *Heraclytus*, tho' he abhorr'd Laughing, the Action that's most peculiar to Man. For who could have forborn? seeing those young Warriors with their Nymphs and Queens so briskly and gracefully advance, retire, jump, leap, skip, spring, fly, vault, caper, move to the Right, to the Left every way still in Time, so swiftly, and yet so dextrously, that they never touch'd one another but methodically.

As the number of the Combatants lessen'd, the Pleasure of the Spectators encreas'd; for the Stratagems and Motions of the remaining Forces were more singular. I shall only add, that this pleasing Entertainment charm'd us to such a degree, that our minds were ravish'd with Admiration and Delight; and the martial Harmony mov'd our Souls so powerfully, that we easily believ'd what is said of *Ismenias*'s having excited *Alexander* to rise from Table and run to his Arms with such a warlike Melody. At last the golden King remained Master of the Field: And, while we were minding those Dances, Queen-Whims vanish'd, so that we saw her no more from that day to this.

Then *Geber*'s *Michelots* conducted us, and we were set down among her Abstractors, as her Queenship had commanded. After that, we return'd to the Port of *Mateotechny*, and thence strait o' board our Ships; For the Wind was fair, and had we not hoisted Sail out o' hand, we could hardly have got off in three quarters of a Moon in the Wain.

CHAPTER XXVI

How we came to the Island of Odes, where the Ways go up and down.

WE Sail'd before the Wind, between a pair of Courses, and in two days made the Island of *Odes*; at which Place we saw a very strange thing. The ways there are Animals; so true is *Aristotle*'s Saying that all self-moving things are Animals. Now the Ways walk there; *Ergo*, they are then Animals: Some of them are strange unknown ways, like those of the Planets; others are High-ways, Cross-ways, and By-ways. I perceiv'd that the Travellers and Inhabitants of that Country ask'd whither do's this way go? whither do's that way go? Some answer'd, Between *Midy* and *Feurolles*, to the Parish Church, to the City, to the River, and so forth. Being thus in their right way, they us'd to reach their Journeys end without any further trouble, just like those who go by Water from *Lyons* to *Avignon* or *Arles*.

Now, as you know that nothing is perfect here below, we heard there was a sort of People whom they call'd *High-way-men*, *Way-beaters*, and makers of Inroads in Roads; and that the poor ways were sadly afraid of them, and shun'd them as you do Robbers. For these us'd to waylay them, as People lay Trains for Wolves, and set Ginns for Woodcocks. I saw one who was taken up with a Lord-Chief-Justice's Warrant, for having unjustly and in spight of *Pallas* taken the *School-way*, which is the longest. Another boasted that he had fairly taken his shortest, and that doing so, he first compass'd his design. Thus *Carpalim*, meeting once *Epistemon* looking upon a Wall with his Fiddle-diddle, or live Urinal, in his hand, to make a little Maid's water, cry'd, that he did not wonder now how the other came to be still the first at *Pantagruel*'s *Lever*, since he held his shortest, and least us'd.

I found *Bourges* Highway among these. It went with the deliberation of an Abbot, but was made to scamper at the approach of some Waggoners, who threatned to have it trampled under their Horses feet, and make their Waggons run over it, as *Tullia*'s Chariot did over her Father's Body.

I also spy'd there the old *Way* between *Peronne* and *St. Quentin*, which seem'd to me a very good, honest, plain way, as smooth as a Carpet, and as good as ever was trod upon by shoe of Leather.

Among the Rocks I knew again the good old way to *la Ferrare*, mounted on a huge Bear. This at a distance would have put me in mind of St. *Jerome*'s Picture, had but the Bear been a Lyon; for the poor Way was all mortified, and wore a long hoary Beard uncomb'd and entangled, which look'd like the Picture of Winter, or at least like a white-frosted Bush.

On that way were store of Beads or Rosaries, coursely made of wild Pine-Tree; and it seem'd kneeling, not standing, nor lying flat; but its sides and middle were beaten with huge stones; insomuch, that it prov'd to us at once an Object of Fear and Pity.

While we were examining it, a Runner *Batchelour* of the Place took us aside, and shewing us a white smooth Way, somewhat fill'd with Straw, said, Henceforth, Gentlemen, do not reject the Opinion of *Thales* the *Milesian*, who said that water is the beginning of all things, nor that of *Homer*, who tells us, that all things derive their Original from the Ocean: For, this same Way which you see here, had its beginning from water, and is to return whence she came before two months come to an end; now Carts are driven here where Boats us'd to be row'd.

Truly, said *Pantagruel*, you tell us no news, we see five hundred such changes and more every year in our World. Then reflecting on the different manner of going of those moving Ways; he told us, he believ'd that *Philolaus* and *Aristarchus* had Philosophis'd in this Island, and that some indeed were of Opinion, the Earth turns round about its Poles, and not the Heavens, whatever we may think to the contrary; as when we are on the River *Loire*, we think the Trees and the Shoar moves, tho' this is only an effect of our Boat's motion.

As we went back to our Ships, we saw three Way-Layers, who having been taken in Ambuscado, were going to be broken on the Wheel; and a huge Fornicator was burn'd with a lingring Fire for beating a way, and breaking one of its sides: we were told it was the way of the Banks of the *Nile* in *Egypt*.

CHAPTER XXVII

How we came to the Island of Sandals, or Slaves; and of the Order of Semiquaver Fryars.

THENCE we went to the Island of *Sandals*, whose Inhabitants live on nothing but Ling Broth. However, we were very kindly receiv'd and entertain'd by *Benius* the Third, King of the Island; who, after he had made us drink, took us with him to show us a spick-and-span-new Monastery, which he had contriv'd for the Semiquaver Friars; so he call'd the Religious Men whom he had there. For he said, that on t' other side the Water liv'd Friars, who stil'd themselves her sweet *Ladyships* most humble Servants. *Item*, the goodly Friar-minors, who are *Semibreves* of Bulls; the smoak'd-herring Tribe of *Minim* Friars; then the *Crotchet* Friars. So that these diminitives could be no more than *Semiquavers*. By the Statutes, Bulls, and Patents of Queen-*Whims*, they were all drest like so many *House-Burners*, except that as in *Anjou*, your Brick-layers use to quilt their Knees when they tile houses, so these holy Friars had usually quilted Bellies, and thick quilted Paunches were among them in much Repute: Their Codpieces were cut Slipper fashion, and every Monk of them wore two; one sow'd before, and another behind, reporting that some certain dreadful Mysteries were duely represented by this duplicity of Codpieces.

They wore Shoes as round as Basons, in Imitation of those who inhabit the sandy Sea. Their Chins were close shav'd, and their Feet Iron-shod; and to show they did not value Fortune, *Benius* made them shave and powl the hind part of their Poles, as bare as a Bird's Arse, from the Crown to the Shoulder-blades: But they had leave to let their Hair grow before, from the two triangular Bones in the upper part of the Skull.

Thus they did not value Fortune a Button, and cared no more for the Goods of this World, than you or I do for hanging. And to show how much they defi'd that blind Jilt, all of them wore, not in their Hands like her, but at their Waste, instead of Beads, Sharp-razors, which they us'd to new grind twice a Day, and set thrice a Night.

Each of them had a round Ball on their Feet, because Fortune is said to have one under hers.

The Flap of their Cowles hang'd forwards, and not backwards, like those of others; thus none could see their Noses, and they laugh'd without fear both at Fortune and the Fortunate, neither more nor less than our Ladies laugh at bare-fac'd Trulls, when they have those Mufflers on, which they call Masks, and which were formerly much more properly call'd Charity, because they cover a multitude of Sins.

The hind parts of their Faces were always uncover'd, as are our Faces, which made them either go with their Belly, or the Arse foremost, which they pleas'd. When their hind Face went forwards, you would have sworn this had been their Natural-gate; as well on account of their round Shooes, as of the double Codpiece, and their Face behind, which was as bare as the back of my Hand, and coursely dawb'd over with two Eyes, and a Mouth, such as you see on some *Indian*-nuts. Now, if they offer'd to waddle along with their Bellies forwards, you would have thought they were then playing at Blind-man's Buff. May I never be hang'd, if 'twas not a Comical sight.

Their way of Living was thus; about Owl light they charitably began to Boot and Spur one another: This being done, the least thing they did, was to Sleep and Snoar; and thus Sleeping, they had Barnacles on the Handles of their Faces, or Spectacles at most.

You may swear, we did not a little wonder at this odd fancy; but they satisfi'd us presently, telling us, That the Day of Judgment is to take Mankind napping; therefore to shew they did not refuse to make their Personal Appearance, as Fortune's Darlings use to do, they were always thus Booted and Spur'd, ready to mount when ever the Trumpet should sound.

At Noon, as soon as the Clock struck, they us'd to awake. You must know that their Clock-bell, Church-bells, and Refectuary-bells, were all made according to the *Pontial* device, that is, quilted with the finest Down, and their Clappers of Fox-tails.

Having then made shift to get up at Noon, they pull'd off their Boots, and those that wanted to speak with a Maid, *alias* piss, piss'd; those that wanted to Scumber, scumber'd; and those that wanted to Sneeze, sneez'd. But all, whether they would or no (poor Gentlemen!) were oblig'd largely and plentifully to Yawn, and this was their first Breakfast (O rigorous Statute!) Methought 'twas very comical to observe their Transactions; for, having laid their Boots and Spurs on a Rack, they went into the Cloysters; There they curiously wash'd their Hands and Mouths, then sat them down on a long Bench, and pick'd their Teeth till the Provost gave the Signal, whistling through his Fingers; then every He stretch'd out his Jaws as much as he could, and they gap'd and yawn'd for about half an hour, sometimes more, sometimes less, according as the Prior judg'd the Breakfast to be suitable to the day.

After that, they went in Procession; two Banners being carried before them, in one of which was the Picture of Virtue, and that of Fortune in the other. The last went before, carried by a Semiquavering-Friar, at whose Heels was another with the Shadow or Image of Virtue in one hand, and an Holy-water-sprinkle in the other; I mean of that Holy Mercurial-water, which *Ovid* describes in his *de fastis*. And as the preceding Semiquaver rang a Hand-bell, this shak'd the Sprinkle with his Fist. With that, says *Pantagruel*, This Order contradicts the Rule which *Tully* and the *Academics* prescrib'd, That Virtue ought to go before, and Fortune follow. But they told us, they did as they ought, seeing their Design was to breech, lash, and bethwack Fortune.

During the Processions they trill'd and quaver'd most melodiously betwixt their Teeth I don't know what Antiphones, or Chantings by turns: For my part, 'twas all *Hebrew-Greek* to me, the Devil a word I could pick out on 't; at last pricking up my Ears, and intensely listning, I perceiv'd they only sang with the

Tip of theirs. O, what a rare Harmony it was! How well 'twas tun'd to the sound of their Bells! You'll never find these to jar, that you won't. *Pantagruel* made a *notable* Observation upon the Processions; for, says he, have you seen and observ'd the policy of these Semiquavers? To make an end of their Procession, they went out at one of the Church-doors, and came in at the other; they took a deal of care not to come in at the place whereat they went out. On my honour, these are a subtle sort of People, quoth *Panurge*, they have as much wit as three folks, Two Fools and a mad man; they are as wise as the Calf that ran nine Miles to suck a Bull, and when he came there 'twas a Steer. This Subtilty and Wisdom of theirs, cry'd Friar *Jhon*, is borrow'd from the *Occult Philosophy*, may I be gutted like an Oyster, if I can tell what to make on 't. Then the more 'tis to be fear'd, said *Pantagruel*; for Subtilty suspected, Subtilty foreseen, Subtilty found out, loses the Essence and very Name of Subtilty, and only gains that of Blockishness. They are not such Fools as you take them to be, they have more Tricks than are good, I doubt.

After the Procession, they went sluggingly into the Fratry-Room by the way of walk and healthful Exercise, and there kneel'd under the Tables, leaning their Breasts on Lanterns. While they were in that Posture, in came a huge *Sandal*, with a Pitch fork in his hand, who us'd to baste, rib-roast, swaddle, and swindge them well-favour'dly, as they said, and in truth treated them after a fashion. They began their Meal as you end yours, with Cheese and ended it with Mustard and Lettice, as *Martial* tells us the Ancients did. Afterwards a Platter full of Mustard was brought before every one of them; and thus they made good the Proverb, *After Meat comes Mustard*.

Their Diet was this.

O' *Sundays* they stuff'd their Puddings with Puddings, Chitterlings, Links, *Bolonia*-Sawcidges, Forc'd-meats, Liverings, Hogs-haslets, young Quails, and Teals; you must also always add Cheese for the first Course, and Mustard for the last.

O' *Mondays*, they were crammed with Pease and Pork, *cum commento*, and interlineary Glosses.

O' *Tuesdays*, they us'd to twist store of Holy-bread, Cakes, Buns, Puffs, Lenten-Loaves, Jumbals and Biscuits.

O' *Wednesdays*, my Gentlemen had fine Sheeps-heads, Calves-heads, and Brocks-heads, of which there's no want in that Country.

O' *Thursdays*, they guzzled down seven sorts of Porridge, not forgetting Mustard.

O' *Fridays*, they munched nothing but Services or Sorbapples; neither were these full ripe, as I guess'd by their *Complexion*.

O' *Saturdays*, they gnaw'd Bones, not that they were poor or needy, for every Mother's Son of 'em had a very good fat Belly-Benefice.

As for their Drink, 'twas an *Antifortunal*, thus they call'd I don't know what sort of a Liquor of the place.

When they wanted to eat or drink, they turn'd down the Back-points or Flaps of their Cowls forwards, below their Chins, and that serv'd 'em instead of Gorgets or Slabbering-Bibs.

When they had well din'd, they pray'd rarely, all in *Quavers* and Shakes; and the rest of the day, expecting the day of Judgment, they were taken up with Acts of Charity. And particularly,

O' *Sundays*, Rubbers at Cuffs.

O' *Mondays*, lending each other Flirts and Fillups on the Nose.

O' *Tuesdays*, clapperclawing one another.

O' *Wednesdays*, sniting and fly-flapping.

O' *Thursdays*, worming and pumping.

O' *Fridays*, tickling.

O' *Saturdays*, jirking and firking one another.

Such was their Diet when they resided in the Convent, and if the Prior of the Monk-house sent any of them abroad, then they were strictly enjoin'd, neither to touch nor eat any manner of Fish, as long as they were on Sea or Rivers; and to abstain from all manner of Flesh whenever they were at Land, that every one might be convinc'd that while they enjoy'd the Object, they deni'd themselves the Power, and even the Desire, and were no more mov'd with it, than the *Marpesian* Rock.

All this was done with proper Antiphones, still sung and chanted by Ear, as we have already observed.

When the Sun went to bed, they fairly Booted and Spurr'd each other as before, and having clapt on their Barnicles, e'en jogg'd to bed too. At Midnight the *Sandal* came to them, and up they got, and having well whetted and set their Rasors, and been a processioning, they clapt the Tables over themselves, and like wire-drawers under their work, fell to it as aforesaid.

Friar *Jhon des Entoumeures*, having shrewdly observ'd these jolly Semiquaver-Friars, and had a full account of their Statutes, lost all patience, and cry'd out aloud; Bounce Tail, and God ha' mercy Guts; if every Fool should wear a Bable, Fewel would be dear. A Plague rot it, we must know how many Farts go to an Ounce; would *Priapus* were here as he us'd to be at the nocturnal Festivals in *Crete*, that I might see him play backwards and wriggle and shake to the purpose. Ay, ay, this is the World, and t' other is the Country; may I never piss, if this be not an Antichthonian Land, and our very *Antipodes*. In *Germany* they pull down Monasteries and *unfrockifie* the Monks; here they go quite Kam, and act clean contrary to others, setting new ones up, against the hair.

CHAPTER XXVIII

How Panurge ask'd a Semiquaver Fryar many questions, and was only answer'd in Monosyllables.

PANURGE, who had since been wholly taken up with staring at these Royal Semiquavers, at last pull'd one of them by the Sleeve, who was as lean as a Rake, and ask'd him,

Hark'e me, Friar Quaver, Semiquaver, Demisemiquavering Quaver, where's the Punk?

The Fryar pointing downwards, answer'd, There.

Pan. Pray have you many. *Fry.* Few. *Pan.* How many Scores have you? *Fry.* One. *Pan.* How many would you have? *Fry.* Five. *Pan.* Where do you hide 'em? *Fry.* Here. *Pan.* I suppose they are not all of one age? but pray how is their Shape? *Fry.* Straight. *Pan.* Their Complexion? *Fry.* Clear. *Pan.* Their Hair? *Fry.* Fair. *Pan.* Their Eys? *Fry.* Black. *Pan.* Their Features? *Fry.* Good. *Pan.* Their Brows? *Fry.* Small. *Pan.* Their Graces? *Fry.* Ripe. *Pan.* Their Looks? *Fry.* Free. *Pan.* Their Feet? *Fry.* Flat. *Pan.* Their Heels? *Fry.* Short. *Pan.* Their lower parts? *Fry.* Rare. *Pan.* And their Arms? *Fry.* Long. *Pan.* What do they wear on their hands? *Fry.* Gloves. *Pan.* What sorts of Rings on their

Fingers? *Fry*. Gold. *Pan*. What Rigging do you keep 'em in? *Fry*.
Cloath. *Pan*. What sort of Cloath is it? *Fry*. New. *Pan*. What Colour? *Fry*. Sky. *Pan*. What kind of Cloath is it? *Fry*. Fine. *Pan*.
What Caps do they wear? *Fry*. Blew. *Pan*. What the Colour of
their Stockins? *Fry*. Red. *Pan*. What wear they on their Feet?
Fry. Pumps. *Pan*. How do they use to be? *Fry*. Fowl. *Pan*. How
do they use to walk? *Fry*. Fast. *Pan*. Now let's talk of the Kit-
chin, I mean that of the Harlots, and without going hand over
head, let's a little examine things by particulars. What is in their
Kitchins? *Fry*. Fire. *Pan*. What Fuel feeds it? *Fry*. Wood. *Pan*.
What sort of Wood is't? *Fry*. Dry. *Pan*. And of what kind of
Trees? *Fry*. Yews. *Pan*. What are the Faggots and Brushes of?
Fry. Holme. *Pan*. What Wood d'ye burn in your Chambers? *Fry*.
Pine. *Pan*. And of what other Trees? *Fry*. Lime. *Pan*. Harkee
me, as for the Buttocks, I'll go your halves: Pray, how do you
feed 'em? *Fry*. Well. *Pan*. First, what do they eat? *Fry*. Bread.
Pan. Of what *Complexion*? *Fry*. White. *Pan*. And what else? *Fry*.
Meat. *Pan*. How do they love it dress'd? *Fry*. Rost. *Pan*. What
sort of Porridge? *Fry*. None. *Pan*. Are they for Pies and Tarts?
Fry. Much. *Pan*. There I'm their Man. Will Fish go down with
them? *Fry*. Well. *Pan*. And what else? *Fry*. Eggs. *Pan*. How do
they like 'em? *Fry*. Boild. *Pan*. And how must they be done?
Fry. Hard. *Pan*. Is this all they have? *Fry*. No. *Pan*. What have
they besides then? *Fry*. Beef. *Pan*. And what else? *Fry*. Pork.
Pan. And what more? *Fry*. Geese. *Pan*. What then? *Fry*. Ducks.
Pan. And what besides? *Fry*. Cocks. *Pan*. What do they season
their Meat with? *Fry*. Salt. *Pan*. What Sawce are the most dainty
for? *Fry*. Must. *Pan*. What's their last Course? *Fry*. Rice. *Pan*.
And what else? *Fry*. Milk. *Pan*. What besides? *Fry*. Pease.
Pan. What sort? *Fry*. Green. *Pan*. What do they boil 'em with?
Fry. Pork. *Pan*. What fruit do they eat? *Fry*. Good. *Pan*.
How? *Fry*. Raw. *Pan*. What do they end with? *Fry*. Nuts.
Pan. How do they drink? *Fry*. Neat. *Pan*. What Liquor? *Fry*.
Wine. *Pan*. What sort? *Fry*. White. *Pan*. In Winter? *Fry*. Strong.
Pan. In the Spring? *Fry*. Brisk. *Pan*. In Summer? *Fry*. Cool. *Pan*.
In Autumn? *Fry*. New.

Buttock of a Monk! cry'd Frier *Jhon*, how plump these
plaguy Trulls, these arch Semiquavering Strumpets must be!
That damn'd Cattle are so high fed, that they must needs be

high metall'd, and ready to winse, and give two up's for one
go-down, when any one offers to ride 'em below the Crupper.

Prethee, Friar *Jhon*, quoth *Panurge*, hold thy prating Tongue;
stay till I have done. Till what time do the Doxies set up? *Fry*.
Night. *Pan*. When do they get up? *Fry*. Late.

Pan. May I ride on a Horse that was foal'd of an Acorn, if this
be not as honest a Cod as ever the Ground went upon, and as
grave as an old Gate-post into the bargain. Would to the blessed
St. *Semiquaver*, and the blessed worthy Virgin St. *Semiquaverera*,
he were Lord Chief President [*Justice*] of *Paris*. Odsbodikins,
how he'd dispatch! with what Expedition would he bring disputes to an upshot! what an Abreviator and Clawer off of Law-
suits, Reconciler of Differences, Examiner and Fumbler of
Bags, Peruser of Bills, Scribler of Rough-drafts, and Ingrosser of
Deeds, would he not make! Well, Friar, spare your Breath to
cool your Porridge: Come, let's now talk with Deliberation, fair
and softly, as Lawyers go to Heaven. Let's know how you Vict-
ual the Venereal Camp. How is the Snatchblatch? *Fry*. Rough.
Pan. How is the Gateway? *Fry*. Free. *Pan*. And how'st within?
Fry. Deep. *Pan*. I mean, What weather is it there? *Fry*. Hot. *Pan*.
What shadows the Brooks? *Fry*. Groves. *Pan*. Of what's the Col-
our of the Twigs? *Fry*. Red. *Pan*. And that of the Old? *Fry*. Gray.
Pan. How are you when you shake? *Fry*. Brisk. *Pan*. How is their
Motion? *Fry*. Quick. *Pan*. Would you have them Vault or
Wriggle more? *Fry*. Less. *Pan*. What kind of Tools are yours?
Fry. Big. *Pan*. And in their helves? *Fry*. Round. *Pan*. Of what
Colour's the Tip? *Fry*. Red. *Pan*. When they've been us'd, how
are they? *Fry*. Shrunk. *Pan*. How much weighs each Bag of
Tools? *Fry*. Pounds. *Pan*. How hang your Pouches? *Fry*. Tight.
Pan. How are they when you've done? *Fry*. Lank. *Pan*. Now by
the Oath you have taken, tell me, when you have a mind to
Cohabit, how you throw 'em? *Fry*. Down. *Pan*. And what do
they say then? *Fry*. Fye. *Pan*. However, like Maids, they say
Nay, and take it, and speak the less, but think the more; minding the work in hand, do they not? *Fry*. True. *Pan*. Do they get
you Bairns? *Fry*. None. *Pan*. How do you pig together? *Fry*.
Bare. *Pan*. Remember you're upon your Oath, and tell me justly, and *bonâ fide*, how many times o' day you *Monk* it? *Fry*. Six.
Pan. How many bouts o' Night? *Fry*. Ten.

Cat-so, quoth Friar *Jhon*, the poor fornicating Brother's bashful, and sticks at Sixteen, as if that were his stint. Right, quoth *Panurge*, but could'st thou keep pace with him, Friar *Jhon*, my dainty Cod? May the Devil's Dam suck my Teat, if he does not look as if he had got a Blow over the Nose with a *Naples* Cowlstaff.

Pan. Pray, Friar *Shakewell*, does your whole Fraternity quaver and shake at that rate? *Fry.* All. *Pan.* Who of them is the best Cock of the Game? *Fry.* I. *Pan.* Do you never *commit* dry Bobs, or Flashes in the Pan? *Fry.* None.

Pan. I blush like any black Dog, and could be as testy as an old Cook, when I think on all this; it passes my Understanding. But, pray, when you have been pumpt dry one day, what have you got the next?

Fry. More.

Pan. By *Priapus*, they have the *Indian*-Herb, of which *Theophrastus* spoke, or I'm much out. But harkee me, thou Man of Brevity, should some Impediment honestly, or otherwise, impair your Talents, and cause your Benevolence to lessen, how would it fare with you then? *Fry.* Ill. *Pan.* What would the Wenches do? *Fry.* Rail. *Pan.* What if you skipt, and let 'em *fast* a whole Day? *Fry.* Worse. *Pan.* What do you give 'em then? *Fry.* Thwacks. *Pan.* What do they say to this? *Fry.* Bawl. *Pan.* And what else? *Fry.* Curse. *Pan.* How do you correct 'em? *Fry.* Hard. *Pan.* What do you get out of 'em then? *Fry.* Blood. *Pan.* How's their Complexion then? *Fry.* Odd. *Pan.* What do they mend it with? *Fry.* Paint. *Pan.* Then, what do they do? *Fry.* Fawn. *Pan.* By the Oath you have taken, tell me truly, what time of the Year do you do it least in? *Fry.* Now.* *Pan.* What Season do you do it best in? *Fry.* *March. Pan.* How is your Performance the rest of the Year? *Fry.* Brisk.

Then, quoth *Panurge* sneering, Of all, and of all, commend me to Ball, this is the Friar of the World, for my Money; you've heard how short, concise and compendious he is in his Answers? Nothing is to be got out of him but Monosyllables; by Jingo, I believe he would make three bits of a Cherry.

Dam him, cry'd Friar *Jhon*, that's as true as I am his Uncle, the Dog yelps at another gat's rate when he is among his

* *August.*

Bitches; there he is Polisyllable enough, my Life for yours: You talk of making three bits of a Cherry! God send Fools more Wit, and us more Money: May I be doom'd to fast a *whole* Day, if I don't verily believe he would not make above two Bits of a Shoulder of Mutton, and one swoop of a whole Pottle of Wine: Zoons, do but see how down o' the mouth the Cur looks: He's nothing but Skin and Bones; he has piss'd his Tallow.

Truly, truly, quoth *Epistemon*, this Rascally Monastical Vermin all over the World mind nothing but their Gut, and are as ravenous as any Kites and then forsooth, they tell us they've nothing but Food and Rayment in this World: 'Sdeath, what more have Kings and Princes?

CHAPTER XXIX

How Epistemon dislik'd the Institution of Lent.

PRAY did you observe, continu'd *Epistemon*, how this damn'd ill-favour'd Semiquaver mention'd *March* as the best Month for Catterwawling. True, said *Pantagruel*, yet *Lent* and *March* always go together; and the first was instituted to macerate and bring down our pamper'd Flesh, to weaken and subdue its Lusts, and curb and asswage the Venereal rage.

By this, said *Epistemon*, you may guess what kind of a Pope it was, who first enjoin'd it to be kept; since this filthy *wooden-shoo'd* Semiquaver owns that his Spoon is never oftener or deeper in the Porringer of Letchery than in *Lent*; add to this, the evident Reasons given by all Good and Learned Physicians, affirming, That throughout the whole Year no Food is eaten, that can prompt Mankind to lascivious Acts, more than at that time.

As for example, Beans, Pease, Phasels or Longpeason, Ciches, Onions, Nuts, Oysters, Herrings, Salt-meats, *Garum* (a kind of Anchovy,) and Salads, wholly made up of venereous Herbs and Fruits, as,

Rocket,	Rampions,	*Figs,*
Nose-Smart,	*Poppy,*	*Rice,*
Taragon,	Sellery,	*Raisins,* and others.
Cresses,	*Hop-buds* ,	
Parsly,		

'Twould not a little surprize you, said *Pantagruel*, should a Man tell you, that the Good Pope, who first order'd the keeping of *Lent*, perceiving that at that time o' Year the Natural heat (from the Centre of the Body, whither it was retired, during the Winter's Cold) diffuses it self as the Sap does in Trees, through the Circumference of the Members, did therefore in a manner prescribe that sort of Diet to forward the Propagation of Mankind. What makes me think so is, that by the Registers of Christenings at *Touars*, it appears that more Children are born in *October* and *November*, than in the other ten months of the Year; and reckoning backwards, 'twill be easily found that they were all made, conceiv'd, and begotten in *Lent*.

I listen to you with both my Ears, quoth Fryar *Jhon*, and that with no small pleasure, I'll assure you. But I must tell you, that the Vicar of *Jambée* ascrib'd this copious Prolification of the Women, not to that sort of Food that we chiefly eat in Lent, but to the little licens'd stooping Mumpers, your little booted Lent-Preachers, your little draggle-tail'd Father Confessors; who, during all that time of their Reign, damn all Husbands, that run astray, three Fathom and a half below the very lowest Pit of Hell. So the silly Cods-headed Brothers of the Noose, dare not then stumble any more at the Trucklebed, to the no small discomfort of their Maids, and are e'en forc'd, poor Souls! to take up with their own bodily Wives. *Dixi*, I have done.

You may descant on the Institution of Lent as much as you please, cry'd *Epistemon*; So many Men, so many Minds: But certainly all the Physicians will be against its being suppresst, tho' I think that time is at hand, I know they will, and have heard 'em say, Were it not for Lent, their Art would soon fall into Contempt, and they'd get nothing, for hardly any Body would be sick.

All Distempers are sow'd in Lent; 'tis the true Seminary and native Bed of all Diseases; nor do's it only weaken and putrifie Bodies, but it also makes Souls mad and uneasy; for then the Devils do their best, and drive a subtle Trade, and the Tribe of canting Dissemblers come out of their holes. 'Tis then Term time with your cucullated Pieces of Formality, that have one Face to God, and another to the Devil; and a wretched clutter they make with their Sessions, Stations, Pardons, Syntereses, Confessions, Whipping, Anathematizations, and much Prayer, with as little Devotion. However, I'll not offer to infer from this, that the *Arimaspians* are better than we are in that Point; yet I speak to the purpose.

Well, quoth *Panurge*, to the *Semiquaver* Fryar, who happen'd to be by, Dear bumbasting, shaking, trilling, quavering Cod, what think'st thou of this Fellow, is he a rank Heretic? *Fry.* Much. *Pan.* Ought he not to be sindg'd? *Fry.* Well. *Pan.* As soon as may be? *Fry.* Right. *Pan.* Should he not be scalded first? *Fry.* No. *Pan.* How then should he be roasted? *Fry.* Quick. *Pan.* Till at last he be? *Fry.* Dead. *Pan.* What has he made you? *Fry.* Mad. *Pan.* What d'ye take him to be? *Fry.* Damn'd. *Pan.* What place is he to go to? *Fry.* Hell. *Pan.* But first, how wou'd you have 'em serv'd here? *Fry.* Burnt. *Pan.* Some have been serv'd so? *Fry.* Store. *Pan.* That were Hereticks. *Fry.* Less. *Pan.* And the Number of those that are to be warm'd thus hereafter is? *Fry.* Great. *Pan.* How many of 'em d'ye intend to save? *Fry.* None. *Pan.* So you'd have them burnt? *Fry.* All.

I wonder, said *Epistemon* to *Panurge*, what Pleasure you can find in talking thus with this lowsy Tatterdemallion of a Monk; I vow, did not I know you well, I might be ready to think you had no more wit in your head, than he has in both his shoulders. Come, come, scatter no words, return'd *Panurge*, every one as they like, as the Woman said when she kiss'd her Cow; I wish I might carry him to *Gargantua*; when I'm married, he might be my Wife's Fool. And make you one, cry'd *Epistemon*. Well said, quoth Fryar *Jhon*; now, poor *Panurge*, take that along with thee, thou'rt e'en fitted; 'tis a plain case, thou'lt never 'scape wearing the Bull's Feather; thy Wife will be as common as the high-way, that's certain.

CHAPTER XXX

How we came to the Land of Satin.

HAVING pleas'd our selves with observing that new Order of Semiquaver Fryars, we set Sail, and in three days our Skipper made the finest and most delightful Island that ever was seen; he call'd it the Island of *Frize*; for all the ways were of Frize.

In that Island is the Land of *Satin*, so celebrated by our Court Pages. Its Trees and Shrubs never lose their Leaves or Flowers, and are all Damask and flower'd Velvet: As for the Beasts and Birds, they are all of Tapestry-work. There we saw many Beasts, Birds and Trees of the same Colour, Bigness and Shape of those in our Country, with this difference, however, that these did eat nothing, and never sung, or bit like ours; and we also saw there many sorts of Creatures which we had never seen before.

Among the rest, several Elephants in various Postures, twelve of which were the six Males and six Females that were brought to *Rome* by their *Governour* in the Time of *Germanicus*, *Tiberius*'s Nephew; some of them were Learned Elephants, some Musicians, others Philosophers, Dancers, and Showers of Tricks, and all sat down at Table in good Order, silently eating and drinking like so many Fathers in a Fratry-room.

With their Snouts or *Proboscis's* some two Cubits long, they draw up water for their own drinking, and take hold of Palm Leaves, Plumbs, and all manner of Edibles, using them offens-ively or defensively, as we do our Fists; with them tossing Men high into the Air in Fight, and making them burst out with laughing when they come to the ground.

They have Joints, whatever some men, who doubtless never saw any but Painted, may have written to the contrary. Between their Teeth they have two huge Horns; thus *Juba* called 'em, and *Pausanias* tells us, they are no Teeth, but Horns: However, *Philostratus* will have 'em to be Teeth, and not Horns. 'Tis all one to me, provided you will be pleas'd to own them to be true Ivory. These are some three or four Cubits long, and are fix'd in the upper Jaw-bone, and consequently not in the lower-most. If you hearken to those who will tell you the contrary, you'll find your selves damnably mistaken, for that's a Lye with a Latchet: Tho' 'twere *Ælian* that Long-Bow-man that told you so, never believe him, for he lyes as fast as a Dog can trot. 'Twas in this very Island that *Pliny*, his brother tell-truth, had seen some Elephants dance on the Rope with Bells and whip over the Tables, *Presto, Be gone*, while people were at Feasts, without so much as touching the Toping Topers, or the Topers toping.

I saw a *Rhinoceros* there, just such a one as *Harry Clerberg* had formerly shew'd me; methought it was not much unlike a cer-tain Boar which I had formerly seen at *Limoges*, except the sharp

Horn on its Snout, that was about a Cubit long; by the means of which that Animal dares encounter with an Elephant, that is sometimes kill'd with its Point thrust into its Belly, which is its most tender and defenceless part.

I saw there two and thirty Unicorns; they are a curst sort of Creatures, much resembling a fine Horse, unless it be that their Heads are like a Stag's, their Feet like an Elephant's, their Tails like a wild Boar's, and out of each of their Foreheads sprouts out a sharp black Horn, some six or seven Foot long; commonly it dangles down like a Turkey-Cock's Comb. When an Unicorn has a mind to fight, or put it to any other use, what does it do but make it stand, and then 'tis as straight as an Arrow.

I saw one of them, which was attended with a Throng of other wild Beasts, purifie a Fountain with its Horn. With that *Panurge* told me, that his Prancer, *alias* his Nimble-Wimble, was like the Unicorn, not altogether in length indeed, but in Vertue and propriety: For as the Unicorn purify'd Pools and Fountains from Filth and Venom, so that other Animals came and drank securely there afterwards; In the like manner, others might water their Nags, and dabble after him without fear of Shankers, Carnosities, Gonorrhæa's, Buboes, Crinckams, and such other Plagues caught by those who venture to quench their Amorous Thirst in a common Puddle; for with his Nervous Horn he remov'd all the Infection that might be lurking in some blind Cranny of the *Mephitic* sweet-scented Hole.

Well, quoth Friar *Jhon*, when you are Sped, that is, when you are Married, we'll make a Tryal of this on thy Spouse, meerly for Charity-sake, since you are pleas'd to give us so beneficial an Instruction.

Ay, ay, return'd *Panurge*, and then immediately I'll give you a pretty gentle Agregative Pill of God, made up of two and twenty kind Stabs with a Dagger, after the *Cesarian* way. Cat 'so, cry'd Friar *Jhon*, I had rather take off a Bumper of good cool Wine.

I saw there the golden Fleece, formerly conquer'd by *Jason*, and can assure you on the word of an honest man, that those who have said it was not a Fleece, but a golden Pippin, because Μῆλον signifies both an Apple and a Sheep, were utterly mistaken.

RABELAIS

I saw also a Chameleon, such as *Aristotle* describes it, and like that which had been formerly show'd me by *Charles Maris* a famous Physician of the noble City of *Lyons* on the *Rosne*; and the said *Chameleon* liv'd on air just as the other did.

I saw three Hydra's, like those I had formerly seen. They are a kind of Serpent, with seven different Heads.

I saw also fourteen Phœnixes. I had read in many Authors that there was but one in the whole World in every Century; but if I may presume to speak my mind, I declare, that those who said this, had never seen any, unless it were in the Land of *Tapestry*; tho' 'twere vouch'd by *Claudian* or *Lactantius Firmianus*.

I saw the Skin of *Apuleius*'s golden Ass.

I saw three hundred and nine Pelicans.

Item, Six thousand and sixteen *Seleucid* Birds marching in Battalia, and picking up stragling Grashoppers in Corn-Fields.

Item, Some *Cynamologi*, Argatiles, Caprimulgi, Thynnunculs, Onocrotals, or Bitterns, with their wide Swallows, Stymphalides, Harpies, Panthers, Dorcas's or Bucks, Cemas's, Cynocephalis's, Satyrs, Cartasons, Tarands, Uri, *Monops's*, or *Bonasi*, Neades, Stera's, Marmosets, or Monkeys, Bugles, Musimons, Byturos's, Ophyri, Scriech Owls, Goblins, Fairies, and Gryphins.

I saw Mid-lent o' horseback, with Mid-August and Mid-March holding its Stirrups.

I saw some *Mankind-Wolves*, Centaurs, Tigers, Leopards, Hyena's, Camelopardals, and Orix's or huge wild Goats with sharp Horns.

I saw a *Remora*, a little Fish call'd *Echineis* by the *Greeks*, and near it a tall Ship, that did not get o'head an inch, tho' she was in the Offin with Top and Top-gallants spread before the Wind; I am somewhat inclind to believe, that 'twas the very numerical Ship in which *Periander* the Tyrant happen'd to be when it was stopp'd by such a little Fish in spight of Wind and Tide. 'Twas in this Land of *Satin*, and in no other, that *Mutianus* had seen one of them.

Fryar *Jhon* told us, that in the Days of Yore, two sorts of Fishes us'd to abound in our Courts of Judicature, and rotted the Bodies and tormented the Souls of those who were at Law, whether noble or of mean Descent, high or low, rich or poor: the first were your *April* Fish or *Makerel*, [Pimps, Panders and

Bawds] the others your beneficial Remorae's, that is, the Eternity of Law-Suits, the needless Lets that keep 'em undecided.

I saw some *Sphynges*, and some *Raphes*, some *Oinces*, and some *Cepphi*, whose fore-feet are like Hands, and their hind-feet like Man's.

Also some *Crocuta's*, and some *Eales* as big as Sea-horses, with Elephant's Tails, Boar's Jaws and Tusks, and Horns as pliant as an Asse's Ears.

The *Crocuta's* most fleet Animals, as big as our Asses of *Mirebalais*, have Necks, Tails and Breasts like a Lyon's, Legs like a Stag's, have Mouths up to the Ears, and but two Teeth, one above, and one below; they speak with human Voices, but when they do, they say nothing.

Some people say, that none e'er saw an Airy or Nest of Sakers; If you'll believe me, I saw no less than Eleven, and I'm sure I reckon'd right.

I saw some left-handed Halberts, which were the first that I had ever seen.

I saw some *Menticores*, a most strange sort of Creatures, which have the Body of a Lyon, red Hair, a Face and Ears like a man's, three Rows of Teeth which close together, as if you join'd your hands with your fingers between each other; they have a Sting in their Tails like a Scorpions, and a very melodious Voice.

I saw some *Catablepas's*, a sort of Serpents, whose Bodies are small, but their Heads large without any Proportion, so that they've much ado to lift them up; and their Eyes are so infectious, that whoever sees 'em, dies upon the spot, as if he had seen a Basilisk.

I saw some Beasts with two Backs, and those seem'd to me the merriest Creatures in the World; they were most nimble at wriggling the Buttocks, and more diligent in Tail-wagging than any Water-wagtails, perpetually jogging and shaking their double Rumps.

I saw there some milch'd Craw-fish, Creatures that I never had heard of before in my Life; and these mov'd in very good order, and 'twould have done your heart good to have seen 'em.

CHAPTER XXXI

How in the Land of Satin we saw Hearsay, who kept a school of Vouching.

WE went a little higher up into the Country of *Tapistry*, and saw the Mediterranean Sea open'd to the right and left down to the very bottom, just as the Red-Sea very fairly left its bed at the *Arabian* Gulph, to make a Lane for the *Jews*, when they left *Egypt*.

There I found *Triton* winding his silver Shell instead of a Horn, and also *Glaucus*, *Proteus*, *Nereus*, and a thousand other Godlings and Sea-monsters.

I also saw an infinite number of Fish of all kinds, dancing, flying, vaulting, fighting, eating, breathing, billing, shoving, milting, spawning, hunting, fishing, skirmishing, lying in Ambuscado, making Truces, cheapning, bargaining, swearing and sporting.

In a blind Corner we saw *Aristotle* holding a Lantern in the Posture in which the Hermit uses to be drawn near *St. Christopher*, watching, prying, thinking, and setting every thing down.

Behind him stood a Pack of other Philosophers, like so many Bums by a Head-Bailiff; as *Appian*, *Heliodorus*, *Athenæus*, *Porphyrius*, *Pancrates*, *Archadian*, *Numenius*, *Possidonius*, *Ovidius*, *Opianus*, *Olympius*, *Selenus*, *Leonides*, *Agathocles*, *Theophrastus*, *Demostratus*, *Metianus*, *Nymphodorus*, *Ælian*, and five hundred other such plodding Dons, who were full of business yet had little to do; like *Chrysippus* or *Aristarchus* of *Soli*, who for eight and fifty Years together did nothing in the world but examine the state and concerns of Bees.

I spy'd *Peter Gilles* among these, with an Urinal in his Hand, narrowly watching the water of those goodly Fishes.

When we had long beheld every thing in this Land of *Satin*, *Pantagruel* said, I have sufficiently fed my Eyes, but my Belly is empty all this while, and chimes to let me know 'tis time to go to dinner; Let's take care of the Body, let the Soul abdicate it; and to this effect, let's taste some of these *Anacampserotes** that

---

* *An Herb, the touching of which is said to reconcile lovers.*

hang over our heads. Pshaw, cry'd one, they are meer Trash, stark naught o' my word, they're good for nothing.

I then went to pluck some *Mirabolans* off of a Piece of Tapistry whereon they hang'd, but the Devil a bit I could chew or swallow 'em, and had you had them betwixt your Teeth, you would have sworn they had been thrown Silk, there was no manner of savour in 'em.

One might be apt to think *Heliogabalus* had taken a Hint from thence, to feast those whom he had caus'd to fast a long time, promising them a sumptuous, plentiful and imperial Feast after it: For all the Treat us'd to amount to no more than several sorts of Meat in Wax, Marble, Earthen-Ware, painted and figur'd Table-Cloths.

While we were looking up and down to find some more substantial Food, we heard a loud various noise, like that of Papermills; so with all speed we went to the place where the noise came, where we found a diminitive, monstrous, mishapen, old Fellow, call'd *Hear-say*; his Mouth was slit up to his Ears, and in it were seven Tongues, each of 'em cleft into seven parts. However, he chatter'd, tattled and prated with all the seven at once, of different Matters, and in divers Languages.

He had as many Ears all-over his head and the rest of his body, as *Argus* formerly had Eyes; and was as blind as a Beetle, and had the Palsie in his Legs.

About him stood an innumerable number of men and women, gaping, list'ning, and hearing very intensely; among 'em I observed some who strutted like Crows in a Gutter, and principally a very handsome bodied man in the Face, who held then a Map of the World, and with little Aphorisms compendiously explain'd every thing to 'em; so that those Men *of happy Memories* grew learned in a Trice, and would most fluently talk with you of a world of prodigious Things; the hundredth part of which would take up a man's whole Life to be fully known.

Among the rest, they descanted with great Prolixity on the Pyramids and Hieroglyphics of *Egypt*, of the *Nile*, of *Babylon*, of the *Troglodytes*, the *Hymantopodes* or *Crumpfooted Nation*, the *Blæmiæ* People that wear their Heads in the middle of their Breasts, the *Pygmies*, the *Cannibals*, the *Hyperborei* and their Mountains, the *Ægypanes* with their Goat's-feet, and the Devil and all of others: every individual word of it by *Hear-say*.

I am much mistaken if I did not see among them *Herodotus*, *Pliny*, *Solinus*, *Berosus*, *Philostratus*, *Pomponius Mela*, *Strabo*, and God knows how many other Antiquaries.

Then *Albert* the great Jacobin Fryar, *Peter Tesmoin*, alias *Witness*, Pope *Pius* the Second, *Volaterran*, *Paulus Jovius* the Valiant, *Jemmy Cartier*, *Chaton* the *Armenian*, *Marco Paulo* the *Venetian*, *Ludovico Romano*, *Pedro Aliares*, and forty Cart-loads of other modern Historians, lurking behind a piece of Tapistry where they were at it ding-dong, privately scribling the Lord knows what, and making rare work on 't, and all by *Hear-say*.

Behind another piece of Tapistry on which *Naboth*'s and *Susanna*'s Accusers were fairly represented, I saw close by *Hear-say*, good store of men of the Country of *Perche* and *Maine*, notable Students, and young enough.

I ask'd what sort of study they apply'd themselves to? and was told, that from their youth they learn'd to be *Evidences*, *Affidavit-men* and *Vouchers*; and were instructed in the Art of *Swearing*; in which they soon became such Proficients, that, when they left that Country, and went back into their own, they set up for themselves, and very *honestly* liv'd by their Trade of *Evidencing*; positively giving their Testimony of all things whatsoever to those who feed them most roundly to do a Job of Journeywork for them; and all this by *Hear-say*.

You may think what you will of it, but I can assure you, they gave some of us Corners of their Cakes, and we merrily help'd to empty their Hogsheads. Then in a friendly manner they advis'd us *to be as sparing of Truth as possibly we could, if ever we had a mind to get Court-preferment.*

CHAPTER XXXII

How we came in sight of Lantern-Land.

HAVING been but scurvily entertain'd in the Land of *Satin*, we went o' board, and having set Sail, in four days came near the Coast of *Lantern-Land*. We then saw certain little hovering Fires on the Sea.

For my part I did not take them to be Lanterns, but rather thought they were Fishes, which loll'd their flaming Tongues on the surface of the Sea, or Lampyris's, which some call *Cicindela's* or *Glow-worms*, shining there as ripe Barley do's o' nights in my Country.

But the Skipper satisfy'd us that they were the Lanterns of the Watch, or more properly Light-houses, set up in many places round the Precinct of the Place to discover the Land, and for the safe Piloting in of some outlandish Lanterns, which like good *Franciscan* and *Jacobin* Fryars, were coming to make their personal Appearance at the Provincial Chapter.

However, some of us were somewhat suspicious that these Fires were the forerunners of some Storm; but the Skipper assur'd us again, they were not.

CHAPTER XXXIII

How we Landed at the Port of the Lychnobii, and came to Lantern-Land.

SOON after we arriv'd at the Port of *Lantern-land*, where *Pantagruel* discover'd on a high Tower, the Lantern of *Rochel*, that stood us in good stead, for it casted a great light. We also saw the Lantern of *Pharos*, that of *Nauplion*, and that of *Acropolis*, at *Athens*, sacred to *Pallas*.

Near the Port, there's a little Hamblet inhabited by the *Lychnobii*, that live by Lanterns, as the gulligutted Friars in our Country live by Nuns: They are studious People, and as honest Men as ever shit in a Trumpet. *Demosthenes* had formerly lanternis'd there.

We were conducted from that place to the Palace by three Obeliscolichnys,* Military-Guards of the Port, with high-crown'd Hats, whom we acquainted with the cause of our Voyage, and our Design, which was to desire the Queen of the Country to grant us a Lantern to light and conduct us, during our Voyage to the Oracle of the Holy Bottle.

---

* *A Kind of Beacons.*

They promis'd to assist us in this, and added, that we could never have come in a better time, for then the Lanterns held their Provincial Chapter.

When we came to the Royal Palace, we had Audience of her Highness, the Queen of *Lanternland*, being introduc'd by two Lanterns of Honour, that of *Aristophanes*, and that of *Cleanthes*, Mistresses of the Ceremonies. *Panurge* in few words acquainted her with the Causes of our Voyage, and she receiv'd us with great Demonstrations of Friendship, desiring us to come to her at Supper-time, that we might more easily make choice of one to be our guide, which pleas'd us extreamly. We did not fail to observe intensely every thing we could see, as the Garbs, Motions, and Deportment of the Queen's subjects, principally the manner after which she was serv'd.

The bright Queen was dress'd in Virgin Christal of *Tutia*, wrought Damask-wise and beset with large Diamonds.

The Lanterns of the Royal Blood, were clad partly with Bastard-diamonds, partly with Diaphanous Stones, the rest with Horn, Paper, and Oyl'd-cloath.

The Cresset-lights took place according to the Antiquity and Lustre of their Families.

An Earthen-dark-lantern shap'd like a Pot, notwithstanding this, took place of some of the first Quality, at which I wonder'd much, till I was told, it was that of *Epictetus*, for which three thousand *Drachmaes* had been formerly refus'd.

Martial's *Polymix*** Lantern made a very good Figure there: I took particular notice of its Dress, and more yet of the *Lychnosimity*, formerly consecrated by *Canopa* the Daughter of *Tisias*.

I saw the Lantern *Pensile* formerly taken out of the Temple of *Apollo Palatinus* at *Thebes*, by *Alexander* the Great.

I saw another that distinguish'd it self from the rest by a Bushy Tuft of Crimsin Silk on its *Head*. I was told, 'twas that of *Bartolus*, the Lantern of the Civilians.

Two others were very remarkable for Glister-pouches that dangled at their waste. We were told, that one was the *Greater Light*, and the other the *Lesser Light* of the 'Pothecaries.

---

* *A Lamp with many Wicks, or a Branched Candlestick with many Springs coming out of it, that supply all the Branches with Oyl.*

When 'twas Supper-time, the Queen's *Highness* first sate down, and then the Lady-lanterns according to their Rank and Dignity.

For the first Course, they were all serv'd with large Christmas-Candles, except the Queen, who was serv'd with a hugeous thick, stiff flaming Taper, of white Wax, somewhat red towards the Tip, and the Royal Family, as also the Provincial Lantern of *Mirebalais*, who were serv'd with *Nut-lights*; and the Provincial of Lower *Poitou*, with an arm'd Candle.

After that, god-wot, what a glorious Light they gave with their wicks: I do not say all, for you must except a parcel of Junior Lanterns, under the Government of a high and mighty one. These did not cast a Light like the rest, but seem'd to me dimmer than any long-snuff-farthing Candle, whose Tallow has been half melted away in a Hot-house. After Supper we withdrew to take some Rest, and the next day the Queen made us chuse one of the most Illustrious Lanterns to guide us; after which we took our leave.

CHAPTER XXXIV

How we arriv'd at the Oracle of the Bottle.

OUR glorious Lantern lighting and directing us to heart's content, we at last arriv'd at the desir'd Island, where was the Oracle of the Bottle. As soon as Friend *Panurge* landed, he nimbly cut a Caper with one Leg for Joy, and cry'd to *Pantagruel*, Now we are where we have wish'd our selves long ago. This is the place we've been seeking with such Toil and Labour. He then made a Complement to our Lantern, who desir'd us to be of good Cheer, and not be daunted or dismay'd whatever we might chance to see.

To come to the Temple of the Holy Bottle, we were to go through a large Vine-yard in which were all sorts of Vines, as the *Falernian, Malvesian*, the *Muscadine*, those of *Taige, Beaune, Mirevaux, Orleans, Picardent, Arbois, Coussi, Anjou, Grave, Corsica, Vierron, Nerac*, and others. This Vine-yard was formerly planted by the good *Bacchus*, with so great a blessing, that it yields Leaves, Flowers, and Fruit all the Year round, like the Orange-Trees at *Surêne*.

Our magnificent Lantern order'd every one of us to eat three Grapes, to put some Vine-leaves in his Shoes, and take a Vine-branch in his left-hand.

At the end of the Close, we went under an Arch built after the manner of those of the Ancients. The Trophies of a Toper were curiously carv'd on it.

First, On one side was to be seen a long Train of Flaggons, Leathern Bottles, Flasks, Cans, Glass-bottles, Barrels, Nipper-kins, Pint-pots, Quart-ports, Pottles, Gallons, and old fashion'd *Semaises* [swindging Wooden-pots, such as those out of which the *Germans* fill their Glasses]; these hang'd on a shady Arbor.

On another side was store of Garlick, Onions, Shallots, Hams, Botargos, Caviar, Biscuits, Neat's Tongues, Old Cheese, and such like *Comfets*, very artificially interwoven and pack'd together with Vine-stocks.

On another, were a hundred sorts of drinking Glasses, Cups, Cisterns, Ewers, False-Cups, Tumblers, Bowls, Mazers, Mugs, Jugs, Goblets, Talboys, and such other *Bacchic* Artillery.

On the Frontispiece of the Triumphal Arch, under the *Zoophore*, was the following Couplet.

> *You, who presume to move this way,*
> *Get a good Lantern, lest you stray.*

We took special care of that, cry'd *Pantagruel*, when he had read them; for there is not a better, or a more Divine Lantern than ours in all *Lanternland*.

This Arch ended at a fine large round Alley, cover'd over with the interlaid Branches of Vines, loaded and adorned with Clusters of five hundred different Colours, and of as many various Shapes, not natural but due to the skill of *Agriculture*, some were Golden, others Blewish, Tawny, Azure, White, Black, Green, Purple, streak'd with many Colours, Long, Round, Triangular, Cod-like, Hairy, Great-headed, and Grassy. That pleasant Alley ended at three old Ivy-trees verdant, and all loaden with Rings. Our inlightned Lantern directed us to make our selves Hats with some of their Leaves, and cover our Heads wholly with 'em, which was immediately done.

Jupiter's Priestess, said *Pantagruel*, in former days, would not like us have walk'd under this Arbour. There was a Mystical

Reason, answer'd our most perspicuous Lantern, that would have hinder'd her. For had she gone under it, the Wine, or the Grapes of which 'tis made, that's the same thing, had been over her head, and then she would have seem'd overtopt and master'd by Wine. Which implies, that Priests, and all Persons who devote themselves to the Contemplation of Divine Things, ought to keep their Minds sedate and calm, and avoid whatever might disturb and discompose their Tranquility; which nothing is more apt to do than Drunkenness.

You also, continu'd our Lantern, could not come into the Holy Bottle's presence, after you have gone through this Arch, did not the noble Priestess *Bacbuc* first see your Shooes full of Vine-leaves; which Action is diametrically opposite to the other, and signifies that you despise Wine, and having master'd it, as it were, tread it under foot.

I am no Scholar, quoth Friar *Jhon*, for which I'm heartily sorry; yet I find by my Breviary, that in the *Revelation*, a Woman was seen with the Moon under her Feet, which was a most wonderful sight. Now, as *Bigot* explain'd it to me, this was to signify, That she was not of the Nature of other Women, for they have all the Moon at their Heads, and consequently their Brains are always troubled with a *Lunacy*: This makes me willing to believe what you said, dear Madam *Lantern*.

CHAPTER XXXV

How we went under ground, to come to the Temple of the Holy-Bottle; and how Chinon is the oldest City in the World.

WE went under ground through a plaister'd Vault, on which was coarsely painted a Dance of Women and Satyrs, waiting on old *Silenus* who was grinning o' Horseback on his Ass. This made me say to *Pantagruel*, that this Entry put me in mind of the *Painted Cellar*, in the oldest City of the World, where such Paintings are to be seen, and in as cool a place.

Which is the oldest City in the World? ask'd *Pantagruel*. 'Tis *Chinon*, Sir, or *Cainon* in *Touraine*, said I. I know, return'd *Pantagruel*, where *Chinon* lies, and the Painted Cellar also, having my self drunk there many a Glass of cool Wine; neither do I doubt but that *Chinon* is an ancient Town: Witness its Blazon; I own 'tis said twice or thrice,

Chinon.

Petite Ville, grand Renom,
Assise sur pierre ancienne:
Au haut le bois, au pied la Vienne.

Chinon.

Little Town,
Great Renown,
On old Stone
Long has stood:
There's the Vienne, if you look down;
If you look up, there's the Wood.

But how, continued he, can you make it out, that 'tis the oldest Town in the World? Where did you find this written? I have found in the Sacred Writ, said I, that *Cain* was the First that built a Town; we may then reasonably conjecture that from his Name he gave it that of *Cainon*. Thus, after his Example, most other Founders of Towns have given them their Names; *Athena*, that's *Minerva* in *Greek*, to *Athens*; *Alexander* to *Alexandria*; *Constantine* to *Constantinople*; *Pompey* to *Pompeiopolis* in *Cilicia*; *Adrian* to *Adrianople*; *Canaan* to the *Canaanites*; *Saba* to the *Sabæans*; *Assur* to the *Assyrians*; and so *Ptolemais*, *Cæsarea*, *Tiberias*, and *Herodium* in *Judea*, got their Names.

While we were thus talking, there came to us the great Flask whom our Lantern call'd the Philosopher, her Holiness the Bottle's Governour. He was attended with a Troop of the Temple-Guards, all *French* Bottles in Wicker-Armour, and seeing us with our Javelins wrapp'd with Ivy, with our illustrious Lantern, whom he knew, he desired us to come in with all manner of safety, and order'd we should be immediately conducted to the Princess *Bacbuc*, the Bottle's Lady of Honour, and Priestess of all the Mysteries; which was done.

CHAPTER XXXVI

How we went down the Tetradic Steps, and of Panurge's fear.

WE went down one Marble Step under ground where there was a resting, or (as our Workmen call it) a Landing-place; then turning to the left we went down two other Steps, where there was another resting-place: after that we came to three other Steps turning about, and met a third; and the like at four Steps which we met afterwards. There, quoth *Panurge*, Is it here? how many Steps have you told, ask'd our Magnificent Lantern. One, two, three, four, answer'd *Pantagruel*. How much is that? ask'd she. Ten, return'd he. Multiply that, said she, according to the same *Pythagorical Tetrad*? That's ten, twenty, thirty, forty, cri'd *Pantagruel*. How much is the whole, said she? one hundred, answer'd *Pantagruel*. Add, continued she, the first Cube, that's eight; at the end of that fatal Number you'll find the Temple-gate; and pray observe, this is the true *Psychogony* of *Plato*, so celebrated by the Academics, yet so little understood; one moiety of which consists of the unity, of the two first Numbers full, of two Square and two Cubic Numbers. We then went down those Numeral Stairs all underground; and I can assure you in the first place, that our Legs stood us in good stead; for had it not been for 'em, we had rowl'd just like so many Hogsheads into a Vault. Secondly, our Radiant Lantern gave us just so much Light as is in St. *Patrick's* Hole in *Ireland*, or *Trophonius*'s Pit in *Bœotia*: Which caus'd *Panurge* to say to her, after we were got down some seventy eight Steps;

Dear Madam, with a sorrowful aking heart, I most humbly beseech your Lanternship to lead us back. May I be led to Hell, if I be not half dead with fear, my Heart's sunk down into my Hose; I'm afraid I shall make butter'd Eggs in my Breeches. I freely consent never to marry. You have given your self too much trouble on my account; the Lord shall reward you in his great *Rewarder*, neither will I be ungrateful when I come out of this Cave of *Troglodytes*. Let's go back, I pray you. I'm very much afraid this is *Tænarus*, the *Low-way* to Hell, and methinks I already hear *Cerberus* bark. Hark! I hear the Cur, or my Ears tingle; I have no manner of kindness for the Dog; for there never is a

greater Toothake, then when Dogs bite us by the Shins: and if
this be only *Trophonius*'s Pit, the Lemures, Hob-thrushes and
Goblins will certainly swallow us alive, just as they devour'd
formerly one of *Demetrius*'s *Halbardeers* for want of Bridles. Art
thou here, Friar *Jhon*? Prethee, dear, dear Cod, stay by me, I'm
almost dead with fear; hast thou got thy Bilbo? alas, poor Peelgarlick's defenceless, I'm a naked man thou know'st; Let's go
back. Z'oons, fear nothing, cri'd Friar *Jhon*, I'm by thee, and
have thee fast by the Collar; Eighteen Devils shan't get thee
out of my Clutches, tho' I were unarm'd. Never did a Man yet
want Weapons who had a good Arm with as stout a heart; Heav'n
would sooner send down a shower of them; even as in *Provence*,
in the Fields of *la Crau*, near *Mariane*, there rain'd Stones (they
are there to this day) to help *Hercules*, who otherwise wanted
wherewithal to fight *Neptune*'s two Bastards. But whither are
we bound? Are we a going to the little Children's *Limbo*? By
Pluto, they'll bepawh and conskite us all; or are we going to Hell
for Orders? By Cob's Body, I'll hamper, bethwack and belabour
all the Devils, now I have some Vine-leaves in my Shooes.
Thou shalt see me lay about me like mad, old Boy. Which way?
where the Devil are they? I fear nothing but their damn'd
Horns; but Cuckoldy *Panurge*'s Bulls Feather will altogether
secure me from 'em.

Lo! In a Prophetic Spirit, I already see him, like another
Actæon, horn'd, horny, hornified. Prithee, quoth *Panurge*, take
heed thy self, dear Frater, lest, till Monks have leave to marry,
thou wedst's something thou dostn't like, as some Cat o' nine
Tails, or the Quartan Ague; if thou dost, may I never come safe
and sound out of this *Hypogeum*, this *Subterranean* Cave, if I
don't tup and ram that Disease meerly for the sake of making
thee a cornuted, corniferous Property, otherwise I fancy the Quartan Ague is but an indifferent Bedfellow. I remember *Gripe-
men-all* threatned to wed thee to some such thing, for which
thou callst him Heretic.

Here our Splendid Lantern interrupted them, letting us
know this was the Place where we were to have a taste of the
Creature, and be silent; bidding us not despair of having the
Word of the Bottle before we went back, since we had lin'd our
Shooes with Vine leaves.

Come on then, cri'd *Panurge*, let's charge through and through all the Devils of Hell; we can but perish, and that's soon done: However, I thought to have reserv'd my Life for some mighty Battel. Move, move, move forwards. I am as stout as *Hercules*, my Breeches are full of Courage; my Heart trembles a little, I own, but that's only an effect of the coldness and dampness of this Vault; 'tis neither Fear nor an Ague, Come on, move on, piss, pish, push on; my name's *William Dreadnought*.

CHAPTER XXXVII

How the Temple Gates, in a wonderful manner, open'd of themselves.

AFTER we were got down the Steps we came to a Portal of fine Jasper of *Doric* Order, on whose front we read this Sentence in the finest Gold, *EN OINΩ AΛHΘEIA*, that is, *In Wine Truth*. The Gates were of *Corinthian-like* Brass, Massy, wrought with little Vine-branches, finely inemall'd and ingraven, and were equally join'd and clos'd together in their Mortaise without Padlock Keychain, or Tie whatsoever. Where they join'd, there hang'd an *Indian* Loadstone as big as an *Egyptian* Bean, set in Gold, having two Points, Hexagonal, in a right Line; and on each side towards the Wall hang'd a handful of *Scordium* [Garlick Germander.]

There our Noble *Lantern* desir'd us not to take it amiss that she went no further with us, leaving us wholly to the Conduct of the Priestess *Bacbuc*; for she her self was not allow'd to go in, for certain Causes rather to be conceal'd than reveal'd to Mortals. However, she advis'd us to be resolute and secure, and to trust to her for the Return. She then pull'd the Loadstone that hang'd at the folding of the Gates, and throw'd it into a Silver Box fix'd for that purpose; which done, from the Threshold of each Gate she drew a Twine of Crimsin Silk about nine Foot long, by which the *Scordium* hang'd, and having fasten'd it to two gold Buckles that hang'd at the sides, she withdrew.

Immediately the Gates flew open without being touch'd, not with a creaking, or loud harsh noise, like that made by heavy Brazen Gates, but with a soft pleasing Murmur that resounded through the Arches of the Temple.

Pantagruel soon knew the cause of it, having discover'd a small Cylinder or Rowler that join'd the Gates over the Threshold, and, turning like them towards the Wall on a hard well-polish'd *Ophits* Stone, with rubbing and rowling, caus'd that harmonious Murmur.

I wonder'd how the Gates thus open'd of themselves to the right and left, and after we were all got in, I cast my Eye between the Gates and the Wall, to endeavour to know how this happen'd; for one would have thought our kind Lantern had put between the Gates the Herb *Æthiopis*, which they say opens some things that are shut; but I perceiv'd that the Parts of the Gates that join'd on the inside were cover'd with Steel; and just where the said Gates touch'd when they were opened, I saw two square *Indian* Loadstones, of a blewish Hue, well polish'd, and half a Span-broad, mortais'd in the Temple-wall. Now, by the hidden and admirable Power of the Loadstones, the Steel Plates were put into motion, and consequently the Gates were slowly drawn. However, not always, but when the said Loadstone on the outside was remov'd, after which the Steel was freed from its pow'r, the two Bunches of *Scordium* being at the same time put at some distance, because it deadens the *Magnet*, and robs it of its attractive Virtue.

On the Loadstone that was plac'd on the right side, the following *Iambic* Verse was curiously engraven in Ancient *Roman* Characters.

> *Ducunt volentem fata, nolentem trahunt.*
> Fate leads the willing, and th' unwilling draws.

The following Sentence was neatly cut in the Loadstone that was on the left.

ALL THINGS TEND TO THEIR END

CHAPTER XXXVIII

Of the Temple's admirable Pavement.

WHEN I had read those Inscriptions, I admir'd the Beauty of the Temple, and particularly the Disposition of its Pavement, with which no Work that is now, or has been under the Cope of Heaven can justly be compar'd; not that of the Temple of

Fortune at *Praeneste* in *Sylla*'s Time; or the Pavement of the *Greeks*, call'd *Alerotum*, laid by *Sosistratus* at *Pergamus*. For this here was wholly in Compartments of precious Stones, all in their Natural Colours: One of Red *Jasper*, most charmingly spotted. Another of *Ophites*. A third of *Porphyry*. A fourth of *Lycopthalmy*, a Stone of four different Colours, pouder'd with sparks of Gold, as small as Atoms. A fifth of *Agath*, streaked here and there with small Milk-colour'd Waves. A sixth of costly *Chalcedony*, or *Onyx* Stone. And another of Green *Jasper*, with certain red and yellowish Veins; and all these were dispos'd in a Diagonal Line.

At the *Portico*, some small Stones were inlaid, and evenly join'd on the Floor, all in their Native Colours, to imbellish the Design of the Figures, and they were order'd in such a manner, that you would have thought some Vine-leaves and Branches had been carelessly strow'd on the Pavement: For in some places they were thick, and thin in others: That Inlaying was very wonderful every where; here, were seen, as it were in the Shade, some Snails crawling on the Grapes; there, little Lizards running on the Branches; on this side, were Grapes that seem'd yet greenish; on another, some Clusters that seem'd full ripe, so like the true, that they could as easily have deceiv'd Starlings, and other Birds, as those which *Zeuxis* drew.

Nay, we our selves were deceiv'd; for where the Artist seem'd to have strow'd the Vine-branches thickest, we could not forbear walking with great Strides, lest we should intangle our Feet, just as People go over an unequal Stony place.

I then cast my eyes on the Roof and Walls of the Temple, that were all pargetted with Porphyry and Mosaick Work; which from the left-side at the coming in, most admirably represented the Battel, in which the Good *Bacchus* overthrew the *Indians*; as followeth,

CHAPTER XXXIX

How we saw Bacchus's Army drawn up in Battalia in Mosaic Work.

AT the beginning, diverse Towns, Hamlets, Castles, Fortresses, and Forests were seen in Flames; and several mad and loose

Women, who furiously rip'd up, and tore live Calves, Sheep, and Lambs, Limb from Limb, and devour'd their Flesh. There we learn'd how *Bacchus* at his coming into *India*, destroy'd all things with Fire and Sword.

Notwithstanding this, he was so despis'd by the *Indians*, that they did not think it worth their while to stop his Progress, having been certainly inform'd by their Spies, that his Camp was destitute of Warriers, and that he had only with him a Crew of Drunken Females, a low-built, old, effeminate, sottish Fellow, continually raddled, and as drunk as a Wheel-barrow, with a Pack of young Clownish Doddipoles, stark naked, always skipping and frisking up and down, with Tails and Horns like those of young Kids.

For this Reason the *Indians* had resolv'd to let them go through their Country without the least Opposition, esteeming a Victory over such Enemies more dishonourable than glorious.

In the mean time, *Bacchus* march'd on burning every thing; for, as you know, Fire and Thunder are his Paternal Arms; *Jupiter* having saluted his Mother *Semele* with his Thunder; so that his Maternal House was ruin'd by Fire. *Bacchus* also caus'd a great deal of Blood to be spilt; which when he is rouz'd and anger'd, principally in War, is as natural to him, as to make some in time of Peace.

Thus the Plains of the Island of *Samos* are call'd *Paneca*, which signifies Bloody, because *Bacchus* there overtook the *Amazons*, who fled from the Country of *Ephesus*, and there let 'em Blood, so that they all dy'd of Phlebotomy. This may give you a better insight into the meaning of an Ancient Proverb than *Aristotle* does in his *Problems*; *viz.* Why 'twas formerly said, *Neither eat nor sow any Mint in time of War.* The reason is, That Blows are given then without any distinction of Parts or Persons, and if a Man that's wounded, has that day handled or eaten any Mint, 'tis impossible, or at least very hard to stanch his Blood.

After this, *Bacchus* was seen marching in Battalia, riding in a stately Chariot, drawn by six young Leopards; he look'd as young as a Child, to shew that all good Topers never grow old; he was as red as a Cherry, or a Cherub, which you please; and had no more Hair on his Chin, than there's in the inside of my Hand; his

Forehead was grac'd with pointed Horns, above which, he wore a fine Crown or Garland of Vine-leaves and Grapes, and a Mitre of Crimsin Velvet; having also gilt Buskins on.

He had not one Man with him, that look'd like a Man; his Guards, and all his Forces consisted wholly of *Bassarides*, *Evantes*, *Euhyades*, *Edonides*, *Trietherides*, *Ogygiæ*, *Mimallonides*, *Mænades*, *Thyiades*, and *Bacchæ*; frantick, raving, raging, furious, mad Women, begirt with live Snakes and Serpents, instead of Girdles, dischevell'd, their Hair flowing about their Shoulders, with Garlands of Vine-branches instead of Forehead-cloaths, clad with Stags or Goat's Skins, and arm'd with Torches, Javelins, Spears, and Halberts, whose ends were like Pine-apples; besides they had certain small light Bucklers, that gave a loud sound if you touch'd 'em never so little, and these serv'd them instead of Drums; they were just Seventy nine thousand two hundred twenty seven.

Silenus, who led the Van, was one on whom *Bacchus* rely'd very much, having formerly had many Proofs of his Valour and Conduct; he was a diminutive, stooping, palsied, plumb, gorbellied, old Fellow, with a swindging pair of stiff-standing Lugs of his own, a sharp *Roman* Nose, large, rough Eye-brows, mounted on a well-hung Ass: in his Fist he held a Staff to lean upon, and also bravely to Fight, whenever he had occasion to alight; and he was drest in a Woman's yellow Gown. His Followers were all young, wild, clownish People, as hornified as so many Kids, and as fell as so many Tigers, naked and perpetually singing and dancing Country-dances; they were call'd *Tityri* and *Satyrs*; and were in all Eighty five thousand one hundred thirty three.

Pan, who brought up the Reer, was a monstrous sort of a Thing, for his lower Parts were like a Goats, his Thighs hairy, and his Horns bolt upright, a Crimsin fiery Phiz, and a Beard that was none of the shortest. He was a bold, stout, daring, desperate Fellow, very apt to take Pepper in the Nose for yea and nay.

In his Left hand he held a Pipe, and a crooked Stick in his Right. His Forces consisted also wholly of *Satyrs*, *Ægipanes*, *Agripanes*, *Sylvans*, *Fauns*, *Lemures*, *Lares*, *Elves*, and *Hobgoblins*, and their Number was Seventy eight thousand one hundred and fourteen. The Signal or Word common to all the Army was *Euohe*.

CHAPTER XL

*How the Battle, in which the Good Bacchus overthrew the
Indians, was represented in Mosaic Work.*

IN the next place we saw the Representation of the Good *Bacchus*'s Engagement with the *Indians*. *Silenus*, who led the Van,
was sweating, puffing, and blowing, belabouring his Ass most
grievously; the Ass dreadfully open'd its wide Jaws, drove away
the Flies that plagu'd it, winc'd, flounc'd, went back, and bestir'd it self in a most terrible manner, as if some damn'd Gad-
bee had stung it at the Breech.

The *Satyrs* Captains, Serjeants, and Corporals of Companies,
sounding the *Orgies* with Cornets, in a furious manner went
round the Army, skipping, capering, bounding, jerking, farting,
flying out at Heels, kicking and prancing like mad, incouraging
their Companions to fight bravely; and all the delineated Army
cry'd out *Euohe*.

First the *Menades* charg'd the *Indians* with dreadful Shouts,
and a horrid Din of their brazen Drums and Bucklers; the Air
rung again all-a-round, as the *Mosaic Work* well express'd it. And
'pray, for the future don't so much admire *Apelles*, *Aristides* the
Theban, and others who drew Claps of Thunder, Lightnings,
Winds, Words and Spirits.

We then saw the *Indian* Army, who had at last taken the Field,
to prevent the Devastation of the rest of their Country. In the
Front were the Elephants with Castles well garison'd on their
backs. But the Army and themselves were put into Disorder;
the dreadful Cries of the *Bacchæ* having fill'd them with Consternation, and those huge Animals turn'd Tail, and trampled
on the Men of their Party.

There you might have seen Gaffer *Silenus* on his Ass, putting
on as hard as he could, striking athwart and alongst, and laying
about him lustily with his Staff, after the old fashion of Fencing.
His Ass was prancing and making after the Elephants, gaping
and martially braying, as it were to sound a Charge, as he did
when formerly in the *Bacchanalian* Feasts he wak'd the Nymph
Lotis, when *Priapus* full of *Priapism* had a mind to *priapise*, while
the pretty Creature was taking a Nap.

There you might have seen *Pan* frisk it with his goatish Shanks about the *Mænades*, and with his rustick Pipe excite them to behave themselves like *Mænades*.

A little further you might have blest your Eyes with the sight of a young Satyr, who led seventeen Kings his Prisoners, and a *Bacchis*, who, with her Snakes, hawl'd along no less than Two and forty Captains; a little *Faun*, who carried a whole dozen of Standards taken on the Enemy; and goodman *Bacchus* on his Chariot, riding to and fro fearless of Danger, making much of his dear Carkass, and cheerfully toping to all his merry Friends.

Finally, we saw the Representation of his Triumph, which was thus; First, his Chariot was wholly lin'd with Ivy, gather'd on the Mountain *Meros*; this for its scarcity, which you know, raises the Price of every thing, and principally of those Leaves in *India*. In this *Alexander* the Great follow'd his Example at his *Indian* Triumph. The Chariot was draw'd by Elephants join'd together, wherein he was imitated by *Pompey* the Great at *Rome* in his *African* Triumph. The good *Bacchus* was seen, drinking out of a mighty Urn, which Action *Marius* ap'd after his Victory over the *Cimbri* near *Aix* in *Provence*. All his Army were crown'd with Ivy, their Javelins, Bucklers, and Drums were also wholly cover'd with it; there was not so much as *Silenus*'s Ass, but was betrapp'd with it.

The *Indian* Kings were fasten'd with Chains of Gold close by the Wheels of the Chariot; all the Company march'd in Pomp with unspeakable Joy, loaded with an infinite number of Trophies, Pageants, and Spoils, playing and singing merry *Epiniciums*, Songs of Triumph, and also rural Lays and Dithyrambs.

At the farthest end was a Prospect of the Land of *Egypt*; the *Nile* with its Crocodiles, Marmosets, Ibides, Monkeys, Trochilos's, or Wrens, Ichneumons or *Pharo*'s Mice, Hippopotami or Sea-Horses, and other Creatures its Guests and Neighbours: *Bacchus* was moving towards that Country under the Conduct of a Couple of horn'd Beasts, on one of which was written in Gold, *Apis*, and *Osiris* on the other; because no Ox or Cow had been seen in *Egypt* till *Bacchus* came thither.

CHAPTER XLI

How the Temple was illuminated with a wonderful Lamp.

BEFORE I proceed to the Description of the Bottle, I'll give you that of an admirable Lamp, that dispens'd so large a Light over all the Temple, that tho' it lay under ground, we could distinguish every Object as clearly as above it at noon-day.

In the middle of the Roof was fix'd a Ring of massive Gold as thick as my clench'd Fist. Three Chains somewhat less most curiously wrought, hang'd about two foot and a half below it, and in a Triangle supported a round plate of fine Gold, whose Diameter or Breadth did not exceed two Cubits and half a span. There were four holes in it, in each of which an empty Ball was fasten'd, hollow within, and open o' top, like a little Lamp; it's Circumference about two hands breadth. Each Ball was of Precious Stone; One an Amethyst, another an *African* Carbuncle, the third an Opale, and the fourth an Anthracites: they were full of burning Water, five times distill'd in a Serpentine Lymbeck, and inconsumptible like the Oyl formerly put into *Pallas*'s Lamp at *Acropolis* of *Athens* by *Callimachus*. In each of them was a flaming Wick of *Asbestine* Flax as of old in the Temple of *Jupiter Ammon*, such as those which *Cleombrotus*, a most studious Philosopher, and *Pandelinus* of *Carpasium* had, which were rather renew'd than consum'd by the Fire.

About two foot and half below that gold Plate, the three Chains were fasten'd to three Handles that were fix'd to a large round Lamp of most pure Christal, whose Diameter was a Cubit and a half, and open'd about two hands breadth o' top; by which open place a Vessel of the same Christal, shap'd somewhat like the lower part of a Gourd-like Lymbeck, or an Urinal, was put at the bottom of the great Lamp, with such a quantity of the afore-mentioned burning Water, that the flame of the *Asbestine* Wick reach'd the Centre of the great Lamp. This made all its spherical body seem to burn and be in a Flame, because the Fire was just at the Centre and middle Point: so that it was not more easie to fix the Eye on it, than on the Disque of the Sun; the matter being wonderfully bright and shining, and the Work most transparent and dazzling, by the Reflection of the various Colours of the precious Stones, whereof the four small Lamps above the main Lamp were made, and their Lustre was still variously glittering all over the Temple. Then this wandring Light being darted on the polish'd Marble and Agath with which all the inside of the Temple was pargetted, our Eyes were entertain'd with a sight of all the admirable Colours which the Rain-bow can boast, when the Sun darts his fiery Rays on some dropping Clouds.

The Design of the Lamp was admirable in it self; but, in my opinion, what added much to the Beauty of the whole, was that round the body of the Christal-Lamp was carv'd in Cataglyphick Work, a lively and pleasant Battel of naked Boys, mounted on little Hobby-horses, with little whirligig-Lances and Shields, that seem'd made of Vine-branches with Grapes on them; their Postures generally were very different, and their childish Strife and Motions were so ingeniously exprest, that Art equall'd Nature in every Proportion and Action. Neither did this seem engrav'd, but rather hew'd out and imboss'd; in *Relief*; or, at least, like *Grotesque*, which by the Artist's Skill has the appearance of the roundness of the Object it represents; this was partly the effect of the various and most charming Light, which flowing out of the Lamp, fill'd the carv'd Places with its glorious Rays.

CHAPTER XLII

How the Priestess Bacbuc show'd us a Fantastic Fountain in the Temple.

WHILE we were admiring this incomparable Lamp, and the stupendous Structure of the Temple, the Venerable Priestess *Bacbuc*, and her Attendants came to us with jolly, smiling Looks; and seeing us duly accoutred, without the least difficulty, took us into the middle of the Temple, where just under the aforesaid Lamp was the fine Fantastic Fountain.

CHAPTER XLIII

How the Fountain-water had the Taste of Wine, according to the Imagination of those who drank of it.

SHE then order'd some Cups, Goblets, and Talboys of Gold, Silver, and Christal to be brought, and kindly invited us to drink of the Liquor that sprung there, which we readily did; for to say the truth, this Fantastick Fountain was very inviting, and its Materials and Workmanship more precious, rare, and admirable than any thing *Pluto* ever dreamt of in *Limbo*.

Its Basis or Ground-Work was of most pure and limpid Ale-blaster, and its height somewhat more than three Spans; being a regular Heptagone on the outside, with its Stylobates or Foot-steps, Arulets, Simasults or Blunt Tops, and Doric *Undulations* about it. It was exactly round within. On the middle Point of each Angle and Brink stood a Pillar orbiculated, in form of Ivory or Alabaster Solid Rings.

Each Pillar's length from the Basis to the Architraves, was near seven Hands, taking an exact Demension of its Diameter through the Centre of its Circumference and inward Round-ness; and it was so dispos'd, that casting our Eyes behind one of them, whatever its Cube might be, to view its Opposite, we found that the Pyramidal Cone of our Visual Line ended at the said Centre, and there, by the two Opposites, form'd an Equi-lateral Triangle, whose two Lines divided the Pillar into two equal parts.

That which we had a mind to measure, going from one side to another, two Pillars over, at the first third part of the distance between them, was met by their lowermost and fundamental Line, which in a *Consult Line* drawn as far as the Universal Centre, equally divided; gave in a just Partition the distance of the Seven opposite Pillars in a right Line; beginning at the Obtuse Angle on the Brink; as you know that an Angle is always found plac'd between two others in all Angular Figures odd in number.

This tacitly gave us to understand that seven Semidiamiaters are in Geometrical Proportion, Compass and Distance, somewhat less than the Circumference of a Circle, from the Figure of which they are extracted, that is to say, three whole Parts with an eighth and a half, a little more; or a seventh and a half, a little less, according to the Instructions given us of old by *Euclid*, *Aristotle*, *Archimedes*, and others.

The first Pillar, I mean that which fac'd the Temple-Gate, was of Azure, Sky-colour'd *Saphir*.

The second of *Hiacinth*, a precious Stone, exactly of the Colour of the Flower, into which *Ajax*'s Cholerick Blood was transform'd; the *Greek* letters, *AI*, being seen on it in many places.

The third, an *Anachite* Diamond, as bright and glittering as Lightning.

The fourth a *Masculin Ruby Ballais* [Peach-colour'd] *amatistising*, its Flame and Lustre ending in Violet or Purple, like an *Amatist*.

The fifth an *Emerald*, above five hundred and fifty times more precious than that of *Serapis* in the Labyrinth of the *Egyptians*, and more verdant and shining than those that were fix'd instead of Eyes in the Marble Lyon's Head, near King *Hermias*'s Tomb.

The sixth of *Agath*, more admirable and various in the Distinctions of its Veins, Clouds, and Colours, than that which *Pyrrhus*, King of *Epirus*, so mightily esteem'd.

The seventh of *Sienites*, transparent, of the Colour of a *Beril*, and the clear Hue of *Hymetian* Honey, and within it the *Moon* was seen, such as we see it in the Sky, Silent, Full, New, and in the Wain.

These Stones were assign'd to the Seven heavenly Planets by the ancient *Chaldeans*; and that the meanest Capacities might be inform'd of this, just at the Central Perpendicular Line, on the Chapter of the first Pillar, which was of *Saphir*, stood the Image of *Saturn* in *Eliacim* Lead, with his Scythe in his Hand, and at his Feet, a Crane of Gold, very artfully enemall'd according to the Native Hue of the *Saturnine* Bird.

On the second, which was of a *Hiacinth*, towards the left, *Jupiter* was seen in *Jovetian* Brass, and on his Breast an Eagle of Gold, enemall'd to the Life.

On the third was *Phœbus* of the purest Gold, and a white Cock in his Right-Hand.

On the fourth, was *Mars* in *Corinthian*-Brass, and a Lyon at his Feet.

On the fifth was *Venus* in Copper, the Metal of which *Aristonides* made *Athamas*'s Statue that express'd in a blushing whiteness his Confusion at the sight of his Son *Learchus*, who died at his Feet of a Fall.

On the sixth, was *Mercury* in *Hydrargyre*, I would have said Quicksilver, had it not been fixed, malleable, and unmovable: That nimble Deity had a Stork at his Feet.

On the seventh, was the Moon in Silver, with a Greyhound at her Feet.

The size of these Statues was somewhat more than a third part of the Pillars on which they stood, and they were so admirably wrought according to Mathematical proportion, that *Polycletus*'s Cannon could hardly have stood in competition with them.

The Bases of the Pillars, the Chapters, the Architraves, Zoophores and Cornishes, were *Phrygian* Work of Massive Gold, purer and finer than any that is found in the Rivers *Leéde* near *Montpellier*, *Ganges* in *India*, *Pô* in *Italy*, *Hebrus* in *Thrace*, *Tagus* in *Spain*, and *Pactolus* in *Lydia*.

The small Arches between the Pillars were of the same precious stone of which the Pillars next to them were. Thus that Arch was of Saphir which ended at the Hiacynth Pillar, and that was of Hiacynth which went towards the Diamond, and so on.

Above the Arches and Chapters of the Pillars on the inward Front a *Cúpola* was raised to cover the Fountain; it was surrounded by the Planetary Statues, Heptagonal at the bottom, and Spherical o' top; and of Cristal so pure, transparent, well polished, whole, and uniform in all its parts, without Veins, Clouds, Flaws or Streaks, that *Xenocrates* never saw such a one in his life.

Within it were seen the Twelve Signs of the *Zodiac*, the Twelve Months of the Year, with their Proprieties, the Two Equinoxes, the Ecliptic Line, with some of the most Remarkable fixed Stars about the Antartic Pole and elsewhere, so curiously engraven, that I fancied them to be the Workmanship of King *Necepsus* or *Petosiris* the Ancient Mathematician.

On the top of the *Cúpola*, just over the Centre of the Fountain, were three noble long Pearls all of one size, Pear-fashion, perfectly imitating a Tear, and so joined together as to represent a *Flower-de-Luce* or *Lilly*, each of the Flowers seeming above a

THE FIFTH BOOK

Hand's-breath. A *Carbuncle* jetted out of its Calix or Cup, as big as an *Ostridge*'s Egg, cut seven square (that Number so belov'd of Nature) and so prodigiously glorious, that the sight of it had like to have made us blind; for the fiery Sun, or the pointed Lightning are not more dazling and unsufferably bright.

Now were some Judicious Appraisers to judge of the Value of this incomparable Fountain, and the Lamp of which we spoke, they would undoubtedly affirm, it exceeds that of all the Treasures and Curiosities in *Europe*, *Asia* and *Africa* put together. For that *Carbuncle* alone would have darken'd the *Pantharb* of *Joachas* the *Indian* Magician, with as much ease as the Sun out-shines and dims the Stars with his Meridian Rays.

Now let *Cleopatra* that *Egyptian* Quean boast of her Pair of Pendants, those two Pearls, one of which she caused to be dis-solv'd in Vinegar, in the presence of *Anthony* the *Triumvir*, her Gallant.

Or let *Pompeia Plautina* be proud of her Dress cover'd all over with Emeralds and Pearls curiously intermix'd, that attracted the Eyes of all *Rome*, and was said to be the Pit and Magazine of the Conquering Robbers of the Universe.

The Fountain had three Tubes or Channels of right Pearl, seated in three Equilateral Angles already mention'd, extended on the Margent; and those Channels proceeded in a Snail-like Line winding equally on both sides.

We look'd on them a-while, and had cast our Eyes on another side, when *Bacbuc* directed us to watch the Water: We then heard a most harmonious sound, yet somewhat stopt by starts, far distant, and Subterranean, by which means it was still more pleasing than if it had been free, uninterrupted, and near us; so that our Minds were as agreeably entertain'd through our Ears with that charming melody, as they were through the Windows of our Eyes, with those Delightful Objects.

Bacbuc then said, Your Philosophers will not allow, that Motion is begot by the power of Figures; Look here, and see the contrary. By that single Snail-like motion, equally divided as you see, and a five-fold *infoliature*, moveable at every inward meeting, such as is the *Vena cava* where it enters into the right Ventricle of the Heart; just so is the Flowing of this Fountain, and by it an harmony ascends as high as your World's Ocean.

She then ordered her Attendants to make us drink: And to tell you the truth of the matter as near as possible, we are not, Heav'n be prais'd! of the nature of a Drove of Calf-lollies, who (as your Sparrows can't feed unless you bob 'em on the Tail) must be Rib-roasted with tough Crabtree, and firk'd into a stomach, or at least into an humour to eat or drink; No, we know better things, and scorn to scorn any man's Civility who civilly invites us to a Drinking Bout. *Bacbuc* ask'd us then how we liked our Tiff; We answer'd, that it seem'd to us good harmless sober *Adam*'s Liquor, fit to keep a man in the right way, and in a word, meer Element; more cool and clear than *Argyrontes* in *Ætolia*, *Peneus* in *Thessaly*, *Axius* in *Migdonia*, or *Cydnus* in *Cilicia*, a tempting sight of whose cool silver Stream caus'd *Alexander* to prefer the short-liv'd Pleasure of bathing himself in it, to the Inconveniences which he could not but foresee would attend so ill-tim'd an Action.

This, said *Bacbuc*, comes of not considering with our selves, or understanding the motions of the Musculous Tongue, when the Drink glides on in its way to the Stomach! Tell me, Noble Strangers, Are your Throats lin'd, pav'd, or enamell'd, as formerly was that of *Pythilus* nicknam'd *Theuthes*, that you can have miss'd the Taste, Relish and Flavour of this Divine Liquor? Here, said she, turning towards her Gentlewomen, Bring my scrubbing Brushes, you know which, to scrape, rake, cleanse and clear their Palates.

They brought immediately some stately, swindging, jolly Hams; fine, substantial Neatstongues, good Hungbeef, pure and delicate, Botargos, Venison, Sawcidges, and such other Gulletsweepers. And to comply with her Invitation, we crammed and twisted till we own'd our selves thoroughly cured of Thirst, which before did damnably plague us.

We are told, continu'd she, that formerly a Learned and Valiant *Hebrew* Chief, leading his People through Deserts, where they were in hopes of being famish'd, obtain'd of God some Manna, whose taste was to them, by imagination, such as that of Meat was to them before in reality: Thus, drinking of this miraculous Liquor you'll find it taste like any Wine that you shall fancy you drink. Come then, fancy, and drink. We did so, and *Panurge* had no sooner whipp'd off his Brimmer, but he cry'd,

By *Noah*'s Openshop, 'tis *Vin de Beaulne*, better than ever was yet tipp'd over Tongue, or may Ninety six Devils swallow me. Oh, that to keep its taste the longer, we Gentlemen Topers had but Necks some three Cubits long, or so, as *Philoxenus* desir'd to have, or at least like a *Crane*'s, as *Melanthius* wish'd his.

On the Faith of true Lanterners, quoth Fryar *Jhon*, 'tis gallant sparkling *Greek* Wine; Now, for God's sake, Sweetheart, do but teach me how the devil you make it. It seems to me *Mirevaux* Wine, said *Pantagruel*, for before I drank, I suppos'd it to be such. Nothing can be mislik'd in it, but that 'tis cold, colder, I say, than the very Ice, colder than the *Nonacrian* and *Deræan* Water, or the *Conthopian* Spring at *Corinth*, that froze up the Stomach and Nutritive Parts of those that drank of it.

Drink once, twice or thrice more, said *Bacbuc*, still changing your Imagination, and you shall find its taste and flavour to be exactly that on which you shall have pitched. Then never presume to say that any thing is impossible to God. We never offered to say any such thing, said I; far from it, we maintain he is Omnipotent.

CHAPTER XLIV

How the Priestess Bacbuc equipt Panurge, in order to have the Word of the Bottle.

WHEN we had thus chatted and tippled, *Bacbuc* ask'd, Who of you here would have the Word of the Bottle? I, your most humble little Funnel, an 't please you, quoth *Panurge*. Friend, saith she, I have but one thing to tell you, which is, That when you come to the Oracle, you take care to hearken and hear the Word only with one Ear. This, cry'd Friar *Jhon*, is *Wine of one Ear*, as *Frenchmen* call it.

She then wrapt him up in a Gaberdine, bound his Noddle with a goodly clean Biggin, clapt over it a Felt, such as those through which *Hypocras* is distilled, at the bottom of which, instead of a Cowle, she put three Obelisks, made him draw on a pair of old-fashion'd Codpieces instead of Mittins, girded him about with three Bagpipes bound together, bath'd his Jobbernol thrice in the Fountain; then threw a handful of Meal on his

Phyz, fixt three Cock's Feathers on the right-side of the Hypo-
cratical Felt, made him take a jant nine times round the Fountain, caused him to take three little leaps, and to bump his A—
seven times against the ground, repeating I don't know what
kind of Conjurations all the while in the *Toscan* Tongue, and
ever and anon reading in a *Ritual*, or Book of Ceremonies, carried after her by one of her *Mystagogues*.

For my part, may I never stir, if I don't really believe, that
neither *Numa Pompilius* the Second King of the *Romans*, nor the
Cerites of *Tuscia*, and the Old *Hebrew* Captain, ever instituted so
many Ceremonies as I then saw performed; nor were ever half
so many Religious Forms used by the *Soothsayers* of *Memphis* in
Egypt to *Apis*, or by the *Embrians*, or at *Rhamnus* to *Rhamnusia*;
or to *Jupiter Ammon*, or to *Feronia*.

When she had thus accoutred my Gentleman, she took him
out of our Company, and led him out of the Temple through a
golden Gate on the Right, into a round Chappel made of transparent speculary Stones, by whose solid Clearness the Sun's Light
shined there through the precipice of the Rock, without any
Windows or other Entrance, and so easily and fully dispersed it
self through the greater Temple, that the Light seem'd rather
to spring out of it, than to flow into it.

The Workmanship was not less rare than that of the Sacred
Temple at *Ravenna*, or that in the Island of *Chemnis* in *Egypt*.
Nor must I forget to tell you, that the Work of that round Chappel was contriv'd with such a Symmetry, that its Diameter was
just the heighth of the Vault.

In the middle of it was an Heptagonal Fountain of fine Ala-
blaster, most artfully wrought, full of Water, which was so clear,
that it might have pass'd for Element in its purity and *singleness*.
The Sacred Bottle was in it to the middle, clad in pure fine
Christal, of an oval shape, except its Muzzle, which was somewhat wider than is consistent with that Figure.

CHAPTER XLV

How Bacbuc the High-Priestess brought Panurge before the Holy Bottle.

THERE the Noble Priestess *Bacbuc* made *Panurge* stoop and kiss the brink of the Fountain; then bad him rise and dance three *Ithymbi*.* Which done, she order'd him to sit down, between two Stools placed there for that purpose, his Arse upon the ground. Then she opened her Ceremonial Book and whispering in his left Ear, made him sing an *Epileny*, inserted here in the Figure of the Bottle.

When *Panurge* had sung, *Bacbuc* throw'd I don't know what into the Fountain, and strait its Water began to boil in good earnest, just for the world as doth the great Monastical Pot at *Bourgueil* when 'tis high Holiday there. Friend *Panurge* was list'ning with one Ear, and *Bacbuc* kneeled by him, when such a kind of humming was heard out of the Bottle, as is made by a Swarm of Bees bred in the Flesh of a young Bull kill'd and drest according to *Aristæus*'s Art, or such as is made when a Bolt flies out of a Cross-bow, or when a shower falls on a sudden in Summer. Immediately after this was heard the Word *TRINC*. By *Cob*'s Body, cri'd *Panurge*, 'tis broken, or crack'd at least, not to tell a Lie for the matter; for, even so do Christal Bottles speak in our Countrey when they burst near the Fire.

Bacbuc arose, and gently taking *Panurge* under the Arms, said, Friend, Offer your Thanks to Indulgent Heaven, as Reason requires, you have soon had the Word of the Goddess Bottle; and the kindest, most favourable and certain Word of an Answer that I ever yet heard her give since I officiate here at her most Sacred Oracle: Rise, Let us go to the Chapter, in whose gloss that fine Word is explain'd. With all my Heart, quoth *Panurge*; by Jingo, I am just as wise as I was last Year: Light, where's the Book. Turn it over, where's that Chapter? Let's see this merry Gloss.

* *Dances in the honour of* Bacchus.

CHAPTER XLVI

How Bacbuc explain'd the Word of the Goddess Bottle.

BACBUC having thrown I don't know what into the Fountain, strait the Water ceas'd to boil, and then she took *Panurge* into the greater Temple, where was the enlivening Fountain.

There she took out a hugeous Silver Book in the shape of a Half-tierce, or Hog'shead of Sentences; and having fill'd it at the Fountain, said to him; The Philosophers, Preachers and Doctors of your World feed you up with fine Words and Cant at the Ears; now, here we really incorporate our Precepts at the Mouth. Therefore I'll not say to you, Read this Chapter, see this Gloss; No, I say to you, Taste me this fine Chapter, swallow me this rare Gloss. Formerly an Ancient Prophet of the *Jewish* Nation eat a Book, and became a Clerk even to the very Teeth; now will I have you to drink one, that you may be a Clerk to your very Liver. Here open your Mandibules.

Panurge gaping as wide as his Jaws would stretch, *Bacbuc* took the Silver Book, at least we took it for a real Book, for it look'd just for the world like a Breviary; but, in truth, it was a Breviary or Flask of Right *Phalernian* Wine as it came from the Grape, which she made him swallow every drop.

By *Bacchus*, quoth *Panurge*, this was a Notable Chapter, a most Authentic Gloss o' my word! Is this all that the Trismegistian Bottle's Word means? i' troth I like it extreamly, it went down like Mother's Milk. Nothing more, return'd *Bacbuc*, for *Trinc* is a *Panomphean* Word, that is, a Word understood, us'd and celebrated by all Nations, and signifies *Drink*.

Some say in your World that *Sack* is a Word us'd in all Tongues, and justly admitted in the same Sense among all Nations; for, as *Æsop*'s *Fable* hath it, all Men are born with a Sack at the Neck, naturally needy, and begging of each other; neither can the most powerful King be without the help of other men, or can any one that's poor subsist without the rich, though he be never so proud and insolent; as for Example, *Hippias* the Philosopher, who boasted he could do every thing. Much less can any one make shift without Drink than without a Sack.

Therefore here we hold not that Laughing, but that Drinking is the distinguishing Character of man. I don't say Drinking, taking that word singly and absolutely in the strictest sense; No, Beasts then might put in for a share; I mean drinking cool delicious Wine. For you must know, my Beloved, that by Wine we become Divine; neither can there be a surer Argument, or a less deceitful Divination. Your Academics* assert the same when they make the Etimology of Wine, which the Greeks call ΟΙΝΟΣ, to be from *Vis*, Strength, Vertue and Power; for 'tis in its power to fill the Soul with all Truth, Learning and Philosophy.

If you observe what is written in *Ionian* Letters on the Temple-gate, you may have understood that Truth is in Wine. The Goddess Bottle therefore directs you to that divine Liquor, be your self the Expounder of your Undertaking.

'Tis impossible, said *Pantagruel* to *Panurge*, to speak more to the purpose than does this true Priest; you may remember I told you as much when you first spoke to me about it.

Trinc then: What says your Heart elevated by *Bacchic* Enthusiasm?

With this, quoth *Panurge*,

> Trinc, Trinc, by *Bacchus*, let us tope,
> And tope again; for, now I hope
> To see some brawny juicy Rump,
> And tickle 't with my Carnal Stump.
> Ere long, my Friends, I shall be wedded,
> Sure as my Trap-stick has a red head;
> And my sweet Wife shall hold the Combat,
> Long as my Baws can on her Bum beat.
>
> O what a Battle of A— fighting
> Will there be! which I much delight in.
> What pleasant Pains then shall I take
> To keep my self and Spouse awake!
> All heart and Juice, I'll up and ride,
> And make a *Dutchess* of my Bride.
> Sing *Iö Pæan*! lowdly sing
> To *Hymen* who all joys will bring.

* *Varro.*

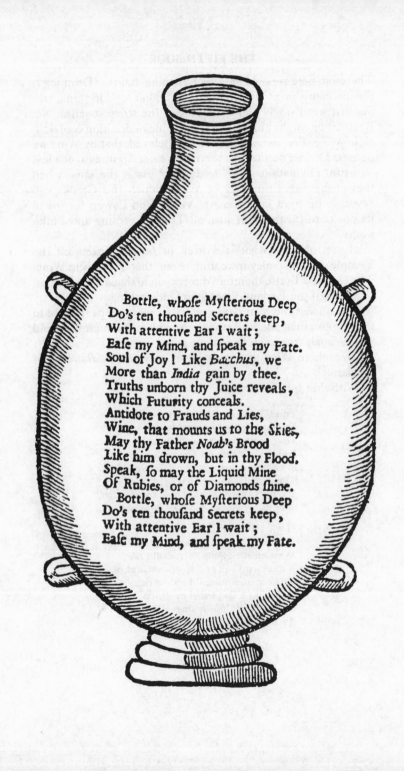

Bottle, whose Mysterious Deep
Do's ten thousand Secrets keep,
With attentive Ear I wait;
Ease my Mind, and speak my Fate.
Soul of Joy! Like *Bacchus*, we
More than *India* gain by thee.
Truths unborn thy Juice reveals,
Which Futurity conceals.
Antidote to Frauds and Lies,
Wine, that mounts us to the *Skies*,
May thy Father *Noah*'s Brood
Like him drown, but in thy Flood.
Speak, so may the Liquid Mine
Of Rubies, or of Diamonds shine.
Bottle, whose Mysterious Deep
Do's ten thousand Secrets keep,
With attentive Ear I wait;
Ease my Mind, and speak my Fate.

Well, Friar *Jhon*, I'll take my Oath,
This Oracle is full of Troth;
Intelligible Truths it bears,
More certain than the Sieve and Shears.

CHAPTER XLVII

How Panurge and the rest rim'd with Poetick Fury.

WHAT a Pox ails the Fellow, quoth Friar *Jhon*? stark staring mad, or bewitch'd, o' my word? Do but hear the chiming Dotterel gabble in Rhime. What o' Devil has he swallow'd? His Eyes rowl in his Logger-head, just for the world like a dying Goat's. Will the addle-pated Wight have the grace to sheer off? Will he rid us of his damn'd Company, to go shite out his nasty riming Balderdash in some Bog-house? Will no body be so kind as to cram some Dog's-bur down the poor Cur's Gullet, or will he Monk-like run his Fist up to the Elbow into his Throat to his very Maw to scour and clear his Flanks? Will he take a Hair of the same Dog?

Pantagruel *chid Friar* Jhon, *and said*,

Bold Monk, forbear, this I'll assure ye,
Proceeds all from Poetick Fury;
Warm'd by the God, inspir'd with Wine,
His Human Soul is made Divine.

    For without Jest,
    His hallow'd Breast.
    With Wine possest,
    Cou'd have no rest,
    Till h' had exprest
    Some Thoughts at least
    Of his great Guest.
    Then strait he flies
    Above the Skies,
    And mortifies,
    With Prophesies,
    Our Miseries.

And since divinely he's inspir'd,
Adore the Soul by Wine acquir'd,
And let the Toss-pot be admir'd.

How! quoth the Friar, the fit Rhiming is upon you too! Is 't come to that? Then we are all pepper'd, or the Devil pepper me. What would not I give to have *Gargantua* see us while we are in this Maggotty Crambo-vein! Now, may I be curst with living on that damn'd empty Food, if I can tell, whether I shall scape the catching Distemper. The Devil a bit do I understand which way to go about it; however, the Spirit of Fustian possesses us all, I find. Well, by *St. John*, I'll Poetise, since every Body does; I find it coming. Stay, and pray pardon me, if I don't Rhime in Crimsin; *'tis my first Essay.*

> Thou, who canst Water turn to Wine,
> Transform my Bum by Pow'r Divine
> Into a Lantern, that may Light
> My Neighbour in the darkest Night.

Panurge *then proceeds in his* Rapture, *and says,*

> From *Pythian Tripos* ne'er were heard
> More Truths, nor more to be rever'd.
> I think from *Delphos* to this Spring,
> Some wizard brought that conj'ring thing:
> Had honest *Plutarch* here been toping,
> He then so long had ne'er been groping
> To find, according to his Wishes,
> Why Oracles are mute as Fishes
> At *Delphos*: Now the Reason's clear,
> No more at *Delphos* they're, but here.
> Here is the *Tripos*, out of which
> Is spoke the Doom of Poor and Rich.
> For *Athæneus* does relate
> This Bottle is the Womb of Fate.
> Prolific of mysterious Wine,
> And big with Prescience Divine:
> It brings the Truth with pleasure forth,
> Besides, you ha't a penny-worth.
> So, Friar *Jhon*, I must exhort you
> To wait a Word that may import you,
> And to enquire, while here we tarry
> If it shall be your luck to Marry.

Friar Jhon *answers him in a Rage, and says,*

> How Marry! by St. *Bennet*'s Boot
> And his Gambadoes, I'll ne'r do 't.

No Man that knows me e'er shall judge
I mean to make my self a Drudge,
Or that Peelgarlick e'er will doat
Upon a paultry Petticoat.
I'll ne'er my Liberty betray
All for a little Leap-frog play,
And ever after wear a Clog
Like Monkey, or like Mastiff-Dog:
No, I'd not have upon my Life,
Great *Alexander* for my Wife,
Nor *Pompey*, nor his Dad in Law,
Who did each other clapper claw.
Not the best he that wears a Head,
Shall win me to his Truckle-bed.

Panurge *pulling off his Gaberdine and Mystical Acoutrements,*
reply'd,

Wherefore thou shalt, thou filthy Beast,
Be damn'd twelve Fathoms deep at least;
While I shall reign in Paradise,
Whence on thy Loggerhead I'll piss.
Now when that dreadful Hour is come,
That thou in Hell receiv'st thy Doom,
Ev'n there, I know, thou'lt play some trick,
And *Proserpine* shan't escape a prick
Of the long Pin within thy Breeches.
But when thou'rt using these Capriches,
And Catterwawling in her Cavern.
Send *Pluto* to the farthest Tavern.
For the best Wine that's to be had,
Lest he should see, and run Horn-mad;
She's kind, and ever did admire
A well-fed Monk, or well-hung Fryar.

Go to, quoth Friar *Jhon*, thou old Noddy, thou doddipold
Ninny, go to the Devil thou'rt prating of; I've done with Rhiming, the Rhume gripes me at the Gullet. Let's talk of paying and
going; come.

CHAPTER XLVIII

How we took our leave of Bacbuc, and left the oracle of the Holy Bottle.

Do not trouble your self about any thing here, said the Priestess to the Friar; if you be but satisfied, we are. Here below in these Circumcentral Regions, we place the Sovereign Good not in taking and receiving, but in bestowing and giving; so that we esteem our selves happy, not if we take and receive much of others, as perhaps the Sects of Teachers do in your World, but rather if we impart and give much. All I have to beg of you, is that you leave us here your Names in Writing in this *Ritual*. She then open'd a fine large Book, and as we gave our Names, one of her *Mystagogues*, with a Gold Pin, drew some Lines on it, as if she had been Writing; but we could not see any Characters.

This done, she fill'd three Glasses with fantastick Water, and giving them into our Hands, said, Now, my Friends, you may depart, and may that Intellectual Sphere, whose Centre is every where, and Circumference no where, whom we call GOD, keep you in his Almighty Protection. When you come into your World, do not fail to affirm and witness, that the greatest Treasures, and most admirable Things are hidden under Ground, and not without reason.

Ceres was worshipp'd, because she taught Mankind the Art of Husbandry, and by the use of Corn, which she invented, abolish'd that beastly way of feeding on Acorns, and she grievously lamented her Daughter's Banishment into our Subterranean Regions, certainly foreseeing that *Proserpine* would meet with more excellent Things, more desirable Enjoyments below, than she her Mother could be blest with above.

What do you think is become of the Art of forcing the Thunder, and Cœlestial Fire down, which the wise *Prometheus* had formerly invented? 'Tis most certain you have lost it; 'tis no more on your Hemisphere; but here below we have it. And, without a Cause, you sometimes wonder to see whole Towns burn'd and destroy'd by Lightning, and Ethereal Fire, and are at a loss about knowing from whom, by whom, and to what end those dreadful Mischiefs were sent. Now they are familiar and useful to us; and your Philosophers who complain that the Antients have left them nothing to write of, or to invent, are very much mistaken. Those *Phænomena* which you see in the Sky, whatever the surface of the Earth affords you, and the Sea, and every River contain, is not to be compar'd with what is hid within the Bowels of the Earth.

For this reason, the Subterranean Ruler has justly gain'd, in almost every Language, the Epithete of Rich. Now when your Sages shall wholly apply their Minds to a diligent and studious Search after Truth, humbly begging the Assistance of the Sovereign God, whom formerly the *Egyptians* in their Language call'd, the *Hidden and the Conceal'd*, and invoking him by that Name, beseech him to reveal, and make himself known to them, that Almighty Being will out of his infinite Goodness, not only make his Creatures, but even himself known to them.

Thus will they be guided by good Lanterns. For all the Ancient Philosophers and Sages have held two things necessary, safely and pleasantly to arrive at the Knowledge of God and true Wisdom; first, God's gracious Guidance, then Man's Assistance.

So among the Philosophers, *Zoroaster* took *Arimaspes* for the Companion of his Travels; *Esculapius, Mercury*; *Orpheus, Musæus*; *Pythagoras, Aclophemus*; and among Princes and Warriors, *Hercules* in his most difficult Atchievements, had his singular Friend *Theseus*; *Ulysses, Diomedes*; *Æneas, Achates*; you follow'd their Examples, and came under the Conduct of an Illustrious Lantern: Now in God's Name depart, and may he go along with you.

The End of the Fifth Book of the Heroic Deeds and Sayings of the Noble Pantagruel.

ABOUT THE INTRODUCER

TERENCE CAVE is Professor of French Literature at the University of Oxford and a Fellow of the British Academy. His publications include *The Cornucopian Text: Problems of Writing in the French Renaissance*, *Recognitions*, and a new translation of Mme de Lafayette's *The Princess of Clèves*.

This book is set in CASLON, designed and engraved by William
Caslon of WILLIAM CASLON & SON, Letter-Founders in
London, around 1740 . In England at the beginning of
the eighteenth century, Dutch type was probably
more widely used than English. The rise
of William Caslon put a stop to the
importation of Dutch types
and so changed the his-
tory of English
typecutting.